A MAN CANNOT CRY

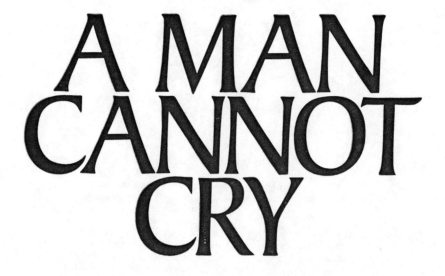

A MAN CANNOT CRY

A NOVEL BY

GLORIA KEVERNE

WILLIAM MORROW AND COMPANY, INC.
New York

Library of Congress Cataloging in Publication Data

Keverne, Gloria.
A man cannot cry.

I. Title.
PR9405.9.K4M3   1984   823   84-22771
ISBN 0-688-01932-3

Printed in the United States of America

First Edition

1   2   3   4   5   6   7   8   9   10

BOOK DESIGN BY ELLEN LO GIUDICE

This book is dedicated to:
the memory of my beloved father,
Thomas William Douglas Keverne,
who was a shining example of love and spirituality in my life . . .
to my husband, John,
without whose unfailing understanding, love, and support,
it might never have been begun . . .
And is a tribute to the dedication of my sister, Brenda,
without whose encouragement, editorial talent, and sheer hard work
it might never have been completed.

ACKNOWLEDGMENTS

I extend my grateful thanks to the many people whose generous contributions of their time, knowledge, and experience have helped me to make *A Man Cannot Cry* as authentic as possible in every detail. They are: the legendary Congo mercenary leader, Colonel Mike Hoare; former district commissioners of Northern Rhodesia and Barotseland, Mr. Seamus Talbot-Phibbs and Mr. George Roche; the former medical officer for the North Western Province, Dr. Tom Hetherington; wildlife expert and my dear friend, the late Mr. Ted Cunynhame Robertson; ex-police officer at Mwinilunga, Mr. John Anderson; mission schoolmaster, Major Tom Howes and his wife, Margaret; Quakers Mrs. Bunty Biggs, Mrs. Pat Blacquière, and other Friends; Luanshya doctors Dr. and Dr. Simons and Dr. Mason; missionaries Miss Jean Reid, Mrs. Gladys Anderson, Mrs. Joan Levengood, Miss Alison Cheesman, and numerous other kindly souls whose names I have sadly forgotten over the twenty years of the book's creation.

Very special thanks go to my friend and mentor, my American agent, Mr. Julian Bach, whose literary vision, wise counsel, and early great belief in my work have been the driving force behind its publication. For invaluable assistance, my sincere thanks also to my British agent Ms. Jacqueline Korn; to my editors Mr. Hillel Black, Ms. Patricia Parkin, and Ms. Laurie Lister, and to all the many other talented people who have worked behind the scenes to help produce this book in its final form.

AUTHOR'S NOTES

There was a transformation in the plain language used among Quakers during the eighteenth century. Instead of "thou," "thee" became the second-person singular, declining as "he." "Thou hast" changed to "thee has," "thou art" to "thee is," et cetera. This quaint form of address continues in some Quaker families to this very day.

Although *A Man Cannot Cry* is based upon authentic territories, tribes, political figures, and historical events, featuring actual situations and circumstances that existed in Northern Rhodesia in particular and Africa in general, it is a work of fiction. I have taken a little license with some languages and locations. The characters, other than those historical, are creatures of my own creation. Any resemblance to any real person, living or dead, is accidental.

PROLOGUE

Before its independence in 1964, Zambia was the British protectorate of Northern Rhodesia. Shaped like a great butterfly spreading immense wings in the heart of South Central Africa, it was a vast land of dense bush, teeming game, tsetse fly, considerable mineral wealth, and a hot tropical climate that annually alternated many months of drought between a shorter spell of torrential rain. Thinly populated by innumerable tribes of as many different dialects, it encompassed the protectorate of Barotseland, a small river kingdom whose powerful paramount chief, Lewanika I, sold the mineral rights along the Great Katanga Arc, in 1890, to the British South Africa Company in return for British "protection." The subsequent exploitation of numerous deposits led to a fabulous copper boom, and as the mining headgear rose in the bush, Africans and Europeans alike flocked to the "Copperbelt." The natives, whose backs were bent in heavy unskilled labor, earned wages below the poverty line; while their children died of malnutrition, they watched the prospering whites and harbored deep resentment.

It was upon this soil of dissatisfaction that the missionaries sowed the seeds of "man's equality." And as the more educated Africans began to understand Britain's original plan for their eventual autonomy, they formed their own advisory and political organizations. But the whites, who had brought advancement and invested money and skills in the land, had also, over generations, put down roots. Now they dug in their heels and refused to let go. In 1953, after much argument from the black nationalists, the British government acceded to the requests of the white territorial governments for the formation of a union between the self-governing colony of Southern Rhodesia and the two protectorates of Northern Rhodesia and

Nyasaland, creating one self-governing colony: the Central African Federation of Rhodesia and Nyasaland.

This political structure consolidated white power and bound Northern Rhodesia to the more racially prejudiced south. The natives saw it as a threat to their hopes for eventual self-rule. They revolted with boycotts and demonstrations against racial discrimination, and with mining strikes and disturbances. The government took effective curbing action, and the people, temporarily thwarted, brooded in their villages and in the towns, in malignant suppression . . .

BOOK ONE

THE RETURN OF
THE PRODIGAL

· 1958 ·

1

SOLWEZI was a small dusty town in the middle of the vast bush. The morning was hot and quiet; locusts clicked in the listless underbrush. And to Matthew it seemed like any other day. If the plane had not come, it might have been. But it did. And at the small airfield two miles out, he watched it descend like a skimming bird over the tarmac strip before trundling to a halt a few hundred feet from where they stood beside the Land Rover.

"Fine landing," he said absently. Then he took Katherine's elbow and they walked into the warm sunshine, squinting against the glare.

"I don't know what I'll say to him," Katherine whispered. "I don't know whatever I'll say."

"Have no fear, my dear, the worst will be over in but a moment," Matthew said calmly. "Remember—of tribulation, peace cometh in the aftermath."

He did not feel as assured as he sounded, but inevitably, he stood up well, like some creaking old beam, under loads that often terrified him. A professor of anthropology, he was a birthright Hicksite Quaker serving as Secretary/Treasurer and Supervisor of Education for the Friends' Central Africa Mission. In his seventieth year, he stood as weatherbeaten and silvered as an old piece of driftwood: his mop of white hair was damp with perspiration, and as he walked out across the sun-scorched field, he tugged nervously at his snowy moustache, straightening his bony frame under gray flannel trousers and a white shirt that was sweat-stuck to his back. Adjusting his faithful old pith helmet over pale blue eyes that squinted somewhat timidly at a Big Bad World, he watched the two occupants alight from the small Cessna. The pilot had climbed out of the cockpit, and around the far wing walked the stranger. And Matthew caught his breath. For, in the full blinding light of the sun, there he stood: The Prodigal Son.

And he was young and fine, in his father's image. Lean and uncommonly tall, he was broad of shoulder and narrow of hip. He had sandy-brown hair that was streaked with sun-bleached blondness and his sunburned skin glowed like burnished copper. He walked with a slow easy gait and carried a suitcase in his hand. His suit jacket was slung over one shoulder and his tight trousers tugged at neat muscular buttocks as he turned to look back at the aircraft. Holding a cigarette in a casually cupped hand, he rubbed absently at an ear that probably still popped from the altitude change. A qualified surgeon of medicine, at the inconsiderable age of twenty-seven he was chief resident of a teaching hospital in San Francisco, but the face was boyish and the body athletic, and to Matthew he looked more like a college boy out to challenge life. (Surely accomplishment came in less frivolous guise?) Oh, he was apt to agree with Tom that the Boy was able and brilliant. He had, after all, achieved phenomenally much for the shortness of his years. And from the States, an uncle in the profession had written that they were saying big things about him in California medical circles. Well, maybe they were, but Matthew was surprised at how little it showed in the Boy's husky appearance. Did brains really come without glasses, arthritis, old age, or stoop? Matthew had always doubted it. But here was the exception that called the lie. For this boy looked no more professional man than one of that philandering breed of fellow countrymen—*The California Surfer*! But no matter. He was American and Tom's boy; in this foreign land he was homefolks!

As he approached, Matthew saw that he was a fine looker, fabulous even, but nice, not offensively so. He had longish hair trailing into sideburns, a sensuous mouth, and smoky veiled eyes, and all this and the catlike carriage of his body had an animal sexuality that was a little embarrassing to a man of Matthew's own advanced years and devout religious bearing.

They stopped a yard apart. The Boy dropped his cigarette, ground it savagely under heel and, with an unhurried motion, set down his suitcase and reached out to clench hands.

"Dr. Livingstone, I presume?" There was a flash of white even teeth in that smoothly tanned face; a gold filling gleamed, the faint bitter smile tantalized some dimples he had, and long dusky lashes caught the sunlight. He came with a faint medical smell, the tang of after-shave lotion and a whiff of clean healthy sweat. Matthew's grand painful smile wracked his gaunt face. (The amusement in the Boy's eyes made him acutely conscious of his old pith helmet for the first time in forty years.) They shook hands easily.

16

"Glad to know thee, son. I'm Professor Tomlinson. Matthew to thee. And I'm mightily pleased and proud to meet any son of Tom's. Thou art set in thy daddy's own good mold."

The mention of paternity made the smile fade from the Boy's face; it was like a cloud darkening the sun. He stood towering a good inch or two above Matthew's own considerable height, frowning warily in the fierce glare. And with the armor of politeness gone, he looked tired and depleted as he stared off into the distance.

Then Matthew turned and there she was: Katherine, looking pale and strained, her eyes, stunned, upon the Boy's face. In her long-skirted Quaker-gray dress with its wide white collar, she was hollow-cheeked and regal, the gentle classical face cupped with bonnet and scrubbed shiny with soap, her sleek platinum hair twisted into a staid coil, the hands primly clasped. With demure mouth and freckles on her nose, she looked about as wholesome and plain as the Sunday School teacher she coincidentally was, and no more likely to be stepmother to this Boy than her own daughter might. There could be no more than seven slight years between them, and to Matthew she looked as easily related to the Boy in wifely capacity as she had been to his father.

The two said not a word. But the Boy's eyes traveled, and Katherine's cheeks turned pink. For a moment he looked innocently astounded, quizzically so. The look was no sooner there than it was guardedly gone, and Matthew detected a faint skepticism, as though the novelty of old-fashioned dress was hard to believe. And in this day and age of immodest attire, maybe it was.

"Son," he muttered lamely, "I . . . I don't guess thee ever did meet thy stepmother?"

"No, sir. I don't guess I ever did."

Matthew cleared his throat uncomfortably. He tugged at his moustache. "Well this is she, son. This is Katherine. Katherine meet Tom. I . . . I mean . . ."

"Than," the Boy said. His fair brows drew together and he stood staring so hard it was embarrassing. "Pleased to meet you, ma'am."

He touched the back of his head and a signet ring glinted gold on his index finger; a silver identity bracelet fell from his cuff. He was full of small touches of elegance and bravado; little flashes of wealth, like a mine veined with its ore. Matthew didn't know whether to be antagonized or impressed; his cautious mistrust of physical comeliness extended, Quakerwise, to material show. The Boy waited. Matthew pursed his mouth and fidgeted. Katherine could not talk. She was devastated and unable to smile. Her slender fingers twisted the plain gold band on her left hand. A frivolous breeze played with her skirt; it worried Matthew's ears and whipped gold-streaked hair across the Boy's tanned brow. Finally she nodded, forcing out words, trying to smile.

"H-how art thee, Than?"

"I'm fine."

They did not touch hands or kiss. Neither smiled. Both kept their own proud counsel. The Boy frowned. Perhaps he had heard the dread in her voice or noticed the tears in her eyes. For now there was a caution in his own and he watched her trembling mouth.

"Kathy," he said, "how is my father?"

She convulsed then, eyes shut tight and mouth clamped against pent sobs. Matthew gave her an awkward arm and stood bolted like rock while she regained herself.

"Thee're too late," Katherine whispered at last. "I'm so sorry." As if it were some fault of her own. "Thy father died seven days ago . . ."

The Boy did not move.

Than didn't know how long he stood there, but for a certain phase of time nothing registered very clearly. He felt the sun strike warm on his back, and somewhere far off a kaffir dog barked. Some natives, walking on the edge of the airfield, were talking, their hands animatedly moving. Beside the lonely gas pumps, inside the jackal-fenced enclosure, the pilot laughed with the town's nursing sister, who had come to open the gates; the sound carried on the wind that filled the fluttering air-sock. The warm bright world receded, dim and distantly heard, and numbed with shock, he stood like a man entranced on that tiny no-account airfield in the heart of Central Africa. He might have stayed that way forever if the old man had not come up and touched him with stiff arthritic fingers, jolting him from his daze.

"Come along, son," Professor Tomlinson croaked. "There's some things that can never be undone, and it's a long ways home."

This was Northern Rhodesia, October 7, 1958 . . .

In a gray hard-topped Land-Rover they left the small civilization of Solwezi far behind, traveling over three hundred miles into the great North Western province. At the tsetse-fly barrier, a bored black attendant sprayed their vehicle with astringent-smelling insecticide before they turned off the main road, passing a dust-trailing dilapidated truck and odd lonely cyclists on corrugated roads and precarious bridges that deteriorated as they went. The sullen, sunburned bush was probably more trees than the disconsolate Boy had seen in his life. The drab drought-stricken foliage smoldered of dust and decay; the dryness of it stung the nostrils, and in the still razing heat it looked deserted of life. But vultures wheeled in the whitened skies and half-naked natives stoically stared from mud-and-thatch villages that broke the monotony of the interminable trees. These were the Lunda of Mwinilunga, a proud matrilineal tribe of hunters and farmers, whose local chief, the Catholic-converted Kadesha, remained politely impervious to the Quaker ideology practiced in his area.

Matthew's back ached as he drove along the familiar weed-fringed twin strips of dirt track that bumped endlessly northward. In the closed cab, the Boy coughed rackingly on the filtered dust as he chain-smoked and scratched irritably at sweat-crawled flesh. With flashes of inspiration, Matthew made pertinent remarks that came out lame and achieved no reply. The Boy was broodily silent. Katherine sat dull-eyed and sleepy-mouthed between them. She fanned her flushed face with a handkerchief, sneezing regularly in the stiffling atmosphere. Matthew said, "Bless thee" each time. The Boy said, *"Gesundheit,"* absently once. They all listlessly stared. It was the peak of the dry season and the gloom of death hung over them like a pall as they passed through a country that was dry, dead, and dying in the dismal ravages of October heat.

In the dense desolate bush near the Congo border, the mission lay in the shallow lap of a river valley. In the soft twilight, its rambling thatch bungalows loomed gracious and tropical, edged with bamboo and banana and bright spilling splashes of bougainvillea, scarlet and mauve. The little tree-shrouded river that snaked through its midst was straddled by a wide concrete span and a swaying rope bridge moored to bark-bumped borassus palms standing high up its steep banks. Barking dogs followed the Land-Rover around the deserted building of the boys' primary school, and at the edge of the playing field they skirted the thorn tree wherein was wedged the mission's old ship's bell—legacy of the Nantucket Quakers who had docked their whalers at the Cape of Good Hope. Beyond the Bible institute and the old printing shop, Matthew drove up the slope toward the row of brick houses that held back the bush. He pulled up before the overgrown garden of a double-storied edifice that was the mission's most ambitious abode.

In the sudden silence, the company climbed stiffly out of the cab. From here the view was panoramic. The river sent up the smells of sun-warmed mud and rotting vegetation. Fish eagles made wild lonely cries along the ribbon of black water. Across it, they heard the lonely bush sound of a generator starting up, and as they watched, the long, low hospital buildings blinked with sallow light. The mission dogs bounded up to investigate: big lopey hounds, excited and friendly, they surrounded the tall stranger, sniffing him shamelessly in the crotch. The Boy pushed them off, disaspassionately smoking. His skin was glistening with sweat and creased with dust; a fine blond stubble had started on his jaw. His collar was unbuttoned and his tie pulled awry.

Kathy hurried off to call Godwin the houseboy, but Matthew, realizing the full significance of the moment, remained beside the Boy. As his tired eyes roved the placid scene, he was suddenly saddened, for he knew what the Boy might see. There was the soiled whitewash, the threadbare thatch, and the rust on the raised iron tanks that held water pumped from the river's flow. The simple architecture was oddly assorted and awkwardly executed. He would see the dirt and the dust and the dim decay, but he would not see the pain and achievement that had manifested within the mission's worn mud walls. Yet, like a good Quaker woman, there was dignity and charm in its austere mein. It seemed to rise with kindly reproach, with a yearning to be accepted and understood. Matthew's breast was flooded with familiar fondness. But when he turned, he saw that the Boy had not heard the spiritual cry of Suseshi. He had seen it, instead, merely as it was, and as the stumbling block that had lain between a boy and his father for fifteen long years . . .

The Boy relinquished his suitcase to the houseboy and stood staring up at the high house. Following his gaze, Matthew realized with shock that the familiar old building, usually so comfortable, looked actually grotesque, like the caricature of a haunted house. He felt himself prickle slightly. Well, what did the Boy expect anyway? Did he not know that out here in the *bundu* every man was his own builder and jack-of-all-trades? Matthew saw by his face that he did not. He coughed uncomfortably.

"Well, I guess I'd best be getting along back to my own good wife."

"Oh please! Stay awhile for coffee and fellowship." Katherine's startled eyes pleaded. (Could it be that she too was afraid of the Boy and his broody silence?) Trapped to the ordeal, Matthew followed the pair onto the cool red-polished veranda and through the screened front door.

"Jayne?" Katherine called in the thin voice of forced cheeriness. "Tom? We're home!"

The silence came back at her like a slap in the face. She untied her bonnet, patting her platinum hair, anxious as a mother hen. "They'll be here someplace. Don't worry. I guess they're just shy."

But the Boy wasn't worried at all. He stepped into that big homey parlor, indifferently staring, looking so out of place, it was disturbing. Matthew shivered slightly. Why, the young doctor had the kind of magnetism that might send a witching stick berserk. It discomforted him acutely, and he had the awful feeling that the old mahogany bureau and the oval oak table might wilt and disappear as the Boy dispassionately stared, eyes lingering on the great kudu horns and the early American clock mounted on the walls. Though the red concrete floor shone with polish, the rugs were threadbare and the faded floral cushions on the native-made settee and chairs, limp and shabby. But Katherine had a feminine flair for framed motifs and flancy flipperies, and in the generator-fed electric light, the big, tastefully arranged living room was clean-swept and uncommonly tidy for a missionary abode. And there was a touch of finesse—company had brought out lace cloths and an artistic arrangement of bull-rushes and berries. Death had set an old framed photograph of Tom on the mantle. Children, with coffee cups and reading books, had spread a little daily disorder. It was the one small homey touch that rescued the house from the complete unhappy aura of strangers and death.

They heard the screened back door slam, and when they turned, Tom junior emerged from the big dark kitchen. A freckle-faced, tawny-haired ten-year-old, he wore an old T-shirt, blue jeans, and a soft gray bush baby like a fur muff around his neck. Katherine let out her breath.

"Tom honey—this is thy brother, Than."

The small boy stared, frowning uncertainly. *This was his brother?* Matthew thought he knew the feeling. Why, even that big-eyed bush baby looked amazed.

The stranger said cautiously, "Which one of you's Tom?"

An involuntary smile started on the small boy's face. Matthew felt the same flooding pleasure, and the tension at last began to dissipate.

"I'm Tom, and this here is Jasper." The child indicated the little raccoonlike African lemur clinging to his shoulders with tiny black hands.

"How do, Tom." They shook hands solemnly. "How do, Jasper?"

Tom smiled shyly, but the bush baby took fright at the stranger's offered hand. It scrambled down its host's shirt, settling around his middle. Tom frowned apologetically. "He's pretty careful of strangers."

The Boy nodded knowingly. "In this world, maybe you have to be."

"Tom, where's thy sister?" Katherine hung her cotton bonnet on the old brass coat rack on the wall.

"Upstairs, Ma." Tom glanced up the dim old, wood-banistered stairway. "Why, here she is now. Come on down, Jayne. Brother's arrived!"

And there she stood at the top of the stairs, a tall little girl turned sullen with grief. She wore a faded checked shirt and ragged denim bermuda shorts. At thirteen, she was an angel-faced child, good and graceful, but, Matthew thought dourly, a little too old to be still running around dressed like a tomboy.

"Come on down," Katherine encouraged softly. "Thy brother's waiting to meet thee, dear."

"He's not my brother," the child said coldly.

Matthew closed his eyes, appalled, and they all stood a moment in the aftershock.

"Well, dearest," Katherine spluttered finally, "a half's nothing to argue about. Come on down and join us, honey."

Jayne came hesitantly down the long stairway, her slight form losing its ethereal look in the reaching light. She had straight silvery-blond hair that fell below her waist, wide guileless eyes, and pale skin the color and glow of purest honey. Her flushed cheeks were lacquered with dried tears, and she stopped halfway down, wriggling her bare toes on a step, thumbs tucked into her hip pockets as she faced the tall stranger, arrogant and contesting, a pint-sized bravado with spitfire in her eyes.

The Boy brought down his shoulder-slung jacket and stared silently back. They both were spellbound by this unexpected stumbling upon another self. For they were as alike as two peas in a pod.

The inherited genes of their respective mothers were barely represented in either of them, and the common blood of their mutual father had molded them in striking similarity. They had the same high cheekbones and soft sullen mouth; she stared back at the Boy from the same defiant eyes.

"Well, aren't thee going to say hello, Honey?" Katherine coaxed gently. "Than has come a long way to be with us in our time of sorrow."

"Yes, Momma." Jayne swallowed. Then she lifted her chin, fair brows haughtily raised, and let the Boy know of the bitterness in her heart with the worst insult she could think of paying him.

"Pleased to meet thee, Dr. Profane," she said with the icy formality of a scornful stranger.

The Boy closed his eyes. *Was this the feeling he had fostered?*

Standing stunned in the silence, Matthew shared his sense of shock.

The dinner drum saved them all. After Than had resisted Katherine's polite persuasions to take supper, claiming no appetite and need of a bath, the old man and she and her small brood left without him. Freed at last from the oppressing demands of strangers and sorrow, Than's first thought was to get out of the house, to be alone in the cool darkness. Two of the mission dogs, a Rhodesian ridgeback and a rib-sprung kaffir hound, followed him down the dark slope to the old brick meeting house. Beyond it, naturally enough, lay a little graveyard enclosed by fir trees. In the dusky moonlight Than had no trouble finding his father's last resting place; it was the only grave without a large stone cross. Crouching before the mound of newly turned earth, he thought of his mother's grave in San Francisco. Beside it was the unmarked plot where his father was supposed to have lain in last reunion with her. But hell, Suseshi was some far cry from that grand American cemetery, and anyway, the man had died committed to a different woman.

Than picked up a clod of earth and crushed it in his fist. He had been twelve years old when he had said good-bye to his father at the big windy San Francisco airport. "Son, you stay here and study hard and one day you'll be a great doctor and a credit to your mother and me." His father had hugged him fiercely, and then Than, so recently bereft of a mother, had watched his father walk out of his life as well. The man never had come back. And he hadn't grieved for long either. Just nine months later, Than received the shattering letter telling him that his father, who had so mourned his mother he had to go off to Africa to find something new to live for, had up and married a twenty-year-old missionary, a mere girl, little more than seven years older than Than himself. And his father a grand old man of forty.

Filled with staunch loyalty to a mother he had deeply loved, Than had been outraged and disgusted. Though his father tried with gentleness and patience to reconcile him to the idea of grief losing its sting and a man growing lonely, he remained stonily unmoved. On his grandfather's insistence, he answered his father's letters, but his replies were always stereotyped and coldly formal. Much of Tom Profane's news necessarily concerned his new family, and that, slowly but surely, had hardened Than's heart till he was left with nothing more than defensive indifference. Other missionaries on furlough, or on completing tours of duty, had called to bring him his father's salutations over the years. But the good man himself, for many years the only doctor at Suseshi, had continually deferred his own respite, and the prolonged separation had compounded their conflict. Sure the old man had never stopped writing, but that wasn't enough. Maybe Than had become a fine physician, but his father hadn't waited around to watch him do it. And latterly, increasingly preoccupied with his own hectic life, the intervals between Than's infrequent letters grew gradually longer. He hadn't written for over a year when the telegram informing him of his father's critical illness brought him down to earth with a jolt. And that had been the beginning of the change in him. Suddenly, after all that time, he cared again. He had no wish to lose a father he had ceased to need. He had no wish to have the needless state indulged.

Oh God, don't let him die!

But he had. And the cold hand of death had a way of making old grudges come home to roost. Now he suddenly saw the whole unhappy affair for the human thing it had been. All those long lonely years he had been nothing but an insecure broody boy, all eaten up with an unwarranted adolescent jealousy and hate. And the worst of it was that he had learned too late. Now there could be no reconciliation with the man he had wronged, and the sadness of it all clung like a burr to his heart. Aching with frustrated feeling, he threw down the fistful of earth. "I'll make it up to you, Dad," he vowed softly, fervently, closing his eyes. "I'll take care of them for you. That's what I'll do. I'll see them through . . ."

2   When the first light began to glow through the curtains, Than awoke to the persistent throbbing call of a ground hornbill. In the dim musty-smelling room he shared with Tom, he found himself fully clothed on a narrow iron bed that his feet overlapped by a good few inches. Someone had removed his shoes and covered him with a quilt. He ripped aside the soft white cowl of a mosquito net and climbed stiffly out of bed. On another bed, his young half-brother lay asleep in the dimness, shaggy-haired as an English sheep dog, freckled nose twitching. Than watched him a moment, then stumbled through the french doors and out onto a crooked little balcony that served both bedrooms of the house. Under a dilapidated wooden awning that sagged with brilliant arms of scarlet bougainvillea, he lit a cigarette and watched the sun rise over Africa. Taking distinction from the shadows, the rustic little settlement emerged majestic and aspiring with willowy palms, spears of sisal, and sprays of frangipani, which burst into starry blossoms at his feet. The missionaries were early risers, and he heard the muted sounds of the household coming to life; the houseboys were up in the cool smoky dawn, lighting fires in the open-chimneyed Rhodesian water boilers in the yards. Along the river, fish eagles had begun their plaintive crying, and from the mission village, the wails of native children forlornly hailed the new day.

Than bumped into Katherine on the landing. Already dressed in her prim long dress and a shawl, she looked surprised to see him.

"Why, good morning to thee, Than. Thee're up early. Yesterday thee looked so tired I thought sure thee'd go into hibernation for a while."

"Thanks for taking care of me." Than started down the stairs beside her. "I guess I dropped off before I meant to."

"Oh, that was no trouble. Afraid the bed is a little short, though; and does thee always sleep with thy pillow over thy head that way?" She chuckled. "Anyway, I'm sure glad thee're up. I dreaded having to wake thee for meeting."

"Meeting?" Than frowned, ducking under a low crossbeam. "I thought today was Saturday."

"Well, it's Saturday all right—or Seventh-day, as we prefer to numerically label it in the old Quaker idiom. But the fact is, out here we hold meeting every morning, mainly for the illiterate villagers, who cannot daily consult their own Bibles. And since the natives have no understanding of silent contemplation as we know it, we sing hymns and preach sermon. We even employ a paid African pastor to help with organizational work. And this morning, in conjunction with thy coming, we are conducting a meeting of thanksgiving for thy father."

"Yes," Than said softly. He went back upstairs to fetch his good suit. Down in the little bathroom, he peeled off his creased sweat-smelling clothing and lowered himself, wincing, into the tepid mud-colored water that filled the narrow confines of the rust-stained, claw-and-ball tub. The mission bell was pealing as he finished shaving, and he pulled on his shirt and walked out into the living room, knotting his tie. The little family stood up immediately, ready and waiting. Tom smiled bashfully, and Jayne, transformed in a long lace-edged pink satin dress with a pink-ribboned bonnet on her head, ducked out of his way. Than strolled to meeting between Katherine and Tom while his haughty young half-sister hurried on ahead. He watched the unconscious female waggle of her bottom as she walked.

They were greeted by the murmurous voices of hundreds of Africans massed around the big thatched meeting house in the early sunshine. In their midst stood a small knot of Europeans, looking queerly white in the milling black throng. The Religious Society of Friends. Than stared in disbelief, struggling to shake off the disquieting feeling that he had stumbled upon a lost civilization, a time-forgotten romantic little world. In the old-fashioned modesty of traditional dress, craning necks to peer at him, they loomed quaint and quizzical. The men wore their hair fairly long, in hacked-off uneven styles that proclaimed theirs a barberless society. The women had made small concessions to the tropical climate with sleeveless bodices and thonged sandals. Earthy and wholesome with unshaven armpits and soap-shiny faces, they gazed at him from their bristling bonnets with a kind of other-world religious ecstasy that chilled his blood. A few of their faces and many of their names were familiar to him from their furlough visits or his father's letters. Now, clamoring to meet him, they clung to his hand.

"Thy father was a find Friend . . . Quaker of the highest order . . . a true disciple of Jesus . . ."

Than stared at them dumbly. He could feel nothing but an aching and bewildering sense of futility. Because he had never seen his father in this setting, he could not fully grasp the loss.

"I can't tell thee how much we'll miss thy father at the hospital."

Than turned to find a sandy-haired, gravely smiling man whose green eyes twinkled with empathy. He felt the smooth confident hand of a fellow surgeon. "I'm Dr. Jerome Dooley. Thy father was one of the finest doctors I ever worked with. Here, meet my wife, Grace."

Than was accosted by a robust, red-haired, and vastly pregnant woman who smiled at him through tears and freckles and hugged him warmly over the hard hump of her stomach. Next he met Lars and Ingrid Wikstrom, a tall young Swedish brother and sister who taught school and nursed at the mission. Denise Smith was a mousy, freckle-faced South African nurse who ran a nurse-aide training course. The Cathcarts he had already met in the States; they taught at Suseshi's two primary schools and were directors of the mission's large orphanage, which they ran with the help of the Misses Hannah Rothchild and Cherish Sinclair, two prim spinsters who blushed at the clasp of Than's hand. Ward Disney was the road maker and trade-school manager, a widower left with two young sons who helped him in his work. The esteemed Quaker evangelist Ezra Peabody turned out to be a balding pompous gentleman, resplendently dressed, who airily inquired if Than had had occasion to read any of his articles presently enjoying worldwide respect in Quaker journals.

Than was glad when Professor Tomlinson, grandly awkward in a bootlace bow tie and threadbare Prince Edward–suit, drew him away from the missionaries' clamoring questions. He began edging Than through the jostling black crowd, introducing him to teachers, headmen, and meeting elders. The unfamiliar African names bounced off Than's confused brain the minute he heard them. And their condolences were another embarrassment.

"I am very compassionate to see thy father he is dying. . . . My heart she is crying for my lovely father. . . . My *baba* he has gone to the Jesu . . ."

The bizarre and passionate wording made Than rankle with guilt. He had the hysterical desire to laugh. For they were saying they had all known and loved a man better than his own firstborn son.

Crowding inside the dim, high, musty-smelling meeting house, the mass of raggedly dressed Africans overflowed the open doors to line the long verandas. In the confined space, the stench of their sweat-stale bodies was overpowering, and they coughed and spat and blew their noses. Grizzling babies were loudly admonished; two mangy dogs meandered the aisles and scrawny chickens strutted in and out, scratching and squawking. It all seemed a fiasco of a Quaker meeting, but according to Katherine, many of these poor primitive people had arisen before dawn and walked many miles in their bare feet to honor his father's memory here today.

The congregation was strictly segregated according to sex, males and females sitting separated in long lines of pews on opposite sides of the meeting house. And in the center of the throng, in the uniquely Quaker square formed by the four facing benches ranging in from the four walls, the missionaries, too, were likewise divided. Than found himself sandwiched between Tom and Dr. Dooley; across from him, he noticed Jayne next to Katherine, staring aloofly down her fine little nose. They were all little more than strangers to him, and he felt alone in the cloying crowd, isolated in his own sense of unreality.

On the elders' bench, Professor Tomlinson sat in erect dignity in his shabby frock coat; the white-haired old gentleman had a look of serenity as if here at last was a place where he felt at home. The congregation fell gradually to a respectful hush as he rose to speak. His gruff, kindly voice rose and creaked like an old ship on high seas as he alternated an eloquent English with Chi-Lunda spoken like a native. Finally Teller, his plump bespectacled little wife, started up the thin asthmatic wail of an ancient Estey organ. Prayer books were creased open and a host of crude voices rose around Than, fervent and sincere, surging with an inborn harmony that raised gooseflesh on his arms. It was something to hear after all: a thousand earnest Africans singing the Chi-Lunda version of his father's favorite hymn, "Abide With Me."

After a small eternity the moving meeting, lauding the life and work of Thomas Elderwood Profane, was finally over. Outside, obeying the rumbling breakfast drum, the missionaries walked across to the small communal dining hut that sat high on the river bank. The rectangular little *chitenje* was nothing more than a pole-pillared open hut with an entrance at each end; roofed with thatch, its crumbling concrete floor was enclosed with a low wall of bamboo sticks. It was furnished with a long central table and benches, an ancient chesterfield sideboard, a vibrating paraffin refrigerator, and a tall, fly-screened safe, stacked with eggs and fresh vegetables. To combat termites, the destructive "white ants" of Africa, every stick of furniture stood with its wooden legs immersed in rusted cans of water, some of which still bore the tattered labels of their previous contents.

Boisterous as a watering herd, the missionaries settled into their seats around the long set table. Professor Tomlinson and Ezra Peabody sat in privileged positions on chairs at either end. The white-capped and aproned cook boy and his disdained assistant scurried around with steaming platters of fried ham and eggs, and Than felt suddenly ravenous. As the missionaries bowed their heads in silent grace, his stomach ached emptily. When he looked up he noticed that a place set next to Katherine was unoccupied. And it struck him: his half-sister, Jayne, was missing.

After breakfast, back at the house, Katherine and Tom sat with Than on wicker chairs out on the veranda. They plied him with cool drinks, coffee, and comfort, and with the help of dim old snapshots, brought him gently up to date on his father's life during their years of separation. Jayne was conspicuous by her absence, and when Than came upon her after lunch, she was up a frangipani tree in the garden. The enforced finery of her meeting dress was hitched up around her thighs, her long golden legs hanging from the bough like some delectable fruit. Reacting instinctively, Than stopped, hands at his hips, and issued a long low animal growl of sensual appreciation. Jayne's legs curled up in a trice; she pulled down her long skirt and glared at him, patently furious at his insolent breach of bereaved solemnity. All that long day, they exchanged no civil word.

With tsetse fly rife in the area, it was impractical to keep cattle and the missionaries subsisted on Klim powdered milk and salt meat ordered from the Solwezi general store or the Copperbelt. They enjoyed an occasional bag of venison supplied by Boniface, the unreliable old mission hunter, who was one of approximately fifty Africans employed by the missionaries to fill positions from the mission-paid pastor, and the houseboys, garden boys, and nursemaids, to the government-paid teachers, nurses, and orderlies. White doctors received monthly grants from the government, but the white nurses and teachers had to rely on small subsidies they received from the mission board.

The missionaries seemed to Than a people of childlike spiritual faith; all afire with enthusiasm for their work, they smiled blissfully, were given to feeble joking, and laughed at their hardships with a lusty courage. He felt something of a misfit among them. It was taking him all his time to settle down to the strange circumstance of a father demised and a new family acquired, but they seemed to have no understanding of his need to be alone and flocked to entertain him. With tight-lipped pride, they showed him the boys' and girls' primary schools, the trade school, the Bible institute, and the printing shop. They conducted him around the citrus orchard, the vegetable gardens, and the chicken run. Lars Wikstrom rushed him down to view a huge bull hippo that wallowed in a muddy pool downriver. Teller Tomlinson, who supervised the culinary department, had the chef bake tasty cookies and honey-dripping flapjacks to tempt his appetite, and the kitchen boys vied to give him the choicest scraps of meat and vegetables.

He knew that they all saw him in his father's shining light, as a living extension of that great man, given them as a gift, and their sympathy for a grief he could not feel increased his sense of guilt. By nature he was a solitary man, happiest when alone. In times of trial words of comfort were meaningless to him, and their smiles of solace and patronizing pats he had to brace himself to endure. For days he steered clear of the hospital. Despite anxious invitations to view its "well-equipped" interior and wealth of patients, he made endless excuses not to cross the bridge to its vicinity. Within its humble brick walls he would find the real spiritual substance of his father's dedication, and like a small boy balking at a corpse, he was afraid to view the final remedy of his father's life.

But out of the solemn vow of obligation to his father's memory a feeling of genuine concern began to grow within him. Every day bound him closer to his newly acquired family. In their humble way, they bared themselves to him, and he watched them in the simple act of living and worried for a future less kind. But what did a man do with a wayward little family happily thriving in the back of beyond? He wished he could simply hand them over to some benevolent organization and pay for their keep, but family responsibility went deeper than that. In his mind it had something to do with giving guidance and direction, with shouldering and sharing troubles, with cherishing and protecting its female and minor members. And this was not just any family. This was his own. Well, he had sworn to take care of them, and he would. But sending them money every month would not be enough. No! He had thought about it and the solution was obvious.

To him, there was no other choice. In six weeks' time they

would have to pack up their humble goods and chattels and return with him to America.

3 When Than had been at the mission a week, Katherine went back to her teaching at the girls' primary school, over which she presided as headmistress. Jayne resumed her private tuition with Professor Tomlinson, and Tom went back to Sakeji, a little boarding school for missionary children near the Congo border. The loneliness of the big house was soothing to Than at first. But after a while the emptiness ached, and at three o'clock, in the sultry heat of the afternoon, he sauntered across the rope bridge to the hospital. He had to stumble across human lines to reach it. In the scorching sun its dry grass yard teemed with the fly-speckled, broken, and diseased children of Africa.

They were a depressing sight, but the sprawling white building was like home to Than. On the first cool veranda the sterile scents of ether and antiseptic filled his lungs like balm. As he cautiously walked the strange corridors, patients and staff alike crammed to the windows to watch him pass. In no time at all the whole hospital was informed of his coming, and he was regaled like his father reincarnate. Dr. Dooley approached with a lopsided grin. He was followed by the Swedish nurse, Ingrid Wikstrom, who strode up, stiffly smiling, nunlike and archaic in a long white Florence Nightingale dress and stiffly starched veil. They were joined by the like-clad Denise Smith and Grace Dooley, whose long white smock was strained to bursting over her enormous pregnant stomach. They crowded around Than grinning foolishly, excited as children.

"We thought thee were never coming!" Grace chuckled throatily. "Jerome's just about eaten up with impatience to show thee around. And he's just about as narrow-sighted as a proud father; he doesn't believe there can be another hospital like Suseshi in this whole wide world!"

And there probably was not. Suseshi Hospital, like most of the mission's recruits, seemed a throwback to ancient times. Almost everything was improvised, antiquated, or in short supply. Furnishings were basic, instruments rudimentary, and everywhere Than looked, dilapidated old mingled with modern addition. Those ap-

31

pliances not powered by the sparingly used generator were operated by hand or paraffin combustion. In the little operating room, the overhead lights shone down homemade cardboard cones lined with silver paper. Instead of cat gut, suturing was done with ordinary sewing thread, and injection needles, a scarce commodity, were sterilized, resharpened, and used innumerable times.

The highly polished red concrete floors shone. Male dressers scurried about on quiet errands. Nurses stood sentry over the long wards. Newly added wings embraced part of the big grassy yard, which was crisscrossed with sheltered walkways. Besides the main wards there were separate rooms for patients with tuberculosis and other infectious diseases. A hut was used for the leper clinic. There was a small kitchen, a dispensary, a large laboratory, and tucked away behind a gloomy old mortuary was an incinerator stack that rose like a factory chimney. And just off the laboratory was a dim little room, clustered with cleaning equipment and a brand new sink, slung with cobwebs.

"This," Dooley announced proudly, "is our X-ray room."

"So where's the machine?" Than said dryly.

Jerome sighed. "Well, we're still waiting for the funds to buy one. An old friend of mine in the States is president of a chemical company. Two years ago his firm agreed to donate four thousand dollars annually to Suseshi, a sum that would do very nicely. Unfortunately, each time the grant has come up, the other committee members have found dozens of 'more important' things that need attending to. But we're hoping that *next year* . . ."

Than frowned. "I'm kind of hard put to understand just what could be more important than an X-ray machine!"

Jerome shrugged. "Well, I'm not the one who decides those things around here. If I had my way, we'd use every spare penny for the hospital. We need more dressing trolleys, obstetric tables, a vacuum extractor and oxygen and resuscitation equipment . . ."

And in the wards, the 210 white steel beds were not nearly enough.

"Only the most urgent cases can be admitted," Jerome explained. "And even then, at the expense of some other poor fellow who's hardly recovered. It's unwise, of course, and in some cases downright dangerous. But what can we do? Those we can't admit or keep for a suitable period we treat as outpatients. Unfortunately, the African is notoriously unreliable when it comes to the regulated consumption of medicine. If they didn't report regularly for small doses,

Lord knows how many might expire from overdose or profit from the sale of their medicines to some other credulous fellow."

There was no incubator for premature babies, and in a small room several of the tiny creatures lay swaddled in baskets, warmed with hot-water bottles, and fed through eye-droppers by nurse-aides. In the maternity ward itself, the newly born lay in baskets beside mothers who must evacuate their beds and trudge home through the bush a short day or two after birth. At the postnatal clinic, some of the new mothers brought their placentas for the nurse to inspect, to rule out the risk of puerperal fever in these unsupervised bush deliveries.

In the children's ward it was toilet time, and two long lines of over fifty small black children sat with white nightgowns hitched up, perched atop stout white enamel chamber pots. Than couldn't help but smile at the rows of little brown bottoms and small solemn faces, all earnest with effort. But some of the children lay fitfully sleeping or silently staring through the white bars of the cots that encaged them.

"Take a look at this little fella." Jerome stopped beside one. The baby, clad only in a diaper, lay listlessly staring. Its scant hair was reddish and straight. Its grayish skin was flaking, and it looked deceptively fat. Through brownishly discolored eyes, it gazed at them apathetically. Than reached down and took hold of the baby's leg. He gently pressed against the plumpened skin and at once the child began to thrash and squall. Than let go. He stared down at the deep indentation left by his fingers.

"Kwashiorkor," he said softly. "Jesus Christ, I've never seen a case of Johnny Red this bad."

Dooley smiled cynically. "This is Africa, Friend. I guess thee'll see many things here thee never saw before . . ."

And he did. What Dooley had crammed into the wards was enough to excite the most seasoned old medic. There was an abundance of exotic tropical diseases; one man lay dying of trypanosomiasis, the dreaded sleeping sickness caused by tsetse fly. Another was grossly swollen, in the advanced stages of elephantiasis. Than was awestruck. He borrowed Dooley's stethoscope and examined dozens of disease-ridden bodies, poring over record charts while his mind ticked over with a thousand theories and plans of action.

Grace Dooley and Denise Smith joined them for a coffee break in the untidy community-cum storeroom. The two freckle-faced nurses stared at Than eagerly.

"So what does thee think of our hospital, Doctor?"

Than set down his coffee cup. "Oh, it's a bit primitive maybe, but the raw material is just beautiful. I can't wait to get started."

The words were out before he could take stock of them. They stared at him incredulously, and he smiled, red-faced, embarrassed by their dawning delight. "Well, I don't exactly have official permission to practice medicine in this country, but time'll be hanging pretty heavily on my hands for the next six weeks—if you'd dare have me."

"*Dare to have thee?*" Jerome hooted. "We'd hold thee prisoner if thee refused. And listen, don't worry about official permission. Thee'd have to apply to be put on the medical register in Salisbury, and thee'd be ready to leave by the time it was granted. So it's not worth worrying about. Out here in the *bundu*, no jasper will be any the wiser, and the medical officer's pretty satisfied we run a responsible show here. Oh, he drops in from time to time to keep us on our toes, and he's a real stickler for doing all things by the book. But if he should show up, just stick thy hands behind thy back and imitate an interested observer. Chances are he won't even notice thee."

The next day they gave Than his father's stethoscope and ophthalmoscope and he picked up a freshly laundered white jacket. This too had belonged to his father; it was tight across the shoulders and short on him. He had outgrown the old man yet. And as he walked down the long fly-screened corridors, the feeling, uncannily, was of walking in his father's footsteps.

4

That first strange day at the hospital, the staggering number of patients was a grim reflection of the nation's suffering. From a cool concrete office, sparsely furnished with a desk, filing cabinet, scales, and a cubicled couch, Than opened his door to find all ailing Africa lining up along the veranda. Arming himself with an antiquated set of instruments and a sketchy debriefing of the most common tropical diseases, Jerome had left him Jeremiah, a gray-haired old dresser, to act as his assistant, interpreter, and record keeper. With a grieving face that was lined and worn with the wages of Africa, Jeremiah led into the office company after company of patients and accompanying relatives who came to challenge and confound Than with strange dialects, alien ills, and intractable bodies adorned with curious charms, skin-imbedded needles, and the festering cuts of the infamous *ngakas*, the prolific medicine men of Africa. With irises so dark it was difficult to detect dilation of their pupils, they all seemed beset by bewildering underlying chills and fevers, all pointing to any number of endemic syndromes.

There were malaria (apparently so common that every patient admitted was automatically treated for it), leprosy, hookworm, amoebic dysentery, relapsing fever, trypanosomiasis, and bilharzia, a parasitic water-snail-borne disease that affected the bladder. However, by far the majority of cases were young children afflicted with the more commonplace tonsilitis, bronchitis, pneumonia, and gastroenteritis. The misery of these pitiful waifs was compounded by malnourishment and neglect. Their continual crying sawed at Than's nerves, and as the day progressed, he was interrupted by the black laboratory dispenser who was forever bursting apologetically into his office to explain that they did not stock some medication or other that he had prescribed. Finally the dispenser compiled a list of the hospital's pharmacopoeia to aid him through the irksome day. Than found some of the most common modern British drugs mingled with a quaint collection of old-fashioned salves that would be at home in any Victorian apothecary. He was puzzling perplexedly at the list when Dr. Dooley swept into his office, cheerfully complaining.

"Hey, kid, I know thee've got first day enthusiasm, but thee've got to stop admitting patients. We'll soon be out of beds. Why don't thee just have them all wait till day's end, then select the more urgent cases? Thee'll soon get the hang of it."

Than was still wincing at the very idea when he was summoned by an agitated nurse's aide. It seemed Ingrid Wikstrom wanted him over at the obstetrics ward immediately. Than arrived at a run. A trail of blood led to an examination couch, where the Swedish nurse was bending over a fully clothed prone figure. Around her were grouped several nurse's-aide trainees, a bunch of clear-eyed and clueless looking young native girls fresh out of some secondary school in the province. When they parted, he saw blood pooled on the floor beneath the couch and dripping off the sheets. The patient's dress was drenched with it.

"Oh, Doctor, thank heavens!" Ingrid Wikstrom spun around, a syringe in her hand. "This woman had a baby about eight hours ago. She was walking home when it happen. I try now to draw a blood sample for transfusion." She began struggling to hitch the saturated dress over the moaning woman's hips.

"For Chrissakes, use a scissors!" Than snapped. "Looks like she'll float right off that couch in another minute!"

Ingrid paused, aghast. "But, Doctor, it is different here! Dese people are poor. Dis is maybe her only dress!"

"This is also her only life." Than snatched the syringe from her hand. "Cut that cloth or we'll be tending a corpse here!"

"Yes, Doctor." The shabby material fell away under the nurse's shakily snipping scissors. Blood, thick as paint, was redly lurid against the black skin. The woman had turned a sickly gray; she seemed disorientated and panted for breath, trying to sit up, plucking at the sheet, staring at them crazily.

While they set up the transfusion, Ingrid Wikstrom was coldly aloof. Once they got the blood flowing into the patient, there was nothing they could do but wait, and Than took a look through the maternity-ward book. It read like a pathologist's journal of holy horrors. Abnormalities listed in about eighteen percent of the cases. Most of the women had anemia. Their blood counts were between forty to fifty degrees lower than the average American's, and the infant mortality rate was horrifyingly high.

After a while, the woman began to rally, and Than left, instructing that he was to be notified at the slightest deterioration in her condition. As he walked back to his consulting room, periodic streams of spittle flew over the veranda's edge, and a man stood on the steps blowing his nose into pinched fingers. Seeing him coming, the people in line stood up along the veranda to beseech him, ignoring the quiet eulogy of a bespectacled black meeting elder who sat amid them, open Bible in his hands, patiently dispensing the Christian gospel to a captive congregation.

"Bwana!" A frantic woman with a distended pregnant belly and a young baby bound to her back pushed a tiny child into Than's arms. In his office, the nineteen-month-old screaming bundle of swollen belly and matchstick limbs tipped the scales at a pathetic twelve pounds. His dull, flaking partially raw skin, discolored eyeballs, and straight scant reddish hair told Than he was in an advanced stage of malnutrition. Apparently, at eleven months, Tanda had been fed a thin corn gruel so that his younger brother might survive on their mother's meager milk. *Kwashiorkor* means, appropriately, "the rejected child." Than could only guess at the damage that the lack of minerals and protein had done to the liver, bones, and brain. But the outer effects became appallingly obvious as he gently examined the screaming child. Little Tanda was blind and in constant pain. The anguished eyes of the raggedly dressed mother implored the doctor to save her child, but he knew there was very little he could do. As he turned away in despair, there was a commotion from the veranda. Jeremiah hurried in to report that a man was convulsing on the floor and an old woman was wheezing with an asthma attack. Than closed his eyes. Singularly unprepared while all Africa fell ill around him, he felt as insecure as an intern again . . .

The day flew like a blur before Than's eyes. There was not enough time to attend to all of the assembled people by late afternoon, so the remaining ones left to reach home by nightfall. By six-thirty, the kitchen boy wheeled out a trolley bearing steaming bowls of vegetables. These would be served with a main staple, usually provided by the squatter relatives, who had begun walking across the veranda bearing, in cloth-covered dishes, *nshima* and *kapenta*, the ensemble of stiff maize porridge and tiny dried fish comprising the country's national dish. Consuming the messy food with their fingers, some of Than's newly admitted patients smiled at him shyly as the staff entourage passed on their evening rounds.

Outside, in the dusk, they could hear the hippo grunting down-river, and there was the smell of cooking fires from the mission village. Pleasantly exhausted, Than took off his white jacket and walked to the dining hut in the awkward company of Ingrid Wikstrom. There, the edge of Than's welcome had worn off; there was plain pressed-beef and overboiled vegetables for supper. Sitting on the hard communal bench, preoccupied with the events of the day, he ate disinterestedly. Finally, Matthew Tomlinson spoke to him. Than looked up with a start, and it was then that he became aware of Jayne, his rebellious young half-sister. Freckles on her nose and acid in her eyes, she was staring at him with an expression as comprehensible as speech. He was floored for a moment. For it was hatred that he saw in her eyes, full-blown and altogether too adult. It quite took his breath away.

That night, when the children were in bed, Than sat with Katherine out on the cool veranda.

"What's eating her?" he said softly. While the mission generator relentlessly throbbed across the distant darkness, he sensed Katherine stiffening beside him. "I mean, Jayne. She's got a kind of murderous look in her eyes, and something tell me it's for me."

"Oh, Than." Katherine faced him earnestly through the darkness. "Thee should not be offended. Jayne is grieving her daddy pretty badly, is all. She can't sleep most nights, and I've caught her out in the garden, fretting up that frangipani tree of hers. And she's kind of shy and doesn't take naturally to strangers. Not white ones, leastways. But she's happy and natural enough with the natives."

"Sure." He stood up abruptly and began to stalk the veranda. "Kathy, I'd like to take you all home, back to the States with me. To San Francisco. I'll set you up in a little apartment and I'll . . ."

Katherine stood up hastily, spluttering: "Please, Than, say no more. Thee has neither the time nor the money to . . ."

"Kathy, listen to me. Yes I have. I have some money my grandfather left me. And it's what I want to do."

"Than, no. I could not let thee." She stood before him, a plain, soap-smelling school headmistress, little older than himself, her blond hair primly coiled, her breasts rising and falling. "It would not be fair to thee to squander thy money on . . . repatriating the likes of us! Thee need not feel responsible!"

"Responsible? Oh hell, of course I should. You're my family now."

"*Now?*" She chuckled. "We are no more or less thy family now than ever we were. Believe me, dear, we can manage on our own."

"Kathy, Kathy," he sighed. "You're only a woman alone."

She looked up at him. "Is that so bad?"

"I think it is." He turned his back on her and stared out across the dark mission. "And there are the children to think of. Tom must have college later on. It's the least my father did for me. And Jayne . . . well, it's fine you and the professor give her lessons, but she needs school with friends of her own age and race. You leave her out in the *bundu* much longer, and she'll be sprouting a tail and teeth and a ferocious canine appetite!"

"Oh, Than dear," Katherine chuckled indulgently, "thee worries too much. Believe me, I know what is best for the children. When Tom finishes his primary education at Sakeji Mission School, he'll go to boarding school in Southern Rhodesia with the Dooley children. And the professor and I can complete Jayne's education right here. There's no need for them to venture further out into the world. Thee see, the decision has already been made for them. *They have been moved by the Spirit!*"

"*Moved?*" Than turned and stared at her, struggling to shake clear of a terrible numbness that had begun invading his bones.

"Yes," she whispered triumphantly, and in the moment she looked lunatic with her proud love. "They have both had a concern placed upon them by the Lord for the redemption of indigenous Africa!"

Than stared at her, unable to speak.

"They want to be missionaries," she clarified.

And right then his worst fears were realized.

5 As the long hot days wore on, Matthew saw the young doctor every morning, blue-jeaned in meeting, sunburned and solemn, and filled with more energy than seemed proper in this awful heat. He was always carefully courteous and polite. But that was not the whole of it. The Boy was a noble fraud, a husky-voiced heretic who healed the sick but crusaded not for Jesus. Matthew noticed that he smoked excessively and swore only a little less. *Goddamn* fell from his thoughtless mouth a hundred times a day with a wild clamor that set the missionaries' ears buzzing. And he had taken to removing his shirt in the worst of the day's heat, a practice which, didn't everybody know, was against their strict Quaker code of personal modesty! Wearing nothing more around his neck than a silver pendant, he walked in plain sight of all the ladies, his tanned, gleaming torso so well constructed it seemed a sinful excess. Completely naked to well down those narrow hips, his decency was just barely rescued by his raggedy old blue denim Levis, which seemed hardly a dignity to the role of doctor anyway.

And yet doctor he was. From the most humble task to complicated surgery, he had a dedication that ran clear through his stubborn backbone and blazed like match flame in those sulphurous blue eyes. He had developed a particular interest in the kwashiorkor babies, and one seriously ill little boy named Tanda had become a personal cause with him. Due to the lack of protein, very often the digestive systems of these children could no longer tolerate food. They vomited repeatedly and their irritability made them extremely difficult to feed, requiring endless time and patience on the part of the already overworked nursing staff. Thus the Boy had devised a system of first intravenously feeding them the protein-rich plasma, then, when their irritability was reduced enough to make mouth-feeding practicable, he had them fed a mixture of skimmed milk and digestion-aiding chemicals. The babies' lives depended upon their ability to retain this food, and in his anxiety, the Boy rose with the dawn each day to feed little Tanda personally, making like a bovine mother and apparently feeling no loss of prestige in doing so.

And his dedication was tempered with a brilliant prowess. According to Dr. Dooley, the Boy had an ableness with the scalpel and a visionary ambition that stimulated revolution on an amazing scale. Matthew was amused and chagrined. Why, that Johnny-come-lately showing seasoned veterans how it was done! And if the Boy wanted to conquer the world and change old trusted procedures in a single breath, Jerome was sufficiently easygoing to acquiesce.

But to those not connected to the hospital, none of this cut any ice. The older ladies saw only the Boy's grosser points and made shocked prissy mouths, averting their eyes when he came to the supper table only half dressed. But despite their nagging complaints and Matthew's own kneading disquiet, he refused to pass judgment. For the Boy was a visitor and a helpful one at that. Also, and mainly, he was Tom's prodigal son come home to a lost cause.

Maybe the worst disillusionment lay in that. For they had all seen him, with that pretty face, in the evangelical role of a choirboy, all clothed in virginal white vestments and prepared to carry on the good causes where Tom had left off. This had been Matthew's own fond dream, but steadily, as time went by, he saw the Boy tarnish before his very eyes. The goodness and glorification seemed to melt with the heat, until all that remained was a blatantly worldly boy with a virility to his lank strong body to make old men pine and a broody look in his eyes that set the spinster ladies skittering like penned donkeys getting whiff of lion.

And he seemed to hold sacred none of the practices most dear to the missionaries. He daydreamed in meeting, ignored the Bible, and wore a pagan pendant. He made no claims on Jesus. He was immodest and blasphemous. And so plain likable, it was disarming. The audacity of his dimpled smile could lay prostrate the birds right out of the trees, and the cast of his eyes made the prim ladies blush. He was goodness and bad all rolled into one, and each part so outrageous and true-blue that he had them all confused. And he brought a worldliness to the mission that smelled vaguely of brimstone and goosed the valiant flesh. He was turned to a touch by the waywardness of the outer world. And maybe it was a blessing that Tom had never seen his son come home to this. As it was, that good Christian soldier must be turning in his grave.

As sure as the framed slogans on the wall, the Profanes were a devoutly religious family and they never let Than forget it. Every evening, on her mother's orders, Jayne, proud as a martyr, came reluctantly down the dim stairway to join the family as they sat in the parlor together with the houseboy, his bovine wife, and a row of eight ragged little children. At first Than had endured the procedure with as much grace as he could muster. But this evening he had medical problems to ponder. He sat impatiently in contained chagrin while Katherine read a text aloud from the Bible and said a simple prayer over their bowed heads. Then, after a long silent meditation, God and the houseboy were finally dismissed. Than let out his breath, and hand sewing and homework books were brought out. Than went to the bookcase and took out one of his father's thick medical books, an elderly tome on tropical diseases. He leafed quickly through the pages and found the subject he wanted, but his attention kept wandering.

And then he saw it—a big black spider that came from behind the African drum hanging on the wall. It was the size of his palm, with eight striped legs that spread flat when it stopped. Than stood up and slowly approached. Taking up one of the old newspapers untidily stacked on the bookcase, he folded it carelessly and whacked. The spider fell crumpled to a stunned silence. Than turned to find all eyes riveted upon him.

"It was a spider . . ."

"Spider?" Jayne stood up slowly, pushing back her chair, her eyes incredulously wide. "Oh, Momma, he . . ."

She came and stood beside Than, staring in horror at the small crumpled mess on the floor. Her hand flew to her mouth: "*Silas!*" she shrieked. "Oh, Momma, he killed Silas!"

"Silas?" Than stared stupidly.

"Momma, he killed him! He killed him!"

"Jayne honey . . ." Katherine put down her sewing. "Than had no way of knowing."

Than shut his eyes, wincing. "Knowing what, for Chrissakes?"

Katherine stood up quickly. She came and put an arm around her sobbing daughter, turning apologetically to Than. "Don't feel bad. Thee weren't to know. It was a harmless wall spider. They do no harm and much good—eating mosquitoes and the like. The children kind of made a pet of him, is all. He was always there behind the drum, and he just got to be so familiar."

Than stared helplessly down at the crushed spider. He felt all kinds of a monster. "Well," he said wryly, "I guess there's nothing I can do about him now. Those legs need more than just splinting . . ."

"Oooooooh!" Jayne gave a little scream of rage and tore away from her mother's comforting shoulder. She stood glaring at Than through her tears. "Thee think it's funny! *Oh, how could thee?*"

"Jayne, that's enough now!"

"No, it's not, Momma," she screeched. "Thee and Tom—thee both think he's so *wonderful*! Thee've forgotten Poppa! Thee don't even *cry* for him anymore. It's sickening the way thee all . . . *the way thee let him take Poppa's place!*"

Her words fell to a horrified silence.

"Jayne," Katherine struggled weakly, appalled. "That's *enough!*"

But the girl, weeping, was inconsolable. She faced Than accusingly, strings of blond hair in her eyes, her vicious little face streaked with tears and spit and sorrow. *"Thee're a murderer!"* she screamed at him. "I hate thee! I HATE thee! . . ."

It was a shock to them all when Katherine's hand streaked out like the strike of a snake, cutting the words from her daughter's mouth. As the red imprint appeared on her cheek, the girl stood a moment in shocked disbelief.

"Thee struck me," Jayne whispered incredulously. "Oh, Momma, *how could thee!*"

"Jayne." Katherine reached out a hand, but the girl turned from her touch and ran from the room, up the dim stairway. For a long time, Katherine stood staring into space.

"That's the first time . . ." she whispered. "I've never struck her before."

"Jesus." Than shut his eyes.

6   One hot November afternoon a native messenger brought word from a Protestant mission station at Kabompo requesting urgent medical assistance for one of its missionaries, Morgan Humphries. Matthew fetched Than Profane and they left immediately. The road struggled wearily through a vast dusty dying land that stood bleached and arid under the harsh African sun. By early after-

noon, the bush rose dismally over shallow undulating hills; an augur buzzard sat on the dilapidated signpost that pointed the way and they finally found the little station—no more than a cluster of old brick buildings huddled at the foot of a tree-shrouded freak of earth: Eshalakali Hill, a lonely sentinel set in spreading miles of flat bush country. Below it, the ground fell steeply away to a wide-banked river that had shrunk like a starved waif exposing ribs of white sand.

Matthew parked the Land-Rover under a grove of flowering mango trees. In the blinding afternoon sun, in the wind-soughing silence, the mission stood oddly quiet, echoing of doom and dust and forgotten lives. A monstrous blue-headed tree lizard ran diagonally around the trunk of a tall tree; otherwise nothing moved. When the buildings seemed deserted, they started down a stony path that crept a gradual descent to the mission's leper colony, which sat in ideal isolation on a great sheltered shelf gouged out of the headland where the river turned off course.

Comprising a teeming outlay of ramshackle thatch huts, its sheer edge was palisaded with natural rock, and directly below, the river boiled whitely over rocks with a distance-compressed roar. A few birds screeched and flew up at their coming, and as the inmates began to emerge from their huts, Matthew felt himself draw in instinctively. *Lepers*. The People of the Dead. It was an old scourge, ancient as the Bible. He had a frightful vision of criers with hand bells and rattles, warning all comers: *Unclean! Unclean!* and he dogged the Boy's confident footsteps, averting his eyes from their crippling disfigurements, from the bodies eroded with oozing ulcers, from their gray, stained bandages trailing in the dirt, afraid of the surly look of resentment in eyes that were dull with long-suffering.

They found Morgan Humphries busy doling out cassava meal from a giant corrugated-iron storage tank. His skin sagging from lost weight, the big, shaggily bearded Englishman stared at them in mortification.

"My dear fellows, I'm most frightfully sorry to have brought you all this way for nothing. You see, yesterday I had a bad turn and I'm afraid my dresser, Paulson, exaggerated the situation somewhat. It's probably just a cold in the liver and this wretched bleeding pyorrhea. I . . ."

He broke off, panting. They had to help him up the incline, and he emerged a completely broken man, nose and mouth streaming blood and eyes filled with humiliated tears. Matthew waited on a bench on the dusty clinic veranda while the Boy examined the man inside. He stood up anxiously when the Boy finally came out ahead of his patient.

"It's bad," he said bluntly. For he had found the lumps of enlarged lymph nodes in the neck, the groin, and under the armpits; the man's spleen was as hard as a rock. "I've taken a sternal puncture, Matthew. Jesus, it's a grind with a hammer and chisel. But he wants to know the worst. And since we have to stay the night, I might as well examine the bone marrow and the blood slides right here."

Later, at the house, they found Jennifer Solomon, the only other missionary there, seated at the supper table. A dark-haired child with calm blue eyes and a gentle grace, she looked to Matthew barely old enough to be an independent worker. In the awkward company of the somber girl and the gravely ill man, eating watery chicken stew served by a fumbling houseboy, Matthew struggled alone to lift the wilting dyspeptic mood. Only he and the girl conversed at all, and drawing conversation out of the shy child was like trying to draw water from a near-dry well. She was polite and abstracted, forever gazing vaguely off into space. The Boy ignored her completely, behaving simply as though she were not there. And she, by some strange ability, seemed to support this illusion.

The next morning, after spending a good deal of the night examining the blood slides and bone marrow by lantern light, the Boy gave his verdict to Morgan Humphries. Matthew saw by the big Englishman's expression that his deepest fears were confirmed.

"Well, Doctor," he said slowly, "I don't suppose leukemia is the worst thing that ever happened to a man. Jesus Christ died on a cross. Now I must face mine. I expect I have some little time."

The Boy looked up warily. "Some little time, Mr. Humphries. And any modern hospital will make it as comfortable as possible for you. I guess your mission board will send out replacements just as soon as they can."

"No," the man said gruffly. "You don't understand. There can never be any replacements. You see, gentlemen, ironically this mission too is under sentence of death. As you know, of course, this is Chief Mulaisho's area, and that decadent old fool has fiercely resisted Christianity because it would mean the end of his evil ways. As a result, our church and the school and the clinic stand empty day after day, so I suppose the church can hardly be blamed for the decision to sacrifice Eshalakali to our more successful station at Luangwa.

"Unfortunately, the treating of lepers is not considered as important as the saving of souls. And it's been argued that the lepers might be absorbed into the settlement near Solwezi or some other leprosarium in the province. The Weatherbys have already left, and I have been given nine months in which to disband the mission and make arrangements for the colony's dissolution. After that the church's support will officially cease. Now, I have no idea what will become of them . . ."

"That's terrible," Matthew said slowly. He swallowed. "And what of Miss Solomon? What will she do?"

"Well, that's up to her, of course. She originally joined the mission through her local church, and she's only been with us for three months. She's grown to love Eshalakali and it will no doubt grieve her to leave her students, but I think she'd best go back to her father in Luanshya. He's a tradesman on the Roan Antelope copper mine. Her mother's dead. And of course it's totally impossible for her to remain here now. This is no place for a young lady alone . . . and unable to see."

"Unable to see?"

The Boy turned from the window; Matthew saw his own astonishment mirrored in that golden face.

"I'm sorry." Morgan Humphries looked uncomfortable. "Didn't I tell you? In the same car crash that killed her mother, Miss Solomon was injured. A splinter of metal pierced her right temple and passed behind her eyes, apparently irreversibly damaging the optic nerves. As a result, Miss Solomon—Jennifer—is blind."

Matthew stood stunned in the silence that followed; he thought with amazement of the girl's extraordinarily beautiful blue eyes . . .

At Suseshi, Matthew drove across the concrete bridge to the hospital, where the ailing Engishman was transferred to a private room. Grace Dooley came with a cleaning boy to collect the man's belongings, and from across the slope, the elder ladies, with unerring perception, flocked like flies to the open sore of morbid excitement. Simpering commiserations, they peered inquisitively at the young girl who waited in the Land-Rover.

"Welcome to Suseshi, dear," Grace Dooley said brightly. "Come on out and meet the gang."

Matthew hurried to help the girl from the cab. The small jagged scar on her left temple scarcely suggested the terrible internal damage done to her flawless blue eyes by some sinister steel projectile,

45

and Matthew said with exaggerated gravity, "This is Miss Solomon, a colleague of Mr. Humphries," hoping that the girl's wooden cane (unfortunately not white but a plain polished one) and the mournful set of his own countenance would convey her handicap as he dared not verbally imply it.

Just then the supper drum rumbled out across the slope. The savory smells of *nshima* and *kapenta* drifted from the hospital wards as Jerome Dooley and Than Profane came out of the building talking earnestly.

"Come, dear," Matthew's Teller said kindly. "Join us for a bite to eat. Then we can bed thee down in our humble home. We'll be glad to have thee."

But Jennifer Solomon stood transfixed to the spot, looking bewildered and lost. Matthew, knowing why, felt unable to call attention to her blindness without great embarrassment, and while he dithered, looking helplessly around for Than Profane, who was already moving off, the moment for speech was lost forever.

"Well, come along child!" Hannah Rothchild snapped. "Are thee waiting for a machila to carry thee off? If thee stand there much longer, thee'll take root to be sure!"

The girl burst into tears. They all stared at her, aghast, and Than Profane stopped dead in his tracks. He turned slowly around, retracing his steps. The company stood in a horrified hush.

Hannah blurted: "She will not move! Just stands there like a lame duck!"

The Boy winced. "Take her hand," he said quietly. "She's blind."

7

Sunday, or First-day, as the missionaries called it in the traditional Quaker nomenclature, came again. With it, recess from the hospital and recurring meeting, a discipline as formidable to Than as school to a tomboy. But desiring the approval of his family, he went uncomplainingly. Then, as they were walking across to the meeting house in the early sunshine, a black nurse came hurrying from the hospital to report that Tanda had deteriorated drastically during the night. Than went to the baby immediately.

In the children's ward, the emaciated little black boy lay in his cot, very still against the white sheets. He wore only a diaper, a snatch of stained gauze sticking out of one side. Despite all their efforts, the baby's system, treated too late, had rejected all forms of food through vomiting and diarrhea; now all that remained was death—the final, merciful release from darkness and pain.

Than settled on a stool beside the cot. He reached over and took hold of one small black hand, which lay limp against the pillow. The sightless apathetic eyes barely flickered, but the tiny fingers, grown so poignantly familiar, curled around his automatically. The smell of ether, permeating the ward, was a comfort to Than, clean and fine, and he felt reverent and strange in his best suit on Sunday, holding the hand of a little dying child. Outside, a small sighing wind dispersed the smells of dry sand and wood smoke. At the edge of the hospital yard, chattering little gray vervet monkeys skirmished in swaying treetops. Someone had gone to fetch the mother from the meeting house across the slope, from whence came a faint radiation of voices singing in English: "Someone's crying, Lord, Kum-baya . . ." The words of the hymn reached Than, sadly appealing, as quietly, imperceptibly, the baby slipped away. As the little hand turned slowly cold against his palm, he listened absently to the far-off fervent "Someone needs you, Lord."

It seemed the anguish cry of all Africa. . . .

The missionaries did not see Than Profane until late supper that night, when afternoon meeting was long since over and the generator had begun to throb. Matthew looked up and saw him approach the *chitenje* through the cricket-shrilling darkness. The Boy was greeted by the sallow lamplight and a stony silence, which he made no attempt to break. He sat down to a table that seethed with animosity. A plate was sullenly laid before him, and he began, listlessly, to eat. Suspecting his motives, the missionaries had tried him and found him wanting. Now they punished him with embittered eyes. Ezra Peabody sat cast in a grievous air of outrage. The elder ladies had greedy eyes for the discerning of sin; now they counted the Boy's trespasses with scornful self-righteousness. Only grave personal ill-ness could excuse the day-long nonobservance of the soul-bread of First-day worship, and casual nonattendance by a white missionary was an undesirable example to the natives, besides being the gravest insult to the Lord.

There were knowing triumphant glances between them, and Hannah Rothchild sniffed contemptuously. Big-boned and bumptious and homely as a broomstick, she was about as barren and dry as the little Nevada town she hailed from. In the insect-fluttered light of the two hurricane lanterns that hung from the *chitenje's* crude eaves, her severe gray dress sagged over a broad-flat bosom, and with her righteous air, austere bun, and hard horse face primly pulled up at the mouth like a drawstring purse, she seemed to Matthew the very caricature of the spinster schoolmarm that she was.

"There's *some* people," she bristled belligerently, "as might regard the keeping of the Lord's word to be of more important sustenance than the bread of the body!"

The indictment was clear. But the Boy carried on slowly chewing. The silence spread fragile as glass between them. Finally, Matthew could endure it no longer. He broke the uncomfortable quiet with a shatter than startled them all.

"We missed thee at meeting," he boomed, but kindly, for he sympathized innately with the torment of a boy standing straddled between two distant worlds.

The Boy looked up. He only toyed with his food, and Matthew half wondered why he had come at all. Despite the good Sunday bounty after a day-long abstinence, he seemed to have little appetite. Now, displaying an unpardonable lack of remorse, he stared at Matthew coldly.

"Yeah," he answered vaguely.

"I hope it was nothing too urgent that held thee back, dear?" Katherine said nervously. Then she thought of something. "How is that little baby, Tanda?"

The Boy stared at her dully. He looked down at his plate. "He died at ten-thirty this morning."

Those at the table sat stunned. Even the older ladies had the grace to look uncomfortable. They had all known how much the baby's plight had meant to the Boy.

Katherine drew in her breath. "Oh . . . I'm so sorry!"

The Boy merely stared. And Jayne slowly put down her fork.

The next night, just as Katherine had told him, Than found Jayne up a frangipani tree at the foot of the garden. Her white nightdress hung like a Halloween hoax in the darkness.

"Hi."

Jayne almost fell off the limb in her fright. The spongy trunk dipped dangerously as Than clambered up and settled solemnly on the broad bough beside her. She sucked in her breath defensively.

"This is *my* tree!"

"Hey, let's not quibble. It's big enough for the two of us."

She opened her mouth protestingly, then closed it again. He knew she couldn't look at him without her terrible words: *I hate thee!* ringing between them. Now, for the first time, she had to sit still and bear the consequences of her behavior. The cool night air was sweet with the peppery scent of the starry white lemon-centered blossoms, and beneath her long cotton nightdress, she swung her legs distractedly on the branch beside him.

"You look like Little Bo Peep," he observed gravely, and she shot him a wary, resentful look.

"I mean it." He smiled faintly, holding a glowing cigarette in the cup of his hand. "You're cute as a button."

He drew on the cigarette, and in the expanding glow he saw that she was staring at his bare chest in unabashed curiosity. And maybe his unaccustomed semi-nakedness and proximity frightened her some, for she looked like some defenseless young animal, mesmerized by a creature of prey.

"You stop looking that way," he said softly. "I don't bite."

She turned guiltily away and he sighed musingly: "My little sister, keeper of spiders and paragon of the bush!"

"Please," Jayne said, fidgeting haughtily. "I want to go down. Thee're in my way. I am very tired."

"So am I. I'm tired of the way you skitter out of my way every morning, tired of the way you can't bring yourself to say a civil word to me. What *is* it with you, anyway? Why do you hate me so? Am I such an ogre you can't stand to be around me? I mean, aside from murdering your favorite spider, what have I done to you that's so bad?"

"It's not what thee've done to *me* . . ." Her words trailed to a charged silence. And the emphasis gave him the clue. Slowly, finally, the truth began to dawn on him. And he cursed himself, for he had known it, without wanting to, all along.

"Not what I've done to you? I guess I see it now. It's *him*, isn't it? You hate me because of our father."

"Because of what thee did to him," she whispered. "Thee made him suffer. Thee wrote awful things. Thee broke his heart!"

She began to cry and it all came tumbling out. About letters that never came, and ones that hurt when they did. About a father who had always waited, and died heartbroken, with the name of a way-

49

ward son on his lips, while there were others around who had loved him more.

"He never stopped talking about thee," Jayne stammered. "He would say to me: 'Jaynie, thee're just like him. Thee have his eyes and cheekbones and his mouth.' He kept going on about that. It was almost as if . . . as if he wished *I were thee!*"

She stared off into space, the tears streaming down her cheeks. Than wriggled a handkerchief out of his pocket and pressed it into her hand.

"I read one of thy letters once. I wanted to know why they always made Poppa so unhappy." She sniffed sadly.

And she knew it word for word, reciting it like a piece of prose, in a dull monotone: "'Why don't we just be a couple of adults and admit we no longer need each other, Dad? Maybe you didn't wait around to see me achieve my medical degree, but at least you paid to make it possible. You've paid off your parental duty—so why don't you quit feeling obligated? Your money did a lot for me. More, maybe, than love could have.'"

She broke off, crying heartbrokenly. Than put his hand on her arm to steady her on the bough. He could not speak.

"Thee said thee were too busy to write more often, and anyway, what was there to say? Thee said . . ."

"I know what I said!" Than swallowed. "I know, damnit!"

Jayne had hated him all these years, and looking back, he could hardly blame her. He sat numbly frozen until gradually her sobbing died down and she blew her nose and wiped her face.

"So you carried out your personal little vendetta," he said hoarsely. "If only you'd known. I got my punishment when he died, honey. That was all the jolt I needed."

She stared at him perplexedly, and he smiled sickly into her wracked little face.

"Oh yes, I loved him. He was my father too, remember? And no writing on any little piece of paper could rub the knowledge of that out of my heart. Have you ever thought that for the first thirteen . . . fourteen years of my life, he was solely *my* father? My mother was dead less than a year when he remarried, and it was hard to reconcile myself to the idea of a new mother—*one I'd never met*, halfway across the world, in that space of time. I felt as if my own mother had been dishonored and my father's love usurped. And I guess time and distance only exaggerated our differences. Maybe he only spoke about *me* to you all the time, but to me it was all you and

Katherine and Tom. I felt like little boy lost. Maybe if I hadn't loved him so much, it wouldn't have hurt so bad."

"But thee never cried!" Jayne shook her blond head adamantly. "Thee never once cried!"

Than swallowed. "Jaynie, I don't know if you can understand this . . . but sometimes *a man cannot cry*! The world expects him to be strong. Sometimes he just doesn't know how."

They climbed out of the tree in silence. He gave her a hand as she came down after him, pulling her nightdress close. As she slid to the cool grassy earth and stood beside him in the moon-dappled darkness, an owl called.

"You're like a butterfly." Than whispered wonderingly. "I watch you. You're wild and free as a part of nature itself."

She lowered her eyes, but he tilted her chin and made her look at him. And suddenly she was in his arms. They embraced like lovers, hearts pounding through the thin cotton of her nightdress. She smelled milky and warm as a pup, and her little pointed breasts, pressed flat against his chest, filled him with a great awkward aching tenderness. Eyes shut fiercely tight, his mouth was in her soft fragrant hair, and he spoke with great effort.

"Hi, little sister," he said huskily. "Welcome to my heart!"

And the way she clung to him, he knew it was the same for her.

"Don't go away," she cried. "Don't *ever* go away!"

8

That small plea, being profound, was all the inducement Than needed. Words, tears, and a girl with more persuasive power than a whole barrelful of TNT. He awoke the next day firm in his resolution. That night, Matthew Tomlinson smiled at his request for counsel.

"Why, surely. Come on inside and have some good old-fashioned Hoosier hospitality!"

Than went up the polished green steps of the wooden-balustraded veranda that surrounded the big old house. "You're from Indiana?"

"Yep," the old man chuckled. "Where else? Small town near Elkhart. Left there just on forty-five years ago with my sister Rainy. We were orphaned young and came out together with a big concern for the godless tribes of darkest Africa. Mighty tough and selfless woman is Eldoraine. Never married, and I guess she took repressed motherhood out on the world. She wanted to take the whole of humanity and pat it on her knee."

He led Than into a big living room that was rustic and homey with dark heavy furniture, faded drapes, and musty moth-eaten rugs. Native art and wooden carvings adorned the walls, and piles of newspapers and old magazines cluttered every corner. The professor took a small framed photograph off a prim little mantel above a cavernous fireplace, and handed it to Than.

"That's Rainy! Six foot two in her bare feet and a temper to match."

Than glanced at the specter of a rigid elderly woman who stared fixedly at him from the dim print, gray hair pulled back in a bun, arms tightly folded across a droopy cotton dress that sagged to her ankles. "Looks like a woman to contend with."

"Oh, she is," Matthew chuckled. "Even today, she surely is!"

"I guess you met Teller out here then?" Than parried politely.

Matthew laughed. "Yes, I married Teller two months after Rainy went home to recuperate from malaria and her bad chest. Teller, just like any motherly woman, took me firmly under her wing. And here I am as thee sees me today. Taken good care of, well fed, and looking just like the cat that took the cream. And blessed with two scurrilous boys to boot. Let's see now, Ralph would be pushing forty now, and Abner not far behind. They've been living with Rainy in Elkhart these past years. The doctor recommended she retire from active service, and the only way we could dupe her into following that prescription was to bemoan the fact we needed someone to take care of our boys while they got educated back home. Now," he settled into a worn wing-backed chair, "what was it thee wanted?"

"Well, sir," Than squirmed a little in his seat, feeling suddenly trapped by the same cozy world the man had just spoken of, "I guess I'd like to take my father's place at the hospital for a while."

The silence in the room grew and engulfed him.

Later, Katherine stared at him as though he were mad, and it was like his own self-doubt staring back at him.

"But, Than . . . I don't understand."

He smiled wryly. "It's perfectly simple. I've got nothing more urgent knocking at my door and I'd like to stay until they get a more permanent replacement at the hospital."

"But, Than—don't misunderstand me—not that I'm not delighted—but what about thy career, thy work at the Arthur Collins Teaching Hospital? Thee were chief resident. Thy uncle wrote us thee were doing so well! Thy father was so proud."

He stared over her head into the distance. "Yes, well that's all over now."

"Why? How?"

His eyes leveled with hers. "Well, there was some problem about me taking leave to see my father. The chief of staff decided to be difficult. But that wasn't all. I disagreed with some of his methods. I'm not exactly a model subordinate, and I just figured I'd be better off without it . . . so I quit. It's as simple as that."

"Oh, Than, I'm so sorry . . ."

"There's nothing to be sorry about."

"But there is, Than. Thee made the sacrifice for thy father. And when thee arrived, it was too late, and all for nothing."

"Kathy, it was worth it to me."

Just the same, it was a wry ironical thing, because giving of nothing when it mattered, he had, in the final analysis, given of everything when it was too late.

"Kathy, don't you see? It doesn't matter anymore, where or why or what. The only thing that's important to me is that I'm here now and they need another doctor at the hospital and until such time as they find somebody permanent . . ."

Smiling radiantly, she gently shook her head at him. "Oh, Than, Than." And it was a look so much like love that he turned away in embarrassment. "Than, thee art so good."

"Oh God, no, I'm not. And I don't guess I even fit in here very well. I'm not . . . too *powerfully religious*, but they do need a doctor and I'll try my best. And I guess if I keep my nose clean and remember my prayers . . ."

"Oh, Than," she said softly, "I'll never mind thee as thyself. I wish that thy father could be here today. To see thee giving a part of thy life to the serving of our poor African brethren."

"Hey, hold on! I'm not that noble. It's just until they get someone to take my place." He hung on to that.

The news spread as fast as Katherine could tell it. At the dining hut, the trade-school manager, widower Ward Disney, shook Than's hand with a certain likable gravity, and the hospital staff crowded jubilantly around him. There seemed no doubt in anybody's mind that the minister of health and the mission board would heartily endorse his temporary appointment.

"But, honey, thee should understand," Katherine warned. "It may take years before the board finds another Quaker doctor willing to take up the call . . . could thee wait that long?"

"I guess," he said casually. But it was only when he saw Jayne again that he felt really sure. Then the ancient biblical words came back to him:

Entreat me not to leave thee or to return from following after thee: for whither thou goest I will go and where thou lodgest, I will lodge: thy people shall be my people, and thy God, my God . . .

It was for Jayne that he was doing this. For all the little Tandas in Africa, for Tom and Kathy and for his father. Most of all for his father. Maybe it was his way of saying sorry—for fifteen years of bitter rejection.

9

As soon as arrangements had been made, Morgan Humphries was flown to England from Solwezi. He left behind the young blind girl, whose continued presence had begun to disturb them all. At the supper table that night, there was a decided feeling of questioning. Over the years of their religious narrowing, the missionaries had become a homogeneous group, jealous of strangers, and now they furtively watched Jennifer Solomon, who sat silent and uneating. She had made no mention of leaving and she could not, after all, remain with them forever. Her one reason for staying had flown with the plane, and although she was twenty years old, it was widely considered that being dependently blind, she belonged at home with her father in Luanshya.

Considering this disturbing fact, Matthew only half listened to Ward Disney's musing discussion of the internal rivalry that had recently riven the country's only black political party, the African National Congress, or Congress, as it was known locally. The increasing popularity of some new young blood, Kenneth Kaunda, a schoolteacher and son of African evangelists, had finally caused the hard-drinking and irascible Harry Nkumbula to resign his post as president last month. When he was promptly reelected by a cheering majority, Kaunda and Simon Kapepwe, a close colleague, broke away to form a new party, the Zambezi African National Congress, which quickly usurped more than a thousand members from the old party.

It was a volatile situation amongst Africans so inclined to the persecution of other tribes and sects, but Matthew at the moment was more concerned with the fate of their blind young guest. Apparently, so was everyone else. As the cook's assistant cleared the table, Hannah Rothchild said halfheartedly: "Anyone for Scrabble?"

For once she had no takers, and she put the box back in the fly safe, tight around the mouth with her annoyance.

At last Matthew cleared his throat elaborately. "Jenny child, I'll be taking thee home to thy father tomorrow."

Her sightless eyes flew up at him, round and shocked. "But, Professor, what about your work?"

"Hush, child, it's no trouble."

"But I don't want to go home!" It burst from her finally. "Oh, please! I need a mission."

So that was it. In the incredulous silence, Matthew was absently aware of roosting guineafowl gabbling like New World turkeys in the adjacent trees. Then, touched by her shy desperation, he chuckled gently.

"So thee wants a mission, does thee, child? And what, pray tell, does thee want one for?"

"I want to teach." She frowned fervently, blind blue eyes imploring. "I want to stay here and teach the blind. I'll become a Quaker if necessary! I'd like that. It makes no difference to me. I think all paths lead to God."

Hannah Rothchild stood up immediately. (She had never forgiven the child her own humiliating *faux pas* the day of her arrival. And now, perhaps the loss of her Scrabble game rankled still.) Seeing the grim set of her face, Matthew winced in anticipation.

"Become a Quaker," Hannah mimicked. "Dear child, may I inform thee that our religion is not a cloak to be taken on and off at the wearer's convenience. It just so happens—has thee ever considered that thee might not have the necessary qualities or qualifications to become a Friend?" She saw the horrified faces and rushed on to more practical considerations. "And what of thy board and keep? Why, already we have a struggle to make ends meet. I say the mission board cannot afford another wage!" She looked earnestly around at her colleagues for support. "There's little enough money as it is! We need . . ."

"Very well, Friend—we'll let the board decide about that." Matthew stood up, shutting her off. She deflated sourly and he stared inquiringly around the table. "Friends, it has been my experience that the board is always happy to welcome workers of any denomination to our fold, but if Miss Solomon has a natural wish to join our faith, well, then I say so much the better. I will write and inform them of her aspirations. In the meanwhile, she'd best remain with us."

And so it was arranged. As Matthew had predicted, the mission board welcomed the girl's services. She was accepted as a probational Quaker, and Matthew and Teller began to arrange their home to facilitate her handicap. And in the evenings, when Matthew pored over his schoolwork, Teller, like some fussy mother hen tucking a helpless chick under wing, began subjecting the child to compulsory lessons of the pacific arts and on the various tenets of the Quakerhood to which she aspired—the whole, Matthew knew, being nothing more than a carefully synchronized program of reform. For besides lecturing on the Quaker saving graces of purity and humility (to her mind, surely neglected in most other religions), the needlework that Teller taught entailed the sewing up of several long dresses that would transform the girl to a matching modesty. But Jennifer Solomon was not long content to be so dependently steered. As the weeks went by, spurning their guidance, she laboriously learned the most common routes and became a familiar sight around the mission, carefully cane-tapping her way to and from the dining *chitenje* and the meeting house, where she meditated devoutly and the congregational chorus was enriched with her sweet vibrant voice, fervently singing . . .

In late November, the Central Africa yearly meeting was camped and convened at Suseshi. Though the sullen skies hung heavy with clouds, the oppressive heat droned dismally on and the delegates poured in over rugged roads that were still passably dry. Here in Central Africa, the annual Quaker conferences were moving mass assemblies with white missionaries and African Friends coming in from as far afield as the Congo. Closer to home, their Barotseland missionaries brought in truckloads of quaintly costumed singing Barotses from the little protectorate, and from Suseshi's surrounding districts thousands of Africans milled in on foot or whatever transport was available to them. Finally fully assembled, some seven thousand strong massed around Suseshi meeting house, an impressive spectacle as they worshiped in the open air.

The following day, amid the threatening grumble of distant thunder, a crowd half the size crammed into the hot stuffy little hall and lined its long verandas to deliberate the affairs of the Society. To Matthew's mind, the most exciting developments were always the recording of new meetings and ministers. This year the recruitment of a young American missionary to teach at Shonona Mission in Barotseland was particularly pleasing. The man's wife was apparently a nurse willing to tend the sick at the little station, and since medical amenities were pitifully few in the little river kingdom, jubilant Barotse members called for a clinic to facilitate her work. Before Matthew knew what was happening, Clara Fotch proposed using their forthcoming grant from Medico Enterprises to help build such an edifice. Well, Matthew reflected wryly, there went the hospital's X-ray machine for another year. And he was right. As usual, the Dooleys' dithering objections wilted under the more aggressive arguments and exuberance of their African Friends. And it seemed to him that the blatantly bored Than Profane, gazing restlessly out of a dusty window, had failed to comprehend this telling consequence. The delegates were still debating the details when outside, blackening clouds obliterated the sun and the day turned suddenly dark. Such was the infectious fervor of the First Rains that the meeting broke up spontaneously and the members massed out onto the long open verandas.

Down at the river, the swaying borrasus palms rustled in the rising wind; lightning snapped, fragmenting the tortured cloud formations while birds winged homeward with panicked cries. As the distant roar of the approaching rains swept across the dry desolate bush, Than Profane, with his tie pulled awry and his shirt unbuttoned, waited with the young Disney brothers and a crowd of Africans out in the open. The first drops thudded into the parched earth, sending up puffs of steam and dust and a fragrance so sweet it seared a man's nostrils. Delighted as a child, the Boy held out an arm, and Jayne ran to him. They huddled together under the swift stinging staccato, flinching and squinting up in silent homage as the deafening thunder rumbled awesomely around the immense, spitting gray sky.

"Come on inside now; we're getting soaked," the Boy spluttered finally. His clothes were drenched, his face glistening wet.

On the packed, gleaming-wet veranda, Matthew caught his breath. For the girl's damp white dress clung to her upper body like a second skin. From under her pink-ribboned bonnet, she smiled up at her brother, unknowing and natural as Eve with the rain dripping off her fine little nose and her pink virginal nipples peeping through the slick transparency. Exultant blacks milled all around them, and the Boy stepped quickly in front of his sister, protecting the secrets of her body with the bulk of his own. Across her bodice he spread a clean dry handkerchief that stuck like glue.

"Baby," Matthew heard him say softly as he bent to tenderly kiss her soft baffled mouth, "you'd best have a little talk with your mother. It's about time you were wearing a bra."

10

After a sporadic start, the rains set in, stormy and torrential, and overnight the drab *miombo* woodland glimmered with sunshot, red and coppery tones of tender new translucent growth. Wild flame lilies sprang up in grasses so green they seemed luminous, and here and there in the bush the spiky round red faces of the striking solitary wildflower, Wife of the Rains, appeared magically over unexplainable distances. Although the mission schools now stood silent, closed for the year, the hospital was still thronged with suffering souls, and for the other missionaries, there was a wealth of work preceding Christmas.

Despite the tropical climate, the mission took on an infectious festive air, with the exuberant white children home from boarding school and the flamboyant and hibiscus trees ablaze with blossoms while the cicadas, or Christmas beetles, screeched from their boughs. When two collapsed bush-pole bridges were finally mended, the stranded, mud-bespattered Central African Road Services pantechnicon belatedly reached them with replenishments for their dwindling food supply and Christmas gifts catalogue-ordered from the Copperbelt.

On December 23, Matthew cut down a small *mukuve* tree to approximate a fir, and the Profanes and the Dooley children and Peter Disney crowded into his big cluttered parlor to help him and Teller trim the branches with their old box of carefully kept trinkets. While they bustled, Matthew switched on his old transistor radio to catch the latest news of the All Africa People's Conference from Accra. His hope that their Northern Rhodesian nationalists would remain aloof from the radical organization had been a little much to expect of a people who unanimously hated the federal structure that bound them to Nyasaland and the more racially prejudiced south. Now, as the white Federal government agitated to achieve complete independence from Britain in a multiracial state enshrining whites as senior partners in a "mutually-beneficial" governmental structure, the African unease was being demonstrated in acts of sabotage, punishable by death. Well, Matthew had long seen it coming. While Federation brought them economic benefits and some political progress, the little autonomy these Africans could yet aspire to as British protected persons was based upon a complicated, limited franchise and allegiance to the queen. Indeed, they had been little mollified by the goodwill speeches of the Federal premier, Sir Roy Welensky, the Polish-descended, stout, and balding "man of the people" whose colorful career included a reign as heavyweight boxing champion of Rhodesia. This thirteenth child of a poor Rhodesian farmer had grown up with the natives. He might profess to understand their psychology, but being obliged to placate the European electorate, could he hope to woo the blacks as well? Matthew doubted it.

As he hung a bright golden bauble near the top of the little Christmas tree, he listened to a direct relay from the conference in Accra. As the newscaster narrated the scene, he could image it all: the air of excitement as Kenneth Kauda, the ambitious young Northern Rhodesian leader, distinctive in a colorful toga with his long crissy hair brushed stiffly erect, mounted the rostrum, and, amid the cheers of the delegates, issued the aspiring cry of a people in bondage.

"Freedom! Freedom! Freedom!"

It was the militant sally of emergent Africa, and Matthew, straining to hear through the harsh atmospherics and the chatter of the busy children, shivered in sudden foreboding. For the natives of this land, yet in tutelage, were not ready for such. In his mind, revolution was synonymous with bloodshed—and Africa had suffered too much already.

BOOK TWO

THE NATIVES
ARE RESTLESS

· 1959 ·

1

IN ORDER to practice medicine legally in the country, Than had applied to the Federal Ministry of Health to be put on the register of medical practitioners. With his qualifications, he expected no trouble getting enrolled, but before he received a reply, the mission had an unexpected visit from the provincial medical officer.

Dr. George Goudie was a gimlet-eyed crusty Scotsman who was patently unamused by Americans. With the omnipotent presumption of his position, the arrogant little man, masked, gloved, and gowned, strode unannounced into Suseshi's stuffy little operating room, where the medical team was busy performing an amputation one hot afternoon. Jerome stammered introductions through his mask and started sweating profusely. Than, caught red-handed, blatantly wielding a scalpel while Jerome assisted him, finished the operation in record time and a ghastly silence. Afterwards, in the anteroom, Dr. Goudie flung off his white robes and stalked through to the staff room. After a moment, Jerome and Than followed him warily.

"Dr. Goudie," Jerome said carefully, "as I informed thee through D. C. Horn, Dr. Profane has applied for permission to practice. We need him here, and as thee've just seen—he's a damn good surgeon. He was a chief resident in the States. So have a heart, Doc. Thee must know it's only a matter of time and red tape before the government gives its permission."

"Mebee." The craggy-faced lean little Scotsman puffed on a worn pipe; he eyed Than's jeans disparagingly. "But ye Americans need to learn that application fer permission is no the same thing as permission!"

He swung around abruptly and strode to the window. "I'll recommend that Dr. Profane serves one month's trial at one o' our government hospitals on the Copperbelt," he decreed remorselessly. Then he turned and glowered at Jerome through bushy eyebrows. "Weel, mon, dinna just stand there gawping! Where's the tea?"

Matthew heard about the incident later, and he was relieved. In these parts, Dr. Goudie's word was law; he was a rigid disciplinarian, if a dedicated man, who was feared and revered and particularly infamous for summarily closing down a mission institution when its operators failed to fulfill his high medical standards. Indeed, the Boy's unsanctioned practice could have reaped a worse forfeiture, and Matthew had no doubt that while he awaited its execution, the defiant Dr. Profane would continue his surreptitious practice, just so long as the formidable medical inspector, whose many duties took him the length and breadth of a province almost as large as Scotland and England combined, was known to be safely occupied elsewhere.

But other aspects boded better. The mission board in America had expressed itself delighted at the Boy's decision to stay on at the mission in his father's place. And it seemed to Matthew that the Boy had fallen to the life as naturally as rain to good earth. He was single-mindedly tackling the new aspects of medicine presented to him, the tropical diseases and obstetrics and gynecology, which comprised a large part of the mission's medical work. And he was learning the language. He had commented wryly to Matthew at the table one day that he was becoming a master at interpreting the animal noises used by the natives to illustrate their discomfiture and pain. And Jeremiah's translation was becoming daily less required, for the young doctor was fortunately endowed of the two basic essentials of a good linguist: a retentive memory and a musical ear. He made a language lesson out of every day, and after supper most nights, when the other missionaries were playing Scrabble, Lars Wikstrom, the young Swedish teacher, would take out a note pad and proceed to polish the Boy's grammar. Thus, in no time at all, applying just the right accent and intonation, he was coming up with idiomatic little phrases in Chi-Lwena, the lingua franca of the many tribes of different dialects in the area.

But his interest extended beyond the African lingua franca or the state of his patients' bodies. He made it his business to know them as people, in order to better understand the other two. And calmly commandeering the mission's recently donated Harley Davidson motorcycle from the proudly possessive Orville Fotch (who had previously timidly ridden the shiny vehicle in ever-widening wobbling circles on the mission common every day), the Boy was off into the bush discovering the people. Matthew had often come upon the vehicle at dusk, parked at some wayside village, where its rider might be found collecting curious black people like honey collects ants: the college-boy scientist, in the thick of life, carrying research to the point of participation, eating *nshima* and *kapenta* with his fingers, listening to the folklore, and getting the feel of the customs.

He had lately acquired a fine white Stetson, one of a whole boxful generously donated from the John B. factory in Philadelphia. Hitherto the hats had been a useless charity in a land where the natives had their own tight wool skullcaps as sun protection and the missionaries lacked the necessary bravado to carry them off effectively. The hats were being cut into squares for mat-making in the women's homecraft class when Katherine rescued one for Than. She set it firmly on that arrogant fair head and that, for Matthew, completed the picture: the Pied Piper in a cowboy suit!

Never shaking off the one-part doctor that he was, he moved through the villages, examining people as he went, searching toddlers for signs of rickets, scurvy, marasmus, or kwashiorkor, unclothing plump bodies in plain sight of all and inspecting suckling babies right at their mothers' breasts. In what shaky command he yet had over their given language, he delivered lectures as he went, stressing the importance of hygiene and diet, ingratiating himself with the people in order to find out what made them tick.

Like cut grass growing wild, he thrived in this new natural freedom, coming to seed sun-bleached and burned and uninhibited as a native. Matthew heard horrifying tales of him trying out the local brew (an illegal sweet-potato spirit that was potent as the very devil), and even (perish the thought) joining the natives in their tribal dances. But Matthew was unprepared to believe these idle stories. After all, the Africans were known for their colorful habit of exaggeration, and the Boy, however uninhibited, would surely not go that far! He moved freely among the natives but remained aloof. They watched with cautious respect while he invaded their homes, their family lives, and their bodies. Allowing no return liberties with himself, he stood superior and set apart. He was always that little tin god—the white man.

2 Each year it was customary for the Quaker mission in Northern Rhodesia and its neighboring states to meet in Katanga so that member missionaries might pool their experience and confer on the special problems peculiar to their religious, educational, and medical programs. This year, Than Profane was assigned to make the trip with Matthew. They crossed into the Congo in the stupefying afternoon heat and reached Lusinga Mission in southern Katanga just as dusk was settling. The mission's functional brick building rose up out of dense bush; set near a river, it was a wild and lonely place isolated in miles of desolate *miombo* woodland. They climbed dust-grimed, weary and stiff out of their Land-Rover to be welcomed by the Spauldings, whom the Boy had met at yearly meeting, and the Dimples, a devoted elderly couple from Ruanda-Urundi.

In the Spauldings' untidy house, they were allotted a cluttered bedroom with a faulty light bulb that seemed to sputter in time with the generator's throbbing, never flaring beyond a certain dim amperage that cast the spider-secreted room into a gloom of worrisome shadows. During supper, Louella Breckenbridge, a firm friend and confidante of Matthew's, came across with her mother, who was confined to a wheelchair with rheumatoid arthritis. With their long braided hair coiled back into staid buns, old Rebecca's snow white to her daughter's mid-brown, the reed-thin pair chattered breathlessly, peering birdlike through identical silver-rimmed spectacles. While the Boy conferred with Dr. Alvin MacLintock from Kasai province and the half-Mexican Dr. Manuel Morehead and his obviously older nurse wife, Agnes, the twittering pair of females cajoled Matthew with teasing affection.

The next day, the early sun burnished the treetops in a strip of gold as Matthew and the Boy walked across to breakfast. Monkeys, warming themselves, set up a conversational chatter in the swaying branches of a great wild fig tree as they passed, and a giant vulture gave them a start when it alighted alongside them with a clatter on the low roof of the generator shed. Hopping from foot to foot, great wings flapping, the grotesque bird eyed them hopefully, as if sizing them up for a meal.

"Allow me to introduce Dr. Jeckle," Matthew said dryly, recovering his composure. "Apparently the mission acquired this genteel feathered friend when some lazy African dresser began leaving amputated limbs out in the bush for predators!"

"No kidding." The Boy chuckled, bemusedly shaking his head. "There's a certain ecological logic to it, I suppose."

"Maybe." Matthew winced at the very thought. "However, our more civilized Friends thought incineration much more fitting. They put a stop to the practice directly. But old Jeckle has a long memory. He's always hopping around with that lean and hungry look, and nowadays he's become the mission's garbage can, disposing of folks' leftovers for them."

After breakfast, while the three doctors were conferring at Lusinga's little hospital, Matthew went across to the school and consulted with the Spauldings, the Dimples, the Breckenbridge ladies, and a new young teacher by the name of Chester Daniels. The missionaries were all helpful and accommodating, and as usual, the Congolese seemed so unaffected and friendly that Matthew found it difficult to believe that here, too, they were having their racial and political problems. But by all accounts they were. In preparation for promised independence, the paternalistic Belgians had encouraged the formation of an African middle class: these emergent educated elite, or *elouves*, as they were locally known, had organized political parties that had begun impatiently pushing for power. Although the Belgians tried to placate them with proper programs of preparation, by January the pent passions of the people had exploded into racial rioting, which left many African casualties and a number of Europeans wounded.

A few days later, coming home from the conference, Matthew and the Boy stopped in the bush in Northern Rhodesia to answer the rude call of nature. Like some exhibitionistic little boy, the Boy urinated casually into a river while Matthew hid modestly behind a bush. They were both barely zipped up when they were come upon by a party of dusty African men on bicycles who asked for a drink from their dusty canvas water bag. Matthew produced a chipped enamel mug and promptly obliged. Then one of the Africans suddenly saw the Boy silhouetted against the glowing horizon in his Stetson, jeans, and embossed Western boots, and a look of wonder and recognition arose in his eyes. Dressed in a city suit, the man carried the ultimate in rural African possessions, a transistor radio, or "Saucepan Special," as they were colloquially called. He was a migrant mine-worker come home from the copper mines to show off his worldliness and wealth. And the bioscopes had obviously taught him a little about the Wild West of old America. Matthew imagined he was visualizing some fine Hollywood classic as he stared at the Boy then, fitting the image. At some time or other, the natives find characteristic nicknames for the Europeans. The Boy met his now. The man tried it on tentatively, raising his hat.

"*Mwapalani*. Bwana Cowboy!" There was no African linguistic equivalent for that breed of men as yet largely unknown in rural Africa. He gave a literal translation: "*Njumbo umwaice!*"

It softened, spread, and stuck. *Njumwaice*. The name was born.

3

On February 26, a state of emergency was declared in Southern Rhodesia. A week later, the drastic measure was repeated in Nyasaland and in Northern Rhodesia, where unrest was now widespread. The leaders of the nationalistic party ZANC, which was opposed to the coming general elections and had threatened to intimidate the masses toward this end, were arrested on March 11 and removed to remote detention camps, far from their tribal homelands. So the hammer blows fell, dealing a crippling catharsis to African nationalism in the three Federal states. While most of the missionaries were scandalized, Matthew's personal view was that the Federal government had acted to contain a runaway fire. Elsewhere, all over Africa, the Soviet-stirred nationalists of Western dependencies, agitating for early independence, had become unwitting Communist pawns. As the old masters were ousted, these new and infinitely more sinister invigilators waited to fill the vacuum, feeding their opposite ideology to impressionable emergent peoples who were conveniently already embittered by the real and imagined crimes of their former overseers. Yet while it happened, Britain and America were apparently so concerned with petty proximities that they could not see the far panorama. While they stood by in gullible gainsay, the battle for Africa, between Communism and democracy—right here and now—was already on.

But this view was hardly shared by the majority. A nationwide outcry against "white suppression" of legitimate black aspirations was followed by an upsurge of vandalism and violence. The ripple of outraged reaction, ever-widening, spread overseas, and amongst pacifist African Friends, who had remained largely uninvolved with nationalist politics, sympathy for the "martyred" nationalists rose like a wave.

At their quarterly meeting, the members united solidly behind Lars Wikstrom's proposal that identical letters, expressing the meeting's earnest disapproval of the acts of arrest and detention, be sent to both the Northern Rhodesian and Federal governments.

It was the custom of their Barotseland missionary colleagues Benedict and Carrie Poe to spend a few days installed at Matthew's house during their quarterly visits to Suseshi to attend the mission committee meetings. The day after their arrival, intimidated as always by Benedict's air of suspicious inquiry, Matthew took him on an inspection tour. As fate would have it, two haughty young black teachers questioned his administration with accusing complaints, the mission's rascally resident honey badger had overturned the garbage cans again, and Benedict spotted Than Profane all set, with his Stetson and medical bag, to go adventuring out into the bush. Matthew tried to steer the stern elder away from such electrical controversy as the Boy's arrogance and ambition might invite, but the good man homed in on him at the arbor of the communal garage.

"Why, Friend, thee going some place?"

The Boy spun around. "If it's all the same to you, man . . . yes I am."

"Well now." Benedict's black eyes narrowed. "If thy casual use of the mission's vehicles has been duly agreed upon by the committee, then I guess it's all right."

There was a deadly silence. The Boy's mouth hardened; Matthew saw the blue eyes begin to smolder, and he hurriedly spoke up. "Ben, I can assure thee our young Friend here has been doing a lot of fine work out in the outlying villages, where he has plans to establish several clinics in remote areas."

"Is that right?" The black eyes gloated upon the faded albeit clean-pressed demin jeans. "Then I take it the committee has approved the appointment of such clinics? And that they are a necessary addition to our already very comprehensive medical service?" He raised a derisive brow. "Perhaps a commendable ploy, Friend, toward the culling of more souls? Or doesn't thee believe in mixing salvation with service?" He affixed the Boy with an odd evaluating eye. "And just where might thee be going this fine First-day?"

The Boy barely stirred; he let go of the Land-Rover's door. It fell softly shut. "Man," he said quietly, "why don't *you* tell me."

They stared at each other for one awful hackle-raising moment. Then Benedict gave a nasty smile.

"Maybe I will at that."

He opened his briefcase and on the Land Rover hood unrolled a hand-drawn map that was fancy with scrollwork. They stood watching in silence as the man's long pale finger coursed a series of colored patches indicative of the differing tribes and chiefdoms. Matthew noticed that a blue cross marked each Quaker converted village, and true to the man's declared advocacy of serving only the "deserving," it was exclusively to these areas that he directed the Boy. Then he pointed to an area shaded in black.

"This place is to be avoided at all costs, Friend," he warned. "This is the chiefdom of the Chokwe chief, Mulaisho. A heathen fornicator, patron of witchcraft and all manner of evil doings. So take my word for it, Friend. *Stay away!* It's the devil's domain."

Than traveled along the main road from Mwinilunga for some miles, stopping at wayside villages and faithfully preaching the gospel of good health while he treated, where he could, the ailments of the people. By early afternoon he was on the road again. Squinting occasionally at the map spread out on the seat beside him, he resisted the sly enticements of a dozen deviating footpaths; he had passed the overgrown turn-off to Eshalakali Hill in the Kabompo district when the rising rebellious blood suddenly hardened his sunburned biceps and he jerked the steering wheel, turning off the known track to follow a stray dry water-course into Benedict Poe's forbidden zone, in the dense bush bordering Angola. A diminutive grysbok, browsing on a shrub, took off at his coming, and he rode the bumpy gully for miles through indifferent *miombo* woodland before braking abruptly on the lip of a short eroded bluff that fell gradually away to an immense forested valley.

Pulling on the hand brake, Than climbed out of the Land-Rover, showering stones and burning his hands and knees on sun-blistering rock as he clambered up a steep escarpment to reach an elevated vantage point where the high gangly trees found precarious purchase among jagged monoliths. At this altitude, the heat-drugged afternoon air was somnolent and still, and he could hear baboons barking from the remote vegetation-shrouded stone cliff faces, which rose up around him. In the thick foliage spread out for miles below, he could just make out the slow shadowy gray shapes of a herd of elephants moving through the trees, while high overhead hooded vultures wheeled in the soft infinity of a cloudless blue sky. Taking off his sunglasses, Than followed the line of smoky blue hills with binoculars for some moments before a series of irregular patches suddenly caught his eye and, staring hard, he puzzled out a distant complex of conical thatch roofs. They were native villages. He had found Mulaisho's chiefdom.

He drove a few miles beyond the lonely escarpment, then, hampered by impenetrable thicket, parked within sight of the nearest village, beneath a huge, grotesquely magnificent baobab tree, the bloated monstrosity of nature, much beloved in African folklore, that looked upside down, as if its branches were writhing roots reaching heavenward. Then he took up his medical bag and set off into the hot listening silence and the thick bush wilderness. As he walked, silent birds flew off, the enmeshed gray thicket fell away, and he came upon a group of women and children tending maize and pumpkin gardens beside a thin stream. At his approach, the women ceased their hoeing and stared at him, oddly still and warily watching.

Than stepped over the stream and raised his Stetson.

"*Mwapalani Magwai*," he greeted quietly, but as he made to advance, the skeletal dogs began to snarl insidiously, and at a signal from a gnarled old woman, the awed naked children, pot-bellied with malnutrition, fled in catapulted panic, their isolated babbling cries thinly battling the great bush silence. Skidding through the dust, they ran into the nearby village. In a while the clamor settled and a group of grim looking half-naked tribesmen carrying sticks and spears emerged through the huts.

Uneasy about the weapons, Than called to them. He tried to explain his mission in halting Chi-Lwena. But the advancing party of men seemed unable or unwilling to comprehend, and their garbled dialect sounded like nothing he had ever heard before.

"Listen." He reverted, exasperated, to the English, wiping a sweaty palm down the seat of his jeans. "Pardon my intrusion, but I don't mean you any harm. Just the reverse in fact. Why, I bet you got enough sick and suffering holed up in those huts to fill a county hospital."

But the men were unmoved. Their faces as malevolent and immobile as wooden *makishi* masks, they were dressed in old skins and rags, and with their dust-powdered bodies they looked as mangy as tree trunks, like parts of the dusty landscape come suddenly alive. Gesturing him off with their primitive weapons, they bore menacingly down on Than so that he was forced to step back across the stream and slowly backtrack in the direction of the Land Rover. In the stagnant afternoon heat, the men stank overpoweringly of stale sweat and kaffir beer, and Than was repulsed as much by their smell as by their spears.

"Listen, you mothers," he said angrily. "Don't crowd me. I'll leave under my own steam. Just back down with those spears a little. I'm unarmed, after all. See—all I have is my medical bag."

He backed abruptly against the trunk of a tree and the men stumbled to a halt, standing before him in debating deadlock. Then a sneering young man moved to the fore. He wore a torn pair of dusty old trousers and seemed unconcerned that his penis was exposed. He leered at Than through vicious narrowed eyes and made a mocking, severing gesture with a finger against his own throat. Then, hissing softly through dazzling white teeth, he threw back his jaw and, with a maniacal glint in his slitted eyes, gave a more concrete demonstration.

"Kah!" Touching the finely honed point of his spear lightly against his skin, he drew a thin shocking red line of blood over the black bulge of his Adam's apple. He laughed at the look on Than's face. Then he spun around suddenly, kicked over a gawky-limbed kaffir dog pup, made a jab with his spear and, with a single contemptuous flourish, slit the hairless underbelly. The animal screamed as the bloody gash opened like a mouth in the soft white flesh, spilling viscera into the dust, letting loose the sickly smell of blood and death into the heat of the indifferent afternoon.

The sneering young man held the blood-smeared spear jubilantly aloft like a trophy of war, and the group of tribesmen, laughing uproariously, turned to look at Than. But if they had expected to find the typical European horror of cruelty, they were surprised. Not a muscle moved in Than's blank face; while the high hurt puppy dog crescendo rang in the air, he stared back at the men with bland blue eyes that were calm and serene as a suburban Sunday. His look cut short the callous laughter, so that it died self-consciously on dust-parched lips.

There was a moment's uncertain bumbling amongst the men, and then, averting their eyes, they turned and began retreating, moving in a file through the listless green maize, leaving the yelping maimed dog behind, to die of its misery.

After they had vanished into the heat-shimmering silence, Than shook himself out of a stealing mesmerization. He forced himself to walk to the wounded animal.

"Easy, boy." He crouched over the frenzied brown bundle of jerking limbs and expanding ribs, snatching back his hand as the animal snapped, baring rotted yellow canines, pain and terror mirrored in the rolling eyes. The dry earth was becoming saturated with its blood and Than worked quickly. Shrugging off his shirt, he tore off a strip of material, looped it over the dog's muzzle, and loosely tied the snapping jaws. Then gently holding in the spilling intestines with one hand, he eased up the narrow body, wrapped it in his shirt, and carefully lifted it in his arms.

He was aware of children surreptitiously watching through the maize stalks as he carried the animal, piteously moaning through its bound muzzle, back to the Land-Rover. Setting it down in the blisteringly hot cab, he walked around to the back and took out the mission rifle. For a while he stood regretfully eyeing the dog as it lay trembling pitifully upon the front seat. A single well-placed bullet would erase incalculable misery. And yet . . . His eyes, as if magnetized, kept returning to the trusty medical bag at his feet. He stood for a moment, torn between terrible alternatives.

Just when the pup raised its frizzy-haired unlovely head, the loose skin on its brow rolled back into sad furrows and it gazed mournfully up at Than with imploring pain-bewildered eyes. Then the muzzle dropped across its outsize puppy paws and a plaintive baby whimper came from the depths of its throat. It shivered spasmodically, sighed gustily through its muzzle, then lay acquiescently still, at the mercy of man.

Than knew then that by the very nature of his being he had no choice. He set the rifle down carefully and took up the bag. Sighing like a matron lamenting her mending, he sat in the stiflingly hot cab and worked, threading needles with sweaty hands that still smelled of blood and antiseptic, sewing up a fine seam of flesh. . . .

4 The dog survived. Despite the additional ravages of malnutrition, it responded to vitamins, antibiotics, good food, and affection. Within two weeks, Cuss, as he was spontaneously christened, was weakly standing and wagging a threadbare tail.

One cool black sweet-scented night, when the ghostly howls of young fishing owls wafted across the river like the lament of lost souls falling into a bottomless pit, Matthew went to visit the canine convalescent at the Profane household. There he found the Boy sitting in the dark on the cool veranda, while Katherine and Jayne tended their mending and math lesson in the lighted living room within. Matthew crouched over an old box wadded with sacking, gently stroking the scrawny-looking dog, whose grateful eyes gleamed up at him in the gloom, brimful of indiscriminate love.

Matthew shook his head sadly, bewildered as always by man's inhumanity. "Such callousness . . ." he whispered. "Such wanton cruelty. It's hard to believe!"

The Boy smiled grimly in the dimness; the expanding glow of his cigarette lit up his watchful blue eyes as he inhaled and said softly, "Maybe now, Matthew, you'd like to tell me more about this Chief Mulaisho's 'Devil's Domain.'"

Matthew sat down with a sigh; the chair creaked under his tense weight, and feeling the faint brush of mosquitoes, he began to fan his hot face with his pith helmet. From the river he was aware of the hippo grunting above the frogs' guttural chorus and he smelled the sweet scent of the wild water lilies. "Well, it's a pocket of the Chokwe tribe, emigrated originally from the Kasai Water Shed in Angola. Mulaisho is one of the most powerful of the independent chiefs in these parts, and he's just about as heathen and ornery as he can be. He crossed into Northern Rhodesia with his people after the Second World War. Originally they were a group of some seventy-five tribespeople. With misery following them like their own bad smell, they traveled from place to place, a troublesome minority, unamenable to taxes, laws, sanitary precautions, and the authority of their senior chief. They are filthy and wild, a law unto themselves. Even their own Chokwe brothers regard them with shame. And the other tribes despise them. Oh, I've heard some pompous opinion that they're superior agriculturists—but that's pure sentimental hogwash! Why, their main efforts consist of nothing more than huge fields of cassava—of little nutritional value—and they keep enormous herds of pigs that root in those pig-pens they call villages! The people dabble in wild orgies—in witchcraft and goodness knows what other manner of evil doings. They are hostile, resistant to change, and irrevocably cemented in their old ways. The district commissioner has endless trouble trying to reason with them. The people shy from schooling and from church . . ."

"I wonder who takes care of their sick."

"Their sick?"

The Boy smiled. "Yes, Matthew, every people, even the 'hostile' nonprogressive heathens, are subject to man's diseases. I'm just wondering what happens to their incurables once the witchdoctors leave off."

"Now, Boy, thee wouldn't be considering . . ." Matthew's eyes narrowed warily. He thought he glimpsed some answer to his suspicions on the Boy's face, and he snapped upright in his seat, blustering in alarm. "Now thee take my advice, Boy, and don't thee go dabbling again where thee're not wanted! Those villages are a veritable wasp's nest of evil intrigue and they will have no truck with missionaries. Thee heard what Morgan Humphries said. Eshalakali Hill lies slap in the middle of that old heathen's chiefdom and for years those missionaries have worn themselves out trying to bring them Christian succor. And to what avail? Even our own evangelists have been insulted and turned away, time and again. Why, the police will tell thee how they maim and murder their own brothers through barbarity and witchcraft. Small wonder that they pick on strangers. They chased thee off with spears, thee say? And in my opinion, if they could mutilate an innocent pet, they fully intended the use of them!" He drew back, shaking his head. "No, I am afraid in this instance Friend Benedict was right! They are the devil's own. They have proven themselves to be a drunken, undeserving lot. Now give me thy word, Boy. Don't thee go messing with them again!"

"Mmmmm mmmmm," the Boy murmured noncommittally. He tucked casually considering thumbs into his belt loops and infuriated an anxious old man with a serene dimpled smile.

On March 20, the country went to the polls. The following morning, Grace Dooley's labor pains started. She was rushed straight from the outpatient department to the delivery room, a pair of scissors and a lint bandage still in her hands. Than shooed away the jittery Jerome, and he and Grace listened to the voting results coming in over a transistor radio, while she bore down and labored mightily, finally delivering in fairly quick succession three tiny, redheaded little girls. The last baby arrived concurrent with the conclusion that the ruling United Federal Party would be comfortably returned to power. However, even the government's drastic curbing of ZANC had failed to win it much measure of African support.

The majority of those eligible abstained from voting, and in the final analysis it was found that the government received only six percent of the black votes taken. It was faint voice indeed from a people whose numbers so vastly outweighed the ruling whites.

Jerome, in his consulting office, was distractedly monitoring the same radioed results when Than burst in.

"You virile son of a bitch!" He smiled wanly, wringing the man's hand. "You just got yourself three beautiful little girls."

A weary-looking Grace smiled triumphantly up at Jerome as he and Than entered her room a moment later.

"Well, honey, looks like we hit the jackpot this time!" She laughed huskily, hugging the three pink-wrapped, squirming little bundles closer to her. "Meet Faith, Hope, and Charity. And stop looking so worried, Papa! We're all fine. Just somebody please give the doctor a sedative. I think he thought they'd *never* stop coming!"

5 The medical officer, Dr. Goudie, was good as his word. After receiving a formal directive from the Ministry of Health, Than drove a Land-Rover through the bush to Ndola, where he had been appointed to serve one month's trial in order to qualify to practice medicine in the federation. Ndola, a part of the Copperbelt complex, was a small thriving commercial and industrial town close to the Congo border. Each day, from the government hostel where he was lodged, Than walked to the hospital, which comprised sprawling buildings fitted with modern amenities. The patients were all white residents of the town; the doctors came from England or South Africa, and most of the white nurses were recruited, on contract, from Ireland.

Than worked hard at the hospital and in his spare time steered clear of all social activities, which, in the light of the natural friendliness of the white expatriate Rhodesians, was hard to effect. Doctors invited him home for dinner; nurses smiled unspoken invitations. In self-defense and with a certain grim devilry, Than began to caricature himself into the religious role that had been typecast for him. The fact that he never went to church and waved no visible Bibles apparently went unnoticed in his self-imposed seclusion. But to his exasperation, despite the fact that he was hard on the nurses, harder than a temporary doctor had a right to be, they were undeterred.

Maybe, like most women, they were putty to the little bit of bastard in a man, for their shameless little mating signals began to come through to him.

When he had been in Ndola for two weeks, five of them ambushed him one evening as he was walking home from the hospital. He walked bravely right into their midst and tried to look suitably perplexed while they controlled their nervous laughter enough to get their proposition straight. It seemed they were all eaten up with anxiety for him; they pitied his friendless state, and since he would not choose one of them . . . well, would he care to be shown the night life of Ndola, such as it was, by them, en masse?

Than turned away from their eager faces in dismay. "Well, thanks, but I'm all tied up with my Bible study."

But just as he was about to move on, the smallest one, a sweet-faced Irish girl by the name of Lucy O'Connor, drew herself up to her full haughty height, like a little bantam rooster getting ready to fight.

"Doctor, there's a rumor it is that's going about the hospital. Maybe ye can put us straight?"

The other girls began to grin and Than grew wary. "Sure," he said uneasily. "Anything at all."

"Then ye'll tell us then." The little nurse smiled spitefully. "Are ye queer?"

Than was floored for a moment. He didn't know whether to laugh or rage. Trapped in his own constricting web of lies, he stared at the nurses in disbelief, red-faced and abashed amongst their irrepressible grins. Wanting to smile in spite of himself, he struggled to arrange the proper stern and pious expression.

"Nurse O'Connor, in light of my status as a missionary, I consider that to be a highly improper and insolent question." He broke off furiously, treating them to the disdain of a pained hurt stare. But little Lucy seemed dauntless. While her companions stared at him seriously, shamed into silence, she smiled blithely.

"Ye don't have to answer that, Doctor."

"You're damn tooting I won't!" Than bent toward her and lowered his voice. "O'Connor, I guess that's something you'll have to find out for yourself."

And find out she did. When he stepped out of his hostel room the next Sunday evening, Lucy O'Connor was waiting for him in the lobby. Looking pretty with her hair down, provoking eyes, and neat figure, she held a Bible in her hands and declared herself willing to accompany him to the church of his choice.

Than smiled at her tightly. "I don't believe they have a Quaker meeting here."

"Oh . . ." She looked crestfallen, then quickly recovered. "Well, how about if we study the Bible together . . . in yer room?"

Without further ado, she led the way back into his room, sat down on his bed, and opened the Bible. He closed the door carefully behind him, and as she chattered merrily, outwardly confident but too wary to meet his eyes, he waited, slowly killing her composure with his silence and an arrogant stare. Finally, flustered, she stood up.

"Well." She gazed at him impudently, daring him. "What are ye waiting for?"

He stubbed his cigarette out in an ashtray and moved purposefully across to her. She gave a surprised little gasp as he bent, lifted her chin, and without otherwise touching her body, kissed her soundly on the mouth. It was a long sucking kiss; he knew tricks with his mouth and tongue that made her buckle at the knees. When he finally drew back, they were both breathing heavily. She stood eyeing him, beginning to smile, her eyes suffused with wonder.

"I guess that's what you wanted," Than said. She put on an affronted look and innocent indignant eyes. But she couldn't hide the little tugging smile.

"I had no such notion! *Ye're a missionary!*"

"Yeah. But maybe you ought to know it—it's a biological fact— I've got balls just like any other guy and little girls who go sitting on big boys' beds ought to expect to find that out. Bible or no Bible."

"Now look here, Doctor." To his intense chagrin, she was laughing. "It's the Bible we are here to study. So come along and sit ye here beside me, and I'll prove to ye the seriousness of my intentions!"

She patted the bed beside her. When he remained slouched against the wall, she snapped the book softly shut.

"Ye're so different outside of the hospital. Inside, ye're all bastard and arrogance! Outside, kind of solemn and shy. Well, ye'd better settle yerself down now and pay attention, Doctor."

"Oh Christ, lady, I'm not in school." Than turned away, annoyed that a nurse who jumped to his whip on duty could mock him in his bedroom. Casually, he kicked off his moccasins and pulled his shirt out of his pants. He unbuttoned the cuffs and began, slowly, deliberately, to unbutton down the front.

"Hey." She stood up indignantly. "What are ye doing?"

"Undressing for bed." He stared her straight in the eye. "And those who don't want to follow suit can leave right now."

She stared at him dazedly, mesmerized by the shocking partial view of his smooth golden chest, the shirt hanging open to reveal one hard sullen brown nipple and his silver medallion. He fumbled nonchalantly with his fly. He was a man well aware of the allure of his own body.

"I . . ." She stared at him helplessly. Then, with an abandoned little sigh, she fell gently against him, sliding her arms beneath the shirt and around the hard smoothness of his body. Wrapped in her arms, he smiled for the first time.

"Ooooh," she whispered rapturously, pressing her face into his bare chest, all pretense finally gone. "It's *beautiful* ye are!"

He changed in an instant. Arrogant indifference turned into controlled savagery. His hands trespassed her clothing, gripping her thighs and bruising her breasts in delicious encounters.

"Oh, it's a wicked, wicked girl I am!" she sighed.

He took her buttocks in his hands and held her tightly against him, making her feel the hard masculine straining of his flesh through his pants.

"And I," he said huskily, "am one very hungry boy."

That was the beginning of a two-week idyll that wore them both out. They slept together regularly, taking advantage of both their quarters, occasionally using her car. One evening, two days before he was due to leave, he found her crying in his room.

"I can tell ye're not a bit sorry to be leaving me. I suppose I'm just like a hundred other girls to ye!"

"Yeah," he sighed tiredly. "You're one in a hundred."

She stared at him, fascinated. "And do they all cry and carry on like this when ye leave?"

"No. Some of them are sports. One of them took sleeping pills."

She stared at him, aghast. "What happened to her?"

"She died," Than said quietly. "And, Lucy, it didn't do her one little bit of good . . ."

Later, as they lay together on his bed, she stared at him warily. "Have ye ever been in love?"

"Well, I was engaged once. To a cute little French med student name of Dominique. I couldn't get over her combination of beauty and brains. We shared a cadaver together, and, man, she was cooler than some of the guys—as if she was carving up a tree. She was the first woman who had ever acted sure of me. And she was a tigress in bed. She taught me to swear in French, and for a while it was pleasant to have her lead me around by the nose." He turned to her. "Christ, Lucy, how'd we ever get onto this depressing subject?"

She evaded his eyes. "Than, I've been thinking. This mission ye work at. Well, I'm about to end my contract here and . . ."

He sat up, spluttering. "Lucy, forget it. There are no vacancies for nurses."

"Oh?" She sat up and eyed him suspiciously. "Ye sure about that? A mission that couldn't do with extra help is a thing I've never heard of. How many nurses do they have?"

"Three—twenty-three," Than amended quickly.

"I mean *white* nurses. Even at a big hospital like Ndola, that seems a terrible lot."

"Well, we're a pretty big mission." He kissed her lingeringly to take her mind off the matter. In a moment she abandoned herself, forgetting everything else . . .

6

The mission, after his brief excursion from it, seemed strangely home to Than and he arrived back eager to continue his work in the hospital and the outlying villages. The encounter with Mulaisho's tribesmen had taken the edge off his nerve but not off his enthusiasm. Matthew Tomlinson's dire discouragements more tantalized than put him off, and his medical appetite, thoroughly whetted now, finally spurred him on to more subtle strategy.

One quiet Sunday, he put the spindly little pup into the Land-Rover and headed out to the distant Chokwe villages. Parking opposite the same patch of maize and pumpkin gardens he had found before, he flushed a group of women villagers from the verdant growth, where they had been keeping foraging birds and monkeys off the immature corn. When he switched off the engine, they took off like shying animals, hiding in the maize, peeping out cautiously from behind the tattered leaves.

Reaching across and opening the cab door, Than gave the kaffir pup an encouraging push that sent it sprawling spread-eagled upon the dry earth. It recovered itself, shuddering dust, and stood for a moment, lifting its frizzy-haired muzzle to sniff the faded scents on the dusty air. Then, getting its bearings, the nervous alertness thawed and there were small squeals of recognition and disbelief as the resurrected pup, all-forgiving, ran across the stream to be re-united with old friends.

Than smiled to hear them. Then he climbed out of the cab and hoisted himself up onto the burning-hot Land-Rover hood and took an old harmonica out of his breast pocket. He rubbed it reflectively against his sweat-damp shirt, pressed it to his mouth, and began to play, making a frail lonesome sound in the desolate bush. He went through a medley of American classics, and as he played, the children crept gradually closer. His heart swelled with the strains of "Sweet Georgia Brown" and he sucked on the tinny-tasting silver instrument, breathed his great aching medical ambition through the metal reeds, and sent a sweet wordless persuasion to the little pot-bellied pagan children across the hot unstirring air. He played until his throat ached and the distant rumble of the dusk drums had begun to sound. And then, when he had made his mark, he set a brown paper packet of sugar cubes on the ground. His visiting card thus dispatched, he turned to take his leave with Cuss close at his heels.

With untiring obstinacy, Than went to the lonely Chokwe villages again and again. Always he found a group of the same dusty pi-canins minding the maize, and each time he parked the Land-Rover under the adjacent thorn trees and proceeded to woo them with sugar and a serenade. He had acquired an old guitar, and this he alternated with the harmonica, sitting on his dusty Land-Rover in the abysmal heat, singing and playing any number of soulful ballads, until his numbed fingers grew slick with sweat and his straining throat grew husky and parched. Cuss, who accompanied him on each visit, became a bond between them, an affectionate envoy who ran happily to and fro across the stream, reassuring both parties with wagging tail and wet kisses.

With each successive visit, Than found that ever more children came to join those few stationed at the stream-side gardens. The dust-wake of his Land-Rover and the shirt-waving signals of some lonely little sentinels who waited on the escarpment brought them hurrying along the converging paths from villages miles around. Always they gathered at the stream-side gardens and stared solemnly. Once, when an old man joined them, Than gave him a carton of cigarettes and asked that these be conveyed to Chief Mulaisho, along with a hastily scrawled note that expressed his respectful regards.

                    *   *   *

To Than Profane's great exasperation, the mongrel from Mulaisho's village developed a dogged devotion to him. It took to following him to the hospital, and when not even the operating room proved sacred to the joyfully romping hound, the animal had to be locked in the house every day to prevent it from doing the ward rounds with the doctor. But unfortunately, the pup was often more wily than its houseboy custodian, and when the Boy talked idly of giving the animal away to some native, Matthew grew concerned.

"Now, now," he chided. "The dog will calm in time. He's only a pup, after all. And a native would not treat him as well. Their poor dogs are left to scavenge what pitiful scraps they may. Besides, it is thy moral duty to . . ." he piously lectured on and on.

"Oh bullshit, Matthew. It's easy for you to talk. *You* don't have him fouling up your footsteps. You're pretty glib when it comes to giving advice, old man, but I wonder if you'd accept the same responsibility yourself. "

"Indeed I would!" Matthew reared up in noble indignation. "If the good Lord had happened such a waif into my care, I would consider it my *embounden* duty."

"Oh yeah?"

They eyed each other for a moment. Then the Boy stooped abruptly and picked up the dog. "Well, that's just fine," he said, "because it has suddenly come upon me in a flash of inspiration . . . that the good Lord's will embodied in me is hereby handing this flea-bitten waif into thy able-bodied care!" So saying, he dumped the squirming hound into a horrified Matthew's arms. For a long time after the Boy had left, Matthew stood helplessly holding on to the scrawny creature. It wriggled fiercely to take after its chosen master. But Matthew did not dare let it go.

"Oh, Matthew Tomlinson!" he moaned in distress. "Thee and thy imprudent mouth!"

The dog was to prove a trial and embarrassment to him forever after. And although he gave the animal impersonal food and shelter, he would never admit to its ownership. In time, the dog developed an attachment to him. Matthew ignored it stonily when it took to following him around. And based upon his own innocent evasions (Who *me*? What, *mine*?), it became common knowledge that Cuss was nobody's dog. He merely owned a few people.

After supper in the evening cool, Matthew and Teller, shining flash-lights, walked with the Poes, who were up from Barotseland for the forthcoming quarterly meeting, across the river to Ward Disney's house for a committee meeting of the Friends' Central Africa Mission. Beyond the boys' school, the house was situated on the trade school campus. The front door opened, releasing two friendly dogs, and Ward Disney, puffing on his pipe, was framed in the lighted doorway.

"Welcome to Disneyland."

Chuckling at the old joke, they trouped, the last to arrive, into the man's untidy living room. As usual, the widower Ward's womanless house was strewn with newspapers and books, with spare mechanical parts, and even stray clothing. With a look of dignified distaste, Benedict Poe removed a grease-stained pair of old undershorts from the settee before sitting down. Matthew discreetly kicked an old chewed shoe under the couch; he had to evict a mangy kaffir dog, curled at home as a cushion, from his chosen chair. As secretary/ treasurer, he efficiently fussed, setting out papers and reports. At first all went well. Most matters on the agenda were lengthily discussed; the ladies had a tendency to ramble on and they had a merry old time dissecting the problems and progress that had checkered their work. Then, during a lull in the proceedings, Ward took off his reading spectacles and looked at Than Profane. At Katherine's instigation, this was the first committee meeting the doctor had been invited to attend.

"Matthew mentioned something about a medical course thee wants to start. Would thee care to elaborate?"

The Boy glanced up. "Well, as you all know, we already train nurse's aides at the hospital. But we sorely need more comprehensively trained staff. Dr. Dooley and I are wasting time and precious capabilities working our butts off doing menial scut work that a few well-trained men could take off our shoulders. What I'd like to do is replace the present nurse's-aide course with a three-year one training men as medical assistants capable of suturing wounds, giving blood transfusions, and diagnosing and treating all the basic endemic diseases, men who would be capable of running departments or manning isolated bush clinics on their own."

"Bush clinics?" Hannah Rothchild quailed. "Pray tell, where would we find those?"

"Well, that's part of my plan, ma'am. You see, the majority of the people live so far from the hospital, it's easier for them to visit the local witchdoctor. They only make the trip to us when their symptoms are very advanced. If we could set up a chain of clinics extending into remote areas and have these manned by the kind of medical assistants I want to train, then the people's diseases and ailments could be detected and treated earlier and it could ultimately mean the saving of eyes and lives."

"Indeed?" Clara Fotch wore a look of wide-eyed wonder. "Why, Doctor, thy ambition never ceases to amaze me. In thy eight months here, thee seems determined to revolutionize our entire procedure!" She paused amid unkind titters of amusement. "I'm sure we all appreciate thy concern to bring all things up to American city standards. But were such schemes truly necessary, I am sure Dr. Dooley, or indeed thy late father, would have long ago introduced them. But perhaps they realized we are not a medical organization, but primarily a religious mission dedicated to the evangelization of heathen Africa. Thee seems to continually lose sight of that fact, Doctor. And I say far too much work has already been done to redeem the people's bodies and not enough to save their souls. A materialist state of affairs which must surely gravely sadden the Lord."

"Yes, yes," Matthew fretted. "I understand thy feelings, Friend, but the new medical course the doctor proposes would hardly make a difference to the present situation. Aside from the curricular materials, it would entail no great financial outlay initially, since we already have a classroom and student accommodation."

"Hold on just a moment there, Friend." It was Benedict Poe, smiling gravely. "Before we go getting heated up over Dr. Profane's proposals, perhaps we'd best consider that old precept of the Friends' mission, that all new recruits be adept in a native language before qualifying as voting members of the mission staff. As I understand it, the doctor has not yet taken such a step to make him eligible."

Matthew stared at the man stupidly. Years ago the language test had been the normal course. What the man had failed to mention was that the practice had died out over the years. In more recent times, none of their new recruits had been held subject to the outdated prerequisite.

There was an embarrassed stirring amongst those missionaries sympathetic to the Boy, and Matthew said in a strangled voice: "Ben, I hardly think the language examination necessary in this case. We all *know* Dr. Profane has developed an unusually able grasp of *Chi-Lwena!*"

"In that case," Hannah Rothchild swiftly countered, "he will surely not be too bothered by a test to establish it."

In the uncomfortable silence that followed, Matthew sat for a moment, irritably aware of the infernal scratching of the Disney dog, Waldo. While others had been discussing his qualifications right over his head, the Boy had said nothing; he said nothing now. And Matthew, while vexed at the petty intolerance, knew from experience that it would be best to have the Boy take the language test and be done with it. Indeed, it would be the least of his worries. Without the support of the majority of this committee, which ultimately dictated all mission expenditures, he could never hope to realize his dream of so dramatically expanding their medical services. Indeed, by the self-satisfied smirks on the faces of Hannah Rothchild and Clara Fotch, Matthew had the uncomfortable feeling they were all set to come up with an inexhaustible supply of excuses to frustrate him at every turn.

Sighing to himself, Matthew finished writing the meeting's minutes. The meeting was brought to a close in a frigid atmosphere that did not thaw even when the Boy left. Matthew, miserably disgruntled, stayed for Ward's usual weak tea and ginger cookies. He listened in frosty displeasure to the cheerful chatter of Clara Fotch and the silly, simpering Carrie Poe.

7

In May the rains stopped and the coming of winter put a thin, chill edge onto early morning and night, sandwiching in between long dry days that were still sallow with frail sunshine. And out in the deep bush, the old life rankled still; through the pacifying veneer of civilization, ancient traditions rose up like ghosts of the past, unwilling to lie down. At a small village near the Congo border, an aged headman, feeling the failing of his exhausted heart, stared up into the scudding winter clouds and was assailed by nostalgia of days gone by . . .

With the cessation of the rains, work in the village gardens had stopped and the villagers were idle. The traditional seven fallow years had now passed since the holding of the last sacred *Mukanda* circumcision ceremony, the most revered of all Lunda life-crisis rituals, and Headman Mbayole, mournful of the breakdown of the traditional way of life, gazed resentfully at the wayward modern youth and longed for the forgotten glories of the ancient tribal rituals. After considering the extent of his small wealth, he called forth the most spirited boy in the village and directed him to approach a powerful witchdoctor who lived in a village some miles away and who possessed the necessary medicines and apparatus to perform a mass circumcision.

The news of the impending ceremony raged across Lunda country. Messengers began to arrive from remote areas, even from senior chiefdoms, asking if they might send their young boys to this *Mukanda*. The parents of the boys began to brew beer and assemble foodstuffs to take along with their children to the village where the *Mukanda* would take place.

Matthew heard the news with a discordant jangling of pleasure. Not for nothing had the natives christened him *Samunyati*, Seeker into the Past, for it was his special torment to find fascination in ancient African rituals frowned upon by the meeting. As an anthropologist, he had recorded practices and events down the years that would have horrified his colleagues, hiding an indecent interest behind the guise of proper ascetic distaste. He wrote occasional papers for the Rhodes-Livingstone Museum, and working in private to compile a history and study of the Lunda-Luvale peoples, he thus considered the promised ceremony with a quickening excitement. It was a complicated ritual, and since the last one seven years ago, he had been left still uncertain of many elusive facets of spiritual significance.

Many of the African converts, chastised to Christian beliefs, had left off their pagan dealings and settled instead for a simple operation performed at the mission hospitals, free of charge, to bring their young sons to inglorious manhood. But despite the missionaries' rationalizations, the spiritual hold of ancient ritual was strong; sometimes, to an old man, the fiery looming of hell seemed no unfair exchange for a last witness of the stirring and powerful Lunda pageantry of the time-honored *Mukanda*, and spurred on by age-old superstition, they sent out tiny feelers of discontent, which sowed seeds in the young, and which, fertilized by the restlessness of an agriculturally dormant dry season, stirred up a massive rebellion. Now the natives from surrounding villages came to flaunt the news almost insolently. After years of calm Christian conformity, they began running mindlessly, like suicidal lemmings, toward the craved excitement of ancient forbidden doings and certain spiritual despoilment. The missionaries' ominous warnings in meeting found no response in ears purposely closed.

Dr. Dooley renewed his offer for free circumcision for all

pubescent boys, and the older ladies howled with effrontery when no takers came. Matthew alone stood miserably exulted. He wore a stern face, volunteering manfully to go into the heathen sin-bath and inject what Christian influence he could. The ceremony, through ignorance and uncleanliness, had been known to cause pathetic suffering and even death, and Matthew, a demeaned double agent, compromised with the natives. With a gleaming eye on Than Profane, he promised a medical overseer to ensure against this.

Although their African mission workers feigned obedient disapproval of the forthcoming initiation, Matthew's preparations to join it severely strained the pious faces. On the day before departure, a number of inordinately helpful men and boys clustered around the Land-Rover, looking longing and bereft as stray starving dogs before a butcher shop window. With desperate martyrdom they offered themselves as harbingers, pathfinders, and bearers of baggage, and it was upon these grounds that Matthew finally selected a fortuitous few. By the next dawn light, when the Land-Rover was finally packed and prepared, Cuss, unabashedly wagging his tail, was illicitly stowed amongst these eager Africans. The Boy took the wheel, and after driving countless miles, they left the main road and headed steadily out through the densely wooded Mwinilunga territory, where the blue grass grew wild and the infrequent villages lay silent and strangely empty; the powerful draw of the *Mukanda* had preceded them, it seemed.

Beyond the tsetse-fly barrier, the thickening bush finally strangled the dwindling bush-track and they left the Land-Rover at a wayside village and, with the Boy's medical supplies and a few home comforts hoisted onto the heads and backs of their bearers, continued on foot. Out in the open, Africa lay basking under a frail honey-pale sunshine, and the stillness was inspiring. Here and there in the drab grayish-green bush, indigenous pink jacarandas blossomed in startling splendor and the scintilating blue-shot grasses were rifled by a light-fingered wind that was filled with the chill fleeting feel of coming winter.

As they walked, a grazing herd of graceful golden impala bounded from their path, leaping and weaving with quick-silver symmetry. A pair of warthogs, running with their yearlings, darted away with tails snapped up like exclamation marks, tossing tusked heads that were nobbled and gnarled as ancient tree trunks. Once there was a sound like a locomotive passing overhead, and they looked up to see the mass beating of wings as trumpeter hornbills crossed the sky in top-heavy undulating flight. The little safari skirted wide, reeded, duck-dabbled *dambos* and splashed through sandy streams. Then they reached a stretch of water too narrow to justify a bridge yet too wide to straddle. The shallow river flowed deep in black, muddy banks.

"*Now* what'll we do?" Matthew looked around fretfully. "We can't wade through that sludge. My land, just look at it, though! It'll ruin our clothes."

But the Boy was unperturbed. He stood in the open sunshine and began to shrug off his denim jacket and kick off his boots. Matthew stared at him with a proper Quaker horror. The Boy, unzipping his jeans, stared calmly back, and Matthew turned away in confusion, feeling ridiculously smitten by his own small shamed sense of Victorian propriety. Why, here he was, an explorer into the awesome annals of time and history. He had crossed a wild land to record a pagan ritual seldom witnessed by the outside world. Yet he stood stumped by nature's first obstacle, defeated by his own almost pathological shyness. Slowly, with a light-headed sense of bodily dispossession, he began miserably disrobing his poor aged body. He turned, and it seemed unfair. With strips of sallow paleness where the sun had not caught him, the Boy emerged sleek, bronzed, and muscular as a young Greek god, so clean and hard and unashamed that there was strangely no offense in his nudity. The Africans around him ripped off their clothes, grinning fiendishly. Matthew turned his head from haired dangling genitals and unpeeled like a shy, shamed flower.

The party, carrying their clothes and possessions above the water line, walked in a single file through the slimy, mud-sucking brown water. Matthew was the last in line. His bony leather-hided body retracted in miserable exposure; his shy pinched buttocks felt vulnerable as butter in the cool open sunshine, and his testes drew up to the nervous knot of his stomach. The cold water made him gasp, tough reeds spiked his tender soles, and he thought of crocodiles. As he moved, shuddering through decomposing masses, fretfully anticipating the silent ensnarlment of reptilian teeth, the water suddenly churned up beside him and he almost fainted clean away. But it was only Cuss, swimming clumsily, coarse hair spiked wet, eager eyes bright and tongue aloll, and Matthew's racing heart subsided slowly. The river, carefully trodden, took forever to cross, and the giggles of phantom maidens rang mockingly in Matthew's blushing ears. It was more than a stream he forded; it was the crossing of a moral frontier, the compromise of a modesty once fiercely upheld. By the time he reached shore, Matthew's face was set like stone. It was a capitulation he would not lightly forgive the Boy.

At the *Mukanda* village, they received a polite but guarded welcome, and the aged headman gave them a hut and sent men to cut grass for their bedding. When they had dispatched their sleeping bags and equipment, he led them to the rudimentary thatch projection of his hut veranda. While they drank mugs of lukewarm *hanyani* tea made from a lemon-scented Angolan grass, they watched the people walking to and fro carrying gourds of beer and calabashes of food. Most of the young wore ragged European clothes, while the elderly wore skins. A blind man sat patiently twanging on the metal teeth of a kaffir piano with his thumbs, and at the edge of the clearing, Cuss, happily integrated with the village dogs, barked at blue monkeys, which shrieked from the trees.

An excited furor of *ululating*, hand-clapping, and kneeling greeted the arrival of a party of African men carrying transistor radios and battered guitars; central among them strode an impressively tall young African wearing sunglasses and blue denim jeans.

"Who's that?" the Boy drawled. "Elvis Presley?"

"That's Jahaliso," Matthew chuckled. "He's senior chief of the Balovale Lunda and, with his powerful following, about the most coveted prize among the missions in these parts. He was brought up on a mission station in the Congo but apparently strayed from the Christian path, and when he became chief here, just about every mission for miles around was after converting him. One time there was quite a tussle between us and the Catholics; matter of fact, we had him all but eating out of our hands until Hannah and Clara chased his brother off the hospital premises because he had venereal disease. 'Course they didn't know he was the chief's brother, and they meant well. Unfortunately, they thoroughly humiliated the poor man, and when Jahaliso heard, he denounced us all over the country! We lost hundreds of probational members, and as fast as the chief's influence works, we're still losing 'em! But the ladies won't admit to their huge *faux pas*, and the official word is, it's *we* who have 'banished' Jahaliso until such time as he gives up associating with the 'criminal elements' among the nationalist politicians he's since taken up with. Naturally, beneath it all they'd give their eye-teeth to win him back and cock a snoot at the Catholics. I'd introduce him to thee, but he doesn't take kindly to missionaries these days. Might be we'll end up in the cooking pot yet!"

After the short African twilight, a chill black cricket-shrilling night fell across the land. Over sixty boys had assembled for the circumcision and the village overflowed with their relatives; their excited chattering filled the air and the night fires reflected on the moving silhouettes of their crouching bodies. The steady monotonous throbbing of the rawhide drums began to sound as the people began to filter through the dark bush to a spot some one hundred yards from the village. There, an expectant hush fell, as first the headman, then the witchdoctor and the "Keeper of the Sacred-Fire," assembled before a line of *nyiyombu* trees, which had been planted as shrines to the village deceased. Holding a ball of white chalk, symbolic of purity, good health, good will, and communion, each man in turn drew three lines on the ground from where he stood to a tree. Then each drew a line upward on his own body from the navel, and finally anointed himself between the eyes. The headman called out each of the village deceased by name, praising them and beseeching them to protect the young novices from misfortune. Then, Mbimbi, the witchdoctor, called upon the shades to witness that he had never previously allowed a novice to die as a result of circumcision. The Keeper of the Sacred Fire, in turn, promised that he would observe the correct customs. Then he gravely knelt and lit the sacred fire with steel and flint, and the people, as if by signal, went wild.

As the drums began to throb and incite, they formed long weaving lines of bodies. The firelight reflected on the sleek ebony of bare jostling breasts and flexing muscles. There was a mass stamping of feet and the rhythmic rattle of dried seed-pods tied around the ankles, and the women began their blood-chilling ululating, clapping hands to their mouths to produce a high-pitched warbling sound that mingled eerily with the shrieking whistles and surging harmony of the men. They danced now to rejoice in the imminent coming to manhood of their young sons.

While bush rats and guinea fowl were roasted on spits, the people passed around great calabashes of food. There were duiker stew and steaming bowls of cassava and *nshima* meal, with relishes of great umbrella mushrooms, sweet potatoes, caterpillars, and wild bananas. The headman approached Matthew with a gourd of murky sour-smelling millet beer, but he disdainfully shook his head. He turned in surprise as the Boy took the beer gourd with both hands, raised it in the traditional manner, and drank like a native. When the liquid ran down his chin, the headman's grave facade cracked in a grin of pure delight.

"*Eureka!*" The Boy, panting exultantly, came up for air. He smiled boyishly at Matthew and wiped his wet mouth on the shoulder of his denim jacket. After that, he drank whenever a gourd came around, and that was outrageously too often for Matthew's liking. He knew that the young man had imbibed much more than was good, when some time later he threw back that blond-streaked head, cupped hands to his mouth, and gave out with a lusty full-throated Commanche war cry that made Matthew's hair stand on end. But worse was yet to come. Matthew closed his eyes, appalled as he stood up and began to wriggle and stamp in expert mimicry of primitive dance. The hip-jerking pelvic movements had strong sexual connotations which he found decidedly discomforting, but he watched, fascinated and enthralled, in spite of himself. It was something to be believed, after all. That tall, tawny, sunburned Boy, moving like a native, with a coordinated in-built grace, was astonishing to see. It was age-old anathema, but Matthew felt a grudging admiration for such as he: the city boy from San Francisco taking Africa like a drug.

The Boy winced, waking up much later in their dim smelly hut. He cradled a tousled head, sitting bare-chested amid his blankets, the silver pendant gleaming in the dimness. Matthew had led him to bed in the early hours, stumbling drunk and confused as a child. Now he was badly hung over and lacking in sleep. Matthew was aloof. But Cuss unfurled off his feet and went to greet the Boy with a cold inquiring nose. The Boy pushed him off.

"Jesus . . ." He gazed blankly at Matthew and a look of extraordinary anguish passed across that handsome face as his throat began to work. "Jesus, Matthew—that food last night. I was so stoned, I swear I swallowed a caterpillar!" There was a scrambling of blankets and he dived naked for the doorway. The sounds of a dreadful dry gagging filled Matthew's satisfied ears. When it was realized that his cigarettes had been stolen, he felt oddly compensated. The Boy was still grumbling about this loss later, while they watched the crowd of young boys perform the symbolic rituals that would culminate in the day-long task of erecting a lodge to house them throughout their seclusion.

By the next morning, the women had been banished from the sacred site, where the men began to chant and drum the *Mukanda* refrain; each boy had an allotted guardian and these now stood behind their trembling, terrified charges as a group of men suddenly cavorted into the clearing, carrying other grown men upon their backs, each holding medicines and fearsome-looking knives. As the drumming grew ominously faster and faster, the guardians suddenly pounced. They threw the small novices onto their backs and held them firmly, while Mbimbi, the great witchdoctor, took a stout knife from a skin receptacle and, amid the traditionally condoned loud screaming and struggling from the boys, knelt over Kambanji, the war leader, and, without anesthetics of any kind, cut and removed the first child's foreskin.

"Jesus," Than Profane whispered with awe as the other doctors began to circumcise the remaining boys, the sound of their agony all but drowned in the singing and drumming of the male relatives.

Awaiting the time when the circumcision novices would be taken to a stream and their congealed blood washed off, Matthew tried to interest the restive natives in biblical parables, and the Boy turned dedicated doctor again. A few sheepish Quaker "attenders" were among the first to seek treatment. Once these had broken down an initial reserve, the majority of the people, away from the intimidating omnipresence of their village witchdoctors, mobbed him. Quaker Friends helped to sort the people into separate groups according to their ailments, and they waited patiently to be doled out aspirins and antibiotics, spoon-fed cough mixtures and purges, and to have their sores and wounds bathed and dressed. Even the surly Jahaliso came to survey the proceedings haughtily; though he ignored the Boy's offer to institute the removal of incipient cataracts that had started to cloud his eyes, he did not discourage others from receiving treatment.

The following day, the novices were led to a stream to clean their wounds. Than examined each shivering boy as he emerged. Then he watched with interest while Mbimbi applied bark pounded in cold water to the fresh scars. The novices were then given *kasanji* leaves to chew, which were subsequently wadded around the gland as a bandage.

No boy had yet died, but if any did, he would not be buried but simply thrown onto a cinder pile near the lodge and gradually covered with the ashes of successive fires. His mother would not be informed until the initiation was over; then she would be silently handed the plate on which she had sent his food—*broken.*

For the next few months, sleeping on the cold winter ground in seclusion in the bush, the boys would undergo tests of extreme hardship. They would be given explicit instruction on sexual matters, on tribal traditions, and on bush- and folklore, thereby befitting them for community life in the role of a man.

8

Two weeks after Matthew and the Boy arrived back from the circumcision ceremony, the annual group of Quaker visitors arrived from the States, and Suseshi was further swelled when the missionaries and a crowd of black delegates came up from Barotseland to attend the midyear quarterly meeting. Finally, a goodly crowd packed the meeting house, and it was a contentious meeting from the start.

The spirit of ZANC, impervious of the government restrictions, had risen up to trouble them anew. As the less important detainees came up for release, they had formed two new parties, which had begun intimidating the masses, while those senior ZANC officials still detained at Kabompo and in Barotseland were disrupting the local people with their pernicious ideology. According to Benedict Poe, they swaggered about in homemade togas of blankets (the uniquely Pan-Africanist garb copied from Ghana) and were sneering and disrespectful to the district commissioners and all whites in general. Well, Benedict had long denounced the nationalists in order to curry favor with the politically aloof, secession-seeking Barotses in whose province he served. Now he stood up to urge the meeting to abstain from all association with such miscreants.

"The people of the Southern province allowed their cattle to die for want of trypanosomiasis inoculations withheld on the say-so of these evil men!" he boomed, tucking his thumbs into a frayed silk waistcoat as he measured the meeting, standing gaunt, grim, and warty-faced in his shabby black Prince Alfred–suit. "And right here in this province we see the example of Chief Jahaliso, whose people have begun denouncing whites and the Christian church since fraternizing with the detained ZANC leaders!"

Before their Lunda and Barotse interpreters could translate such hearsay, Matthew stood up, immediately censorious in his role as senior elder. As missionaries, they occupied but honorary roles in the country; in the meeting their agreed capacity was to guide opinion rather than lead it, he reminded quietly. But he knew his words would be little heeded, and he was troubled. For the benign influence of their pacifist Quaker members could be immensely moderating in the country's nationalist political parties, which seethed with militant radicals. Furthermore, the unnatural neutrality Poe advocated was a provocation to the very intimadating violence their members so feared and decried.

Matthew was relieved when the meeting moved on to more mundane matters, and Sakapuchi, an influential leader in their district, stood up to decry the dearth of medical facilities provided by the Friends' mission in this province. Since the man had hitherto expressed little concern for the people's health, Matthew suspected Than Profane's hand in enlisting this outside "enthusiasm" to back up his cause. Whatever the case, Sakapuchi felt strongly enough about it to call Benedict Poe, who had converted him years previously, into account on the issue.

"Thou means bush clinics?" Poe looked uncomfortable, and Matthew understood his distress. In face of the headman's churlish annoyance, their work was fast losing face in front of their annual contingent of weighty visitors from the States, who peered from the pews. Also, Benedict had in attendance two carefully nurtured Lozi royals who were in direct contact with their paramount chief, Barotseland's powerful monarch, whose kingly conversion Poe had long coveted. Now he stared helplessly at Jerome Dooley, who stared helplessly at Than Profane, who sat on a front-facing bench nonchalantly chewing on a toothpick.

"Impossible," the Boy said mildly. "We don't have the trained personnel to man such isolated clinics."

"Theny you must train some!" the headman called contemptuously. "The Baptists and the Catholic missions take heed of the people's needs!"

"Er . . . thank thee for the suggestion, Friend," Benedict muttered fretfully, obviously irritated and bewildered to find himself taken to task on an issue that did not even remotely concern him. Still avoiding Than Profane, he turned hesitantly to Matthew. "Er . . . Friend, does thee think we might make some resolution to fit Mr. Sakapuchi's suggestion? Some recommendation?"

"Well, that's a little difficult." Matthew raised a questioning brow at the Boy, who, as the silence stretched on, became a suspenseful focal point.

"Well, I don't know," the Boy finally allowed. His face was a study of reluctance, and Poe, leaning forward, looked under strain to choke some sense out of him. The Boy was clearly acting up in order to egg on an already avid audience. But being guilty of having previously debunked the project, Benedict was helpless to call the Boy's bluff now, not while their weighty white Friends looked on and the Lozi princes waited to be impressed.

"Well," Poe subsided unhappily, tugging at his tight collar. (The concession must be killing him.) "Perhaps, Dr. Profane, at some future date thee might see thy way clear to . . ."

And having lured him this far, the Boy suddenly dropped all subterfuge and came right out in the open with it.

"Mr. Poe." He stood up and looked around, talking loudly to secure the attention of all the meeting. "Let's get this straight. As I understand it, you're suggesting we begin advanced medical training as soon as possible at Suseshi? That we set up a circuit of out-clinics extending right to our new clinic in Barotseland?"

Benedict stared sickly at the Boy. He was suggesting no such thing, of course. But he was stuck with the sly supposition.

"Er, yes . . ." Grimacing, Benedict rubbed a hand over his mouth so that his reluctant words came out muffled. "I suppose thee might say so."

"Well," the Boy said, smiling slowly, "*I* sure have no objection. Does anyone else?"

All the Boy's allies gave loud blessings, and even the elder ladies, trapped to demonstrate generosity in front of their overseas guests, mouthed sweet smiling affirmations, which after their earlier irked objections Matthew found ironical to hear.

Later, an examination conducted by Matthew proved the Boy to be adequately adept in Chi-Lwena, and he was present when the Friends' committee officially sanctioned his scheme to upgrade the present medical training and start a chain of clinics extending into Barotseland. After their elaborate farcical support to impress their visitors, the originally opposing members now had no option but to accede and gave grudging way, having made the one premise they could still legitimately make—that Than Profane himself raise the funds to cover any additional expenses accrued by his projects. Well, the Boy seemed little ruffled by this detail, but Matthew, with the wisdom of long experience, was worried. Oh, if the schemes were approved by the government, they would most certainly be grant-aided by it; however, the government paid only a percentage, and the outstanding costs of his clinics alone could be prohibitive. Even supposing the villagers, using local materials, helped with their construction—local materials, if cheaper, were not free—the large round huts lined with verandas that the Boy had designed would ultimately need furnishing with benches, cupboards, an examination table, desk, chairs, besides rudimentary medical instruments and basic medications. But the Boy wasn't about to let any grass grow under his feet. He made it clear at the outset that he would shortly need to take off for Salisbury, in Southern Rhodesia, to present his plans to the Federal government and otherwise agitate to raise the funds.

9

One abysmal afternoon there came out of the still bush the melodious plinking of a lone xylophone player. It was an old man carrying his long *olimbo* suspended on leather thongs around his scrawny neck. As he walked, solemnly playing, across the school playing field, the magical jingles wove a spell and the man, like some indigenous Pied Piper, drew behind him scores of vagrant adults, children, dogs, and the whole of Orville Fotch's science class, while the teacher himself hailed feebly after them. Matthew, witnessing this blatant mutiny, winced. He did not suffer fools gladly, and although he tried to overlook many of Orville's shortcomings, it was his unhappy feeling that the man was a bumbling incompetent, an ineffectual buffoon who was scorned by his students and colleagues alike. As science teacher, he was an academic disaster and only Quaker fellowship in the cover of his colleagues' and Matthew's own tender hearts lent him a kind of uneasy immunity against recall.

But this was no time to take the man to task. Matthew hurried ahead of the *olimbo* player to round upon and challenge him. As he stepped up breathlessly, barring the musician's path, the playing stopped abruptly and the trailing audience massed around him.

The solemn old man fumbled in the pocket of his torn, dirty bush jacket. (Despite the shabbiness of this European attire, he wore copper bracelets and anklets, a kilt of jackal tails swung around his waist, and Matthew sensed in him the innate pride endowed the consort of a chief). Without saying a word, he thrust out a grubby scrap of paper at Matthew.

There was an expectant hush as Matthew unfolded the note and felt for his reading spectacles. But he had left them behind, and the writing, in blunt pencil, was an illegible scrawl. Then in one corner he espied the faint stamp of a chief. It was a legacy of the early days of widespread illiteracy, when the colonial administrators had issued each chief with a stamp depicting some animal, to serve as that man's identifying seal of authority. This one depicted a crocodile, and Matthew had to wrack his brains before the long-ago-learned code came back to him. "The crocodile! Why, I do believe the crocodile was the seal of the ancestors of . . . of Mulaisho's clan!"

A murmur of awe rippled through the crowd, and when Matthew focused again, he saw that Hannah Rothchild had joined the throng and Clara Fotch was hurrying up some way behind.

"Mulaisho!" Hannah gasped. Her eyes were wide in disbelief. "Come calling on *us*? Clara, come hear thee this!" She giggled with exhilaration as Clara joined them. "This here's Mulaisho's man. Looks like all our efforts sowed seed on that stony ground after all! Mulaisho! My, won't the Catholics and the Baptists be vexed that he's chosen *us*!"

The crowd clamor fell to an excited hush as the old musician, clearing a wheezy throat, began to speak. He had a lisping speech impediment, and after a short guttural outpouring, Matthew was left still trying to fathom the gist of it. Then the headmaster said quietly, "Professor, this man is an *olimbo* player of Mulaisho's band. He has brought word from his chief's capital. The chief wishes to see Dr. Profane. As he is himself too old and ailing to make the trip to Suseshi, he invites the doctor to his village."

In that moment of revelation, the aghast faces of Hannah Rothchild and Clara Fotch were etched forever in Matthew's mind.

Jealous of the Boy's license, the Friends' committee decreed that Matthew, in his official capacity as mission secretary, should accompany Than Profane and his dresser, Cosmo Mlongoti, to see Chief Mulaisho. The following day was cold and overcast in winter's wake. Optimistically laden with medical supplies, they left the Land-Rover beyond the escarpment before setting off on foot to the chief's village. They took directions from surly men who were busy lopping off tree branches that would be burned to fertilize their cassava fields, and as they trudged past isolated ancestor shrines and dirty derelict villages, Matthew took the opportunity to prime the Boy on the protocol deemed proper for such a privileged personage.

"Friend Profane," he said with formal severity, "I would ask thee simply to mind the Light, but having become a little dubious of late as to just what amperage thee adheres to, I will ask thee simply to stick by me and do as I do. Thee don't have to say a single solitary word. I'll do all the talking. And wipe that grin off thy face. This is no laughing matter."

"Yes, Daddy."

"Oh, thee may laugh." Matthew drew up severely, offended by his levity. "But I know these people better than thee. Thee might think that after years of taking example from the white man they are reasonably civilized. Well, that's where the deception lies, Friend. Amongst these backwoods people, still so riven with superstitious devilry, thee never can tell what heinous deeds are simmering behind their smiling faces. It was not so long ago that they had necrophagy down at Barotseland!"

That shocked the levity out of him!

"*Necrophagy?*" The Boy's head snapped up and he stared incredulously. "Jesus! I thought that was a barbarism that went out with the Stone Age."

"Not in these parts. Couple of years back, a whole conspiracy of ritual grave robbers and corpse eaters was brought to brave British justice! And that in genteel Barotseland amongst the progressive Lozis. Some of them have even gone so far as to eat their own relatives. Well, we all know about the African craving for meat, but that's taking it a little far. So thee see, Boy, if seemingly civilized natives could make a meal of their own . . ." He shuddered squeamishly at the very thought. "Well then . . ."

He fell silent as they approached the chief's sprawling village. It was thickly fortified with enmeshed thorny thickets. The gray tangles of dead foliage had to be negotiated through a long tunnel. Cosmo led the way. Next the Boy, in his durable jeans, managed the crawl on all fours with admirable dignity. But the awkward scramble unnerved Matthew completely; the thorny brush scratched his face and snagged at his frock coat, the wet sand staining his scuffed knees. He finally scrambled up at the opposite end, feeling foolish and disoriented, to be grimly greeted by a surly array of skinclad tribesmen.

The region's rotational months of famine had not yet arrived to restrict the brewing of fermented beverages, and the beer-blousy men, some of whose dark eyes were dazedly dilated (doubtless due to the indigenous weed dagga), staggered a little as they led the way through the untidy village squalor while drums ominously rumbled and dogs, pigs, chickens, and children scattered from their path. A group of ragged, shivering young men, busy moving beans in a set of little holes gouged in the ground, looked up from their draftlike indigenous game of *chisolo*, and as they meandered, people all around them left off their labors and sullenly stared.

A filthy apathetic child defecated where he sat. He, like most of the children, was naked and caked in cracked gray mud to ward off the bitter bush cold. While they wandered in aimless existence, unfed, unclothed, and uneducated, their uncaring mothers sat in idle vanity, patiently painting each other's faces in horrific heathen patterns or intricately plaiting hair in the ancient tribal fashions. At one point a filthy woman suddenly pushed through the throng to confront them pleadingly; even her own people shrank back, repelled by her presence, and Matthew could hardly blame them. She stank unspeakably, and there was about her shamefully bowed head and shabby skins a pathetic persecuted humility. She might have been young, but her black face was creased with ceaseless suffering and her dead despairing eyes appealed to them with an ageless anguish that stopped the Boy in his tracks. He scientifically sniffed her odious odor before she was banished by the sticks and shouts of their scornful entourage. Matthew was about to protest when he realized they had arrived at Mulaisho's hut. And then he was impressed. Compared with the other ramshackle hovels, it was a spacious and commanding edifice with a large veranda around it.

Inside, the smoke of a small fire stung his eyes. (How did they learn to live with it?) And Matthew felt his stomach contract; herein, in the firelit gloom, Mulaisho, evil-doing old disciple of the devil, was finally confronted. In the smoky dimness, Matthew squinted to appraise the preposterous spectacle of a wizened figure ludicrously reclined upon an elaborate brass bedstead. His first thought was that others had exaggerated. *Why, he's just a feeble old man!* Then he remembered the heinous deeds attributed to this man, and his cautious nature whispered: *there is no smoke without fire!* And amid so much poverty, surrounded by flamboyant possessions, the old man exuded a despotic wealth. Formally appareled for this audience, his grizzled gray head was bedecked with a bead coronet and a filch of flaming feathers. Amulets and charms and a beaten snuff spoon hung around his scrawny neck. A fine cape of leopard skin covered his thin shoulders and a length of brightly patterned *chitenga* cloth was wound around his lower body. A group of his councillors squatted to his right, while behind him three witchdoctors stood in aggressive attendance. Awesomely arrayed in cowry-shell necklaces and kilts of skins and tails, they stared through faces horrifically smeared with soot and white paste beneath fantastic headdresses of beads and colorful feathers and antelope horns. Bedeviled by drowsily buzzing flies, only their facial muscles twitched as they stood in ebony immobility; with their oiled torsos gleaming in the firelight, they looked to Matthew as inanimate and grotesque as carved wooden statues, and he sensed in their proud presence a jealous guarding of traditional rights.

He took off his pith helmet to initiate the greeting, but to his surprise the Boy, touching him with a restraining hand, moved ahead of him. Advancing toward the ornate brass bedstead, he went down on his knees before the old chief, and producing a piece of chalk from his jeans pocket, he proceeded, while Matthew looked on in astonishment, to regale the old man with an elaborate greeting.

"*Euleyi!*" He clapped his hands softly three times. "*Kalombo.*" He clapped again. "*Euleyi . . .*"

Cosmo, squatting behind him, joined in with the clapping with a calm readiness that implied a complicity, which indeed there must have been since the pagan ritual, preserved in the ancient archives of unfailing tribal memory, was a grand antiquation reserved for personages of great honor and was today seldom seen. As the ritual continued, Matthew could scarcely believe his eyes, for in the ancient tribal way, the Boy ripped open the studs of his jacket and opened his shirt and began drawing a chalk line upward from his navel upon his bared golden skin. Then he hobbled on his knees over to the chief while the entire company stared at the strange spectacle of a white missionary making like a primitive black man. For an awful moment, Matthew feared that the chief, suspecting mockery, might refuse to cooperate, but after a moment's stunned hesitation, the chief pulled aside his own cloth, leaning forward while the Boy drew a speckled white line across the thin rib-beveled coal-black chest. Then, leaning back on his haunches, the Boy scraped a handful of dirt from the hut's earthen floor; this, in final desecration, he sifted over his own head and body. Matthew sat breath-stilled, enthralled in his own bland disbelief; there was a hushed deliberation, then the chief nodded with a distant smile of proud approval. He gestured to a stunned henchman, and immediately two stools were brought forward upon which Matthew and the Boy sat.

"*Mutende, Ba-Mulaisho. Mwa-kosa-tu bulongo?*" (Greetings to Mulaisho—are you strong?) The Boy continued his dialogue.

"*Ee mwane, twa-kosa-tu bulongo,*" the chief replied in solemn sequence. (Yes, indeed I am strong.)

They rattled easily back and forth, and Matthew, long since left behind, looked on in amazement. Through his chagrin, it was obvious to him that the Boy had the notorious old man eating right out of his hand. He sat stupefied while the doctor, easing into the more familiar Chi-Lwena, parleyed with the chief.

The chief informed the Boy that he had received his present of *sekeleti*, cigarettes, and explained that it had taken him some time to trace the missionary, since he was a stranger to them. He thanked the Boy for his generosity and confessed that he was puzzled by it.

"The gift was a gesture of my goodwill," the Boy explained quietly. "To honor you as chief and acknowledge your authority. Now, as it happens, I am a medical doctor, and if there are any of your people who are ill or injured, I will be happy to treat them."

Mulaisho thought over this proposition for some moments. Finally he announced irrelevantly that he often felt cold at night; he wondered if the doctor had seen the long coats such as soldiers wore in the white shops? Matthew drew back disapprovingly. It was suddenly plain to him that the old scoundrel had summoned them here merely to further try his luck; the rascal was simply greedily grasping for more gratuities. However, the Boy was unruffled. He replied with calm dignity that he knew of such greatcoats and would try to secure one for the chief. In the meanwhile, he reiterated, would the chief care to call forth the sick?

"That is not necessary," the chief said shortly. "Here we have our own doctors who take care of the sick."

"Well, I do not doubt their prowess," the Boy said carefully. "But would you not agree that even as some men are good at hunting and others at fishing—it is the same with medicine? In my own case, it has been acknowledged that I have particular skill in the repairing of internal organs. But I have no doubt your own doctors are good at yet other things. Therefore, would it not be desirable for one doctor good at one thing and another good at some other to work together? For example, I have heard of the skill of your medicine men in healing surface wounds. And since I have only this morning suffered such a wound upon my own person, I would be grateful to receive the attention of one of your doctors."

Matthew stared in amazement as the Boy ripped open the studs of his denim shirt, pulling it out of his jeans to reveal on his side a broad Band-Aid, which he pulled off to expose a deep lateral cut. It was the beginning.

Much later, when they left the village with Cosmo leading a scrawny bone-humped cow, followed by a group of curious children and the vile-smelling woman who had earlier confronted them, Matthew gave finally full vent to his day-long fermented fury.

"That was *outrageous*!" he whispered. "I see it all now! Of all the un-Christian, un-Quakerly . . . why, it was as much as a missionary doing deals with the devil! Thee deliberately inflicted that wound upon thyself!"

"Shucks, Matthew, does that sound like the way of a disease-fighting doctor to you?"

"Indeed it does not." Matthew drew up haughtily. He patted a handkerchief fretfully to his perspiring brow. "And I seriously doubt it would seem that way to others either. So to save a lot of scandalous controversy, I advise thee not to divulge the means of thy *inducement* to our more genteel mission Friends!"

"Why, Matthew." The Boy looked up innocently, his face oddly endearing, still smeared with the desecrating dirt. "I don't know what you're so sore about. He gave us a milk cow, didn't he?"

"He gave us *a* cow," Matthew said disconsolately. "And a more sick and sorry looking beast I have yet to see. Why, it looks about to drop dead with sleeping sickness at any moment. That evil old despot had a nerve to offer it as a gift. Thee're a doctor, not a vet! And even were it not such a sickly tick-infested specimen, with the tsetse fly so rife around Suseshi, we'll have a difficult task keeping it alive."

The Boy shrugged. "Some of the natives manage to keep cattle on the open plains. And it might be nice to have fresh milk in our coffee again."

But Matthew was not consoled. He did not like the look of the creature's funny freckled udders, and anyway, years of consuming the tins of Klim powdered milk had altered his palate.

"It's plain to me," he sniffed haughtily, "that the sly, greedy scoundrel merely wanted to secure more of thy gratuities. A greatcoat, to be specific! And since he happened to have that dying old cow and that poor smelly old hag, who everyone wants shed of anyway, it struck him to humor thy medical appetite!"

"Well, look at it this way, Matthew. If I can do something for the poor woman, who's been given up as hopeless by their own medicine men, Mulaisho's chiefdom will be pretty much open house to the mission."

Matthew eyed the Boy warily, beginning to thaw. *"He said that? When?"*

"While you were reading the children those Bible stories." The Boy's smile faltered and he coughed, looking so guilty that Matthew was immediately alerted. "He made one little proviso, though."

"Oh?" Matthew stiffened suspiciously. "What proviso?"

The Boy smiled sickly. "I had no choice, so don't get mad, Matthew. The fact is I kind of gave Mulaisho my solemn word we wouldn't try to convert the woman to the Christian faith."

"Thee what?" Staring at the Boy in outrage, Matthew stopped dead in his tracks. One of the oncoming children collided with him, and the Boy caught and steadied the mud-covered little mite.

"Hey now, simmer down. What else could I do, Matthew?"

"What else could thee do? Would thee sell thy soul to the devil for the sake of the Hippocratic oath?"

"Now, Matthew, that woman needs help pretty bad. And what's one soul among thousands? Just as soon as I get her fixed up and we get a foot in the door, then you can go in there and go around converting souls to beat the band!"

"Thee had no right!" Matthew exploded. The roused blood pounded in his temples and he could scarcely speak for the ferocity of his feelings. *"No right,* thee hear me? That woman's soul is her own possession and it is our sworn Quaker duty to spread the Gospel to all who come within our Christian walls!"

The Boy winced. Glancing uncomfortably around at their curious entourage, he lowered his voice urgently. "Hey now, can't you understand? It was the only way I could get the chief to let her go. Otherwise, she was as much doomed to die by inches of her own rotten smell. I examined her and, Matthew, you ought to have seen it. When she was slow in giving birth to her baby, one of the witch-doctors, some knife-happy butcherous bastard, cut her some to ease its passage. Well, he eased it all right, cutting so deeply into the birth canal she can no longer retain her urine or her bowel contents. Now she just naturally smells so bad that her husband and family have shunned and disowned her. The poor creature has a severe vesicovaginal fistula. Well, old Mulaisho couldn't have handed me a tougher test if he tried. It's a damn difficult condition to heal. Sometimes, in spite of repeated corrective surgery, the walls keep breaking down and the tissue refuses to heal. She . . ."

"Spare me the details." Matthew winced distastefully. He glanced disgustedly at the preposterous-looking bark poultice on the Boy's midriff, partially visible through his opened shirt. "Butcherous, thee calls them, yet I notice thee has no compunction in prostituting thy own body—thy sacred temple!—to the dispicable means of these same evil sorcerers!"

"Matthew, it was to win their confidence. And besides, it just may be that *some* of their methods may have merit. We'll never know unless we try them. And as for old Mulaisho—put yourself in his place. He regards Christianity as some kind of a social disease. The old tribal traditions are ingrained in him like the very salt in his skin, and he's afraid the influence of the church will extinguish the old ways and ultimately usurp his power. And he's right in some respects. He's seen the conversion of old tribal dynasties into Western-oriented monogamous upright Christian societies. Rightly or wrongly, it's what he fears, and in order to secure his confidence and cooperation, I have to honor my word and ensure that that woman gets no Christian indoctrination while she's with us."

"*Thee* may have to!" Matthew snorted vengefully. "But I do not."

"Hey, now." The Boy eyed him uneasily, footsteps slowing. "You wouldn't . . . you *couldn't* do that to me, Matthew. I gave the chief my word!"

"Couldn't I?" Matthew triumphed. "Well, it just so happens, *I* gave the Lord *mine!*"

Smoldering impotently, the Boy would not speak to Matthew the rest of the way home.

10

Matthew knew that Than Profane's casual coup of Chief Mulaisho's coveted confidence had put a few noses out of joint when an angry group of the elder ladies, in their capacity as the meeting's overseers, came to caustically complain that against Dr. Dooley's advice, the Boy was treating venereal disease, advocating contraception, and administering pain-killing drugs to ease childbirth. Well, they all knew that such ministrations were the common practice of the more worldly Quaker doctors back in the States, but out here, through comprehensive Bible study and the inspired ministry of Clara Fotch, Suseshi meeting had formulated a strict puritanical policy that specifically forbade such dispensations.

Matthew was up a ladder supervising the rethatching of an old storage hut when the ladies arrived, staring up at him, huffed and disgusted, requesting haughtily that he "elder" the erring Boy on the matter immediately. Matthew climbed down the ladder. He did not relish trying to lovingly labor with the Boy or anyone else for that matter in this fierce heat. (It was significant that the explosive human emotions aroused by October's daily soaring temperatures had lent it the legendary label of Suicide Month, with considerable statistical justification!) However, the ladies were right, of course; such contrary activities could be enormously confusing to the natives. Thus, without even taking the time to change from his old working dungarees and frayed straw sombrero, Matthew, feeling gauche and apprehensive, went directly across to the hospital to set the Boy straight. There he learned that Dr. Profane was busy conducting an autopsy in the mortuary hut, and having no intentions of braving some grisly investigation to make his point, Matthew was fondling his sombrero, idling indecisively on an adjacent veranda, when the Boy came out of the building. He was wearing nothing more than his moccasins and ragged old Bermuda shorts, and for once, in this weather, Matthew envied him the license that allowed such levity.

"What do you want?" He eyed Matthew darkly.

At first, not understanding, Matthew spun around to see who else might be waiting in line for this suspicious salutation. Then it dawned on him that he had been innocently venturing into the vicinity of Mrs. Mapanya, the woman from Mulaisho's village, whose unpronounceable first name had forced them to christen her Mary. On the pretext of protecting others from her odious odor, the Boy had placed her in a private room. But Matthew wasn't fooled. What the Boy really hoped to protect in this unusual arrangement was the woman's heathen soul. And although aided in this by her very smell, the mission's daunted evangelists had become ever more ingenious and brave. Pastor Peter Mwanza had latterly been caught regaling her with the Gospel with a clothes peg on his nose! The Boy attributed all such insidious assaults to Matthew, but in truth his pagan pact with Mulaisho had made him hypersensitive to a dogged indoctrination that was commonly practiced upon all mission inmates. Now, trailing on the Boy's hurrying heels as he strode purposefully down a screened corridor, Matthew spluttered out his story.

"Thee should understand, Friend," he explained earnestly, "by such practices thee appear to the natives to condone illicit sexual activity. Why, their tribal courts are already inundated with paternity and adultery cases! They are already lacking in moral conscience, and when thee takes away the responsibility of the life seed they were born with . . ."

"Oh come now, Matthew." The Boy stopped dead. "Immorality has nothing to do with contraception! In San Francisco, I saw the little girls filing into the O.B. wards with bellies as big as their innocent eyes. Boys will be boys. And as long as there's some female with sweet joy between her legs . . ."

Matthew shuddered.

". . . there's some guy who's going to give it to her, come baby or bastard. And prostitution, I might remind you, is as old as the Bible."

"Well, I'm sorry thee feels that way." Matthew raised reproachful eyes. "Friend Jerome and thy father always respected the meeting's guidance."

"Then they were damn fools!" the Boy said softly, with such vehemence that Matthew drew back defensively.

"Perhaps they understood more than thee," he floundered. "Why, on the matter of childbirth, the Bible tells us there are divine reasons for nature's apparent cruelty. Thus, when thee counteracts the pain, thee interferes with divine ruling itself. The pain is woman's penance for Eve's original sin. The Lord has said: 'In sorrow thou shalt bring forth children.'" He raised his eyes and quoted further from the Bible: ". . . and woman, being deceived, was in transgression. Notwithstanding, she shall be saved in child-bearing.'"

"Matthew," the Boy looked exasperated, "don't you think that's a smug attitude in view of noninvolvement?"

"Might I remind thee that Friend Jerome's wife has set the good example in this matter!" Matthew spluttered indignantly. "We ask nothing of the natives that we do not expect of our own."

"Well, it seems to me it's pretty easy for Friend Jerome's wife to be so all-fired advocating, considering she drops babies like a rabbit."

There was an uncomfortable silence. "As a member of Suseshi Meeting, we naturally expect thee to perpetuate its policy," Matthew said quietly.

"Matthew, you go to hell. I refuse to have my work molded to the dictates of a deluded bunch of people, misguided by a narrow and outdated religious handbook!"

Matthew stared at the Boy, aghast. "I don't understand. Don't thee believe in the Bible?"

"Sure I do. It's a fair historical record, although sometimes a little too emotionally clouded and interpreted too many times to be altogether scientifically reliable."

Matthew was stunned. To doubt the Bible's infallibility! "Why did thee not," he managed, dry-mouthed, "say this before?"

"Nobody asked me. And I guess I wouldn't like Kathy to know. It might hurt."

Matthew nodded woodenly. Of himself, he wouldn't like *anyone* to know. The fact was too dangerous. It might upset the applecart.

"Now, if you'll excuse me, I have work to do," the Boy snapped.

For a long time after he had left, Matthew stood feeling numbed and devastated, forced at last to accept the fact of the Boy's heresy. And now that he had the truth, what must he do with it? Expose the Boy and deprive the sick of their staunchest medical champion? Could he do that? Did he wish to? No, he did not, could not. And if it was impossible to bind the Boy to the meeting's puritanical principles (merely sectal tenets of their particular meeting, which the more broad-minded mission board and certainly the district medical officer were unlikely to support), the ladies, he knew, would never forgive the defiant deviation . . .

II

With the troubles continuing all over the Federation, the British government proposed a royal commission of inquiry into conditions in the three territories. And while away in England this commission was being set up to investigate the state of their existence, oblivious schoolchildren at Suseshi were preparing for their year-end examinations. For the standard 5's, weeks of intense cramming finally culminated in rows of desks in the long school hall. And since thousands throughout the province would be denied access to the pitifully inadequate number of secondary schools, no cheating could be chanced: a rifle-slung black policeman stood impassive guard over their collective integrity, while Matthew, a strict but compassionate invigilator, watched over the bowed black heads from his desk on the dais. In the dry November heat, it was stuffy as an oven in the steel-roofed building, but after months of unrelenting drought, Matthew's barometer bones had been beset with vague shooting aches since dawn. Cumulonimbus clouds were gathering, and with the elusive, indescribably sweet scent of damp earth feverishly infecting him with the yearning for rain, he found it hard to concentrate on his weekly mail batch and sat dully perusing a letter from the mission board in America. The board had finally decided to sponsor secondary education at their stations in Northern Rhodesia, he read, and a couple of British teachers, Norman and Eileen Townsend, had been recruited to run the first school.

Matthew sat stunned. After years of tedious negotiations among the board, tribal leaders, and the local education authorities, the concession would surely open up wonderful new dimensions in the lives of some of the very seedling souls now sitting before him. In a daze he read the rest of of his mail. Morgan Humphries had passed away peacefully in England, he learned, while another letter, from the government, informed him that the Ministry of Health felt unable to take over the man's abandoned leper colony. (With an estimated thirty thousand sufferers in the protectorate, how miserly must seem Eshalakali's thirty-odd?) The suggestion that they be absorbed into other, already overcrowded, institutions far from their clung-to home ground was hopelessly impractical, and Matthew sighed. He had promised poor Morgan that he would do what he could, and of the lepers, he had seen their hopeless eyes and little doomed children. Now, feeling responsible by mere virtue of knowing of their plight, he began tentatively to toy with the possibility of the Friends mission itself adopting the station. And now that the board had sanctioned secondary schooling, the possibilities suddenly blossomed. He thought of the empty school buildings, and a rising excitement made him restlessly stride down the hall to stand in the open doorway.

Outside, swallows dipped and cried and the towering black thunderheads suddenly swallowed the sun, trapping an unnatural light that basked the earth in a vibrant and glowing peach-colored gloom. As the hall turned dim, the children looked up and secretively smiled. Now even the bored black policeman stood reverently hushed in a breath-bated waiting. Matthew stood out on the step, mindlessly exulted as the accelerating rain patter swept across and sounded a musical carillon on the corrugated-iron roof above him, the cool kissing drops smacking into the hard dusty earth. Appropriately, today was the American Thanksgiving Day. Matthew raised his silver head and silently gave thanks.

In the fresh stillness following the roar of the rainstorn, when millions of termites, temporarily winged for this their annual nuptial

108

flight, were turning the dying day into a fairy-land fantasia, Matthew heard again the compelling tones of a xylophone. He turned and out of the glimmering green bush stepped Mulaisho's musical emissary. Trailed by a shabby entourage, he looked as quaint and familiar-grown as some fairy-tale figure. Matthew, on his way to discuss the leper colony with Than Profane, led the little troupe to the Profane house. There the tinkling chimes lured first Jayne, then the doctor from the house. He came through the cherry-pie hedge, gnawing on a kidney mango snatched from a tree. The strain of prolonged surgery had caused the relapse of an old basketball injury, and he wiped the juice from his mouth with the sprained crepe-bandaged wrist, his golden chest sweat-gleaming through an unbuttoned pink shirt.

This time the old musician was accompanied by an interpreter, a shabbily dressed youth who conversed with the doctor in inelegant English while picking at a fever blister on his lower lip. Than was able to report that he had finally operated on the woman from Mulaisho's village after weeks spent antisepticizing her urine; however, the success of the delicate repair might not be ascertainable for weeks. The youth conveyed the chief's thanks for this care of his subject, also for the fine greatcoat the bwana had sent. He explained that the chief was now keeping warm at night and, in gratitude for the doctor's help and generosity, had sent a gift of his own. The youth turned and beckoned two young girls who were busy catching the "flying ants," popping the wriggling African delicacies whole into their mouths. Suspended between them on a shoulder-slung pole they carried a small bark cage. This gift, the interpreter explained, was chosen on the chief's knowledge of the white man's fondness for animals.

Animals? Matthew and the Boy exchanged uneasy looks. They became suddenly aware of the excited barking of Cuss and the ridgebacks who circled the cage in darting offensives. Shooing them off, the Boy bent and peered thorugh the bars. Constructed of tree sticks, it was the type commonly used to transport fowl. But from this crude receptacle no homely clucking came. Jayne gave a squeal of maternal tenderness. The Boy snatched back a claw-lashed hand, and seeing an incredulous look cross his face, Matthew drew apprehensively closer. Cramped within the cruel confines of the little twisted cage there fiercely hissed what looked to him like some dark and strangely marked tortoise-shell kitten. It took a moment's stupefied staring before he realized that the silently snarling, weak, watery-eyed, big-pawed, and barely alive little creature was of the species *felis pardus*. It was a leopard cub.

With a strained air of ceremony, the little creature was carried into the Profanes' big kitchen. The strangled kitten cries brought the houseboy quizzically peering, and the bush baby on Jayne's shoulder leaped for a high shelf. For once, his clambering among the crockery went unchallenged as Jayne scrambled in a cupboard for an old rubber glove to fashion into a serviceable teat. Katherine stood warily watching.

"It's a present from Mulaisho," the Boy explained, plainly embarrassed. Breaking open the cage, he tipped the feebly tottering kitten onto the table. Despite its size, it rounded upon him, fiercely spitting.

Seeing the milky blue eyes in the little whiskered face, Matthew exclaimed: "Why, what a spunky little critter. He's just a few weeks old."

The Boy lifted the tail and inspected clinically. "It's a she, and she's got rickets and mange. Looks like a pretty sick little cat." He saw Katherine's face and hastened: "We've got to get it well again—but, Kathy, I won't keep it, of course!"

"Of course not!" came her firm reinforcement of the furthest thought from their horrified minds.

12

As Matthew had expected, once the furor over the cub had died down, Than Profane readily agreed to oversee the leper colony, in order that he receive Esalakali as one of his clinics. Matthew narrowly quashed the heated objections of the other missionaries with the argument that the takeover would give them an important evangelical foothold into Chief Mulaisho's heathen stronghold.

Thus, a sanction-seeking proposal was sent to the mission board, and Matthew began feeling out the possibilities of purchasing the station. But before these tentative arrangements could be finalized, their hand was forced by circumstance. The government medical officer came to report that the African dresser left in charge of the colony at Eshalakali Hill had deserted, leaving the lepers helplessly stranded. In light of this disastrous development, the man urged that Suseshi consider stepping into the breach until more permanent arrangements could be made. Without hesitation, Matthew assured the man that the Friends' Africa Mission, ever ready for service, would send someone at once.

Than left with the old dresser, Jeremiah, the next day. They found the mission in a shambles. The top clinic and two of the classrooms stood window-smashed and defaced with excrement. They stared down at a colony that was crippled with chaos and insurrection. One fire-gutted hut still smoldered in the sun; several others were collapsed in ruins. At first the grounds seemed deserted; loathsome with leprous tissue, the inmates had crept like roaches out of the sunlight, and now, as if sensing surveillance, they came silently out of their huts, watching the wary descent of Than and his assistant with unmoving insolence. Walking among the people, Than grimly surveyed the scene while Jeremiah gleaned information from reluctant sources. It seemed that the dresser had taken with him the dispensary blankets, some allotted money, and what remained of their grain. And the lepers, left without medical care or sustaining manna, had gone wild in their liberation. It was a senseless and ungrateful rebellion and now, bearing the scars of ugly in-fighting and turned surly with guilt, they grumbled unintelligibly, deriding the doctor's late arrival with their sallowed eyes. Long-pampered by Christian benevolence, they had come to regard help as their due, the lack of it their injustice. They blamed the Europeans for this, as for everything.

They had broken into the food store and looted the mission houses. The storeroom door gaped emptily onto shattered glass, and the crude colony streets, edged with stands of bananas, stood quaintly aggrandized with antique articles of missionary furniture, which stood monumental as streetlamps outside dilapidated huts too small to admit them. Righteously sulking, the lepers, trailing filthy bandages in the dirt, came out to stare at Than as he and Jeremiah walked in stony silence through the meandering avenues. They passed a mirrored washstand that bore the feather-bloodied remains of some slaughtered chicken, and as they walked along, more and more lepers emerged from their dark hovels, some to occupy a stuffed sofa and erect missionary chairs, like convivial small-town folk come out to watch the world go by beneath the shaggy thatch overhangs of their huts. But there the cozy resemblance ended; with dead eyes and disfigured faces, the lepers stared malevolently.

Around them the ground was littered with broken bric-a-brac, with scarcely recognizable household utensils, and magazines and books that lay incomprehensively riffled and defaced. Squashed behind a benched school desk, three small boys sat making dodging steering-wheel motions and revving engine noises that suggested the hell-raising driving of some hot-spit vehicle. Feasting flies and an unspeakable stink lingered over piles of human excreta. A decrepit crone, with congealed blood matted in her woolly skull and two fingerbones protruding the weeping ulceration of one abbreviated hand, wore upon the fingerless other the decorous adornment of a once-white glove, the empty cotton fingers hanging macabrely limp, with little finger cocked in a flippant gesture that was absurdly genteel. Wearing a lady's old pink corset perched, crownlike, upon his nodule-thickened face, a morose Luchazi man sat sullenly drinking water through the spout of a teapot; he had only one eye, and with infected mouth eaten away to a rim of pink gum, he gazed at Than with a lunatic leer. A heinous old hag with no nose and a toothy skull grin exposed in the gaping hole of an ulcerated cheek wore the mad millinery masterpiece of a daintily rose-painted chamber pot upon her dreadful head. It seemed that every hovel revealed more horrors. The whole spectacle had a nightmarish quality that gave Than the creepy feeling of having stepped straight into some kind of a theater of the absurd. He took off his sunglasses, wincing with awe. "Holy shit! This is *dee*-lightful. Looks like the Mad Hatter's Tea-party. Only Alice never had it this good!"

13 The following night, when Than Profane, on his way home late from the hospital, called at Matthew's house with a comprehensive list of Eshalakali's requirements, Matthew knew that his one visit to the colony had been bait enough. Although clearly disgusted by the dirt and degradation, Matthew could tell that the very difficulties that had so infuriated him were fuel to the flame of the Boy's voracious medical appetite. Matthew plied him with coffee and warmed-over pumpkin pie as he examined the long list. Mentally scratching around in Suseshi's scant supplies to supplement the government's meager subsidy for the colony, he assured himself that the looming difficulties would be met as they came. It was the way in which the good Lord took care of his own.

"Well, I see there's a lot needed and much to be done."

"You're damn right," the Boy growled. There were thin scab-threaded scratches across his collarbones and the bridge of his nose (that playful cub!). Sitting sprawled on the faded floral cushions of the sagging old settee, he absently ruffled Cuss's ears as the dog wriggled fawningly between his long hairy legs, licking the golden knees and indecently sniffing. "And how did Morgan Humphries ever come up with that cock-eyed figure of thirty lepers? Huts, maybe—but lepers? Jesus, that poor Jack must have been hallucinating. They tell me a few have run off and what's left is more like seventy-five, and with seven women pregnant, the number's rising all the time. And it's not just medical attention those Jaspers need. It's complete rehabilitation. I'm going to have my work cut out just reviving their self-respect!"

"Why, that's terrible!" Matthew dutifully intoned, suppressing a smile. He looked up earnestly. "More pie?"

"No thanks." The Boy brushed crumbs off his shirt. "I guess Kathy's saved some supper to force on me, and I'd better be going now. It's getting pretty late."

And indeed it was. The electric light was suddenly warningly flickered to signify the imminent ten o'clock switch-off. Even as Matthew hastily fumbled to light a lamp, the throbbing generator choked and died, and they were plunged into darkness. The African operator, eager to get off, was never a minute late! The Boy came to Matthew's aid with a lighted match. As the flickering oil lamp flared the room with its sallow light, Cuss pricked up his ears and they heard distant cheery voices as the dispersing Quaker instruction class drifted down from the meeting house. Teller came home, sweetly resounding "Lead Kindly Light." A patter of footsteps sounded on the porch before she came up the passage, warding off the joyful dog. Behind her, with slowly measured footsteps, outstretched hands, and a look of frowning concentration, came Jennifer Solomon. The girl was proud of what little independence she had painstakingly gained at Suseshi, but Teller's absentminded untidiness was an old habit that died hard, and the house was often unthinkingly rearranged, fraught with unchartered changes. They had all learned by now not to add to Jennifer's difficulties by disturbing her silent counting with premature greetings. They waited politely as the dark-haired girl approached the open doorway, feeling along the doorframe with shy, sensitive hands. When she stopped questioningly on the threshold, Matthew took her arm and led her inside.

"Jenny, Dr. Profane's with us here. He was out at the Hill yesterday, visiting thy old stamping ground."

"Oh?" As if trying to sense his location, the girl tilted her head with the quizzical look of alert listening so characteristic of young animals. "Dr. Profane?"

He stood up noisily, guiding her gaze. "Jennifer Solomon."

The girl pushed the dark hair with its elusive Titian undertones off her face and gazed unseeingly in his general direction, her long-lashed, beautiful blind blue eyes suddenly alive with expressive animation. "*The Hill!* Oh, it seems so long since I . . ." She stopped, checking her enthusiasm, hesitating shyly. "How is Eshalakali, Doctor?"

The Boy was quiet for a moment. Then he said huskily, "I'm sorry to disenchant you, Miss Solomon, but the Hill . . ." he weighed the word distastefully, *"the Hill is an abomination."*

In the sudden quiet they could hear the water in the Ascot heater gurgling around the walls like some full-bellied giant with gastronomical problems. The lamp hissed and sputtered on the heavy oak table, and Matthew saw the eagerness die in Jennifer's eyes like a light going out. For a moment they all stood mesmerized, then Teller took a lamp off the mantel.

"Well, we'll say good night now if thee'll just excuse us, Doctor. Jenny was about falling asleep in the meeting house as she sat. Come along, dear." She lit the lamp, then took the girl's arm and began leading her off, holding the lamp aloft in one hand. "I'll just settle thee down with thy lamp for the night."

When they had gone, the Boy turned to Matthew with a slight puzzled frown. "Isn't that a little crazy? Lighting a lamp for a blind girl?"

Matthew chuckled. "Oh, didn't thee know? Jenny's not totally blind. Apparently she is able to make some dim distinction between light and dark. And her daddy wrote us about her nighttime fears. It seems she's afraid of the dark. And perhaps that's only natural. Afraid to lose what little light she can yet perceive. But there is little else that sets her back. She's starting Braille classes here in the meeting house next week, and just as soon as thee returns from Salisbury, she wants to accompany thee on thy weekly service trips to Eshalakali to resume her old classes with the blind there."

Matthew smiled fondly. But when he looked up, the Boy was staring at him with a face like thunder. He set down his coffee cup and stood up abruptly.

"Look, Matthew, maybe you should know this. I'm not going to Eshalakali for any picnic parties. The lepers are a godforsaken, wretched people and I'd just as soon not be further hampered by a . . . by a helpless little blind girl who's afraid of bogeys in the night!"

Matthew drew up in wounded surprise. "Well, I must say, I am surprised at thy pettish ungraciousness, Doctor! Jennifer Solomon is not an invalid or a helpless child. She happens to be a particularly courageous and determined young woman who, in spite of her handicap, can still find the heart to help others less fortunate. It's a charity thee might learn for thyself."

They stared at each other in contesting anger. Then the Boy strode to the window, pulled aside a drape, and stared furiously out into the darkness.

"Maybe that's just it, Matthew. Maybe I just don't think that girl should be encouraged to throw away her life. Just because she's blind doesn't mean she has to bury herself alive out here. She could lead a pretty near normal life. Jesus—isn't it bad enough as it is?"

So that was it. Matthew reached out a stiff comforting hand and touched the Boy's shoulder. He felt him heave under his touch. "Is thy mother throwing away her life?" he said gently. "Or thy sister?"

"That's different!" The Boy spun around on him. "You know it is! *They're* different! *They* can see."

He was about to take his leave when three barefoot children appeared up the passage. It was Tom, fresh home from boarding school, their houseboy's shy, tattered little daughter, and Jayne. Cuss scampered up to sniff the leopard in the little girl's arms. That little cub, once so stricken with rickets and mange, had grown big as a young dog now, bright-eyed with good feeding, heavy and softly furred, the exquisite jet-black rosettes standing out like ink splashes on a honey-clear coat. She had been vaccinated against feline enteritis, and the mission garden boys supplemented her diet of powdered milk, calcium, and vitamins with craftily caught lizards, wagtails, and mole rats, which she played with, dead, for hours before finally devouring.

"Shoo!" Jayne admonished as the dog eagerly frisked. But Cuss, battle-scarred as the rest of them, had yet to learn: he came away from the feline's playful swat with a piteous yelp and a bloodied nose.

"Bathsheba!" Jayne scolded, shaking the lank silver hair back over her shoulders as she struggled to contain the wriggling bundle in her arms, raising one slim thigh to keep the clawing cub from slipping through her clutches. Both she and Tom were burned brown by the sun; they, like the Boy, were engagingly stippled with the cub's thin scratches.

"Good evening, Professor. Sorry to disturb thee at this hour." With characteristic quaint formality Jayne addressed Matthew, but her gaze, like Tom's, hardly left their elder brother. Matthew had noticed that in his company the two children had eyes for little else and no other. Now she looked at the Boy expectantly. "Momma's just finished her home-craft class. Thee coming?" she said, soft as a caress. "We kept water warm for thy ablutions and Momma was wondering . . ."

The Boy dropped his Stetson on the girl's head and, taking the cub from her arms, stooped to kiss her mouth with a hushed tenderness so unexpectedly poignant that Matthew felt intrusive. As he followed them down the passage with the lamp aloft, the Boy gathered the slender girl under his arm. She was shivering slightly, but whether from his proximity or the weather Matthew could not tell. For distant dying thunder still faintly grumbled and it was cool enough out in the rain-refreshed air to raise a crop of goosebumps on bare arms.

As the little group walked away into the darkness, Matthew hesitated uncertainly on the veranda. "Er, Jennifer's banking on resuming those Braille classes at Eshalakali Hill, Doctor. May I tell her thee'd be happy to take her?" he called.

The Boy stopped dead. Without looking back, he said: "Well, you're the boss, Matthew. If you insist, then I guess I have no option."

"I do," Matthew said. And watching them go, he nodded staunchly to himself, feeling fully justified. Perhaps Jennifer Solomon's handicap did render her a little helpless; indeed, she was afraid of the dark. But it was indicative of the girl's sweetness and courage that despite her affliction, the natives found reason to call her *Maseccasecca*—One Who Smiles . . .

14

Taking Jayne with him in the Land-Rover, Than left for Salisbury, burdened with two overnight bags and a long list of Christmas shopping for the bush-bound missionaries. They traveled through the sweltering hot Northern Rhodesian bush and finally crossed the Zambezi River into Southern Rhodesia at Chirundu, after which the character of the bush changed abruptly. Here, game became scarcer and, interspersing the stunted thorn bush, cultivated cattle-cropped hills signified the control of tsetse fly.

Reminding Than of many American cities, Salisbury, the clean new palm-lined capital of the Federation, broke the African skyline with aspiring skyscrapers.

On the city's outskirts, Than dropped Jayne off at the home of the Carltons, an American Quaker couple who, despite six boisterous children, regularly accommodated missionary Friends on their excursions this far south. A fine meeting house adjoined their neat suburban home, and they were as welcoming as old family. They tried to induce Than to accept their hospitality as well, but he wanted no haunting hosts and no inquisitive sister to monitor his movements. Avoiding the disappointment in Jayne's crestfallen face, he extricated himself as politely as possible from their possessive clutches and booked into a modest hotel in the heart of the city. Here, after an exhilarating cold shower, a glass of fresh milk, a mixed grill supper, and the first beer he had enjoyed in the eight months since his medical stint at Ndola, Than felt good, back in civilization again.

The following day, dressed in his best suit and carrying the substance of his dreams in a bulging briefcase, Than located the building of the Federal Ministry of Public Health. After waiting half the morning for an interview, he found the secretary general politely enthusiastic about his plans for advanced medical training. The man listened intently to Than's requests that the course be granted immediate government recognition; that due to the critical shortage of secondary schools in the territory, there be an initial period during which pupils with less general schooling than was required elsewhere would be eligible for enrollment, and further that the informal mission training of their existing black hospital staff be formally recognized. Advising Than to present his blueprints and plans in time for consideration during the forthcoming meeting of ministers, the man secured him an appointment with the Federal medical education inspector the following week.

In the interim, Than went across to the Ministry of Foreign Affairs to secure a permanent residence permit for himself. Armed with his expired visa and passport, he began a tiring round of standing in lines and going back and forth from the Ministry of Foreign Affairs to Immigration, all the while endlessly explaining. After almost two days of this tedious toil, he spent an exasperating afternoon at Immigration, only to be sent back to the Chancery, as his papers had not been properly processed. There, the same man who had sent him to Immigration in the first place, now packing up to go home, hastily ushered him out, promising to make the applications presentable by Monday. Than felt hot, vexed, and totally frustrated as the department's doors finally closed in his face.

A storm had begun to blow up, and walking back to the hotel, tired and disgruntled, he almost bumped into a young girl whose skirt was suddenly whisked over her head when she stopped to retrieve a wind-snatched hat. The reviving vision of her shapely long legs and neatly filled panties helped to mollify his mood some.

Later that evening, after having showered and changed for supper, Than passed a slender brunette impatiently tapping one high-heeled foot on the shabby scarlet carpet of the hotel's palatial entrance lobby as he walked across to the reception desk to inquire about a pair of sunglasses he had lost. There was a vague familiarity about the girl that stopped him, frowning, in his tracks. When he looked back, he found her looking startled, also staring at him. It was the girl whose dress had blown up, and she recognized him too. While the receptionist made an idle search for his sunglasses, Than stared beyond her into the wall mirror, watching the girl in the lobby watch him. She seemed to hesitate, then as he turned from the counter, retrieved sunglasses in hand, she broke her stationary vigil and walked briskly toward him with a careful casualness.

"Excuse me . . ." she faltered, flashing him a gay, engaging smile. "I'm in a bit of a spot, and I was wondering if you'd be good enough to help me."

Her Rhodesian accent was obviously tutor-trained, intriguingly attractive in its classic correctness, and up close, she turned out to be fresh-faced and pretty enough to attract attention without accosting it. "I . . . uh . . . hate to ask this of a perfect stranger, but you see I'm waiting for someone . . . he's late as usual . . . might be some time . . . and it's just so . . . *embarrassing* standing here on my own with all these men *staring*. . ." She broke off, shrugging inanely, gazing pleadingly up at him.

Than said nothing.

"What I mean is . . ." she struggled, ". . . would you mind escorting me to a table in the lounge?"

"Well, ma'am, I don't see as to how you're in any danger of being attacked right here in the lobby. But if you're the nervous type, well, who am I to refuse a lady in distress?"

"Oh, thank you," she trilled delightedly, instantly at ease. "You're a gallant gentleman."

She followed him through to the adjoining lounge. They sat at a table near the doorway, and Than signaled a waiter and ordered drinks.

"You're American," she bubbled at him over her port and lemon. At her insistence, he gave a brief sketch of his circumstances.

"Oh . . . a *doctor*!" She eyed him in undisguised awe. "I've never met an American doctor before!"

"You've met one now."

"It's so exciting meeting people from different countries."

"Isn't it?" But he was gazing off disinterestedly, wishing her friend would come. By her gushing affected speech, he had guessed she was younger than she looked, and he had no desire to get mixed up in some cradle-snatching boyfriend-baiting affair. But untouched by his dispassion, she prattled gaily on while he sat thinking about his own appetite and the hotel's dining hour ebbing away. When the friend finally arrived, he reared with relief, and the girl, looking distinctly disappointed, hailed the young man, who came striding toward them dressed in a police uniform, peaked cap in hand, and hair shorn in the "short back and sides" cut that was currently conventional. Glancing belligerently at Than, he stopped at their table. By the grim set of his face, Than guessed at his serious romantic involvement with the girl.

"Mandy—what are you doing in here?"

"Oh, Gavin! You promised to meet me in the lobby straight after work, an hour ago. Where have you been?"

"Delayed," the policeman snapped. "I see you didn't wait very long."

"Oh, Gavin, don't be so unreasonable. Sit down and meet my friend." She smiled spitefully, obviously enjoying his jealousy. "This is Dr. . . ."

"Profane." Than stood up and briskly shook hands with the surprised young man.

"Oh . . . a doctor. . ." His anger seemed to melt as if a medical degree automatically ruled out lechery in a man. "Well, I'm Gavin Woodcock. I'm pleased to . . ."

"Yes. Now, if you'll excuse me . ." Than started to sidle off. "I have things to attend to." When he looked back, the girl was staring bereftly after him. He hurried thankfully off.

The next day, guilty at having so long neglected Jayne, Than postponed all mission business and took his sister to town on a shopping spree. After their long sojourn in the bush, they were as innocently awed as children as they toured the big city department stores, all festively bedecked for Christmas. His long hair and Levis and her quaint Quaker bonnet and old-fashioned long dress attracted curious stares wherever they went. She looked on shyly in starry-eyed excitement, faintly protesting while he bought her anything that caught her fevered fancy. Afterward with Jayne all dressed up in new shoes with a rainbow-colored tulle-and-lace stiff petticoat billowing out a wickedly short floral sundress she could never hope to wear at the mission, Than jealously contested the speculative stares of other admiring males. Leaving their pile of purchases locked in the Land-Rover, he took her to lunch at an expensive restaurant, then to a movie theater in the city center. *The Five Pennies,* starring Danny Kaye and Louis Armstrong, was the first feature film Jayne had seen in all her fourteen years of life. She sighed, cried, and laughed so continuously that Than, warned by experience, began to worry that her Coke-bloated bladder might not hold out. Finally, at bursting point, toward the end of the film, unable to bear the strain a moment longer, she stumbled out to find the ladies' toilet. After the film's conclusion, Than found her. Having lost her way in the dark, she had groped out of a side exit. Outside in a side street, she stood helplessly crying in a puddle of her own making, being comforted by two overdressed old ladies. Politely shooing them away, Than put his arms around his sister while she wept in vexed humiliation against his chest.

"Hush," he said huskily. "You're beautiful."

"Oh, I am not! I'm a disgrace to thee. Such a baby."

"Honey, you can't help having a weak bladder. It's a thing that could happen to anyone. So why'n't you just stop saturating the front of my shirt and go clean up. Tell you what, you go blow your nose, arrange your hair, and do whatever it is you females do and maybe I'll take you someplace for a milk shake and fill you in on the movie's ending."

Moments later she came out of the ladies' toilet, recovered, smiling bashfully, looking self-consciously coy in her new dress. He whistled admiringly. "Hey, lady, you going my way?"

"Oh shoosh!" She squinted dubiously around at the back of her dress, sighing. "My shoes are all wet."

He smiled, taking her hand. "Hey, I guess it's not every day you have new shoes to christen."

Wending their way through the homebound crowds, they happened upon a group of young nurses advancing from the opposite direction.

"*Than Profane!*"

Both parties stopped short in surprise. Unable to believe his eyes, Than stared at the shortest girl for several seconds before finally finding his voice.

"Lucy O'Connor." Acutely conscious of Jayne's incredulous stare, Than had to steel himself to resist the magnetic pull of sexual electricity that crackled between them. "God, what're you doing here?"

Lucy raised a saucy brow. "I might ask ye the very same thing." The catty look only left her eyes when he introduced Jayne as his sister. Then, properly placated, she grudgingly introduced her own eager entourage, and Than invited them for a drink at an adjacent hotel. In company with the nurses, he drank brandy and Coke. His mind full of the sexual facets of their affair, he held Lucy's thigh under the table, and starved by the eight long months of enforced celibacy in the bush, this sudden free association with un-church-bound females had him so susceptible, he was afraid to stand up for fear of thoughts telling. Hardly aware of Jayne's sulking as she sucked a milk shake through a striped straw, he gazed at Lucy in dumb longing, scarcely registering the conversation of her companions, whose subtle suggestive looks gave him the feeling that given the proper time and place, he might have his way with any one of them. But Lucy was the only girl among them who needed no foreplay; it was this rather than any real preference or loyalty that made him stick to her. The niceties of courtship were a little beyond him

121

right at that moment, and as they sat sipping their drinks, he stared at her in hot anguish, thinking only, wildly, of some way and somewhere to get her alone. Finally, he stood up abruptly, cutting short the conversation, only then aware of the words left in mid-air, of the flushed quizzical faces, of Jayne's surprised stare. He blurted without thought: "Excuse me. I have to attend to . . ." Incapable of coherent explanation, he gazed lamely, lastly, at Jayne. "I mean listen, baby, we won't be long."

So saying, he grabbed Lucy's hand and abruptly left, pulling her in front of him to hide the embarrassing visible manifestation of his arousal. Eyes shining with anticipation, Lucy came with willing obedience. They left a pained silence at the table which bothered Than vaguely, but the urgency in his loins demanded answer *now*.

Spiriting her into the men's toilet, Than pushed Lucy into a lavatory booth. Still impatiently fully dressed, in a blind thrall of passion, he made frantic love to her standing up against a wall. Afterward, they clung together in their crumpled clothing, trembling, wet, and weak at the knees.

"God, Lucy, I sure hope you're protected."

Her eyes dancing with satiation, she stared up at him through disheveled hair, dispelling his doubt with a blissful uncaring smile. "I'm sorry," he croaked, and she chuckled.

"So it was rape?"

"Well, there are more genteel ways of saying hello."

He pulled carefully away from her. Glancing at each other, they straightened their clothing self-consciously, he smiling a little, frowning a lot. Scrawled on the wall above her head, four-lettered graffiti loomed in sordid epitaph; it made him feel slightly sick.

"Listen, Lucy . . ." He kissed her in shamed gratitude.

On the way out, they surprised an elderly man at the urinal. Lucy, a hardened nurse with an incurable wicked sense of humor, greeted him cheerily. Than had to hurry her out to prevent a scene. Despite his thunderous frown, she still shook with suppressed laughter when they got back to their table.

There, the blighted silence and searching stares sobered her considerably. Than ordered another round of drinks, and gradually, to his relief, the insulted atmosphere softened and the conversation started up again. It was only then that Than learned that at the end of her contract at Ndola Hospital (the little town had seemed "boring and dull" without him!) Lucy had applied to take up a position at the much livelier Salisbury General Hospital.

At the Carlton house later, Jayne barely bid Than good-bye. Watching her stalk up the garden path, fine nose in the air and long white hair trailing beneath the correct Quaker bonnet she had furiously tied back on, Than hung hands on his hips in amused exasperation. Sisterly jealousy yet!

"Hey!" he called contritely after her, surprising himself. "Listen, baby—I'll see you tonight."

"What for?" She turned aloofly, glancing reproachfully up at him with wounded gray eyes.

"Well, that meeting you mentioned." He squirmed at this undesired concession. "I'd like to come, is all."

That night after supper, feeling hot in his suit in the sultry evening air, Than went to the hotel cocktail bar for a quick beer before setting out for the meeting. At the counter, the brunette curls of a familiar female form made him look twice. Then he stared in surprise. For it was demure little Mandy Mansfield, looking unbelievably sophisticated in a clinging black sheath with a halter neckline that dipped low over a softly molded bosom. Her skin was tanned a glowing brown and she sat alone at the bar, looking uncertain and shy with a drink in her hand. Her searching brown eyes expanded at the sight of him. He looked quickly away, ordering a beer, and after a moment's hesitation, she came quickly across to him.

"What's a sweet little girl like you doing among the wolves?" he said without looking around.

"Oh, Doctor, thank goodness you're here!" She had the grace to sound sheepish. "Oh, I know it's my own fault, but I've never been so embarrassed!"

"I guessed you might."

"No, really." She climbed up onto the stool beside him and looked around expectantly. "Do you have a cigarette?"

He lit one for her and she held it with a shaking hand, inhaling amateurishly. He waved away the cloud of smoke. "Does Momma know you're smoking?"

She gave an intoxicated giggle. "No. How did you know? Am I that obvious?"

"You don't inhale properly. I bet your healthy young lungs are all but innocent of nicotine. Why don't you try keeping them that way?"

"Oh, what for? I want to have fun." She gave a sassy little laugh, drawing up her slender shoulders in a gesture that compressed a fine swelling cleavage between her full golden breasts. He stared a little avidly.

"What're you drinking?" he said as the barman handed him a foaming Lion lager.

"Whiskey," she giggled. "On the rocks."

"I don't think so." He studied her skeptically. "That's a little strong. Seems to me you're high already." He turned to the barman and ordered her a port and lemon.

"Oh!" She pulled a petulant face as the drink was passed to her. "You're treating me like a child, Doctor. Just like my father and six brothers."

Than sipped his beer. "You have six brothers?"

"Yes! And believe me, it's a positive bind being the only precious daughter. Oh, it's nice to be spoiled. But it's simply not worth the hyper-surveillance. My parents own a tobacco farm out in the sticks and it took me a year to persuade them to let me take a flat and a job here in Salisbury."

Than shook his head bemusedly. Putting his own stub out in a novelty ashtray, he took the girl's cigarette away from her, drawing on the lipstick-smeared filter tip. "Well, maybe they were right. Something tells me you shouldn't be out alone. Where's that boyfriend of yours tonight?"

"Oh—you mean Gavin? Well, we were going to a party, but we had an argument and I walked out on him." She smiled maliciously. "And good riddance, too. He's just so pigheaded! Do you know, he resented the way you were looking at me yesterday?"

"The way *I* was looking at you?" Than turned on her in indignant surprise. His eyes traveled guiltily down to her cleavage. "Maybe you know something I don't. *How* was I looking at you?"

She flushed slightly, shrugging. "Oh, you know . . ."

He looked abruptly away. Maybe he did. Her fresh eager face was beginning to have an effect on him. He flinched slightly when she suddenly reached out a hand and touched his hand over his glass, her trailing fingers caressing him tantalizingly. His skin tingled pleasantly, but he made no move to respond, sitting tensely beside her for a full five minutes before he took her hand and gently replaced it by her side. When she retracted in wounded surprise, he leaned closer, hungrily eyeing her wet, baffled mouth.

"Listen," he said tightly. "You're pretty yummy. But I eat little girls like you for breakfast. Maybe I ought to take you home."

"Oh no!" She stared at him appealingly. "I don't want to go. As a matter of fact, there's something I've been wanting to ask you."

124

"Yeah? What's that?"

She blanched under his searching stare. "Uh . . . well . . . I was just wondering whether you'd be good enough to give me the benefit of your . . . uh . . . of your professional opinion!"

"Jesus!" Than smiled, shaking his head, exhaling smoke.

"Did I say something funny?" She drew back, offended.

"Oh no, ma'am. That's a familiar question to most doctors, I believe. I just never figured it from you, is all. Reminds me of my wild intern days. Then it seemed I never bumped into a girl without she had some pressing problem she wanted urgently looking into. Why don't you see your own M.D.?"

She let out her breath. "Oh, I know I should. But he's just so old and fatherly, it gives me the creeps." She shuddered affectedly. "I'm shy, I suppose."

Than smiled, unconvinced. "Oh, come now, Mandy Mansfield. In my book, any girl brought up in a brood of six brothers shouldn't be shy of anyone."

"Well, if you don't *want* to help me . . ."

"I never said that," he sipped his beer. "Maybe we can talk about it. What's your problem? You're not pregnant, are you?"

"Oh no!" She looked so horrified that he believed her. "It's just . . . well . . . I think I have a lump in one of my breasts."

Than was ready for it. In his experience, most lovesick women who begged a doctor's professional favors pretended an affliction in areas easily erotically stimulated by manual exploration. "Well, ma'am, that's not exactly a hypothetical thing. I don't know how you imagine I can help you. I have no hospital privileges here and no surgery in which to make a physical exam."

"I know." She turned and looked him directly in the eye. "But what about . . ." She licked her lips nervously. "I mean . . . couldn't you do it in your . . . your hotel room?"

Than's mouth turned dry. After a moment, stubbing out his cigarette, he said carefully: "Mandy, you can hardly expect any degree of professional objectivity from a guy with a young girl in his hotel room, doctor or no. It's not exactly the classical dehumanizing setting."

She looked up at him earnestly. "But I trust you."

"Believe me, lady, such touching belief is no guarantee." He shook his head, smiling. "But if you're prepared to take the chance . . ."

Up in his room, she sat on his bed and nervously undid her halter top, unclipping her bra front to reveal a fine pair of breasts, which, in contrast to her bronzed body, hung pale and bigger than he had imagined. He made her lie down with her arms behind her head. Kneeling beside the bed, he wiped his sweaty palms on his trousers before dutifully going through the motions of examining one beautiful breast after the other. While he worked, her nipples stood erect, her breathing quickened, and her eyes never left his face. As he had suspected, he found nothing even vaguely suggestive of a mammary lump. As this became increasingly obvious, his own breathing pattern changed and his professional palpitations turned into a sensual caressing that made her close her eyes and silently gasp. Then she reached out and snapped off the lamp, and before he realized what he was doing, he was lying on top of her on the bed, kissing her wildly, ravenously, devouring her eager opened mouth with his own. But still, despite her obvious eagerness, his mission-tamed conscience insistently kicked. Finally, forcing himself to stop, he whispered: "Mandy, I don't want to ruin you. You're still pretty young and sweet. You done much of this before?"

"Only with Gavin," she murmured against his throat. "But I'm through with him now!"

"Oh, Jesus!" He tried to pull away. "I don't want to break up your little romance! You have to help me. We can still stop."

"Oh no! Please. . ." She clung to him, her hands slipping under his shirt, caressing his back sensuously. "Not now!"

It was all the persuasion he needed. He had her long skirt half-way up her thigh and was frantically trying to make further head-way when there was a knock at the door.

"*Shit!*" They both fell still, their hearts agitatedly beating, breath shrilling in their ears as they lay panting and entwined, listening acutely. After a moment, the knocking continued, light but insistent. Finally, filled with guilty trepidation, Than raised himself, drawing slowly away from her. "Gavin?" he whispered, but she shook her head.

"He doesn't know I'm here."

"Well, maybe it's a maid to turn down the quilts or something. I'd better check before they use the master key."

Disentangling himself from her arms, Than stood up, straightening his clothing and smoothing down his hair. He unlocked the door and opened it a crack. "Yes?"

"Hello, Than."

"*Lucy!*"

In the glaring light of the passageway, Lucy O'Connor stood

smiling sweetly up at him. "What took ye so long? I managed to swap shifts with a friend and I thought . . ." Her voice trailed off as she noticed his expression. Her eyes narrowed. "Hey—I'm not disturbing ye, am I?"

"Uh . . . well, as a matter of fact, Lucy . . . the truth is. . ." He rubbed guiltily at his lipstick-smudged mouth, hanging on to the door, blocking her entry with his body. "I was just dressing to go out."

"Dressing?" She raised a cool, skeptical brow. "In the dark?"

"Uh, well you see . . ."

Before he could stop her, she had pushed past him into the room, quickly feeling along the wall to switch on the overhead light. The stark glare flooded down on them.

Quickly pulling up her bodice to cover herself, Mandy Mansfield gave a small gasp and sat up on the bed, wide-eyed with shock, her thick dark hair disarrayed and her cheeks guiltily flushed.

"Well, well, well . . ." Lucy demurred, smiling cattily as she took in the scene. She turned and gave Than a hard, haughty look. "I see it's still lusting after ye lost vocation, it is ye are, Doctor—practicing gynecology! And I have to hand it to ye, ye don't waste much time, do ye?"

Than sighed, shutting the door behind him. Disgruntled, he leaned back against it, gesturing with exaggerated gallantry. "Lucy O'Connor, meet Mandy Mansfield."

"How do ye do?" Lucy greeted with sarcastic sweetness.

Mandy, struck speechless, looked bewilderedly from her to Than. He folded his arms resignedly and watched them both. When it became apparent that neither girl was prepared to desert him indignantly, he went to the telephone and called room service, ordering them drinks. Then he dialed Jayne at the Carltons' house.

"Jaynie," he said testily. "Listen, honey, I'm sorry I won't be able to make meeting tonight. It's just . . . well, I have this headache and my stomach's a little queasy. Yeah. Maybe it's the different water. Whatever, don't worry about me. I'll take two aspirin and I'll be fine. No, you go ahead without me. There's absolutely no reason for you to come over here. I'll be fine. Yeah . . . good night, baby."

He put down the phone and turned around to find both openly eavesdropping girls staring at him.

"My, my . . ." Lucy tut-tutted, with a spiteful smile. "I must confess ye have my unqualified admiration, Doctor. What an adept liar it is ye are. And ye with such true-blue eyes and all. It's a wicked deception they are, I'm finding to me cost. A wicked, wicked deception . . ."

15

It was eleven o'clock in the morning when Jayne suddenly burst into Than's room. Filled with concern and straight from morning meeting in her pink gingham Sunday bonnet and dress and little white gloves, she sailed right in, still panting and pink in the face from her rush up the stairs.

"Than!"

Standing shaving at the washbasin, wearing nothing more than his denim jeans and a face full of lather, Than froze, acutely aware of the fresh, bloodied scratch marks that raked his bare back. Razor in hand, he turned slowly around and stared at his sister in horrified disbelief.

"Jaynie!"

"Than . . . I . . ." Her eyes slid sideways and she was struck dumb by the sight of the two tousle-haired young women asleep in the twin beds. Her eyes followed the discarded feminine clothing draped over a chair and dropped on the rug, the empty liquor glasses, and the cigarette stubs that littered the ashtrays. She dropped her head, baffled and embarrassed, knowing she had unwittingly done wrong.

Than swallowed with an effort. He knew she had taken in the whole sordid scene and he didn't have a thing to say to her.

"Jaynie," he said huskily. "Honey—you should have knocked."

"I . . . I'm sorry." She began to back away, tears filling her despairing gray eyes.

He grabbed a towel and wiped the lather off his face. "Baby, how did you get here?"

"Poppa . . . Poppa Carlton brought me. H-he had to come into town. And I was worried about thee . . ."

"Worried about me?" He stared at her blankly.

"Yes." She nodded, her head hung, her voice barely audible. "Thee said thee were sick, remember?"

"Butterfly, listen to me! I can explain!"

"Thee doesn't have to explain!" She raised a proud face that was a tragedy of disillusionment and hurt. A small sob escaped her and her face crumpled in crying. "It's really none of my business." She spun around to flee.

"Jaynie!" He caught her arm at the door and she grew rigid in his grasp, her fiercely averted face hidden in the pink gingham bonnet. "Honey, listen to me. I know how it looks, but you don't understand. They just . . ." His mind worked fast. "Well, they're both nurses I knew in Ndola. They stayed too late visiting me and got locked out of the nurses' home. They had nowhere to spend the night. I couldn't leave them out on the street, could I? And in case you're wondering, I—uh . . ." he swallowed, frantically searching the sparsely furnished room. "I slept on the rug!"

"Oh, indeed he did!" He turned gratefully to Lucy's confirmation. His relief lasted just until he noticed her naked nipples clearly impressing the tightly wrapped sheet she sat up in, and the now-familiar look of spiteful mischief stirring in her eyes. She hadn't yet forgiven him the inclusion of Mandy in their little love nest!

"The poor fellow speaks the truth." She smiled sarcastically at him, speaking with soulful overearnestness. "He's a proper gentleman, yer brother. He just did not have the heart to leave two helpless little maidens out on the street. So he sacrificed his own comfort to sleep on the rug on the hard, bare floor. And though he might have passed the entire night in the very same room as two unmarried females, ye need not fear for yer dear brother's virtue. Oh, no. For like the good Christian soul that he is, he prayed through the long dark hours, asking the Lord to preserve his cherished purity."

"Lucy—cut it out!" Than warned. She was taking it too far, even for Jayne. He turned to his sister. "She's only kidding, honey."

"Oh?" Jayne stared from one to the other, her solemn gray eyes big and round with her growing befuddlement. "Well, I . . . I think I'd better be going."

"Oh don't go yet, dear. Ye've only just arrived. Stay awhile and tell us all about yer dear brother. We were just having some coffee sent up."

"Well, I . . ." Jayne hesitated.

"She can't stay," Than snapped. He grabbed a shirt and shrugged it on, anxious to get her out of there and away from Lucy's wicked wiles. "Come on, honey, I'll walk you downstairs."

"Oh no, don't ye be such a bully." Lucy eyed him petulantly. "Let the little girl stay if she wants to. I thought the more the merrier was yer motto, after all. Or don't ye want her to get friendly with yer girlfriends?"

"*Lucy!*" Than glared at her in impotent exasperation, but it was too late. A look of incredulity had passed across Jayne's sweet face.

"*Girlfriends?*" she whispered. Sexual dalliance might yet be a vague notion, but girlfriends were definitely a known quantity in her naïve little mind.

"Heck no." Than's forced chuckles were a little off-key. "Lucy and Mandy are just . . . just old colleagues . . . is all. I couldn't leave them in a spot."

"That's right." Obviously sumptuously enjoying his discomfiture, Lucy nodded, making big innocent eyes. In the bed beside her, Mandy giggled. "We're not his girlfriends. We just slept with him, that's all. Isn't that so, Mandy m'dear?"

"That's right." Mandy smoothed back her hair and smiled.

"Will you girls kindly keep out of this?" Than struggled to contain his vexation, hopping from foot to foot as he hastily pulled on his boots. He fumbled to light up a cigarette as he buttoned his shirt with one hand, unzipping his fly and tucking in the tails, while tears and the very substance of her faith in him trembled in his sister's eyes. "Come on, baby. Let's go!"

"Dearie, before ye go, pass me my underthings on that chair, will ye?" Lucy smiled appealingly.

Than stopped at the door. "*Jaynie*, come on!"

But she hesitated, torn between obedience to him and common courtesy. Courtesy won. When she moved woodenly to the chair, Than stormed out without her.

"Thanks, dearie," Lucy smiled. Taking the flimsy underwear, she pushed back the bed clothing and stepped out of bed, stark naked. Shocked witless, Jayne turned red with embarrassment; she began to back away.

"I . . . I . . . good-bye!" she gasped, polite to the very last. Then she turned and rushed through the door, pulling it shut after her. For a moment, she stood in the passageway in a terrible turmoil, gasping and whimpering.

"Jayne, what's wrong?"

She started, surprised to find Than waiting for her, arms folded and leaning against the wall, furiously smoking. She shrugged helplessly, bursting into grieving tears. "I . . . I . . ." she struggled. Then: "Oh, Than! She had no clothes on!"

"Hush, honey. That doesn't matter. You're a girl too, aren't you?"

She fumbled in her drawstring purse, pulling out a little lace handkerchief, dabbing her eyes as he led her to the elevator. "Oh, Than," she mourned afresh. "Tell me the truth. What do those ladies mean to thee?"

"Baby, those were no ladies!"

"What does thee mean?"

"Nothing," he relented with a sigh. "It's just the way I told you. They're old colleagues, nothing more."

"Oh." But she still sounded unconvinced. He pressed the elevator button, and while they awaited its arrival, he lifted her chin, turning her head, forcing her to face him.

"Look at me, baby. Would I lie to you? Don't you believe in me?"

She stared at him, mesmerized. Put like that . . . She swallowed. "I . . . of course . . ."

"Well then, what are we worried about?" He smiled at her beatifically, and she fell into his arms, oblivious of his look of sick relief. His legs still quaked and he felt as emotionally wrung-out as if he had just been fractionally missed by a speeding train.

"Oh, Than," she murmured against his shirt. "When I saw them there in thy room, I . . . I just did not know what to believe, especially after thee behaved so strangely with Lucy yesterday."

"Oh that." Than drew away and smiled at her sickly. "Well, maybe I should have explained about that. I had just remembered a personal message I was asked to pass on to Lucy . . . by a . . . a dying friend . . ." The lie came so glibly, he surprised himself.

"Oh?" She gazed guilelessly up at him with great gray eyes. "She had a friend who died . . . at *Suseshi*?"

"Yeah," he coughed uncomfortably. (The story wouldn't stand too much scrutinization.) "Didn't I tell you about that? It was an . . . an African girl she had known in Ndola. Anyway, it was a very sad and private disclosure."

"Oh, I see." Jayne struggled with a growing puzzlement. "So then . . . when she came back to the table . . . and I thought she was *laughing* . . ."

"Yeah!" Than nodded quickly, gravely. "In reality, she was crying. It's hard to tell with some females. But it was a great shock and the poor girl was almost beside herself . . . quite . . . quite hysterical for a while there."

"Well, she acted so cheerful. I think she was very brave." Jayne frowned dubiously.

"Yeah. Listen, honey—do we have to talk about those two all the time? Tell you what—if you're real good and promise not to spread that story—well—I'll take you for one of those milk shakes you're so crazy about!"

"Really?" Her eyes lit up. As they stepped into the elevator together, she started to laugh.

"What's so funny?" He growled good-naturedly, by now totally unnerved by the morning's hilarity at his expense.

"Oh, Than. Thee has whiskers all down the one side of thy face. Thee never did finish thy shave."

16

On Monday morning, when Than returned to the Ministry of Foreign Affairs, blank-faced officials, unable to find his forms, directed him back to Immigration again. However, the clerks in this building seemed to have no better idea of where his documents might be. Finally, thoroughly exasperated by red tape and an apparently boundless apathy, Than gave up the effort and went to the American embassy. There, in a spacious checker-tiled reception lobby, he waited to see the ambassador while the pretty raven-haired receptionist, busy typing behind a large neat desk, occasionally engaged him in casual conversation. Finally, a door opened along a dim passage and a dark-suited man strode out, rifling through a handful of papers.

"For Christ's sake, Cecille," he growled, "when I ask you to type out a memorandum, I expect . . ." Reaching her desk, he stopped and, catching sight of Than, his eyes seemed to sharpen in suspicious dislike. He smiled automatically, moderating his tone. "Cecille, you never told me . . . what's this gentleman waiting for?"

Blushing, the receptionist flustered. "Well, Mr. Profane's waiting to see the ambassador, Mr. Steiner. He works on a mission station in Northern Rhodesia, and he's hoping for some financial assistance for . . ."

"Is he, indeed?" Steiner smiled coldly at Than. "Well, I'm sorry to disappoint you, sir, but I doubt you'll have much luck. You got problems with Immigration or visas, we can help sure. But financial aid, well, I'm afraid you fellows will have to begin motivating the natives to help themselves. It's a sad story, but our A.I.D. program is already committed. So take my advice, young man, and don't waste your time."

"Thanks," Than smiled. "but I think I'll take my chances with the ambassador."

Steiner's expression changed. Contriving a cynical smile, he shrugged. "Have it your own way. But if you must, take my advice and go get a haircut."

"Oh no!" the receptionist wailed involuntarily. "I think it looks . . ." She caught Steiner's look and subsided into silence.

"Maybe not for you, honey," Steiner smiled sarcastically, "but for his own sake. Ambassador McQueen's hardly likely to favor bohemians."

"Is that right?" Than said innocently. He snapped his fingers. "Doggone it, goofed again." He touched his jaw tentatively. "Say, how am I off for a shave? When you fellows offer advice, you surely do give it!"

"Very amusing, Mr. . . . er . . ." Steiner fumbled for his name as the main embassy doors swung open, admitting a stocky man with a balding head who strode across the foyer, briefcase in hand.

"*Ambassador!*" Steiner and Cecille rang together.

"Carl, Cecille," the man smiled pleasantly. "Sorry I'm late. Got a little tied up. Are there any . . ." He noticed Than and turned around.

"Oh yes," Cecille spluttered at once. "Ambassador, this gentleman wants to see you about . . ."

"It's all right, Cecille," Steiner snapped, eyeing her reprovingly. "There's no need to bother the ambassador. I told you I'd take care of Mr. . . . er . . ."

"Doctor." Than stood up and walked across to the ambassador, extending his hand. "I'm Than Profane. I believe you knew my father."

"*Profane?*" Shaking his hand, the ambassador looked blank for a moment. Then: "Oh, yes! Now I remember. Thomas Elderwood Profane. You look a lot like him, in fact. He used to come up from the bush from time to time. But wait a minute. I seem to recall reading an obituary a while back."

"Yes, sir. He died in '58."

"Well, I'm sorry to hear it, son. We only had a kind of passing acquaintance, but he came across to me as a fine man and I liked him a lot." He put a companionable arm around Than's shoulders. "Why don't you come along into my office and we'll reminisce over some coffee?"

"But, sir!" Steiner squalled in outrage. "I can handle that. You're behind in your schedule as it is."

"Peace, my good man," the ambassador said, smiling stiffly.

"There are some things more important than schedules. I'll trust you to arrange a little room for me the next half-hour or so."

Later, Ambassador McQueen telephoned Than at his hotel to invite him home to dinner. When Than inadvertently revealed that two possessive girlfriends took up all his free time, the ambassador, amused, insisted that he bring both girls along. But embarrassed about taking them both or choosing between them, Than escorted Jayne instead.

Set in parklike gardens, the ambassador's house was an elegant mansion in the most elite suburb of Salisbury. The tinkling door chimes brought a dress-suited black butler, who relieved them of their jackets and hats before ushering them into a spacious drawing room hung with original Renoirs and Soutines. There the ambassador introduced his wife, an attractive, chestnut-haired Frenchwoman in a striking African-print kaftan, who greeted them warmly. In a palatial dining room that dripped with diamanté chandeliers, at a banquet-sized table that glowed with flowers and real silverware, they dined on roast guinea-fowl and stuffed onions with red wine.

Aaron McQueen was jovial and inconsequential throughout; Jayne, overawed, scarcely spoke, and it was left to Than and Magdalena McQueen to carry along a meaningful conversation. After supper, retiring to the "intimate" lounge, they drank coffee and liqueurs while Than, prompted by his hosts, began to expand diffidently on his plans for an advanced medical course and bush clinics. But it was obvious the couple had little idea of what this entailed, and after a time, drowsy on the unaccustomed wine, Than, stifling his yawns, had just begun to plan a polite escape when the ambassador's daughter and her beau arrived from a theater show in town.

Instantly recognizing the man, his hackles rising in remembered resentment, Than stood up to greet them while the ambassador turned to pour more drinks from a well-stocked liquor cabinet.

"Dr. Profane," he said pleasantly as he measured and poured, "I believe you met my secretary, Carl Steiner, at the embassy. And this is my daughter, Suzannah."

Accepting a martini from her father, the girl turned and smiled aloofly at Than. She wore a full-length dark blue clinging sheath set off with a blue-feathered wrap, but by the effect she had on him, she might have been standing there stark naked. For she was breathtakingly beautiful, with honey-gold skin, a lithe voluptuous body, and the fine-featured face of an angel, encircled with a soft halo of short honey-blond curls. Than's mouth turned dry; losing his voice, he nodded politely. When Jayne was introduced as his sister, the girl's clear cat-bronze eyes widened in derisive surprise.

"Sister?" She looked inquiringly at Than. "Why, Dr. Profane, whatever happened? As I recall it, Daddy said you were bringing two girlfriends." She smiled musingly, sipping her drink. "Rather a surprising excess, I thought, for a pious Christian missionary."

"I . . . uh . . . well, cheers!" Damn her! Than raised his glass and sat down abruptly. But Jayne, ever doting, rushed to redeem his honor.

"Oh, but they're not girlfriends!" she innocently insisted, her anxious voice engaging the attention of the entire room. "They just got locked out of their place and had to sleep the night with him, is all."

Than almost choked on his drink; eyes wide, he spilled cherry liqueur down the front of his shirt, spluttering: "That's not what she meant! What she meant was . . . I mean . . ."

"How quaint." Carl Steiner, sipping neat whiskey, savored Than's embarrassment with a satisfied smirk, while the ambassador's wife, suppressing an amused smile, fussed ineffectually around him, dabbing at his shirt with a handkerchief. Suzannah McQueen, obviously evilly entertained by his dire predicament, blatantly smiled.

"You don't *have* to explain, Doctor."

"Oh, but you don't understand," Than rushed on. "My sister's not used to the wine! You see, she . . ." Feeling the futility of it, his words trailed. And Jayne, uncomprehending, stared at him in bewildered distress.

"But that's what thee said!" Not even her subsequent lapse into an incriminating bout of hiccups helped to vindicate him then. . . .

Back at Immigration the next morning, Than charmed a senior woman supervisor into taking up his cause. His elusive documents were finally unearthed, and the lady promised to have them processed by the following day. Heartened by this belated progress, Than went back to the hotel for a beer before finally giving in to his day-long urge to call Suzannah McQueen. He had to ring back twice after supper before finally catching her, and then the coolness in her voice was enough to spoil his digestion.

"Dr. Profane?"

"Than's the name," he reminded, and by this time, uneasily anticipating the unannounced arrival of Lucy O'Connor and/or Mandy

Mansfield, he launched straight into his objective without polite pre-
amble. "I'd like to see you again."

There was a short silence. Then: "Oh, Dr. Profane, you can't be
serious! What about your girlfriends?"

He caught his breath. "Listen, that's not funny any more. I told
you, my sister . . ."

"Oh come now, Doctor—of all the unchivalrous excuses. You're
not going to insist on blaming your little sister's inebriation, are
you?"

"Hell." He was disgusted now. "Can't we be serious? I'm asking
you to come out with me tonight."

"Why?"

"Why?" Angry now, he spoke acidly. "Well, let's see now. First
of all, I like your buck teeth! Then there's your hairy legs and that
wart on your nose. Gives you that witchy-bitchy look that kind of
goes with your temperament. Know what I mean?"

"Very funny," she seethed sarcastically.

"Well, touché. *Now* will you come out with me? I thought maybe
a movie or . . ."

"Well now," she contrived a surprised tone. "Don't you missionaries get around! Well, I'm sorry to disappoint you, Sir Galahad, but
I've had a pretty hectic time this week. I was planning on a quiet
evening at home."

"Well," in the face of this unflattering lack of enthusiasm, Than
struggled to rerally his flagging confidence, "as it happens, I'm a
pretty quiet guy myself. How about if I come over and make it even
quieter?"

"Oh, the Lord bless us all—a clown!" she simpered. "Well . . . I
suppose, if that's what you'd like."

"I'd like." Before she could change her mind, he slammed down
the receiver, picked up his jacket, and was out the door before the
telephone had grown cold. Taking the stairs two at a time, he just
narrowly missed Mandy Mansfield coming up in the elevator.

At the house, Than found Suzannah out in the garden, sitting at
the edge of a big kidney-shaped pool, legs dangling in the water, in a
stunningly brief imitation-leopard-skin bikini.

"Hi." He stared down at her gleaming golden body in open admiration, watching the round breasts bob with the kicking of her
legs. "I got a pet back at the mission, looks almost as good as you do
in that spotted fur."

"Oh?" She looked up at him with soft amber eyes. "Aren't leop-
ards dangerous?"

He smiled. "So are some girls."

"Well," she shrugged her fine shoulders impatiently, "the change rooms are over there. I'll get one of the spare trunks we keep for guests."

He watched her long glistening wet legs as she walked past him to the change room. She stopped halfway, as though a thought had suddenly struck her. "Oh, by the way, you *can* swim?" she asked, looking appealingly wide-eyed and dubious. A bitchy one. Than had long ago categorized her: a butter-mouthed little tease.

"Hell, no." He played her game, gritting his teeth in an apologetic smile. "But don't worry, I'll stay near the shallow end."

The first pair of trunks she handed him were very obviously produced out of sheer sarcasm. Than gave her his most adorable smile. "Those are boy's trunks," he told her sweetly. "Now *me*, lady, I'm a man. I got a whole lot more to fill it out with."

"You don't say?" She raised her perfect brows at him before producing a more suitably sized pair she had kept hidden behind her back.

When he returned, she was already in the pool, a flowery pink bathing cap on her head. Seeing him, her eyes widened in admiration; his lithe, muscled body was fetchingly lit up in the light of the tall lanterns that skirted the pool.

"Well now, Hercules!" she murmured, her voice hollow against the lapping water. "Aren't you just a darling boy?"

He did a running dive into the wafting, blue, icy-cold water, surfacing beside her in a ticklish foam of bubbles.

"Goodness!" She blinked at him through droplets of water. "You're a regular tiger, aren't you?"

"Yeah." He smiled at her, unable to keep his eyes off her bobbing breasts. "And I eat females. They're my natural diet."

"Really?" She raised her brows coyly. "Well, would you like to take a bite?"

"Don't tempt me. My momma never did get me properly weaned. I'm still on the breast."

Suzannah made big eyes. "Your momma's?"

He grinned at her devilishly. "Hell, no."

They swam leisurely and at first he kept his hands right where they belonged. Then she began to bait him, ducking him and diving through his legs. He let her play, feigning good-natured surrender, until she got confident. Then he turned and attacked. He pursued, easily caught, and gently wrestled her. But she was a dirty little fighter and it was all he could do to keep his gentlemanly reserve.

She kicked, pounded with her fists, and pulled his hair. He grabbed at her as she lunged to escape and her leopard-skin bra came away in his hands. He stared at it in surprise, the implications making his cheeks burn. She spun around with a spitting fury that surprised him.

"*Give that back! How dare you!*"

"Come and get it." He smiled sadistically, warm with his sense of power.

"I will not! You give it back here, right this minute!" Treading water, she bobbed below the surface, but the pool lights gave him a tantalizing glimpse of shimmering white breasts. She saw the direction of his gaze and clutched at herself cross-handedly. "*You bastard*! Give that back to me or I'll call my father."

But he was unintimidated. "Tell you what—we'll work a trade. A kiss for your bra. That fair enough?"

"Why, you . . . you *sex fiend*!"

"Just one little kiss, is all. A platonic little peck on the cheek. Just like I'd kiss my own sister."

"If you think for *one moment* that I . . ."

"I don't," he said softly. "One kiss is all."

She waded to him grudgingly, standing where the water came up to her chin. "All right, wise guy," she gave him a brittle smile. "But if you try anything . . ."

"Won't try a thing. Scout's honor, cross my heart and hope to die. I won't but brush your little pink cheek."

She eyed him dubiously. "Well, all right . . ."

And still holding on to her overflowing breasts, she stretched out her neck obligingly, her cheek aloofly poised. But cheating unashamedly, he ignored it and went straight for the mouth. Then he grabbed her wrists and pulled her toward him. She fretted and twisted in his grasp, her angry objections muffled in his mouth. His hands went around her slender back, and his arms tightened, pulling her soft buoyant breasts full against him. He felt her nipples prick his bare chest, and he went wild. He kissed her savagely, until she could scarcely breathe, and she tore at him with her nails, shaking her head in an effort to be rid of him, her legs squirming against his in the water. When he finally released her, she swung around away from him, holding on to the edge, panting and shivering. Her cap had come half off, and she glared at him through short wet strings of hair.

"You *bastard*!" she said softly, vehemently, but he could see the

138

secret flash of excitement in her angry eyes. *"You mean, low-down, son of a bitch!* Ooooh!"

"Yeah," he smiled maliciously. "That's me all right."

She made no answer. They were both breathing hard and fast, and he draped the leopard-skin bra carefully across her right shoulder before turning his back like a gentleman. "Go on," he said gruffly. "Put it back on. Be a spoilsport."

"Just you keep . . ." she was half crying with her anger now, ". . . keep away from me!"

When she had it back on, they climbed out of the pool without a word. Draped in a giant towel, she ripped off her cap and fluffed out her blond curls. Than stood dripping on the slate, watching her.

"You know something," he said musingly, "I can't help wondering about how easily that bra came off . . ."

Eyes wide, she stared at him with a look of surprise. "You don't think I . . . for goodness' sake, you don't think I would *deliberately* . . ."

"It did occur to me." Then something imperceptibly guilty about her expression reinforced the opinion. "Yeah, I do. All that fine spitting anger—but you like teasing men, don't you, Suzannah McQueen?"

She hesitated in the act of drying her legs, her breasts hanging full. For a moment, she did not speak. Then she stood up and threw the towel at him. He caught it against his stomach and looked questioningly up at her.

"Maybe I do." She eyed him haughtily. "Maybe I do and maybe I don't." Then she smiled a tiny tight catty smile. "Oh by the way, Dr. Profane, I notice you've injured yourself. Those scratches on your back. Tell me, how did you happen to come by them?"

Than smiled sweetly right back at her. The little bitch knew very well how he had come by them! "Oh," he said casually, "nothing much. I got them crawling under a hedge to rescue a schoolmarm's cat."

"A schoolmarm's cat?" She broke into a peal of derisive laughter. "That's a good one! What on earth was the cat doing there?"

"Stuck in a gopher hole," Than glibly supplied. "It didn't like the schoolmarm."

"Oh brother." She smiled at him sweetly. "Your audacity, Doctor, is exceeded only by your imagination."

"And your beauty," Than snarled through an equally sweet smile, "is exceeded only by your sweet nature!"

"Well, touché!" she purred. "Maybe we'll get along."

"Maybe we will . . ."

17

The following evening, fresh from the triumph of finally receiving his permanent-residence permit, Than phoned Suzannah McQueen again. "How about a movie or a nightclub?"

"I don't know," she demurred. "I need to wash my hair and get a few things done."

"Well listen, I wouldn't get in your way. How about another nice quiet evening at home? They're the best kind."

"As you please," she sighed, her tone still tantalizingly indifferent.

Two hours later, he arrived just in time to see her, looking stunning in a low-cut evening gown, leaving the house on Carl Steiner's arm.

"Why, hello." She smiled sweetly up at him as they met on the stone driveway, arching her perfect brows innocently up at him. "You come to see Daddy?"

With an enormous effort, Than swallowed his bitter anger. He ignored Steiner's stiff greeting, dropped his freshly lit cigarette, and ground it savagely under his heel. "Sure," he said sarcastically. "I've come to see your father."

In the early hours of the morning, through the vague layers of sleep, Than heard the insistent ringing of the telephone. After an exhausting night spent diffusing his anger in frenzied sexual activity, he tried to escape the sound, burying his head deeper under the pillow. But still it bewailed him, shrilling intrusively, until finally, unable to settle back into sleep, he began to resurface and reached groggily for the instrument on the bedside table. But reaching out over him, her bare breasts pressing into his back, Mandy Mansfield, fumbling sleepily, preceded him fractionally.

"Hello . . ." He heard her sleepy voice with ill-founded relief just before the star-bursting shock of realization hit him with her words. "Yes . . . this is Dr. Profane's room . . ."

"Mandy!" Whispering fiercely, he leaped up, bumping her jaw with his head, clumsily wrestling the receiver from her. "For God's sake . . ."

"Ooooow . . ." She was bewilderedly rubbing her jaw. "What'd I do?"

"Will you for Chris . . ." He clapped his hand belatedly over the receiver, glaring at her through the dark. ". . . For Chrissakes keep your voice down!"

"But . . ."

"Jesus! What did you do that for?"

"What?" She stared at him brokenly, hurt tears beginning to gleam down her cheeks. She sniffled. "I . . . I just didn't think. And you bumped me with your head!" She touched her chin and started to whimper.

"For God's sake!" Than clapped a hand over her mouth. "Don't cry now! You understand me? Don't make a single damn sound!" Crouched naked on the bed beside her, he sat glowering at her in the dimness, not satisfied until she flipped over and suppressed her silent weeping into her pillow. Only then, feeling his heart pounding furiously in his chest, he removed his hand from the receiver and spoke tentatively into the phone.

"Hello?" There was a stony silence, but the line was still open. He tried again. "Hello?"

"Hello," Suzannah McQueen said with sarcastic sweetness, "and good-bye."

The line went dead in his hand. For a long time afterward, Than didn't move. While Mandy Mansfield's weeping grew increasingly vocal, he sweated in silent sufferance. Finally, he thawed; still in a dreamlike daze, he settled back onto the bed beside the convulsively shaking girl, reaching absently out to her. "Hey, what are you crying about?"

Her heaving stopped abruptly. After a moment, she raised a tear-streaked face and stared pathetically at him in the dimness. "You hurt me!" she whispered submissively, and in that moment he remembered remorsefully just how young she was. Not yet out of her teens, and here he was cold-bloodedly corrupting her, using her body, teaching her techniques that would make a practiced whore proud. He closed his eyes, groaning to think of it.

"Come here," he said gruffly, holding out an arm to her. Whimpering and grateful as a whipped pup, she crawled to him, snuggling desperately against him. "Now—where does it hurt?"

Pushing her back against a pillow, he held her head tenderly in his hands, kissing her all along the contour of her jaw. "Does that feel better?"

She nodded, smiling through her tears. "But you seemed so angry!"

"I'm sorry." He took her in his arms. "But I'm not angry anymore."

"I know," she whispered rapturously against his throat. "Oh, I know . . ."

At ten o'clock in the morning, still torn between anger at himself and Suzannah McQueen, furious that the previous night's fiasco should so acutely intrude upon his sacred medical preoccupation, Than went to the Ministry of Public Health to keep his appointment with the inspector of medical affairs. In their preliminary discussion, the man was disturbingly evasive and noncommittal, his questions exacting and probing.

Finally he asked Than to leave behind his portfolio, requesting that he remain available for further discussions during the next few weeks, in which time the details of his plan would be studied and assessed. Than left the office in a daze of doubt. The inspector had given him no reason to expect a favorable decision, and while the inadequate hospital staff struggled to shoulder his additional load at Suseshi, he wondered how much longer he could afford to stay away.

That evening, on the impetus of his gnawing anxiety at the project's outcome and his own growing anger at Suzannah McQueen, he went unannounced to the ambassador's house.

The ambassador's wife greeted him warmly. Her husband, ushering him into the study with a stiff smile, seemed more cautious. "Well, Doctor—to what do we owe this unexpected pleasure?"

"I'd like to see Suzannah, please."

The couple exchanged meaningful looks. Finally, Magdalena smiled. "I will call her."

Moments later, Suzannah McQueen came through the study doors. Her stepmother had evidently not revealed the identity of her caller, for she looked surprised, then outraged, when she saw him. "Maggie, I thought you said . . ." She turned accusingly, but Magdalena and the ambassador had already beat a hasty retreat, the double doors just closing behind them, and she turned haughtily back to Than. "Well, Dr. Profane, what do you want?"

"I want to know what the hell game it is you're playing."

"The game *I'm* playing?" Her amber eyes went wide with indignation. "Why, you've got a nerve. I should have thought the shoe was on the other foot."

"You mean last night? Well you stood me up, remember? What'd you expect me to do? Sit all alone in my hotel room faithfully pining for you?"

"I never expected anything of the sort. Your behavior is your own business."

"You're damn right it is!"

"But . . ." Her eyes narrowed spitefully. "For a pious Christian missionary, I find your habits highly questionable."

"Now listen, she only came up for a drink!"

"A drink? Oh come now, Doctor! You must think I was born yesterday. A drink at two o'clock in the morning?"

"Is there a law against it?"

"Well whatever, I doubt your missionary colleagues would be charmed by it. Personally, I couldn't care less. So, if you've finished having your say, Doctor, I'm expecting Carl at eight. Now, if you'll kindly excuse me . . ."

Than caught her arm as she turned to stalk off. "No," he said quietly. "As it happens, I'm not finished having my say. And like it or not, you're going to hear me out."

"Oh really, Doctor! If you imagine I'm interested in hearing your excuses . . ."

"Jesus, I'm not trying to make them! I'm a grown man, and my private relationships are just exactly that. The only reason I'm here at all today is because I think—I *hope*— you were calling last night to apologize for your unprincipled behavior."

"*Unprincipled?*" She snorted indignantly, trying to wriggle out of his grasp.

"Fortunately for you, though, I'm a pretty forgiving fellow and I'm willing to forget all about it, providing you do the polite thing and give this guy Steiner decent prior warning that you're putting him off tonight."

"Putting him off?" She gaped at him in high indignation.

Than turned to the cream-colored telephone that stood on the large desk beside him. "What's his number?" He smiled grimly at her, handing across the receiver. "You can tell him right now."

"You're outrageous, you know that?" Suzannah told him later.

"And you smoke too much." Sitting beside her on the sofa, Than

143

took the cigarette from her hand and ground it out in the ashtray. "I never could stand to see a woman smoke like a man. It looks cheap."

"Is that a fact? Well, while we're about it, is there anything else you'd like to change about me, Doctor?"

Than gazed at her skeptically. "Well, I don't know yet. I still know so little about you. Have to first feel my way around a little, so to speak." He drew her toward him and kissed her softly, testingly, just brushing her lips. "Hmmmmmmm . . ." There was a deliberate doubtful quality in his musing assessment that brought up her brows.

"Well?" She looked up at him, innocently wide-eyed. "What's your verdict?"

"Welllllll . . . it's hard to say." He breathed against her neck. "A woman's physical assets can be pretty deceiving. Guess I'll have to try again. And again. And again . . ."

Her indignant reply was smothered by his passionate mouth.

18

The days went by with no word from the Ministry of Public Health. But despite his increasing anxiety over his absence from the hospital and the acceptance of the medical school, Than went ahead with his plans to provide for it. During his daily shopping expeditions with Jayne, he found a medical supply depot, where hours of rapturous browsing resulted in the optimistic purchase of a number of teaching aids. His daytime preoccupation with these and other mission supplies helped to dull his disquiet, and during the evenings he found a more delicious distraction in the person of Suzannah McQueen. Her earlier aversion to him seemed to have worn off completely and he was seeing her most nights now. Their most ambitious date so far had been a visit to a nightclub, where they had watched a cabaret show and dined and danced until the club closed.

But Than's financial resources were limited, and with his masculine pride disdaining her suggestion that they go Dutch, they had begun to spend most evenings at her father's house, usually at the poolside, where under the lantern lights, pleasantly cool and half-naked, their relationship had progressed rapidly, their teasing horse-play quickly turning into amorous exchanges. In between their compulsive kissing, Suzannah talked freely, and during one such evening beneath the stars Than learned a little about her background. It seemed that one of the most basic banes of her life was her own mother, who had run off with another man when Suzannah was just three years old, declining to take custody of her small daughter in the subsequent divorce.

"That's tough," Than sympathized as they sat side by side, swinging their legs in the clear chlorine-smelling pool water. She sniffed disdainfully, but despite this brittle bravado, he could tell that she was more affected by the memory than she pretended.

"Oh, I couldn't care less. She was nothing but a whore. My father and I were better off without her." She swallowed visibly. "Until Magdalena came along, that is. They've been married just eighteen months, you know." Suzannah looked at him. "And already she's got her claws into Daddy."

Than shrugged, embarrassed by her bitterness. "I thought she was pretty nice."

She spun on him with a spitting fury that surprised him completely. "Oh, you would. You men are all the same. All you see is a pretty face or a good body. But she's not good enough to be an ambassador's wife. Behind that sweet smile she's a scheming, money-grabbing little tramp. She hates my guts and I hate hers. She deliberately tells Daddy things to put him against me." She paused to stub out her cigarette on the flagstone at the pool edge, breathing heavily, her amber eyes sparking with outrage.

After a moment's acid silence, Than tried to sidetrack her. "What do you do when you're not hating your stepmother?"

To his relief, she subsided, laughing shakily. "Well, Daddy provides me with a generous monthly allowance. But I like to keep busy, so I model for a living. And I'm pretty good at it, too. I was in great demand in the States before Daddy was shipped out to this hick place." She smiled haughtily at him. "I once graced the centerfold of *Playboy* magazine."

He smiled lewdly at her, pleased at the thought, his avid eyes frankly wandering over her beautiful bronzed body, his growing admiration affirmed in his face. "Well, I can believe that. But I'd like to see the evidence just the same."

Without any argument or false modesty, she brought out a few of the magazines for which she had modeled. With indecent directness, Than sought out the *Playboy* among them, and for several stunned moments gazed lustfully at the titillating color photographs of her scantily draped, perfect female form. Finally, he looked up, blandly smiling. None of what he felt showed in his face.

"Pussycat, you're pretty nice. Your daddy's got a lovely daughter."

"Oh . . ." She gathered up the magazines, preening with pleasure. "Well, Daddy doesn't exactly think so. At least, at the time he didn't think it quite proper for a senator's daughter to appear in the nude. Even now he doesn't like to mention it around too liberally. Thinks it might disgrace the dignity of his diplomatic position or something, and yet his beloved Magdalena . . ." She stopped short, smiling maliciously at him. "I once stumbled upon a sordid little scrapbook, categorizing her earlier days as a French strip-dancer. Well, it seems that everybody but Daddy knows how those little two-bit tramps used to give it all away after the show."

"Well, you could have fooled me too."

"Oh, Doctor. Don't act so innocent! You're starting to sound just like Daddy. As far as he's concerned, she has a lily-white past no matter what her occupation. She's got him eating right out of her hand, completely fooled with her helpless, butter-wouldn't-melt angelic air. But she can't fool me. And she's frightened of me. You know that? Of what I'll do next. She's forever throwing up her manicured hands and saying, 'Whatever will that child do next!' And poor Daddy doesn't know whom to please; he's caught right in the middle. You know, I once brought home a black man. Oh, you should have seen their faces. Magdalena almost had a coronary! She's gotten as reputation-conscious as Daddy, and I had the pair of them running around like chickens with their heads cut off. I told her I intended to marry him, and I swear she almost fainted. Daddy just about turned gray overnight. But at least he realized I was around for a change."

"A *black* man?" Than was still staring at her incredulously; he hastily stubbed his cigarette out on the flagstone. "You don't mean . . ."

"Oh, he was nobody's gardenboy," Suzannah assured him. "He was the intellectual type, educated at Cambridge in England, and he's a lawyer here, full of civilized airs and graces."

"*Shit.*" Than swallowed. "How long did . . ."

"Oh, only a few weeks." She giggled gleefully. "Just long enough to scare the shit out of them both before Daddy finally *begged* me to stop it. I only broke it off to please him. He said it would ruin his career, and he was so sweet to me then. He's been suitably adoring and attentive ever since."

146

"Jesus Christ." Than shook his head disgustedly.

"What's the matter, Doctor?" Suzannah stared at him haughtily. "Don't you like Africans?"

"I don't like little white bitches who flaunt it in their faces!"

She drew up aloofly, her eyes narrowing. "If you don't like the way I am, Doctor, why do you come here?"

It was a good question. He stared at her dumbly for a long moment, considering it. He had learned early on that she had no great spiritual virtues; she was the typical rich bitch, selfish and spoiled and all screwed up with a sensuous self-pity. But her beauty was a great consolation. Disease and death awaited at Suseshi, and sometimes, to the weary soul, there was no balm so great as frivolous love.

"I come here, I guess, because I'm as dumb as all the rest of them. I'm only a man, a poor clay morsel, all flesh and blood and aching balls. I might not think much of your manners, but your body—well, ma'am, I'd sure like to be a full beneficiary of your ample charms."

It was the honest sum of his regard for her, and he knew that knowing this, she only lured him on to hold him at bay, delighting in his torment, alternately alluring then aloof, so that he always left her feeling frustrated and mad, only to return meekly for more of the same treatment the very next day. In this respect, Lucy O'Connor and Mandy Mansfield became the safety valve for his pent-up passions. Although they must guess at his new involvement and were still fiercely jealous of each other, they hung hopefully on just the same, tripping to his beck and call, allowing the use of their bodies to abate his hunger for another girl. It was what kept him so patient around the ambassador's daughter. With their help, he could face Suzannah reasonably unravenous, although his nerves wore thin as the long hot summer nights wore on, and he sensed that Suzannah was instinctively aware that his secret love life, fed at impossible hours, was still fully flourishing.

"How do I measure up to your *other* girlfriends?" she said suddenly, as if reading his thoughts.

Than drew away from her testily. "Now, let's not start that again. You don't seem to realize I'm a conservative kind of guy. I'm not much interested in girls right now."

"Oh?" She put on a hurt expression. "Well, how would you describe me?"

"You? Well, you ought to know it—I only come here to see your father."

"Ho, ho! Very funny." She smiled icily at the old joke. "However, despite your noble lack of interest in the fairer sex, there is one sweet maiden who seems pretty worried about you."

"Oh?" Than looked quickly around at her and maybe the apprehension showed in his eyes, for she laughed at his expression.

"Oh don't look so worried, Doctor. It's just that you seem to have made a pretty big hit with my stepmother. Yesterday, she actually broke her stony reserve and asked me to invite you to spend the rest of your stay as a guest in our home. I'm not sure Daddy thinks it's wise. He's a little anxious about my neglecting Carl lately. But Maggie, as always, has the upper hand. And it seems she finds you such a personable gentleman, she just can't abide the thought of you remaining in that dreary old hotel room a day longer!"

"Oh?" Than started to smile.

"Yes. She told me not to take no for an answer, to beat down your reservations and quash your objections until you submit."

"Hell." Than shook his head, smiling. "Providing it brings me closer to your . . . uh . . . er . . . *father*, who's protesting? When can I move in? Tonight?"

"Now, hold on just a moment there, Doctor. I appreciate your flattering enthusiasm, but it's already ten-thirty, and aren't you a little underequipped? Won't you need at least pajamas and a toothbrush?"

"Oh hell, I'm like a Boy Scout. I always come prepared. I figure my birthday suit and a toothpasted finger should substitute very well."

Tantalized by the knowledge of Suzannah's nearness in the bedroom along the landing, Than was unable to sleep. At around two-thirty in the morning, when the ashtray at his bedside was almost full of cigarette stubs, he turned at a sudden slight sound, watching in vague surprise as the door soundlessly opened to admit a shadowy form.

Through the dimness, Suzannah stood silently appraising him for a moment before the white mist of her long nightdress wafted across to the window, where she opened the drapes so that the bright moonlight fell on her in a dazzling nimbus. Then she turned to face him, head held high as she began to deliberately untie one of the shoestring straps that held her gown together at the shoulders. Hardly daring to move lest it break the spell, Than reached out blindly and extinguished his cigarette, watching in fascination as, with all the practiced coquetry of a stripper, she undid first one strap then the other, shaking her slender shoulders so that the soft chiffon shivered and with a faint whisper fell down the length of her perfect naked body to lie pooled at her feet. Feeling strangely dispossessed of his actions, Than tumbled out of the bed and found himself kneeling naked before her, humbled and awed as a religious devotee worshiping at a shrine.

"Jesus," he whispered reverently. "I swear you're the most beautiful woman I ever . . ."

Before he could finish, against the bleached backdrop of moonlight, their two reaching silhouettes merged and became one, his words cut off under the cloying crush of their passionate kiss.

19

They were just sleepily stirring in the morning light, rediscovering each other with searching reverent hands and long searing kisses, when there was a polite knock on the bedroom door. Snapping out of a sweet sucking kiss, Than turned in time to see the ornate doorknob turn and the door open to admit the apologetic ambassador.

"Good morning, Than. Sorry to disturb you so early, but . . ." He stopped dead, stunned at the sight of his daughter in Than's arms, their two tanned bodies obviously naked beneath the sheets.

"Daddy!" Her amber eyes widening, Suzannah pulled out of Than's embrace and struggled up on one elbow, the sheet pulled taut across her heaving bosom.

Than felt the blood rush to his face. Sick with shame, he removed his hand from her bare breast, staring at the ambassador, too shocked to speak.

But Suzannah quickly recovered herself; her eyes narrowed in defiance and she smiled with sarcastic sweetness, gazing saucily at her father. "Why, whatever's the matter, Daddy? You've never seen a man and a woman in bed together before?"

"Suzie!" Than recoiled in horror, and the ambassador's face hardened into a mask of cold contempt.

He whispered viciously, "You little tramp!"

"Well, I have to keep up my bad old reputation, don't I, Daddy dear? Did Magdalena send you in to spy on me?"

"No, missy. I'm sorry to disappoint you, but Maggie has long since grown tired of your outrageous little attention-getters. On the contrary, your boyfriend here left his Land-Rover parked behind my limousine and I . . ."

"Oh yes, sir," Than spluttered anxiously. "I'll move it."

"If you wouldn't mind, Doctor. I have to go to the embassy this morning and . . ."

"Right away, sir." Than swung his legs over the side of the bed, reaching for his pants.

"And as for you, missy!" Ambassador McQueen turned back to his daughter.

"And now comes the pious lecture." Suzannah stared airily at her pearly-pink fingernails. "Now listen, Daddy, I'm over twenty-one. If you think . . ."

"No! *You* listen, missy. I'll speak with you later. I'll see the pair of you tonight."

He left abruptly, pulling the door shut behind him. For a shocked moment, Than could only stare at the door. Then he turned on Suzannah angrily. "Now, what the hell'd you have to go and do that for?"

"What's the matter?" She raised a cool perfect brow at him. "You afraid of him?"

"Jesus, I've accepted the guy's hospitality! I feel something of a heel caught in bed with his daughter the first night out!" Than pulled on his undershorts and wriggled into his jeans. "Couldn't you have been a little more contrite and considerate of his feelings? For Chrissakes—you're his daughter, after all!"

"Oh, wow," she smiled at him cynically. "Don't you have a lot of puff and piety! Seems to me all that burning passion has been somewhat diverted. Don't take it so seriously. You've never been caught in bed before?"

"No, have you?" he snapped savagely, zipping up his pants. Then he saw her face. "On second thought, for God's sake, don't answer that. I couldn't stand any more of your sordid confessions right now. From practically the first day I met you, you've been telling me what a raw deal you've been getting from your father and stepmother. Well, from what I've just seen, they both have my deepest sympathy!"

Her face changed instantly. "A lot you know!" she hissed at him scathingly, her amber eyes filling with tears. "You don't have those two *self-righteous* senior paragons scrutinizing your every act!"

"Seems to me," Than grunted viciously, shrugging on his shirt, "a good, clean-living girl shouldn't have too much trouble showing a little modesty and humility once in a while!"

"Say, whose side are you on, anyway?" She gazed at him angrily through her tears. The sheet slid off her heaving pink-nippled perfect breasts, and sitting there like that, she looked so helpless and beautiful that he relented with a sigh.

"Oh hell, yours, I guess. You're just so goddamn beautiful, I don't guess I have much choice." He smiled, stooping to kiss her soft mouth. "I'm sorry, baby. I guess I . . ."

They jumped apart at the blast of a car horn outside.

"Whoops. Guess I'd better not keep the man waiting. I've never faced an enraged father before. Jesus, he might decide to whip my ass!"

Snatching up his Land-Rover keys, he blew her a kiss as he hurried out of the room, shutting the door behind him, his quick footsteps muffled on the carpeted stairs.

That night, after a strained family supper, with a chastened Suzannah sitting ominously swollen-eyed, silent, and uneating following a private reckoning with her father, the ambassador took Than aside to his study. As the man fiddled with bottles and glasses, pouring brandy with his back to Than at the liquor cabinet, he said quietly:

"I want you to know, Doctor, that I hold you entirely responsible for the seduction of my daughter."

Than stared uncomfortably at the man as he turned and handed him a drink. After a moment, he let out a sighing breath and sat down on the settee. "Well, sir, I guess that's your prerogative. I'm just sorry you had to find us that way."

The ambassador nodded stiffly. Taking the seat across from Than, he sipped speculatively at his drink. "Thank you for your sympathy. Now, the crucial question is, what do you intend to do about it?"

Than almost choked on his brandy. He put down his glass and coughed politely into his fist. "Uh, sir . . . I don't get you. I realize it must have been pretty rough on you finding us that way, but at this point there doesn't seem much I can do beyond offering my profuse apologies."

"*Apologies?*" Ambassador McQueen snorted derisively. He took a handful of fresh peanuts from a silver side dish, tossed them into his mouth, and chewed aggressively as he talked. "Come, come, Doctor. Surely you can do better than that? You're supposed to be a Christian missionary, after all, a man of integrity and honor, and yet accepting our hospitality, you come in here, practically rape my daughter, ruin her romance, and . . ."

"Practically *rape?*" Than felt his hackles start to rise. "Isn't that a little strong, Ambassador?"

"I don't think so, Dr. Profane. Not from what my daughter's told me. You're obviously a highly persistent man, used to having your way with women. All I know is that two weeks ago she was happily in love and engaged to be married to Carl Steiner. I find it hard to believe that in that short space you could have turned her head so drastically as to . . ."

"*Engaged?*" Than frowned incredulously.

"Well, practically. Carl had already bought the ring." Ambassador McQueen put down his glass. "You mean Suzie never told you?"

Than drew in his breath. "So that's what's really bugging you? Carl Steiner." He put down his glass and stood up. "Listen, Ambassador, I'm sorry if my liaison with your daughter has upset you. But what's done is done and I just don't see the point in going over old ground. As far as I can see, there's nothing more to be said."

"Not from where I sit, boy!"

Than stopped. "Meaning?"

The man smiled tightly. "Sit down, Doctor. It's a long story. Have a cigar."

After a moment's hesitation, Than took one of the thin Havanas the ambassador offered him from an ornate silver box, stooping to draw deeply on the lighter flame the man held for him. He sat down uneasily.

"Now, Than." Taking a cigar himself, the ambassador smiled at him, suddenly congenial. "Please don't misunderstand me. I'm not a narrow-minded man. I understand all about the powerful urges you young fellows feel. God knows I raised enough dust myself once. But it's the motive that counts. Now, if you have any genuine feeling for my daughter—well, that just about puts a whole new complexion on the matter."

"If you mean am I in the market for marriage," Than smiled tightly right back, "then the answer is no."

"You're very blunt, Doctor. I take it, then, you were just casually dabbling with my daughter's affections, having a little fun fornicating before you go back to your mission and teach the natives how to live a good clean moral life?"

"Jesus!" Than laughed bitterly, breathing out cigar smoke, shaking his head. "This is the twentieth century, Ambassador. Premarital coitus is no longer considered the moral crime it once used to be."

"Not to the world at large, perhaps," the ambassador said meaningfully, and Than stopped smiling. "But would your mission board consider the matter in quite the same casual light as you apparently do?" The ambassador flicked open his lighter and drew on the flame with his cigar.

"Listen, Ambassador—that's just crazy. Quite frankly, I don't give a damn what they think!"

"Oh, and I take it your family feels the same way?"

"My family?" Than squirmed. He was starting to sweat slightly. "Well, my family's feelings don't come into it either."

"Oh?" The ambassador smiled cannily. "I guess they—that is, your little sister and your stepmother—won't be too upset then to hear about your amorous little . . . *escapades*, shall we say—through your mission board?"

"My . . ." Than stared at the man incredulously. "Jesus, Ambassador—just what are you getting at?"

"I mean, Doctor, if you walk out on my daughter and leave her in the lurch, as a doting father I might just feel compelled to send a letter to your mission board, complaining about the questionable activities of one of their . . . shall we say 'officers in the field'?"

"That's blackmail," Than stared incredulously. "You'd go that far?"

"Doctor, I'd go as far as I deem it necessary to secure my daughter's happiness or avenge her honor. As American ambassador, I'd say my word carries a fair amount of weight. Now maybe you don't care one way or another, Doctor, but wouldn't it be a shame for your family if you were recalled under such shady circumstances?"

"Jesus!" Than stared. "You mean you'd be prepared to go to such lengths—to farm your daughter out in marriage to some guy . . . who didn't want her?"

"Don't you, Doctor?"

"That's beside the point."

"On the contrary, Doctor, it's the whole point. After ruining Suzie's romance and . . ."

"Yes, I do care for your daughter—if that's what you want to hear! I care for her and I desire her. I just have no particular wish to get married right at this time. And I'm damned if I'll be pushed into anything before I'm good and ready!"

"Now look, Doctor." The ambassador raised a placating hand, looking grave. "Nobody's trying to push you into anything. As I explained, I would just feel compelled to complain to . . ."

"*They'd never believe it!*" Than said vehemently, averting his eyes.

"Who wouldn't?"

"Nobody. They have faith in me."

"That just about spells it out then, doesn't it, Doctor? I guess it would naturally come as something of a shock to them to hear about your numerous affairs."

"*Numerous?*" Than started to look indignant.

"Why, yes. Being an astute man, I checked on your little sister's touching story about those two dear friends."

"*You had no right!*"

"As a concerned father, Doctor, I believe I had every right. I did a little *undercover research,* so to speak—and I discovered you've been having two young ladies up to your hotel room on a regular basis. Well, those poor nurses sure must have been having trouble getting into their dormitory by the sound of it. I believe you had them in there, sometimes both together and overnight. Which makes you something of a tomcat, Doctor. And whichever way you look at it, that'd make pretty scandalous reading to your mission leaders and the board!"

Than closed his eyes.

"What's the matter, Doctor?" Ambassador McQueen said coldly. "Suddenly you don't look so well."

"You bastard," Than growled under his breath, looking up. "Isn't this a little out of your league, Ambassador? Spying on me? Oh, I guess I know what your story is. I heard it all from Suzannah. Suzie's been making trouble between you and your new wife, and you want her out of the way so you can enjoy a little peace and privacy in your new nuptial bliss. So you figured to pass her off on the first guy fool enough to . . ."

"Hey now, Doctor—don't push it. Any fellow 'fool' enough to get Suzie would be in a pretty enviable position. My daughter has dozens of men just panting to be honored with the pleasure of her company."

"Oh yeah? Well what's the big deal, then?" Than glared at the man. Goaded into it, he said angrily, "As far as I am concerned, once I move out, even old Carl Steiner is welcome to her!"

"Well, Doctor, since you seem to so persistently fail to get the point, let me enlighten you. Suzie's mother left us when she was just a little girl, so I've been mother and father to her most of her life. And I guess I spoiled her pretty badly to make up for the mother she never had. She always was a little charmer, so it was easy to let her have her own way. She can twist me around her little finger, I guess. The upshot of it is, my personal weakness has always been in the policy of what Suzie wants, Suzie gets. Whether it was a new doll or a new car or . . ."

"So?" Than smoked impatiently.

"So, Doctor, what you have failed to understand is that in this instance my little Suzie no longer wants Carl Steiner, or for that matter, any other guy. *Suzie wants you.*"

20

After the ambassador left him, Than stayed in the study, silent and stunned, struggling to sort out his feelings, to make sense of the seeming insanity that had suddenly turned his life upside down. He was perched, slumped, on the edge of the desk, sipping brandy, when the double doors suddenly opened and Suzannah stepped in. He swiveled on the desk, turning his back on her. She hesitated on the threshold for several moments before he heard the door click shut.

"So we're going to be married," she said in a high little voice.

"Aren't we just?" He swallowed a mouthful of brandy, staring sullenly at the wall of books as it seared down his gullet.

"Well, it could have been worse," she chuckled bitterly, trying to be flippant. "I haven't lost my allowance, and your testicles are still intact! And I guess it might turn out for the best. After all, I may be pregnant!"

Than swung around at her, so angry now he could scarcely contain himself. "Oh sure! But then again you might not be. I tried to be careful. Seems to me the least we could do is wait and find out!"

"Don't talk to me in that tone!" she flashed at him, suddenly equally angry, her tawny eyes filling with tears. "Don't shout! I can't stand it."

"And I can't stand this whole damn stinking setup!"

By the change in her expression, he could tell his words had hit home. She stared at him, seeming suddenly uncertain. Then she strode to the liquor cabinet and filled a brandy glass almost to the brim with whiskey. She took a great swallow of the golden liquid, shuddering as it went down, eyes tightly closed, mouth compressed. "Oh Jesus, I needed that." She walked toward him with a strained little smile tremulous on her beautiful face. "To our marriage," she chuckled shakily, holding up the glass.

"Jesus! You've got half a bottle of whiskey in there. Next your father will accuse me of plying you with liquor."

"Well." She drew away from him, measuring him coolly. "Whatever happened to the ardor of the night before? Last night I could have sworn you were ready to capture the moon and the stars for me. What's the matter? You miss your old habits? You still want to kiss and run?"

He stared at her acidly. "Well, lady, doesn't seem like I have much choice in this instance."

"Oh bullshit." She eyed him cannily with her cat-yellow eyes. "If you weren't so unsure of what it is you want, don't you think you'd fight this thing a little harder? Well, I think you've just got a short memory, honey lamb," she purred soothingly at him, smiling haughtily. "Here, let Mama refresh your memory some."

She set down her glass and came up against him as he sat, embracing him, snuggling against his body, her questing mouth moist against his neck. He kept rigidly still, afraid of his reflexes, held so perilously, tightly, in check. "Suzannah," he growled, not moving. "Leave me alone."

But she ignored him. With a wily understanding of the tricky biological mechanism of his body, she pressed herself against him, sighing with pleasure, her hands caressing his back. Her hips undulating slowly between his spread thighs were all the trigger he needed.

"Jesus!" he cried. Betrayed by his body, he grabbed at her, his hands clawing at her buttocks, jerking her tight against him between his thighs. He bit her mouth as he kissed her and his hands, rough and searching, gripped hurtfully into her flesh. A moment later the dizziness descended, and he thrust her distractedly away from him, disgusted at his own lack of control. Well, maybe she was right after all. Maybe he would have kicked harder if deep down inside he didn't really want to keep her. He might as well face it; even if he didn't care much for the idea of marriage, he was crazy about the girl. "Keep away from me," he growled, standing up and moving away, infuriated by her triumphant smile of self-assurance as he fumbled to light up a cigarette with shaking hands.

*   *   *

Two days before he was due to be married, Than was finally summoned by the Ministry of Public Health. Still stunned by the bewildering whirl of activities preceding the wedding, he went to the office of the medical inspector to be given conditional consent for the formal upgrading of the mission staff and for his advanced medical training course, final approval to be dependent upon subsequent on-site inspection. He was issued a confusing array of documents, teaching aids, and curricular materials, and wished good luck.

Back at the ambassadorial mansion, dressmakers, florists, caterers, and wedding presents had begun to arrive. Whatever guilt the ambassador might feel over his inducement of the marriage, he handsomely compensated with magnanimous gifts, giving the couple as a wedding present a spanking new yellow Ford Thunderbird, which, in spite of Than's prickly pride, served to mollify his mood some.

Due to the lack of time for preparation, the wedding was to be a relatively small and discreet affair, confined to a few close friends and important diplomatic colleagues. But the ambassador's original registry-office plans had grown more ambitious; the wedding service was to be conducted in the family's traditional Methodist church, and the bride, in accordance with her father's cherished dream for her, was to be traditionally veiled in white. A close modeling friend and Jayne were to be her bridesmaids. In this capacity, Jayne was now in residence at the ambassador's house. Shocked by the news, she was quiet and withdrawn, and contrary to Magdalena McQueen's optimistic expectations, not even her beautiful new pink bridesmaid's dress served to lift her wilting spirits.

Although worried by her reaction, Than had little time to comfort her as the hectic days flew by. Then, finally, on the day of the wedding, during the rush of last-minute preparations, Jayne mysteriously disappeared. Worried sick, Than helped Magdalena and the servants search the house and gardens. Finally, as the precious moments ticked on, Magdalena pushed him into his room to dress, silencing his anxious protests with comforting platitudes.

Helplessly trailed by the flustered Myron Carlton, who had agreed to act as his best man, Than hurriedly dressed in his stylish new navy-blue suit, compliments of the ambassador; Magdalena, glowing in a pink chiffon dress, was still struggling to fit his carnation buttonhole as she pushed him into the ambassador's satin-scolloped black limousine.

Later, in the stained-glass elegant atmosphere of the Salisbury Methodist Church, Suzannah trailed up the aisle on her father's arm, breathtakingly beautiful in white Chantilly lace. She and Than exchanged gold rings and were duly married by the smooth-talking minister. Outside in the warm sunshine, social reporters scribbled on pads and cameramen scurried around them, lightbulbs flashing. Suzannah was radiant. The ambassador looked dignified and proud. Magdalena and Mrs. Carlton both shed wistful tears, and in the shower of confetti and congratulations, it seemed to Than that he alone was unmoved. He stared at the empty space where his sister should have stood, and his heart was as cold as stone.

21

"Kathy, this is my wife." Than stood on the threshold feeling smitten and shamed as an errant dog caught bringing a dug-up old bone onto the living room carpet.

Forewarned by radiograph, Katherine stiffly smiled. Awkward in their newlywed presence, she was obviously disarmed by this striking blond girl and the streamlined car she had driven in convoy with Than's Land-Rover. Jayne, in her old sunbonnet and long pink dress, tagged along behind, dusty and creased, quiet and remote, shy with her mother and aloof to the company.

"Pleased to meet thee," Katherine enthused politely, touching her bonnet self-consciously.

"Y're welcome, I'm sure." Suzannah, patently amused, flexed her bright mouth in a quick frosty smile and stifled a bored yawn. "God, I'm all stuffed out. I hope you have soap and hot water in this place. I'm about to suffocate under all this dust."

"Of course." Katherine averted her eyes.

Than felt he could read her mind; a grown woman in boy's blue denim jeans, sinfully tight and outrageously endowed of fly! Kathy led the way into the house. Everything stood orderly and neat; the dark furniture shone. It was dim and quiet in the hot listless thrall of afternoon. Than didn't remember it as depressing or oppressive. The old stairway, smelling of polish, creaked as they went up, and in the room he had shared with Tom, Kathy had discreetly removed Bathsheba's sandbox and smelly bedding, along with the leopard itself. A bowl of fresh frangipani decorated the dresser, and an ornate brass bedstead stood in place of the two divans. Covered with a faded blue candlewick quilt, it took up much of the room, the ungainly antique that Katherine and his father had shared in wedlock.

There was a frigid silence while Suzannah icily eyed the humble effort. Than turned finally, embarrassed by his bride's pointed disdain.

"I hope it wasn't too much trouble," he said carefully, killing the awkward quiet.

"Oh no." Katherine shook her head briskly, forcing a smile.

"How about Tom?"

"Well, Tom can sleep in the study when he's home from school."

"Listen, Kathy." Than stood humble. He wanted to explain about everything, to apologize, but he didn't know how. He shrugged helplessly. "Thanks, Kathy."

When they were alone at last, Suzannah fell back onto the big quilted bed. She threw back her arms and her breasts rose under her checkered cotton shirt. "Oh, Jesus!" she wailed. "What a hick place!"

"It's not so bad," Than said guardedly.

"Not so bad!" She sat up, spluttering with indignation. "It's a throwback to Victorian times!"

Than shrugged, perspiring in his shirtsleeves. "You'll get used to it."

"I don't want to get used to it." She jumped off the bed. After a while, she came and put her arms around him, purring like a cat. He heard the warning bells clang in his head and remained stiff in her embrace.

"Oh, honey," she appealed to him with huge amber eyes. "We don't *have* to stay in this awful backwoods. You're not bound by any contract. We could take off someplace."

"We'll stay." He pulled her arms down deliberately. "And you'll like it!"

She stepped back and glared at him balefully, quietly furious. "Why?" she demanded.

He turned his back on her and went and stared through the window at the hot sallow afternoon. The mission was festive with the red dazzle of flamboyant blossoms, and down the slope, the sullen green river was suffused in heat waves, the borassus palms rising still and regal from the tangled growth on its banks. Floating listlessly in the hot stillness, an emerald-spotted wood dove uttered its sad, dripping, monotonous call.

"Because," Than said quietly, "you're my wife. And this is where I'm at!"

*   *   *

Matthew stood scandalized, for the renegade Boy had shocked them all by bringing home such a wife. The indolent woman and his new yellow car were unseemly ostentations at the staid little station; both of them were flashy and fabulous, a mockery to the simple Quaker state of being, and Matthew, in his lonely loyalty, felt oddly betrayed. The woman, particularly, was a beautiful creature, suggestive of summer and lightness with her smooth sunburned skin and hair and eyes saffron and tawny as the bleached summer grasses. She had a rosebud petulant mouth that could pout like a baby's or smile like an angel's, but her eyes, like a cat's, were seminal with latent wickedness. She was a wild, wily female who matched the Boy with her beauty, and Matthew watched them together and saw that she consumed him with earthly lust. She chained him with her beauty and guile, drove him to distraction with her teasing wiles. Oft-times, Matthew was to see the Boy seethe with exasperation. For she was his worldly counterpart, and what he was in plain honesty, judge as thee may, she flaunted in the missionaries' faces like red rag to a bull.

She had come to them with a painted face and improperly clad body. Matthew remembered his first uneasy liking tempered with fright. For her dress was so short! The slim smooth legs moved freely, and in common decency, Matthew had to look away when she stooped. The prudish elder ladies stood bolted with shock at first sight, tight-lipped and white-faced with their mortified distaste. And she had laughed at them all, Matthew realized with horror. Those light-flecked tawny eyes took them all in as a huge joke and not even grim Matthew escaped lightly. Feeling her derision, he could never be in her presence without feeling self-conscious of his battered old pith, but he struggled to keep it on as a gesture of immunity he could not quite feel. For that beautiful, willful, spoiled child had a way of making her presence felt. Even during the long hot sulky afternoons, her slinky body, coming with its hip-jerking cat walk, had a way of making a man feel his lost manhood, old though he may be and pure and unlecherous though he may struggle to feel. For she was the old womanly evil of Eve, and she flaunted this power before all men in a manner that infuriated the sterile older ladies and made them hate her unreservedly. Taught that good looks and comeliness were no reliable measure of equal good, they comforted their own homeliness by believing it to indicate a matching degree of the reverse. (They cited movie stars, notorious for immorality, as just illustration!) And the Boy, their old bone of contention, lost priority to this new worldly carrion. They fed on the girl's faults like scavaging vultures, until all that was left were the bare bones of her scant virtue. For there was precious little they could credit her for, and lots to condemn.

She had no redeeming features, as the Boy did, and she hated the life. She was squeamishly afraid of insects, snakes, and the Boy's pet leopard. She complained endlessly about the lack of social recreation, the plain food, and the primitive plumbing (the spider-secreted bucket latrines located in dim smelly back-houses at the foot of each missionary garden being the bane of her life). She was blatantly jealous of the Boy's solicitous affection for his stepmother and Jayne. What was more, she disdained working with the natives and begrudged the Boy his chosen duty, pulling him one way while dedication pulled another. With airy sighs and restless summer-yellow eyes, she played the martyred wife, and during the long lonely hours that the hospital forced them apart, they saw her sulkily wandering around the mission. In her unhappy boredom she came to taunt the mission men, displaying those long perfect legs and pouting sultrily. In Matthew's less noble moments, he considered that a good old-fashioned spanking would do her no harm. But she held the Boy in a powerful thrall, and he seemed helpless to stem her willful ways. There existed between them an embarrassing attraction that was hard not to notice; in his eyes, a naked sulphurous longing that was blatant and incriminating as a vague whiff of semen.

Matthew had come upon them unwittingly in the bush one Saturday afternoon when the Boy was off-duty. Pressed up against a tree like a couple of rutting animals, that long, lean rangy Boy in his faded blue jeans, had his legs braced apart between hers, his hands right up the short pink skirt to engulf her buttocks, her thighs forced wide to his intruding hips. The Boy was all gilded brown skin, glossy as grape, darker than she, his muscles straining, mouth hunting, enveloping. They were fused in a searing kiss, the Boy's sun-bleached head bent, his tortured Adam's apple and strong chin presenting. She seemed lost behind him, small and golden, arms entwining. There was a large birthmark on his left shoulder blade, a dark mole that she caressed with her pearly-pink fingernails. Racked like animals, they grunted and groaned. Matthew, on a calm bush excursion, had been shocked half out of his kilter. He froze on the leaf-crackling path as, before his stunned gaze, they pulled apart. Then he closed his eyes, dumbly relieved to realize they were not as yet exposed or sexually joined. For a moment, he had thought . . .

161

he shuddered. Now he was afraid. Feeling like the worst nasty kind of Peeping Tom, he wanted to get away from there before any such inevitable consummation took place.

He began to back away, stealthy as a cat, down the grassy path, so terrified of discovery that his old bones were locked rigid, so mesmerized by what he saw that he could not look away. It was then that she saw him. Those tawny terrifying eyes blinked open, then widened in surprise over the Boy's hunched shoulder. She twisted her head so that Matthew could see her face and then, staring straight at him, she smiled. It was a terrible smile, flagrantly mocking; Matthew watched in a spellbound rigor. But she did not give him away. She moved instead as if to taunt him, digging nails into the Boy's bronzed back so that the red blood welled. Then the Boy was laying his disarranged wife down in the bed of grass, and Matthew, finally abandoning all caution, turned and blundered away through the bush.

For a long time Matthew could not forget the incident. It pained him afterward to submit to the girl's taunting presence. Judging by the Boy's indifferent eyes, he had no doubt that the secret remained between him and the young woman alone. In his dislike of guilt and nasty secrecy, he half wanted to confess the stumbling accident for what it had been, but shyness and shame and the girl's laughing eyes held him back. What was the matter with that little wench anyhow? Had she no shame? No womanly decency? Matthew was powerless to the conclusion that she had not . . . and that poor ham-strung hankering Boy was cuckold to her teasing mockery.

The first Wednesday following his return, Jennifer Solomon accompanied Than to Eshalakali Hill. By now the Friends' mission had officially adopted the derelict little station. Matthew Tomlinson and Ward Disney were presently cleaning up and repairing the buildings that would accommodate the new secondary school when the two English teachers arrived to run it next year, and the little stained-glass church, a potential meeting house, had been aired and swept for Jenny's use. Than found it hard to forgive her presence, and although she was quiet and uncomplaining, he struggled to find inconvenience in her simplest act. He begrudged the use of Jeremiah to transport her Braille machine and text equipment and resented having to lead her to the church and wait upon her while the stiff wooden door was pushed open and the dim interior aired and inspected. When a snake was found coiled under a musty pew, he blamed the risk on her too, swearing under his breath as he sliced off its head with a spade from the anteroom.

He tried to dissuade her from continuing, but she raised a face of gentle dedication that blasted him to silence. And he stood oddly rankled as, calm and steadfast, she began to feel around, lying out her bulky Braille books on the dusty vestry table. No blind came and all the long day she sat alone in the dim old building, surrounded by nothing more than her hopes and a faulty Braille machine. When Than joined her to eat their sandwiches in the church, she said quietly:

"I know they'll come when they hear I've started again."

He turned exasperatedly away.

But she was right. The following week they found a small group of blind Africans awaiting them outside the church. A week later, their numbers had doubled. Led by patient relatives, they were a motley group of children and adults. After cursorily examining and questioning them, Than realized with horror that most had been blinded by the caustic preparations used by ignorant witchdoctors to treat normally curable cataracts, trachoma, and glaucoma. . . .

22

"Do you really have to go?" Suzannah sat on the edge of the great bed, pulling on a pair of fluffy pink slippers. "It's barely dawn outside!"

Than closed the wardrobe door and looked at her in blank surprise. Fresh up from the bathroom, he unwound a bath towel from around his hips, shaking his head at the naïveté of her selfishness. Pulling on a clean pair of jeans and a fresh white jacket, he smiled ruefully. "Of course I do. I'm a doctor. I don't just truant out when I feel like it."

He bent to pull on his boots, glancing up as his wife swept by, pacing the floor in a flowing honey-colored negligee and an aura of expensive French perfume. She was smoking furiously.

He straightened slowly. "Suzie, like I said before—why don't you come with me to Eshalakali? Jennifer Solomon teaches Braille there; she's got together quite a good class now. If you found something worthwhile to do, maybe you wouldn't mind being here so much."

"Sure! All my life I've wanted to play nurse to a bunch of rotting lepers!" She turned on him furiously. "And what else is there to do in this stinking hole? There are crocodiles in the river, wild animals in the bush, spiders in the john. And a bunch of old fogies who watched over my manners like a network of spies. I can't even show an ankle without those old biddies reaching for the smelling salts."

Than shook his head bemusedly.

"Find something to do, he says. But don't swim in the river; you'll catch bilharzia. Don't wear your shorts, you'll excite the natives. And don't swear or you'll give the old ladies apoplexy." She glared at Than. "Pray tell, what *is* there for me to do?"

At the dresser, Than stooped to brush his hair in the reflection of the cracked mirror. "Suzie, there's always plenty of work to be done on a mission. Maybe Katherine can find you something at the girls' school."

"You mean scut work, don't you?" She eyed him angrily through the mirror. "A little teacher's helper. Oh, how could you expect that of me? Have you forgotten . . . my father is an ambassador!"

Than spun around at her. "Oh shit, pussycat. That doesn't make him royalty. And sweet and pink as your little ass is, it's never sat on any throne other than the john. You're so busy keeping your nose in the air, you're missing out on a whole lot of life going on around you."

They stared at each other, seething. Then, relenting, he bent to kiss her mouth. She twisted her head away and he planted the kiss on the side of her neck.

"Suzie," he said warily. "How about the hospital? There's nothing lowly about helping the sick. Why don't you give it a try?"

She eyed him cautiously, a tiny tight smile beginning to tug at the corners of her lush mouth. "Would I see more of you then?"

"Some," he said evasively. "You might even get to like it. Maybe you could help out in the dispensary or at outpatient clinic. I'll talk to Ingrid today."

"I haven't said I would yet!" She grabbed his arm as he turned to go.

He eyed her darkly, pushing off her hand. "No, I don't guess you have. Call me when you decide to start thinking about it."

She sidled seductively up to him with a coy little smile, sliding her arms around his neck. "I'll think about it now," she purred, cleaving her lithe body to his, her firm pushing breasts divided by a cleavage as golden and smooth as poured honey. "*If* you persuade me."

"Dammit, Suzie! You don't listen good, do you?" He took her and threw her angrily down on the bed. Lying there, disarrayed and panting, her blond hair sprawled out around her, she smiled provocatively up at him, lifting her arms above her head and moving her legs apart in an inviting "V" beneath the honey sheerness of her gown. Her flesh-pink nipples starred her bodice, and he could clearly see the pale triangle of hair at the apex of her pubis. And he was lost. Pulling up the gown, he crawled between her legs, unzipping his pants.

"Good boy!" She wrapped her arms around his heaving shoulders, murmuring against his ear. "Oh my, that's a good boy."

The next day, Suzannah began work at the outpatient department of the hospital. But her attitude doomed her to failure from the start. Unskilled and overconfident, she was careless and presumptuous; lack of sympathy gave her the necessary coolness of a nurse, but she was disgusted and disinterested, indulging her feelings completely, going green and threatening to vomit at the sight of blood, sores, and secretions. She bossed the African nurses and orderlies around on minor errands, drawing them from more pressing duties, and above all she developed a cloying attachment to Than. She wanted to watch whatever he was doing, to follow him down the corridor every time he passed. The only place he could keep her from was the operating theater, and that was because she feared she might faint at the sight of "exposed organs." In fact, she would only deal with minor casualties and was annoyed when Than insisted he could not do the same. Left alone with Ingrid, she made herself unpopular by passing critical comment upon whichever patient she was currently ushering to a cubicle. She was too unskilled to act as anything more than a junior nurse's aide, and there were times when she got so careless passing medications or lint that the exasperated Swedish nurse disregarded her completely and called for the assistance of an African trainee.

"How's she doing?" Than approached Ingrid later, in private.

"Not so good," Ingrid said shortly. "She is careless, critical, unwilling to learn. And I'm afraid I cannot allow her to disrupt my work any longer."

Than sighed, drawing on his cigarette. He had thought as much. He turned and watched guiltily as Suzannah came toward them. It was after five and time to retire, but Suzannah had been in and out of the coffee room all day. She looked tired and wan and Than kissed her as she came up. They walked home slowly, smoking, as they dawdled on the swing bridge together.

"How'd it go?" he said carefully after a while.

"Oh, it was awful!" she snapped. "The smell and the filth and the blood and the dirt. I could hardly stand it. And that Swedish girl lording it over me all the time. Who does she think she is, anyway—Ingrid Bergman?"

"Oh come on, Suzie! She's a pretty good nurse. She's okay when you get to know her."

Suzannah looked at him sharply. "What'd she say about me? I saw you two together."

"Oh, she said she didn't think you—uh—liked the work too much. Thought maybe you ought to let it go."

"She would," Suzannah snapped. "I knew it! She's just the type to carry tales. Well, she needn't worry. I've already decided to give it up. I was pretty bored anyway! And I've had this backache all day. Guess it's my period coming on. And I get terrible cramps once it starts. I don't guess I'd be fit for work for a while anyway." She stared at him coldly. "So you can tell your little nurse that I resign!"

"Okay," he nodded, sighing. "So you resign."

23 Since his return from Salisbury, Than's workload at Eshalakali's clinic and colony had increased. He had to cope now without Jeremiah, whom Suseshi Hospital could no longer spare, and by midafternoon, the once empty veranda of the top clinic was clustered with suffering souls. But before he could treat them, he had to finish medicating, bathing, and bandaging the lepers, who then cried to be doled food, fuel, and soap, dogging Than with multitudinous complaints. Finally, in desperation, he recruited as a medical assistant and overseer for the lepers an earnest pug-nosed youth who had the unlikely name of Teapot and a jinxed tendency to mishap. An ex-houseboy of Morgan Humphries, he was a former inmate of the leper colony, where his condition had been arrested in the early stages. He claimed to have achieved the prized "Cambridge" status at one of the few secondary schools in the province and was ready, willing, and available—this last being the greatest qualification, when the disconsolate youth, pining his past employ-

ment, had appeared on the scene, where hitherto no other vaguely literate soul was to be found.

On the first day of his employment, Teapot Kapendula, nervously murmuring hymns under his breath, gave some echo of calamities to come. In his pathetic eagerness, he succeeded in knocking antiseptic off the treatment table, dropping bandages in the dust, and misplacing the scissors. Then, while searching for them, he tripped over the wicker chair and broke its leg. He stood up, dusting off his large clumsy hands and struggling vainly, with a look of baffled piety, to fit the chair back into one piece again.

Than winced, gazing appealingly heavenward. "All right, Teapot," he said carefully. "You must take your time and *think*. Now, leave that chair alone. I want you to go up to the top clinic and fetch me . . ."

He ran off with impressive alacrity to achieve the errand. Five minutes later, he trailed sheepishly back, dragging his feet, hanging his head. "Bwana . . . what was it you would have me fetch?"

But he endured. After that first calamitous day, Than and the lepers were committed to the eager hapless youth, by labor shortage alone. He bestowed upon himself the grand title Captain of the Lepers, and gradually, by his very unwitting appeal, he grew on them.

Passing through the bush after a conference with the education officer at Mwinilunga Boma, Matthew spotted the familiar mission motorcycle parked at a wayside village where Than Profane had set up one of his new clinics. On an impulse, he stopped. The Boy's pioneering enthusiasm always intrigued and inspired him, and besides, he might be able to assist by taking any overly ailing persons to the hospital in the Land-Rover. Too late he realized that the Boy was not alone.

Suzannah Profane, in blue jeans and a sweater, sat sulkily on a tree stump while her husband tended the swarming village sick inside the newly built open thatch shelter. As he worked, the Boy kept up a conversation with her, explaining about his patients' problems as they came up, obviously trying so hard to engage the young woman's elusive interest that Matthew felt for him. Whatever their physical attraction for each other, spiritually they seemed poles apart, and outside of their bedroom she was a continual tribulation to him. Her trial stint at the hospital had been a dismal failure. She

167

was still fiercely jealous of Katherine and Jayne and was so terrified and intolerant of his pet leopard that the adolescent cat had been summarily banished to an outdoor pen. Now, it seemed, the Boy was vainly trying to involve her in his out-clinic work, doubtless in order that he might be the freer to pursue it.

Matthew, uneasy as usual in the young woman's scornful presence, decided to cut short his visit; he might have managed an early escape had it not been for an exhausted African youth, who came running in from some distant village, panting that his pregnant sister was desperately struggling to give birth.

The Boy hastily closed up his clinic, and to save time, Matthew took him and his wife and the native youth bounding through the bush in the Land-Rover. When they finally reached the village, the smoky dusk was already deepening into night and they were regaled by flickering fires and scores of curious children with fat-smeared smiling faces. A stony-faced elderly man came forward to greet them, identifying himself as the girl's grandfather. Around him were assembled the village inhabitants. In their integrally communal lifestyle, they all awaited the girl's deliverance with hushed expectancy. They were led to a dilapidated thatch hovel, and pulling aside the flimsy stick door, the Boy stooped and entered. There were no windows and the interior of the low hut flared with firelight; it was choked with dampened smoke and crammed full of gabbling crones. In a moment, all the old women came out grumbling, dismissed by the Boy while he examined the girl. A moment later, he came out frowning in the dusk.

"Suzie," he looked at his wife. "You can help me. Birth is a pretty moving and exciting experience. It's something every woman should see. You can just watch and pass things across as I need them."

But the young woman was staring at him in consternation. She began to shake her blond head, backing away, her face stiff with distaste. "No I couldn't! I couldn't bear to!"

"Suzie, there's nothing to be afraid of." The Boy stared at his wife in surprise.

"That's easy for you to say!" she wailed, and as they stood dumbly watching, she turned and ran off to the Land-Rover.

"Well," the Boy turned to Matthew, frowning. "Looks like *you'll* have to help me."

Matthew stood shocked to the core; his pained eyes disbelieved: *Who, me?*

"Yes, you," the Boy said.

Looking frantically around, Matthew mumbled weakly, "I'll go find some women."

"No, Matthew. You know these people would be more hinderance than help. You can assist me. And stop looking so shocked." The Boy's blue eyes mocked. "You're a married man. You know what a woman looks like."

"It is not that," Matthew groaned, passing a handkerchief across his perspiring brow, ". . . *entirely*. It's the other thing also. I am afraid to see a child birthed. . . . Why, I have no inkling of what to do. I have no idea of the process."

"Well, I'll tell you where it'll come out." The Boy smiled cynically. "Not her mouth. Nor the backside. And we don't cut the tummy open unless absolutely necessary. That leaves you but one guess. And Matthew, they sure as hell don't come by the stork!"

In no time at all Matthew was in his shirtsleeves, boiling water over the small smoky log fire in the center of the circular hut. Above it, in the path of the ascending smoke, hung a grain-drying rack. In a corner, scrawny chickens roosted. Cured animal skins scattered the cold bare ground and a fiber bag containing gourds and calabashes hung from the rafters. The flickering firelight threw live leaping shadows from an obscenely grinning baboon skull and a fixedly horrific wooden mask.

Outside, in the black night, hyena, the hump-backed scavengers of the night, jibbered and eerily howled. With his white hair all awry, Matthew knelt knobby-kneed on the hard earthen floor of the hut, quaking with fright as he sterilized instruments that were as foreign to him as a witchdoctor's bones. Clumsy and flustered, he silently entreated the Lord as he worked. They heard the murmurous humming of the voices of the waiting relatives as the Boy knelt on the reed mat, his sandy-blond head bent, reverent as a lover, over the young girl's slender spread legs.

"Christ." When he tried to stand up, his head brushed the low smoke-blackened roof, showering sooty spiderwebs and cindered thatch. His tanned face was gilded with sweat and his narrowed eyes intense. "She's pretty immature. Her pelvis is narrow as hell. Jesus! I don't know that I can do it. She should have forceps at the very least."

The girl moaned. Matthew was sick with fright.

"Don't look so worried." The Boy smiled faintly. "I guess I'll have to do something. Only I'm not all that expert in this field.

Jerome's the O.B. champion. I only do it when I have to. And then I'd rather be cutting. Screaming women make me nervous. I'd rather have them out cold."

And scream she did. In a while, Matthew thought he had never heard such a sound. It assaulted his eardrums and left his knees weak. He was mute with sympathetic suffering. She could be no more than fifteen or sixteen years old. A mere girl with a belly like a mountain and a blue-duiker's horn of witchdoctor's nonsense around her neck to ward off ill-fortune, while a white doctor with his more scientific methods ran his hands and a stethoscope over her poor bloated body. As she lay, sweeping muscular reverberations took her body and she moaned and cried out, twisting her head from side to side, her eyes dull and anguished, her dusky skin glistening with perspiration. Matthew watched and was struck with an outraged surprise. How could the Boy remain so calm? He was the one who cried so indignantly for the pain of child-bearing. Well, why wasn't he doing something about it now when it counted?

The Boy looked up with shrewd, answering eyes, resting back on his haunches for a moment. "What's the matter, Matthew?" He smiled bitterly. "Screaming got you? Well, I wouldn't worry about that too much. It's a woman's lot, remember? Like the millions of others before her, she's taking Eve's rap. Only I wonder where it will ever end, don't you? Where a cardinal sin like a disobedient apple-bite finds its equivalent in pain. I'd say it's just as well Adam was only an accessory after the fact. They say if men had to endure the agony of child-bearing, the whole human race would come to a dead full stop. We simply couldn't endure that much pain the way women can."

Matthew was flabbergasted, amazed and exasperated that the Boy could sit there smiling, using this moment of truth to rub in his argument.

The Boy stared at him pointedly. "But don't worry, Matthew. I know how you feel about pain-killing in childbirth. I won't violate that meeting principle in your presence."

Matthew stared in consternation, perturbed with a vague indignation. *But what of the girl's feelings?* Were *they* not to be considered? Dropping his eyes, he said gruffly, "That's—most considerate of thee. Only thee has thy *own* feelings in the matter, and similarly, I cannot expect thee . . . of course," he added hastily, ". . . I cannot condone. Far from it. But all men have their own . . ." he swallowed ". . . beliefs. And far be it for me . . ."

"Well, that's very big of you, Matthew," the Boy said, looking noble, with just the hint of a smile in the twitching indentation of dimples held firmly in check. "But no. I couldn't possibly suffer you the mental anguish."

"Oh no, no . . ." Matthew waved an airy hand. "I am not that important. If it would strain thy medical ethics . . ."

"Matthew!" The Boy put on a pious, shocked expression. "You're not *suggesting* that I use a pain-killer and thereby stand guilty of balking God's justice?"

"I am not!" Matthew wrung his hands vexedly. He lifted his eyes hopefully. "Anyway, thee wouldn't have such a drug handy, would thee?"

The Boy, grinning fiendishly, already had a hypodermic fitted to a vial. He drew off the desired dose as Matthew watched and fumed inwardly. Why, he had intended using the drug all along but had waited instead for Matthew, provoked beyond endurance, to betray his own principles in asking. Now he seethed miserably between anger and gratification. He watched as the Boy swabbed alcohol on the side of one silky brown buttock, then swiftly injected. "Okay, Mother, that'll ease you . . ."

With the lack of equipment at hand, the Boy could not perform the Caesarean he would have preferred. As it was, he risked natural childbirth without the aid of forceps. "Remind me, Matthew, never to venture out without them again." He had no mask either, but wore cream rubber gloves, and his hand at one time seemed to disappear right inside the girl's body.

Matthew saw a tight look come across the Boy's face and he asked for the scissors in the boiling pot, which Matthew swiftly extracted, scalding his finger. He watched in horror, holding the flashlight and sucking his hand, while the Boy nicked the taut skin, cutting in a straight line down from the vagina, laying wide the yawning pink cavern of flesh from which life would erupt. Red blood welled, and Matthew felt sick. The mother, however, still moaned softly; she seemed oblivious.

"That'll give us more room to work in, Mother," the Boy said softly, preoccupied. His eyes flickered up at Matthew. "Episiotomy. I've cut through to the perineum before she has a chance to tear. Poor little thing. I guess this will rip all hell out of her internal organs. I'll have to patch her up way down into the uterus. She'll have a sore tail for a month if she survives this."

Matthew was horrified. Did such things really happen? They

did. In a moment, he was to find out that this was the least of it. The morphine seemed to have only temporary effect. As the baby's head began to crown, the girl's anguish was terrible to hear. Her screams jarred at Matthew's vertebrae like hammer blows that traveled all along the taut timbre of his strained nerves. "Is there nothing more thee can do?" he blustered in consternation.

"I've done it, Matthew. Short of putting her right out, I can't risk too much morphine. It would travel in the bloodstream and drug the baby. It would also impede the mother's performance. She has to work to get the baby out in good time. Too long a stay in the birth canal and he would suffocate. That is, assuming the pelvis opens wide enough to release it. My guess is, even with a little luck in that direction, I'm doing to have to haul this babe out bodily."

Matthew nodded mutely. He felt close to tears. The sight and sound of this little native girl screaming her agony was wearing at his nerves. She seemed unreached by his clumsy attempts to give comfort in *Chi-Lunda*, and in a moment she began to fret and toss around like a wild thing, pulling away from the Boy.

"Jesus, Matthew, grab her!" the Boy grunted angrily. "Hold her hands. Make her lie still."

But in the next moment, just as Matthew fumbled to take hold, she gave a small sigh and slumped in a dead faint, limp as a rag doll. Matthew was terrified.

"Thank God for that." The Boy sounded pleased. "That'll quiet her for a little while. Now I can work a moment in peace."

Matthew couldn't quite make out what he was up to, but it appeared difficult. Desperately gripping with his fingers at the vaginal orifice, the Boy seemed to tug and twist and pull, at the same time trying to be as gentle as possible. The girl came conscious, screaming.

"For Christ's sake, Matthew, shut her up!" the Boy implored, face twisted, veins straining in his own anguish of intense concentration. And then it happened. In a little bubbly wash of liquid and blood, the baby's head popped out in his hands. Matthew had never seen a sight more welcome or preposterous in his entire life. A body with two heads! And the little one all puckered for a crying—which did not come.

The Boy inserted a finger and began to draw mucus from the tiny snuffling mouth. Matthew was amazed. How could two bodies support that queer joining for any length of time? But the girl was contracting again. The Boy slid his hand underneath the baby's head and, amid the mother's exhausted gasps, delivered the small shoulders. "Jesus, that's good." The Boy was panting, eyes glazing with concentration, sounding oddly like a man receiving sexual gratification. "Good. Good. Come on, Mother, push. You're making it."

There was a slippery *whoosh* and then . . .

He held a tiny honey-soft, honey-pale scrap of humanity in his hands. A miracle that Matthew could scarcely credit. (Where had the mountainous belly gone?) Without detaching the twisted multicolored navel cord, the Boy raised the baby feet first in a one-handed grip. He whacked the small backside a mighty blow. Although somewhat stupefied by overlong birth, the baby drew in a great breath and came back with a raucous cry that was more sweet and terrifying than any Matthew had ever heard.

In the grimy little hut, the young man held the tiny bloodsmeared baby gently, reverently, in his spread hands, looking enormously surprised and so confoundedly young, his eyes shining with an innocent wonder.

"Jesus God, Matthew," he whispered in awe. "Isn't he beautiful?"

24

For a long time Matthew could not forget the touching interlude. In that dim smoky hut he had glimpsed a side of Than Profane he hadn't known existed, a disarming boyish innocence that somehow made up for much of his worldliness. And if his Christian zeal was dubious, he could at least be depended upon to go to any lengths for medicine. Although Dr. Dooley had automatically succeeded his father as medical director of the Friends' mission, it was the Boy who traveled to Barotseland to inspect Shonona's new clinic, while the Dooleys, encumbered with their crawling triplets, remained behind to run the hospital. Since his visit coincided with yearly meeting, to be set at Shonona this year, he joined the mission convoy into Barotseland. All whites had to obtain official permission to enter the exclusive little protectorate, and the mission vehicles traveled from dawn to dusk along bumpy boggy roads that skirted the partially flooded great Barotse Flood Plain, traversing endless grassy reaches and the coarse white Kalahari sands. In this region, most of the infrequent, isolated villages they encountered were neatly palisaded with reed fences, the huts roofed with the impressive Norfolk thatching taught by the early English missionaries.

Shonona Mission, aflame with vivid splashes of bougainvillea and blossoming flamboyant trees, sat on headland that overlooked the distant blue Zambezi River and sweeping vistas of the flood plain. The great grassy wastes looked sleepy and uninhabited, but around the paramount chief's northern capital, Lealui, were situated the greatest number of mission stations per square mile in the world. Upon this Central African battleground, where the differing denominations fought to win the heathen souls, an elusive man-eating lion, the Kazungula Killer, had begun making meals of the dispersed population. And although the paramount chief, Mwanawina Lewanika III, bent upon the secession of his little protectorate from Northern Rhodesia, had banned all political parties in his province, agents of the newly formed United National Independence Party (UNIP), had begun calling on his people, an African mafia selling party policy like the product of its trade.

In these tsetse-fly-free parts, the natives kept cattle, and the missionaries enjoyed fresh beef stew before being bedded down in the Poes' big house and a number of out-huts. The following morning the Congo clan arrived, followed shortly by the Haskels, from nearby Mambundi. Homer was a hard-working and unacademic man who ran a trade school and supervised primary classes at the little station, situated on the Musheketi swamp at the edge of the flood plain. The kindly little fellow shook Matthew's hand as warmly as a long lost friend. His big grim wife nodded curtly, and Loreley-Salome, their long-locked teenage daughter, curtsied childishly in her blue-sashed white satin frock. Behind them loomed Elliot Moke, a spare-looking middle-aged man with a narrow, melancholy face and evasive gray eyes, a dour and narrowly religious person who was forever to be found tagging along behind the Haskels. Having been unable to attend the last yearly meeting, they were introduced to Jennifer Solomon and looked expectantly around to meet the young Dr. Profane and his new wife. To Matthew's embarrassment, the entire family followed him up the passage to Katherine's allotted room, where the couple might be found getting spruced for yearly meeting. Tom junior opened the door to a scene of hustled domesticity; while Katherine, at an ironing board, pressed two starched cotton bonnets with a hissing charcoal iron, Jayne sat on a bed brushing tangles out of her long blond hair. The Boy's wife was absent, but the Boy himself, in a well-cut navy-blue suit, was knotting his tie before a mirror. With a surprised cry, Katherine set down the tilly iron.

"Edith! Homer! How nice." She hugged them all warmly, kissing the squirming Loreley full on the mouth. They had not met since Tom's death; now they babbled awkward commiserations. She shrugged off their furrow-faced concern. "Oh, hush thee. I'm fine now. Here, meet Tom's eldest son."

Their excited laughing stilled as the Boy turned around.

Hubert and Zelda Clayton were the new young couple from Baltimore. He taught at the school while she ran the new clinic, a fine four-block building with a small dispensary. Unfortunately, all the neat new beds stood empty. Than Profane was nonplussed to learn that in her two months there, the zestful Zelda Clayton had treated only the mission staff, and these for only minor ailments. Since the three hundred thousand inhabitants of this protectorate were served by only seven white doctors and twenty-three dispensaries, only nine of which were staffed by white nurses like herself, Matthew could understand the Boy's anger that Nurse Clayton seemed more interested in the tennis court she was building than in soliciting the sick. The pair had words over the issue at the start of a particularly stormy yearly meeting.

To Matthew's astonished distress, Benedict Poe, citing the cruel intimidation of UNIP agents on some of their Quaker members, and with one coal-black eye upon his two pet secession-seeking Lozi princes, reinforced his call that all the meeting's members remain uninvolved in their nationalist politics and, incredibly, that all mission amenities and ministrations be withheld from those who did not. Well, since the main body of the meeting comprised Lunda who had no such separatist aspirations, the policy Poe proposed to implement country-wide would be unrealistic beyond Barotseland's borders.

While the meeting simmered in considering inanition, Clara Fotch calmly declared: "I unite." Orville mumbled the same. An elbow in Cherish Sinclair's ribs elicited agreement, and when Hannah Rothchild and Carrie Poe agreed, Benedict began to smile.

Then the meeting stalled in uncertain silence, and Matthew croaked with some sarcasm and little hope: "May we have the opinions of our African Friends?" Whereupon their paid pastor, Peter Mwanza, immediately affirmed. (The fool had taken Matthew's query for prompting.) There followed a string of approvals from other Africans, which came with snowballing confidence. Mesmerized, Matthew turned his head to follow the faces. The dread confirmation fell from one mouth after another like so many axes: "*I unite! I unite! I unite!*"

In desperation, Matthew searched for an objection from one of his remaining white colleagues. Unfortunately, the outspoken Grace Dooley was absent, and the others seemed not to comprehend the drastic policy pledging that was taking place. Ward Disney sat, eyes closed and mouth agape, in a suspiciously snoozelike meditative pose. Homer Haskel was hunched, miserably mute, under his wife's directive eyes. Katherine Profane gazed dreamily into space; the Wikstroms looked mildly uncomplaining, and Than Profane sat aloofly apart and judging them all. On these depended the meeting's rescue. Matthew wanted to shake them all. He stood up wearily, raising a tired voice that came out creaking and decrepit as an old wheel turning.

"Friend Poe, inasmuch as thy proposal calls for discrimination against others who have also that of God in them, I cannot unite."

There was a low murmur of surprise. Pastor Peter stared at his hands in shamed dismay. Matthew felt for him; the poor man, holding Matthew in the light of a mentor, had as usual bumbled from grace.

Traditionally, no votes are taken in Quaker meetings. Instead, an effort is made to reach harmonious consensus. And while a member might not impose his views on the meeting on the strength of his own voice alone, it required but one objection to effect a deadlock that could continue indefinitely, until all opinions could be brought to common accord. It was an awesome individual power that should be judiciously used; now it pained Matthew to be the one to so disrupt the meeting's harmony. He knew he had long been regarded by some of the missionaries as a doddering sentimentalist; no doubt their secession-seeking Barotse members would resent his intervention now. But there was no help for it. However, if the meeting's attitude to nationalist politicians was thus successfully set aside until next year, Matthew knew that the attitude of their impressionable African members could endure no such unnatural suspension: He knew that many would leave the meeting house thoroughly prejudiced against their own political leaders . . .

BOOK THREE

AFRICA YEAR: THE DARK CONTINENT BEGINS TO STIR

· 1960-1961 ·

1

SUZANNAH'S HABITS of swearing, smoking, and wearing short skirts (this last even despite Katherine's awkward offers to loan her long dresses) increasingly cooled the community's feelings. It seemed to Than that ever more often one or other of the elder ladies, "moved by the Spirit," found occasion to stand up and decry the sinfulness of "indecorous dress and behavior," and if the Africans innocently assumed this referred to the heathen habits of bare breasts and blasphemy, Than was not fooled. If Suzannah listened at all, it served only to cement her defiance, and as the days went by, she showed no signs of softening. She had been at the mission a little over a month when Than's own uneasy feelings came to final fruition one January night after supper, when he answered Katherine's hesitant knock at their bedroom door to find her looking abashed and embarrassed. Averting her eyes, she murmured something about Suzannah being wanted downstairs before hastily disappearing into her own room. Warned by her distress, Than snatched up his shirt and shut the door behind him before he started barefoot down the stairs, to find Hannah Rothchild, Clara Fotch, and Cherish Sinclair awaiting him at the foot.

"Well, good evening to thee, Friend." Hannah squinted up at him from within her floppy cloth poke bonnet. Seeing his bare chest, she hastily lowered her eyes, the thin smile congealing on her face as she rigidly addressed the banister post. "I trust thy good wife is in? As overseers of this meeting's morals, we have come to lovingly labor with her."

"Yeah?" Than stopped halfway down the stairs, shrugging on his shirt, starting to button it. "Well, I don't guess she has anything to say to you."

"Be that as it may," Clara put in caustically, her smile a trifle strained, "we have a great deal to say to her."

Than hesitated, tucking in his shirt. "Then maybe you'd better say it to me."

But as he started down the stairs again, a door opened along the landing and Suzannah emerged in a filmy pink negligee. She raised a brow when she saw their company, and after a moment came sensuously floating down the stairs with an exaggerated wiggle and a haughty little smile on her face.

"Suzie." Than turned.

"Oh I know, honey." Her smile spread sarcastically. "The Gestapo have arrived. No wonder Katherine disappeared in such a frightened flurry. Looks like a regular witches' convention."

"Listen, Suzie," Than said quickly, barring her way, "we don't have to hold still for this."

But she shook her head at him, smiling deprecatingly. "On the contrary. I wouldn't dream of disappointing all these good ladies. Looks like they're all puffed up with something more than air. It might ease them some to let it out."

In the living room, with exaggerated graciousness, she gestured them all to sit. Eying her nylon negligee with mortified distaste, the three women stiffly complied, sitting in a row on the dust-dulled damask cushions of the Kaffir settee. Taking a pack of Matinee cigarettes off the oval oak table, Suzannah offered it around with a wicked flourish. The three women snatched back their noses as if seared with sin, and as Than sat on the bottom step pulling on the boots he had earlier discarded there, he inwardly groaned. Did she have to bait them so? There were Katherine's feelings to consider, after all. When he looked up again, she had lit herself a cigarette and took a long, loving draw on it before flopping down on a seat close to the settee. She crossed her bronzed shapely legs and discharged the smoke, sighing pleasantly. "Well, let's hear it then."

The three women stared at her stupidly. Then Clara collected herself. "Friend Suzannah," she said huffily, "we wish to speak with thee *alone*."

"Oh come now." Suzannah drew back. "Let's not get picky about this. I have no secrets from my husband."

"Very well," Clara conceded severely, glancing meaningfully at her colleagues. "Be it upon thy own head."

But disarmed by Suzannah's candor and obvious derision, she and Hannah took some time warming to their subject. Lighting up a cigarette on the step, Than winced to hear their stumbling starters. Finally, Hannah resorted to irrefutable biblical law. She quoted from St. Paul's Epistle to Timothy, in a thin high quavering voice that was furious with conviction. "'. . . *that women,*'" she marshaled the words like so many soldiers, stiffly disciplined and bent on vengeance, "'*adorn themselves with shamefacedness and sobriety; not with braided hair or gold or pearls or costly array!*'"

The injunction was clear, and with a hand dramatically clasped to her low-bodiced bosom, Suzannah drew back with a wide-eyed look of mock innocence. "Well, merciful goodness! I get the feeling you're trying to tell me something, ladies!"

"That we are, Friend!" Hannah snapped, slapping shut the book. "It grieves me to point this out to thee, but it is my common Christian duty to inform thee that thy immodest dress and behavior have become a source of most grievous embarrassment to us all!"

"Is that so? Well, I'm real sorry to hear that." Suzannah smiled, unperturbed, and Than turned on the step.

"My wife doesn't have to stand for all this," he said quietly. "She's not a Quaker. She's not bound by this meeting's rules."

"Be that as it may," Clara sniffed. "As a resident of this mission—albeit a stagnant one—she is representative of our kind to the natives. As such, I suggest it is her common civilized duty to conform to our . . . er . . . to our more modest modes of dress and behavior! Thus far, I must say that aside from setting a most distressing example to our African Friends, the length of her skirts and her use of devilish facial makeup have served to make a most scandalous spectacle of the female form!"

Than opened his mouth indignantly, but Suzannah waved him silent. She let Clara and Hannah talk on, calmly hearing out their cutting criticisms with smiling disdain; while little frizzy-haired Cherish Sinclair sat meekly blinking and nodding her agreement, Suzannah mocked her accusers with an oooohing mouth and wide, surprised eyes. And even as they were decrying her "distressing habit of tobacco consumption," she leaned forward and deliberately aimed a discharge of smoke at their disgusted noses.

"Well, it seems like I'm a real bad little girl," she said finally. "The question is, what do you intend to do about it?"

Her unexpected poser stopped the women in surprise; they stared from each other to her in puzzled pique.

"Well, the fact is, Friend," Clara sputtered finally, "we had hoped *thee* would do something about it."

"Is that so?" Suzannah said lightly. "I guess you'd like me all prim and proper—conformed in one of those long Victorian gowns

181

with nary an ankle in sight! Why, if you all had your way, I guess you'd stop me having intercourse with my husband as well!"

There was a shocked inhalation of breath. Than almost choked on his cigarette. He recovered, smothering coughs, spluttering: "Dammit, Suzie!" He stared furiously away, and Hannah struggled, red-faced and staring-eyed, to her feet.

"*Friend!* We have not come here to be insulted! If thee continues to make a mockery . . ."

"Oh, fiddle-faddle!" Suzannah laughed derisively. "If you old biddies think you can turn me into a shriveled up old carbon copy of yourselves, then you are sorely mistaken."

"*Well!*" Clara Fotch leaped to her feet. She was narrow-eyed and heaving. "I must warn thee, Friend, if thee continues to be offensive, we shall be forced to take this matter higher! And that would be most regrettable. I am sure the mission board has far more important matters to occupy them without our having to inform them of thy noncompliance in this matter. I assure thee it will be far pleasanter all around if thee will simply cooperate now, while this is yet a 'family affair,' so to speak."

"Ho ho! And wouldn't you just love that." Suzannah's smile was so flagrantly mocking that the three women, affronted, finally blew up in exasperated rage.

"*Well!*" they exclaimed in unison and began to babble. "As if it weren't enough to cast shame on the female form!" Hannah burst, while Clara cried: "We only came to lovingly labor with thee! And *this* is our thanks for our sympathy and tact, why . . ."

It was finally too much for Than. "Ladies," he growled in a tone that brooked no argument, standing up. "I guess that's enough now."

As they stood up, huffily collecting their Bibles and tracts, drawing tight their shawls and fussily straightening their bonnet bows, Suzannah, still gleefully smiling, started back up the stairs with a contemptuous flourish of her negligee. It was a clear dismissal, but insulted and incensed, the three women took a while to trail off, muttering furiously among themselves.

"Shaming her husband's position as a doctor!" was Hannah's irrepressible parting shot, and that, reaching some unknown depth, finally stopped Suzannah. She turned, derisively laughing.

"Listen, you old cows, I am what I am. Do what you like about it! See if I care." Then, while Than looked on in horror, she committed the ultimate outrage and stuck out her tongue at them.

"Christ!" Than winced, closing his eyes.

The women, scandalized, began to back out, babbling in outrage. Than herded them onto the veranda and closed the screened front door on their insistent last words. When he returned, he looked up to find Suzannah gone, their bedroom door along the landing shut. Feeling the suppressed anger beginning to boil inside him, he gazed beseechingly at the ceiling and counted to ten. Then he tore up the stairs and burst into their room. He stopped on the threshold, staring in surprise. Suzannah, lying face down on the bed, was weeping brokenly.

"*I hate them!*" she sobbed with rage, pummeling her fists into her mascara-smudged pillow, looking up at him with a wracked wet face and tear-filmed eyes. "*Snotty old bitches!* Oh God, how I hate them!"

All his outrage deflated, Than released his pent breath.

On a dull damp rainy-season day, Matthew sat in his musty little rondavel office, watching wearily after the departing backs of the latest in a long line of schoolboys who had come with their parents to apply for enrollment at the mission's new school. Well, the sorely sought treasure of secondary schooling had come at last to this remote little outpost of Northern Rhodesia. And, in political spheres, change on a more national scale seemed finally set to snowball: the recently released Kenneth Kaunda had been elected president of the new United National Independence Party, which was swallowing up new members at a ravenous rate, making so much noise in the process that the British government had no option but to listen. And listen it would. The royal commission of inquiry into conditions in the Federation, to be headed by a certain Lord Monckton, had been formed, and the British premier himself was presently touring Africa. Here in Northern Rhodesia, the leaders of the two rival black nationalist parties had reiterated to him their parties' intentions of boycotting the coming commission. And that was the way it went, Matthew mused. The same Africans who had squealed long and loud for change turned suddenly reluctant and aloof when it finally showed signs of coming.

"Send in the next one, please," he called wearily. After almost a week of interviewing these candidates, he felt decidedly fretful and fatigued. For the task of elimination was for him a heart-rending one. Each hope-harrowed boy came with parents who would badger and harangue him should their child be refused. And of the two hundred and thirty students allocated by the local education authorities, only a double class of seventy could be accommodated by their new secondary school. The lack of boarding facilities helped to whittle down their numbers, automatically disqualifying those who did not live within walking distance of Eshalakali, where the school was to be sited. But since many more must, of sheer necessity, be denied acceptance, Matthew strove to be as practical and unemotional as possible in his pruning.

"Good morning, sir."

Matthew looked up and there in the doorway, sitting on the shrunken remnants of his crossed legs, was a paraplegic schoolboy. As Matthew watched, he propelled himself into the room, awkward and toddling as a dwarf on short tomato-box quasi-crutches, supporting his swinging weight on uselessly dragging withered feet and callused knees. He stopped on the straw mat before Matthew's desk, and rearing from the crumpled spider legs, the sturdy torso looked queerly detruncated, the arms hanging apelike in their developed length. By some obscure nerve reaction, his one knee spasmodically jerked, and sitting there expectantly, he reminded Matthew oddly of some tail-thumping tame seal, excited to perform.

"Sir," the boy said hoarsely, "my name is Bernard Kanangu. I did not bring my parents because they were both killed in the Kasenji bus smash of 1955."

Matthew was ashamed that his first reaction was relief that at least in this instance a refusal would not be met with the customary parental pleadings and recriminations that usually followed discriminatory selections of this nature. To stifle a stealing sympathy, he launched quickly into his standard list of questions. The youth answered with pathetic earnestness, finally fumbling in a crude cloth satchel worn around his neck to volunteer, as added inducement, two carefully kept exercise books. By this time, painfully aware of what this meeting's outcome must be, Matthew accepted the books and sat inwardly writhing in a dull distress. For no matter how deserving, how could this handicapped boy, living beyond several rivers, possibly drag himself over ten miles to and from school every day?

"Bernard, please understand that there is nothing I would like more than to see thee enrolled. I admire thy spirit, but . . ."

Matthew's voice trailed as the expectant face fell, devastated, into a look of dawning dread. The boy swallowed visibly. His nose dribbled, and setting down one of his crude crutches, he fumbled to pull a pathetically grizzled handkerchief from his patched pocket. He blew awkwardly into the crumbled rag and, sitting there in his mud-splattered khaki clothing, his bare black arms goose-rippled in the damp cool, there was a pathos about the struggling humility that seared like a flame at Matthew's heart. He had a sudden dim conception of stomach-aching poverty, of endless dogged difficulty, of lessons longingly learned and homework painstakingly penned in cramped conditions by cruel candlelight. All this in the heroic attempt to raise a thigh-high head to the head-high level of an uncaring world.

Matthew glanced, flustered, down at the exercise books lying before him. Slipping on his reading spectacles, he wet a finger and opened one. He began to turn the pages and sat staring incredulously, silently considering as page after page of perfect penmanship was revealed to his astonished eyes. And it occurred to him with growing conviction that perhaps there might be a way after all . . .

"Ahem. Well, Bernard, perhaps I might speak with thy headman and arrange for some bedding to be donated; perhaps, in these exceptional circumstances, we might arrange accommodation for thee at Eshalakali Mission . . ."

The boy's wary black face broke into a gum-gaping guileless smile of pure joy, and Matthew sat warmed anew with the shining worth of it. For here, for him, in one grateful schoolboy, was fittingly rewarded all the long weary years and months spent struggling to secure and install the frustration-fraught seeming madness of secondary school. His effort and disgruntlement finally fully paid, he felt a millionaire . . .

2

When Suzannah had been at the mission for almost two months, she fell ill. She caught a cold and developed a severe streptococcus infection of the throat that kept her laid up in bed for days, listless and irritable and swallowing with pain. Than's departure to a camp bed seemed the final outrage and she turned her back on him, refusing to understand his doctorly duty to avoid germs that might incapacitate him or be transmitted to his patients. Sickness had a way of exaggerating her bad points, and Than missed the solace of their marital intimacy. He worked with a will to get her well. When she complained about hardly ever seeing him, he had the study desk moved into their room so that he could be with her in the evenings, when, by the subdued light of an oil lamp, he worked to compile the entrance examination for his new medical course. But city sickness seemed part of her illness, and she failed to pick up. Knowing how her father's letters left her moody and depressed, Than put her prolonged prostration down to pining. Then one night when he was undressing for bed, he bent to locate a wayward sock under their bed. Pulling the brimful chamber pot out of the way, he stared at it in shock. The urine inside it was red with blood.

"For Chrissakes, Suzie," he looked up at her, aghast. "Why didn't you tell me?"

She shrugged unconcernedly. "I meant to. Forgot, I guess."

"Well I'd better take a look at you." Than drew back the bedclothes and stared. Suzannah's face was puffy and her ankles markedly swollen. This, coupled with the blood in her urine, was a serious indication. Than covered her up again, frowning to himself, disturbed that he had been so preoccupied with his patients at the hospital, he had failed to notice curious symptoms in his own wife.

"Go to sleep now, baby. I guess I'll have to take some tests first thing tomorrow."

Later, in the early hours of the morning, while Than sat engrossed in the intricacies of the entrance exam, Suzannah suddenly stirred on the bed and called out to him in a small frightened voice:

"Than, I feel funny."

He turned in his seat, instantly alert. "What's the matter, honey?"

"My chest is tight. I can't breathe. *Help me!*"

He was off the chair and at her side, leaning over her as her eyes began to move rhythmically from side to side, the pupils finally turning upward until only the whites showed.

"Oh God, Suzie!" When he took her up in his arms, her face contorted and she clung to him with a desperate strength, her clawing hands scratching and biting into his flesh.

Shaking unprofessionally, he felt frantically along the bedside table until he found a comb. Then, prising her jaw apart, he slipped it between her teeth in case she should bite her tongue in the spasm. Then he held her in his arms while her jaws clamped shut, her teeth bent the plastic comb, and the muscles of her face distended grotesquely. She breathed in gasps, making wheezing sounds as her tongue jerked backward, almost cutting off her air. He forced her head over the side of the bed, chin up and head down to ensure a good airway.

He could feel her body growing rigid in his arms as the spasm spread through her entire body and she jerked and twisted against him. Her back arched, her legs kicked rigidly, and her arms struggled and pushed. Her strength was suddenly extraordinary. It was all he could do to hold on to her, to keep her from injuring herself.

Then as suddenly as it had come, it was over. She relaxed like a rag doll in his arms, her breathing peaceful and easy. Her eyes flickered open and she stared up at him in dull puzzlement. He pulled the comb out of her mouth.

"What's the matter?" she mumbled thickly, her eyes bewildered. "What are you doing? Why are you holding me so tightly?"

"Am I?" He smiled down at her, his heart still beating furiously. "Pussycat, you nearly fell off the bed, that's all. I had to grab you." He laid her against the pillow again and pulled the bedclothes up to her chin. She stared at him in exhausted puzzlement.

"What did you put in my mouth? Why were you . . ."

"Hush, honey." He ruffled her hair affectionately. "You go to sleep now. It's late . . ."

But for a long time afterward, he couldn't sleep. He sat cross-legged on the camp bed and smoked in the dark. His hand was shaking so hard, he could scarcely bring the cigarette to his mouth.

Suzannah had acute nephritis, a serious disease of the kidneys. Under Jerome's more objective care, she was confined to bed in a private room in the hospital. A heating pad was applied, and she was put on a high protein diet and given penicillin injections every three hours.

"I guess I don't need to remind thee that one of the most distressing side effects of the disease is the danger in child-bearing," Jerome said gravely when he and Than were alone in his office.

Than nodded. He looked tiredly away. He hadn't slept much through all this. "I know and I won't subject her to that. Suzie's more important than children. I'd like to have her permanently sterilized."

"Hey, now." Jerome smiled gently. "Don't be so hasty, kid. You know how the disease sometimes works itself out? Well, maybe in a few years . . ."

"Maybe." Than looked up. "But I wouldn't like to take the risk. You saw the size of the casts that came away from her. Any more strain on the kidneys could push her through to the chronic stages. Even if she didn't die, she could end up an invalid the rest of her life. And you know Suzie—that's just not her style. As it is, I antici-

pate trouble getting her to be extra cautious about her health . . ."
He looked away, shaking his head. "I just don't ever want to see her
take a fit like that again. Jesus, not ever!"

Jerome nodded understandingly. "Convulsion is a pretty scary
phenomenon. It's most unusual for an adult to have that reaction."
He looked at Than gravely. "Thee knows I'm going to the Missionary Alliance Conference in the Congo with Lars Wikstrom tomorrow. Will thee tell her about the children?"

Than stood up. "I'll break it to her."

But the tears and trauma Than anticipated never transpired. That
night, when he told his wife she should never bear children, she
looked at him as though he had just told her the price of butter.

"Oh," she said simply, her eyes placid as a child's. All built up to
console her, Than gazed at her stupidly, not understanding.

"*Oh?*" he croaked. "Is that all you can say?"

"Well there's nothing I can do about it, is there?"

He stared at her, baffled; he could see that if she had any reaction
coming, he would have to shock it out of her. "Suzie! Do you know
what this means? Can you imagine what it's like to *never* have children?"

"Yes," she said simply, contentedly. "I understand."

"Just like that, Suzie?" he whispered incredulously. "For
Chrissakes! Just like that?"

"Well, what do you expect me to do? Throw a tantrum? Scream
for a sedative? I won't be the first woman who'll never be a mother,
you know! So you can stop looking at me as if I were a criminal.
What'd you expect me to do—break out crying?"

"Yes," Than said, nodding slowly, sadly, his voice suddenly
tired. "I guess something like that . . ."

It occurred to him vaguely then that her indifference toward having children might have something to do with her repulsion at childbirth, but in that moment, instead of being relieved, he felt he had
never been more disappointed in anyone in his life. He began to
back distastefully away from her.

"Where are you going?"

"Out . . ."

"Well, you come back here!" she shrieked at him. In sudden insane rage, she grabbed the vase of wildflowers at her bedside and
threw it with all her might. It struck his back and fell to the ground
in shatters.

He turned slowly around. Water dripped off his shirt and flowers lay scattered at his feet. There was glass everywhere. He was cut; he felt the wet seeping blood on his back, but no pain. He felt he wanted to take her and strangle her.

"Do you know what it's like to have a child?" she wailed at him, heaving. "Do you know? Do you know about the pain? What it's like to have your body pull open like a vise? To lie for hours screaming in pain that won't go away?"

He walked slowly back into the room. "Be quiet, Suzie. You're getting hysterical."

She was crying now, sobbing hugely.

"Do you know?" she shrieked heartbrokenly. "Do you know?"

"Suzie . . ."

"DO YOU KNOW?"

"No," he said softly. "Do you?"

"Yes," she wept, her pretty face a distorted mask of anguish. "Oh yes!"

He couldn't move. She bowed her head on the bed and just sobbed. "When?" he croaked at last when he found his voice. He felt like a zombie, curiously without feeling. He cleared his throat. "How long ago?" His voice had a hollow ring.

"Seven years," she whispered. "When I was fifteen."

Than walked away in a daze. Curious how he had never noticed before. But maybe not surprising. He had had no reason to suspect; her nipples were still uncommonly pink for a woman who had undergone the metabolic changes of child-bearing, and there wasn't a stretch mark on her beautiful body; the baby couldn't have torn her any, either. But maybe Dooley had found evidence of it when he examined her for nephritis, evidence that his wife had given birth to another man's child. . . .

"Why didn't you tell me before?" he asked her later, when he was composed enough to go back to her. "Suzie, I know all about human nature. I would have understood. I always knew you weren't a virgin. I wouldn't have expected any gory details. Just a little straight honesty." He sat numb and pained, and asked again. "Why . . . ?"

"I don't know why!" She rolled abruptly away from him. "So help me, I don't know. I just wanted to forget about it. It was just something too *horrible* . . ."

"Horrible?"

"Oh yes, yes! You're a doctor. Don't you know that?"

"No, Suzie, I don't," he sighed tiredly. "But maybe you'd like to tell me."

And then it all came tumbling out. About a frightened fifteen-year-old girl in a home for unmarried mothers. About two teenage boys and their hot denials, and her senator father's disillusionment and fear of scandal. "I've always given you everything you wanted and this is what I get for it," he had raged. "Cheapness and deceit, your mother all over again!" But even more than her father's fury, she had been afraid of the alien being that was growing inside her. A friend had told her about a whore who had borne a one-eyed monster. And she had been bad, hadn't she? Wouldn't God punish her too? She cried at night, terrified as it grew and moved inside her.

And she got little sympathy. The elderly matron had taken an instant dislike to her. "You little rich girls want to play with fire, you got to expect to be burned! And you'll pay for your ways when the baby comes, little Miss High 'n Mighty. Let me tell you, I've heard some women scream in my time!" Then, when at last her labor started, the old matron was there, smiling craftily. "Oh, Nurse, please couldn't I have someone else?" she babbled desperately, starting to cry. But it had been the wrong thing to say. "Shut up, you little bitch." The woman had slapped her face. "Stop that squealing! You're feeling nothing now. It'll be a thousand times worse in a while!"

She pushed Suzannah up onto a gurney and wheeled her down the corridor to the administrative wing, into a secluded storeroom, before she turned with a demented look. "You just stay here awhile till you learn to quiet down and behave!" Then she closed the door and left Suzannah alone in the dark room. The trolley bed was so high, she was afraid to climb down and by now the pains were acutely cramping. She cried and screamed, but for a long time nobody heard her. By the time they finally found her, she was hoarse and exhausted and the baby's head had already crowned. She was delivered right there in the stuffy little room. And then, worn out with her pain and fear, she had turned away from the blood-smeared child, sobbing hysterically. "I don't want to see it! *Take it away! Take it away!*"

For a long time Than couldn't move. The implications of Suzannah's story echoed numbly through him. She seemed suddenly, terribly, a child to him then. Her aversion to childbirth was suddenly explained and he felt a pity and rage, understanding so much about her that had eluded him before.

190

"Why weren't you there?" She looked at him with tear-filled eyes, illogically accusing. "You could have helped me, couldn't you?"

"Yes, baby, I could have helped you."

Maybe that old matron had subsequently been dismissed, but that did not appease him. For how could retribution give his wife back the lost spark of maternal feeling? How could it erase the scars of a terrified young girl, alone for five hours in the throes of her labor?

After a while, she raised a wondering tearstained face at him. "You don't hate me now?" And this sudden naïveté after her usual wordly sarcasm was unbearably appealing to him then.

"No, baby, I don't hate you."

And how could he? People in glass houses couldn't throw stones, and at a more responsible age, he had accumulated more guilts than she would ever know about. As an intern, he had used abortion to eliminate one mistake, and before that, he had committed a worse crime. He had a little illegitimate daughter in the States who knew him only as a family friend, and it was his own nagging feeling that to deny love to a child already born was maybe worse than to deny life to one that wasn't.

3 In the sweltering midday heat, Matthew walked down the steep rocky path to Eshalakali leper colony. From beyond the rocky palisade of the greater ridge he could hear the continuous rushing roar of the rapids far below, and staring over the splendid sweep of the river and out across the gray-green wooded lowland that stretched in lonely desolation to the blueing infinity of faraway Angola, Matthew was filled with an exhilarated pride of possession. This fair Eshalakali was a fine prize engineered by him, a fledgling Quaker institution in the heathen Kabompo. At this hour the leper clinic was finally over, but a group of the lugubrious lepers still malingered around the veranda. They exuded a dead-mouse odor, and Matthew greeted them frigidly as he walked up the steps.

"Hi." Than Profane turned as he entered. Dressed in a white jacket and his rugged bermudas, he was busy with his dresser, setting up a microscope.

"Sorry to interrupt thee." Matthew took off his pith. "Ward's gone to look over the colony, but I've seen it before. Thought I'd stop off and greet thee." He cleared his throat uncomfortably. "How's that poor woman from Mulaisho's village getting along?"

The Boy sighed. "Unfortunately, her tissues have refused to heal. We'll have to operate again in another few weeks." He stacked some medications into a small paraffin refrigerator and turned. "Once I start Teapot on these Ziell-Nielson tests, I'll join you and Ward for lunch. Why don't you take a seat while I finish up?"

"Oh, no thanks," Matthew said hastily.

Closing the refrigerator door, the Boy turned and studied Matthew skeptically, one silvery brow quizzically raised. "Hey, you're not still worried about contracting the disease, are you? Like I told you, contagion is through an inherited susceptibility you're unlikely to have."

"Oh no," Matthew said, waving his pith airily, "it's just that . . ."

But the Boy's knowing amused smile dried the feeble evasions on his tongue, and Matthew sat hurriedly on a knot-holed bench beside a raw-looking young native woman who carried a sleeping baby, cloth-bound, upon her back. His prim greeting raised dazed, dispirited eyes. Turning to the other side, Matthew was equally disconcerted by the sullen scrutinization of a youth who sat slouched in the doorway, his face smeared with the yellow juice of a fibrous mango pit he was busy gnawing. Rebuffed by such dispassion, Matthew sat uneasily eyeing the lumpy examination couch, whistling sketchily under his breath. The small low-walled hut was enclosed to the corrugated roof with fly-screening reinforced with jackal-mesh; the outside awning kept the sun off the open veranda, where the lepers gathered once daily for Teapot's casual care and once weekly for the Boy's more comprehensive ministrations.

"Hope I'm not interrupting thee," Matthew spoke up hopefully. His sensitive nostrils shying from the stench of stale sweat and suppurating sinuses, he shifted in distress.

"Not at all," the Boy smiled tantalizingly. "These people are just waiting to be tested for leprosy. This woman here arrived last week. According to Teapot, she was newly married in a strange kraal. In her tribe, leprosy is regarded as an indication of adultery, so when the village elders noticed the telltale skin discolorations, her husband's family just threw her out."

"How terrible." Matthew mopped at his sweating brow with a handkerchief. "I surely sympathize. Leprosy is a formidable disease."

"Well, we're still not sure it's what she's got. Thus far, I've found the village elders pretty canny diagnosticians, but we have to make sure." The Boy turned abruptly. "Teapot, will you hurry up."

He fumed impatiently as the young dresser, with quaking fingers, placed a drop of cedar oil on a slide. He was trembling as he slid the slide onto the microscope's stage. His round black face was beaded with sweat and Matthew felt for him. It must be bad enough being imbued with a natural puppy-dog clumsiness without having that specter of perfection personified glowering behind him. The continual strain of a sick, unsympathetic wife and the late-night toil preparing for his new medical course and the bush clinics was surely telling on the Boy.

"Those new huts thee've built here," Matthew said slyly, trying to ease away some of that stern surveillance, "they look real nice. I was admiring them from the top of the ridge."

"Yeah, well I want to eventually get rid of all those old huts. They're a dilapidated slum, infested with termites and ambrosia beetles. But first we need enough huts to house the present population."

"Well, the D.C.'ll be pleased," Matthew said lightly. "We bumped into him on the way up here. He was kinda perturbed about a cache of Communist propaganda the police have discovered in the bush. *The Thoughts of Mao Tse-tung*, no less!" His voice trailed and he strained forward, watching apprehensively as Teapot fitted his eyes to the microscope's eyepiece and fiddled with the adjustment knobs.

"*I see dem! I see dem!*" The dresser's triumphant peal made him jump. "*Da led lod-shapped bacirricus!*"

"Oh, the red rod-shaped bacillicus," the Boy qualified in a bored tone. He caught Matthew's look and shrugged. "He's still new to the thrill."

"Is that good news?" Matthew asked eagerly.

"Decidedly not," the Boy said flatly. "That's leprosy." Hustling the dresser aside, he stared down the eyepiece himself. After a moment, he murmured regretfully. "Yeah. There it is."

He glanced meaningfully at Teapot. The dresser turned, looking awkwardly at his hands. It was a profound moment. The woman on the bench stood up with a rod-straight back and an expressionless face.

"It is *tembwe*," Teapot said softly.

The woman nodded. Untying the patterned cloth knotted across her chest, she shrugged the baby bundle higher up her back, retying it more tightly. Then she turned and left the hut without a word. Teapot sat down to fill out the government report on the case. In a moment, another anxious applicant entered, and the process was painstakingly repeated. While he worked, Teapot endlessly mumbled the chorus line of the hymn "Jesus Loves Me."

Every now and then a strong wind from the plains gave them dubious relief, blowing dust and debris through the fly screens, the fine gauze sieving out dry foliage that collected like insects against the wire, while overhead, a giant jacaranda tree creakingly shifted against the roof. Well away down in Cape Town, the visiting British premier had spoken of the winds of change blowing through the African continent. And he was right. The All-Africa Peoples Conference had just ended in Tunis; Tanganyika had been given an African majority; Nigeria was nearing independence; and Britain was holding a constitutional conference for Kenya. The wind of change was blowing indeed. Yet out here, who would know it? Flies drowsily droned around the dusty screens and the sickening sharp sterile scents had given Matthew a headache. In the suffocating atmosphere, he thought the day's dispensations would never end. . . .

It was an embarrassment to Than that his own wife was the hospital's worst patient. She demanded daylong attention, which could scarcely be afforded, and continually badgered the staff with petty complaints. Her chief gripe was that she saw so little of her husband, and twice she refused her shots so that he was forced to visit and remonstrate with her. She was behaving like a spoiled child, and with Jerome away at the Congo conference, Than scarcely had the time to humor her. When the man finally arrived back a day late due to fighting between the Baluba and the Lunda tribes in Katanga, Than was relieved to see him. He was even more relieved when Suzannah was finally well enough to be discharged.

But that was hardly the end of his troubles. The seriousness of her illness did not worry or interest her, except as a means to worry and infuriate him. She had a simple childlike belief in her own indestructibility and in Than's infallibility as a doctor. She refused to be a slave to the disease and played senseless games the moment his back was turned: washing her hair too late in the day, walking barefoot on the cold concrete floors, running unprotected in the rain. Finally, when she caught a chill and the ensuing blood in her urine proved him right and forced her back to the bed-ridden days she hated, a measure of reality returned and she would be frightened and coy, nervous of his wrath. Over the weeks she was in and out of hospital a dozen such times. Each chill precipitated an attack; each attack did irreparable damage to her kidneys. And knowing the dangers of her disease, her health became an obsession with Than. He took to watching over her like an anxious mother hen.

On a clear sunny day in early February, Eshalakali secondary school was finally begun. Matthew attended the simple inauguration, which was graciously officiated by the district commissioner of the Balovale. The seventy schoolboys, uniformly outfitted in serviceable khaki bush shirts and shorts, were divided into two groups, which filled up the mission's block of two classrooms. Their teachers, the Townsends, a pale timid couple straight from some correct white school in the south of England, were patently overawed by the advanced ages and heights of their big African charges. That first day, obviously unnerved by the silent inscrutable stares and the total lack of relieving laughter at feeble jokes that must previously have wrought them ready roars, the disconcerted couple dithered and erred, trying, with ingrained English ethics, to reach and interpret the alien African mind. . . .

4

Suzannah came out of hospital like a colt on new legs and stared at the mission dispassionately. She turned vague eyes to Than and he felt his heart lurch, she had grown so pale and thin.

"I want to go home," she said in a mesmerized voice, and he turned cold with sudden apprehension.

"Home?"

"Well, I'd like to spend some time with my father in Salisbury."

"Yes," Than said numbly. He knew he should let her go, should even recommend it. She needed some recreation, some change of interest to pick up her waning spirits. And God knew he needed time away from her and her continual carping to devote to his clinics and the new medical course. But he didn't want to let her go. Possessive and obsessed by her and her illness, he wanted to make her stay with him, to watch over her, to keep her careful. She had become such a feature of his life at the mission, albeit a troubling one, that the sudden thought of being without her seemed intolerable. "How would you go?" he said slowly. "It's too far; there's no way."

"There is," she said quickly. "Daddy has chartered a private plane to pick me up at Solwezi in a week. I got his letter yesterday."

"A chartered plane?" Than frowned, hurt that all this had been arranged without his knowledge. He turned away, sick at heart. Yet he should hardly be surprised. Intent upon keeping Suzannah in the luxury to which she was accustomed, the ambassador still sent her a generous monthly "allowance" she could not hope to spend at Suseshi.

"Daddy's worried about me being stuck out here in the bundu, what with the troubled situation and all," she said flatly. "He's heard about the cars being stoned on the Copperbelt, and I guess he's afraid for me. Also, after my illness, he thinks I should come home and have some rest."

Than turned and stared at her coldly. There was no place he could think of more restful than a mission. And no wife he could think of more eager to get away.

"Don't you want me to go?" she said petulantly, giving him a pained stare.

"No. You go," he said deliberately. "No sweat. It's all the same to me. Maybe then I'd get some work done around here without getting nagged at. Maybe I'd prefer it."

He couldn't look at her then, but if there was hurt in her eyes, it was echoed inside him.

The following week, the completed written entrance examination papers for Than's medical school began to come in. Eager to get down to the marking and selection of suitable candidates, he wanted Suzannah to go now and be done with as quickly as possible. He was relieved when Matthew Tomlinson, due to go up to Solwezi to collect the schoolteachers' salaries, agreed to drive her to the airfield.

In the early morning pending her departure, he watched Suzannah pack while he dressed for work. She was happy and so bright and talkative, he was surprised. There was pink in her cheeks and a glow in her eyes, and he hadn't seen her this carefree and excited since leaving Salisbury. She went through her collection of expensive clothes hanging cramped in the dim old wardrobe, deciding what to take, holding glamorous garments against herself as she preened before him and the mirror.

Than stared at her sullenly, saying nothing. He didn't remember when he had had the power to make her sparkle the way the idea of partying obviously did.

In the dusky cool of early morning, he stood beside the Land-Rover and kissed her stiffly. "Tell your father I'm counting on him to push through that A.I.D. grant for my bush clinics." He caught at her arm as she turned to go. "Oh, and remember you're a married woman now. No more wild parties or nude modeling—hear?"

"Oh, honey, is that any way to say good-bye?" She sighed, seeming suddenly unsure of herself and reluctant to leave him. Falling into his arms, she hung on to him then, beautiful in a pink tailored suit, her face pressed against his cheek. Full of hurt pride, he held back for just as long as he could. Then suddenly her going dawned painfully in him, her proximity worked its old magic, and he groaned and closed his eyes and held on to her so fiercely that the old professor turned away in embarrassment. Moments later, as he watched the vehicle roar away in the dim early light, a heavy sadness enveloped him; the desolate day stretched interminably before him, and he sat on a tree stump and smoked a cigarette, brooding with his sense of loss.

For a while after she left, Than missed his wife. Although he had initially married her and brought her to the mission against his will, she had become a drug to him physically, and without her, without her tantrums and her turmoil, without her disconsolate wandering over some part of it, the mission was suddenly empty for him, a desolate and depressing place. He ached for her stimulating company and the sweet solace of her body, and without the accustomed sexual release he had found in her, the nagging need gnawed at him and he grew bad-tempered and as tense as a coiled-up spring. But gradually, as the days passed, the emptiness dissolved. At the hospital during the day, he buried himself in his work, and at home he had time at last to turn his undivided attention to the organization of his clinics and the new medical course. He liaised with the medical officer and Denise Smith, who would be in charge of the new course when he was not lecturing, and worked feverishly through the evening hours, cautiously marking the pile of examination papers he had received, carefully considering all factors before finally selecting twelve students for the school's first year. It was only now that he began to appreciate fully his new peace and freedom. But always, late at night, he needed Suzannah. After crawling into bed exhausted, he often awoke reaching for her in the early hours, troubled by his own conditioned appetite, haunted by her lingering smell.

His family and the other missionaries were less bereaved. He knew that Jayne and even Katherine loved having him to themselves again. At the house, their loving attentions, although constricting, were as healing as time. And it seemed to Than as if at Suzannah's going, everyone else at the mission suddenly let go of their breath. And although bereft, life for him was less troublesome. Katherine's sensitive Quaker feelings were less frequently offended; Jayne became his indulged little sister again. And the leopard, Bathsheba, came back to his bed . . .

Than's first bush clinic was completed. Sakapuchi sent word that the new hut to accommodate it had been built by his people at Than's specifications. Than arrived at the village to find the large edifice neatly plastered and thatched, the thatch projecting to form a narrow sheltered veranda, which was lined with crude wooden waiting benches. The villagers clustered around, excited and proud, as Than, accompanied by the headman, approvingly inspected the clean-swept interior. The large unglassed windows let in plenty of light and air, and two handmade wooden chairs and a little crooked table comprised the furnishings. It was barely adequate, and once Than was able to attain his ideal of a medical assistant, two dressers and a cleaning boy to run the clinic independently, shelves and a lock-up cupboard for medications would be needed, as well as a sink, an examination couch, basic instruments, and even, ultimately, a bed or two. In the meanwhile, Than planned to service the clinic once a fortnight, bringing with him what drugs and equipment he might need.

While Than took tea with the headman in his hut, the village drum began to throb, spreading the news of the clinic's first session. By the time they returned to it, the long veranda benches were already crammed with hopeful patients and ever more were trickling in from the surrounding villages. They came with pneumonia, bronchitis, malaria, bilharzia, enteritis, eye infections, toothaches, and threatened miscarriages. Gratified by the knowledge that without this clinic many of them would have waited until their ailments were far more advanced before undertaking the journey to the nearest hospital, Than worked happily through the long afternoon. Then a young boy was brought in by his father and all Than's work and skill seemed suddenly futile. For the man begged Than to restore to his son sight in eyes that had already been irreparably ruined. Than turned away, sick at heart to hear how a witchdoctor had spat chewed bark into the boy's eyes, causing them to swell up horrendously before finally bursting amid unspeakable agony. He quietly chastised the man for not having taken the boy to a proper hospital in the first place and was nonplussed to learn that the man had in fact originally taken him to Suseshi. It was only after being referred to the eye specialist in Kitwe, to have the cataracts removed, that he had decided to try a traditional herbalist first.

"Kitwe is a long way, and I am a poor man," the man said simply.

For a long time after the despairing pair had departed, Than could not stop thinking about the scores of cataract patients he and Jerome regularly referred to Kitwe; how many of them, daunted and discouraged at the idea of such a journey, wavered in their faith and went away to be blinded by the blundering witchdoctors?

On his return to Suseshi late that night, Than went across to the Dooley house and woke up Jerome. In his striped pajamas, the man stumbled, yawning, onto the veranda; he stared stupidly as Than unfolded his story.

"Thee woke me up to tell me that?" he croaked. "Thee knows we've always sent the cataract patients to Kitwe."

"Yeah, but I've been making inquiries and it seems there's usually a long waiting list. These people have to travel hundreds of miles there, usually on foot or bicycle, only to be told to return again, weeks or months later, for the operation. Why can't we operate on them here?"

"Why?" Jerome stared at him in exasperation. "Because we're not ophthalmologists, that's why. We're already busy enough, and at the Kitwe mine hospital they'll get specialized attention. In the old days, mission doctors chanced it, sure. But that was before the advent of eye specialists in the next province!"

"Then the people were a damn sight better off in the old days!"

"Well, we can't help that. We explain that the condition is completely correctible and give them a referral note. And that's where our responsibility ends!"

"I don't think so. While we know there's the remotest chance that someone could lose their sight for life, I think our good intentions aren't good enough. Sure they should go to the Copperbelt and be operated on by an expert. They *should*, but sometimes they won't. And so long as we know that any kind of delay can precipitate a visit to the witchdoctors, I believe it's our duty as doctors to perform the operation ourselves."

Running a hand through his rumpled hair, Jerome sighed wearily. "Kid, it's a delicate procedure. You could go through life carrying the responsibility of the eyes you've ruined."

Than shrugged. "Oh shit, my shoulders are broad; I've *buried* my share of mistakes before."

"Well, in that case," Jerome opened the screen door to usher Than out, "don't let an old fuddy-duddy like me deter thee!"

The next day Than read up on the operation and sorted through the instruments on the surgery shelves. He picked out a few and went across to see Ward Disney at the trade school, where the man, working with other mechanical oddments, laboriously fashioned a serviceable set of cross-action lens capsule forceps. In the meanwhile, Than requisitioned the government for several sets of the powerful "plus 10" spectacles, which would act as temporary artificial lenses until the recovering eyes of cataract patients had sufficiently adjusted to be tested for permanent glasses.

By the time the spectacles finally arrived, Than already had a backlog of twenty cataract patients. He immediately operated on the worst, an aged man who was totally blind. There were currently two principal methods of removing the clouded lens. Than chose the more difficult intracapsular extraction, since it excluded the risk of a secondary membrane forming postoperatively.

Under Jerome's inhibiting anxious eye, with slightly shaking hands, he made a bold limbal incision superiorly into the sclera, then carefully reached in with the makeshift forceps and, with disarming ease, grasped and extracted the opaque lens intracapsularly. In ten days, when it was clear there was no infection and he was sure of the operation's success, Than operated on the other eye. In another two weeks they unbandaged the first eye operated on and fitted the patient with the thick convex glasses. The old man's tearful unbounded joy at being able to see again after several years of increasing darkness touched Than deeply. He urged the man and all the hospital staff to spread the news of the successful surgery. But he knew they hadn't yet seen the end of eyes ruined by ignorance.

5

The day came when Than Profane's workload overtook even his time for worship. When he began missing First-day meeting to service his several outlying local clinics, Matthew was apprehensive. When one such Sunday Ezra Peabody snidely inquired as to where the young doctor might be found, he was instantly on his guard. From the first, the Boy had treated Ezra to the contempt of ignoring him; whenever the man began to go off into one of his effervescent religious tirades, the Boy would gaze off into space as if the man were a bad joke that was hard to believe. And Ezra, used to being pandered to, was a vindictive Friend who did not suffer the slight kindly. But if he had a Godside manner as enthralling to elderly women as the heaven and hell he perpetually preached of, Ezra's uncanny charisma was a complete mystery to Matthew, whose Quakerly quietude had made him chary of the man's loud ostentation from their very first meeting two years ago. Unfortunately, Ezra's wondrous way with words was enshrined in countless publications and a frightening fame, which had preceded him to the mission, securing him a privileged infallibility in the minds of the adoring elder ladies before ever they laid eyes on him. When even Teller began airing the man's views, it had been for Matthew the final straw. Deprived of domestic deity, he had rankled disconsolately. *Ezra Peabody!* Why, even the name sounded stage. The man was a mockery, but who else could see it? Of the other missionary men, only Than Profane was noticeably antagonized.

Now, honesty compelled Matthew to reveal the Boy's location, but filled with misgivings, he decided to accompany the pompous principal of their Bible institute, his black students, and an entourage of admiring missionary ladies on their next Sunday School sojourn into the native villages. As he had feared, the man planned, as his venue, the very village of the Boy's Sunday ministrations. They arrived after lunch to find the village meeting house deserted. Not even the headman was there to greet them.

"Didn't anyone tell them I was coming?" Ezra quailed. He seemed to feel a responsibility to justify by popularity the extent of his fame.

They finally found half the village surrounding the doctor's leopard cub beneath a spreading muSaka tree. For a few pounds a month, Boniface, the mission's spry old hunter, kept the young feline fittingly fed on regular bags of wild fowl and small game. Now, chained to a low branch, she looked sleek and healthy as she licked her own almond-eyed reflection in a rain puddle. And the medical team was obviously taking a lunch break; Matthew looked up to see Than Profane and one of his dressers approaching through the village trees. When the cub saw the Boy, she left off lapping and splashed straight through the puddle, yowling piteously, stretching the chain to its fullest extent as she waited, golden eyes big and soft, filled with young yearning. Reaching her first, Cosmo Mongotti crouched to untie her. He tried to pet the little cub, but hearing the Boy's soft signaling whistle, she countered the caressing black hands, craning her head around his blocking body, impatiently clambering over one white-clad knee. When the young dresser unleashed her, she was instantly off, gamboling across the damp earth with a single-minded purpose set like steel in the butter-soft eyes.

Laughing lightly, the Boy went down on his haunches to greet her. Echoing affectionately, she bundled straight into him, kissing him fulsomely on the face, setting him off balance so that he fell backward onto the ground. His hat tipped off and he lay with his long blue-jeaned legs sprawled out in the grass, chuckling huskily while the little cub climbed eagerly all over him. With a head-hung hunting nose, she sniffed, nuzzled, licked, and tenderly chewed on him. When he finally pushed her off, his white jacket was mud-smudged with the perfect rosette arrangements of the little paw pads. He retrieved his Stetson and stood up. Dusting off the hat, he seemed to suddenly digest the silent company of missionaries, who stood frigidly aloof among the mesmerized village population.

"Afternoon," he called politely, and Ezra nodded stiffly, starting to walk warily across.

"Good day, Doctor. I trust thee'll be joining us in meeting today," he said haughtily, removing his fashionable dove-gray hat.

"Afraid not, Mr. Peabody." The Boy replaced his Stetson. "I have a crowd of sick people to tend back there."

"I see." Ezra drew himself up aloofly. He stared disdainfully down at the little leopard. "I see thee have that animal with thee again. I'm afraid a lot of Friends feel it's a pretty dangerous practice with it growing so large. Thee made arrangements to have her shipped off to some zoo yet, Friend?"

There was an uncomfortable silence. Matthew looked away in

distress. Oh that Ezra! He must be mightily stung by the Boy's usurpal of his congregation and absences from meeting to so publicly challenge him to a formal commitment on what had obviously for him long since become an unspeakable subject. With a soft look of love, the Boy stared down at the little shaggy cub, which was blissfully purring, rubbing itself against his long blue-jeaned legs, staggering lopsidedly as it furled back and forth around him.

"Sheba's not going to a zoo," he said quietly. But his defiant words were belied by innate sadness in eyes that nevertheless knew no other answer. "This big open country is her birthright. She has more right to be here than you."

Ezra colored and glanced meaningfully at the haughtily aghast ladies. "Well, I don't believe that's up to thee to decide, Friend. She's a dangerous wild animal, prone to parasites and mangy diseases. I am very much afraid thee'll have to make some arrangement and put her where she can't harm innocent people, before very long."

He was holding a ream of printed Sunday School treatises in one hand; a sudden wind furled up the top few pages, and in his effort to catch the flutter, the man dropped his expensive gray hat. It rolled on the ground in front of Bathsheba. Ezra saw what was coming and gave a shout as he pounced to grab the hat first. They reached it simultaneously, and with a furious yell, Ezra pulled back the hat with a claw-lashed hand. He slapped the cat copiously with his wad of papers and the aghast young animal reeled in fright. It rounded on him, and before their very eyes, that deceptively soft-eyed, big-pawed, and baby-shaggy little cub was completely transformed. Ears flattening, the whiskered lips curled back in a sneering show of curved canines, it reared up with a deep, rumbling, incredibly vicious growl and a feral ferocity that shocked them all into frozen fear.

"Call it off . . ." Ezra managed hoarsely. And the Boy hauled off the spitting cub, dropping to his haunches to pacify her.

But the ladies, infected, squealed with anxious outrage and the cowed little cat crawled behind the Boy's haunches and crouched there, spitting and sneering at them.

"Hush, now. The man's no friend, but he sure can't hurt you," the Boy soothed. And Ezra, cradling his scratched hand, swelled up like a frog, reddening angrily.

"I believe that animal just proved my point, Friend, and I reiterate! In keeping her thee're treading mighty dangerous ground. To say nothing of thy practice of missing meeting lately. So take heed of my words, Friend. There are none among us can afford to miss the soul-breed of meeting. *Don't thee be the one to tempt the burning fates of hell!*"

The Boy pulled on a weed and stood up, chewing on the stem. It waggled insolently from the corner of his mouth as he gazed at the man for a long measuring moment. His thumbs went to the empty belt loops at his hips, and he raised his jaw to better see the man beneath the brim of his white hat.

"Mr. Peabody," he said deliberately, "I'm a big boy now. If I want to tempt the burning fates of hell, then I guess it's my own goddamn business."

From that moment on, it was out and out war. They split the village population between clinic and meeting that day. Back at Suseshi, in the combat ring of the dining hut, they sparred daily with words or the lack of them. It seemed to Matthew the Boy's every act was calculated to antagonize the man in some way. For the first time he saw the young doctor fully roused, and it was an awesome spectacle. The Boy had a blistering contempt that could wither like a lightning bolt; the sulphurous flash of those belligerent blue eyes could give an innocent bystander psychological powder burns that stung for a week.

6

The Monckton Commission of Inquiry arrived in Northern Rhodesia to a string of placards citing the "sins" of Federation. According to reports, one amply-padded black matron hoisted the ludicrous legend: FEDERATION KILLS! WE ARE STARVING! The commission received a mixed reception; while the whites gave freely of their opinions, the majority of the black population, respecting the boycott of the two nationalist parties, remained stubbornly silent. But in the North Western province, the district commissioners managed to encourage the opinions of a group of chiefs, who charmed the English delegates with their full ceremonial dress.

In the meanwhile, in the urban areas outbreaks of violence escalated daily. Along the Copperbelt roads, stone-throwing bands of hoodlums terrorized passing motorists, and all over the country there were riots and incidents of arson, vandalism, and assault. And in the

African compounds, blacks were hideously maimed or burned alive when crude petrol bombs were thrown into their little boxlike houses in the dead of night. When it became apparent that the victims were mostly outspoken members of the more moderate "Congress" political party, the rival nationalist group, UNIP, began to take on an aura of vicious brutality. Arrogantly screaming *"Kwacha!"* its members struck terror into the hearts of detractors when they rode around the country, crammed into dilapidated trucks that were riotous with ripped green foliage, mockingly saluting all wayfarers with the fluttering UNIP wave.

In the wake of reports of increasing nationalist canvassing around Mwinilunga, Matthew was acutely discomforted when three swaggering, grandly dressed UNIP agents arrived at the mission, declaring their intention of selling UNIP membership cards to the "fortunate" populace. Matthew could trace their course by the dribble of agitated teachers, houseboys, and even hospital staff who came to report a veiled intimidation. Unfortunately, there was nothing Matthew could peaceably do about it. When the politicians' battered car finally roared away into the thickening dusk, he felt something of a feelingless fool going around adjuring their workers to "be not intimidated." While their African employees could decline UNIP membership on the security of the mission ground, away from it they were defenseless, and they were all poor, frightened human beings. The houseboys failed to turn up for work the following day, and the teachers reported discrimination on the sale of fish at the river; their wives returned with frightened faces, empty baskets, and a sure indictment of the power of the United National Independence Party. Matthew, as usual, bore the brunt of it all. The missionaries and natives alike nagged him as if he were God misbehaving, ordering him with outraged eyes to put the position right, just the way he might with equal ease bring the seasons to order.

In the wake of the British premier and the Monckton Commission, the colonial secretary, Iain Macleod, was one of a flurry of important British personages who arrived in the Federation to consult on the troubled state of the three component territories. In Northern Rhodesia the man was met at Lusaka Airport by a screaming, stick-brandishing mob, which surrounded his car. Police eventually managed to extricate him, but later, hundreds more Africans gathered to demonstrate outside Government House. It seemed that the whole nation was in an uproar, a mutinous mood which Matthew saw reflected at Suseshi in the continued absence of their houseboys and the increasing disobedience of their primary-school seniors, who staged a strike in the dining room. When Matthew and the headmaster confronted them, they were surly and evasive; they registered several complaints, which were easily quashed for lack of validity, and still they silently stalled. Matthew called in their African pastor and a village headman to reason with the children. But these measures were hopelessly immaterial. A trip wire was placed across the road to the mission, and the boarding master's house was stoned. Matthew immediately summoned the suspected ringleaders and issued stern warnings of expulsion and police action. But the boys merely stared at him, surly and unmoved. And since they comprised some of their most promising boys, Matthew stopped short of making good the threatened expulsions. Neither could he take the serious step of calling in police aid. It seemed like conceding defeat somehow and would ultimately work against them, driving pupils and teachers irrevocably apart. Yet he could think of no other way.

Every night he went to his carelessly straightened bed, anxiously straining to detect riot in the ever-loudening rabble of raised voices emanating from the boys' dormitories across the river. Finally he summoned the executive staff of the two schools to his house. They arrived looking anxious and nervous as mice.

While Jenny sat at the living room table placing a Braille puzzle and Teller prepared tea, groping around the piles of unwashed cups and saucers in their unserviced kitchen, he consulted with Katherine, headmistress of the girls' intermediate school, and Mr. Katima, principal of the boys'. The seventeen other African teachers filled his living room with their lines of trousered legs and obvious unease.

Matthew was trying to pacify their fears when Jenny gave a sudden shout. As they turned to stare at her quizzically, she clutched the table, vacant eyes wide. Her horror so communicated itself that there was a stunned silence and they watched her as she stood up slowly, shaking her dark head, visibly swallowing.

"Professor . . . there's a fire somewhere. I see it burning."

Katherine looked aghast; she and Matthew looked at each other. Why, the poor child must be hallucinating.

Matthew blustered, "Now, Jenny dear. Do not be distressed. There is no fire. Thee is mistaken."

But the girl would not be pacified.

"No. It's true. I can *feel* it. I *know*." And so impressive was her conviction that Matthew stopped to look around and sniff. A few of the teachers did the same. But there was nothing to bear out her strange illusion.

Then Teller went warily to the window. She pulled aside the drapes and gasped.

"Matthew." She whirled, ashen-faced. "She's right! *The school is on fire!*"

While the black teachers craned to see, Matthew stood galvanized with shock. He could not see beyond the deranged stranger who was his wife. "How can that be?" he thundered disbelievingly. "Are thee out of thy mind?" But her dumbstruck expression answered him more effectively than words. Matthew dragged himself to the window and stood sick with horror. Down the dark slope, a fire crackled and raged. He pushed open the window and heard the distant thunder of spreading conflagration. Red leaping flames had begun to eat away at the old brick and thatch of two of the buildings.

"The boys' school," Matthew moaned, fascinated by the dancing firelight. "Dear Lord—the precious school!" Then he was outside, bellowing at the top of his lungs: "*Fire!* FIRE!"

And suddenly the night was filled with running figures given ghostly prominence in the rosy glow. Scores of natives milled around the roaring spectacle with transparent rapture. The missionaries had begun running up and down the slope with containers of water, but in all the panic, more was spilled on the ground than ever reached the fire. Little Cherish Sinclair, flustered and foolish, made the classic gesture with a cupful. To Matthew it all seemed some hideous nightmare. Although the Cathcarts kept back the pajama-clad huddle of black orphans, the schoolchildren and mission workers milled mindlessly. The cloying crush of the crowd hampered their progress, and Ward Disney, that questionable Quaker, with customary brute bluntness, thumped the idle Africans out of the way. Dragging a brimful bucket from the house, Matthew tripped and ended up bruised and drenched in water meant for the fire. Teller fussed and berated him, and Matthew jammed his pith back on and began to limp fiercely back up the slope. Then he saw a unanimous relief expanding on the surrounding faces and, turning, he understood.

For suddenly, silently as shadow, Than Profane was among them, materializing out of darkness and panic, as seraphically alluring as the Son of God. In all that hot havoc he had a stabilizing presence as solid as rock, the solemn sunburned face ballasted with a tranquil strength, his bare sweat-glazed torso looking like some tall copper-hewn statue, standing in odd tribute to himself. Matthew wondered how they had ever managed without him. For he had a drawing power that stilled the frantic scurrying, a look that shut off the futile wails and screams for water, a pointed questioning that stopped dead the useless single effort. Responding to his animal magnetism, the missionaries clamored pathetically around him. The Boy shuffled them all with the inimitable ease of an adept; like some seasoned hustler, he dealt out duties like a rippling pack of cards. In a voice of calm gravity that made even the flames seem less intimidating, he appointed one delegation to fetch spades and containers, another to drag out what furnishings and books could be saved. The African schoolchildren and spectators he organized to form a human line to the river.

In no time at all they were all paring off on their respective ways, moving with constructive haste. Matthew stood on the top of the river bank and supervised the collection of water. And every spare moment, with infinite anguish, he stopped and watched the buildings burn. Even when the swinging buckets of bouncing river water began arriving along the chain of human hands, he knew that it was too late. As the flames fanned out with their deadly appetite, making nonsense of their frantic human efforts, resignation spread through them like a malaise. It left them standing defeated, watching the buildings go. As the crackle and roar gradually died down, even the chattering schoolchildren fell silent. But even as the missionaries acclimatized to a dull disbelief, their mood was rudely shattered.

"The meeting house!" A cry went up. "The meeting house goes too!"

They turned and there it was, the interior blown with leaping light, wooden beams etched in licking flame.

In the morning only charred piles of smoking debris remained of the two schoolrooms and the cherished meeting house. A drizzle, too light and too late to be useful, drearily drenched the steaming mess. Besides a quantity of school textbooks, scores of precious Chi-Lunda prayer books had perished. So much was lost that had taken years to attain, and the people, without adequate accommodation for the schoolchildren or their God, were desolate and acidly angry.

Although subsequent police investigation failed to prove the schoolchildren's implication in the arson, Matthew by this time knew the identity of the culprits beyond doubt.

Though it sorely grieved him, wretched with his rage, he called in the six ringleaders among the boys and summarily expelled them. Two of them broke into bitter tears, at last confessing as to the political instigation that had all along been feared; they revealed that the visiting UNIP agents had threatened to beat them if they disobeyed, entreating Matthew that there was nothing else they could have done, imploring that they had not realized! But it was too late now, and Matthew, mourning the meeting house, hardened his aching heart. For it had not been fear but defiance he had seen in their eyes, and he knew they wept now not for the lost schools or the church, but for their own lost opportunity. To allow them to remain now would only further compromise an already teetering authority. He sent them off. And if their subsequent last-minute switch to insolent name-calling: "Kaffir coward!" and "racist pig!"—might seem to justify his action, it gave him no comfort.

The rest of the day, the other students seemed uneasy and strangely quiet. That night, fearing revenge for remaining in school, they went to bed protectively armed with sticks. By the next morning it was found that more than half of them had run off. By nightfall, anxious parents came to withdraw still more. The Townsends, in a tizzy, arrived from Eshalakali Hill to report a similar exodus. Matthew consulted with the education officer at Mwinilunga boma, and it was conceded that with even the remaining few students poised on the edge of fleeing, they had no recourse but to close the schools until the trouble subsided.

Left stunned in the ensuing silence, the missionaries became aware of the enormity of the outbreak. That month, theirs had been only one in a series of disturbances that broke out in schools all over the country. And there was no doubt as to which of the two nationalist organizations was behind it all. In the Luapula province, outbreaks of arson were so severe that all UNIP meetings were banned. Obstructions were placed on railway lines and more cars were stoned. There were numerous clashes between the rival nationalist parties, and hysterical black crowds and the police. Yes indeed, Matthew soberly reflected, the dynamic new United National Independence Party was emerging as a force to be reckoned with.

Without the meeting house, they had commandeered the empty school hall to hold worship. But the hall had not the same *feel*, and the members were discouraged. They elected a committee to raise funds to build a new one, but with the oppressive political climate, there seemed little hope of realizing the money soon.

7
When Than went to Barotseland to inspect the progress of Shonona's clinic, Matthew Tomlinson, at loose ends with the closure of their schools, accompanied him to inspect the Friends' educational centers that were still fully operative in the little protectorate. They took with them Peter Disney and Bathsheba, who pined too long without Than. The leopard rode in the canvas canopy of the Land-Rover roof, and on a clear morning in late April, armed with official permits, they crossed into the vast flat country.

Although the rains had now stopped, the central plain was still massively inundated with the annual flood of the Zambezi River; they were frequently bogged down on soft sections of the previously submerged sand road and were obliged to cross stretches of the swollen Kabompo and Zambezi rivers on crude log hand-hauled pontoons. Crossing the limitless lake of the Zambezi flood into Barotseland, the African pullers chanted rhythmically, their sweat-oiled ebony muscles rippling as they worked in marvelous metronomic unison to haul the large flat ferry with its cumbersome load of their Land-Rover, one car, and two trucks across to dry ground, where an elephant on an ant hill was feeding on the pungent-smelling fruit of a marula tree. The receding flood had left uncovered a vast landscape littered with a sodden havoc of slimy debris, writhing roots and rank grass, which had grown with the rising water to reach a height of twelve feet in places. Now the air-exposed rotting vegetation stank unspeakably in the stewing sun. But although the missionaries found it foul, the natives seemed not to mind. But then they had bigger problems to ponder. In this little river kingdom, the Barotse people, comprising twenty-five different subject tribes, which had largely intermarried with the dominant Lozi, were still being preyed upon by the ferocious man-eating lion despite all the efforts of government-appointed hunters and rangers.

Reaching Shonona Mission that afternoon, Than dropped Matthew and Peter off at the school and went straight across to the little clinic. There he found that Zelda Clayton was making some progress. Several Africans awaited attention on a bench in the sun. Than learned that they were all inhabitants of a village whose principal crops had been destroyed by elephants. Since they had been existing on nothing but dried corn and water, they were all badly constipated and sickly, and Than was horrified to learn that three babies had subsequently died. He dispensed strong purgatives and a tonic and then went across to see the Poes, who were relaxing on their veranda after the day's work. Carrie promised to see what food could be spared from the mission's provisions for the malnourished villagers, but Benedict seemed loath to donate any of the citrus from his orchard.

"It's the government's job to take care of the people in times of famine," he said shortly. "They bring in truckloads of grain. The D.C. will arrange it if'n they just approach him."

"We don't have time to put this thing through the proper channels," Than snapped. "If these people don't get some protein and essential vitamins soon, many more may die!"

"They meeting members?" Benedict rubbed at his furrowed brow.

"No, I don't think so." Than stared at the man strangely. "What difference does that make?"

Benedict stared at Than with eyes as cold as black marbles. Sitting between them, partially in the path of that icy regard, the professor seemed to shrink in his seat.

"The fruit is not ripe," Poe said finally.

"Now, listen—it hardly matters if the fruit is still a little sour!" Than spluttered.

"Thee heard me: there's none ripe," Benedict said shortly. He picked up a newspaper and stared at it concentratedly, closing the subject.

Than stared at the man angrily. The orchard belonged to the mission, after all. It comprised trees cut from Matthew Tomlinson's own lovingly grafted hybrids, and Carrie Poe's meal table was always abundant with her home-preserved marmalade and juice prepared from the fruit.

That night after supper, Matthew was approached by Than Profane in their bedroom. "Pete and I are going for a little walk, Matthew. Would you mind coming along with that carpetbag of yours? It might come in handy."

Thus, spluttering in indignant mystification, Matthew, clutching the moth-eaten old bag, found himself hurrying after the two young males, who strolled across the dark, treacherously bumpy mission yard, with eyes like cats. Out here, clear cold Barotseland seemed to watch and wait. From somewhere far distant, the thin eerie howling of scavenging jackals bestirred the great stillness, and from the swamp nearby the continuous tinkling of Egyptian reed frogs overlaid the periodic peculiar "popping" of the lazy sludge lapping in the rushes. Shivering in his shirtsleeves in the sharp night air, Matthew sniffed distastefully; with the cessation of the rains, there was no escaping the gluey stench of the sodden vegetation exposed to the air and elements on the river-receding great Barotse Flood Plain. He heard the creak of a rusted gate, and before he knew it, they stood before the low bushes of the citrus orchard. As the Boy began feeling around in the clusters of leaves, plucking off several fruit, it struck Matthew with a chill: he was stealing Benedict Poe's forbidden fruit!

"Give me a hand," the Boy said, calm as you please. "Pete's keeping watch. We have to work fast."

Matthew tried to protest, but as fast as he talked, the Boy fumbled and ripped and little oval lemons and small hard oranges dropped into Matthew's open carpetbag with dull, regular thuds. Finally, out of sheer urgency, glancing guiltily around, Matthew bustled to help him, plucking sweet-smelling limes with his arthritic old fingers. If he did not help, they would surely all be caught in the ensuing delay. Thus, flinching in constant fear of a flash-lit discovery, Matthew rushed from tree to tree, frantically fumbling. But his shabby old bag seemed endlessly to swallow up the fruit he dropped inside. He stubbed his toes and cracked his head; the sense of nightmare slowness turned his bones to lead. And through it all he felt a mounting anger at the Boy. Such outrageous acts were part of his repertoire, of course! An infernal foliage drawn to his casual infamy as naturally conglomerating as trees following water!

Suddenly, just when the bag seemed finally full, they heard Peter Disney's amateur owl hoot. Matthew tried in vain to urge the Boy away, but he carried on, busily pilfering, stuffing citrus into his pockets and shirt and down his long jacket sleeves. Hurriedly closing the carpetbag, Matthew struggled to lift the dadblamed thing. It weighted a ton, but propelled by fear, he stumbled through the rusted orchard gate on amazingly limber legs. Then, through the clear night air, he heard his own name called. It was Benedict Poe! *The Pharisee wanted him!* Wobbling alarmingly, Matthew scurried toward the lighted house. He heard the gate creak behind him and was relieved when, just before he and Peter reached the house, the Boy joined them. Coming into the radiated house light, Matthew blanched guiltily as Benedict, on the veranda steps, spun around at their tread. He peered at them peevishly.

212

"There thee are! Where the dickens have thee been?"

"Why, uh . . . er . . ." Matthew, a wretched Robin Hood, looked helplessly around at his accomplices. Peter Disney, blushing furiously, was a dead giveaway; the Boy, in his fruit-bulging jacket, looked impossibly muscular. Matthew's white hair, uncommonly unkempt, hung in strings before his eyes. Together, the three of them must be a glaring advertisement of gargantuan guilt. Matthew smiled feebly.

"Uh, well, Ben . . . we went for a walk."

"A *walk?*" The man stared at Matthew as though he had never heard of such a thing. His eyes brooded dubiously on the three of them.

"Was there anything you wanted, Mr. Poe?" the Boy said casually.

"Well." Benedict frowned, reluctantly diverted. "Carrie's fixing some hot chocolate. She thought maybe thee'd . . ." His eyes narrowed suddenly.

"Matthew Tomlinson," he said sourly. "Out for a walk—what on earth'd thee need that silly old carpetbag for?"

Matthew's sick smile froze on his face. His legs seemed to seize up like wet cement drying. Feeling suddenly every one of his seventy-three years, he stood staring at the man like a prize simpleton. No answer would form in his dread-dry mouth. He might have stayed that way forever, hair in his eyes and fossilized with foolishness, had not the Boy suddenly turned to him.

"Yeah," he said in a curious voice. "That's a good question, Matthew. What *are* you doing with that silly old bag?" Then his face broke into an eye-dancing grin of wicked delight as he answered himself. "Why, you suspicious old devil! Hefting that luggage with you all over the place! Don't you trust *anyone?*"

In that moment, if it weren't for the seemliness of things, Matthew might have cheerfully strangled him.

8

Back at Suseshi, the political temperature gradually subsided; the houseboys came cringing back, as pitifully aware of their own odious odor as mangy dogs come in from the rain, and several patients who had fled in panic during the arson reappeared at the hospital, climbing back into bed as if nothing had happened. The schools were reopened and their outlying local and monthly meetings began to pick up.

But Susehi's midyear quarterly gathering was a decidely wet affair. The Townsends, having made little religious headway on Mulaisho's stony home ground, joined them with a small tentative team of probational attenders, but this hardly made up for their own missing members. Since the April arson, their meetings had never quite regained their former strength. But while other missionaries blamed nationalist intimidation, Matthew got wind that many of their former Friends were becoming voluntarily involved in politics. Even their respected black teachers (the needed intelligentsia for the Brave New Adventure) were having their heads turned, for the UNIP leaders detained at Kabompo had spread an infectious political and ethnic awareness. In guilty defiance, they now allowed political alignment to replace religious fervor, forced by the disapproval of the missionaries to make an exclusive choice when there need be none. In Matthew's view, the only way to combat this steady erosion of their membership was to begin living up to the neutrality they ostensibly stood for. And here they might do real good, by inspiring in politically active members a Christian conscience, which might serve to dampen the violent overtures of more militant party fellows.

But Matthew might as well talk to the walls as effectively convey this view to his colleagues. For, deprived of their beloved meeting house, they had become emotionally incensed at the radical UNIP, whose nationwide campaign had promoted its destruction. By comparison, their stern regard for the older and more moderate Congress Party had softened considerably, but even this mellowing was a far cry from neutrality. But there was no telling *them* that. When the school hall proved too small to house even the drastically reduced quarterly crowd, they were doubly disgruntled. Convened in the open, around the Nantucket-bell-bearing thorn tree, the meeting's congregation had neither the necessary numbers nor the mental frame to inspire proper survival in the outdoors. The people fidgeted continually and their ministering words seemed lost to the air. In time, the tedious meeting began to take on a disturbing political tone, and Matthew sensed a sharp swing to nationalistic feeling among their members. Now there were no more complaints of intimidation, and indeed it seemed to him that even their more devout members seemed less concerned about religious duties than racial discrimination, social inequalities and, more especially, the recent banning of UNIP on the Copperbelt.

The government order had come following a period of violence, when the stoning of cars on the important Copperbelt arteries culminated in the killing of Lilian Burton, a young white woman, on the Ndola road. Stopped in her car by a band of incensed UNIP dissidents dispersing from a banned political meeting broken up by the police, the woman's children were injured and she was saturated with petrol and burned alive. Although she nobly forgave her killers with her last breath, others were less forgiving. As shock waves at the senseless, savage murder resounded throughout the Federation, infuriated white miners in Northern Rhodesia threatened to form vigilante groups to retaliate and protect their families. A special police strike force, the mobile unit, was formed to put down riots and twenty-eight more detention camps were being built. On the federal level, Welensky announced plans to strengthen the armed forces.

But at Suseshi, the majority of their quarterly members seemed far less incensed with the tragic crime than its outcome. And this apparent indifference of their "pacifist" African Friends aroused in Matthew a dull disbelief. Was the civilized facade that shallow, the underlying racial hatred that deep?

By the first of June, all the students for the advanced new medical course had arrived. On the day of its inception, while Than worked in surgery, Denise Smith led them around the outpatient department, lecturing while she worked. That afternoon, in the spacious classroom adjoining the hospital, Than faced the twelve earnest young African men who sat behind wooden desks, looking clean and uniform in royal blue shirts and shorts that Katherine had designed and ordered from the local Asian seamstress who made the schoolchildren's uniforms.

Than had decided to begin getting to know the students and their general intelligence by testing their knowledge of the human body. A chart illustrating the skeletal frame was pinned to the blackboard, and a model female pelvis and baby's head stood on the new demonstration table specially constructed by the mission carpenter. With these few aids to prompt them, Than asked each student in turn what he knew. As one after the other stood up and falteringly responded, he began to understand that most had acquired a sketchy knowledge of the human physiology by comparison with wild and domestic animals, which they had seen dissected since childhood. Using local names and vague descriptions, they told Than something of the respiratory, digestive, and circulatory organs. However, they

215

seemed to know little of the nervous system, the brain, and the spinal cord; they could not describe the function of any of the principal organs of the body and were unaware that the circulation of the blood caused the beating of the heart.

Finally, Than singled out a student to whom he transferred his stethoscope. "This is an instrument by which you may detect the heart's position through its beat," he explained. "You have told me that the heart lies within the chest. Now, listening through this device, I want you to tell the class of its exact location within your own chest."

"Yes, sir." Fitting the earpieces to his own ears, the awed youth unbuttoned his shirt and placed the bell of the stethoscope against his black skin. With a look of frowning concentration, he listened to a spot near his navel for several moments. Then, while the class waited in suspense, he moved it to one side and listened again. Again he seemed dissatisfied, and moved the bell up. When this spot seemed equally unrewarding, he moved it down again. A look of increasing puzzlement and unease was beginning to furrow his features. and finally, after several more futile tries, he looked up, ashen-faced and aghast.

"Doctor, sir!" he blurted in distress. "It is not there! *I have no heart!*"

In the shocked silence, Than stared at the youth in awe; this, then, was to be the level of their launching . . .

9

On June 30, the neighboring Belgian Congo went to her independence. At the inaugural ceremony to celebrate this summary transfer of power, King Badouin of Belgium ended his eulogy with the words: *"May God help the Congo."*

In light of what had latterly transpired, his words took on the tone of a fearful plea rather than of a blessing. For unlike the more progressive British, who encouraged the increasing political participation of her colonies' inhabitants, Belgium, governing from afar with an old-fashioned paternalism that deigned the "child" seen and not heard, had suspended the political participation of both blacks and whites within the Congo. All local power was invested instead in the gigantic mining and industrial concerns that conducted its thriving economy. Consequently, the Congo was awarded "freedom" with an African parliament that had never sat and black leaders without ministerial or political experience. Patrice Lumumba, its first premier, shccked the world with his inaugural exhortation, calling on his compatriots to: ". . . *remember the blows we had to submit to because we were black!*"

On such sufferance was an untried and long-enchained nation let suddenly loose. And bred on ignorance and ignominy, long starved of any autonomy, it rounded upon its former feeder like a ravenous dog. Within days, the gendarmerie formations of the formerly well disciplined Force Publique mutinied against its Belgian officers. Whipped up by the pre-independence incitements of aspiring politicians, they took the initiative and began rampaging through the towns and cities, routing whites, looting, raping, and killing as they went, the main criterion for such unspeakable atrocities being their victim's tribe or color. It was evil, avenging racism as the whites had never known it or shown it . . .

Although they were shocked at this outcome, the missionaries had had some warning of what was to come. Friends from the Congo Gospel Mission wrote worried letters, and the district commissioner at Mwinilunga had deployed district messengers in plain clothes across the Congo border; these had sent back disturbing reports of the readying lawlessness and license. For, freed at last from the old European administrational restraints, old long-suppressed prejudices had come to the fore. Serious tribal fighting had broken out in border towns, and watching helplessly while all semblance of civilized order began rapidly disintegrating around them, large numbers of whites had packed up their possessions and were poised for flight.

Then, six weeks later, on a public holiday, some four thousand white refugees poured over the border in bush-battered, blue-number-plated big American cars, descending on Mwinilunga in desperate need of food, water, fuel, and medical attention.

Shivering in his mangy old deerskin jacket in the winter cold, Matthew took his place beside his wife at the head of the long laid table, in the light of the two hurricane lanterns that hung from the *chitenje's* eaves. At seven o'clock it was already deeply dark, and gathered for supper, most of the missionaries sat straining to hear the evening news through a crackling transistor radio. And though it would no doubt unsettle his stomach, Matthew steeled himself to listen as well, nodding at Than Profane, who materialized out of the night darkness. And chilly winter had chastised the Boy as disapproving missionary eyes never could; he had stopped dropping his white jacket off at the laundry before supper and wore it now, shivering, at the table. His tanned arms were stippled with goosebumps and his breath condensed in steamy gusts as he sat listening to the grim newscast with distant blue eyes that were filled with sadness and anger. And he was not alone in his feelings.

The Congo Republic's post-independent disintegration had drenched the entire Federation in a reflective pall or morbid dread. In a matter of a dozen days, all essential services had collapsed and the ineffectual Central Congolese government was faced with the mutiny of its troops and the declared secession of the copper-rich Katanga province, whose provincial president, the principled and intelligent M. Moise Tshombe, struggled to restore order in a sea of carnage and chaos. While a caring white community and the concerned federal government (hamstrung by international protocol) looked on in helpless horror, the whole apparatus of order was collapsing across the border, the veneer-thin fabric of imposed civilized standards ripped asunder as tribe rose against tribe and the mutineering Congolese soldiers, joined by civilian thugs, systematically singled out whites, tracking down missionaries and the settler Belgians, who fled in terror and trepidation across the Congo River into Brazzaville, and from there, over the border into Northern Rhodesia. All American missionaries were ordered to evacuate, but although not all chose to, scores of other white civilians did, and refugees in the thousands continued to pour across the border to reach safety. The road from Mwinilunga was clogged with cars, and the missionaries, aiding the refugees with food, fuel, water, and medical care, heard their horrific reports of unspeakable atrocities, which surely grew worse and more numerous with each dread day slowly passing. Matthew was grateful when the newsreader's deadpan dialogue finally ended, just as the cookboy and his assistant staggered into the *chitenje* bearing their food-laden trays. But he could not forget those forsaken souls suffering untold tortures just miles away across the dark bush. Under Teller's mothering eye, he dutifully filled a plate he knew he'd scarcely touch; as usual, he and Teller came jointly to Jenny's aid, dishing up a piled plate despite her plea of lack of appetite. Matthew described the fare and its location in a clockwise sequence, while all down the long table the sense of shock was finally thawing to a bristling indignation.

"Well, I don't know!" Ward Disney muttered on a mouthful of food. "Those dadblamed fool Belgians handing that country over to an untrained bunch of ignoramuses! Why, that's tantamount to giving Cadillac keys to a two-year-old tyrant!" He looked up disparagingly.

"Well, don't look at Matthew," the snide Clara Fotch sniffed disdainfully. "He's the one always advocating we encourage our own African Friends to join the nationalists of this country in their quest for the very same!"

"Oh now, Clara—that's unfair!" Matthew looked hurt. "I have merely urged that our Friends go with the times!"

"That's just precisely it, Matthew Tomlinson," Hannah Rothchild interjected, tossing a haughty bunned head. "*The times! The times* in Africa has come to mean unruly premature rule—with the killing of innocent white missionaries and settlers, the very people who brought them Christianity and the prosperity they now flaunt! Why those UNIP officials here are promising the people the very same as did they those . . . *inhuman animals* over in the Congo—the white man's women and possessions! So what does thee suppose would happen to we poor lambs if *all* the natives were to heed their wishes and join the pressure for black rule?" Her words fell to an accusing silence, and Matthew spluttered to correct her.

"Oh now, Hannah! Thee has it all wrong! I am no more in favor of premature independence than any right-thinking person would be! But at this very time, resentful radicals are pushing for power, and if any are to rule—albeit prematurely—then let them be responsible men of God and not as much as . . . as that *paranoic Communist pawn*, that Patrice Lumumba of the Congo!"

It was enough said; Matthew continued eating in wounded silence while the ladies, having no answer for this, changed conversational course, lapsing into their usual morbid dissection of the atrocities committed upon their counterparts in the Congo. They had kept newspaper clippings to send home to frighten friends, and now they vied to horrify each other with tales of the tortures of gentle nuns and the Christian missionaries who least deserved it, citing their "despicable desecration" (as the unspeakable act of rape was indirectly referred to), dwelling so graphically upon the gory details of dismembered bodies that Than Profane, glancing at his sister's aghast face, had to tell them to stop. He was angry; it was common knowledge, after all, that the young girls had begun having nightmares on such sadistic stories. Yet Matthew could hardly blame the ladies for their perverse preoccupation; he endlessly evaluated the same incredible horrors himself. It was a compulsive reiteration motivated by a natural fear. They shared a common frontier with the Congo, after all. The economy of the adjacent Katanga province was complementary to Northern Rhodesia's; both straddled the mineral-infested Great Katanga Arc; for the production of its copper, Katanga bought Northern Rhodesia's coal and coke; it used her railways for export. The two countries were divided only by geographic boundaries that followed no logical course, taking no account of the tribal dynasties, kindred clans, and even family groups divided in its wake.

Indeed, Katanga was the ancestral home ground of the Lunda tribe, whose people comprised the main beneficiaries of the Friends' Mission in this part of Northern Rhodesia; Katanga's President Tshombe was himself a Ka-Lunda who had married into the Lunda house of chiefs. And goodness knows, the natives of Northern Rhodesia were no less aggressively eager to be given their pledged autonomy than had been their kindred Congolese. Indeed, on his return from a fund-raising overseas tour, Kenneth Kaunda, the leader of UNIP, was greeted by the uncompromising roar of a crowd of thousands: "INDEPENDENCE BY OCTOBER—NO CHANGE!" UNIP militants, antagonized by bannings and incited on by the rapid developments in the neighboring Congo, had whipped up the people with an infectious fervor. And while they screamed and ululated, the whites apprehensively waited, their worst fears reflected in the plight of the thousands of Belgian refugees who poured over the border in their big bullet-riddled cars, making an endless convoy on the Copperbelt roads, families who had narrowly escaped death or even lost some of their members in coming. Haggard, unshaven, and hurriedly dressed, many had brought household pets and come with little more than what they stood up in.

But they were comforted and kindly received at the isolated bush stations and beyond, in the little Copperbelt towns, where the white expatriates, known for their friendliness, magnanimously heeded the call for temporary accommodation. They opened their hearts and their homes, for they had long lived under the same threat themselves. Their own massive black population, outnumbering them by many hundreds of thousands, and at present fired by nationalism and the false promises of its perpetrators, was ripe for the same revolution. There was a sobering similarity, and the settlers and missionaries alike looked at the Belgain refugees and those Christian workers killed and defiled and saw in horror:

There, but for the grace of God, go I. . . .

10

Matthew was as surprised as everyone else when, at their next meeting for business, Ezra Peabody suddenly stood up and began berating them all for not yet rebuilding their meeting house.

"It has come to my notice," he said testily, glancing pointedly at Matthew, "that a sum of money eminently suitable for such a project will be shortly at hand. It only remains for the Lord to influence the hardened hearts of those responsible for dictating the use of this mission's funds!"

He sat down directly, leaving the stunned members with incredulous eyes, innocently asking: *What money?* After a moment's dull deliberation, it suddenly occurred to Matthew that the sum he referred to could be none other than their forthcoming annual grant from Medico Enterprises, which was finally pledged to purchase the hospital's long-awaited X-ray machine. He had no doubt that Ezra Peabody and the Fotches had connived to infect the meeting members with this seditious incitement. And this time they had really stirred up certain trouble, for Than Profane was dead set upon obtaining the X-ray unit, and while it might be just possible to reiterate the importance of the machine upon the other missionaries, convincing their hundreds of African members why a new house of worship was not their most cardinal commitment would be entirely another matter.

A staff committee meeting of the Friends' Africa Mission was summarily gathered to discuss the matter at the Fotches' house that very night. Matthew, feeling as if the sky were about to fall, and nursing influenza to boot (a scratchy throat, hammering head, and achy joints), arrived to an atmosphere that smoldered and snapped like a brewing storm. Prissily house-proud, Clara Fotch scurried around, placing seats, hanging antimacassars on the backs of her worn chairs, and settling coasters on the little side tables. Her long dust-dulled maroon velvet curtains, usually so gloomy by day, looked almost cheery in the sallow lamplight, and her cluttered living room was lively with almost every white face known to Matthew. The two spinsters smugly smiled, and the Fotches posed superior. But others looked worried and strained, and as the government inspectors had arrived today to evaluate the new advanced medical course and the informal training of their hospital staff pending formal recognition, Than Profane had not yet arrived. Matthew had no idea how this meeting might end, and wanting the worst to be over and done as soon as possible, he settled immediately down into meditative silence, earnestly praying that the Lord might deliver them all from bigotry and blunder.

Ward Disney, in his capacity as chairman, slapped at a mosquito and called for the reading of the last meeting's minutes, and Katherine, as assistant secretary, read them aloud. When these were approved as accurate, Clara Fotch immediately stood up to reiterate their need for a new meeting house. She spoke of a sum of money that had been "discovered," as if their annual grant from Medico Enterprises was something shocking that Matthew had kept secret.

Matthew flushed angrily. "Now see here, Clara. Thee were told the truth inasmuch, as this year's grant, being pledged to the purchase of a radiology unit for the hospital, is not open to being tampered with."

"Indeed?" Clara countered. "But that pledge was made before the destruction of our house of worship, which completely alters the situation! I propose the money be used to rebuild the meeting house!"

She broke off as the living room door opened and Than Profane entered. Coming straight from the hospital in his white jacket, he apologized that he had been held up by the medical inspectors. Well, nobody could deny that he was hard pressed for time. Even when he did not have inspectors to show around, in between his hospital work he was sandwiching lectures to his students and trying to start up and service his hopeful little out-clinics with the help of the local people. And he had operated again on the woman from Mulaisho's village; according to Jerome, the delicate vesicovaginal repair, of such importance to the spiritual salvation of Mulaisho's people, might have to be repeated many times before the wound properly healed, if at all. Meanwhile, it was another pressing problem that helped distract the Boy from the anguish of a wayward, worldly wife who had deserted him these many months past without word or sign of returning. But if the work and worry of weeks showed in the young doctor's tired face, he got little sympathy from some committee members, who eyed the bloodstains on his jeans with sneering distaste. He sat down on a little dark-wood carved elephant table, the trunk curving up between his thighs like some monstrous phallus. As he stubbed his cigarette on the heel of his boot, Matthew spoke up hurriedly:

"Dr. Profane, it has been proposed that the annual Medico grant, already pledged to the purchase of an X-ray machine, be used instead to rebuild the meeting house. Would thee care to comment?"

"Sure. I totally oppose such a proposal inasmuch as the X-ray machine is a sorely needed commodity that could mean the saving of lives and limbs," the Boy said gravely.

"I agree." Matthew nodded. "I feel . . ."

As he paused to measure their faces, Hannah Rothchild suddenly leaped to her feet, struck a dramatic pose, and with eyes cast fervently heavenward, piously prayed aloud: "Dear Lord, protect us now from the diabolical diversions we are about to hear from the mouth of our misguided Friend!"

Matthew, outraged, opened his mouth to protest and promptly exploded into a fit of coughing, which perfectly suited the woman's purpose.

"Thank Thee, Lord," she righteously declared, "but go easy on him. He means well."

As he convulsed in the fit, Matthew's glasses were knocked askew and papers went flying. A meaningful look from Clara sent Cherish Sinclair scurrying for a glass of water. Straightening his spectacles, Matthew took it gratefully, gulping it down. He subsided, patted a handkerchief to his sweat-beaded brow, and hastily collected his strewn papers. Still irked at Hannah, he nodded with exaggerated dignity. "As I was saying before being so *hysterically* interrupted by Friend Hannah—there can be no question of using the Medico grant for the meeting house since it has already been pledged."

"Oh come, come, Friend." Ezra Peabody chuckled with such gentle amusement that Matthew felt a prize fool. "Me thinks thee're too tied by a misguided sense of duty. Oh, a pledge is a pledge to be sure. But loyalty to the Lord surely cancels out all others. It saddens me to think that any might deny this."

"No, no . . ." Matthew managed fretfully. "Do not misunderstand me, Friend. There is no cause dearer to my heart than that of the meeting house!"

"Well, I am relieved to hear thee will then raise no objection to its rebuilding," Ezra purposely misunderstood him. "It is clear to me there are two choices before us. The need to properly glorify the Lord—and the desire to furnish the hospital with an outrageously expensive little gadget, which, I feel, has been proved unnecessary by long survival without it. Oh, I grant that in its absence there's a little more head scratching to be done, a little more palpating, as the doctors call it. But I most gravely doubt that any good done by such a machine could ever exceed that of housing the people that they might fittingly receive the Lord's instruction and thereby inherit eternal life! However, if there are any here who agree with Dr. Profane that a mere mechanical aid is more important than the Lord, let him now speak. . . ."

Put like that, his pompous, pitying words degenerated the committee meeting into a witch hunt. Now, any who might speak in favor of the X-ray would be summarily branded *Judas!*—a stigma that would surely follow them all the days of their service. Matthew waited anxiously for some word at least from the hospital staff, but as the minutes ticked on, it became increasingly clear to him that Dr. Dooley and the nurses were, like most of them, shamed speechless, inhibited by Ezra's awesome influence and, even more ominously, by the One Most Paramount. Thus, they must all be mentally passing the buck, tensely waiting for someone with reckless courage enough to second Dr. Profane's objection, thereby futilely risking the wrath of the Lord and the displeasure of the meeting.

The last-minute reprieving bid was sadly ineffectual when it finally came. For the speaker was Jennifer Solomon, and other than shaming others with her courage, she achieved little in this lonely allegiance. For although she spoke fluent Chi-Lwena and had become a "language-tested" committee member, she was a self-conscious, only sporadic user of the traditional Quaker plain speech that gave devout distinction to their meeting, remaining for some a suspect Quaker, artificially spawned, who, while formally accepted in the Friends' fold, seemed yet a dubious Free-Churcher, whose eerie psychic sensibility and teaching of Eastern yoga postures to help exercise her blind students, seemed to them to signify an eccentric acceptance of the occult that was totally disqualifying.

11 But Than Profane surprised them all. The government inspectors had granted a formal recognition of his advanced medical course and agreed to appropriately upgrade the status of their informally trained black hospital staff. And the hospital would have its radiology unit. It transpired that the Boy was arranging to have his own money transferred from the States to the little bush bank in Solwezi, and it was his avowed intention to see the X-ray bought

and installed before the year was out. Although undeniably thrilled by the gesture, Matthew was nevertheless ashamed and embarrassed that the Boy had been so unfairly provoked to such action. He suspected that a donation on this scale would leave the young man with little to start the new life he spoke of realizing when he left the mission. However, the hospital staff had no such reservations. They were jubilant. But knowing of the resentment this generosity would cause among the Boy's antagonists, Matthew did not make much of it. And if they heard of it at all, Ezra Peabody, the Fotches, and the maiden ladies did not speak of it.

By this time the missionaries were plunged into the controversial business of planning the new meeting house, and in their fevered preoccupation, the rude realities of the Congo terrors finally began to fade. Their relief grew when they received word that all their Congo colleagues had thus far come through the troubles unscathed; those deployed in the worst hit Kasai had fled to their station in the more stable Katanga province, to wait out the worst of the fighting. The news was an immense consolation to them all, and the ladies, anxious to believe that all would be well, were further comforted by the fact that the United Nations was sending in increasing numbers of troops and civilians to control the anarchy. But Matthew, more politically astute, was less easily assured. For the world body had sent in its "peace-keeping" patrols at the request of the blatantly Communist Patrice Lumumba of the Central Congo government, whose very adherents were committing the worst atrocities, incited by inflammatory broadcasts inspired by Lumumba himself. Thus, with the various contingents of foreign troops of no certain loyalties entering the country under such dubious direction, it was not hard to imagine the kind of chaos that might ensue. As things stood, there was very little sign of the troubles abating. Lumumba-loyal Congolese soldiers were on the rampage, while elsewhere old tribal rivalries, smothered by years of imposed civilized standards, had begun to resurface in cruel competitions for dominance, so that wide areas of the country seethed with myriad wars within wars.

By contrast, with the aid of Belgian and local forces, the competent Moise Tshombe had succeeded in restoring order in Katanga. As a result, more and more Europeans were returning to the province, copper production was back to normal, and the disrupted trade was beginning to refunction. Yet although Tshombe and the government of the neighboring Federation urged Britain's recognition of the pro-Western Katanga secession to strengthen its position lest the pro-Communist Central Congo government call in United Nations troops to challenge the unilateral independence, the British government, not wishing to antagonize world opinion or to encourage the break-up of the Congo, vainly temporized.

And in Northern Rhodesia, it seemed no more sure of its actions. With the specter of October and all that it stood for to the nationalists looming up, the African pressure for action suddenly began to crack the stony facade of British stated policy. Just weeks after the new governor of Northern Rhodesia had stressed that no constitutional changes were planned, the British colonial secretary announced that a conference to consider such changes would be held in December, concurrent with the Federal Review Conference. The nation was amazed, the Federal government enraged. A new constitution just granted to Nyasaland guaranteed an African majority. Now this new proposal for Northern Rhodesia reduced the Federal Review Conference to a battle for survival. And, temporarily appeased, the clamoring demands of the black nationalists for immediate self-government fell suddenly silent, compromised at the eleventh hour. Yet even so, uneasy Europeans awaited developments with a wary apprehension. For the silent echo of the incited crowds still lingered in the air. *Independence by October . . .*

With the promise of a new constitution, this coveted ideal, although positively denied for the immediate future, had become a distinct feasibility for the year to come . . .

Than Profane's continuing operations on the woman from Mulaisho's village had thus far been only partially successful. Matthew knew that the poor woman's uncomplaining fortitude would keep the Boy trying, but it might be months before he had real results to reveal to Mulaisho. In the meanwhile, he was kept increasingly busy with his out-clinics and the new medical course, which, after some initial problems, was going well. Matthew helped where he could, advising the Boy on the ambiguous African mind, and printing out curricular material. Taking a pile of such printed text over to the Profane house one evening, he found the Boy busy marking a pile of his students' test papers on the living room table. Katherine and Jayne sat beside him, engrossed in their needlepoint and English essay, and Matthew set down his pile of papers and leaned hopefully across to the Boy.

"How are thy charges coming along?"

The Boy winced. "See for yourself."

He handed a wad of the test papers across, and Matthew settled onto the kaffir couch to read them. Some were penned in impeccable handwriting, but the answers revealed the students' ineptitude with English and lack of sophistication in a few howlers, which made Matthew's moustache wuffle.

For snake bite, one wrote, *bleed the wound then rape the patient warmly for shock.* Another asserted: *For fainting, rub the person's chest. If it is a woman, rub between the chests.* Still another advised: *For fractures, to see if the limb is broken, wiggle back and forth and listen for the noise.*

Matthew was so engrossed in their quaint originality that he jumped with fright when Jasper, the bush baby, suddenly launched from a curtain rail and sailed through the air at him. He hastily set the papers aside as the saucer-eyed appealing little gray imp settled matter-of-factly upon his lap, stretching out on its furry back, arms raised above its head as it waited to be scratched. While his pounding heart subsided, Matthew stifled his fastidiousness and stiffly obliged. Then, at a sudden noise from the top of the stairs, the little creature sprang to its feet, hackles rising and chattering excitedly. Matthew looked up to see the young leopard come bounding down the stairs, dragging in its mouth the chewed-up old leather jacket of the Boy's upon which she had cut her canines. Near the bottom she stepped on a trailing leather arm, tripped and tumbled head over heels down the last few steps, landing at the bottom in a yowling mass of spotted fur. When the company laughed spontaneously, the young leopard gathered herself and rounded upon them, spitting fiercely in a defensive show of wounded pride. A suspicious swirl of feathers sailed down the stairs in her wake and Katherine rose from her chair.

"Oh no! Did we leave that demolition squad upstairs by herself?"

"My stuffed rabbit!" Jayne wailed, jumping up. She and her mother collided at the stairway; they scurried up the stairs together. From their ensuing cries, Matthew guessed that the leopard had wholesomely enjoyed itself. The Boy winced. And Matthew shifted uncomfortably. For he had his own problems. Bathsheba had come up to challenge the bush baby and the small creature took off from Matthew's lap in one frantic bound; chattering cheekily, it hung swaying from the curtain rail, and the leopard, left with Matthew, sniffed him instead. No doubt disliking what it sensed, the animal, all of three feet tall at the head now, flattened its ears and stood inches away, hissing at him threateningly.

227

"Nice cat," Matthew simpered sickly, not daring to stretch out a stroking hand. "Nice kitty, *please!*"

But he sat alone in a crowd. The Boy had gone back to his marking at the table where Katherine and Jayne were engrossed in their occupations again. The cat might silently shred him to pieces, but who would notice?

12

Just when Matthew had begun to hope that order might be restored in the Congo in time for them to stage the yearly meeting in Katanga as planned, the unilateral secession of South Kasai province set off rumors of a new war waging, and Matthew, full of fears for the safety of Dr. MacLintock, who had returned alone to his station there, went to Mwinilunga boma to contact their Katanga mission by radio. After wasting half the morning waiting for radio time, he finally contacted Chester Daniels, the young schoolteacher at Lusinga, who was surprisingly optimistic. According to messages regularly received, Dr. MacLintock was alive and well and working hard in his Kasai hospital. Their own province of Katanga, Chester assured Matthew, had been completely stabilized, and Friends in the area saw no reason to change the venue of the forthcoming yearly meeting.

Well, that may well be, but Matthew left the boma feeling uneasy with misgivings. At Suseshi, he met his clamoring colleagues with a fainthearted sigh.

"Poor folks! I guess we should have broached the subject of moving the yearly meeting when the troubles first started, but at the time it seemed a little cruel to be fretting about mundane matters while their very lives were at stake. Anyhow, seems like they're pretty determined to host it there now. Although Chester did beg off to delay it a while to give them time to pick up the pieces, so to speak. Well, it's just out of the question, of course; we have to be realistic. . . . I'll go across to the permanent board now. Maybe we can draft out a tactful letter." He sighed again, picking up his helmet. "It'll be a shame to disappoint them, though."

"Well, I should say so too!" Orville Fotch quailed. "Shame on thee, Matthew Tomlinson . . . after all their trouble to prepare for the meeting, thee're too scared to go out and join them. And since when does thee speak for yearly meeting?"

Matthew prevaricated. "Well, I have a duty to advise the permanent board; also, as senior elder and spokesman of the Friends' mission here, I have a responsibility for the safety of thee all, and according to the newspapers, just next door to Katanga, South Kasai is headed for big trouble; apparently Lumumba is readying to overthrow the secession. All in all, I'd say it'd be blatantly unwise for us to go over there and stand in trouble's way. It's the ladies I'm most afraid for."

"Well, speak for thyself," Clara said haughtily. "Those poor folks will have made months of preparations! The Congolese Friends will doubtless regard it as desertion on our part. Perhaps *thee* would so disappoint them, but not all of us so miserably doubt the Lord's ability to protect our witness!"

Matthew swallowed. He wanted to point out that the good Lord had apparently not seen fit to so insulate those misfortunate missionaries so recently butchered and defiled, but it seemed in bad taste. Also, he was completely disarmed by the Fotches' uncustomary fervor over the issue; Clara was not naturally given to indisposing risks that reaped no financial rewards, and as for Orville, he was a pettishly timid man who normally shied from mice and moths, let alone savage civil war! Well, if even these two chary crusaders felt such clear faith in facing those distant terrors, he must be getting overanxious and old. Thus, feeling shamed and shown up for a faithless laggard, all it needed was Katherine Profane's gentle persuasion to make him waver in doubt of his own judgment. She took his arm, solacing him with a sweet smile.

"Matthew dear, I understand thy concern for us, but I feel we should respect the wishes of our Congo Friends. Surely the Lord has spoken His Will through them? Our visit would only be for a few days; think how it would strengthen their faith to know that we are willing to share, even momentarily, the perils with which they have lived day by day these past months."

"She's right, honey lamb." Teller took his other arm. "A big rousing rally might be just what those poor folks need right now to wipe away all the horror of these past months."

"Hear, hear!" Hannah Rothchild joined in the bombardment.

"All right, all right," Matthew muttered fretfully, mopping his brow. "We'll see . . ."

It was not until it was much too late to change the venue that Matthew realized the true reason for the Fotches' outspoken courage. Then it struck him like a thunderbolt. Of course! They did not expect to be present at this year's yearly meeting, wherever it was held. By the time it was convened, they should be safely on their six-month furlough back home in the States. But not before having misled their colleagues into dangerous pastures, like lambs to the slaughter. . . .

The building committee, comprising most of the missionaries and several of the yearly meeting's field staff, set to the formidable task of planning the new meeting house. Since the building would have to be completed before the rains began, there could be no time lost; their natural materials must be prepared and the necessary processed items ordered from the Copperbelt. The committed poured nightly over Ezra's tentative blueprints, working out specifications, arguing, and airing ideas. Then the district commissioner was consulted, requisitions were sent off, and things began to happen. To Matthew and Ward fell the task of recruiting and supervising the labor. At this time of the year, many of the African men were busy burning felled trees and fertilizing their fields with the ashes, searing the hot bush with the acrid smoke of hundreds of fires, but with the prevailing poverty there was no lack of willing workers, and from early each morning they were besieged with hopeful local tradesmen. The project was also incorporated as a practical part of the trade school's brick-laying course, and initially they employed two teams of hourly-paid soil diggers, sand carriers, water bearers, and mud paddlers, who were set to work in the brick field behind the trade-school campus. Here the sandpit was surrounded by a whole range of clay anthills. Some of these tree-covered minor mountains were upward of twenty feet high and forty feet wide, the incredible architecture of a species of ant now reputedly extinct.

Well, Matthew reflected, at least the extra labor distracted them all a little from politics, although there was no getting away from that entirely. Through the nightly broadcasts from Radio Elizabethville, they heard with horror of the fall of the unilaterally seceeded South Kasai. Menacingly advancing in Russian-supplied Zim trucks and Ilushyin transport aircraft, the Congolese army had engaged in a systematic slaughter. As reports of thousands of dead and wounded filtered through the bush, Lumumba's excesses proved finally too much. On September 5, State President Kasavubu, using powers invested in him, dismissed Lumumba from office on the grounds that Lumumba had governed arbitrarily and engaged the country in civil war.

At Suseshi, the news came as an immense relief to the missionaries, who had followed the "unleashed lunatic's" monstrous career with helpless horror.

And now here in Northern Rhodesia the whole country was amutter with news of a new law that made it mandatory for European proprietors to admit Africans into their business premises (previously a privileged domain where blacks could only be served through hatches segregated from white entrances). The removal of this social color bar had been a totally unexpected major concession toward the "multiracialism" that was ostensibly Welensky's ultimate ideal. Coming in the wake of massive African boycotts of European-owned businesses, it was seen by the whites as an act of appeasement, and outraged proprietors put up their prices when jubilant blacks flocked to cafés and cinemas to sample the hitherto forbidden delights.

Although the missionaries were scarcely affected out in the rural areas, they heard a little about the chaos this new license was creating in the towns, when D. C. Horn stopped by to inspect their amended building plans. He stayed for lunch and told a few tales about how urban blacks, with uncouthness, filth, and disreputable dress, were infuriating restauranteurs by crowding up dining tables to buy Coca-Colas and stale three-penny buns. The way the D.C. heard it, the men smoked cigarette stubs left in ashtrays, snotty-nosed children licked out the tomato-sauce lids, and women bared their breasts to suckle soiled babies.

Matthew stopped sipping his soup right there! He winced squeamishly at the classic tale of a native woman who dipped her elongated breast into the sugar bowl before passing it across her shoulder to her suckling child . . .

"It's a sad thing." Matthew grimaced, discreetly setting aside his spoon. "I guess they still have a long way to go. They're still mighty raw around the edges." He took his fob watch from his trouser pocket. "Well, thee'll have to excuse me, Mr. Horn. Guess I'd best be getting along. I'm afraid the kindly elves won't build the meeting house if'n I don't keep those work-shy scallywags with their backs to the wheel. Why, the minute my back is turned . . ."

He hurried away, horrified at the very thought. Setting these natives to work was one thing; keeping them at it, entirely another.

But gradually, miraculously, amid sweat and frayed tempers, work was seen to be done, and double lines of bricks began to grow along the ground in front of the brick makers. Matthew shared much of the load with Ward, and it was a thankless task. The Fotches, dogmatically recording their jealous opinions before reluctantly leaving the meeting house's construction to lesser mortals, had gone off to America on furlough. But followed around by the carping criticisms of other inactive colleagues, Matthew was grateful to hear Than Profane had finally received news from his father-in-law that the American self-help program (A.I.D.) had approved his application for financial aid for his bush clinics. The clinics would have to be built by local voluntary labor, and since another of the conditions stipulated that they be completed in good time, the Boy's need of a fluent and knowledgeable guide to help him go out and begin establishing his out-clinics in Barotseland lent Matthew a graced excuse to escape for a while . . .

By now Than Profane had built seven clinics and obtained the franchise to set up several more. Now, with the financial aid finally secured him, he was anxious to scout out still more in Barotseland to realize his dream of extending a chain of such isolated infirmaries in a vast circle to and from their new clinic at Shonona. Thus, one hot October day, he and Matthew crossed into the little protectorate, taking with them Cosmo and Peter Disney, who was convalescing from chicken pox (enlivened with a lingering itch and a budding evangelism), with Bathsheba traveling in the canvas hammock of the cab roof.

Out on the sun-baked, drought-dry central plain, the red-breasted cuckoo called sadly, and goliath herons, yellow-billed storks, marabous, and pelicans congregated to make easy pickings of the writhing whiskered catfish caught in the dwindling mud puddles and shrinking oxbow lakes. They skirted straggling *mukusi* bush and great forests of *mutemwa* thicket and Rhodesian teak, and finally, after midday, arrived at a little native village beside the Musheketi swamp. Most of the able-bodied men had migrated north and south to work in the mines, but a few gangly youths, eyeing the hissing leopard nervously, climbed aboard the mission's barrel-buoyant little log ferry and helped the missionary men pull the Land-Rover across the sluggish swamp to Mambundi Mission on the opposite shore. Nudging an erratic path through a multicolored mosaic of wild water lillies and algae-dripping floating green islands of Nile cabbage and sedge, they hauled on the twin steel ropes with their bare hands, disturbing a wading flock of spur wing geese, which took off, whistling on wing. As they heaved and strained, gliding herkily across, Mambundi loomed up in the heat-hazed everglades: a long line of bungalows, looking Victorianly vaudeville on long-legged stilts.

Loreley Haskel and some little black boys were sitting on the wide wooden reception jetty.

"Hidy, Uncle Matthew." The grubby, childishly dressed seventeen-year-old girl jumped up and waited as Peter Disney drove the Land-Rover onto the jetty, across the bumpy poles, and onto level ground. When he had parked the vehicle in a dilapidated spider-web-shrouded arbor opposite the jetty, Matthew hauled out his old carpetbag and Than Profane coaxed the young leopard off the cab roof.

"Dr. Profane, thee's like Mary hadalittlelamb, tagging that tiger with thee ever'where thee goes," Loreley chastised, squinting at them from the jetty with a screwed-up frown.

Tiger? Matthew's educative instincts shrieked. He walked slowly up to the girl. "Why, Loreley-Salome! That's not a tiger. That's a . . ."

"Oh, it is too!" She stamped a small bare foot. "Thee can't fool me! Lookit he's spots!"

Who could argue with such native naïveté? The child had been known to throw up over lesser issues. Matthew gave a tiny tight how-could-I-be-so-stupid smile and turned to go.

"Hey, wait up a minute there!"

They turned and she was standing astride, motionlessly poised and staring down, her feet placed apart over a crack between the jetty planks. At first Matthew was puzzled; then he heard a faraway watery trickle. The piccanins began to furtively snigger and he stood sick with his shame.

Loreley-Salome looked up proudly. "See that? I piddled myself right in that crack. A little more practice and I'll be able to do it through the eye of a needle." She scooped her skirt under her crotch and wiped herself matter-of-factly. Matthew and the Boy looked at each other; Peter turned away, blushing furiously.

"Why, Loreley-Salome!" Matthew managed. "That's disgraceful! Thee should be ash . . ."

"Aw, Matthew, save your breath," the Boy said wearily. "You might as well remonstrate with a brick wall."

And he was right, for all the good it would do.

"Poor child," Matthew murmured. Then, with more feeling: "Poor Homer!"

But for all her shortcomings, the child seemed happy. She skipped along behind them, giggling and humming, her erratic attention catching randomly, like some long lagging tail, on small irrelevant things as they passed.

Homer was delighted to see them; he suggested the use of their primitive thatched meeting house for a temporary clinic here and promised a guide to take them out onto the plain to introduce them to influential headmen with a view to setting up more remote clinics the first thing in the morning. His wife, Edith, was less accommodating.

"When they told me some crazy men came up with a leopard, I might a known it was thee." She eyed them narrowly. "Now, Tom," (she meant the Boy), "just thee leave that overgrown tabby in the old henhouse. I've heard how he beds with thee, and I'll have none of that shenanigans in my house."

The Boy spent an industrious afternoon conducting an impromptu clinic. Then that night, after supping on a succulent stuffed spur wing goose shot by a local villager, Homer took out an old fiddle and played some stirring country music, much to the delight of the servants, who had stayed for the evening Bible-study hour. Matthew, cheered with a little homemade sweet cider, enjoyed it immensely. Then Edith surprised him completely by swinging into a jaunty square dance with Elliot Moke. They made a ludicrous spectacle. He lanky and loose as a sack of potatoes, and that big bulldog-jawed woman stomping around on flat heavy feet. Matthew was glad when it was over. It was a gaiety he couldn't quite believe in, somehow, that wooden pole of a man coming disjointedly to lilting life and the dour dismal woman suddenly switched on to a light-hearted lurching. Loreley-Salome sat looking scrubbed and spruced, her long blond ringlets done up in lilac satin ribbons. Sleepy-mouthed and sullenly watching, she dipped a finger into her sweet cider and sucked on it thoughtfully.

At ten o'clock the thudding racket of the generator cut out, and Matthew and his two companions used candles to guide them to a room off the long veranda that Edith had allotted them. They had just blown out the candles and settled into their beds when there was a scattering of stones against the window pane. After a moment, Matthew saw the Boy's naked silhouette at the window as he peered into the moonlit night.

"*Jesus!*" he whispered. "It's Loreley Haskel out there. She's cavorting with a veil across her face. Maybe that little Salome's enacting the biblical tableau in King Herod's court. She's doing a seductive dance."

"Why, that foolish child," Matthew clucked indignantly. "She can't do that. What'll thee do?"

"Do?" The Boy chuckled. "Well, I sure won't hand her the Baptist's head on a platter." Then he strained forward. "She's kicking off her shoes. There goes her shawl. Holy cow, she's taking off her clothes!"

Matthew sat bolt upright in bed. He spluttered: "She can't do that! The trade-school dormitory is right near here. *Thee've got to stop her!*"

The Boy sat on his bed and began pulling on his jeans. He stopped suddenly. "What about her parents?"

"There's no time for that!" Matthew snapped. "Homer sleeps like a dormant volcano; it'd take a live one to wake him. And as for her mother . . ." He shuddered at the very thought. "That woman would never believe it!"

"Well, you and Pete better come with me, Matthew. The last thing I want is for Kathy to hear on the grapevine I've been violating young girls down in Barotseland."

Peter was up in a jiffy, pulling on his clothes, and Matthew, flustered and flabbergasted, flung on his robe, yanked the quilt off his bed, and followed them. Outside, the screech of crickets and the thin liquid piping of frogs in the swamps punctuated the great night silence; the sweet scent of water lilies mingled with the fungoid stench of the feculent waters. He found the two young males standing in the garden, peering through a bush.

Peter Disney spun away, clapping hands over his eyes, groaning. "She's got it all off now, Uncle! Cover thy eyes!"

The Boy whistled softly. "Yeah. Don't look now, Matthew. You'll ruin fifty years of pure thinking."

Matthew held out the quilt, fretting. "Here, I brought this to cover her."

"In a minute." The Boy held up a hushing hand and Matthew waited obediently. After some moments he grew suspicious. Looking up, he found the two young males avidly gaping (that rascally Peter peeping through his fingers), and it was no wonder. Matthew caught an accidental glimpse of the girl and it sent sinful shivers all down his spine. For in the phosphorous night she looked beautiful, a woodland nymph with her fair ringlets unleashed, her boyish body marble white, her small breasts bobbing as she postured and pirouetted with a classical grace, her slim legs shamelessly high-kicking, a pale triangle of hair dimly discernible at the junction of her thighs. Cheeks burning, Matthew tore his eyes away.

"For goshsakes!" He turned and shakily vented his guilt on the Boy. "Remember thyself! Thee's a doctor and here's young Peter taking example from thee!"

"Okay, okay." The Boy reached back a hand for the quilt. He shook it open and, holding it outspread before him like a bullfighter's cape, cautiously approached the young girl. At first she took off, and looked like getting away, before she suddenly turned. Then she ran on tiptoe to the Boy and, before their disbelieving eyes, reached up and clung on him with a searing kiss. The Boy dropped the quilt, dumbly defenseless while her hands, as attacking as crabs, were intimately groping. There was a sudden shocked stillness. Matthew could have sworn the Boy, head craning toward to follow her melting mouth, hesitated on her lips a shade longer than his stuporous thrall insisted. Then suddenly he snapped out of it. He was all business, disengaging her, pushing away her hands, snatching up the quilt, and wrapping her tightly to still her feeble fighting. While she kept up a muffled token show of kicks and squeals, he lifted her easily in his arms. "Matthew, you better call her mother."

Just then a lamp flared up in the house. Strangely, it was Elliot Moke who met them in the passage. Matthew, struck by the man's flushed furtive look, had a sudden vision of him brooding in the dark house, watching their charade. Gaunt as a stick, with thin hairy legs sticking out beneath a worn satin brocade dressing gown, the man listened, tight-mouthed, to Matthew's explanation before turning to morosely appraise the Boy, who stood, blue eyes defiant, shivering slightly, staring back. Without a shirt, the chill had got to him; his tanned torso was stippled with goosebumps, the brown nipples hardening. The goosed hairs standing erect at his temples gave him a curious hackle-risen look, and Elliot, outstared, turned with a vague air. He ordered the girl to her room, and to their surprise she went meekly, bundling away in the trailing quilt, frowning sulkily at them over one lily-white shoulder that was shockingly bared to the glare of the lamplight.

When she had left them gaping vacantly after her, Moke said simply: "It's the company, keeps her awake. I'll go in the kitchen; some warm milk should settle her."

Afterward, back in their room, the Boy sat restlessly smoking on his bed. "Whew, I'd better think of something else. That crazy female sure shook up my juices. Something tells me her momma better keep a right rein on that little filly, else she'll be broken in and pregnant before the year is out."

236

Of one accord, Matthew and Peter Disney looked up incredulously. Peter's eyes and mouth were soulfully round with delicious horror. Swallowing hard, he said hoarsely: "Thee think so?"

"I know so. By some callow black youth or that Elliot Spook or whatever his name is, lurking there so queerly in the dark. Well, whoever gets to her first, if indeed none yet has, will find her easy pickings. That little swamp angel is just looking to get laid." He looked up grimly. "She really went for me, you know that? I mean really *touched* me, like she knew what it was all about. Oh man! That little cookie's got a pea-sized brain in an adolescent body that's just too hot for her to handle!"

13 Early the next morning, after packing up the Land-Rover, they found Loreley-Salome at the old chicken coop teasing Bathsheba. Now simply a tiresome girl (her small-eyed mean sullen face put a body off), Matthew hardly recognized her for the wanton beauty of the night before. Yet he felt uncomfortably aware around her just the same.

The Boy untied the coop gate and gave his special whistle. As he clicked his tongue and patted his blue-jeaned thigh, the cat gave an affectionate grunt and tunneled out into his arms, bowling him over. She *owled* at him softly, and in their special language the Boy *owled* back, while the prematurely weaned little cat settled down and started sucking on his shirt, paws kneading and purring contentedly. Huskily chuckling, the Boy played with her a moment, teasing her with her own tail, mystifying her mischievous eye with a sleight of hand and a tender tussling. Peter laughed and Matthew watched in fond fascination as the spotted little cat tangled, then withdrew pussy-footed, then pounced, biting and nuzzling, chewing and clawing, the outsize paddy-paws playfully pattering. Finally there was the inevitable loud rip as the Boy's shirt tore. And evidently mindful of Katherine's exasperated admonitions, the Boy sat up hastily, slipping on the cub's leash. He scrambled up, dusting the grass off his spilled Stetson.

Loreley-Salome followed so longingly after them as they walked away that Matthew felt reluctantly sorry for the sullen-faced girl. Suddenly the Boy stopped. Without looking back, he said: "Keep your pants on, Loreley. And for God's sake, stay around your mother."

Bathsheba bounded unbidden onto the Land-Rover roof, and the girl watched wistfully from the jetty as the Boy, Matthew, Peter, and an old Lozi guide Homer had procured once more strained on the twin steel ropes to pull their vehicle across the limpid swamp on the ponderous little mission pontoon.

The heat was already intense, and they were all hand-chafed, perspiring, and heaving with exertion when they finally reached the opposite bank. In the Land-Rover, the Boy took the wheel and they drove up the wooden ramps and followed a stray dry track into the great grassy valley. In the dust-filtered cab, Matthew broiled in his own sweat, and the old Lozi guide, pointing the way through the dusty windshield with one gnarled black hand, was powerfully pungent. Before them lay a wide and withered featureless waste of grass and sand, burned wheaten and gray as an old lion's hide. No differentiating landmark loomed to give directional bearing and the Land-Rover plowed up a pale spume of dust, bumping through mile after mile of tawny tussocks that rolled endlessly into dust-shrouded distance.

For twenty miles the only living things they saw were a solitary secretary bird stalking the savannah and the distant specter of a giant nubian king vulture, symbol of death with a nine-foot wing span, slowly circling the pale sun-shrieking skies; a few flies buzzed feverishly. Otherwise, nothing stirred in the sun-shimmering symmetry and the sameness was as mesmerizing as snowblindness. They seemed swallowed up in a strange soundless vacuum of space, heat, and light, which Matthew could tell was like nothing the Boy had ever known before.

"The Living Museum" some cynical white administrator had christened this intractable tract, and Matthew was apt to agree. Some seventy years ago, King Lwanika I, fearing internal overthrow and a Matabele invasion from the south, had bought the queen's "protection" guised in the unscrupulous imperialism of the riches-hunting British South Africa Company, which had failed to fulfill its entreatized undertaking to develop the protectorate. Thus the multitude of settlements in this rhythmically flooded river kingdom had long stagnated; in the final analysis, somewhat in vain, the king had traded his title, much of his prestige and power, many of his tribute tribes and tribal lands, and the entire mineral wealth of the Copperbelt to preserve for his people and posterity this fiercely loved lonely hinterland in which time has stood still . . .

Than was just beginning to feel they might never find the plainspeople when he suddenly spotted the heat-hazed humps of human settlements on the vast straw-grassed savannah. Built on man-made mounds that would render them water-lapped islets once the great river rose with the rains, the palm-tree-tassled tufts peppered the plain, rising like distant desert islands on a tawny sea. The guide led them to a village bounded by a low mud wall that was cannily contrived to trap fish in the waters retained each time the annual flood receded; it huddled beneath the skimpy shade of gangly oil palms, stark gray-scaled trees, and a great "sausage" tree, which presently dripped with sumptuous sprays of exotic wine-red trumpets, some of which lay in a trampled carpet beneath.

The only sound was the soft sad *swizzling* of a red-billed teal, and at first the place seemed uninhabited, solidified in the hot listening silence. Then two dogs began to bark hoarsely and several figures came unstuck from rectangular huts, whose palm-plaited walls were interwoven with rectilinear designs. The men wore their traditional pleated-cloth *seseba* skirts; the children wore belly-burst loincloths or skirts, while the women flounced, quaintly Victorian, in full blouses and long floral skirts; these, though tamer tunics than the Sunday splendids seen at the mission centers, were yet bustled and bunched in faithful facsimile of the missionary fashion of half a century before.

The sun-squinting faces creased into grimaces of disbelief at the sight of the tall young white man and his tame forest leopard. They warned off the agitated dogs as Bathsheba leaped to the ground, rubbing her slinky body affectionately against the Boy. After drinking thirstily from the dirt-dripping canvas water bag, he cupped a handful for the cat, then he chained her to the cab, put on his hat, and stepped over the low mud wall. Matthew and Peter joined him, and the people immediately dropped to one knee, giving the respectful *kandalela*, the traditional Barotse greeting of soft clapping into the palm of one hand.

Shaking hands with the headman, Than Profane wasted no time communicating his commodity. "I am *Njumwaice*, Quaker missionary physician, famous healer of countless hundreds in the North Western province."

"*Manare ngaka?*" (Missionary doctor?) Echoing his awesome credentials, the people crowded around. While Cosmo boasted of his bwana's prowess, a man began to pound the village drum and the Boy set his instruments and medications out along the thick rim of the mud wall. After some time, the drum's steady thunder was taken up at the next isolated village island; from there it echoed out, relaying the news of the clinic on and on in an ever-widening web across the lonely plain.

In the privacy of the headman's hut, Than examined malnourished people who were beset with endemic diseases, parasitic infestations, and the puzzling paraphernalia of their local witchdoctors. Most wore skin charms around their necks or wrists; there were usually several concoction-covered festering cuts over the site of any pain or inflammation, and needles, often of the ordinary sewing variety (perhaps a symbolism intended to duplicate the efficiency of the European injections!) were imbedded in the skin in various parts of their bodies. All of these charms seemed to have had little effect on their pathetically advanced ailments. Than examined a woman who carried a pumpkin-sized tumor in her uterus. One man had a goiter so advanced that his struggling breaths whistled through a grotesquely swollen strangled airway. A small girl, incredibly still alive after she had fallen open-mouthed onto a stake an amazing four months before, lay on a crude log litter, staring listlessly, critically close to death.

As more and more people trudged in from the surrounding villages, Than worked feverishly. Impeded by bad light, sweat, flies, dirt, cramped conditions, elusive drug vials, finicky needle packets, and a faulty ophthalmoscope light, he grew hot and vexed. He dropped gauze bandages into the dirt, burned his fingers trying to snatch sterilized instruments from scalding water, and cracked his head on a bound bundle of clay pots hanging from the rafters. While he conducted examinations on a papyrus mat on the earthen floor, a pet mongoose, curiously peering, rummaged through his medications. Unnerved by his white face, babies screamed at his stethoscope. The Barotse women were coy about their intimate anatomy and old folk stared at his questions in stony incomprehension. All in all, Than managed to work himself into a steaming frazzle trying to practice flawless medicine under pressure in a primitive setting.

At Shonona, vivid splashes of bougainvillea shimmered in the cooling dusk silence, and the Poes awaited them with the news that the finally released report of the Monckton Commission had appealed for the abolition of all discriminatory practices based on color or creed

240

and recommended a new constitution for Northern Rhodesia. It claimed that the black majority's abhorrence of the federal structure had become almost pathological, and it was Professor Tomlinson's opinion that its recommendations, if instituted, constituted the death sentence of the Federation. However, the commission had supported the preservation of Barotseland's special status, and the Barotse National Council, apparently panicked by the possible release of Northern Rhodesia, had formally requested that Britain allow Barotseland to secede as an independent protectorate.

Than left Matthew and the Poes discussing the awesome omens and drove across to Shonona's little clinic. There, Zelda Clayton triumphantly preened her own small coup; there were several cases of bronchitis and enteritis in the wards. The people were beginning to come around, it seemed. At any other time, Than might have been pleased to see them. Right now, with his own jeep full of the chronically ill, they presented an accommodation crisis that was only solved by placing some two abed. Zelda and her junior aides washed and fed Than's new patients while her new assistant, a supercilious fellow named Francis Mbeze, made out record cards. Than and Cosmo, their trousers still darkly coated with the fine Kalahari dust of the plain, did tedious work-ups with fearful and suspicious patients and relatives who, accustomed to having their symptoms volunteered by witchdoctors, were confused by Than's lack of clairvoyant ability. They haggled about signing consent forms for surgery the next day, and the uncle of a small boy with a broken arm that had turned gangrenous refused to give legal authorization for amputation of the life-endangering putrid limb until the child's grandmother had been consulted the next day.

It was eleven-thirty by the time the last patient had been settled down for the night. Finally, after administering injections, prescribing medications, requisitioning tests, and writing out diet orders, Than fed Bathsheba and settled her in the mission's garden shed. Then a surprisingly solicitous Zelda Clayton forced a light supper on him, and Carrie Poe ran him a hot bath. He was just climbing out of it, dripping wet, when the generator-fed light suddenly flickered and the house was plunged into darkness. Than emerged from the bathroom with a towel around his hips to find Carrie awaiting him with a lighted lamp. The inner house lay in darkness; Benedict, Matthew, and Peter had long since retired, and to Than's mortification, Carrie, lighting his way, hurried after him with a glass of warm milk, right to his room. Feeling her awed old eyes caressing his back

241

all the way down the long veranda, he wondered wryly if she would tuck him in and kiss him good night. To his relief, he managed to shut her out almost immediately. Groping in the dark, he stripped the blankets off his narrow bed, unfurled the damp towel, and crawled between the crisp sheets. Snuggling down, he burrowed under the lumpy pillow. And the unexpected solicitude of the ladies had cracked his defenses and affected him more than he liked to think. He thought of Suzannah, and for the first time in weeks, uncomfortably tumescent, fell into a drugged sleep, physically aching for a woman's soft love. . . .

14

Suffused in sweat in the dark dawn, Than awoke to the distant thunder of the royal drums from Lealui, endlessly proclaiming that the Barotse king was alive and all was well. He crawled out of bed feeling shaky and sick, unaccountably depressed, and strangely homesick for San Francisco. His first cup of coffee, creamy with condensed milk, made him feel nauseated. The long hours of cramped examinations on a hard hut floor had strained and stiffened just about every muscle in his body and he limped over to the washstand and washed up and shaved in the cold water, pulling on a clean pair of jeans and a fresh white jacket before hobbling out into the raw white light of the new-broken day. He found Zelda Clayton already busy at the clinic, filled with a cheerful zest that was hard to take in his sensitive state.

He looked around distractedly. "That kid's uncle get back with the consent yet?"

"No. I guess it'll take him some time cycling across the plain. Cosmo's busy drawing blood for the typing and cross-matching. He's persuaded some of the relatives to give blood." Zelda indicated a dressing trolley laid out with a sphygmomanometer, thermometers, and swabs. "I was just about to take specimens and tests, but if thee wants to start rounds . . ."

"Fine," he said shortly. "We'll do it together." And feeling stiff and strained, filled with distracting fears and neuroses, he had a struggle to smile and talk, to reassure fearful patients with a contrived confidence and calm he scarcely felt. He turned away from crying babies, spent moments staring unseeingly at record charts, and had to concentrate hard to formulate simple courses of treatment.

Later, while Zelda supervised the prepping and premedication of patients, Than did urine and hemoglobin tests in the laboratory. Finally, with the aid of Cosmo and Zelda and two of her more competent aides, he prepared to operate on the scrubbed lab table. Cosmo had connected a spotlight to a twelve-volt battery and hung a lamp on its cord suspended over the table.

Than's first patient was the critically ill little girl who had fallen open-mouthed onto a stake. Without an X-ray to guide him, Than had spent long moments carefully examining the child's throat and palpating and percussing her thin little chest; her apparently undamaged pharynx convinced him that the steel stake had somehow entered her mouth at such an angle that it had perforated her esophagus. Now, lying pitifully small under the spotlight, she eyed him woozily with stricken eyes as her little body sagged into a drug-induced submission. While Zelda strapped a blood-pressure cuff onto one thin little arm, Than worked on the other. But her veins were impractically small and he injected a local anesthetic, did a cut-down on an ankle, and got an intravenous drip going. Finally unconscious, the child was dehumanized with drapes, just a small square of dark skin left visible through a hole in the cloth. Cosmo watched over the vital signs, and one of the nurse's aides, little more than a wide-eyed schoolgirl with only the faintest notion of surgical instruments and the procedure they were designed for, blundered to pass them across.

Than made a long exploratory incision and began snapping off bleeders in the cramped confines of the child's neck, while Zelda, defensively rash and know-it-all, got in Than's way with surgical sponges and let blood vessels slip through his knots before he could completely tie them. Then, unreconciled to her own imperfection, she eyed him acidly over her mask and told him how it was done where *she* came from, citing the more accommodating ways of other doctors she had worked with.

Smoldering with a fervent desire to strangle the insufferable bitch, Than dissected out the esophagus, found the perforation, and repaired and replaced it. Then, warned by the child's shallow wheezy respiration, he made another exploratory incision, this time into her chest. He cracked off a rib to reach the pleura, the glistening transparent membrane that covered the lungs, and found that as he had feared, the infection had traveled down and, in a pocket half behind the heart, formed a badly suppurating messy abscess that had burst into the pleura. After aspirating out much of the thickened

243

empyema, he let in a rubber drainage tube and closed the wound around it. A glass collection bottle was taped into place and the wound covered with a large gauze dressing. Finally he sent the little patient, breathing more easily, back to her ward, fully three and a half hours after leaving it. It had been a long haul for him on such a surgical procedure; the fact that it was a success was no thanks to his fuming and fumbling first assistant.

Zelda left with the patient to supervise the post-operative care; after each operation she would have to leave to make checks on all post-operative patients. Each time, upon return, she would have to rescrub scrupulously. Meanwhile, Than would be left to assist himself. In the stagnant heat, his pounding head kept neurotic time with the throbbing of the generator outside. Over the prone body of the woman who carried a pumpkin-sized tumor in her uterus, he found himself staring at Cosmo, while a distinct possibility began to firm in his mind.

"Cosmo," he said slowly, "whyn't you let that aide watch over the vital signs. You come over here and help me out."

Cosmo's white mask expanded with the pull of a smile, his dark eyes seemed to coalesce with something like joy, and he came un-hesitatingly. Following Than's needs with surprising coordination, he quickly grew so edge-quick and eager that Than had the feeling that should he flag, Cosmo might quite competently take over. Obviously, in the long hours spent as secondary auxilliary in Suseshi's surgery over the years, the young dresser had quietly taken in a good deal more than had been realized. He might not fully understand the disease and traumas they worked with, but he instinctively knew what needed to be done and how, with just what instruments, it was to be achieved.

It was past three-thirty in the morning by the time the last operation was completed. Anxiously awaiting his wife, a pale Hubert Clayton peered through a window. After more than nineteen and a half hours of straight surgery, when there seemed no more reason for it, Than suddenly started shaking. Untying his scrub suit, Zelda Clayton looked at him strangely. Barely able to walk on legs turned quaky, he stumbled out onto the veranda and sat down on the cold steps while Zelda tried vainly to coax him to accept a helping hand he was too proud to consider.

Their old battling relationship was back in full force again, and thus demoralized before the avaricious I-told-you-so eyes of his arch antagonist, Than was mortified and embarrassed. He struggled to brace his body against the compulsive shuddering, but for the life of him he couldn't stop it. His teeth chattered, and unaccountably cold, he couldn't hold his hand still while he smoked. Still pride-stung at having her position usurped by a mere black assistant, Zelda muttered bitterly about him driving his body beyond endurance. She tried to give him a sedative, but he wanted to stay alert lest any postoperative complications occurred.

"I'm staying here the night in case I'm needed," he said defiantly.

After they had left, Than, too wound up to think of sleep, sat smoking alone, watching the first pale blush of dawn begin to lighten the night sky. He felt feverish and sick, aching in every bone, and so exhausted he could scarcely see straight. Fragments of the surgery tumbled through his mind and through it all he felt a rising excitement that filled him with an anticipatory joy he could scarcely contain. He met the new day raptly aware of one wondrous thing: *Cosmo Mlongotti had the makings of a surgeon. . . .*

By the next day, Than knew he had malaria. For two days he raged in a delirium that kept him in bed, solicitously tended by Zelda Clayton who pointedly complained about doctors who took care of others while neglecting themselves. On the third day, aided by injections of chloroquinine and anxious about his medical students and the work awaiting him at Suseshi, he ignored Zelda's protests, crawled onto the mattress in the back of the Land-Rover, and had Matthew Tomlinson drive him back. Feeling weak and sick after the long nauseating ride, he arrived home to be faced with a formidable accumulation of work, twelve nonplussed students, and a worried and overtaxed Denise Smith.

15

The meeting house roof was completed in the nick of time. Suseshi's gracious flamboyant trees were already bursting into dazzling red blossoms, the high-pitched screech of cicadas had started to stun the hot silence, and it seemed to Matthew that the rainy season politely, impatiently waited, like an exuberant child holding its breath, until the last slate tile was fitted into place. And then it let fly. Although they were at least able to finish off the interior in dry comfort, as usual the damp brought on Matthew's rheumatism, mildew, mosquitoes, and the winged termites on their annual nuptial flight. The violent storms bruised the ripening mangoes hanging heavy on the trees, leaked through dilapidated roofs, turned the bush roads into quagmires, and disrupted their radio reception with turbulent atmospherics.

Not that there seemed much news worth hearing about these days. Indeed, what little they gleaned through the static was mostly bad. Over in the Congo, for instance, Patrice Lumumba, who had been placed under a lackadaisical United Nations guard, was constantly escaping; after his latest recapture, his ally Antoine Gezinga broadcast ominously that many hostages would be killed if any harm came to him.

And here in Northern Rhodesia, the political future seemed no less uncertain. In London, the long-awaited Federal Review Conference had been reduced to a desperate battle between the federationalists and the nationalists, while the British government, striving to effect a compromise, was miserably torn between the two.

It was enough to upset Matthew's delicate digestion. Fortunately, the rush to complete the meeting house largely relieved him of undue speculation. They had hoped to have it finished by Christmas, but when this proved impossible, the New Year seemed a good objective, and Matthew worked hard to meet this deadline, chivvying the African workers and taking up hammer and nails to do many of the finishing touches himself. He tried to entreat Ezra Peabody, who came every day to watch the proceedings, to take a more active role, but the illustrious gentleman immediately developed a more pressing errand and limped affectedly off, complaining of lumbago. But finally, unbelievably, it was all done. Verging on physical and mental exhaustion, Matthew stood spellbound when, on the first Sunday morning in January 1961 he watched the meeting members stream starry-eyed through the entrance doors just as a gentle rain began to christen the virgin gray slate roof, glistening on the vibrant plain blue stained glass, melting on the stone facade.

Indeed, only Ezra Peabody had the necessary pomp and opinion to master its awe that first shiny rain-trilling day. As he stood triumphantly at the elders' bench, firmly in possession, Matthew's own prideful joy miserably melted in the same degree as Ezra's ego rose. For the pride of achievement positively swelled the man's portly frame till it seemed about to burst the seams of his fine seersucker suit. Swaying importantly on his feet, his booming voice bouncing off the walls, he offered the meeting house to the Lord. Then, his tone dropping to effect humility, he reminded the meeting that it was *he* who had instigated and argued for the simple grandeur that now seated and surrounded them; *he* who by his faith and persistence had ultimately made it all possible. Although Ward and Matthew had strained their backs, minds, and emotions in its erection, Ezra Peabody, appearing briefly at the inception and the ending of the project, had, by some odd magician's trick, yet made the house wholly his.

The Northern Rhodesian Constitutional Conference in London was characterized by fury and high feelings. The Federal government bitterly condemned the colonial secretary's draft constitution. While it was now apparently resigned to the revolutionary new constitution granted Nyasaland, it would not surrender Northern Rhodesia to the same kind of secession-promoting scheme without a fierce fight. In Northern Rhodesia itself, UNIP, encouraged by its recent diplomatic successes, was boldly branching out into forbidden Barotseland. The nationalists detained in the little protectorate last year had apparently sewn seditious seeds in sections of the Barotse people, grown disillusioned with a paramount chief who, besides autonomously accepting the hated Federation, had transformed the Barotse National Government into little more than a favored family consortium. Thus, while the ruling Lozi royals stoutly denied the growing popularity of UNIP, its illegal meetings were springing up like mushrooms around the country. The Litunga employed *indunas*, headmen, to go around villifying the party, breaking up its meetings, and fining the participants. Paul Jabuo, an esteemed young Lozi prince and a respected Quaker elder of Shonona Meeting, was one such *induna* who learned tragically the extent of his people's swing to nationalism. His attempts to break up a UNIP meeting ended when the incensed crowd turned on him and stoned him to death.

16

Paul Jabuo had been a well-liked member of their yearly meeting, and shocked to learn of his tragic death, as many of the Suseshi missionaries who were able made immediate plans to attend his funeral. Accompanying Than Profane on a clinic-servicing and scouting tour into Barotseland, they traversed a land vastly inundated by the rising Zambezi waters. They were frequently bogged down on the rain-sogged secondary roads, and Than Profane's low yellow car was damaged when a subsiding bush-pole bridge scraped his sump; badly leaking oil, it barely limped into Shonona with the other mission vehicles.

At the meeting for burial, much of the Quaker service went beyond the comprehension of the simple elderly relatives who finally relapsed, grief-stricken, into the traditional moaning soliloquy of their heathen heritage. Since Bartoseland's elusive man-eating lion had recently carried off its forty-fifth victim, the heartrending howling had become increasingly common on the plain. In the listless heat, the dispirited wailing had an indescribable desolation. That evening while the missionaries, still stiff in their formal funeral attire, gloomily drank hot chocolate around a single candle on the Poes' long veranda, Matthew was still struggling to shake off the haunting horror of the sound as Benedict's fear-feasting temperament was exercised in terrible tales of the man-eating monsters that had plagued Northern Rhodesia—a country reputed to have the largest and most ferocious lions in all Africa.

Uncomfortably mindful of the impressionable young girls and the timid elder ladies, some of whom must later sleep in isolated outhuts, Matthew tried to change the subject. But the man seemed unstemmable once started; and his captive audience, caught in funereal mood, grew quickly addicted to the delicious shudders his macabre anecdotes invoked. Indeed, sixteen-year-old Evangeline Dooley, a tomboy redhead in her mother's lusty mold, constantly egged the man on, eager to hear ever more of his grisly tales.

"The natives believe the Kazungula Killer to be a reincarnation of the evil old Chief Marumahoko from Senenga." Benedict's black eyes brooded morosely. Through a tracery of rebounded black shadow, the flickering flame caught on prominent bone and lit up his gaunt, pallid face, giving his words a hair-raising disquiet. "But I say it is the criminal political dalliance and the animist idolatry practiced by the plainspeople that had provoked the Lord's wrath and unleased this evil as a punishing pestilence to plague them! There can be no doubt that the incredible intelligence of this creature is beyond that normally possessed of mere animals, and the more I hear of its malfeasance and cunning, the more I am convinced that this 'Kazungula Killer' is the very devil incarnate come to reap more souls to fill his flaming nether kingdom!"

Startled at the very idea, Matthew drew back. It was typical of Benedict's warped thinking that he blamed both God's wrath and the devil for the phenomenon. The latter suggestion was preposterous, of course, but in the gloom right there in the heart of the monster's hunting ground, Matthew suppressed a shudder. The stealthy rising wind, carrying the fetid stink of the swamps, whistled mournfully through the flimsy fly-screens in gamey gusts, uncomfortably reminiscent of the hot hoary breath of some mangy man-eater come to sniff out the scent of more human blood on the eerie night air.

17

The following morning, in one of the mission's garages, Than had been tinkering with a flashlight and tools beneath his ramp-raised car for over an hour when the daylight suddenly dimmed and the heavy double doors creaked slowly shut. Lying listening incredulously in the dank grease-smelling gloom, he heard the doors being bolted from the inside. Then there was a light scampering and a gusty giggling as Loreley Haskel wriggled up between the ramps beside him. As he lay still stupefied with surprise, she came over him, swarming his skin with little hot kisses, whispering dark secrets, unselfconscious as a child as she unbuttoned her blouse to press her bare breasts against his grimy chest.

"*Hey!*" Momentarily stunned into submission, he felt her start to straddle his blue-jeaned hips before he could gather his wits to stop her. He struggled to counter her wily hands, sitting up to push off her cleaving body, his hampered head bumping against the undersides of his car. He was whispering furious chastisements when they heard voices and the garage doors being rattled and pounded upon. Frantically shushing the girl's demented giggles with a hand across her mouth, Than crawled out from beneath the car, dragging her out after him. Panting and shaking in his guilty haste, he fumbled to button her back into her blouse before slinging on his own shirt. Then smoothing down his hair, he struggled to open the doors, finally pushing them open onto bright daylight and a row of puzzled faces.

While a sizable group of Africans consulted agitatedly in the background, Elliot Moke stood glowering at him; Katherine and Jennifer Solomon, seeming set for some out-meeting outing with prayer books in hand, stood looking stunned, and by Professor Tomlinson's look of sick shock, Than realized too late that he had rebuttoned Loreley's blouse all wrong; her erectile nipples clearly impressed the thin cloth, which, along with her arms, was incriminatingly covered with the smudged fingerprints of his own grease-grimed hands. Speckled with damp ground debris, both of them stood looking disgracefully disheveled, the blatant bulge of his own—albeit rapidly subsiding—reactive erection felt acutely conspicuous, and Loreley-Salome turned suddenly petulant and dumb, eyeing him hungrily through her tumble of fair ringlets, was no help at all.

For a shocked moment, no one said anything. Then Matthew managed: "We . . . uh . . . came to call thee . . ."

"Hey! Now hold on, Matthew—stop looking at me that way!" Than hastened, shaking his head sickly. Unable to bear the embarrassed old man's hurt disillusionment and the shattered look of betrayed trust on Katherine's disbelieving face, he blurted desperately: "I know how it looks, but I was just minding my own business, fixing my car, when Loreley . . . listen, *I can explain!*"

"Maybe thee'd better," Elliot Moke sneered sourly. "Fixing thy car, thee says? With the doors locked, alone in the dark with that girl, and the two of thee all covered in grease like two peas in a pod? Thee expects us to believe that?"

"Hey now, listen . . ." But with the evidence stacked so hopelessly against him, aware of how it must look, Than flamed guiltily. Even as he spluttered to explain, Katherine, unable to endure the evidence of her eyes, turned and silently fled. Sick with humiliation, Than watched her go. Then he turned angrily on Elliot Moke, hackles rising in defensive defiance. "Now you listen to me, Mr. Moke. I don't give a shit what you do or don't believe. I don't have to explain myself to you or anyone else. I'm no kid and you're not Loreley's keeper."

"Oh?" The man's stony face cracked in a queer crumpled smile and he measured Than morosely. "Well, sir, it just so happens—maybe thee ain't heard, but Loreley and me are likely getting betrothed. 'Pears to me thee have some pretty hefty explaining to do! Seems to me thy story's a little difficult for even Kathy to swallow!"

Than saw red then; he grasped the man's shirt front in his fists, dragging him up to a fierce face-to-face confrontation.

"Now you listen to me, man, and listen good!" he snarled. "You can think what the hell you like, but you go spreading your slanderous smut and I will personally break your worthless neck." He shook the man wrenchingly. "Hear me now? You got that?"

"Doctor!" Shocked out of his stupefaction, Matthew spluttered indignantly. He said with chilling gravity: *"Unhand Mr. Moke this instant!* Get a hold of thyself!"

Slowly, with an effort, Than subsided, releasing the man, who sagged back, grown pop-eyed and red in the face. Evading their eyes and self-consciously straightening his shirt, Elliot turned and bumbled away. Watching after him, Matthew said uncomfortably, "Well, with the way things look, boy—what are we expected to believe?"

"Yeah?" Avoiding Matthew's eyes, too proud to plead, Than tucked his unbuttoned shirt furiously into his jeans. "Well, you can take it as you see it, Matthew. Just so *he* has that straight." As he swerved past the bewildered Jennifer Solomon, starting to stalk off, Matthew caught at his arm.

"Where are thee going?" he demanded. But his gruff voice had softened; as if remembering Loreley Haskel's wanton amoral propensity, he seemed suddenly uncertain. "We came to call on thy help."

Than's footsteps slowed; he turned sullenly around. "Yeah? Who needs it?"

"A man mauled by a lion." Matthew's shoulders sagged. "It's a terrible thing. Seems like that Kazungula Killer has struck again."

"The Kazungula Killer?" Than frowned. "You mean that man-eating lion Benedict Poe was trembling about last night?"

"The very same," Matthew nodded grimly. "In fact, probably at that very time, the animal was measuring up this victim." He indicated a seseba-skirted Lozi man who stood patiently awaiting them, staring stoically beyond his tall spear amid a group of natives who were still excitedly gabbling with the horror of this latest statistic. "This man's just come in with the news; wants us to pass the word on to the district commissioner in the hopes they'll send out a game scout on the morrow. For what little good that will do! Apparently, the D.C.s in these parts have been demanding effective action from the game department for some time now, but it seems like that cantankerous cat is just too crafty for them. Uncanny creature just refuses to be baited by traps. He won't return to the kill and keeps moving around and changing his tactics, displaying superhuman intelligence." Awkwardly dusting off the stained brim of his pith, Matthew looked up at Than. "I guess it's no wonder these natives figure he's the reincarnation of old Chief Marumahoko, come back to settle old scores. To make matters worse, most of them are afraid to inform on his whereabouts for fear the old chief's spirit will take them in reprisal, which kind of helps perpetuate his blood-thirsty career. Anyhow, the upshot of it is—like Ben says—the people hereabouts are living in a state of continual terror, spending the nights under siege, barricaded in their huts, with even the men afraid to go out after nature's call! Not that that's any insurance. This time, apparently, it leaped twenty feet onto a stilted hut, breaking through the grass door to take the man right off his sleeping mat."

"*Jesus!*" Than stared incredulously.

"Yes," Matthew agreed. "Well, what with all the commotion, as soon as dawn began to break, the villagers took courage and came out with their muzzle loaders, taking potshots, throwing rocks, banging calabashes, and by the sounds of it, generally making enough puff and storm to scare up the dead. Well finally the lion made off and they found what was left of the man; seems likely he is dead and beyond the help as the man says, but Benedict says it's as likely a ruse simply so's they can bring in the witchdoctor to tend the victim without the interference of the D.C. and the medical officer. So maybe thee'd best go out and see if the poor fellow is still alive. Thee might at least be in time to ease his end before they bring in their heathen juju men to finish him off. Elliot was to accompany thee, but I guess thee can manage on thy own. I'm afraid I don't have much stomach for that kind of thing; but this Lozi man will show thee the way." He hesitated awkwardly, glancing around at Jenny. "Ah . . . and perhaps, afterwards, thee'd be good enough to allow Jenny to spend a little time with a blind family I was taking her to see. Their village is in the vicinity. I'm sure this Lozi would be glad to guide thee there after thee has inspected the victim. I promised Jenny we'd go today . . . but, well, under the circumstances I feel it might be more prudent if I were to go counsel Kathy right at this time."

"Yeah," Than sighed. "Under the circumstances, maybe you'd better."

18

Across the desolate miles, at a squalid village lost in the lonely infinity of the plain, the anguished howling of women hung like horrendous holes in the surreal silence. Following a grim group of seseba-skirted Ma-Lozi men to the scene, Than lifted the bloodstained blanket to stare awesomely down at the remains of a man who had long been beyond his ministrations. With its entrails eaten out, the rib cage exposed, and patches of skin licked raw in places, the corpse had already begun to putrefy in the heat. The face was crawling with metallic-green bloated blowflies, the glazed eyes and mouth set in an expression of unspeakable terror. Dropping the blanket, Than backed away from the stinking spectacle. He could almost feel the fear simmering in the air all around him; he saw it in the people's terror-tightened faces. And he could scarcely blame them. During the long lonely night hours, above the dying victim's diminishing moans, the natural acoustics of the plain had forced them to helplessly endure the sound of the cat's callous crushing on his bones. Now they stood staring down at the huge paw prints in the soft sand, pointing out the dragging marks of one maimed forepaw, an old healed wound that indelibly identified the Kazungula Killer. According to the headman, the lion, true to Northern Rhodesian form, was an exceptionally large black-maned male of inordinate audacity, a formidable foe to face in their flimsy grass huts. Than shivered in the sun to think of it. From way out across the heat-hazed plain, as uncannily attendant of death as the predatory vultures, he saw migrations of mourners, with assegais and ancient muzzle-loading muskets weaving through the tall wind-waving grass.

Their guide mysteriously disappeared at this juncture, and unable to coerce another to take his place, Than and Jenny set off alone. Following Matthew's ambiguously marked map further into the remote reaches, they crossed a rain-engorged river on a shaky bush-pole bridge and splashed through two swollen streams. They drove uncomprehendingly from one isolated village to another before Than was ready to concede they were hopelessly off course. It was late afternoon by the time he had retraced their route into the vicinity of the lion-victim's village. Confused by the stark symmetry of the landscape, he was relieved when the remembered river at last loomed up, distantly distinguishable by its escorting belt of thicket, which wound like a green snake across the treeless terrain.

Than was driving slowly across the bumpy poles of the trussed tree-trunk bridge when he suddenly realized it was a mistake. The recent rains must have undermined the foundations, for the heavy supportive poles began to buckle and sway like old knees bending. Even as he sat, stupefied with surprise, the log floor rolled drunkenly loose beneath the tires as the structure lurched. It collapsed sideways in a fitful curtsy, and before they knew what was happening, the surging waters had swept the vehicle into the river, where, slowly sinking, the engine drowned abruptly. The Rover listed and rolled, bobbing like a boat, the rising waters glugging and gurgling around the submerging sides. Jenny gasped with shock as the cold water squirted through the crevices, staining her long lilac dress with mauve splashes.

"*Jesus!* Hold on, Jenny." Than burst his door open with a shoulder, letting in a wave of water, which swamped the cab floor, surging around the gear lever and their legs. Snatching up his medical bag, he reached for Jenny's hand. Stepping diaphragm-deep into the river, he yanked her out after him into the shockingly cold water, which came over her breasts. Her copious gathered skirt rose around her in air-trapped billows, and the turbulence crested her chin, leaving her gasping.

In the sluggish slipstream of the sinking Land-Rover, she clung to him, floundering in sightless terror while he tossed his medical bag into the plumed bamboo reeds on the sloping river bank. Then, leading Jenny sprawling along beside him in her long dragging dress, he began to wade for the shore through the crystalline-clear waters that were characteristic of Barotseland's sand-sifted rivers. Feeling for firm footing across the slimy bottom as they moved through sun-warmed underwashes and tugging eddies, they fought to stay on their feet while the swift surging current caught at their clothing with compelling strength. Finally, as the river shallowed, they emerged, dripping wet.

They had almost made it ashore when Jenny suddenly slipped and submerged. Than caught her and hauled her, spluttering, into the reeds. There, entangled in enmeshed slimy roots, he over-balanced backward and sat down in the shallows among the bristling stems with Jenny in his arms. Gasping and panting, his jaw smarting from a percussive collision with the back of her head and, in sudden awful equality, unable to see with his Stetson slipped down over fiercely shut eyes that stung from splashed water, Than felt Jenny, coughing and crying, squirming around against him. He pushed up his hat and sat blinking and surprised as she reached out and clung to him with hysterical ferocity, nuzzling against him with all the frenzied yearning of a stray starving kitten at last finding home, pressing her face into his chest with such uncharacteristic abandon that he was touched and embarrassed.

"*Oh please, don't leave me*—I can't swim," she whispered fervently, with furtive shame into his wet shirt, and he closed his eyes, humbled, pressing his throbbing chin against her brow, smoothing the wet tresses off her temple. She couldn't swim, to say nothing of the fact she couldn't see too well either. The bridge had gone so fast, he hadn't had time to explain. It was no wonder she was scared witless.

"It's okay . . . it's okay . . . you're safe now . . . I won't leave you," he murmured, holding her awkwardly in his arms, feeling preposterous sitting calmly comforting her with his pants on in eighteen-odd inches of water, not a little unnerved by the idea of cruising crocodiles as he cradled her head, stroking the wet dark hair that streamed from her lavender bonnet. "The bridge just collapsed under us. But we'll be safe now. Just the same, I don't think we should sit here playing *From Here to Eternity* for much longer; if we don't get out of these reeds pretty soon, some hoary old crocodile might decide to make a meal of us. . . ."

They stood up unsteadily together, streaming water. Pushing through the rasping reeds, Than found his medical bag, then they splashed through the sedge, up the bank to the relatively dry shelter of the river-huddling undergrowth. They tried to wring the excess moisture out of their clothing, and Than made Jenny put her finger down her throat to bring up some of the impure water she had swallowed. Watching her regurgitate delicately (even then trying to stay ladylike!), the events of the day took sudden toll of him; his own stomach heaved and he turned and vomited vengefully into the reeds. Afterward, starting to shiver, feeling shaken and weak and acutely cold, he reached down to help Jenny up. And he was amazed anew at how tiny she was; she must be a mere five feet to his six feet three, and her hand felt small as a child's in his grasp.

"Hey, stop looking so worried." He picked up his medical bag. "I guess there are any number of natives hereabouts who'll give us shelter till the mission sends help. There's no need to be afraid."

"No?" By the gravity in her great blue eyes, he knew she was thinking of the man-eating lion.

"No. You got me to take care of you, remember? And even if I say so myself, you sure do have your luck, lady, getting stranded in the African bush with so hardy a hybrid as a cross between Albert Schweitzer and Tarzan of the apes!"

But the joke failed to bring a smile and for a moment she stood swaying, staring at him so seriously he thought at first she hadn't heard him. Then her grave eyes cleared.

"I won't be afraid," she murmured dully, lifting her chin with sudden simple conviction. "Not if you stay with me."

"Yeah." He looked away, disconcerted by a calm clear faith he could not quite share. "Well, right now I guess we'd better start walking. Maybe we can hitch a ride in all this traffic. . . ."

But caught without compass, weapon, or creature comfort, a sojourning stranger with a blind dependent in this land of unintelligible languages, a mystifying landscape, and a lascivious lion, he did not feel as assured as he spoke. The tinkling of Egyptian reed frogs rose like Chinese windbells as the swift African dusk descended around them. Beyond the swollen river, Shonona Mission, their closest link with severed civilization, lay untold miles away. Casting one last look back at the half-submerged Land-Rover, Than straightened his hat and fitted Jenny's hand to his arm, so that, in the manner of the blind, she might feel the lie of the land through his body movements and so facilitate her own. Thus, dripping wet and shivering in the cooling air, they started out, following one of the myriad footpaths that traced the course of human passage through the long-grassed lion country.

19

Out on the open veld, spiraling shafts of sunlight, flashing pink and gold off the reeded stands of stagnant water, sank with frightening swiftness. As the cold black night settled across the great valley, the distant darkness was tantalized with the eerie howls and insane jibbering of hyenas, and the vast still swamplands came alive, pulsating with clouds of mosquitoes and the screech and croak of multitudinous crickets and frogs. Away in the east, a storm played itself out with soundless flares of sheet lightning; the stark white stage light reflectively flickered among the mountainous clouds, momentarily suspending the two fugitives like players on a set. Jenny's bedraggled bonnet bobbed against her back and her drenched dress dragged in the sand as she clung to Than's arm, struggling to keep up with his long-legged strides along a path that furrowed through six-foot-high grass, growing spongy and often pot-holed with the heavy tread of hippopotamuses when it veered to skirt dimly perceivable patches of marsh.

After almost two hours, Than's shivering suddenly subsided. His head began to pound painfully and a strange stealing lassitude spread warmth through his chilled bones. It dulled his desperation to a dreamlike detachment, so that he was conscious of little other than the ceaseless loping of his aching legs, the rhythmic squelching of their wet shoes through the sand, and the whip of the tall grass as he held his dimming consciousness desperately focused on the directional draw of the drum, until it seemed to him that the persistent petition pitted his mind like a woodpecker's tattoo. At last the hyenas ceased their hideous howling. Than was aware of Jenny's frail weight lurching out of step against him when the path turned suddenly boggy and, her shoe stuck, she stumbled, sprawling and splashing into a deep sedgy pool.

Startled to life, Than pulled her, dripping wet and muddied, from the long clutching grasses. Stooping to retrieve her lost shoe, he was overcome with dizziness. As he shook his head to steel himself against its sinister suck, it struck him that he was in the grip of a shock-induced recurrence of malaria. Suddenly terrified that the beckoning black oblivion might beat them to the nearest native village, he felt frantically along the dark ground. Locating Jenny's shoe, he fitted it clumsily to her small cold foot while she clutched at his hair to balance herself. Then, as they straightened unsteadily together, the clear night air was suddenly assailed by a queer mournful moaning. At first it seemed incredibly too much like the morbid manifestation of their worst fears to be anything more than overwrought imagination.

Then it came again, and this time, as they stood listening in scalp-prickling presentiment, there was no mistaking the malevolent moaning that rumbled across the flood plain. There was only one species of animal capable of such powerful resonance, and although Than tried to pass it off as the howl of a hyena, a sudden reverberating roar shattered the illusion. Numb with cold and dread, they walked in spine-tingling terror as the restless bawling resounded through the night, seeming to reach ravenously after them like some sinister claw-hooked paw. Then gradually the moans petered out and the drum suddenly stopped beating as the lion fell into the ominous searching silence that was said to precede an attack. In the precarious quiet, their every action seemed suddenly conspicuous and strangely magnified; their labored breaths sawed noisily, the sand-scratching trampling of their feet sounded inordinately loud and the slightest snap and shiver of the tall grass took on sudden sinister significance. By now Than's body felt on fire with a dry heat that ate at his entrails; the fever sapped at his strength, and desperately fighting the desire simply to succumb, he kept moving mechan-

257

ically, holding on to his medical bag and supporting Jenny's increasingly weary weight through the sheer will of his mind.

Then as the fever began to burn into his brain, the horror was suddenly all around him; every shadow was inhabited and his eyes played tricks on him, so that looking back, he felt he could distinctly discern the skulking shape of some leonine animal stalking them through the grass. Desperately holding on to the diagnosis of delirium, he fought to deny this nightmare manifestation. Then a swift shuttered flash of lightning bleached Barotseland blue, and for a brief blinding moment, bathed in its ghostly glow, he suddenly clearly saw it.

The yellow eyes leaped to evil incandescence, and the massive, magnificently maned animal was given indelible dimension before being obliterated into the grass. Praying under his breath, Than stumbled on, too weak to run, while it seemed to him the awful apparition hankered after them, the deadly padded footfalls taking on the dull thudding tempo of his own racing heart, his spooked spine fairly prickling in expectation of the raking claws. Then, with Jenny and his medical bag starting to slip through his weakening grip, when he felt at the end of his endurance, he looked up and suddenly saw it: a village fire, flaming blessed refuge through the tangle of a thorn boma directly ahead.

On a great fallen tree trunk that was twisted and gnarled, leprous with long-whiskered lichens and fantastic fans of fungus, they sat before a huge, badly smoking, wet-wood fire, a blue-jeaned cowboy and a little lilac-clad Dresden figurine, straight from some old world *Vanity Fair*, marooned in a primitive African village. Dazed and exhausted, they were watched by poor fear-craven creatures who had crept down the crooked ladders of their tall stilted huts, braving the lion-haunted night with antique guns to offer them this humble hospitality. The headman, a thin, dignified personage in a faded seseba skirt and a surprisingly formal shabby Western shirt and tie, propped aside his old tower musket to broadly communicate with expressive hands and a broken Chi-Lwena. He welcomed them gravely and offered them food and water.

Neither felt able to face food, but Than took the offered gourd of water eagerly. After Jenny had sipped sparingly, he slaked his own feverish thirst, pouring a little water over his head to reduce his rocketing temperature. Clusters of children, with bare navel-knobbled bellies bursting from ragged seseba skirts, crowded forward to stare intrigued while he injected himself with chloroquinine. Regular doses of the drug generally brought malarial attacks under control within twenty-four hours, but within this time he was likely to get worse. One gourd of water had not been enough, and when Than indicated again his insatiable thirst, a nervous-looking youth brought forth a large calabash with a long-handled gourd dipper. Than lifted the dripping ladle to his lips. But this time the murky liquid was no common water; by the strong smell alone, he recognized it as ka-tchipembe, a bubbling fermented spirit with the deceptive mild taste of skimmed milk and a kick like a mule. He came back from a swallow with a seared throat and a fiery gullet; the sharp rising fumes first cleared then clouded his head and he sat silently gasping while the first fierce effects faded to a fuzzy euphoria. Regardless of its alcoholic strength, the drink was a refreshing febrifuge. Than downed another dipperful before offering some to Jenny, who sat looking dreamy and dazed, her wet lilac dress beginning to steam in the fire's heat.

"Here," he said, closing her hand around the gourd dipper. "A little firewater to warm you."

As she gazed trustfully up at him with great blue eyes, her sweet face glowing pink in the firelight seemed suddenly, unaccountably, acutely kissable within the circular brim of her Quaker bonnet. A fine-chained tiny gold cross hung around her neck, and her long, curly wine-burnished hair trailed across her wet bodice. The top buttons had burst open to show him the virginal white swells of her small breath-stirring breasts, and Than's stomach tightened uncomfortably. His recently roused blood still sensuously smoldered from his brief inflammatory brush with Loreley Haskel and the hallucinatory lion, and he looked away, disconcerted. Steadying the ladle in her hands, he held it to her mouth. And it was a token of her innocence that she took it like tea. The raw spirit seared her unsullied constitution like a lick of naked flame. She gasped, eyes wide. The dipper was almost knocked from his hands and she nearly toppled from the log as she exploded, spluttering, in a paroxysm of coughing.

"Whoops." He steadied her. "Hush. It'll warm you once it settles."

The fit subsided at last and she finally shocked him: with her blind eyes still bright with liquor-burst welling tears, she raised her mouth, ready for more.

"Hey, go easy; this is potent stuff." He began to rue his rash encouragement as she demurely glugged down the whole dipperful. But this time, with a tremendous effort of will, she stifled the protesting spasms of her gullet and resolutely did not cough. Shaking his head with amused admiration, Than handed the ladle back to the youth. He fumbled for the crumpled pack of damp cigarettes in his back pocket; offering one to the headman, he puffed impatiently, trying to light his own sagging filament on a firebrand the man offered. Finally catching a light, he drew deeply and turned to find Jenny's sightless eyes regarding him vaguely.

"Does thee believe in God?" she whispered dreamily.

For a moment he was taken aback. Since he was a missionary, ostensibly sworn to all the common Christian precepts, it was an odd, profound, and untimely question. Something in the way she said it made him stare at her dimly, appalled that he might be so patently transparent that this quiet young blind girl could see right through his defensive facade. And maybe the potent *katchipembe* had stiffened her spirit some. For despite his hesitation, she remained searchingly silent, her blue eyes staring solemnly straight through him with such candid questioning that he felt uncomfortably bound not to act on his first impulse to lie. He felt worn out, sick, and depressed; with his defenses down at this lowly ebb, he said dyspeptically:

"Do I believe in God? Well, lady, if you must know it—not usually. Being a scientist at heart, I am loath to believe in anything I cannot personally prove. But there are a few rare times when I see some of His supposed handiwork that I am moved, by awe, to imagine there might just be some great overriding intelligence after all."

"Oh?"

"Yes, ma'am," he said acidly, stubbing out his soggy cigarette on the log between them. In his sickness and disgruntlement, suddenly resenting this unsolicited prying, wanting sadistically to shock her with his personal truth, he said deliberately: "Like when I see a mighty mountain range . . . or a baby born . . . or more particularly, the naked body of a beautiful woman. Then, if He designed this—and who else could?—it's praise heaven and hallelujah. Right then I'm ready to kneel."

"Oh," she murmured, gazing at him with a look that was so glassily enthralled that he began to understand that she was starting to haze over in what was probably her first encounter with some of the same warmly delicious inebriation that had begun to fog his own senses pleasantly as well. But if the fumes had risen to his head, the liquid went straight to his bladder. Abruptly excusing himself, Than urinated covertly in the black shade of a palmyra tree. On his return to the fireside, judicious inquiry revealed Jenny to be silently suffering in the same bloated condition. Standing with his back respectfully turned, Than guarded her privacy while she crouched, skirts huddled, in the shadows beneath the scrawny boughs of the same benighted tree. Then he consulted with the headman, who assured him that although every hut in the village was crammed with resident families, he and Jenny might be squeezed into one or another of these communal huddles.

It was a hospitable proposal, but although his own jeans had dried on him, Jenny needed to get out of that wet dress, and wary of the lice, bedbugs, and disease that so often inhabited the bodies and abodes of these poor primitive people, Than stubbornly haggled to secure separate accommodation. But glancing nervously into the night darkness, doubtless anxious to be off into the relative safety of his hut, the headman explained that the only other shelters comprised a large mud grainery and a series of small chicken coops. Well, the big blind tower of the cereal-filled granary was out of the question, and the chicken coops, little wicker-woven rondavels with conical thatch roofs like miniature stilted huts, looked a trifle small if more promising. However, the headman's coop, built to accommodate a goodly flock, was larger than most.

Their trip into the protectorate had necessitated the uncustomary carrying of money, and a damp five-pound note salvaged from Than's back pocket helped the headman realize the feasibility of turning his chickens out to roost in the open for the night, encouraging him to have the small entrance hole enlarged to admit his two guests. The man also arranged fresh straw for them to sleep on, two bottles of water, a box of matches, and the only covering the impoverished villagers could spare—a large shaggy kaross made of the skins of *sitatungas*, the seldom seen shy swamp antelopes.

While a youth went to clean out the coop, Than fetched Jenny and they followed the headman, stepping over scattered utensils and through and around the long knobbled hut legs in the darkness. By now the fires were dying down and most of the villagers had evaporated into the high hunddles of their stilted huts. The little village stood eerily quiet and deserted. The pungent smell of trampled cow dung drifted to them along with the nervous lowing of cattle from an adjacent kraal, and a marsh owl startled them, swooping low overhead with a weird cry.

Once the youth had shooed out the squawking chickens, cleaned their debris, and spread the coop with clean dry straw, the headman held the rickety log ladder steady while Than helped Jenny scale it, guiding and supporting her as he climbed up beneath her. To escape the rising river waters, the coop, like the huts, stood sixteen feet up on a log platform, where the querulously clucking evicted chickens sat perched along the rim, white blobs disgruntledly fluffing their feathers in the darkness. Through the ragged entrance hole the coop loomed dark and smelly, and Than reached across Jenny's shoulder, holding out a lighted match to inspect it. In the dim glow, he judged there would be enough room inside for both of them to sleep comfortably curled up on their sides.

Once Jenny had climbed in, her long skirts trailing as she groped on her hands and knees, Than pushed in his medical bag, then the bottles of water and the *sitatunga* robe handed up to him by the headman, and crawled in after her. The ragged wicker weave scratched against his back as he squeezed through the enlarged hole that was barely big enough to admit him. The headman called after them, wishing them a safe night, and they felt the structure shiver slightly on its spindly legs as he descended. Far below, he shuffled away into silence and they were alone.

After his eyes adjusted to the dark, Than drew in his legs and sat up. The sloping thatch roof brushed against his head, tipping off his Stetson, but he found there was enough room for him to sit comfortably upright in the center of the coop, where the wheel-spoked log beams rose to about four feet, its highest point. The smells of stale chicken feed and dried bird droppings were strong in his nostrils, making it unpleasant to breathe, but the fresh grass covering the pole platform beneath them was clean and dry. After a while, he began to distinguish shapes in the dim glow of the moonlight that seeped through the entrance hole and the regular cracks in the wicker weave, falling across them in specks and slithers of shining light. The night wind rustled through this ventilation, touching them with fingers of ice.

Jenny sat crouched a little apart from him, her teeth quite audibly chattering by now. Although Than gave her his shirt to wear and explained the necessity of keeping dry, he had the devil's own difficulty parting Jenny from her wet clothes. Finally, assured that it was too dark for him to see in here, reminded of his immune status as doctor, and under threat of pneumonia and his rising temper, she shyly succumbed. First taking firm hold of his shirt before she would relinquish a single item, she sat with her back to him while she awkwardly disrobed, the rickety coop rocking slightly on its stilts as she crouched as far away from him as was possible in its cramped height. Even then she gave in reluctantly, arguing successive points as they came to mind. Finally, shamed into it by his stony silence, she meekly slipped off her wet panties and fell still, softly panting, clad only in his blue denim shirt, which swamped her small frame, reaching like a short nightdress to her thighs. Even then it was a terrific ordeal and she held the shirt pulled carefully taut around her and jumped like a startled baby when he innocently touched her.

"Jesus Christ." He shook his head in exasperation. "Calm down. I'm not Brer Wolf, and unless I'm sadly mistaken, you've got no physiological parts I haven't seen a million times."

He began to pile up the straw, spreading the *sitatunga* skin in the center of the coop, muttering: "Guess this old skin's not too soft or clean or sweet-smelling, but it'll keep out the cold and we can huddle together for warmth." He shook out the robe and it crackled hollowly, settling down. "Now all we have to worry about is diphtheria, dysentery, and the Friends' committee ever finding out."

He blew out the match, hunkering down on his side and wriggling to get comfortable in the prickly straw. Then he reached out to her. "Here's my hand, Jenny. Come on over here and lie with your back against me. That way I can cuddle around you and we might keep halfway warm. And stop worrying—I promise not to try and get back into my shirt while you're still wearing it."

But despite the joke he deemed their situation to be, they both knew how the Friends' committee might very well view this necessary liaison in the cold light of day. Now Jenny sat in the dimness, looking so wide-eyed with horror that he had to laugh.

"Hey, take it easy—not a word of your wanton ways will pass these lips to sully your lily-white reputation, ma'am. So come on now."

"I don't think I should," she murmured uncertainly. "You were right about . . . how it might look."

"Oh, Jesus," he groaned in vexed exasperation. His whole body ached, and feeling hot and sick, desperately in need of rest, a conscience-stricken female was more than he felt he could handle right now. He sat bolt upright in the straw, whispering urgently: "Hey! Did you hear that? Jesus! I hope it's not the Kazungula Killer!"

That did it; with a small squeal, she tumbled around and fell on top of him. Ready for it, he caught her and pulled her down beside him, proclaiming stoutly: "Don't worry, Jenny—I'll protect you!"

But captured in his arms, her priorities had instantly shifted; she promptly forgot the lion in her frantic struggle to keep the shirt decently down as he pulled her back against him. By the time she realized it was a false alarm, she was inescapably snugly pinned in his arms.

20

In the dead of night, Jenny's urgent shriek brought Than conscious with a terrifying start. Through the soporific fog of his fever, amid the thin abysmal whining of mosquitoes, he lay for a moment paralyzed with fright, sweating and shaking, listening to his own feverish breathing as he stared up into the moon-softened darkness. For a moment he didn't know where he was or what was happening. Then the all-pervading stink of the chicken coop and the feel of Jenny in his arms gave him back his bearings, and he whispered above his pounding heart:

"Jenny—what is it?"

"I don't know . . ." she breathed, shuddering unendurably, all wound up in a tense knot and clinging to his arm. "I think it was a rat or something. It ran right across my hand."

"A *rat?*" he quailed in disgust, sagging back with relief. "Jesus, the way you yelled—I thought we had the Kazungula Killer in here."

His heart was still pounding painfully and he lay for a moment trying to interpret the light rattle of rain against the thatch roof above them. His mouth was so dry he could scarcely raise the spit to swallow, and besides his raging thirst, he felt sick and depressed and drenched in perspiration; his bare chest dripped with it, and his jeans, which had shrunk snug as a second skin while drying on him earlier, felt decidedly damp again. His arm beneath Jenny's head had begun to tingle and he had little feeling in one frozen foot, which he had kicked out through the entrance hole during his drugged sleep; it must have lain there exposed for some time, sprinkled by the light falling rain.

"Jenny," he croaked. "Would you mind easing off there a little? My arm's going to sleep."

264

"I'm sorry."

She sat up and Than dragged himself up in the prickly straw. Cursing under his breath, he bent his stiff leg and hauled up his bare foot; he sat fiercely chafing it till it gradually thawed, then he began rubbing his arm to get the circulation going, grumbling ungraciously: "Jenny—for such a little girl, you got a head like a rock."

He felt around in the straw, found the box of matches, and lit one up, squinting in the dim flare as he peered around the little circular coop. Clustered along the outer perimeter, a beady-eyed collection of scrawny white fowl blinked belligerently back at him.

"Jesus. I don't know about any rat, but it looks like we got the whole goddamn barnyard back in here. We'll be lucky if we're not crawling with lice and some godawful poultry disease by morning."

Moving the match, he began to search for the bottles of water the headman had given them. Catching a glimmer of glass in the straw, he blew out the match and unearthed one of the labelless whiskey bottles; wiping his sweat-slippery hands on his jeans, and with fingers trembling with eagerness and haste, he twisted off the lid and tipped back his head, gulping down a great greedy mouthful. His eyes widened and he came back immediately, explosively coughing and spluttering, showering Jenny with liquid.

"Jesus," he gasped, holding a hand to his seared throat. "This is some more of that scorching moonshine we were served up earlier. Goddamnit—what was that guy thinking of? Where's that other bottle?"

"Is something the matter?" Jenny asked hesitantly as she distressfully scratched at her mosquito-bitten arms.

"Yeah. My mouth's so fucking dry, I can scarcely raise the spit to speak." He glared around at her, slapping at mosquitoes, defying her to object to his unthinking obscenity. "I'm dying of thirst, this goddamn roof keeps decapitating me, these goddamn bottles keep playing hide and seek and . . ."

Suddenly losing the train of his thought, he stared at her dumbly, swallowing dryly, sitting motionless while the perspiration dribbled in ticklish trails down his face. For in the dim glow as she knelt anxiously upright beside him, her long-lashed beautiful eyes in that guileless angelic face looked strangely compelling, artificially alive, mirroring the match flame that flared like fiery passion in their dead dark depths. As she waited expectantly, she looked unconsciously as coyly sexy as a schoolgirl pin-up in his blue denim shirt. Her rich, dark, Titian-tinged hair, disheveled during sleep, tumbled womanishly across her slight shirt-swamped shoulders, and for the first time in their acquaintance, he got a good hard look at her slender, shapely legs. She still had the shirt pulled carefully taut around them, as if she kept hidden between her thighs some sinful secret it might shock him to suspect. She had the kind of easily bruised soft, sensitive skin that never seemed to take a tan, and compromised by the husky male attire, which emphasized her untouchable quality, her puritanical properness, fairness, and fragility, she had an alluring big-eyed baby innocence, which by its very nature challenged corruption, aggravating the animal in the male.

The match flame burned down to Than's fingers and he hissed, shaking it out, catching himself staring. Then, feeling confused and disgruntled and sick, aware of Jenny still politely waiting, he turned away and tried to collect his thoughts.

"Now where in hell is that damn bottle . . ." After a moment's frantic scrambling, he came up with the second bottle. When this too turned out to contain more of the same *katchipembe*, he lifted it, resigned. At least it was wet. Driven by his desperate thirst, he had drained half the bottle before he knew what he was doing. When he finally came shuddering back to his senses, he looked around, wiping his mouth, suddenly aware of Jenny's sightless eyes still watchfully trained on him in the dimness. Feeling oddly uncomfortable with the recent picture of her smooth white thighs still indelibly imprinted in his mind, he rankled guiltily.

"Listen, don't wait for me. Why don't you go back to sleep. That pussy cat's probably miles away and a little rat won't hurt you."

"Are you all right?" She blinked at him solemnly in the shadowy gloom. "You were breathing so strangely, Doctor; sweating and tossing and groaning in your sleep."

"Doctor?" he echoed irritably, recapping the bottle. "Will you for Chrissakes quit that? My name is Than, little Miss Solomon! And if I'm not mistaken, I've known you for some time now. Normally I wouldn't bat an eye at your quaint formality, but you happen to be sleeping with me, for crying out loud!"

"I . . . I'm sorry." She turned away and sat so still he knew his angry words had affected her deeply. He felt her withdrawing, bewildered and hurt, and he was instantly ashamed; it must be tough enough being blind and shy without his taking exception to its outcome.

"Hey, it's okay," he said softly, setting aside the bottle, touching her arm. "Don't mind me. It's just a little spooky, is all—sleeping with a girl who keeps calling you Doctor. Feels like I just crawled

266

into bed with a patient. Besides, we irascible old sawbones don't like being reminded of our profession once we're off duty."

"Yes," she said, but she sounded sad and strained and unconvinced. He wanted to take the time to reassure her, but the *katchipembe* had settled ill on his queasy stomach, and feeling suddenly nauseated, he turned, and scattering crazily-cackling chickens in his wake, crawled hastily out through the entrance hole.

As he sat crouched over the edge of the narrow platform in the night darkness, it started to rain hard and he shivered violently, feeling the gooseflesh rise as the stinging drops pelted his bare back while he dryly gagged. After he had managed to expel a little bitter bile, swaying unsteadily over the dizzy drop, he unzipped his jeans and urinated the sixteen feet down to the ground. Then he crawled weakly back inside the stuffy coop, slumping shivering beneath the crackling *sititunga* robe while the rain rattled on the thatch above them and a drunken dizziness descended upon his painfully pounding head. Wet with rain and sweat, he felt freezing cold and he opened his aching eyes and searched out Jenny in the dimness. Feeling wretched and weak, he wanted comfort so badly that the words were out before he could stop them.

"Jenny, I'm sick."

That reached her; she straightened instantly and turned slowly around, a shadowy figure in the gloom. "I know," she said softly.

"It's nothing too bad." He tried to be light. "Just a recurrence of malaria, but I feel pretty rough."

"I'm sorry." She sat perfectly still in the dimness. "Is there anything I can do?"

He didn't speak for a moment; then he stirred listlessly. "Well, I sure wish you could procure me a serviceable cigarette . . . but since that's kind of impossible . . . Jenny, sometimes there's nothing a man needs so much as . . ." he swallowed ". . . as a soft body to hold."

After a moment, he closed his eyes, whispering huskily, "Jenny, you're so sweet and little and good. And you're a woman. Comfort me, Jenny."

For a small eternity there was no sound but their breathing. She sat so silent and still that he began to think she was either offended or asleep sitting up. Then she turned all the way around to face him. In the dusky light her sightless eyes regarded him strangely, and he guessed that even in her innocence, she must have some dim, if ambiguous, idea of the different kind of contact he now wanted, for she dropped her head, confused and irresolute, lifting her hands helplessly.

"I . . . I'm not properly dressed."

"Hush." He reached out and touched her hand, humoring her modesty. "That doesn't matter to me. I'm a doc—remember?"

But he knew it was a qualification of immunity he only felt compelled to repeat because it was suddenly invalid. He took her small cold hand and she felt the trembling need that wracked his body and instantly forgot her own fears. Gradually, groping blindly, guided by his hand, she crawled to him on her knees. He opened the kaross to admit her, urging her around to face him, and slowly, tremulously, keeping the shirt pulled carefully down around her, she settled tensely on her side beside him.

"I'm pretty sweaty," he apologized, but she shook her head, smiling nervously.

"I don't mind."

"No, I didn't guess you would." Smiling tenderly back at her, he touched her cheek softly, almost shyly, before he reached out and gathered her in his arms. The denim shirt soaked up the sweat that gilded his bare chest as he held her against him, her face pressed to his collarbone. Then he bowed his head to find her face, nuzzling her cheek comfortingly with his sweat-slickened bristled chin.

They listened for a moment as the clicking staccato of the rain suddenly ceased, trailing to a fitful pattering on the low thatch above them, and a sweet waft of clean fresh air momentarily alleviated the stifling stink of the cold coop.

"Honey," he croaked gently, struggling to suppress the shivering spasms that racked him. "Put your arms around me."

Slowly, shyly, trembling almost as much as he was shaking, she reached up and slid her arms around his neck.

"Yeah," he murmured approvingly. But she lay stiff in his arms, and before he knew what he was doing, he began automatically seeking out her erogenous zones, awkward in his inebriation, gentling her with a trained and restrained tactile persuasion, massaging the nape of her rigid neck with his fingers, stroking her hair with his shaking hands, clumsily smoothing her cheeks, blowing on her closed eyes, and whispering in her ear. The shirt had pulled up when she raised her arms to embrace him, and she gave a small start of shock when he put his arm back around her and accidentally touched her bare behind.

"Hey, it's okay," he whispered, catching her quick hand before she could adjust it; as he talked, he slipped his other hand unobtrusively up her back beneath the shirt. "It's okay . . . it's okay . . . leave it be."

Nuzzling the side of her neck, he felt the agitation gradually die down inside her, until her body relaxed against him and she lay, eyes closed and acquiescent, beside him, mesmerized by his touch, her sweet face, in the moon glow, racked with a look like love. He bit softly at her neck and earlobes. Then, staring woozily down at her in his own dizzy darkness, struggling to properly focus his clouded mind, he brushed her lips with his own, tenderly tantalizing, tracing their shape with the tip of his tongue, kissing the corners of her mouth, till, finely primed, she sighed and pouted for the full promise of his mouth, following his teasing touch like a sensuous cat preening to a stroking.

Then, suddenly too weak to sustain his sensual assault, he sagged back, bereft and disabled at the point of conquest, feeling frustrated and helpless as a beetle on its back. It was more than he could bear, and he whispered hoarsely, "Kiss me, Jenny."

She stared dully beyond him and he lay dazed and dissipated, a mute plea communicating itself through his touch, his urgent need magnetically drawing, until she raised herself, and shyly, uncertainly, came hunting for him with her quivering mouth. And although it must be against her very nature to initiate in this intimate contact, in her intuitive empathy, doubtless instinctively understanding the tormented months in a lonely bed that had culminated in this desperation, she reached out her shy hands, finding his face, locating his mouth, giving of herself so selflessly that he felt a wave of gratitude and, regaining his strength, came up to meet her.

He took her mouth tenderly at first, sweetly sucking till he felt her reticence fade and she too was straining fervently toward him for fuller contact, her lips opening to receive his probing tongue in a flushed fever of feeling. Then he slid his hand down and found one small breast. And after the months of deprivation, the feel of it all but lost in the thick denim folds of his shirt unleashed the animal in him. He gnawed at her mouth and caressed her breast with resurgent strength and a bruising lust that shocked them both. She twisted her face away, bursting breathlessly from his kiss, suddenly flustered and frightened.

"Oh . . . please no," she gasped, shivering, catching at his hand to still his frantic fondling, trying to pull it from her breast, staring at him with wild wide eyes. "Please don't!"

But there was no way in the world he could stop himself now, and resisting her efforts to ward him off, keeping his hand still possessively clinging to her breast, he choked brokenly, "Jenny, please—oh God, I need you! Love me, please . . ."

And staring in anguish up at him, moved by the raw emotion of his plea, by his sickness and suffering, her struggles fell finally still, her faltering fears silenced by his overwhelming greater need. As her blind eyes stared intensely through him, her urgent hand fell still at his wrist, sagging weakly away, leaving him free access.

"Oh God . . ." he sighed with gratitude. "You're so sweet and beautiful . . ." Struggling to suppress his violent shivering, he moved to kiss her with his shaking mouth, his hands all the while furtively fumbling as he ripped open two of the stubborn shirt studs, slipping his hand inside. At the first touch of his fingers on her naked flesh, she stiffened reactively, eyes opening wide. But this time he was ready for her.

"Jenny, don't worry. I just want to love you . . ."

Cuddling her head against him, he smothered her uncertain protests against his chest and began nuzzling her neck and caressing her breasts until the little nipples stood out stiff against his palm and she lay fretting sensuously, as peaceably pliable as clay in his hands. And unable to restrain himself a moment longer, he hooked his fingers in her shirt front and ripped it all the way open. Then he slipped his other arm around her, inside the shirt, holding her little limp body fiercely tight against him. She gasped at the contact, and the feel of her small breasts pressed flat against the hard muscle of his bare chest filled him with a great awkward aching tenderness, exciting him unendurably. Aching for consummation, he pressed his swollen groin to her prim little pubis, caressing her silken flank with his hand, his palm lingering tantalizingly on the angular bump of her slender hip.

She made no move to stop him when he pushed her over onto her back, but lay anguished and acquiescent, staring up at him with great dark eyes that frightened him strangely with their pain. He was glad when his own black shadow blotted them out of the faint dusky light as he climbed unsteadily on top of her. Even in his confused intoxication, he understood the need to take great caution with her, and he struggled to discipline his desire-driven blundering body to a finesse and a patience and restraint he felt drunkenly incapable of. He smoothed back her hair and kissed her throat and breasts as he gradually eased apart her tightly clamped trembling thighs with a

270

rough insistent knee. His painfully pulsating powerful erection was threatening to burst the cramped confines of his jeans, but holding her close, straining to contain his own restless impatience, he bided his time as long as he could. He comforted her tenderly, whispering ageless endearments into her ear as he wriggled in his other knee, wedging wider her thighs. Then, afraid to take the time to undress fully, he fumbled hastily at the front of his pants.

At the first probing touch of his flesh, she reared up beneath him, startled to reality, reacting like a frightened filly first feeling the whip. He withdrew at once, hurriedly reassuring, kissing, and caressing her until, soothed by the pleasurable sucking sensations and his sensitive stroking of her breasts, shoulders, and throat, she began to quieten again, the tension seeping out of her loins until she lay limply receptive beneath him. This time she did not pull away, but as he eased himself gently into her tight virgin body, she began trembling violently and the tears of lost innocence burst through the thick enmeshed lashes of her tightly closed eyes.

"Oh God, Jenny—don't cry. Jenny, Jenny . . . love me, please. Don't cry."

He tried to kiss away her streaming tears, but already engrossed in his own increasingly pleasure-pain, his consideration for her, like everything else, was fast losing substance in the narrowing realm of his reality, and he was only dimly aware of her when the tough resistance of her hymen brought him dazedly back to more practical considerations and he whispered anxiously against her cheek:

"Baby, I'll be as gentle as I can; it'll only hurt a moment. Just bear down against me as I push up . . ."

Then, staring down into her widening, tear-filled, anguished eyes, he plunged brutally and he was through. She gasped and cried out, yet even while softly, heartbrokenly crying, weakly bucking at him, rejecting him with her loins, she clung to him with her arms and mouth like someone sweetly drowning. And insulated in his high fine intoxication, in that moment there was no right or wrong, no Katherine-conscience, no Suzannah-spouse, and no censorious Friends' committee. And while he moved, rapt in the bittersweet hurting ecstasy, her soft crying gradually died. She might have fervently whispered "*I love thee,*" or was it just her breath in his ear and the soft susurration of the wind in the plain, singing dizzily around their wicker womb, whispering to them the long-forgotten secrets of the eternal savannah . . .

21

The ardent carousing of a cockerel heralded the dawn on the pole platform outside, dimly penetrating Than's drugged slumber as he lay bruised and burned out after his night of fever and passion. As the sun rose, the village drum began to sound, jerking him fitfully awake. He lay for a moment, twitching inertly, stultified in the stuffy atmosphere, at first too stupefied to function or feel anything much beyond the pounding pain in his head and the ache in his spleen. By the time he was sufficiently roused to ease open his aching eyes, he squinted against the searing light that seeped into the cloistered little coop, soft, white and cynical, bristling with accusation.

He shook his head and closed his eyes again, trying to orientate himself, becoming gradually aware of each of his stiff aching limbs, of his body lying loosely sprawled half across Jenny, who lay limply pliant beneath him. As he raised himself groggily, their fused flesh, glued by his dead weight and his feverous sweat, came reluctantly unstuck. Looking down, he was horrified to realize that the shirt was pulled open so that Jenny's nude body was exposed before him; his own fly was open, his genitals hanging out. Even as he stared, stunned, down at her sweetly sleeping form, Jenny's dark lashes flickered open and her vague blue eyes stared up at him blankly. Then her face twisted with horror and he felt her growing rigid with the same sense of shock as she too remembered what had happened between them during the night.

With a wrench that stung their flesh, Than rolled abruptly away from her. Left uncovered, naked and vulnerable, Jenny cowered in sudden helpless horror, frantically feeling for some cover, while he hastily stuffed his penis back into his pants. Scattering squawking chickens, he crawled backward and lay with his back pressed against the wicker wall of the coop. Scorched by his shame and self-recrimination, he closed his eyes, devastated by his own despised role of violator, wanting to die of remorse.

"Oh God . . . Oh Jesus! What have I done?" he whispered. His throat ached and he felt like crying; he covered his bowed head with his crossed arms and shook his head, unable to endure it. "Oh God," he choked. "Please tell me I never did what I know I've just done. I must have been crazy, half out of my mind! Please tell me it never happened."

When he looked up she had crawled away and was sitting on her haunches against the wicker wall opposite, stiffly erect in the straw, her pale thighs tautly clamped and his blue denim shirt wrapped tightly around her as she sat hugging her waist beneath her crossed arms.

"Oh God, Jenny. What can I say? Believe me, you're the last person on earth—the *very last*—I would have wanted to . . . to do *that* to! Believe me. The very last!"

"Why?" she whispered dully, still sitting very still, her sightless eyes staring stonily.

"Why?" Interrupted in his anguish, the question threw him for a moment and he stopped and stared at her stupidly, trying to figure it out himself. "Why? Well . . . I guess because you're *blind* . . . and . . ."

He knew it was a mistake the minute he said it, when he saw the raw pain break in her despairing face, and trying to undo it, he babbled desperately, "No! I didn't mean that! Believe me, please . . . hey, if you think for one moment that I . . . well, it's not true! Listen, whatever you think, I don't pity you . . . I . . ."

But taking cue from her eyes, his trailing words lost conviction, and he knew she must know as well as he that his righteous denial was only half true. Because in spite of what he wanted to feel, pity for her was partly the reason he so regretted his cruel seduction. But it was more than that; it was Jenny herself—kind, considerate, gentle Jenny, whose very high-mindedness and pure and principled nature were anathema to the kind of searing sexual dalliance he had mindlessly subjected her to.

"Oh God," he groaned helplessly. "Forgive me, forgive me . . ."

But his unrightable wrong lay irrevocably between them; there was no comfort for either of them in his anguished apology, and he watched in pain as the tears slowly swelled in her stricken sightless eyes, which looked very big and blue in her pale shocked face in the faintly infused daylight. Yet even in her own anguish she found the feeling to comfort his, shaking her head, absolving him of blame, trying to smile as the tears burst through her dark lashes and began to stream down her colorless cheeks.

"It's not your fault," she whispered, a little quirk of pain catching perplexedly in her smooth brow. Then she turned away and pressed against the wicker wall, struggling to suppress the grief that rose on soundless breath-caught sobs, finally covering her face as she wept brokenly, stammering through her anguish and shame: "It's all right . . . it's all right."

But staring sickly at her in his own torment, Than knew innately that now it never would be. For somehow, carnal knowledge of her had sullied his soul. And now, feeling contemptible and contaminated, unable to face her or himself, he had to escape. Snatching up her sodden dress, he tossed it to her before pulling on his clammy boots, jamming on his Stetson, and crawling hastily out into the raw light of the cold and overcast dawning day.

Spread out below him, the mist-shrouded panorama of the partially flooded plain resounded faintly to the hushed booming of hornbills. The village drum still rumbled monotonously, and as he scrambled, shirtless and shivering, down the tall crooked ladder, someone shook sleeping mats over the edge of a pole platform, while in the little jesse-enclosed village beneath, a baby wailed and women clattered dirty cooking pots, tossing the lumpy dregs of stale maize porridge to the snapping village dogs.

As he tumbled hastily to the ground, a passing woman threw down her hoe and immediately sank to a knee in the traditional greeting. Hastily acknowledging this courtesy, Than turned to find to his dismay that still others were leaving off their chores and hurrying up to follow her example. In his desperate desire to be alone, the prospect of people was claustrophobic. As they approached from all directions, he began backing off, looking helplessly around, mumbling inane apologies. But misunderstanding, gabbling unintelligibly and smiling like simpletons, they began to swarm around him, and he gave up all pretext of politeness and fled.

His panicked haste through the spindly hut-stilts was enough to send the shy children clambering like monkeys up the long pole ladders. As he hurried, scattering chickens and goats in his wild wake, knocking over utensils and swerving around a giant pet tortoise in his desperate search for an outlet in the thorn boma, the forsaken villagers turned baffled faces to follow his flight. Finally finding a break in the bush, Than burst breathlessly through, almost stepping into the path of a balefully bawling herd of the big-horned Barotse cattle, which thudded past on their way to pasture in the misty grasslands.

By the time the last piebald cow had ambled off amid the whistles, slaps, and shouts of its young spear-carrying attendants, Than's panic had started to subside; as he stood slumped, breathing hard and regaining his senses, he heard a shout and looked up to see the village headman hailing him urgently from amidst a group of men who were consulting agitatedly amongst themselves, hanging on spears as they pointed, pouring earnestly over the earth. As Than trudged up to join them, they greeted him and the headman gestured for him to inspect pug marks that pocked the rain-firmed sand. The prints were indistinct and overlaid in places where some large animal had evidently several times encircled the village during the night.

With his head still pounding and his aching eyes blurring at the effort of concentration, it took Than a moment to properly digest the implications of the sketchy trail of spoor. Such was his anguish over his illicit liaison with Jenny that the realization took him by complete surprise. He stared, further stunned as the headman found a clearly impressed set of prints and pointed out the dragging lighter tread of one incriminatingly twisted wounded forepaw. Over on the bark of a nearby *mkusu* tree, another man called his attention to a damp stain that was clustered by a cloud of bright yellow butterflies. Than stooped to sniff the unpleasantly ammoniac cat urine, pulling a face as he straightened up slowly. Well, the Kazungula Killer had clearly left his calling card.

"Jesus," he whispered incredulously. "I guess I really did see it, after all . . ."

22

Matthew, Homer Haskel, and the redoubtable Ezra Peabody comprised one of the search parties that set out at daybreak to scour the countryside for the missing pair. Village drums relaying news of the strays had been throbbing since dawn, and after enlisting the directional aid of several wayside natives, it was ten-thirty in the morning by the time they finally traced them to a small swamp-skirted village on the great Barotse plain. Parking the Land-Rover before a boggy patch, they entered the village on foot, surprised to find the village full of dancing and jubilation. The stranded couple sat on a log in the sun among the long-legged huts, looking, even at a distance, so sick and dispirited that Matthew felt a vague disquiet.

Homer called a cheery greeting as they strode across the village amid the kneeling decorous greetings of the clamoring natives, and the marooned pair turned to meet this robust rescue as dejectedly as if it signified the imminence of the world's end. Than Profane got stiffly to his feet, unfolding slowly to his full height, dusting off the seat of his crumpled blue jeans as he reached down to help Jenny up. As she rose and turned, a small, soft puppy dog spilled from her lap. She stood looking so inexplicably vulnerable and afraid that Matthew, on reaching her, took her cold hands in his.

He stood for a moment anxiously searching the wan wistful face under the limp lavender bonnet, alarmed to realize that for the first time in their acquaintance, her expression bore the indefinable blankness he always expected to find in the eyes of the blind. Yet although he sensed in this some soul-deep hurt, the only visible signs of anything amiss were the mud stains on her skirt and a faint oval bruise starting to surface on the side of her neck.

"Jenny child," he croaked anxiously. "Is thee all right?"

"She's fine," the Boy answered for her, but his narrowed blue eyes were impenetrably distant in the shadow of his Stetson, and he didn't sound any more reassuring than she looked. As Matthew stood there taking silent stock, Homer jostled up to greet the girl, and feeling her fretting to pick up the ousted pup, which tumbled, whining, around her ankles, Matthew let her go and took the Boy's clammy hand. Shaking it diagnostically, he studied the pale perspiring handsome face skeptically, while beyond them, waiting officiously in an immaculate frock suit, Ezra Peabody stood holding a big leatherbound Gideon Bible.

"We came upon the wreck of the mission vehicle in the river," he said in a voice of grievous gravity. "It's a pity thee thought to chance such a fragile bridge, Doctor. Seems to me it's rather an ignominious end to thy glorious crusade—and the vehicle seems likely seriously damaged. I'm rather afraid the board will want some answer to such sorry destruction."

"Well now, Ezra, I don't know about that!" Matthew was instantly defensive. "It could happen to anyone. The vehicle's a trifle overwet perhaps, but I've no doubt we'll be able to have it pulled out and overhauled. I'm just grateful to the good Lord to find them both safe." He turned back to the Boy, releasing his hand. "It must have been a harrowing experience. Thee sure thee're all right? Thee both look kind of . . . *strange.*"

"Oh pshaw!" Homer grinned brashly. "If thee asks me—they look disgustingly healthy. Why, we rushed out here expecting to find them in the lion's belly or somebody's cooking pot. And here they stand, not a mark on 'em, the two of 'em looking as if they've just taken a tumble in the hay!"

Matthew knew what he meant; the pair were covered in bits of dry grass, which implied some such idle activity. But under the circumstances, the innocent remark was embarrassingly open to crude interpretation. The Boy was apparently likewise acquainted with the sexual significance, for he stared at Homer in stupefied disbelief; the perspiration popped out on his temples, and he shut his eyes suddenly and swayed on his feet.

"Here now—hold on there." Matthew caught at his arm, alarmed. "Is thee all right?"

"I'm fine." The Boy shrugged off his hand. But when he opened his eyes they were an unnatural indigo against the pallor of his tan. He stood for some moments self-consciously staring, awkwardly dusting the stray flecks of grass off his creased denim shirt. "I'll be all right. It's nothing too serious; just a recurrence of malaria."

"Malaria!" Matthew exclaimed. "Nothing too serious, thee says?"

"Now, don't thee go getting all excited, Matthew," Homer interjected levelly. "The doctor should know, after all. Seems to me he's big and bad enough to take care of himself!"

"Quite," Ezra agreed shortly. "And the good Lord sometimes acts in mysterious ways. Why, this may very well have been a heaven-sent opportunity for the doctor to get through to some of the pitiful heathen souls hereabouts." He turned a cold, inquiring smile onto the Boy. "Tell me, Doctor—did thee put the previous wasted hours of this estrangement into good employment?" Wetting his pale lips, he smiled thinly. "I trust thee were able to reach a few souls?"

Matthew stared at the man in incredulous exasperation. But if he were so ignorantly inconsiderate of the debilitating effects of malaria and a motor accident, the Boy would not waste the time it took to enlighten him.

"You got it, Mr. Peabody," he answered ambiguously, but his tired tone belied the inference that he was a veritable superman, indefatigable even by disease, an illusion which Matthew, for once, direly doubted.

"Well, I'm not so sure about that," Matthew said lamely. "Just the same, I thank the Lord thee's not injured any. I could not have withstood another shock."

"Another shock?" As he stooped to pick up his medical bag, the Boy's fair brows listlessly lifted. "Why? What else has happened?"

"Well, I'm afraid it's Dr. MacLintock over in the Congo. Thee remember how he returned to his hospital in Kasai province once the independence troubles started to settle down? Well, we've just got word from our Friends in Katanga that a militant band of Patrice Lumumba's supporters have invaded the mission and taken him prisoner along with a number of other whites in the area. Apparently they fear Lumumba will come to some harm now that he's been transferred to Tshombe's jail in Katanga, and they're holding them hostage—threatening to kill them should anything happen to their idol."

"Yeah?" The Boy eyed him darkly. Beside him, Jenny looked up with a dazed despairing face, and the Boy swallowed visibly. "That's tough; how about his family? Mary and the girls?"

"Well, they're still safe back in Katanga. Fortunately, Alvin had the good sense not to allow them to . . ." But following Ezra's distasteful stare, Matthew broke off, suddenly seeing the unsightly sores, the fly-bitten ears, and the fleas that crawled thickly beneath the bedraggled soft fur of the thin little pup that Jenny fondled obliviously in her arms. He addressed her gently: "Jenny child, that little dog looks kind of unsavory. Maybe thee'd best set it down."

"Aw, save your breath, Matthew," the Boy said cynically. "I already tried to tell her that, but seems like she believes in giving her love to any poor stray starving jasper that comes her way, regardless of the consequences. She . . ." He stopped abruptly as if suddenly shocked at his own unwarranted sarcasm. Then, avoiding the girl's stricken bewildered look, he said impatiently, "Matthew, would you mind coming with me to see the headman? I have some unfinished business to attend to."

"What? Oh yes . . ." Matthew trailed, vaguely disturbed because, despite his advice, Jenny still absently nursed the malodorous little mutt, which had started sucking one of her fingers with sleepy slurping sounds as if desperately trying to draw sustenance from this dry digit.

Leaving the little group, Matthew strode with the Boy through the towering hut stalks to a thin Barotse gentleman who came solemnly to meet them, surrounded by a lively hoard of dusty children. After waiting out the man's decorous *kandalela*, Matthew thanked him for his hospitality on the Mission's behalf. The headman had evidently never heard a white man talk *sikololo*, the local Lozi language, so fluently before. So intoxicating was his astonished admiration that Matthew's vanity did not allow him to leave it at that; as he drifted along beside the man and Than Profane, he touched nonchalantly on the weather and Christianity, becoming so caught up in his eloquent effusing that before he knew it, he had followed the pair out of the village through the thorn boma. They were out in the open in the cicada-shrilling heat and silence of the great sun-shimmering plain, where the distant blue spread of the rising Zambezi stretched to the infinity of the horizon.

Just outside the village, a group of tribesmen were gathered beneath a big-boled tree. Dressed in skins and seseba skirts, they carried sticks and spears and muzzle-loading guns. It was not until they neared that Matthew, noticing a colorful figure heathenishly clad in a black fiber wig and a kilt of mongoose tails, began to unhappily suspect the nature of the Boy's "unfinished business."

"Here, now . . ." he began uneasily in English. "What's all this?"

"Well, near as I can make out, this fellow's a witchdoctor from the Congo." The Boy paused while he and Matthew, waving away the lazy flies, acknowledged the greeting of the group. Then he sighed, "He pitched up here after the news went out about our little adventure last night. If I've got the gist right, according to the headman, he wants to "throw the bones" for me. You arrived just in time to interpret, Matthew."

"*Now, see here!*" Matthew gaped at the Boy, nonplussed and incredulous. Aware of the uncomprehending headman staring at them in innocent awe, he whispered furiously. "Thee mean, with Mr. Peabody right here—thee had the almighty nerve to drag me out here to officiate in some *noxious heathen doings!*"

"Now hold on, Matthew." The Boy stared at him sickly. "Right now I don't feel up to playing these games any more than you do— but we can hardly offend these people and it might just be we have something to learn from it!"

"I don't care what we have to learn," Matthew snorted, throwing up his hands, growing red in the face with the force of his feeling. "It'd not make a jot of difference to me if the queen of England herself ordered thee to . . . to . . . *thee had no right!*"

Suddenly catching the headman's bewildered look, dimly aware that he was making a spectacle of himself before a bunch of susceptible heathens, Matthew broke off, subsiding huffily, hardly consoled when the headman began introducing them to the witchdoctor and his entourage. At this point in the proceedings, he might have petulantly refused to cooperate (if anything, the Boy's goading nudge and appealing gaze only steeled him in his opposition!), but stirred by the headman's stricken face and his own common good grace, he reluctantly responded, albeit snappily and with a great show of wounded pride. When the witchdoctor, staring stonily at them through festooning flies and the thin ringlets of his black fiber wig, began to address the Boy in his native Chi-Lunda, Matthew swallowed his gall and translated the gist. But with the indignation still seething within his breast, he hardly registered the meaning of the man's words as he mechanically relayed them.

"This man says that as one medicine man to another, he salutes thee. He concedes that thee must indeed be a powerful doctor, for even Chief Marumahoko in the person of the man-eating lion sensed thy power and was afraid to attack thee. He says that by thy presence was the lion repulsed and the village saved. He says the lion . . . *lion?*" Suddenly registering the dread word, Matthew stopped dead, staring at the Boy in trepidation. "What does he mean?" he quailed like a man in pain. "Lion? *What* lion? Thee don't mean to say . . ."

Taking off his Stetson to run his fingers through his sandy-blond hair, the Boy sighed tiredly. "I guess you never got to hear the latest drum broadcasts, Matthew. Well, I'll tell you—the fact is the Kazungula Killer paid us a little visit last night. Judging by the spoor, the village trackers figure it must have actually been stalking Jenny and me when we came in from the plain. I guess I even saw it once. We were in no shape to hold it off, so God knows why it never attacked. Anyhow, the upshot of it is . . . like the man says, these people now regard me as some kind of powerful *ngaka;* they feel I have somehow saved them and granted their village immunity from future attack. They've been pretty cheerful ever since, dancing and singing, and I've had to refuse any number of grateful gifts. Anyhow, you can stop looking so worried; the lion's gone now." Replacing his Stetson, he nodded toward the witchdoctor. "Looks like our man is about ready to begin, so maybe we'd better get it over with before I start throwing up again."

He sank to the ground, sitting in the bleached grass opposite the *ngaka,* who sat with his back against the tree trunk. As the man spread the pernicious paraphernalia of his trade in the tree's dappled shade, the hoarse barking of the village dogs jolted Matthew from his stupefaction and he turned to find, to his horror, that Homer Haskel and Ezra Peabody were briskly approaching with Jenny in tow. It was a coming confrontation that Matthew, caught red-handed in embarrassing context with a denizen of the devil, dreaded almost as much as the man-eating lion.

"Well, there thee are!" Homer panted up. He stopped, squinting in surprise when he saw the witchdoctor all set for the performance of his evil art. "Here now—what in the world is all this?" he said warily. Then, half-joking, as if unsure how to take it, he trumpeted tactlessly, "Now, Matthew—don't tell me thee're about to fraternize with the likes of this heathen fellow?"

"What? Oh no . . . not at all. This man has simply asked to meet Dr. Profane," Matthew managed. But acutely mindful of the Boy's reputation for indulging in just such dubious doings, he was horribly embarrassed by the repulsive gizzard-hung hoary creature uncovered in their midst. As Ezra joined them, he took out his handkerchief and fretfully patted his perspiring brow. Lest, by his tongue-tied trapped compliance such sacrilegious skulduggery be indeed construed as complicity, he qualified cautiously: "Er . . . as thee has earlier so aptly reminded us, Friend Ezra, opportunities to give out the gospel come in many guises, and it has occurred to me that if we hold still and hear out this fellow, he's likely to afford us the same courtesy."

He paused, looking hopefully at the Boy. But if he had expected any grateful aiding allegiance from this instigator of his dilemma, he was sorely disillusioned. The stonily staring ingrate, seemingly indifferent to his discomfiture, merely left him to welter. Matthew looked up earnestly, his faded eyes anxiously asking an understanding which Ezra, for one, seemed unwilling to give. The man's aggrieved look of offended morality chilled Matthew to the bone. And if loyal Homer said nothing more, his continuing innocent amazement made Matthew feel even worse. Then, turning away, his eyes lighted on Jenny. Seeing her blind blue eyes brimming with inexplicable tears, Matthew promptly forgot his own distress and took her arm. As he drew her gently forward, the Boy looked up; seeing her, his squinting face seemed to soften suddenly and he reached up and took her hand, urging her down. She settled shyly in the grass beside him just as the witchdoctor raised his great amulet-adorned arms for silence and attention.

Such was his command that even the group of tribesmen who had discreetly withdrawn to stand out of earshot beneath a far tree fell still, turning to watch in idle curiosity as the *ngaka* took a flat winnowing basket from his assistant. Noticing his choice of receptacle, Matthew knew at once that the scoundrel had no intention of "throwing the bones," as the Boy had understood it. No indeed. It seemed that this was a *ngaka ya buloi*—a "big" doctor—who would divine by means of his *ngombo yakusekula*, a practice made infinitely more awesome and maledictive by the sinister requirement that each novice training in the art should kill a close relative as a prerequisite of success.

Innately grateful that he was probably the only European in league of this horrific little fact, Matthew nevertheless sweated guiltily in unchallenging complicity as the witchdoctor began an eerie chanting incantation, inviting his ancestral spirits to influence the fall of his symbols as he began shaking the little object-filled basket from side to side, like a woman sifting wheat. The seeds in his python-skin amulets rustled in time to the shaking of the inflated animal bladders attached to his ringlet-wriggling fiber wig, which flopped obscenely forward as he worked, leaning over the basket to watch the bouncing mass of small sticks and stones, bits of root and bone and even tiny balls of beeswax, which shivered and shifted at the agitation, falling to form and reform in myriad patterns. At length, seeming satisfied with a particular arrangement, the man suddenly stopped. Placing the basket on the ground, he leaned forward to examine minutely the pattern of its contents. As his hesitation stretched on, Matthew strained instinctively forward; out of the corner of his eye he saw Homer and Ezra edging closer. In that fly-droning, smoldering stillness, so malevolent was the witchdoctor's aura and so mesmerizing the suspenseful silence, punctuated with the liquidly dripping sad repetitive call of an emerald-spotted wood dove, that Matthew jumped visibly when the *ngaka*, staring straight at the Boy with his inscrutable black eyes, began to speak.

Wincingly aware of the silent displeasure of his two colleagues, who stood censoriously a little removed (no doubt craning necks to take avid account of this heathen fiasco in which he was by now so inextricably complicit), Matthew cleared his throat and began to translate.

"Ahem . . . Dr. Profane, I am asked by this . . . this *heathen gentleman* to inform thee that he sees thee have come across a great water to this land. He predicts for thee a long and successful life. However, he warns thee to beware of certain persons who pose as thy friends, for they will eventually conspire to have thee banished from this land." He stopped, waving away the worrisome flies, waiting impatiently while the witchdoctor finished studying his symbols before continuing his forecast. Though Matthew and his ilk were fond of denouncing such "divination" and all associated sorcery as being supernormally inspired by the devil, at the same time they usually doubted its validity, deriding the natives' respect and fear of clairvoyance and magic, and attributing occasional ostensible successes not so much to supernatural agency as to freak accident, clever psychology, sly confabulation, or the blatant fraudulency of the witchdoctors, who were notorious village snoops. Now, incredulously digesting the uncanny accuracy of the forthcoming facts, Matthew began to prickle uncomfortably with a strange stealing chill that assailed him in the heat-swollen stillness, filling him with foreboding lest this man indeed be truly empowered of the Devil.

"Matthew?"

At the sound of the Boy's voice, Matthew snapped to and continued his interpreting. "Er . . . well . . . this man chances to suppose that thy natural parents are both now lost to thee. He . . . uh . . . *conjectures* that a woman might be standing in as thy surrogate mother. He says he also sees a young girl and boy sired by thy father of this woman . . ."

This time even Ezra Peabody's low muttering was horror-hushed in the background as the diviner began to talk again.

"He says thee will have five children, one of which will die in early life," Matthew said with some relief, for the bad kidneys of the Boy's wife made at least this prediction unlikely to come true. "Furthermore, he says there have been many women in thy life. However, only three will be of lasting importance to thee, and of these, only one will be thy true love. This woman, he says, will have, like thyself, *mehiokazulu*, the eyes of heaven."

"The eyes of heaven?" The Boy squinted quizzically up at Matthew.

"Blue eyes!" Matthew scoffed with feeble satisfaction. "Of course they know that many Europeans have that coloring, and this is just where his trickery and clever conjecture are shown up for what they are! Why, if I'm not mistaken, thy wife has brown eyes, whereas he says thy love will have eyes like . . . like . . ."

Drawn by some queer questing compulsion, his eyes, like the Boy's, suddenly turned to Jenny, who sat with her dark head bowed, listening silently. At the same instant, as if sensing their surveillance, she looked up, and the brilliant blue of her sightless eyes struck Matthew with a strange sensation.

He was still wrestling with the unfathomable feeling when the witchdoctor set aside his divining device and asked his assistant for a skin bag, which hung from the tree. His face suddenly secretive, he ferreted within the bag to come up with a small wooden figurine that was attached to a long skin thong. He held the artifact aloft, reverently fondling it before handing it across to the Boy. The little carving with its white-painted slit-eyed human head and the black body of a snake looked to Matthew suspiciously like a depiction of *Ilombo*, a malevolent Lunda familiar, an evil-looking little fetish he would not have touched with a barge-pole. But the Boy, apparently not so fearfully fastidious of ill-luck and evil emanations, took the figurine, examining it with squinting interest as the *ngaka* spoke.

"He says this token is a very powerful charm, which, if worn upon thy person, will protect thee and symbolize to the natives thy powerful prowess." Matthew spoke with grim disapproval. "He says it is part of a heritage passed down to him from a much removed grandfather who was a powerful *sitondo*, or rain-doctor, at the time before the whites entered Africa." Matthew paused to blow his nose. In the muffling folds of his handkerchief, he whispered a stern aside. "Thee will not accept it, of course!"

The Boy merely smiled. "Tell him I regard the gift as a great honor. And I thank him."

Matthew stood horrified. In order to save face with their fellow missionaries, it was imperative that the Boy denounce the thing as being evil and un-Christian! However, since he could scarcely argue the point in their company, in an effort to hide and override this crucial Christian lapse, he hurried on.

"Ahem. Well, doubtless later, when thee has had time to scientifically study the thing, thee will have it destroyed. Aside from its un-Christian associations, of which I feel constrained to warn thee, the man asks of thee an impossible exchange. He feels thy escape from the lion clearly shows thee to be a great *ngaka wa litau*—doctor of lions—and while he is familiar with such men, thee are the first white man he has known endowed of such powers. He feels that thy methods and magic will be unlike those of his own kind and he asks that thee impart to him the secret of thy magic, as lions are a scourge in his home country."

Matthew paused, considering the matter as he mopped his brow. "Old fraud," he sniffed scornfully. "I'll bet he was imported into this area to take care of the man-eating lion himself. Aside from exploiting the people's fears for his own gross gains, he clearly has no faith in the very ability he is supposedly selling!"

"We don't know that, Matthew," the Boy said patiently.

"Maybe not," Matthew snorted. "But I know the likes of these scoundrels and the lengths they will go to profit their own skins. Anyhow, I'll tell them thee refuses his proposition."

"Not so fast," the Boy said, and Matthew stiffened, suddenly realizing the horrific potential that lay in the Boy's reply. Now taking suspicious stock of the young doctor's narrowing eyes and slow smile, he sweated apprehensively, expecting the Boy now to deliver the *coup de grâce* and dash them both irretrievably into damnation. But after a moment's silent considering, seeming to savor Matthew's suspense while he chewed on a weed stem, Than Profane made of his reply a vindicating riposte, which he delivered to Matthew with a flourish.

"Tell him," he said softly, in a husky voice which held an odd ring of truth, "tell him my only method was to pray to the Christian God. If anything protected me, then it must have been Jesus."

23

On their return to Suseshi, Matthew liaised by radio with Lusinga Mission in Katanga. There was no further news of Dr. MacLintock, but Chester Daniels revealed that in Katanga, Dr. Morehead had sustained a broken leg and a "hurt" hand during a small fracas with Baluba rebels at an isolated out-clinic. Now the full burden of Lusinga Hospital, overloaded with sick and starving refugees, was left on his wife and Louella Breckenbridge, at a time when they were drastically short of drugs, as Dr. MacLintock had taken much of their supplies with him to the stricken Kasai; unlike the Catholic institutions there, Protestant missions were not subsidized by the government, and due to the present confusion, there was a serious drug shortage. In addition, famine and disease, the two specters of war, stalked the villages. In the past months, there had been two Baluba uprisings in Katanga, and Lumumba-loyal soldiers, advancing from Stanleyville unimpeded by the U.N. "peace-keeping" force, had crossed the Katangan frontier. But Tshombe's gendarmes and mercenary contingents were effectively containing this far-flung feudal warfare, and with their Lusinga mission situated close to the "safe" capital of Elizabethville, snug in the heart of Tshombe-loyal Lunda country, Chester Daniels stressed that he and his colleagues, feeling the situation to be completely safe, were anxious that the long-deferred yearly meeting should still take place in little over a fortnight's time as originally planned.

Just the same, it seemed a daring decision to Matthew.

He left Mwinilunga boma grave with concern. Their Friends had not bemoaned their lot or called for help, but the message was clear—drugs and medical assistance were urgently needed. Back at Suseshi, Matthew went immediately to the hospital to consult with Jerome Dooley and Than Profane. There he found the staff exhilarated by the arrival of the new gasoline-fueled X-ray machine. However, the news of the circumstances in the Congo quickly sobered the doctors. They sorted out what medical supplies could be spared, and the Boy volunteered to cross into Katanga with Matthew on an errand of mercy. So as not to unduly worry the ladies, Matthew neglected to tell them of the more worrisome aspects of the circumstances in Katanga, mentioning only the critical drug shortage and Dr. Morehead's injuries. He suggested that in two weeks' time the male members of the all-Africa yearly meeting permanent board might follow them to attend the yearly meeting. However, there was no need for the others to make the trip; the schools, in session, should not be left, and together the group would surely constitute an adequate delegation.

In another two days they were ready to leave; in their laden Land-Rover they crossed the Congo border into the calm but tense secessionist state, which proudly flew a new red, white, and green flag emblemed with three copper crosses. Katanga's own currency notes, issued against the old Congolese franc, were already in circulation, and along the tree-lined avenues of Elizabethville, gigantic posters of the sad Sambo face of Moise Tshombe compelled patriotism from every edifice. As they turned off into the bush, the tall talking drums began to rumble of their arrival; at Lusinga, the missionaries boiled out of the buildings and fell on them with relief; although their morale was yet high, the Boy found that Dr. Morehead's right femur had been broken and his right hand severely crushed. Silencing the man's anxious fears, the Boy left him to inspect the sprawling hospital, which overflowed with refugees. There was a pitiful shortage of black staff, and with the help of other unqualified missionaries, under the supervision of Agnes Morehead, the overburdened institution had limped along on its meager supplies. Many operative cases needed urgent attention and the next morning, preparing for surgery, the Boy assessed what drugs and instruments they had on hand. While Matthew inspected the recently reopened schools and visited lengthily with the distressed Dr. Morehead and Mary MacLintock, the Boy and the stalwart Agnes Morehead operated in the spacious, new, well-equipped surgery clear through the day and well into the night.

286

*   *   *

On the evening of February 12, the day before yearly meeting was due to commence, a convoy of vehicles arrived at the mission. Expecting the yearly meeting's permanent board, Matthew and the Boy went down to greet it. As they approached, Matthew realized there were too many Land-Rovers for the Board's entourage and his heart quickened; perhaps more refugees come across from Kasai? But even at a distance there was something worryingly familiar about the travel-grimed passengers who alighted in the twilight. As the group came up to meet them, he realized these were no war-ravaged refugees; they laughed and chattered as gaily as tourists.

"SURPRISE!" came the party chorus. "We've come for yearly meeting!" And there, besides the permanent board's male African members, stood almost their entire Northern Rhodesian missionary contingent; they babbled that the Poes and the Claytons would fly in on the morrow; otherwise, only the children in school, Grace Dooley, the Townsends, and the Haskels were absent. Even Than Profane's wife, having flown up from Salisbury after all these many months, had extended her surprise visit to join him here. And to most of these travel-hardened apostles, it had no doubt seemed a trifling escapade. Elizabethville was only an hour's drive across the border; Lusinga lay closer to Suseshi than their stations in Barotseland, and there was no doubt in Matthew's mind that his own carefree communications, denouncing the "exaggerations" of the press to reassure anxious Friends, had encouraged this excessive confidence—why, even the intrepid Fotches, fresh home from furlough, having arrived unwittingly in time to meet this long-deferred date, seemed pleased to be present. And the group had entreated through several charitable institutions on the Copperbelt a mountain of medical provisions and foodstuffs for the relief of Katanga. It was symptomatic of their innocence that the greatest danger they could see and all they could talk of was the "sticky" situation back in Northern Rhodesia, where feelings were running high; five hundred white miners had threatened to strike if the British government's new constitution proved "unfavorable," a circumstance which, rumor had it, might cause the Federal premier to seize independence unilaterally. These fears, if legitimate enough, seemed to Matthew strangely frivolous over here in the far graver frame of the Congo.

Followed by the shyly smiling Katherine and Jayne, the Boy's wayward wife, the beautiful blond Suzannah, pressed forward to greet her stunned husband. Teller, looking silver-haired and vulnerable, dearly familiar with her faint fragrance of Mitchum's Old English Lavender, smiled tenderly up at Matthew through the deepening dusk.

"Well, dear heart." She took off her spectacles to puzzle at him fondly. "Aren't thee pleased to see us?"

But, innocent as children, they had cheerfully traversed what was today one of the world's most troubled states. Matthew and the Boy stood stupefied; sick with foreboding, they could only silently stare.

24 The following morning at Rutshura, forty-seven miles away on a great granite-strewn grassy hillside that opened onto an idyllic daisy-scattered meadow, yearly meeting was finally set to convene. Parking their vehicles before a massive buttress of rock that ended the road, the missionaries walked up to the meeting house to make preparations. They awaited their black Friends with some trepidation, but contrary to Matthew's fainthearted expectations, the local Congolese people, unbowed by the adversity that plagued their compatriots further afield, came in prodigious numbers, from miles around. The wealth of their mineral-rich province was evident in their slick suits, colorful calicos, and city shoes, all of which made an impressive array as they gathered on the immense flat clearing around the homely meeting house.

Although too small to contain them, the picturesque thatch building seemed to hold out smiling welcome; backed by a forest of tall blue gums, it commanded a panoramic view of misty hills across a bush-shrouded valley. As the streams of incoming Africans thickened the congregation, European members from Elizabethville brought news that the American consul had managed to ascertain through the United Nations that Dr. MacLintock was unharmed and well. Although the poor man, still at the mercy of Lumumba's power-hungry incompetents, was by no means out of danger, the news that he was alive at all was enough to boost the sagging spirits.

And as they awaited the congregation's assembly, Teller and Katherine passed around photographs of their new meeting house to brighten the proceedings, while the Fotches competed for the attention of the weighty Friends with pictures and anecdotes of their furlough, dramatically breaking the glad news that Miss Molly Dibb, a young English nurse who had previously worked in East Africa, was to join the Friends' Central Africa Mission this year. When Benedict Poe presumptuously claimed the young woman for their Barotseland clinic, the issue, before their wide-eyed Congo Friends, grew embarrassingly contentious, with an equally adamant Than Profane charging that Zelda Clayton had little enough to do as it was, claiming the experienced nurse to help run the leper colony and clinic at Eshalakali. It was a sticky situation that Jerome Dooley, as medical director, would doubtless come under heavy cross-pressures to sort out later.

Under threat of rainfall in this season of sudden storms, the business of worship was quickly consummated; a Katangese Friend read deliberately in French and Chi-Lunda from the big Quaker Book of Disciplines, and in the soft ensuing silence, Matthew was seduced to sermonize on the cultivation and expression of the "missionary spirit." Thereafter, testimonies were given of the courage and dedication of Dr. MacLintock and Friends of both races, who had been called upon to prove their Christian mettle in the current Congo catastrophe. It was amid this stirring salute that Benedict Poe, as if not to lose limelight for their Northern Rhodesia delegation, came up with a surprising tribute to the "exceptional" medical work, "fine dedication," and "exemplary decorum" of one Zelda Clayton. Unable to believe his ears, Matthew stared at Poe in stupid indignation.

After all, no one had ever so cited Than Profane—a far worthier candidate for this awesome accolade! Coming amid the legitimate testimonies of the sterling heroism of their Congo colleagues, such praise of the commonplace paid endeavors of one of their own seemed like the prejudiced panderings of a parent, embarrassingly narcissistic and excessive, more especially since if Than Profane's opinion was accurate, the young woman was coldly impersonal, indifferent, and undedicated. But slowly, as Matthew digested the implications, he began to understand it. Their earlier argument then had not been set aside. For this was nothing more than a cock on the snoot at the Boy, a calculated gesture to discredit his implied criticism of the young woman's work, in a pointed praise, which must by comparison overshadow his own far greater effort into insinuated insignificance. Sickened by the sneaky unfairness of it all, Matthew stared from Poe to Zelda Clayton. Avoiding the Boy's cynical smile, she at least had the grace to look embarrassed. In the prickly silence that followed, Matthew, by some devious subject-jumping, tactfully set the matter aside.

In the late afternoon, the meeting was engrossed in legitimate meeting business concerns, when a talking drum began to pound persistently. The complicated cadence carried unexpected news of Patrice Lumumba, the deposed Communist Congolese premier, who had been imprisoned by Kasavubu's Central government before being recently transferred to the custody of a protesting Tshombe right here in Katanga.

Out of a meditative silence, the interpreted gist burst from an aged African elder: "LUMUMBA IS DEAD!" And there, out in the sunshine amid the friendly butterflies, the shock waves engulfed them like an icy wind. On the elders' bench, aghast mission ladies gazed dazedly from bowed bonnets. Sitting among them, Matthew, staring unseeingly at the frivolous flutter of a bright yellow butterfly, thought of Dr. MacLintock, his very life held hostage to just such an eventuality, and he could not speak. And massed around the small nucleus of white missionaries in the open air, their Katangese Friends, wanting the same separate tribal and territorial identity and integrity that had so recently provoked the deaths of thousands in South Kasai, were sobered and stunned by the shocking demise of this, the feared enemy of their cause. Surrounded by a world hostile to their secession, and now vulnerable to the avowed vengeance of the man's followers, the lonely league of Katangese were spontaneously stirred to a moving rendition of their new national anthem; their hope-hung, earnest voices charged the open air with a fervent feeling that stippled Matthew's flesh.

> *"March, march, brave Katangans,*
> *The sun is risen on your ancestral home . . ."*

25

Back at Lusinga Mission, the missionaries learned that Lumumba had "died in the bush" after escaping with two other prisoners. Chester Daniels, still single-mindedly set on a successful session, dismissed the Lunda fears of reprisals as being idle and exaggerated. But in the inexorable African mind, the foreboding still clung; the following day, the temporary camp stood deserted, while from the nearby villages a mere five hundred followers pressed to fill up the meeting house. It was less than a tenth of the thousands who had draped half the hillside the previous day, but the fact that any came at all was heartening to the despairing missionaries. For along with Lumumba's life had gone the one guarantee on Dr. MacLintock's. After having lain awake half the night praying and waiting for some word of their colleague's fate, the missionaries arrived looking tired and strained.

But for all their fears and harrowed hopes, their dignity was doubled, their witness to the natives an impeccable example. Struggling on his wife's arm and a single crutch, the half-Mexican Dr. Manuel Morehead, with his broken leg in plaster to the groin, had risen from his sickbed to be here today. And surrounded by her solicitous daughters, Mary MacLintock was gracious and smiling, sustained by her son, who had flown in from Swarthmore College to be with the family at this trying time. And if the congregation numbered less, the spirit of these faithful few inspired them all.

The speakers gave forth divine epithets; the three-tiered tithes receptacle was quickly filled with copper coins, and all items on the agenda were arbitrated without argument. In fact, except for the occasional rumble of distant thunder, the day seemed set for a surprisingly peaceful session. Then suddenly, during the reading of the Queries, a single drum began to sound. Matthew, heat-dulled, snapped out of a light illicit snooze. The speaker faltered and looked up, and Matthew was dazedly trying to decipher the instrument's total talking when he heard a man shouting hoarsely in the distance. Then, from far off, the ominous rumble of approaching trucks. The shouting grew louder as the man approached and his agitated words, in the Lunda tongue, burst in upon them, washing Matthew cold.

"*BALUBAS!*" The word echoed urgently out across the great valley. "*YOU HEAR THIS? RUN! RUN! THE BALUBAS ARE COMING!*"

The sense of shock fell, a sinister shadow, through their midst, closely followed by intoxicating fear. *The Balubas are coming! The Balubas are coming!* The phrase, whispered and wailed, rippled through their ranks, disseminating a deathly dread that disrupted the meeting in a flash. Before the presiding officers could call for order, the congregation had surged to its feet and the missionaries' despairing appeals were hopelessly drowned in the shuffling roar of mass evacuation. Stampeded by panic, there could be no stopping them now. For the Balubas, a primitive minority tribe whose political body, the BALUBACAT, fearing domination by Katanga's Lunda government, had, unlike their kindred clansmen in Kasai, taken up allegiance with Lumumba. His imprisonment in Katanga had already given rise to their random reprisals; now, on his death, how much worse would be their wrath? Corralled like cattle in a church, the pacifist people would not wait to find out.

The outlets of the meeting house were quickly clogged with writhing black bodies as they struggled to escape; trodden heedlessly underfoot, children and the elderly screamed and cried, and bursting from the doors, the people streamed down the hillside, running in fear for their very lives.

In the meeting house, among the disseminating dregs, the missionaries stared at each other in frozen fright. Joseph MacBurney and Jim Sutton, two valiant visiting Friends from Philadelphia yearly meeting, stared in astonishment. With the mark and memory of his assault still so vividly upon him, Manuel Morehead raised a sweat-beaded face. Pale Mary MacLintock gathered her three long-locked daughters feverishly around her, reaching back a hand to clutch that of her son. Teller, her dove-gray bonnet knocked askew when she was jostled by the departing throng, stood blinking dumbly through the magnifying lenses of her spectacles, reaching for the clammy comfort of Matthew's gnarled old hand. As the silence stretched on, Cherish Sinclair began to whimper like a child; Katherine Profane comforted her dazedly while Carrie Poe started to sniffle threateningly. Stupefied with shock, they all stared beseechingly at Chester Daniels, who stared blankly back. For reality had at last caught up with the man; finally found out in his foolish faith, he could give them no answer. But reason had not yet deserted them all. Rheumatoid arthritis may have crippled Rachel Breckenbridge's bones, confining her to a wheelchair, but her good sense was still intact. A calm, capable woman during normal times, she apparently saw no reason to change now. She spun her wheelchair to face the men. "Will somebody for pity's sake go out there and see what's happening? If it *is* the Balubas, we'd best get out!"

It was just the jolt they needed. But before they could act, it was suddenly too late. Outside, the blackened pall of some gasoline-fed conflagration hung like a flag of anarchy against the far horizon, and pushing through a side door, Matthew saw a distant string of battered trucks beginning to swarm up the sand road, discordantly hooting, strained engines screeching as they labored up the steep incline. Crammed with riotous Balubas dressed in skins and feathers, they droned up the tortuous mountain road, their frenzied cargoes dropping off before they could stop at the gigantic barrier of palisaded rock. Here the scrambling human ants began to boil off the trucks converging to form an incensed black mass, which began advancing up the hill to the meeting house, giving the Lumumba salute, shouting political slogans and screaming of vengeance.

As they drew nearer, Matthew discerned in the distant riot of their voices the dread words: *"Ciyuga! Ciyuga!"* Kill! Kill! and his blood ran cold as he saw the steely flash of sun-glinting spears and butcherous-looking pangas. His first foolish thought had been to place his life in God's hands and go out among them in peace and placation. But out here in the open, with the heat of their hatred searing his senses, he saw the terrible futility of it. These men were in no mood for conciliatory talk, but being unable to face them, neither could they flee, for three of the dust-dulled mangy-looking men had already reached the edge of the meeting house meadow. They were so close he could all but make out the cruel barbs on their slung arrows, almost smell the alien animal stench of them as their splayed black feet trampled the wild white daisies and the violent green of the rank rainy-season grass. With a wild sinking heart, Matthew knew then they could never reach their transportation before the Baluba reached them. The distant dreaded doom of Armageddon was suddenly upon them, right here and now . . .

Indeed, at the rapidity of the Baluba approach, the foremost escaping Lundas reeled in terror, making for the forest. The tail end of the throng screamed and did an abrupt turn, doubling in upon itself, pushing back into the meeting house, taking Matthew with it, frantic hands pulling the main double doors in on the scrambling bodies. Many might have been mangled or left outside had not Matthew forcibly intervened; one distraught child, weeping piteously, wanted to go out after its mother, from whom it had been separated, but with their attackers so near, Matthew could not allow it. The missionary men called for calm, and along with a ludicrously speckled white goat, which bounded right in, ever more fugitives were pulled back into sanctuary before the side exits were finally closed. In the deepened gloom, the doors were quickly locked and bolted while two African Friends hurried with long hooked sticks to close the fanlights set in the high latticed windows. Feeling finally secured, enclosed in the suffocating atmosphere, the people, reduced to about a hundred in all, fell back, panting and trembling. The blacks stared desperately at the whites for some sign of leadership; the whites stared helplessly back.

Outside, the isolated cries had increased to an incensed shouting crescendo, which rose in volume as the hoary mob advanced up the hill. Amid the mangle of shouts, screams, and cries, Matthew, sickened to his soul, chilled at what mindless madness must be overtaking those fleeing Friends outside. Very soon, by the harsh hubbub of incited voices surging all around them, they sensed the meeting house surrounded. While the fearful hostages cowered, shocked and terrified among the rustic pews, screaming Baluba pounded on the stout wooden doors, till, vibrating and bulging, it seemed they must burst. Heavy wooden cupboards and an ancient Bible box were hastily pulled across to further fortify them. By now the situation was considered too frightening to arbitrate openly before "innocent" ears. On Matthew's shouted instruction, the meeting's leaders pushed through the congregation to confer at the rostrum, filtering in through the pews, which, in typical Quaker outlay, came in from all four walls to meet at this central point. Benedict Poe, Gerald Spaulding, Chester Daniels, Ward Disney, Matthew, and several African elders and permanent board members gathered anxiously around the little paper-strewn rostrum table to deliberate the ramifications of their fate. Straining to hear themselves above the commotion, they had consulted for only a few moments when Than Profane, distinctive in his white Stetson, pushed through their ranks, his blue eyes darkened with dread.

"Jesus, Matthew—what in hell's happening?"

"Well, thee'll have to ask Mr. Daniels about that." Matthew turned to the agitated young man in a pale checkered shirt and plain tie who stood beside him, guiltily evading their eyes. "Apparently the administrator sent an urgent message to Mr. Daniels early this morning urging us to cancel the meeting. Seems like, in retaliation for Lumumba's death, his supporters have been ransacking the countryside; Lunda and whites have been beated up and imprisoned all over the country. Unfortunately, Mr. Daniels decided not to worry us with such details."

The Boy turned slowly to the young man, who shrugged weakly.

"You can understand, we've already had so many delays and false alarms, I didn't want to spread unnecessary panic. What with all the trouble we've had lately, the administrator's become a rather skittish man. He's cried wolf before, so I decided . . ."

"*You* decided?" The Boy's voice cracked incredulously as he stared at the young schoolteacher in outrage. "*You goddamn fool!* You insisted it was safe to hold meeting out here! We trusted your judgment when all the time you were keeping the truth from us! Good Christ, you had no right to decide for us and take a chance on our lives!"

"Now, Friend, keep your voice down. There's no sense getting emotional and blasphemous." Chester glanced uncomfortably, covertly around. "You don't seem to understand—with the natives so suspicious and jittery, I naturally wasn't too worried when . . ."

"*I bet!*" The Boy's face was terrible with his outrage. "With your family safe home in the States, I don't guess you were. You son of a bitch—you don't have to watch your wife and your sister and your mother get . . ." Unable to finish, almost in tears with the intensity of his feelings, the Boy grabbed Chester's shirtfront and began to shake him furiously. "*I ought to kill you, crazy bastard!*"

"Here, now!" With amazing limberness, Matthew was around the rostrum. He grabbed at the Boy's arm and tried to pull him off, his anxious eyes indicating the wide-eyed women and children who peered from the pews, watching them in fright. "Hush, Boy! This's no time to lay blame," he whispered through his moustache. "Think of our African Friends; of our own ladies and little ones!"

But his words were drowned in the rising deafening din of their tormentors. He had just braced himself to shout when quite suddenly it ceased. The Balubas' incensed screaming fell to a sinister surcease, to an absolute unearthly quiet that was somehow more frightening than had been the full force of their fury. The precarious hush fell on them like some baneful occult power, so that their voices faded and they stood transfixed, scarcely breathing, hackles rising, wracked in a watchful waiting, in a stunned limbo of listening. Slowly, his cheeks flushed with high feeling, the Boy subsided; he released Chester Daniels, and all around the dim meeting house the people stirred, eyes darkly dilated, stricken faces pale with dull dread as they stared at each other, acutely aware of the weakness of the walls and the flimsiness of the reed roof, all that separated them from the malevolent madness, which brooded, dark as a malignant growth, all around them.

In the uncanny quiet, Matthew almost jumped out of his skin when Maddy, one of the MacLintock girls, gave a sudden shrill scream. Crouched on the floor, she sat in the pool of her long brown dress and shook a frantic hand, pointing wordlessly. Following her riveted gaze, they found framed in the small square of a windowpane a disembodied head which had risen up, silent as a ghost, the slit-eyed tooth-filed evil black face of a Baluba leering at them grotesquely beneath a shading hand. Evidently raised on the backs of his brothers, he tottered for a moment before dropping out of sight onto the collapsed bodies of his supporters. Hushed to an alert listening, they could actually hear them out there, jumping up and down like blood-crazed hunting dogs hot on the scent, struggling to climb each other's backs to spy on them through the high windows. It was a nightmarish experience which unnerved them completely. Children sat wide-eyed while grown men and women cringed, cowed and trembling, in the pews. Then suddenly the explosion of a window riveted them all in a catalytic shock; even as they all sat still stunned out of their wits, more and more of the sectioned panes burst around the meeting house, showering stones and shattered glass upon them.

"EVERYBODY TAKE COVER!" the immense Gerald Spaulding, his silky mane of wavy white hair bobbing in their midst, shouted urgently. But with squeals and cries, the people, in instinctive self-preservation, were already sinking to the crumbling concrete floors, where they sat crouched behind the protective pews. Jerome Dooley lifted the frail Rachel Breckenbridge from her wheelchair; Matthew saw her braided white bun disappear behind a pew. Likewise, Than Profane and Agnes Morehead lowered the cast-legged and wincing Dr. Manuel Morehead to safety behind a bench, while the bobbing heads of unwary black children were bowled over by anxious adults. Finally only one was left standing.

"Girlie, GET DOWN!" Mr. Spaulding cried, and with a sense of shock Matthew recognized the blue dress and ribbon tied dangling blue bonnet of Jennifer Solomon. Somehow, in all the confusion, she had been separated from Teller. But even as he started toward her, other caring hands tugged at her long skirt, pulling her down. And right then, Mr. Bayusa, the clerk of the meeting, was struck by a stone on the brow; holding a blood-dripping hand over one eye, he shrieked and palpated like a pup impaled on a spear, while all around the rostrum, groveling in animal indignity on the ground, the suit-straining ungainly elder men stared at him in fright. Then Than Profane, scrambling on all fours amid the fusillade of spraying glass, dived down the aisle to tend him. Katherine Profane ripped a frill from her calico petticoat to serve as a bandage, and someone passed up a carafe of water. As the grimacing African sat, eyes tightly shut, hissing and neighing under his breath while the Boy cleaned the wound, the Balubas' bombardment petered to a paltry pattering of pebbles, and people all around the meeting house stared cautiously around.

"Listen . . ." The Boy grunted as he furiously tore the calico into strips with his teeth. "There's a door onto the forest from the ante-room at the back! If I could just get at that rifle in Mr. Spaulding's jeep . . ."

"*Never!*" Benedict Poe's voice rang out in outrage, and he struggled to stand at the rostrum, rising up, black-suited among them, a pale specter of biblical doom, with his gaunt warty face grim and hypnotic black eyes fanatically afire. He stood for a moment heaving speechlessly. Then, staring surreptitiously around lest any innocent African overhear, he suppressed his voice to a sibilant seething: "Friend, by thy bigotry and blasphemy, thee challenges the very fundamentals of our faith before our impressionable African Friends—and as a senior elder of this meeting, responsible for their spiritual welfare, I will hear no more of thy heresy in this house of the Lord. I will not stand by and see our blessed Peace Testimony violated in the taking up of arms!"

"I unite with that!" Hannah Rothchild, with her peculiar talent for long-distance eavesdropping, shrilled from the pews. And if she had indeed overheard the complete context of Poe's stifled outburst, Matthew could only marvel that while other women might cower in palpable fear and trembling, this incorrigible soul could not, even now, see the blacks as anything other than bullying brash children, as infuriating brats who had only to be punished with privation or frightened with hell's doom to bring them scurrying to heel.

Than Profane finished tying the bandage before he turned around. And then he seemed merely immensely irritated, as if he found the upholding of their cardinal religious principle to be in de-plorable bad taste at this terrible time; a childish playacting simply too tiresome to entertain seriously right here and now amid the des-perate demands of real ravaged life.

"Oh come now, Mr. Poe," he snapped deprecatingly. "Get off my back. Maybe you want to be a martyr, but there are people here—women and children—who deserve a choice. It's our duty to protect them in whatever way we can. Now at any other time you can go imposing your fine Quaker ethics on the meeting, but right here and now, with innocent lives on the line, the act of self-defiance is a personal right and a group responsibility."

He said it with flat finality, as if his word were law, and Poe, demeaned by such presumptuousness, was perilously provoked. He opened his mouth to speak, but was too infuriated to formulate a fitting reply. Matthew closed his eyes, agitated and appalled. While their very lives were at stake, the centuries-old Quaker quandary yet rose to taunt them, their discussion degenerating to a clashing of wills which would surely wrack asunder their already wavering meeting. He did not know what un-Quakerly confrontation might have ensued just then had not an awesome roll and reverberation of thunder suddenly shaken the little meeting house on its foundations. The people looked at each other, and Matthew looked up in a breath-bated hush, with a kindling of hope. The brewing storm was about to break—one of those violent African deluges by the sound of it. Although it might only serve to complicate matters, Matthew never felt more the power of the Lord than when a great tree-lashing storm was erupting all around him. Coming right now, it seemed like the Lord's voiced disapproval of their heathen attackers. Lightened by his leavening faith, Matthew felt revived in his belief in the Boy. If anyone could do it, *he could*! But just then a cry went up.

"*Smoke! Smoke!*" Pastor Peter Mwanza leaped to his feet, pointing upward. "See—the roof is burning!"

And so it was. With a corporate anguished moan, the people stood staring entranced, up at the thick smoke that filtered through the thatch, a vision of hell among the rough eaves. Although the dessicated grass had been drenched in the previous night's downpour, Matthew knew that by now the sun must have sufficiently dried the uppermost layers for the smoldering flame to take hold. Now, intimidated by the encroaching crackle, by the streaming searing smoke, they had little choice. They had either to go out there and seek that of God in the dim humanity of the Baluba or remain to be enshrined as martyrs, burned alive as they stood.

It was a terrible realization. Suddenly, their calm shattered, the people, in primal panic, began to hurl themselves against the barricaded doors, grown men and women screaming and crying while little children wandered, wailing. Even missionaries, caught in the crush, infected by the fear, began to wail and cry beseechingly to God. Orville Fotch was blubbering like a baby; Ezra Peaboby hung on a pew, fanning his face, as pale as paper; and the distraught Carrie Poe stood wretchedly tearing at her thin hair in hopeless anguish.

Amid this mindless melee, the harlequin goat, butting at bodies, bleating pathetically, darted skittishly in and out of the tangled legs, adding to the confusion, and an African woman began a ghastly keening that went right through the hall like a funeral lament. Two overseers ran to calm her, but there seemed no way of silencing the poor soul. By the pathetic naïveté of her orange floral frock, ensembled with pink and purple beads and a bilious blue hat, Matthew remembered her as the elder's wife who had so civilly served him tea and devil's cake during recess the day before. And all around him, more and more of their genteel African Friends were reverting to the nature of their recent roots; the calls of rallying elders and overseers were drowned in the desperate din and for a moment it seemed all would be lost in the seething insanity. Then Than Profane slapped the face of the hysterical Zelda Clayton, and the shock of this unthinkable affront spread like an electrical current. In the sick surprised silence that ensued, he turned to address them angrily.

"Stay quiet, all of you. You're frightening the children. It seems you're all forgetting your fine Quaker faith! Now, just stay calm and get a hold of yourselves."

It was enough; African Friends stood stunned in silent resignation, and the missionaries, caught on the brink of abandoned faith, looked up in shamefaced contrition. With trembling mouths and tear-filled eyes, they squared their shoulders and straightened ties and bonnets to rebolster their composure.

Feeling claustrophobic at the acrid infiltration of smoke that streamed in increasing billows through the thatch, Matthew clawed loose his ribbon tie and gently adjured, "Remember, we are in the power of the Lord. He will deliver us if we but believe. If we go in calm faith, in brave belief, way will open and we will find safe conduct through the Baluba ranks."

It was a fine speech, but thinking of those he held dear, and watched by the wide upraised eyes of trusting little children, in particularly by two abandoned little black boys who perched on a bench in petrified silence, nervously nose-picking, appraised of their innocence, Matthew's throat constricted with emotion, and he gazed, full of love at his black and white brethren. Unable to continue, he looked helplessly at Gerald Spaulding, who spoke up gruffly.

"Friends, it appears we might just outwit and confuse our Baluba brothers if we exit through the three sets of doors. So kindly form a line up the aisle. Stay calm, and no pushing. And gentlemen first, please. There's plenty of time for us all to get out. It's still smoldering up there, more smoke than flames."

The people milled in confusion, then with some nudging persuasion the women and children stepped back into the pews and the men moved, somnolent as sleepwalkers, as Mr. Spaulding grasped their shoulders and pushed pliant bodies into line down the long central aisle.

"Men up front, please," he reiterated, "and ladies, join up with families and friends behind. Then once we get out there, watch me and do as I do. At first opportunity, those of us who came in vehicles make for the transport. It may be they have been too preoccupied with us to tamper with them, so, drivers, have your keys at the ready. The rest just disperse through the forest or down the hill, whichever seems best. And remember, don't be distracted or intimidated. Let us go out now and show them a fine witness of our faith. And remember the Peace Testimony. If a man strikes one cheek, then turn the other. We have to think of the ladies and little ones and take what they give us . . . or . . ."

He broke off in mute anguish, his tormented eyes touching his thin little wife, the MacLintock girls, and Jayne Profane. Matthew understood his anxiety. All the men did. While the sheltered mission ladies bolted themselves with faith, hoping it was all that was necessary, their menfolk cringed in knowing fear for them. For the white female form, incitement in itself, was that much more the vulnerable. The formidable task of keeping their women undefiled loomed even more frighteningly than death itself.

There followed some confused hand-clasping, fleeting anguished hugs, and wordless good-byes. None of the fatherless MacLintocks wanted to be further separated; the girls clung to their mother and each other and the tall young son embraced his congealed family before he left them. Matthew noticed Than Profane taking leave of his wife and family while Peter Disney stood staring at Jayne, his childhood sweetheart. Then, with unspoken anguish in his eyes, the young boy turned and silently took his place up front with his father and Virgil, his elder brother. Chester Daniels, relieved of his leadership, took his place in line, looking sheepish and shaken. Jerome Dooley, ever gallant, had elected to remain behind to look after Dr. Morehead and the redoubtable Rachel Breckenbridge, who, for all her inhibiting incarceration, sat in her wheelchair looking about as arrogant and unafraid as Boadicea poised to ride her chariot out to battle. Matthew almost bumped into Lavison, the bespectacled young clerk of the permanent board, who was pushing to join the line of men. The young man was sniffing, wiping his running nose on a frayed suit cuff, and Matthew saw with concern that he was crying quietly, a silver tear dripping off his broad flat nose.

He patted the young man comfortingly before turning to seek out Teller and Jenny. Teller found him first. "Dear, thee see to Jenny," she called anxiously, herding a group of frightened native children before her, carrying a wailing toddler on her hip, and leading another chubby little cherub by the hand. Following after them like a little lost lamb was the frizzy-haired Cherish Sinclair. Sprawling, as usual, in shoes and clothes that slapped and flapped, by far too large for her diminutive person, she was sobbing fitfully into a lacy handkerchief.

"Now, now," Matthew offered lamely. "It's not that bad."

But it was and Cherish knew it; she latched onto Matthew's arm and clung to him, pressing her face into his black-frocked shoulder. Entrapped, Matthew craned his neck, frantically scanning the hall for Jenny; amid the confusion, he finally spotted her standing uncertainly near the Fotches. He put a hand to his mouth and called urgently across the crush of bodies and the clamor of voices.

"Orville! Thee coming up front?"

Starting guiltily, Orville spun around, spluttering defensively: "Indeed not! *Somebody* has to stay behind and take care of the Lord's tithes!" He quailed scornfully as if about to make a sacrifice that others had not thought of. But Matthew was not fooled; there was nothing noble about Orville's intentions. Pushing through the people to reach the tithes as fast as his blundering bulk could move them, the man was glassy-eyed and intent, in grip of a grim avarice that conveniently coincided with his customary cowardice; no matter that lives were in the balance, his resolution not to leave the tempting tithes to the barbaric Baluba offered a graced opportunity to shelter safely behind the skirts of the women. Even as Matthew watched, Orville struggled frantically to lift the large tithes receptacle off the shelf. An especially fine one, carved from a tree trunk, it had three circular tiers and a handle shaped like a wing-spread dove. As he staggered under its unwieldy weight, the tall object, see-sawing uncertainly, slipped sideways, showering pennies.

"ORVILLE!" Matthew shouted again. "Since thee're staying behind, thee and Clara take care of Jenny, please! Hold her hand and keep her with thee!"

Orville grunted a grudging affirmation, but for all the action it evoked, Matthew might have spoken to the bare brick wall. The next Matthew saw of the man and his wife, they were tracing spiraling coins through the forest of legs across the dusty floor. To beat it all, stepping on to a bench, Matthew saw Orville slipping some of the recovered change into his own pious pockets. Exasperated, he was about to give uncharacteristic vent to his disgust when Hannah came up. Prim in her paisley-print dress and bonnet, she looked, with her annoyed air and her purposefully clutched purse and umbrella, about as indignantly inconvenienced as a suburban charlady who has just missed the last bus.

"Hannah," Matthew gasped. "Am I pleased to see *thee!* Teller's helping out with the babies, so here, thee take Cherish, and quick, the pair of thee go across and fetch Jenny across the hall there. I have to take my place up front, so mind her carefully, now; and stay behind with the Fotches."

He watched with relief as the formidable woman, looking pettishly put out, took the hand of her friend. As they moved obediently off, pushing forcefully through the bundling bodies, Matthew felt himself jostled by the urgent crowd; for the flames, settling in, were licking through the thatch now, the smoke pouring down, black and noisome among them, convulsing them in coughing. Still craning his neck to see that Jenny was safely escorted, Matthew was pulled along with them. Then, as the men made to push aside the heavy cupboards blocking the doors, the front-line men, missionaries and blacks alike, began to filter frantically back; it seemed no one wished to form part of the vulnerable wall that would first face the Baluba. Matthew found himself and the Boy pushed directly in front of the double main doors. They glanced at each other in dull recognition, the Boy shrugging resignedly; somebody had to be first. Hearing the muffled weeping of the women, Matthew sought to inspire them with the legendary larghissimo: "Abide With Me." But his gruff baritone cracked timorously, failing him, and it was left to Hannah Rothchild to take up the strains. Her forced soprano wobbled perilously, as in pathetic self-seriousness she led the throng like a shepherd with uncertain sheep, until finally almost every voice was raucously raised in a stirring and spirited rejuvenation of floundered faith, and they were carried along, sustained on a surging sea of soul-felt singing.

By now the cupboards had been removed and the bare doors stood before them, the last barrier between them and whatever bestial aberrations the rampaging Baluba might care to commit upon them. In the stifling atmosphere, breathed by a hundred fear-sweating humans and one stinking goat readying to meet their adversaries, the men, notwithstanding the clammy heat, were shrugging on their jackets. Gerald Spaulding struggled to pull back the heavy rust-jammed bolt of the main double doors. It seemed impossibly set, then he and Than Profane heaved together and in a moment, after the oppressive dimness, the doors flew open onto the comparative dazzling light of the overcast day, onto blessed cool fresh air and the breathtaking sight of scores of swarming black Balubas.

The foremost of them leaped back with shrieks and yelps as the bursting doors slammed back, striking brick. Then in a nightmare daze, with Peter Disney and Drew MacLintock standing nervously ranged on one side of him, Matthew stepped out onto the top step beside Than Profane. Blinking and coughing, he looked out across the immense hillside and he knew that for the rest of his life he would never forget the awesome, terrifying stricture of it, the all-consuming terror as the tumultuous mass of men rose up with bestial hungry moans, like a pack of ravenous animals, baying to reach them . . .

26

From the womb of the meeting house, it was a brutal birth. The overpowering stink of sour sweat, moldering animal hide, and the hot halitosis of beer-bilious breath hit the missionaries like a physical force. The full-throated enraged roar of the swarming Balubas exploded in their ears as the European-aping alien impi of the new independent African order, in shredded shirts and shorts, shaggy with scabious skins, hung with horns, rattles, and feathered fetishes, rushed to menace them with a bristling fusillade of upraised spears and pangas. Kilts and karosses flying in a frenzied kaleidoscope, they swirled in feinting skirmishes, soot-smeared fiendish black faces leering through shocking cicatrices of white and red ocher paste. It was a terrifying spectacle; the Friends' brave supplication died instantly on fear-dried lips and it seemed to Matthew that the Lord deserted them then. The light went out of their lives, split seconds swelled and distorted like the delayed frames of a film, and stalled in a strange serialized succession of separately focused sequences, stunned witless in abject terror, the little Quaker party stood in sudden dark adjournment, in the Valley of the Shadow.

For a time it was too much to take; beleaguered and bedeviled, there seemed no respite from the stupendous sight and sound, no refuge from the terror of their teeming black tormentors. Matthew's very senses seemed to waver and warp till every fearsome flourished face took on the fixed ferocity of a wooden *makishi* mask. Then, frighteningly, above the turbine pounding of his heart, his mind seemed to dim and diminish all exteriors, so that with nightmarish magnification, he became aware of a single tribesman who stood apart from the rest with an intrinsic authority that went beyond his superior size. Young, with a brutal, haughtily handsome face, the Baluba leader, smeared with soot and matted mud, was beetle-browed and bestial as a baboon in a long-tailed headdress of a mangy monkey skin and a kilt of mongoose tails. As the jeers of the unruly rabble died down, Matthew realized that he was haranguing the whites contemptfully. Malefic fetishes swung around his neck, and his BALUBAKAT badge was a ludicrous propriety among the ragged skins and tossing tails as, crowded by several demonic-looking henchmen, he strode up and down before them, chasing back his brethren to forge a passage along the packed bodies. And then it occurred to Matthew that, being steeped in a crude political order that presently adhered to this man as its leader, the mob was not driven on purely reactionary instincts; although that leader was presently little more than animal in inclination, he was yet one of God's souls. The fact that he held in check the rage of this unruly rabble like reins in his hands narrowed their target to a single focal point; in short, it gave them some slight chance.

By now surrounded by the swarming Balubas, they stood before the smoking meeting house, a tightly packed company of Quakers, their front line extended by the massing out of fearful Friends fleeing the radiating flames, the ranged men, stubborn elder ladies, and African Friends shielding from salacious sight the covey of comely young white girls who cowered within. As the Baluba leader and his henchmen strode restlessly along their ranks, switching their pangas threateningly in their faces, laughing derisively to see them flinch, Matthew was still numbly wondering how they might go about reaching out to such a man, when Gerald Spaulding, who knew the language, suddenly spoke out, ostensibly entreating the men with their personal innocence in the matter of Lumumba's death. (Amid the incomprehensible tirade, Matthew heard specific mention of the inflammatory name.) The big Baluba stopped, and their stifled hopes rose as he seemed to soften and consider, smiling sunnily.

Then he swirled in a vicious backhanded blow that caved Gerald Spaulding's lips in a mouthful of blood and broken teeth, knocking him off his feet, backward into the packed throng of Friends. All around him, Friends stifled their horrified gasps; clutching hands eased his spasmodic slither to the ground, and he panted there, crumpled and bleeding, spitting out teeth. He sat up shakily, dusty and dazed, wavy white hair in his eyes. And with their leader so easily reduced to such sorry insignificance, it was a sobering moment. As the Baluba continued his pacing as if nothing had happened, the dazed missionaries looked up and stood in sudden awful understanding, their worst fears finally confirmed. They knew now without doubt the awesome caliber of their enemy. These demented men cared little for proven complicity; their racial and tribal identity was crime enough. Matthew knew their likes. Like the perpetrators of the recent atrocities all over the Congo, their ultimate intention was horrifyingly obvious.

But first, cold-bloodedly, like cats with caught mice, with all the teasing sporting instincts of fickle felines, they had a predilection for malicious maiming; they would alternately ravage then release them in a cruelly prolonged foreplay, holding out hope only in order to watch them squirm half-wounded away, deriving sadistic pleasure out of pulling them back with a playfully pattering vicious claw-hooked paw. One thing Matthew understood about such barbarous bullies was their inexplicable need for some flimsy excuse to act as a catalyst on their bated barbarism. Aware that any reactionary action would be construed grossly provocative, he tried to warn Teller and Gerald Spaulding's wife as they bent to the poor man's aid. But he was too late; the big Baluba had turned at the end of the line. He stared at them, his face darkened with outrage, and with a furious shout, he raised his panga and readied to rush at the women, who stared at him, transfixed in terror.

In that moment Matthew's legs turned to water. His heart was pounding the breath out of him, but without forethought, in sudden rash rectitude, he pushed forward to block the blow from the womenfolk. But even as he waited to meet his Maker, struggling to summon the serenity to die with dignity, tremulous breast miserably bared for the murderous maiming, he felt the brush of something hard and hairy from behind. In a moment the harlequin goat, spooked by the smoke, catapulted through their legs. The cantering creature, with horned head menacingly lowered, charged straight at their aggressor; Matthew heard the forcefully ramming horns connect with his shins in a compacted crack that sent the big Baluba leader sprawling.

A howl of outrage rose from the ground. Amid the resultant

melee of tangled bodies, a multitude of weapon-bearing black arms lashed out and there were sickening fleshy thwacks as successive lunging, slicing blows quickly spotted and striped the speckled body with blood-spurting stab wounds and slashes. The animal went down flailing in its death throes, the half-severed head falling forlornly forward, nose first into the grass, an amazed expression on the benign bearded face. Although many of the missionaries shrieked and looked away, Matthew, in mesmerized masochism, could not tear his eyes from the squirting jet of bright red blood; as the demented natives fell away, in a sick daze he watched the last convulsive kicking of the animal's limbs. He saw its slowly glazing eyes upturning, standing in strange speculative detachment as the bowled Baluba leader scrambled to his feet and with a belligerent bellow added his own hacking punishment to the goat's twitching carcass, wreaking his vengeance in a terrifying display of ferocious brutality that left the creature unrecognizable, a blood-gory mutilated mess.

When it was over, Matthew, sickened by this sadistic foretaste of their callous capabilities, waited in breath-stifled suspense, to meet his own end. But when the Baluba turned, the insanity had gone, like a cloud cleared from his face. The butcherous act, it seemed, had climaxed a pinnacle of rage. Now, with his blood lust suddenly sated, symbolically spent on the supine spine of the sacrificial animal, he dropped his panga and returned to them, dully dispossessed of the raging demons that had rent his reason a moment before, a grizzly apparition, dripping with the sprayed blood of his victim, his face and hands horrifically red. As he came toward them, Matthew heard from behind Jayne Profane's horrified hiss, and the susceptible Peter Disney, who had averted his head from the goat's carnage while standing steadfastly in line helping to hide her, suddenly sagged in a blood-sighting swoon. Before anyone could stop her, the anxious girl had pushed through the packed throng and was on her knees at the young boy's side. She crouched over him, cradling his unconscious head. Even as her brother caught at her arm, a shadow fell over her. As the Boy drew her up, she looked into the terrible face of the towering Baluba.

It was an awesome moment; face cautiously controlled, careful not to convey any sign of emotion, the Boy put his arm around his sister and gathered her possessively against him. With a small sob, she buried her bonneted head against his chest while he faced the Baluba leader, face expressionlessly set, jaw defiantly raised, and legs braced apart in the defensive male attitude of protection.

But, if anything, the native seemed challenged by this spirited defiance; in a kind of inverted voyeurism, he seemed sexually incited by the Boy's jealous surveillance as he appraised the young girl with open insolent lust, his black face inflamed, dark eyes coalescing with carnal excitement as he pulled off her pink bonnet so that the lustrous blond hair tumbled free. Running his bloodstained black fingers through the silken tresses, he gave a sudden gleeful giggle, which infected his fellows, so that a rising ripple of laughter spread around him like the ever-widening wave in a pebble-dropped pond. The mirth seemed to signal a growing license that spread to the common ranks, so that all along the beseiged company of Friends, black hands began to plunder. The few stalwart elder ladies who had pushed bravely forward to stand beside their men in the front line had their prayer books snatched and dashed to the ground; their purses were rifled and the watches and rings torn off their hands; they were tauntingly touched, while the men, likewise pillaged, were prodded and provoked.

Amid this petty purgatory, Peter Disney stirred on the ground only to look up at the blood-drenched Baluba and faint again. Kneeling to surreptitiously reach him through the tangled legs, Katherine and Louella Breckenbridge slipped their hands beneath his shoulders; they began edging him back into the relative shelter of their midst, succeeding unnoticed while the Balubas were gleefully preoccupied in the cruel provocation. Amid their growing aggression, a strangled squeal escaped Teller and the diminutive Elizabeth Spaulding started to tremulously sing: "Lead Kindly Light" to keep up their courage. She was summarily silenced, gasping for breath, punched in the stomach for her pains. As the mouselike little lady, clutching herself, slowly sank to the ground, her husband reached over to console her. Matthew, murmuring with pity, patted her shoulder. The others, enthralled in their pacifist indoctrination, knowing full well that any overt aiding action would be invitation to further effrontery, remained outwardly enduring, holding firm in their faith.

Not that these men needed any invitation now. Matthew sweated in silent apprehension as beside him, the big Baluba began to play intimately with Jayne Profane. The girl stood rooted to the spot, stupid with shock, as he pawed at her dress; her soft pink mouth fell open, her anguished gray eyes widening with unbelieving outrage as he began suggestively stroking her flat female crotch through her skirt, the bestial black fingers leaving obscene smears of goat's blood on the clean cloth.

"*Jesus God!*" The Boy, aghast, grunted through clenched teeth. He took the young girl by the shoulders and wrenched her around against him, holding her protectively enfolded within his arm while the Baluba's crude laughter exploded in their faces. The insistent hands continued their exploration of the child's innocent body, pulling up the long rosebud peppered pink skirt and frilly white petticoat, so that Matthew had to look away; innocent bloomers exposed in the daylight, defiled by big black bloody hands insolently petting the small behind.

"*Leave her!*" the Boy snarled. He pushed the skirt down, spreading his own open hand across the small buttocks, clutching her possessively. Then Jayne gasped; when she pushed away from her brother, leaving his trouser leg drenched wet with her urine, Matthew realized the extent of her fright. As she sagged back, weakly crying against him, the Boy's enraged face was constricted with pain; the small muscles flickered furiously in his clenched jaw, and Matthew feared that with much more provocation, he would explode and became a raving lunatic to be dragged down by a mob hungry for just such a display. But worse was yet to come. For the tall Baluba, peering over their shoulders into the Quaker convoy, had spotted the beautiful Suzannah Profane. His powerful black arm reached in and, against her shrieking protests, the young woman was dragged through the crammed bodies to the fore. As she erupted beside him, the Boy, still holding on to his little sister, caught at his wife's hand. Faced with the kind of odds that made mouse flesh of a man's flexed muscles, powerless to help her, he stood gripping his wife's fingers till the bones must break.

"Hold fast, Boy," Matthew groaned weakly. Out loud, addressing them all, he cried: "*Remember, Friends, we are in the power of the Lord. We suffer now in His cause; our humiliation, passively endured, is here glory to His name!*"

But in the awful immediacy of the moment, words were an empty solace. Dazed with disbelief, the Boy seemed not to hear, his blue eyes filled with a dull hot anguish. And Matthew could scarcely blame him. For the Boy held the fairest prizes: sensuous Suzannah and the young sweet Jayne. Without them he might move mountains; with them he was hopelessly handicapped, sick with the fear that they might be despoiled. His tormented face convulsed with pain at his wife's tear-burst shout.

"DON'T TOUCH ME, YOU STINKING BASTARDS!" She slapped at hands that crawled tantalizingly up her short skirt. But her reaction was just what her tormentors wanted. Giggling insanely, one of the henchmen suddenly grabbed at the neckline of her dress; with a tremendous wrench, he ripped it half off her so that one luscious pink-nippled breast was shockingly exposed. The white-faced young woman reacted quickly, holding the torn material clasped tight to her breast. Her amber eyes sparkling with tears, she yet faced them defiantly. But it was too much for the Boy. His eyes went dull and glazed, and he quivered and reacted like a man having a convulsion, swearing at them savagely in the neutral French, spewing up his impotent hatred and rage with an unmissionarylike venom and vocabulary that stunned his fellows and stopped the noisily disporting Baluba in incredulous surprise.

"SALAUDS! MACAQUES! MERDE BALUBA! YOU MOTHER-FUCKING SONS OF HYENAS—I SPIT ON YOU!"

So saying, almost in tears with his torment, he hawked up and ejected a spume of spittle. Reaching target, it mingled with the congealing goat's blood and dribbled slowly down the big Baluba's tail-tassled chest. In the shocked silence, as the obscene vilification echoed in scorched ears, Matthew closed his eyes, anguished and appalled. The Boy's pain apparently went beyond the bounds of human decency. His devilish denunciation drastically besmirched their faithful Christian witness, doubtless doing mortal moral damage to the already listing morale of listening Friends. Now a strange hush settled over all the hillside. Finally it was so still they could hear the distant cries of sand grouse fleeing the coming storm as the fresh wind blew the refreshing scent of damp earth in their flushed fevered faces. Overhead, blackening banks of towering thunderheads tumbled across the sky, the twisting vapor furling thick as smoke to trap the day's diminishing light in an eerie illicit twilight that was like the metaphoric darkening of their lives in the sinister stillness. And seeing the Baluba leader's dagga-dulled black face slowly suffusing with an incredulous climbing outrage, Matthew knew with sudden sick certainty that Than Profane, having sewn the wind, would now reap the whirlwind.

Matthew sensed the Boy silently rueing his own rash reaction as he stood heaving on his receding rage. Then, bundling his frightened females behind him, he braced himself to face alone the burly Baluba leader, who suddenly lunged at him with a horrendous howl, his pink-gummed mouthful of filed white teeth bared like a mad monkey about to bite. He brought down a brutal black fist in a side-swiping backhanded blow, which evoked shrieks from the cowering Quakers and flung the Boy's head sideways, knocking off his hat, glancing off his temple and chin. But his braced body had absorbed the jarring momentum, and when Matthew looked again, the Boy was still standing his ground, bloodied but unbowed, sucking in the blood that seeped at the crushed corner of his mouth, shaking his head to restore his senses. Still unrepentant, pushed to the brink of desperation, he was doubly defiant. Swiftly stooping to retrieve his Stetson, he set it jauntily back on his head and faced his foe with a fine high rebellious pride, somehow managing to epitomize magnificent majesty with his swollen lopsided mouth twisted in a positively suicidal smile of courageous contempt.

The Baluba, frustrated and infuriated, immediately began searching for his discarded weapon. As it was obligingly restored to his grasping hand, Matthew heard the distraught screaming and crying of the Boy's family mingling unmusically with the babbling desperate pleas of Friends all around. But as the sneering native advanced with his panga menacingly raised, the Boy's reaction was somewhat strange; wrenching down his tie, he ripped open his collar, fumbling in his shirt to bring forth some obscure object that hung from his neck on a long string of dried leather. This he held intimidatingly aloft before the advancing Baluba. It took Matthew a moment's stunned staring to realize what it was. Then, dully recognizing the carved wooden protective fetish presented to the Boy by the Congolese shaman in Barotseland, he suddenly understood the look of sick shock that had transformed the unreasoning rage of the native's face. Mouth agape, the man lowered his weapon and stood irresolute for a moment, staring stupidly.

And pressing his advantage, blatantly exploiting the notorious African susceptibility to supernatural sorcery, face twisted with hate, the Boy screamed at the man in Chi-Lunda:

"I *NJUMWAICE*—POWERFUL *SITONDO* OF THE MAL-UNDA—CURSE YOUR WIVES AND YOUR SONS AND YOUR MOTHERS WITH STERILITY AND SICKNESS! I CALL UPON THE LIGHTNING TO STRIKE YOUR FOULNESS FROM THE FACE OF THE EARTH!"

His rage-catapulted words burst like bullets in the stillness. And coupled with this occult intimidation, his charisma was such that Matthew saw the eyes of his assailant and the foremost Baluba suddenly shadow with superstitious dread. They began to back off, mumbling darkly among themselves, flinching fearfully, as in uncanny compliance, as if to verify the validity of the Boy's *vandililo*, or spiritual power, a vicious whiplash of forked lightning suddenly brilliantly split and splintered the immense brooding black sky. Their sudden uncertainty was contagious, and while ever more of the natives struggled to regain their equilibrium in face of the Boy's fearsome threatened damnation, an awesome contusion of thunder further unsettled the milling men. The rumbling, booming detonation cowered the craven creatures, bearing down upon them like a deafening bombardment of boulders, quaking the very earth beneath their feet before the shock waves ebbed away into the stunned stillness.

In the echoing aftermath, the Balubas, superstitiously spooked with their fear and fright, stood perilously poised between rapine and retreat. And aware of their see-sawing unstable state, the Boy, reckless with despair, suddenly grabbed his women and heedlessly plunged.

"MOVE, YOU BASTARDS!" he growled, and miraculously, like the Red Sea to Moses, the way opened up for him, the wall of stupefied natives falling away in infectious unfoldment. It all happened so quickly that Matthew, in his staring astonishment, was a little slow on the uptake. By the time he grabbed Teller and Cherish to follow suit, the crowd had swallowed up the Boy and his women, leaving no trace. He tried timidly to shoulder his way, but the natives stood dumbly debarring; the wall would not open for him; he had not the same gumption.

"What does thee want of us?" Matthew moaned, almost weeping at the missed opportunity. Then, looking wildly around, he spotted Orville Fotch, crying copiously, drooling like a baby with his palpitating self-pitying fear, still cuddling the tithes receptacle like a pacifier in his arms, and inspiration hit Matthew in a blinding flash.

"*Money?*" he exclaimed, turning to the mob, amazed and delighted at his own ingenuity. "Is that what thee needs? *Francs, centimes, pennies?*"

So saying, he reached back a hand and, amid Orville's howled protests, began to scoop up handfuls of the coins, flinging them out across the heads of the Balubas. Their leader, recognizing the ruse, tried to warn them, but it was too late. His people subsisted in piteous poverty; the dissemination of so much money, theirs for the taking, was too much to resist. Caught up in competitive cliques, they fell fighting, groveling on the ground to capture the spiraling coins. Before Orville could recover himself to stop it, Matthew had thrown handful after handful among the swarming natives. While their leader, enraged, ran vainly up and down trying to stop them, the natives fell on each other, dropping spears and pangas in their efforts to take hold of this elusive wealth.

Finally, with the last tier of the tithes all but empty, Matthew turned to catch the eyes of his fellows. Ahead of them, the Baluba leader was actively embroiled with his men, trying to shout and shake them to sanity, but very shortly, all pennies found, the opportunity would be lost. Thus, extracting nervous nods from Gerald Spaulding and several of his fellows, tugging Teller and Cherish behind him, Matthew moved forward and began to bodily battle his way through the brawling Balubas. But very shortly, bogged down in their midst, he realized it was a dangerous mistake; these men, tearing at their own brethren, could just as easily turn on them.

But the Lord was on their side. At that moment, from above, a strange explosive sound rent the air; it seemed to Matthew that the heavens opened and fell in on them, the rains cracking like a contusion of thunder, falling in cloudburst capacity, in such vengeful velocity that it stunned them, the stinging drops striking them like needles, reducing the world to a blurred quagmire in a matter of moments. In the midst of it, cringing and huddled together, there was little they could do but blindly bumble along. But if it blinded and disabled them, it did the same to the Balubas. With their hair plastered to their faces and the relentless rain spitting in their blinking eyes, Matthew and the two women almost blundered into the bloody carcass of the goat.

They stumbled around it through the grassy tussocks of the meadow, twisting and turning to avoid writhing black bodies that were barely visible through the deluge. Then, just when they had begun to fear that this nightmare would never end, suddenly, miraculously, the way opened up; lifting his head to squint through the stinging silver sheets of rain, Matthew could see his way clear across the blurred brilliant green of the hillside. Behind them, the Balubas, like swamped ants, were scurrying for shelter, and with a sudden swell of bubbling exhilaration, Matthew knew that they were free. His heart sang out with joy and lightness. Miraculously, by the Lord's incredible grace, they had been spared . . .

27

At Lusinga Mission, as they awaited the arrival of a mercenary contingent of the radio-alerted Katangese army, the last truck of their mission convey limped in, carrying less than half of its original load of Lunda locals. Even long after dusk had fallen and several exhausted stragglers had begun stumbling in to reach them on foot, many were still ominously missing. The dumb despair in the searching black faces almost broke Matthew's heart. But beyond tending the shocked and wounded, holding meeting for the missing, and giving sustenance and shelter to the survivors, there was little they could do but wait for Tshombe's militia to rescue, or at least retrieve, what mortally remained of those still unaccounted for.

Except for the shock, the missionaries themselves had escaped remarkably lightly. Gerald Spaulding was worst off, having lost two front teeth and a great deal of his dignity; severely shocked, Jayne Profane had been put to bed under sedation; and Peter Disney, his masculine pride publicly compromised, had slunk off like a tail-tucked dog to mourn his humiliated manhood. Gloomy with his guilt, Chester Daniels stood on the veranda outside the radio room waiting word from the administrator, who was liaising with government authorities in Elizabethville on the situation. The others had changed their rain-drenched clothes, and as they completed their ministering tasks, they took supper, then drifted up in the rain-washed night to join Chester's tense vigil.

Even Suzannah Profane came with her husband. Her torn dress had been changed, but refusing bed rest, she would not be parted from the Boy, who stood with his arm around her, continually nuzzling and caressing the beautiful blond girl, holding her so compulsively tight drawn against him that Matthew had the feeling he might never again be induced to let her go.

It was past nine o'clock and there was still no sign of the army convoy when Teller and the Fotches came hurrying across the grassy yard, flashlights bobbing in the black drizzle-sprinkled night.

"*Matthew!*" Teller gasped as she stumbled up the wheelchair ramp to reach them. Her gray hair glistened with drizzle drops, and Matthew's heart turned cold at the desperate anxiety he saw in her face. "Dear heart, it's *Jenny*! We can't find her anywhere, and it

313

seems no one has seen her since . . ." She swallowed, ". . . not since *Rutshura!*"

"*How say thee?*" Matthew stared stupidly at his wife; the woman must be overwrought to be sure! Why, everybody knew all the missionaries had escaped unscathed! Had he not himself handed the child into Hannah's capable keeping? Why, they would have missed her in a moment. But would they? Stopped by the chilling thought, a wave of panic dissolved his stomach and washed him weak. For chaos had reigned, and that shy and unobtrusive girl, never wanting to put anyone to extra pains, had a way of making herself seem absent even when she was not. Now, blinding foolishly at Teller, aware of the other missionaries staring at them both in fright, Matthew tried to chuckle off their fears, but his chest felt oddly constricted and he struggled to hold on to his own waning faith.

"Now, dear, thee has it all wrong! Of course Jenny's here! Before ever we left the meeting house, I made sure she was in good hands." He turned to the tall woman who stood stony-faced beside him. "Why, Hannah'll tell thee! I left them together!"

But instead of giving the confirmation he desperately desired, the horsefaced woman reared up in reactive guilt, spluttering huffily, "Well, don't look at me, Matthew Tomlinson! How am I to know where the child is? I am not her keeper! Heaven knows with that mob it was difficult enough to hold one's own body and soul together without . . ." Suddenly unsettled by the stirring horror she saw in her colleagues' staring faces, she blurted out righteously, "And besides, I had to help Orville with the tithes. They had spilled all over the floor, and with everyone else just mindlessly fleeing, *somebody* had to . . ."

"Orville!" Matthew, remembering, switched his focus to the plump pale little man who stood with his wife, belligerently bristling up at him beside the veranda. "*Thee* too! Thee waited behind with the womenfolk! I entrusted Jenny to thy care!"

"Now see here!" Clara flared in defensive indignation. "It's all very well for thee to start picking on Orville when things go wrong, but he risked his life trying to preserve the tithes—and it's thanks to thee they're now lining the pockets of those murderous men! He might have succeeded in saving them if thee hadn't thrown it all away like swill to a herd of hogs!"

"That's right," Orville pouted, pink-faced and petulant with his guilt. "And what thanks do I get? That girl's not my responsibility if she wants to go wandering off! The Lord's our first duty, and the tithes, being his tribute . . . well, I had my hands full enough without . . ."

"*Jesus Christ!*" From behind, Matthew heard Than Profane's scathing hiss. "I don't believe this! You trying to tell us when all hell was breaking loose out there, you considered money more important than . . . why, you sniveling little worm! Call yourself a man? You got less balls than a fucking sewer rat! I'm gonna kill you—you know that?"

Before they could stop him, the Boy had sprung off the veranda at Orville, tearing his shirt as he grabbed hold of the man, shaking him senseless like a terrier with a rat. But even while Matthew stood dully digesting the Boy's emotional discharge, and as the other men rushed to drag him off, they heard the growing growl of the army convoy rumbling into the mission.

The knot of dissension instantly dissolved and the missionaries turned and ran across the clearing to greet the machine-gun-mounted jeeps and the open lorries packed with uniformed black infantry. While cheering black Friends massed around them, white men alighted from the jeeps and emerged in the headlights. They were Belgian mercenaries, *les affreux*, the frightful ones. Disheveled and unshaven, in Belgian berets, bare-chested under camouflage jackets with shabby shorts, they looked to fully deserve their derogatory nickname. But Matthew, gentle pacifist though he was, was never more pleased to see anyone in his life. Quaking with his anxiety and haste, he and Gerald Spaulding pushed through the throng to explain the situation and confer with the stocky commanding officer on the logistics of Rutshura. Even as they were impatiently poring over the man's flashlighted map, they heard the slam of a vehicle door and an engine revving up. They looked up dumbly as a Land-Rover roared past them with a furious squealing of tires. Than Profane was at the wheel.

28

Shortly before midnight, the bravest among the remaining missionary men came to join the Groupe Mobile of the Force Territoriale Katangaise in their apprehensive search in the soft rain around the still sadly smoking semidemolished mess of the meeting house. The Balubas had long since fled, leaving a bloody trail. Pitting feeble flashlights against the cloud-eclipsed bitter black night on the mud-churned clearing and the dark daisy-trampled meadow of Rutshura, between them the misfitted party of missionaries and mercenaries found a scattered radius of ravaged human beings—seven lying dead, six more barely breathing.

In between helping Jerome tend the wounded, Than frantically scoured the surrounding countryside searching for Jenny. Haggard and exhausted, his jeans splattered with mud and blood, his throat hoarse from calling, and his senses numb with the icy anxiety that had frozen his mind since he had first learned of her loss, he was just beginning to believe the white-haired old professor's distraught rambling that it might all be a terrible mistake, that she was likely safe back at Lusinga, fallen asleep in some overlooked corner, when he heard the signaling shout of Drew MacLintock, who had stumbled on a shoe. Only a short way behind him, Than was second on the scene. At six-thirty in the morning, when the ground hornbills had begun their muffled booming through the bush and the first pearly pink flush of dawn was breaking luminous light through the clearing clouds, they found her in the blue-gum wood behind the meeting house.

And amid the pale peeling trunks of the towering trees, she looked so small somehow, as small and still as a sleeping child, lying half-naked in trampled grass that was littered with her panties and petticoat, sprawled awry amid shallow shales of dead leaves and sloughed bark. She was so brutally beaten that it took them a time to realize it was really her, to recognize the blue dress stained brown with mud and the bruised swollen face smeared with dirt and streaked with tear-trails and scratches. Sightlessly staring up at the sky, her big blind blue eyes were still brimful of unshed sorrowing tears, her long dark hair torn out in brutal bunches, spreading in a tangled skein across her soft open anguished mouth. But left for dead, she was yet alive. Through the rip in her bodice and the ragged tear that split open her long Quaker skirt, Than dazedly discerned the feeble flutter of resurging breath beneath deathly white gleaming wet flesh that was fast blueing in the cold rain. Scoured with bleeding abrasions, her slight slender body was unmercifully mottled with smoky contusions and raised red welts; her one exposed tiny tender breast had been cruelly crushed by clawing fingers, and beneath the dark patch of pubic hair, which seemed an absurd maturity on the childish figure, he saw that she was hemorrhaging, the back of her skirt beneath her parted legs soaked dark with her blood.

Drew MacLintock, shocked sick to his stomach, turned instantly away, retching hoarsely. But even amid his own sick stupor Than's training took control. Numbly assessing her injuries, he reacted automatically on the instinctive urges to shield her vulnerable nakedness from irreverent eyes, to stem the bleeding, and to warm and conserve her waning life. Hastily tumbling off his Stetson to cover her groin, he ripped open the studs of his denim jacket, tearing it off with his shirt, quickly wadding the folded shirt up between her thighs. Then, tucking the jacket around her, he gathered her up in his arms, holding her insensibly tumbling head pressed to his bare chest. As the trapped tears tipped and silently streamed her bruised battered cheeks, he was smoothing the disheveled hair tenderly off her vacantly staring face with a shaking hand when he looked up and suddenly saw her Quaker hat abandoned in the bush. And somehow that broken blue bonnet, reminding him of Jayne, had a powerful poignancy that finally cracked his defenses, stopping him dead as a great sickness descended upon him, painfully spreading to touch and reverberate his stony cold heart.

And there, somewhere in the southern Congo, amid the shadowy soaring spires of the cool green cathedral forest, with the soft rain pattering on the bouncing leaves and the astringent scents of mildewed earth and wet eucalyptus filling his nostrils, staring stoically, dazed with his grief, he held the unconscious girl cradled in his arms, willing the warmth of his body to radiate and thaw the cold uncaring feelingless shell, wherein the gentle and blind *Maseccasecca*, One Who Smiles, had once so warmly dwelled . . .

BOOK FOUR

A REDEEMER
IS BORN

·1961·

1

THE TRAGEDY at Rutshura had been only one of many savage reprisals by Lumumba's supporters all over the Congo. It quickly reached world headlines that Dr. Alvin MacLintock had been among numerous hostages executed in Stanleyville. His desecrated body, retrieved by United Nations troops, was returned to the Friends' Congo Gospel Mission. The heroic doctor's death would affect the lives of hundreds of Africans, yet incredibly, the very maniac whose tormented life had caused this and countless other atrocities had overnight become a shining martyr. Even as the stunned missionaries at Lusinga conducted the moving mass burial for the American missionary and the African Friends who had died at Rutshura, outrage at Lumumba's death reached hysterical proportions and spread beyond the Congo's borders; the Belgian embassy was sacked in Cairo and there were riots in Washington, London, Paris, and Moscow. Thus, with its members bewilderedly shaking their heads over the wider world's strange sense of values, the Central Africa yearly meeting concluded its historic tragic session. The inconsolable, conscience-stricken Chester Daniels returned to the States with the bereaved MacLintock family, leaving behind courageous colleagues who talked constructively about "repairing their losses," and the Northern Rhodesia delegates, stunned and subdued, bereftly bundled up their belongings and went home across the border.

And back in Northern Rhodesia, they were met by a sinisterly similar atmosphere of violence and impending premature change: It seemed that overnight, African speech was predominantly peppered with the chant "*Kwacha*" (loosely interpreted to mean freedom), and even along remote bush roads the missionaries were mockingly met with the fluttering UNIP wave. In London for the constitutional talks, Kenneth Kaunda had warned that unless Britain capitulated to the black nationalists in the protectorate, trouble would ensue that would make the Mau Mau look like a child's picnic. Sir Roy Welensky, equally unsatisfied with the constitutional proposals, had battalions of white territorials carrying out "show of strength" maneuvers through African townships on the Copperbelt. It seemed that whichever way the British decision went, Northern Rhodesia was set to erupt into the same savage civil war that had so recently disrupted the neighboring Congo.

Unsettled by these awesome omens, the mission board in the States raised funds for a new short-wave radio for Suseshi, and Suzannah Profane scurried back to the safety of her father in Salisbury. For the rest of them there was no such refuge, and the missionaries, emotionally wrung out, settled uneasily back into their old lives. But the new radio, linking them with the police post at Mwinilunga, gave them a sense of security, and gradually, as the same old tedious tasks gave them back some semblance of normalcy, without visible signposts to remind them, they might almost imagine that this country's constitutional conflict and the terrible trauma of the Congo had ceased to exist.

For Matthew at least, the deception lasted just until the day's end, when necessity forced him home to the tragic sight of Jennifer Solomon, pathetically clinging, trailing on Teller like some insecure child inseparable from its mother. But although this distressed him, he was at least immensely grateful for the return of her reason after the long weeks when she had lain unmoving, silent, and staring, mechanically fed and cared for, in a dazed apathy of emotional shock. Although the doctors patched up her body and pried into her mind and the other missionaries plied her with kindness and encouragement, for a long time neither pressure nor persuasion penetrated.

Informed of his daughter's desecration by Matthew's awkward anguished letter, Jenny's father arrived at Suseshi. An English South African who had immigrated to Northern Rhodesia sixteen years before, after the death of his wife in the same automobile accident that had blinded Jenny, Douglas Solomon was a fitter and turner on the Roan Antelope copper mine at Luanshya. Matthew found him to be a quiet and intelligent man who was deeply shaken by his daughter's defilement. His first fierce instinct was to take her back to "safe" South Africa, away from any environment that might foster such awful acts. But teaching the blind was Jenny's chosen vocation; in Jerome's opinion it would be immensely therapeutic if she were to resume her work, and obviously, having put down deep roots in his adopted country, Mr. Solomon seemed relieved at a solution that allowed him to stay. But embittered by his daughter's debasement and the whole Congo debacle, he was cynical of black aspirations and angry at what he saw as Britain's "weak-kneed" unwillingness to continue its obligations to the politically floundering protectorate.

The British colonial secretary had by this time dissolved the constitutional conference, and while the entire country tensely awaited the release of the revised constitution, a bitter cross-continent battle was raging behind the scenes among the British government, the Federal government, and the nationalists.

"The British seem to be doing everything in their power to appease the nationalists!" Douglas Solomon commented angrily. "Perhaps Northern Rhodesia was built on the backs of the black man, but by the same token it was built on the minds of the whites! Oh, the nationalists whine about inferior social conditions, about inequality and the color bar, yet little over fifty years ago the white man rescued them from a mere stone-age existence, from barbaric cruelties at the hands of their own chiefs and rival tribes. And as the Congo fiasco has so clearly shown, no white man has ever treated the blacks as cruelly as their own kind. We have at least provided them with education, civilized standards, Christian morality and relative relief from starvation and disease. Left to their own devices, I am afraid most of them would soon revert to the law of the jungle, the survival of the fittest! I'm sorry if I sound bitter, Professor. I suppose my daugther's attack has darkened my outlook, but it appalls me to think of turning this wonderful country over to people who are still little more than savages."

"Maybe so . . ." Matthew sighed. Although the view was rather extreme, he understood the man's bitterness against the unleashed lawless forces that had transformed his sweet smiling daughter into the sad, staring stranger who faced them now. On the whole, the man's visit was a harrowing unhappy time, with Jenny remaining unresponsive, fretful, and withdrawn, and finally, after three strained days at the mission, Douglas Solomon left them with obvious relief, gratefully entrusting his daughter to the missionaries' more objective care.

And gradually, tentatively, they began to reach her. As she began to find coherence, Jerome's searching assessment of her convinced him she remembered nothing of her defilement, and as her body healed, coaxed by kindness and normalcy, she learned to live with the frightening blank of this merciful amnesia, coming increasingly to her senses. But in the dark depths of her mind, mortally wounded, she was never quite the same. Her old ready smile was gone, and although she might have no conscious recall of her physical abuse, her body, instinctive as an animal's, remembered it well. Around all men, black men in particular, she became uneasy and anguished, acting so fretful and frightened that they had to keep her from company most of the time. And haunted by the horror, sensing sinister substance in the slightest shadows, shapes, and sounds, the nights became terror-filled times, when craving comfort, company, and light, she clung so pathetically to Teller that Matthew moved his wife's bed into the young girl's room so that she might stay at Jenny's side during the long lonely night hours when her restless sleep was wracked with recurrent nightmares of vague vicious horrors that left her staring with terror, saturated with cold sweat, shaken with sobs.

And during the days, her self-confidence completely shattered, she was incapable of any small task or even self-reliance; Than Profane went alone to Eshalakali Hill, where the faithful blind ever waited, and Teller's daily chores piled up as she stayed home to console an incapable child who had become irrationally afraid of pitfalls and of falling, of even familiar places and people, standing helpless without a hand to hold, suddenly blunderingly blind and accident-prone. And there was no medicine to cure this crippling paralysis; the two doctors shook helpless heads over her, as, eating little and saying less, she remained wan and pale, sad, silent, and insubstantial as a shadow.

2

On February 21, Britain released the new constitutional proposals. When it appeared to compromise the white position, Welensky made a scathing radio speech attacking the British government and called up four battalions of territorial troops. A rumor-rife nation tensed for the premier to seize independence unilaterally. But the man commanded white and black police and armed forces of conflicting allegiances. The troops were stood down and Welensky vowed to contest the elections by what precarious constitutional means were available to him. For the new white paper revealed a tricky scheme in which the national seats could go either way, a condition conducive to the election of a "middle" or anti-federal party. It was therefore just conceivable that a coalition with the rival Congress Party or the white Liberals might win a majority for UNIP. Obviously seeing their slim chance, the nationalist leaders accepted the plan while the embittered Welensky rushed through a Defense Amendment Bill to allow the Federal government to call up all white men between the ages of eighteen and fifty.

Over in the Congo, the situation seemed no more settled. The very day that M. Moise Tshombe called for a meeting of his fellow Congolese leaders to settle their differences, the United Nations Security Council called for the withdrawal of all foreign military and paramilitary personnel from the Congo and authorized the use of force by U.N. troops to "prevent" civil war. It was a cunning move clearly calculated to deprive Tshombe of his Europeon officers, advisers, and mercenary contingents.

When the new English nurse arrived, Jerome Dooley avoided the thorny question of her designation by summarily abdicating his medical directorship to Than Profane. Matthew was hardly surprised; the man had been a reluctant successor to Tom Profane from the start, an uncertain leader who shied from decisions and dissension, and the Boy had never disguised his eagerness to take total control. Now, installed in his new authority, he promptly delegated the care of the lepers and the little clinic at Eshalakali Hill to Molly Dibb. She was initially to spend some months at Suseshi getting to know the people and their language. But once she took charge of Eshalakali's clinics, the Boy's own heavy workload would ease, leaving him more time to solicit and service ever more of the little outclinics he was encouraging the people to build in the outlying villages. And he was currently set to conquer new territory; the way Matthew heard it, after seven unsuccessful operations on the woman from Mulaisho's kraal, involving eighteen months of fortitudinous suffering and of physical and social rehabilitation, the Boy had finally succeeded in getting her urethral walls to knit, converting the bowel and vagina into one sac. Although this unnatural arrangement was as much as they could do for her, it was a vast improvement, since she now at least had some control over her natural discharges and her disagreeable smell was likewise diminished. It also made her eligible for discharge, and Matthew, remembering the Boy's promise, was quick to include himself in the Boy's triumphant return to Mulaisho's chiefdom.

Their trip into the Balovale coincided with the hunger months of the year, when the grain harvest had fallen too low to allow for the brewing of beer. Since a contingent of district messengers had also recently confiscated a communal cache of dagga, arresting many found in its possession after discovering the hemp weed growing under camouflage of tobacco plants, they arrived to find an agreeably chastened, sober, and hunger-humbled populace who seemed genuinely pleased to see them; the scrawny village curs clambered to follow the Boy's alluring leopard smell and indeed, even the reticent Mulaisho, doubtless disconcerted in the midst of his seasonal hangover, agreed to see them. Looking sick and dissipated as he lay, ravaged with syphilis and senility, on the skin-covered springs of his old brass bedstead, the old scoundrel, having doubtless only released the "hopeless case" to get rid of the missionaries once their usefulness to him personally had ended, sniffed skeptically at the woman he had obviously never expected to see again, let along minus her offensive smell. Matthew suspected that a great many of the old fellow's henchmen had been among those apprehended in the district commissioner's blitz on his village, for this time his counselors were conspicuously few, and in the absence of his intimidating retinue of witchdoctors, the old man was easily cajoled into keeping his promise. He agreed that Matthew might assemble whoever wished to listen to introductory lectures on the Christian faith and modern education, while the Boy would be free to solicit the sick.

But first, to demonstrate his new benevolence, the old chief struggled up to sit with them out on his thatched veranda and had tea served them in a surprisingly elegant cracked china tea service. The Boy's bounty of a penicillin injection and a pack of cigarettes had a quick psychological effect, and now, full of bonhomie, the old man ordered that the "mutilated people" be shown to them. Before they knew what was happening, while they fastidiously sipped the weak weed tea, a pathetic specimen of a man, crippled and minus nose, fingers, and toes, with the scars of old cruel wounds gouged deep in his chest, was dragged before them by two youths; released, the poor creature fell to the ground, and amid the callous laughter of his fellows, began to chitter like a monkey. Matthew turned away, sick to his soul. Well, he might have known something as odious as this would constitute entertainment to these people; historically infamous for their brutality as brigands and slave dealers in days gone by, this clan, less progressive than other elements of their tribe, had obviously changed little with the advent of the white man. The awful spectacle reconjured the recent barbarism of the Balubas, and while the Boy set down his teacup and stared stonily, Matthew rose up with his outrage, surprising even himself with his brave belligerence as he upbraided the people and shooed them off before any more of their broken "exhibits" could be so cruelly paraded.

Then, while the chief, contrite and curious, looked mildly on, he erected his portable folding table, setting out the Quaker Book of Disciplines and a large Bible. Still too angry to canvass a congregation or to directly address the errant chief, Matthew lifted his old white head and began to talk to the Lord in *Chi-Chokwe*. As he talked, a strange thing happened; a hush fell over the village, and the people, unbidden, began to creep up, settling down to listen. Before he knew it, Matthew was earnestly talking to a sprawling crowd that sat crammed around him on the bare earth before the chief's hut. Although less receptive to the idea of schooling, with their childlike love of folklore and legend, grateful for this sanctioned distraction in their careworn lives, they sat entranced while Matthew told the classic tale of Jesus Christ. The romance and gentleness of this God of love was obviously something new to them, and despite the frequent interruptions of wailing babies, rooting pigs, and barking dogs, so receptive were they that while the Boy, with the sensitive antennae of a skeptical eye and his stethoscope, surreptitiously sniffed out sickness in their ranks, Matthew talked until his throat turned dry and the day had darkened into dusk. They had planned on spending the night at Eshalakali Hill with the Townsends, but when the chief magnanimously invited them to remain at the village, anxious to cement this tentative inception, they accepted.

As they sat around the night fires with the village elders, companionably supping off a frugal meal of *nshima* and mushrooms and some more of the weed tea, Matthew noticed a certain child with the matchstick limbs and bloated belly of kwashiorkor sitting alone in the shadows at the edge of the firelight. As time went on, he observed that the little fellow, wearing nothing more than a perfunctory skin G-string, would wait, crouched expectantly, until someone shouted and tossed him a scrap of food. Then, scrambling on all fours, slapping off the scavenging dogs, the child would devour the food like an animal. When one of the tribal elders apologetically explained that his people only tolerated and fed the blind and orphaned boy, because he would surely shortly die and they felt it best not to mistreat him overtly lest his spirit return to bring them misfortune, Matthew's horror was compounded. Well, this was one little candidate for care Than Profane had obviously missed. He came across now and cursorily examined the cringing little creature in the firelight, confiding to Matthew that the poor mite had evidently been blinded by some witchdoctor's poisonous potion (one eye was completely seared from its socket, while the other was a disfigured white orb). His young soft bones showed signs of old healed fractures, he had broken teeth, a suppurating burn on one foot, a badly septic throat, and a touch of bronchitis. Looking about three years younger than the seven years the elder had accredited him for, the thin, dirty, starving little waif was frightened and shy; he shrank back, terrified of the doctor's touch, cringing pathetically to ward off expected blows. While Than Profane rummaged in his apothecary for pills and solvents, Matthew, sick at heart, ignoring the suspicious stares of the elders and the child's filth and fulsome smell, lifted the awkward bundle of belly and bones onto his knee.

"Child, what is thy name?" he said in Chi-Chokwe.

At first the small boy seemed too afraid even to move, and it was only after Matthew gently persisted that the trembling little creature finally responded.

"Bwana," he whispered in a hoarse scratchy voice, covering his face with his hands, "my name is Africa. I am as the earth—as nothing."

Staring in sorrow at the pathetic little soul, Matthew felt a slow pain begin to rise in his breast. The name seemed oddly appropriate: Were not the continent's sins of omission and commission seen in the child's great suffering?

He said gently, "Tell me, little fellow, does thee know of Jesus Christ?"

"Yay, Master. Did I not hear you talk of this God today?"

"Indeed. Well then, thee will have heard that Jesus loves the little children."

"Yay, Master. The other children. But he cannot love me. For I am as the dogs, useless and unclean, and I have no sight. Who could love such a thing?"

Exchanging looks with Than Profane, Matthew stared at the child for several moments, unable to speak. Finally he swallowed against the uncomfortable lump that had begun contracting his throat. "Jesus can," he croaked. "And he does. Jesus loves thee, child . . ."

The child's hands dropped away and he slowly turned his head. As the dull sightless little face puzzled at him incredulously in the flickering firelight, Matthew saw a single tear swell in the corner of his eye at the one undamaged tear duct; as he watched, it splashed down and began to stream a glistening path across the dark dusty little cheek.

The next day, Matthew and Than Profane rose early; after an uncomfortable night spent sleeping in the Land-Rover, they breakfasted briefly on bitter black coffee, brushed their teeth in the murky river water, and went to take their leave of Chief Mulaisho. They found the old man turned querulous and evasive; furthermore, the chronically ill whom the Boy had arranged to take back to Suseshi failed to appear. They had gone into hiding and their relatives shook sullen heads as the Boy walked from one smelly smoking hovel to another, uselessly entreating while a hyena-trailing mangy-looking witchdoctor, wearing a dangling monkey-tail headdress, vertebrae necklace of dried birds' heads and a short wildebeest-skin cape, triumphantly gloated.

Since the tragedy at Rutshura, the Boy had been about as prickly and unapproachable as a cornered porcupine. This obstructiveness in the face of his care hardly improved his mood, and finally, infuriated, he damned them all to die of their discomforts and prepared to leave without them. Then, at the Land Rover, crouched beside a wheel almost as big as he, they found the little blind boy, Africa. He held in his hands a broken wooden spoon and a filthy scrap of cloth, the pathetic sum of his worldly possessions. Now, at the scudding of their footfalls, he lifted his ravaged little face expectantly. Their unaccustomed care had obviously affected him deeply, yet Matthew felt innately that it was more than the promised benediction of physical repair that had lured this little orphan to follow faithfully in the footsteps of strangers. No indeed. The sad sightless little soul followed a dream that shone like a beckoning light in the dreadful darkness of a hitherto lost lonely life. The dream of a benevolent deity who promised the priceless rare gift of undiscriminating love . . .

3 It was First-day and they arrived home in time to attend afternoon meeting. Matthew found Teller and Jenny at the house all dressed up to attend. Teller fell silent when she saw the little blind boy he led into the living room. Her soft eyes filled with tears at Matthew's tragic tale, but she refused to let sentiment, suppurating

sores, or a septic throat get the better of her practical nature. Within minutes she had the child naked, in a tub of warm water; she dunked him in disinfectant, scrubbed and deloused him, shaving off his tight wooly curls. Then she dressed him in some ragged clothing entreated from the houseboy's children, and they started out for meeting.

Cutting through the Lantana hedge, gay with its miniature pink and yellow posies, they came upon Than Profane at the open arbor of the communal garage. He was still unpacking his traveling apothecary, with the aid of his houseboy. He greeted them, frowning when he saw Jenny. Though he seldom saw her these days, one glance at her pale despairing face and her hold on Teller's arm must have told him the old story. Looking wan in her pale bonnet and patched lilac dress, she nodded distantly at his greeting, breathing nervously, barely mouthing a strained reply.

"Well, we're taking little Africa off to meeting," Matthew explained brightly. The Nantucket bell, announcing meeting hour, had just begun to peal. "Figured thee wouldn't mind him meeting the other orphans and worshiping before thee take him off to the hospital."

"Matthew," the Boy said abruptly, "there's something I'd like to discuss with you and Teller. It may take a while. But Jenny can go ahead and take the boy over to the meeting house."

"*Jenny?*" Matthew stared at the Boy in disbelief. Had the fool lost sight of the fact that she had been incapable of going anywhere by herself since Rutshura? "Now, Doctor . . ." he accused uneasily. "Thee *knows* . . ."

But while Matthew and Teller stood still bewilderedly blinking at him, the Boy led the bald little blind child across to Jenny and placed one small black hand on her arm. He said coolly: "Jenny, this is Africa. He's blind too. Africa, this *dona* will take you to the church."

"No!" Jenny whispered, aghast, shaking her head, her blue eyes wide within the lavender bonnet. "Oh please, I *can't* . . ."

"Yes you can," the Boy defied quietly. "You've done it a hundred times before."

"Oh now!" Teller wailed.

But the Boy described Jenny's whereabouts to her, then took Teller's arm and hustled her off, beckoning Matthew. At last digesting what he was trying to achieve, Matthew reluctantly followed. They reached the Fotches' hedge before they turned. And at first the

330

child's fearful bewilderment and the young girl's terror were so palpable that Matthew could hardly bear to watch. Jenny stood, wiping at her eyes, struggling to suppress silent rising sobs. Unable to endure it, Matthew was about to rush to comfort her when the Boy caught at his arm and pointed. Jenny's stance was subtly changing. Facing up to the little blind boy's utter dependence on her, she had squared her shoulders. Then, tremulously feeling the uneven path with careful feet and her long cane, her frowning face intense with concentration, she began to walk unsteadily, leading the little blind boy slowly along beside her.

And to Matthew it was a remarkable sight: *the blind leading the blind!* He sniffed and wiped at his eyes as they followed some way behind, monitoring the brave denouement. He and Teller, jostling together down the slope, joyously chuckled to themselves. They endured some suspenseful moments watching the blind pair falter frequently. But barely bearing it, they held back and were rewarded.

Near the meeting house, a few children and some African women saw them coming. Warned off by Matthew's urgent signals, they stood aside. When the pair finally reached the milling crowd around the meeting house, Pastor Peter, Katherine, and Grace Dooley came out to meet them. They were softly laughing and silently weeping with joy. The precarious pilgrimage had been an immense achievement, after all. After the long lonely weeks of her incapacitation, Jenny had at last walked alone again.

When Matthew reached them, Jenny turned; she stood, brow furrowed and head tilted, acutely listening. Through her unseeing gaze, she seemed to be reaching out, silently communing across the slope, searching for someone. Following the uncanny radar of her sightless stare, Matthew found him. The Boy, who had slowed up and stopped some way behind, stared solemnly back. Then he turned and walked slowly away. Later, when Matthew heard Jenny's sweet vibrant voice, which had so long been silent, join in the chorus of "Amazing Grace," he knew that she was truly getting well at last.

Africa, the seven-year-old blind foundling, had been discharged from the hospital but a few days when he suddenly turned up at Matthew's office. On all fours, he was minus the shirt and shoes they had given him, and though he confessed that his back longed to feel the sun and his feet, like his hands, the earth, Matthew realized that whatever had brought him here, over strange ground in an alien environment, was something more serious than mere physical adjustment. He took the reluctant little fellow back to the orphanage, where he found Hannah Rothchild in the dining room serving luncheon at the long laid table surrounded by the twenty-two well-behaved black orphans who ranged in age from four to seventeen. She looked outraged when she saw Africa with Matthew.

"That young rascal has been banished to his bed!" she snorted.

Matthew echoed innocently, "Banished? For what possible reason?"

"For stealing from the kitchen, the ungrateful little wretch!" Hannah set down the soup ladle. "I found sugar and crackers, twisted in leaves, beneath his pillow!"

"But . . ." Amazed to realize his indignation was expected, Matthew stared at the woman incredulously. "The little fellow is accustomed to starving! Surely thee can understand his instinctive desire to set aside provisions for future want! Remember, the Lord himself extolled us: 'Suffer little children . . .'"

"Exactly! And thee would do well to remember, Friend Matthew, that the operative word is *suffer*, not spoil! And there is another commandment: *Thou shalt not steal!*"

"But the child has only been here a few days," Matthew spluttered. "Surely thee can . . ."

"Very well," Hannah gave an exasperated sigh. "Since he is new here, I will give him one more chance. But woe betide if he repeats his disgraceful behavior!"

Taking the child roughly by the arm, she ushered him to his seat. She thrust a spoon into his hand, placed a steaming bowl of soup before him, and commanded him to eat. Then she stalked back to the head of the table, clapping her hands for silence.

"Come, come, children, eat up thy soup!" Suddenly she peered suspiciously across the table. "Mary Mduma! What has thee there? Come show me, child, before I take a switch to thy behind!"

The little black girl left her seat and came hesitantly to the head of the table; she stood before Hannah looking terrified, with her hands behind her back.

"All right!" Hannah held out a hand. "Hand it over!"

Cringing fearfully, the child gave Hannah a dried corn husk with a face caricatured with soot and clothing contrived of leaves.

"Aha!" With contemptuous disregard for Matthew's presence, Hannah ripped the little effigy to pieces, finally dashing it to the floor in the stunned silence. Then, wiping her hands with satisfaction, she sent the child to stand in the corner pending corporal punishment and turned to Matthew with a defiant stare. "I was never allowed a doll myself! Frivolous playthings take attention from the Lord. Dolls especially are as much as idolatry! I am gratified that I have at last got Merry Cathcart to understand that! She and Ratchet are altogether too soft with the children. Why, the minute my back is turned, they pamper the little beasties. I have all my time cut out just trying to instill a little discipline around here!"

She looked around suddenly. "Saul! I saw that! Elbows on the table! How dare thee!" She strode around the table to a small boy, and while Matthew looked on, horrified, stood twisting the little fellow's ear till he shed tears, which dripped into his soup. Matthew could stand it no longer. He stumbled out of the dining room aghast to realize they had a barren-souled monster playing mother to their orphans.

The following day, Hannah Rothchild turned up at the dining *chitenje* waving a little wooden box in one hand and dragging a weeping Africa with the other.

"Well, Matthew Tomlinson, I hope thee're satisfied! See what thy lenience has led to? Now, not content with stealing from the hand that feeds him, this young beastie has begun thieving from others! Why, he's a veritable magpie; one of Mulaisho's crooked kin to be sure!"

The object turned out to be a musical box she had discovered in the child's possession directly after morning meeting. She was just extolling the ungrateful sinfulness of the wretched child when the Profanes arrived. Jayne Profane came forward looking perplexed.

"Why, Miss Rothchild, didn't he tell thee? That music box belongs to me. I gave it to him after meeting. Since he can't see, I thought it might pleasure him some to listen to the pretty strains."

Hannah turned beet red; it seemed to Matthew it was the first time in their acquaintance that she was struck speechless. Unfortunately, the paralysis in her larynx did not last long. In a moment she was spluttering furiously about the child having deceived her in such a manner. By the strained silence of her audience, it was evident to Matthew that he was not the only one skeptical of the domineering old spinster's guilty gush. Clearly, she had been so eager to incriminate the flabbergasted little fellow that she had allowed him no chance to explain.

4 Returning from his clinic run into Barotseland, Than arrived back at Suseshi after dark, all buoyed up with the news that the Kazungula Killer had finally been killed by a white hunter. After devouring over fifty human beings, the battle-scarred irascible old lion had died of three bullet wounds in a lonely thicket near the Musheketi swamp, disconcertingly close to Mambundi Mission. Katherine was waiting for Than outside the house, and one look at her face drove all thought of the man-eater from Than's mind. Her eyes were wide and pain-stricken, the freckles standing out dark as pepper on her pale complexion. When Bathsheba jumped off the canvas cab to greet her, she ignored the cat's affectionate furling around her skirts, wailing:

"Oh, Than, it's too terrible! It's Jenny, and just when she was recovering and starting to teach the blind again! Jerome found out today: *she is with child!*"

Than stared at her in dull disbelief; after a moment, in a daze, he stooped to clip on Bathsheba's chain.

"Apparently, she's taken it very badly," Katherine mourned, wringing her hands. "I'm just about to go over and help Teller counsel the poor child. The committee is meeting to discuss the consequences at the Dooleys' right now."

The muscles in Than's clenched jaw had begun to flicker furiously, and Katherine whispered anxiously: "Than, now don't go getting all riled up . . ." She grabbed at his arm as he moved past her, but he gave her Bathsheba's chain and shrugged her off, stalking furiously across the grass toward the big rambling Dooley house, which stood sallow-lit in the darkness, the long fly-screened veranda animated with visitors.

Jerome sat in his shirtsleeves, looking stubble-chinned and haggard; a little red-haired girl was curled up in his lap, and around him, on wicker chairs, come homing in like wasps to the treacle of tragedy, sat Hannah Rothchild, the Fotches, and Ezra Peabody, looking important and pitying, while Professor Tomlinson, the girl's proxy parent, sat looking dazed and disconsolate.

Than burst up the steps in a storm. Jerome, seeing him coming, pushed his sleepy daughter off his lap and stood up, looking nervous.

"Now, kid! Don't go getting excited! If thee thinks I would wish . . ."

"Jesus, Jerome," Than talked angrily through gritted teeth. "What the hell would have been wrong with a simple preventative D. and C.?"

"*Friend!*" Matthew Tomlinson struggled to his feet. "We're all upset about this, but there's no sense getting riled. It's no fault of Jerome's, and thee has no right to go making recriminations now, when it's too late!"

"Too late?" Than growled, shrugging off the old man's hand. "I made that little recommendation weeks ago, when it first happened." He turned fiercely away. "Unfortunately, Jerome felt differently. And Jenny's not my patient."

"Well, now!" Matthew admonished, as if to a child. "That just about sums it up then, doesn't it? Jenny is Jerome's charge, and he has to do as *his* ethics dictate."

"Indeed!" Hannah Rothchild declared, face drawn up in a stern knot. "And the child has suffered nothing more than our sisters in Christ have endured in the Congo and in other primitive lands. It's an occupational martyrdom we female missionaries risk in the serving of the Lord!"

"Well, hot diggity dog! That just about comforts the hell out of me!" Than growled, and Matthew interjected earnestly:

"Now, son, there's no need to get uppity! We all feel as badly about this as thee does, but what can we do?"

Now all eyes were riveted on Than, and a unanimous questioning quivered in the air.

"Well, I can suggest an old ugly solution," he said brutally. "It's called abortion."

"*Abortion!*"

Than stood unwavering amidst the outraged babble that rose up around him. There were low cries of *Murder! Blasphemy!* and *Criminal!* and Clara Fotch shrieked furiously: "As a Christian, how can thee even suggest so shameful a solution? It's unthinkable, inhuman!"

"Inhuman?" Than said acidly, raising a cynical brow. "On the contrary, ma'am, it's the only human thing to do. That girl . . . is unfit, both physically and emotionally, to carry that child. Any psychiatrist would second that opinion."

"No matter," Hannah Rothchild proclaimed pompously. "It is the will of the Lord!"

Than looked infinitely pained. "Rape is the Lord's will?"

"Doctor!" Orville Fotch rose up, palpitating in blustering indignation. "Besides thy terrible blasphemy, would thee kindly moderate thy language in view of the ladies here present?"

"Swell! What should I do? Frame my points in nursery rhyme prose?" Than said bitterly, looking around at them. "Any woman here who understands my words is old enough to hear them, and rape is rape! I didn't invent the word or the practice!"

In the mortified silence, he continued quietly: "Jenny was abandoned out there—blind and helpless. You all left her while you saved your own skins! The least you can do is help her now!"

His words fell to a self-conscious silence, which grew more prickly by the moment. Then Hannah Rothchild, patently wrestling with her own great guilt, rose defensively, arms in their leg-of-mutton sleeves accusingly akimbo. "How dare thee!" she whispered scathingly. "How dare thee make such a slanderous accusation?"

"I'm just telling it like it happened," Than said grimly.

"Have thee forgotten, Doctor, that the Lord's justice works in many ways? There is none among us fit to question His punishment for untold wrongs."

"Punishment?" Than snorted. "Miss Rothchild, are you telling me Jenny deserved what she got?"

Hannah raised a contemptuous chin; in a voice that gloated with malicious meaning, she said haughtily: "I can only say that in all my long years in this country and during many solitary excursions through the bush amid many tricky political situations, *I* was never once likewise accosted or abused in any way. After all, they had no quarrel with us whites; *we* all escaped the encounter unscathed. It is not our fault if she chose to wander off, and it's my own considered opinion that the child must have done something foolish . . . or indeed *provocative* to encourage such . . . such . . ."

There was a bloated pause. Than stared at the woman, white with fury, so outraged that he could scarcely speak. "Ma'am," he finally snarled softly, "you can go to hell. Have you ever considered that the reason you never tempted a man to ravage or rape might be the same one you never tempted one to matrimony?"

Then he stepped backward down the steps and fled into the night darkness, radiating his rage.

A light glowed on the veranda of the Tomlinson house, and Than found Katherine and Teller crouched outside the boxroom door, looking furtive and anxious.

"She's locked herself in there," Katherine whispered anxiously. "She won't talk to anyone! Teller's managed to retrieve the key on a piece of newspaper under the door!"

"That's right." Teller got heavily to her feet, bones creaking as she straightened up, wiping plump palms on a polka-dot pinafore, her face creasing with anxiety as she stared up at Than through her magnifying spectacles. "I'm real worried; she's been acting so strange since Jerome broke the news and told her what was done to her. Hasn't eaten or said a word! Seems to me like she's relapsing back into her mind again. I tried to talk to her, but . . . well, I guess I wasn't much help. I'm still pretty shocked myself . . . and the next thing I knew, she rushed off and locked herself in there. Doctor, maybe thee can talk to her in thy professional capacity. I know she thinks highly of thee."

Than nodded. He waited while Teller unlocked the door and Katherine took up the hissing oil lamp, leading light into the little dark room. As she set the lamp down on a small cluttered table, the sallow glow spread and enveloped the forlorn figure of Jennifer Solomon, who sat on the bare floor among piles of old newspapers and Quaker journals, amid the dusty discarded bric-a-brac of years of missioneering. Tightly hugging knees that were drawn up beneath a faded cotton dress that was patched damp with perspiration, she sat with her head slightly bowed, her long dark hair hanging forward and her face expressionless as she stared sightlessly into space.

"Jenny dear." Katherine reached out, then drew back in anguished surprise as Jenny shrank from her touch, wailing distraughtly.

"Don't touch me! I'm *dirty* . . . don't you know that?" She covered her face with her hands and began to cry. "How can you bear to touch me?"

"Oh now, dearest." Katherine's own eyes filled with tears, and she shook her fair head. "Don't say that. Don't even think it! Remember, they may trespass thy body, but they *never* can touch thy good clean pure Christian soul!"

But Jenny had broken into wrenching sobs, and scalded by this great grief, Katherine stood up slowly, glancing at Than.

"Get my medical bag," he said, and she nodded and hurried out, closing the door behind her.

For a while, Than let Jenny cry. Pushing aside an old box of litter and a dusty broken lampshade, he eased down and sat cross-legged on the cold concrete floor, lighting up a cigarette and smoking silently, watching with dispassion while in the dull desolation of that stale-aired, forgotten little room of the ill-built big brick house her small frame shook with broken sobs. Finally the ferocious tremors began to lose intensity through sheer exhaustion, and as he watched, a great tear dripped off the edge of her chin and splashed down into the pale cleavage at the unbuttoned top of her bodice, where the tiny fine-chained gold cross lay against her fair skin.

"Whoops." Digging a clean handkerchief out of his hip pocket, Than dabbed at the splashed tear. Then, when she drew back in surprise, he leaned across and began to clean up her face; he hadn't had time to wash up since coming in from his clinic run, and now he caught the reek of his own sweat and the gamey leopard smell of Bathsheba as he tenderly patted dry her flushed cheeks and wiped her nose.

"Blow!" he commanded gruffly, and she obeyed automatically, saying listlessly:

"Thank you . . ."

"Don't mention it, ma'am." He pressed the bunched handkerchief into her limp hand. "I'm a knight in shining armor and it's my calling to wipe the noses of pretty ladies in distress." When she giggled hysterically and began to cry again, he said huskily, "And you are one beautiful lady."

"Oh no. No I'm not!" she whispered sickly, turning away. "I'm so ashamed, I could die!"

"Now, you hush that now," he growled, suddenly angry, stubbing his cigarette furiously out on the concrete floor. He took her reluctant chin in his hand, tilting it up, forcing her to face him. "I don't want to hear you talk that way ever again, hear me? You have nothing to be ashamed of, and I want you to act so people will know it—to walk with your head held high, as erect as your principles! Hear me now. I want you to be proud you're Jennifer Solomon and good and clean and fine as you are!" He broke off furiously, chest heaving, staring at her scathingly, vaguely surprised at the intensity of his feelings. Although her irrepressible tears still slowly streamed, as surprised as he, she was silent. Her huge suffering blue eyes stared at him solemnly, and after a moment he could bear it no longer and he released her chin, thankful when she turned the afflicted gaze from him.

"W-What will it do to my father?" she stammered softly.

"Your father's a grown man," he said gently. "I think he can take it, if you can." After a moment he said cautiously, "Listen to me,

Jenny." He broke off and drew in his breath. "It'll be all right. When you come to Eshalakali with me next week . . . I'll abort you."

There was a small sound and Than turned to find Katherine standing in the doorway, her tanned freckled face aghast, breasts still heaving from her hurry as she held the medical bag out to him.

"You heard that?" he said, quietly defiant, taking it from her.

She nodded, her face ashen; then she wailed softly: "Oh, Than, *Than*, thee can't do that! Thee must not talk that way."

"Why not?" He unclipped the bag. "I'm a doctor; it's my job to ease suffering."

"Thee are also a Christian missionary! The Bible clearly says *Thou shalt not kill*—and besides . . ." She came further into the room and quickly shut the door behind her, leaning back against it, her body rigid in her long gray dress. "*They* would never allow it."

"Listen, Kathy, I don't give a shit what they would or would not allow. I can't *not* do it. And nothing you or anyone else can say will change my mind."

Outside, Matthew Tomlinson had joined Teller's anxious vigil, pacing the veranda like an impatient caged cat, white hair awry and eyes wild, looking like a man demented. When Katherine led Jenny off to her room, he reached out and gripped Than's arm with fingers like claws.

"Now, Boy, I don't know what thee're up to, but I'll give thee warning right here and now. Thee leave that girl alone! Understand? Now, I appreciate the way thee feels. I guess thee're more hot-blooded than the rest of us. But thee must learn to take the unhappy pitfalls of life and turn the other cheek. Thee must learn to accept what *is*!"

Than shuddered and wrenched away his arm. He stared at Matthew with a look like hate. "You're telling me?"

The old man drew in a mighty breath and rocked back on his heels, silver-haired and magnificent in his righteousness. "I'm telling thee, boy, not to go getting outlandish ideas! Not to go committing acts justified by thy medical ethics! Remember that here it's Christian ethics we go by, and not . . . well, what is done is done, and anything thee can do to reverse it would be cardinal sin! Against the will of God! Against the principles of this mission. Against thy and the Africans' interests. Why, the taking of the life of an unborn child—feticide—is *murder!* Just as much as the taking of any other fully-fledged life. And don't thee forget that, boy! Thee go playing around, influencing that poor child and tampering with the course of nature and God's will—thee go interfering with what is Jerome's and none of thy province—then, boy, there is nothing I could or would do for thee in the event of . . . God's wrath, *or the mission's reprisal!*"

"Matthew!" Than snarled softly in the darkness, "you go to hell! If that's Christianity—to force an innocent young girl to carry the child of her rapist—then I want no part of it." He turned and stalked off down the steps. Matthew, sounding suddenly unsure of himself, called timidly after him in the darkness.

"Son. *Son?* Now thee hear me! Don't thee go . . ."

Than laughed bitterly. "Just you try and stop me!"

"Boy!" Matthew stormed, thumping his fist on the wooden balustrade. "They would have thee recalled, thee know that! Don't thee have any regard for thy work, to so jeopardize thy presence?"

Than stopped dead then; seething, he spun around, staring at Matthew through the darkness. After a moment, he drew in his breath. *"Don't they?"* he said softly. And then he was gone.

5

The following Wednesday at Eshalakali Hill, Than left Jenny at the church with her blind students and went down to the leper colony. By mid-morning, the father of one of her pupils hurried past the line of lepers and stuck his head through the doorway.

"Bwana Doctor, there is something wrong with the blind *dona.*"

Than found her sitting motionless, silent and staring. Explaining that she was sick, he dismissed her students and took her to the Land-Rover, where she sat silently the rest of the day. Than finished his work at the leper colony, then treated the collection of sick who waited at the top clinic as quickly as he could. He had developed a bad headache by the time he finally dismissed Teapot and locked up the clinic. Then he took Jenny down to the lepers' treatment hut, where they were less likely to be disturbed. Ignoring the puzzled stares of Teapot and the lepers, he locked the door and helped Jenny onto the freshly sheeted examination couch. With the door closed, it was dim in the freshly scrubbed hut, and he lit up a Tilly lamp and filled a clean kidney bowl with equipment he had brought in his medical bag.

"Listen, Jenny," he said gently. "I want you to take off your pants and draw up your knees. If anything happens, I'll stay here with you at the Townsends' tonight. Then we can go back to Suseshi in the morning and tell Jerome you've started a miscarriage. He'll fix you up at the hospital."

As he turned to get a clean towel off the shelf, he heard her wriggling on the couch; when he turned back, she was frantically pulling down her long skirt.

"Okay, Jenny." He handed her the towel. "Put this under your behind." While she busied herself on the high table, he turned to the kidney bowl and held a hypodermic syringe up to the light. He had an ampule of oxytocin and several ampules of scopolamine and pethidine ready in the kidney bowl. Since only the European staff had access to the drug cupboard at Suseshi, checks on the contents were consequently slack and it had been a simple matter for him to extract his haul.

But right now he wasn't worried about official consequences; he was feeling a little shivery and sick and the very real dangers inherent in the procedure he was about to attempt worried him more. Because reaction varied in the individual, he knew that too little oxytocin might not be enough to start contractions to expel the fetus. Too much, however, could rupture the uterus and cause massive hemorrhage. In this event, he would immediately inject the scopolamine and pethidine, but there were no guarantees that the depressants would bring the contractions under control, and she might go into severe shock and die. His hand was shaking slightly when he injected the oxytocin.

Jenny closed her eyes tightly. Than passed a hand over her abdomen. After a while, he felt the faint quiver of a contraction starting. Another started up, then another and another. But they were weak and irregular and gradually petered to nothing.

"Oh, Jesus!" Than closed his eyes. When he tried to examine Jenny for blood, she sat up with a start and rolled aside, legs tightly clamped in fierce modesty. He found only a small stain of blood on the towel. "Jenny," he sighed. "I don't guess it's any good."

She stared unseeingly past him with desperate, disbelieving eyes. "Can't you try again?" she said in a tiny tight voice. "Can't you give me more?"

"No, Jenny. I don't dare give you more. A bigger dose could be . . ." He let the implication hang in the air and shook his head slowly. "I can't, Jenny."

"Oh please," she whispered, starting to cry. "Please try! I can't . . . can't shame my father . . . everyone, this way!"

"Oh God, Jenny, don't cry." Remembering the fatal results of other illegal abortions he had seen gone wrong, he turned sickly away. Of course he was more knowledgeable and accomplished than the average back-street abortionist. He could try once more. But if things went wrong, it was a long way back to Suseshi Hospital, where the bleeding could be controlled. And even then the ruptured uterus could become infected, and she could die.

"Listen, Jenny, I'll do it another way. I'll rupture the bag of waters manually. That'll be a little uncomfortable, but not bad or dangerous. Only I'll have to have very sterile conditions. I'll have to do it at Suseshi. Maybe we can sneak it in the dead of night, and once the bleeding gets started, I'll persuade Jerome to give you a dilation and curettage. Maybe he won't take the life, but he surely wouldn't deliberately perpetuate it."

Jenny's crying had trailed off, and Than extinguished the lamp and they sat for a moment in dull digesting silence in the dimness amid the sterile sweetish odors of the cloistered little hut. Then Than helped her down from the high couch. Outside, the air was cool and sweet in the hour preceding dusk and Jenny stood self-consciously straightening her long dress, tying on her bonnet while Than locked the clinic door. Above the muffled roar of the rapids far below, fish eagles screamed along the wild lonely river as it lay reflecting pink cloud-scudded sky in the unearthly frieze of flaming sunset, panoramically unfolding within the pale spits of sand across the bush-shrouded remote reaches extending to ancient Angola. The trees were already etched in inky shadow, and they could smell the lepers' cooking fires as they started across the colony clearing.

As Than helped Jenny to negotiate the steep stone-cobbled path, Teapot, clumsy and eager as a pet pup, hurried up to carry his medical bag. While they disjointedly toiled to the top of the ridge, a stray kaffir dog wandered in their wake, apathetically sniffing at their heels. Jenny was crying silently, her face pale and distraught, and below, among the meandering lines of the dilapidated thatch huts, a few crippled and disfigured figures hobbled out of the shadows and stared perplexedly after them.

After supper, Matthew was startled from his customary perusal of a pile of week-late newspapers by young Jayne Profane, who stumbled breathlessly into his parlor.

"Uncle Matthew, come quickly! My brother's just got in from the Hill and something's wrong with him."

He leaped up at once, hurried to the house next door, and found the Boy on the living room floor, struggling to raise himself. Katherine, cradling a swollen eye, knelt beside him.

"He collapsed!" she wailed. "When I went to help him, he struck out at me! He's not himself!"

And she was right; he stared at Matthew with the dull hot eyes of an injured animal, unseeing and defensive. He was fighting blind and delirious. Matthew took one look and shouted for Jayne to fetch Dr. Dooley. How they ever got him up the stairs Matthew would never know, but between them, he and Katherine battled to do it, fighting the Boy every inch of the way. In his room, exhausted, they dropped him on his bed like a sack of grain. And they left him there. In his wild state, it would have taken more strength than Matthew possessed and more objectiveness than Katherine's modesty permitted to get him undressed. They left him fitfully shivering, writhing, and moaning on the big double bed. Moments later, Jerome Dooley burst in.

He proclaimed it was malaria again, this time a particularly vicious attack, which made him shake his head in disbelief. "Will thee look at that kid! Laid out cold with malaria, and just completed a full shift at Eshalakali bordering that condition." He turned to Matthew. "Well, roll up your sleeves, old man, and get ready to fight. Help me get the pants off him."

"Wait up," he called after Katherine, who had begun to tiptoe discreetly out. She stopped at the door. "Set out his pajamas and make some coffee, sister. I'll be down in a while and give thee something for that black eye!"

6 "Good morning to thee." Katherine breezed into Than's dim room. Setting a tray of orange juice and scrambled eggs at his bedside, she drew the drapes, opening wide the windows, letting in the sunshine and a breeze. "Now just thee sit up and eat thy breakfast!"

"Kathy!" He rolled over, frowning fiercely at the intrusive light. "I'm not hungry. I want to get up and work. What'd you do with my clothes?"

"Now, Than, Dr. Dooley said at least another day or two. Thee're still weak!"

"Oh Christ, Kathy! Another day in bed would drive me crazy. How long has it been?"

"Six days," she said brightly, and he groaned.

"Six days! Jesus, what have I missed?"

"Well, let me see now. The hospital and the rest of the world have managed to survive without thee, although not awful well. Merry Cathcart sprained her ankle. Matthew Tomlinson broke his spare spectacles, and Cherish Sinclair was terrorized by a gaboon viper in her outdoor privy. Lewanika of Barotseland was refused the secession of his protectorate over in England, although in compensation he has been restored the traditional title of *Litunga*, or "The Earth." Oh, and Moise Tshombe's been imprisoned in the Congo; poor man went to another conference in Léopoldville in all good faith, only to find that the United Nations had managed to influence his fellow Congo leaders. They went back on just about everything agreed upon at the previous conference, and without so much as a by-thy-leave, arrested him at the airport as he was leaving. The Lord only knows what will happen to him now!"

"Yeah? That's tough." He stared at her blankly for a moment. "Kathy, what the hell are you wearing those dark glasses for?"

She stiffened, turning quickly away to fiddle flusteredly with a vase of frangipani on the dresser, shrugging evasively. "The sun, of course. It's so bright out. That's what dark glasses are for, are they not?"

Than looked pained. *"In the house?"* He struggled to sit up in bed. "Kathy, come here."

After a moment she hesitantly obeyed, and he reached across and snatched off the spectacles. "My God." He whistled softly, eyeing her plum-colored bruised puffy eye. She tried to avert her head, but he took her chin and jerked her back to face him. "Did I do that?"

She floundered, "Well, I . . ."

"Jesus," he squinted at her incredulously. "Fist or open hand?"

"Well," she gave an embarrassed little laugh. "I don't rightly remember. Kind of a blind sideways swing, as I recall it."

He winced. "Sent you flying, huh?"

"Laid me out against the wall." She laughed girlishly. But he didn't think it was so funny.

"Oh God, Kathy, I'm sorry."

"Don't be. It wasn't thy fault." Fitting the glasses back into place, she burst into a cheery smile. "It's not as if thee're always doing it."

"No, I guess not." He flexed his mouth in an irked automatic smile and they stared at each other searchingly for a moment. Then she turned away, suddenly bashful.

"Why, whatever's this?" She stopped to pick up a pile of clothing on the floor. He turned and defiantly stared as she eyed him sternly. "Thy father's pajamas! Now why . . ."

"Kathy, I told you! I can't abide those damn things. I'd like some clothes. Now, what'd you do with my things? All my drawers are empty!"

"Well now, thee should not have been up to discover that! Dr. Dooley was right. He said to withhold thy clothing till thee were well enough to wear it."

"Well, maybe I'll just damn well get up naked and find something!"

"Not while I'm around," Katherine said firmly, folding her arms. "And I intend remaining right here till thee have finished every scrap of thy breakfast."

"Oh yeah?" Than eased himself back down on the bed, lying solemn and sallow, his bare chest uncovered, staring at her broodily. Then suddenly, feeling the defiant devilment rise with his dimples, he said: "Well, you know something, Kathy? Maybe that's not such a bad idea. You're pretty nice. If you weren't my father's wife and so all-fired precious good, I might get hot for you."

She stared at him, aghast. Honey-skinned and platinum-blond, she was pretty with surprise, younger and sweeter than some women he had loved, laid, and left, and suddenly horrified at the unlikely truth of his joking words, he rolled fiercely onto his stomach, pulling the limp pillow aggressively over his head.

"Get out of here, Kathy," he growled through a curiously aching throat, fists clenched on the pillow slip. "I'm naked and wifeless and getting healthy as hell!"

Katherine needed no second warning. With hands clasped to her bright burning cheeks, she fled, heart beating like a captive bird against her ribcage, horrified at her own perverse secret surge of pleasured delight. After she had hastily tossed him a pair of clean-pressed jeans, a redeeming thought fixed itself in her mind and she hurried to the study. Sitting at the big littered desk in the small dusty room where the streaming sunshine made rays of dust motes, she searched among the disordered papers, found a clean sheet and a pen, and with a trembling hand fervently wrote:

"Suzannah dear, please come home! Thy husband has been ill and sorely needs thee . . ."

7

As soon as he was able, Than approached Jenny again. But he found her flustered and evasive; her attitude had changed so radically during his illness that he stared at her suspiciously, suddenly cautious.

"Jenny, who's been talking to you?"

"Nobody!" she said quickly. Then she turned away and mumbled with embarrassment, "It's just that I've had time to think about it and I realize I had no right to ask such a thing of you."

"Jenny," he growled. "Let's get one thing straight. You never asked a thing of me!"

"I know that," she sighed. "But you offered because you felt sorry for me. And I had no right to allow you to risk your position that way."

"Risk my position?" Than frowned. "Hey, come on, Jenny, who has been talking to you?"

"Nobody," she repeated. Then she sighed resignedly. "Mr. Peabody told me what you said about . . . about *abortion* that night. He said it was a terrible sin and if you ever approached me with such a suggestion, he wanted me to tell him so they could have you expelled from the mission."

Than stared at her dumbly for a moment. Then he closed his eyes. "Oh, that goddamn son of a bitch!"

"Well," Jenny said, turning away, "it doesn't really matter. I've always felt abortion was wrong. I had no right to countenance such a thing and to allow you to risk everything that way. *It* has a right to life, too. And no matter how hard it is for me to bear, I can have it adopted. I know now that I was selfish thinking only of myself and my shame. Selfish and cowardly."

"Selfish? Cowardly?" Than snapped. "Listen, Jenny, you're the most selfless girl I've ever met, so don't let them go telling you right from wrong. No one has the right to expect you to carry the child of . . ." He couldn't bring himself to say it. After a moment, he raised her chin and made her face him.

"*Let me do it,*" he implored. "Jenny, let me please."

"No!" She pulled away from him, her breath quickening with distress. "I can't let you! It *is* wrong! And they would have you recalled and then all the sick would suffer."

"Jenny, they needn't ever find out. And even if they did, I don't give a damn what they'd do to me."

"Maybe you don't," Jenny said softly, frowning, staring earnestly up at him with her soft sightless blue eyes, "but I care. *I care very much . . .*"

8

Over the months of necessarily infrequent visits, Than developed an unusual friendship with Chief Mulaisho. In a country that presently seethed with political intrigues and the jealous rivalries of opposing parties, the old man's small dynasty remained innocently untouched by the advance of nationalism. The fact that Sir Roy Welensky and the two black nationalist leaders had recently flown back to Britain in a desperate last-ditch bid to influence the British colonial secretary before the imminent release of Northern Rhodesia's new constitution was lost on the beffudled old man, whose latest brew of honey beer seemed of more important consequence.

Mollified by Than's gifts of O.K. cigarettes and *chibuku* beer from the Copperbelt, the old man grew increasingly accommodating, and his people, encouraged by this trust, shyly began to congregate to have Than treat the aggravated ills that their own medicine men had failed to alleviate. Jealous of this growing respect for his *muti* and methods, the witchdoctors themselves were less easy to win over, but despite their surly disdain, Than patiently paged the chief's personal hyena-trailing *ngaka*, asking his advice and the sources and effects of the tribal herbal remedies until, flattered by this intense interest, Furanswa began to grudgingly respond.

However, due to the infrequency of Than's visits, progress was slow and in the meanwhile Than had nightmares over the fates of the malnourished children, and the child-bearing women, whose prodigious births had left many of them worn out and old before their time. Although the witchdoctors apparently pandered some kind of herbal contraceptive, this had so often proved fatal (doubtless due to the African tendency to overdose), that most women simply succumbed to uncontrolled successive pregnancies, which resulted, in many of them, in relapsed wombs, painfully displaced organs, and pendulous bellies and breasts with no elasticity left in the muscle fiber. And Mary Mapanya, he found, had been no isolated incidence of the mishandling by the tribal midwives. Almost all the women he examined showed signs of having been brutally handled, and even hacked; often their offspring bore the scars of the same brutality. Than found one baby minus a foot that had been summarily amputated by a novice witchdoctor, who was superstitiously spooked by its unexpected appearance during a breech birth. Other children displayed signs of congenital brain damage, while at least one infant had been stillborn with a broken neck, after being too vigorously wrenched into the world.

Not surprisingly, the infant mortality rate was appallingly high, and mothers who were unfit to give natural birth simply died in the process. Yet the people were fatalistic. Encouraged by their chief, the women allowed Than to examine them, but superstitiously instilled in the traditional ways and fed sinister suggestions by the jealous witchdoctors that the whites desired their babies to produce powerful medicine, they stubbornly refused to come to Suseshi to be delivered. They met Than's reasoning with the stoic customary credo: *It is not the custom.* Even Mulaisho could not be persuaded to allow the confinement of his latest wife at the hospital, politely evading Than's heated argument that besides being outrageously young, the girl had a T.B. spine and a deformed pelvis, which would make natural birth impossible. According to Than's calculations, the heavily pregnant fifteen-year-old was due to give birth in less than two months; after vainly pleading with the chief to at least bring her to Suseshi at the onset of her labor, he left the village, deeply concerned about the young girl's life.

9

On June 22, M. Moise Tshombe was suddenly released. He emerged from sixty days' incarceration, calmly smiling but looking sick; his signed statement repudiating the secession of Katanga was dismissed by his Katangan parliament on the grounds that it had been coerced under extreme duress. Since Tshombe was a committed anti-Communist, representing the democratic Western and Christian ideals, Matthew found it ironical that his undermining was being encouraged by the West itself. He sat discussing the situation with Ward Disney and Ratchet Cathcart during supper in the dining *chitenje*.

"It seems the poor man cannot win." He shook his head sadly. "Rejected by the West, he is hated by the Communists for his Western outlook, and his peculiarly un-African propensity to recognize African shortcomings and the value of whites has alienated him with the Afro-Asians and the Pan-Africanists. And now that new United Nations representative to Katanga, Dr. Connor Cruise O'Brien, seems to be doing everything in his power to break his spirit and the resistance of Katanga!"

As they sat forlornly speculating on Tshombe's fate, sipping black bean broth in the chill winter night, Teller arrived belatedly with Jenny. The girl was big with child now, her belly swelling out one of the long cotton smocks Teller had sewn her. Matthew stood up hastily to guide her to her seat.

"Friend Matthew, *if* thee please! I must inform thee it will no longer be necessary for Miss Solomon to attend table with us!"

In the ominous hush evoked by Clara's belligerent tone, the generator relentlessly throbbed into the night. After settling Jenny in her place beside his own chair at the head of the table, Matthew turned and stared at the woman in bewildered surprise.

"In future it has been arranged that all her meals be conveyed to her room," Clara said severely.

As Matthew sank, stupefied, to his seat, Hannah Rothchild rigidly reinforced: "That's right. So hurry along now, child! Lenius will take thy food to thy room."

"Yes," Jenny murmured dully. As she stood up, looking bewildered and confused, she knocked over a glass of water, which drenched the table and splashed her dress; stammering apologies, she fumbled to retrieve it, feeling along the table as she edged around the end of the bench. Then, trembling slightly, she felt for her cane and began to make her slow cane-tapping way out of the *chitenje*. When Teller, face furrowed with concern, stood up to give her assistance, Clara shouted her down.

"The child knows her way! And it's about time thee all stopped babying her so! There are many people worse afflicted. And sympathy only encourages self-pity!"

Matthew was flabbergasted; if they had taken to helping Jenny lately, it was because her heavily pregnant state made them fearful lest she take a fall. And as for having her take her meals in her room, why, that was one form of "babying" Jenny definitely did not need! Matthew patted a napkin to his moustache and glared at the woman indignantly. He waited until he was sure Jenny was out of earshot before he ventured darkly:

"Friend Clara, I think somehow that the child would prefer to eat in company. And whilst I might understand thy concern for her comfort, I contend that we should allow her to make her own decision on the matter."

Clara drew back as if stung. "Friend Matthew! I would have thee know it was neither the child's comfort nor her feelings I was considering in arranging this banishment from table! Are thee aware that our children—our *innocent* children—are shortly due home from boarding school?"

Matthew nodded stiffly. "I am aware of that, Friend."

"Well, Friend," Clara sniffed contemptuously, "in that case I am at a loss to understand thy complacency! Has thee no concern for the moral welfare of our children that thee would have them witness that . . . that girl's awful shame? Her body proclaims her condition most strongly now, and it would be *monstrous*, indeed *indecent*, for the older children to witness her that way! One would expect her to have more shame of her own accord, but as she appears to be devoid of any modest incentive, it is our imperative duty, as parents in this community, to protect our children from . . ." she eyed the company daringly . . . *"from the corrupt sight of her!"*

"Friend!" Matthew rose up with a growl of outrage. "Might I remind thee that the poor child's condition is hardly her fault!"

"Be that as it may, Friend—a little shame and consideration for others who must be subjected to the sight of her ungainly form, would still be in order! Granted her blind students are spared the painful picture, but does she think we are all blighted in the senses?" Clara threw back her head, eyes like pinpricks as she eyed Matthew measuringly. "Perhaps thee has no concern for thy children, but our Sidney is important to us. He is eighteen this November. In our opinion, it would be unfitting, indeed *distressing*, for a boy so young and undespoiled to be subjected to the witness of so . . . so *ugly* a fact of life! And think how it must look to the natives!"

It was enough said, and as her venomous words settled satisfied into the stupefied silence, fortified by the smirking nods of her clan, Clara continued calmly and with victorious gusto to clear her plate. Ranged on either side of her down the long table, Orville, Ezra Peabody, and the maiden ladies were artificially merry, unconcernedly clattering the cutlery, laughing and joking with exaggerated vigor to cover the stony silence that faced them from the opposite side of the table. But Matthew was not through; after ruminating a moment, he stood up resolutely.

"Friend Clara," he said gruffly, "if thy boy, at eighteen, has no knowledge as yet of the misfortunes and unpleasantries of this life, it is my humble opinion it is about time he was given some taste. Furthermore, at eighteen, he is not too young for a little compassion either."

He pushed back his chair, carefully replaced it, and departed in a haughty huff, followed shortly, in a show of support, by Teller, Katherine, Jayne, and Grace Dooley. Looking back, Matthew saw Than Profane, silently seething, push aside his untouched plate to leave as well.

The following night, at the roll of the supper drum, Than Profane skipped up the veranda steps of Matthew's house. With a dimpled insistence, while Matthew and Teller looked gratefully on, he prised Jenny from the shamed sanctuary of her room.

"Jenny." He put a smile into his voice. "I've come to take you dining."

Her sightless eyes stared at him blankly for a moment. Then she turned away, flustered and confused. "I don't mind staying here."

"No buts, Jenny." He took her chin and gently turned her to face him. "I'll be your beau for tonight. And I won't take no for an answer. So go put on your cape and your gloves or whatever, and do me the honor."

Slowly and with great ceremony, they walked together down the slope, Jenny's small hand tucked shyly into the Boy's arm, a hesitant smile on her face as he coaxed her with charm and cheeriness.

At the table, Jenny faltered at the hostile silence that met them. But the Boy urged her on and, warning their opponents with his eyes, sat her down. He sat beside her and gave her his plate (hers had already been sent off with Lenius), dishing up her food and describing it and its arrangement in the usual clockwise sequence, as he watched over her comfort with an aggressive protectiveness that scared off any would-be remarks. And now, in a reversal of roles, it was Matthew, Teller, Katherine, the Dooleys, and the Disneys who outdid themselves being noisy and merry; chattering cheerfully, passing condiments haphazardly, making silly jokes to make Jenny smile and to cover the frozen displeasure of the Fotches and their clique. But it was a strain on them all and Matthew was glad when at last Jenny pushed her partially cleared plate aside and looked expectantly around.

"Well, child," Matthew said, standing up with an unhurried air, "guess it's bed for us all now. Been a long day . . ."

Teller slipped Jenny's hand into her arm, and with a show of family unity they started back up the slope. Katherine and Jayne left with Ingrid. The Dooleys and Disneys drifted off, and Clara's needlepoint and the Scrabble set came out while the kitchenboys began to clear the table. Glancing back, Matthew noticed that Than Profane was taking his time leaving, arranging his knife and fork and carefully folding his napkin before stepping back over the bench. As he began walking away, the pent-up indignation, bursting irresistibly forth from the ladies still at the table, stopped him in his tracks and he turned and slowly retraced his steps. Clara and Hannah froze when they saw him. He stopped at the low bamboo wall of the *chitenje* and stared at Hannah viciously.

"Don't say it," he said softly, menacingly, his face twisted. "Lady, don't you say it. *Not one single word!*"

And then she couldn't. She deflated with a small faint sigh of outrage.

When Suseshi's school closed for the term, the missionaries' children came home from boarding school, boisterous and fit, filling the quiet mission with carefree young voices, games, and gaiety. On the first day of their arrival, the Fotches' son, Sidney, a slender sallow boy, as ferret-faced as his mother, was escorted early to the supper table by his doting parents. After Clara had dished him up a bountiful plate, he sat silently eating until Jenny arrived, and just as Teller was helping the bulky-bellied girl onto the communal bench, the youth stood up.

"Mother," he said loudly, his sneering voice carrying clear across the crowded table, "for some reason I feel suddenly nauseated. If thee'll excuse me, I don't think I'll attend this table again!"

There was a stunned silence as he threw down his napkin and stepped back over the long bench. No one could have missed his timely implication. Jenny sat, head bowed over her big belly, her eyes slowly filling with tears. Matthew, too stunned to react, turned instinctively to Than Profane, who had arrived just in time to take in the cruel fiasco. The Boy stopped on the threshold of the *chitenje*, thumbs tucked into his empty belt loops as he leaned speculatively against one of the wooden entrance poles, taking in the scene. As the sneering Sidney made to stalk huffily past him, the Boy, staring absently off, as innocently artful as some schoolboy scamp, stuck out a vengeful waylaying leg. With a squeal of surprise, the youth tripped and fell heavily, flat on his face on the hard concrete floor; in an instant, winded, his dignity demolished, he rose up on his grazed hands, gasping and spluttering.

"Whoops." The Boy turned with a mild tut-tutting look of mock concern. "You all right, Sidney? You ought to watch where you're walking, fella."

Clara Fotch, doubtless infuriated at a complicity she was powerless to prove, leaped to her feet and stood impotently heaving within her limp paisley-print bonnet and dress, while her son, in tears of rage and humiliation, scrambled to his feet and hurried, furiously snorting, out of sight.

"Well." Than Profane settled onto the bench between a bewildered young Tom and a smile-suppressing Katherine, dimpling disgracefully as he looked questioningly around in the uncomfortable silence. "Nice weather we're having. Matthew, pass the carrots please."

In July, the British colonial secretary's revised constitution for Northern Rhodesia revealed to a breath-bated nation that the constitution had swung in favor of the United Federal Party. Under the new scheme, both races would need four hundred each of the votes of the other race. While such a concession was conceivable for whites among a black roll of ten thousand (the UFP had hopes of winning over the "moderates"), the same task for the nationalists from the small three-thousand-strong white electorate seemed impossible.

Again, as the facts became clear, an ominous quiet fell over the country. The pressured governor tried to placate the nationalist parties and warned that security forces were ready to deal with trouble from any source. And trouble there would be. Kenneth Kaunda, outraged, threatened that his party would not allow the enforced constitution to survive; he denounced the British government's "betrayal," and four thousand delegates at UNIP's annual conference empowered him to put into action his emergency master plan to "paralyze the country."

Now the whole country awaited the unleashing of the nationalist wrath . . .

10

Like a distant rumble of thunder presaging a storm, the threatened disorders began: on the Copperbelt, there were beer-hall boycotts, telephone wires were cut, and government property was burned; when an attempt was made to blow up the important Kafue Bridge on the Ndola-Kitwe road, police reservists and troops were deployed to guard all the important installations. During a tour of the troubled Northern province, the UNIP leader, Kenneth Kaunda, interlaced inflammatory statements with appeals for nonviolence, and the people, interpreting his words in their own way, rose up and marched chanting through the bush in groups of up to a thousand strong, chopping down trees, blocking roads, and destroying bridges and government schools and workshops as they went. The government moved in riot police, and when the clashes intensified, these were reinforced with troops and spotter planes and UNIP was banned in the Northern and Luapula provinces. Kaunda flew off to London, claiming the only hope of stopping the violence lay in persuading the British government to change the constitution once more. In the meanwhile, the governor insisted there could be no negotiations under duress.

It was difficult to assess what might happen next, and with the increase of nationalists canvassing in their own North Western province, Matthew, expecting trouble, was apprehensive when one day after lunch a government Land-Rover roared into the mission. Hurrying to greet it, Matthew stopped in surprise when Mr. Hargreaves, the district officer from Mwinilunga boma, opened the passenger door to emit . . . Suzannah Profane. The man diffidently explained the circumstances as he shook Matthew's hand. Apparently, the girl's father had arranged for this prestigious delivery after she arrived by chartered aircraft at the boma's dusty little airfield.

"Well, this is indeed a surprise," Matthew said, although in truth he was getting used to the young woman's periodic unannounced appearances. It was patently obvious to him that while she was wildly in love with the Boy, she had not the same affection for his life-style. For hers were the wanton ways of the world. Lavish shopping sprees and frivolous partying might be her most passionate pastimes at Salisbury city, but here at Suseshi, the Boy waited with the pleasures of the flesh. And since, like most folks, the girl wanted to have her cake and eat it too, she seemed doomed to dash insatiably back and forth, never for long satisfied with one without the other.

"Er . . . my dear, I believe thee'll find thy good husband still at the *chitenje* having a late lunch." Matthew managed a weak smile. "Mr. Hargreaves, perhaps thee'd join us there for some refreshment before returning?"

They found Than Profane consuming a plate of chicken salad, sitting alone amid the dregs of the lunch table. He glanced up as Matthew called for tea, then suddenly seeing his wife, his eyes narrowed and he set down his fork and slowly stood up.

"Reckoned thee'd be surprised," Matthew chuckled as the girl stopped on the threshold, looking, in this rustic setting, too clean and beautiful to be true with her coiffeured corn-silk hair, wearing a tailored beige suit over a pink chiffon blouse.

"Well." She measured her tall, tanned young husband with a tantalizing little smile. "Aren't you going to say hello to your little old wife come home to all this heat and hardship?"

"Hi," the Boy said softly. He nodded at Mr. Hargreaves and then sat down again, took up his fork, and resumed eating.

"Well!" The girl, aghast, stood with hands on her shapely hips while Matthew, flustered at this uncertain reception, hustled Mr. Hargreaves to a seat and shouted loudly for Lenius to hurry up with the tea tray.

"Is this all the welcome I get?" Suzannah Profane wailed. "I've come hundreds of miles to surprise you! I'm your wife, remember?"

"My wife." The Boy turned with a frown of mock perplexity. "Doggone it! I almost forgot about that. But then it has been six months, and of letters, one miserable little postcard!"

"Well, what did you expect? A day-to-day itinerary? I told you I'm a poor correspondent!"

"And I told you," he said softly," to come home."

"Home?" She looked at him despairingly. *"This is home?"*

"Home is where the heart is. And if yours is elsewhere, you better go back there, baby."

"Ooooh!" she raged at him, the pair apparently oblivious of the anguish of Matthew and Mr. Hargreaves, who sat inescapably audient to this family feud, uncomfortably clearing throats and staring stupidly while Lenius laid a clattering tea tray before them.

"And I came back to you, you bastard." The girl's eyes were sparkling with tears now. "I might have stayed in Salisbury and had the time of my life! But Katherine kept writing those tragic little letters about how sick and lonely you were, and I . . ."

"Katherine?" The Boy's face hardened; but in his eyes the pain leaked through and he sat half smiling, shaking his head. "Oh God . . . so it was Katherine . . ."

Obviously realizing her mistake, the girl receded into uncertain silence, and Matthew, fussing, red-faced, with the tea things, was immensely relieved when Jeremiah came hurrying up.

"Bwana Doctor." The grizzled old dresser stood panting in his starched white uniform. "The wife of Mulaisho, she come now to the mission."

The Boy's eyes narrowed; he wiped his mouth with a napkin and stood up. "Mulaisho's wife? Is she . . ."

"She labor for one and half day." The old man looked agitated. "Now she velly sick."

The Boy nodded and stepped quickly over the communal bench. As he strode past his wife, she caught at his arm.

"What about me?" she wailed. "I've just arrived! Why can't Dr. Dooley . . ."

He stared at her coldly. "Well, you've made it this long without me. Try and hold out through the afternoon."

Matthew heard her outraged catch of breath as the Boy left her.

Than found Mulaisho's wife surrounded by the chief and a noisy entourage in the hospital yard. Lying on a primitive pole litter, the bare-breasted young girl, belly bulging beneath a shabby cloth sarong, was sweating profusely, her dilated eyes dull as she fretted weakly, half delirious with pain and exhaustion.

After taking one look at her, Than sent for Jerome and they prepared for immediate surgery. In the stuffy little operating room, he performed a hurried Caesarean section, hardly glancing at the breath-gasping grotesque little scrap of humanity that was brought forth and hastily set aside while they worked to save the mother. When her precarious condition had stabilized, Than turned back to the tiny male infant. Only then did he realize the full extent of its inadequacy. Surrounded by his anxious colleagues, he examined the pathetic little creature in a cold thrall of shock. Stunned, he looked up to find all eyes upon him, intent above the white masks. He stared dazedly back, his mind dimly grappling with the awful implications. There was a strange roaring in his ears, dulling his senses as he soaked a wad of absorbent cotton with liquid chloroform and started purposefully toward the feebly squirming infant.

"No!" Grace Dooley moaned, catching his arm; her hazel eyes were blurred with tears. But he knew what he had to do and, his anguished eyes imploring complicit understanding, he shook off her hand and advanced relentlessly.

11

An afternoon radio newscast revealed that the continuing violence erupting around the country had resulted in over three thousand arrests and a dozen deaths; it was uncomfortably reminiscent of the onset of the Congo crisis, and after finishing his work for the day, Matthew, filled with grief at the racial bitterness and the needless loss of life and property erupting all around them, trudged despondently across to the meeting house to ruminate the matter with the Lord. For over an hour he sat alone in the empty bethel, and at dusk, when the day had deepened to a chill silence, the slight squelch of rubber-soled moccasins interrupted his prayerful reverie, and he opened his eyes and stared in surprise as Than Profane came sauntering down the long aisle, wearing a creased white jacket, blue denim Bermudas, and a wistful look. His bare arms were stippled with goose bumps and his breath steamed lightly in the chill air as he sat on the hard pine bench beside Matthew.

"Don't get up, Matthew. I've come to relate my good deed for the day."

And he told it all as casually as a country outing, all the while concentrating on rolling shreds of bush tobacco in a scrap of paper (the old C.A.R.S. van was late as usual with such essential supplies!). Matthew might have taken indignant umbrage at this absent sacrilegious occupation had not the Boy's story so distracted him. As it was, he simply stared.

"Thee *what?*" he croaked finally.

"You heard right the first time, old man." The blue eyes flashed up and he gave Matthew a faint bitter smile. "I anesthetized Mulaisho's child and put it painless, permanently, to sleep."

His tanned face glistened with cold sweat and his hand shook slightly as he stuck the improvised cigarette into his wet mouth; then, as if remembering his whereabouts, he took it out again and sighed. "And then I substituted the healthy baby of a woman delivered by Caesarean section a short while earlier. The woman was still groggy with the anesthetic, and when she came around it was a simple matter to tell her her child had been still-born. So you see . . ."

Struggling with an enourmous outrage, Matthew gripped the pew in front of him and ineffectually squeaked, *"Thee can't be serious!"*

The boy sighed again; he tugged at a piece of white cotton at the frayed edge of his Bermudas and earnestly frowned. "You're damn right I am."

It was too much to believe. The Boy winced as Matthew sprang to his feet; anguished and outraged, the air seemed too big for his lungs as his voice crackled out like the wrath of God: "WHO GAVE *THEE* THE GODLY RIGHT OF SOLOMON'S JUDGMENT?"

The Boy stared him straight in the eye. "Who gave it to Solomon?"

It was a preposterous presumption, so infuriatingly like the Boy, that Matthew was temporarily struck speechless. Finally he subsided, almost weeping with his rage and grief.

"Feticide!"

"Euthanasia," the Boy corrected quietly.

"It lived, thee said, and breathed. It must have been constitutionally sound!"

"I don't think so, Matthew."

"Thee don't *think*? Did thee bother to verify that?"

"Well, I gave it the routine examination. Aside from the fact that the face was hideously deformed, I found that the fontanelles—you know, the soft spot in the head—was closed. There was a faulty heart sound and narrowing of the aorta. He had a deformed spine and the liver was abnormal. Respiration was impaired, the reflexes sluggish, and the head was abnormally enlarged. It was as mixed up inside as out, and it's my professional opinion that the child—if you can call it that—was mentally no more than a vegetable; a monstrous mutation, which nature, left alone, would never have allowed to survive the trauma of birth."

There was a shocked silence. Finally Matthew managed, *"But it did!"*

"Yeah," the Boy bowed his head. "But its safe delivery, even as much as its death, was due only to my intervention."

"Be that as it may, it was a God-given life!"

"Yes. But without artificial aid, it would have died at birth. Afterward, in a few days, maybe less. I had to be cruel to be kind. Don't you see, Matthew, that baby was the death sentence to countless other babies. Had I handed Mulaisho that doomed monstrosity, he and all his clan would have been superstitiously spooked. They would have taken off like scared rabbits and never set foot in a hospital again. It was the cardinal test. And because I was responsible for saving its life, it became my moral duty to destroy it. Just the same as I would destroy any other plague that threatened human life."

There was a strained silence. Then the Boy said humbly, "I regarded it as a small sacrifice to odds so great."

"*Small?* A human life? The life was never thine to sacrifice! And it's only thy personal theory that Mulaisho's people would suffer by it, thy personal conceit!" Matthew charged miserably, blustering through his moustache, his wracked face wet with tears.

The Boy's eyes flashed up then, suddenly responding, darkening with their outrage. "Goddamn you, Matthew, it was a very real risk! One I couldn't afford to take. I *had* to do what I did! Jesus, I might have turned away and shirked the responsibility! But there was no one else who would do it! I took the rap for them all!"

"And what of the other child? To deprive the natural mother!"

"She's a poverty-stricken, worn-out old woman who already has more children than she can feed. As a matter of fact, she came to Jerome a while back, begging to be surgically sterilized. He passed the buck to me; I would have tied her fallopian tubes right then if she hadn't been pregnant with this child at the time! So you see, she didn't want the baby any more than it needed her. If you ask me, it was an immense relief to the poor creature."

"Thee can't be sure of that! And what thee did was without legal warrant! Against God's laws and man's! It would never stand up in a court of law."

"It won't need to. Out here in the bush, who will ever know?"

"The Lord does." Matthew turned away, aloof and forsaking. "I do. But I suppose thee considers me nothing more than a naïve old man. Thy Christian conscience has been eroded by the false values of the wider world. I suppose it was the kind of thing thee saw all the time back home in the States."

The Boy turned. "As a matter of fact, it's an unwritten ethical standard, the kind of thing that goes on from time to time behind the scenes of any big hospital. No doctor with any self-respect or sense of responsibility would allow a vegetable to live."

"Well." Matthew stood up wearily, exhausted by his grief. "I can see it is useless trying to reach thee with Christian ethics. Thy valuation is, to say the least, peculiarly heathen. But since it is not God but heathens thee wishes to appease, I imagine it was a simple matter for thee."

The Boy stood up abruptly, blocking Matthew's way. His face was set like stone, and so radiating was his rage that Matthew, startled, stepped back, as if from fire.

"No, Matthew," the Boy growled. "Contrary to what you may think, it was the first time for me, and I can't say it gave me any great personal charge! But I did what I thought was right under the circumstances, and if that will damn me to hell, then I guess it was worth it to me!"

His enraged eyes glowed with a strange pain, and in that moment Matthew had a sudden dim conception of the underlying anguish that had urged the Boy to so casually confess his festering sin in the first place. But his tentative forgiving hand touched only air, his inadmissible comforting words remaining repressed beneath a grieving breast as the Boy suddenly turned and left the pew, striding down the long aisle, his tall figure dissolving into the dimness of the deserted meeting house. Left alone in the stillness, Matthew sank to his knees, his clasped hands wrung in imploring supplication; he was weeping now with compassion.

Oh, Lord, forgive him; he knows not what he does . . .

12

Later, returning from the hospital and remembering that Suzannah was back, Than forgot their quarrel in an overwhelming rush of gratitude, as if simply being with her would obliterate the raw pain of his conscience and make everything all right again. He had missed supper, and at the house, he found her upstairs in their room. Shivering in a sheer nylon nightdress, she lay under the quilt of their big double bed, indolently rifling through an old magazine. But if her visible nipples and seductively sprawled body signaled invitation, she stared at him in surly hostility, and confused at the contradiction, he stared back in mute anguish; then, abandoning his pride, he cast off his clothes and crawled to her like a child craving comfort.

In a purely puerile need, he nuzzled at her breasts with the seeking insistence of an infant at feed. But she twisted aloofly in his arms, teasing his desperation with her voluptuous body and a haughty petulance, wailing so commandingly for a glass of water that finally, exasperated out of his need, he shrugged on his robe and went downstairs to fetch one. The electric light flickered and the generator was switched off en route, and stubbing his toe and spilling the water, he stumbled back up the stairs in the dark to find their door locked. Suzannah responded to his knock with a muffled snarl; still angry at his earlier rebuff and misinterpreting his need, she was punishing him with sex.

"*Jesus!*" Feeling grim and foolish, he stormed down the stairs again. Fumbling in the crammed linen closet for a spare pillow and rug, he finally settled on the lumpy settee in the living room. Unable to sleep, he was still restlessly smoking in the dark when Katherine returned from a preparatory meeting. She lighted the oil lamp on the veranda and came tiptoeing in, breathing steam in the cold air, flinching in fright when she found him there.

"Why, Than, thee startled me!" She set the lamp shakily down on the cluttered oak table, eyeing him with concern. "Oh, honey, a marital quarrel so soon?"

"Suzie's punishing me." He shrugged abashedly, avoiding her eyes, siting up bare-chested under the blanket, resting elbows on his raised knees as he smoked.

"Oh dear." She stared at him searchingly as she untied her bonnet, gentle gray eyes intuitively sympathetic of his long lonely months in a cold empty bed. "I'm sorry!"

"Don't be." He stared speculatively at the cigarette that smoked from the cup of his hand. "If she thinks I'm suffering, she's living in real high hopes. The fact is, I'm pretty harmless; I haven't been able to make it with my wife since the day they raped Jennifer Solomon."

The words were out before he could take stock of them. Now, digesting his impotence, Katherine stared at him sadly in shocked commiseration. "Oh, honey, *I'm so sorry!*"

"Yeah." He turned away to crush his cigarette stub in an ashtray. "Aren't we all?"

The next day, awaking angry, Than made no attempt to change his schedule, and without saying good-bye to Suzannah, he left for Eshalakali Hill. When he returned that evening, a lot less angry, she was having supper with the other missionaries at the dining *chitenje*. Barely acknowledging his greeting, she finished eating in aloof silence; she stood up when Katherine and Jayne were ready to leave, and feeling unable to face his own food, Than left a full plate and went after them. He stopped in surprise when Suzannah began to veer off before they reached the house.

"Hey, where are you going?"

"For a walk in the bush." Her eyes flashed spitefully at him in the moonlight, and he winced. She was making him pay for his neglect in painful pennies. And she knew his vulnerability; since the Balubas' attack, the safety of his family had become a nightmare obsession with him.

"Suzie, now you know that's just foolish! Especially in this cold. Come on home to bed now."

"You go. I'll see you later." She smiled vengefully back at him, and after a moment's silent fuming, he sent the surprised Katherine and Jayne into the house and followed Suzannah into the thick scrub that bordered the back of the houses.

"Suzie, will you for Godsake quit playing games. You know you can't walk out here alone in the dark. You don't even want to."

"I'll be the judge of that."

"Jesus! *Women!* Sometimes I'd rather have the extra rib!" Tired and depressed, Than gazed beseechingly up at the night sky. *Please, not this now!* As she stumbled, twigs snapping, further into the shadowy bush, he caught angrily at her arm. "Listen, you little bitch, you stop this silly little game right here and now! I'm in no mood for your childish dramatics. You come home this minute, hear me?"

Gripping her flesh painfully tight, he swung her around to face him. She stared up at him aghast, and regaining his composure, he loosened his grip and moderated his tone.

"Suzie, this's just dumb! There are snakes and spiders out here. And you know what happened to Jennifer Solomon when she was left in the bush!"

"Oh sure. And maybe that's not such a bad fate! Why should you care anyway? You can't do it anymore!"

He shut his eyes, appalled. Now she knew his Achilles heel, she surely intended using it to wound him. After a moment he drew in his breath.

"All right, Suzie, I meant what I said. Come on home now."

"Make me! Or don't you have the balls to do that either? I don't need you, you know that? There's plenty of other men just panting to take your place back where I come from."

"Oh yeah?" Than snarled, stung and smarting now. "You little

362

whore. For all I know, you've been having yourself a real swell time down in Salisbury! If that's all the activity you care about, why'd you bother to come back? For a rest?"

"*Why you* . . ." It was too much; with an impotent cry of fury, she catapulated at him through the leaves. He stumbled backward with the impact, hanging on to her small body as she pounded furiously at his chest with her fists.

"For Chrissakes!" he gasped, taken aback.

"I *hate* you! I *hate* you!" she shrilled hysterically, bringing up her hand to rake her long nails across his cheek. He felt the stinging welts and was suddenly incensed with fury.

"You bitch!" He took her by the hips and rammed her brutally against the trunk of a tree. And then he was all over her, like raging flood waters let loose, one hand wriggling up her skirt, the other crushing her breast.

"Stop it!" she gasped, pushing against him in proud contrariness, panting and shaking her head to get the hair out of her eyes.

But something had snapped inside him; his eyes were unseeing and smoky with desire, and he was hurting her, pressing against her with brute strength, his hands clawing at her skin, tearing down her panties.

"I guess this is what you want, any way and any where it comes!" he snarled.

"Leave me alone, you horny bastard!" she wept with fury. "I don't need it from you! I never want to see you again!"

But he was thrusting convulsively with his pelvis, his fingers wriggling between her thighs, and in her pride-stung demented rage, she brought a knee up, hard, against his testes. And the world, suddenly rocked crazily beneath him.

"*Jesus God!*" A surprised hollow look of agony passed over Than's face, dulling his eyes. He swung at her in a blind white-hot rage, and she went sprawling into the grass. The agony traveled up from his loins like sheet of flame, and his legs caved and he groveled on the ground, clutching at himself and gasping and groaning with pain.

"*Bitch!*" he grunted. "Bitch! Bitch." And then he let fly with a spate of four-letter words, which must have burned her eardrums. She sat up slowly in the grass, shocked, touching the stinging welts his open hand had made across her face, beginning to cry as the pain ebbed and left him and he convulsed and vomited in the grass. When he was finally done, he wiped his wet mouth on his sleeve and rested a while on his bent knees, panting to get air back into his lungs.

Then he stood up slowly and stared heavily down at her in the moonlight. She struggled to her feet and stood staring awesomely up at him, looking cowed and frightened as a wide-eyed child. There was horror on her face, disheveled blond hair in her eyes, and her heaving bodice was streaked with dirt.

"Lady," he said carefully, savagely, biting off the words. "Let me give you a little friendly advice! Don't you ever—*ever*—try that again!"

Then he turned and walked away. After a moment, whimpering submissively, she came hurrying after him.

Than did not touch her that night; he slept in the living room again and got up at dawn, working at the hospital through his lunch and supper hours. That night, when the house had settled into darkness and silence, he finally went home, trudging wearily up the dim stairway. In their bedroom, Suzannah was startled awake as he opened the door; she sprang out of bed and stood in a lacy black negligee, staring at him, aghast. As he closed the door and advanced upon her, she stared up at him uncertainly, looking scared and submissive as a child.

"Listen, you," he growled softly, touching his clenched fist lightly against her chin. "The next time you knee me in the balls, I'm going to beat your sweet little ass till you're blue!"

She stared at him for a breath-caught moment before falling into his arms, crying hard. He nuzzled her neck beneath the soft fragrant hair. Then, with a lascivious growl, he took her frail body and threw her across the bed. He crawled on top of her, grunting like an animal.

13 On September 13, the British government announced its decision to reconvene the Northern Rhodesian constitutional talks once the violence had ceased. The pressure of UNIP had apparently been successful, and the United Federal Party, infuriated, denounced this familiar British succumbing to nationalist "blackmail." However, the furor was swamped to relative insignificance by events in the Congo on the same day. There, a comparatively unknown political figure, M. Cyrille Adoula, had been appointed prime minister in Lumumba's place; he immediately vowed to end the secession of Katanga. It seemed incredible to Matthew that while the rest of the Congo languished in lawlessness, the Central government and the United Nations concerned themselves with badgering its one peaceful state, but after occupying strategic points in Elizabethville on August 28, United Nations troops began an all-out offensive to crush Katanga in the early hours of the morning. The Elizabethville post office and the city's radio station were taken with excessive brutality. A cordon was thrown around Tshombe's house, but the premier managed to escape, while his people, conveniently rendered without officers or advisers to facilitate this shameless U.N. coup, rallied in a courageous defence. Rumbling war drums brought thousands of tribesmen converging on Kamina military base; they prevented its use by U.N. aircraft; electricity and water supplies were cut off, and a handful of Katangese volunteers destroyed U.N. vehicles, ammunition, food, and fuel.

To Matthew's mind this spirited defiance proved that the tribes of Katanga would never willingly submit to the rule of other tribes, a thousand miles away, who could not even speak their language. And Tshombe, far from being the neocolonialist and the capitalist pawn his detractors had branded him, emerged as the fiercely loved legitimate leader of his people. But his freedom was precarious, and Matthew, fearing for the premier's safety, dogged the radio for the next three days until news came through that he had contacted the U.N. representative through the British consul in Elizabethville, urging an immediate meeting to discuss a peaceful solution to the moral and military mess that the United Nations had created in his state. Dag Hammarskjöld, the U.N. secretary-general, presently in

Léopoldville, haggled over the terms of a ceasefire, but agreed to meet the Katangan leader in the neutral Northern Rhodesia. The Federal premier, Welensky, an obvious ally of the beleaguered Tshombe, welcomed the plan offering, to facilitate the meeting. Thus, flying in ahead of Hammarskjöld, Tshombe, together with a British representative, anxiously awaited the arrival of the Swedish secretary-general, upon whose weighty word so many Katangese lives were presently so horrendously hinged.

By 9:30 that night, Hammarskjöld's aircraft, after briefly communicating with the Ndola Airport control tower, had failed to arrive. By now Tshombe and the British representatives, magnanimously provided with Federal security and hospitality, had been wearily waiting for many hours, and in the shroud of secrecy that surrounded the U.N. secretary-general's flight, fears for his safety were mounting. The Federal Broadcasting Corporation was standing by to bulletin his arrival, and Matthew, unable to retire while the survival of Katanga hung on the man's security, remained in the dining *chitenje*, huddled around his radio set with Ward and Virgil Disney while the ladies indulged in their customary Scrabble and Than Profane, fresh from the hospital, ate a belated supper. So intense was Matthew's political discourse with Ward that he failed to notice Jenny's approach till she suddenly appeared at the *chitenje* entrance, walking cautiously behind her tapping cane. She had earlier declined to eat, and Hannah stared at her now in churlish exasperation.

"Well, thee're a mite late, child! Supper's been over and done an age ago. If we were all so wishy-washy about our appetites, I doubt the kitchenboys would ever get off. As a Christian, thee might consider that they are human too, with the same need for rest!"

Than Profane set down his fork, and Matthew, remembering the dry old spinster's own pointed lack of concern for the same staff she now argued for, was irked by her hypocrisy.

"But I don't want to eat." Jenny stared vaguely around. "I'm looking for Dr. Dooley. I . . ."

But waving aside her protests, Hannah stood up and stode to the fly safe with a martyred sigh. "Well let this be a lesson to thee! No doubt there'll be some scrap left to suffice thee." She extracted a knife and fork from the cutlery box and reached across to thrust them into Jenny's hands. "Take a place at the other end of the table, girl; we're playing Scrabble this end. Thee're a great nuisance, to be sure!"

Matthew was about to guide her to a cleared spot when Than Profane stood up and took her by the arm.

"I'll go call Lenius," Virgil offered earnestly. He climbed over the bench and flattened sideways, walking nervously around the girl's bulky belly as if she were a bomb that might go off at any moment. When she suddenly stopped midstride, the expression on her face was so strange that Virgil, having glimpsed it in passing, paused to squint curiously back. She gasped, and all eyes were upon her when her cane and the cutlery clattered to the concrete floor.

"Jenny?" the Boy said cautiously. He crouched to retrieve the knife and fork, and in the next instant they all heard a great washing explosive sound, and a pool of liquid spread around her skirts like the nightmare unpardonable of an erring child. The Boy's boots were wetted by the amniotic fluid and he stared up at her in horror. For some moments there was no sound save the croaking of frogs and stone curlews from the darkness. Then, standing guiltily aghast in the unexplainable puddle, Jenny began to cry. Matthew could evict no words from a dread-dry mouth and the Scrabble players and Ward, embarrassed beyond the narrow scope of their modesty, sat stupidly staring in transfixed hysteria. Virgil, frozen mid-flight, looked terrified.

The Boy straightened up slowly. He put the cutlery on the table and took Jenny's arm; she stood rigid in his grasp, whimpering distractedly.

"It's all right, Jenny," the Boy said gently. "I guess your time's come a little early. The bag of waters just ruptured. We'd best get you over to the hospital right away."

14

Later Than learned that Jenny had been having contractions since before noon but, in her shy uncomplaining way, had waited until the increasing urgency of the pangs had forced her to seek out Jerome Dooley. He waited with her at the hospital until the Dooleys and Ingrid arrived. Then, urged by Grace to take his sorely neglected rest, he went home, bathed, shaved, and lay in bed, silently smoking in the dark. Suzannah, sulking because he had come home late yet again, lay stiffly beside him. For several moments,

367

unable to sleep, he endured her frigid aloofness, embalmed in his own pride. Then the thin thread of endurance suddenly snapped within him and he turned with a growl and pounced on her like an animal, prying apart her clamped thighs with a brutal knee.

"Baby," he snarled, holding her down against her pushing protests. "You're my wife, and this is my goddamn marital right!"

He made angry love to her, quickly and viciously, and afterward they lay side by side, panting slightly, oiled in sweat, nothing resolved between them but physical passion. He lay unmoving until the anger gradually melted, and his mind went back to Jennifer Solomon. By ten o'clock, still unable to sleep, he could endure the silent waiting no longer. He got up and hastily shrugged on his jeans and jacket in the dark, leaving his unloving wife to her proud sleep, skipping down the dark stairs two at a time.

Outside in the moonless night, Jenny's night-light no longer shone from her room, but the Tomlinson house radiated lamplight, and before the big living room window, the white-haired old professor made a rythmic silhouette as he paced the floor in anxious anticipation of imminent birth.

Long before Than reached the labor ward, Jenny's lonely despairing wails told him that nothing was resolved. Just as he was going up the veranda steps, Jerome stepped out of the delivery room. He looked at Than quizzically.

"Any news about Hammarskjöld yet?"

Than shook his head. "How's Jenny doing?"

"Not so good," Jerome sighed. "It looks like this little baby is going to be a tough little cookie to extricate. It's a full breech; right sacram anterior, near as I can work out."

"*Jesus!*" Than shook his head. "RSA? That's pretty rare. Poor kid. Listen, Jerome, have you thought about doing a section?"

Jerome laughed shortly. "The trouble with thee, kid, is thee've got a fixation with the scalpe!. Thee refuse to acknowledge that birth is a natural function."

Than kept staring down at his cigarette. "Well," he said defensively, "RSA is a damn difficult procedure. I think a caesar would alleviate a lot of danger and discomfort."

Jerome smiled wryly. "Listen, kid, stop worrying. I know my obstetrics. And out here, we're so used to abnormal procedures that RSA is practically run-of-the-mill to me!"

They turned as from inside the delivery room Jenny's breath-caught gasping and crying rose to a wrenching full-throated scream. Than turned away, wincing.

"Christ!"

"Well," Jerome said casually. "Guess I'd better get back. Sounds like she's getting ready for the big performance."

Than nodded numbly. Then he spun and stopped the man as he was about to enter the annex off the delivery room, awkward and wracked, for a moment not knowing what he wanted to say. Finally he croaked: "Listen, man, tell her, tell her I said to keep her chin up. I'll be holding thumbs."

Jerome looked up at him quizzically. "Well, kid, she's about ready to deliver now. I believe she'd place great store by thy presence. From personal observation, I'd say she thinks the sun shines out of thy big blue eyes, so why don't thee throw away that tobacco, come scrub up with me, and give her the message thyself?"

"Yeah," Than sighed. He sent his cigarette stub spiraling away into the darkness. "Why don't I?"

A moment later, they entered the delivery room together, cloaked in white and cautiousness. Ingrid was just covering Jenny up. She said crisply: "She's coming along nicely, Doctor."

On a high white obstetrical table, Jenny lay looking small as a child, lost somewhere in an overlarge hospital nightgown, which rose in a snowy peak over her pregnant abdomen. As Jerome pulled back the sheet and bent over her, Than went to the head of the table.

"Jenny?" He fumbled for her small cold hand. "Hi. I hear you got a tummy ache."

But her eyes were dark and exhausted, blank beyond blindness, her face white and bewildered amid the sprawled tangled mass of her perspiration-damp hair.

"Tummy ache?" Grace Dooley chuckled. "Well isn't that just like a man? Didn't any woman ever tell thee, Doctor, the real bad pain is mostly in the back."

"Jenny!" Than shook her hand. "Can you hear me?"

Gradually her features sharpened as if she were listening for something far away. Then something moved in her big blank eyes and they lifted and stared straight through him.

"*Njumwaice,*" she whispered perplexedly.

"Yeah, Jenny, it's me."

Then the bewildered look melted suddenly and she began moaning softly, exhausted and panting. "Oh, I can't stand it anymore! The pain's so bad."

"Honey, it'll be over in a little while. Just try to hold out." But her eyes had gone wild and panic-stricken.

"*Oh no!*" she whispered in horror. "It's starting again!"

And she was right; the contraction came with a powerful force. As it wrenched through her small body, her back arched and she screamed piercingly.

"*Jesus!*" Than stepped back. He stood there appalled, as Jenny, gasping and crying, tore at her hair, beyond hearing, beyond knowing, as she lay in the lonely dazed delirium of a woman in excrutiating childbirth.

"Now, honey," Grace was saying gently. "Thee have to try and concentrate above the pain. Just now Jerome's going to tell thee when to hold back and when to bear down. Thee have to cooperate if we are to get that little baby out safely."

But she might have reasoned with the walls. Jenny stared dementedly, eyes woozy and wild as another contraction hit her like a thunderbolt. She gasped and cried out, and Than was horrified. Finally, as the contraction receded into the comparative sweet silence of her exhausted panting, he forced himself to mouth the words.

"Jerome," he said haltingly. "*Jesus!* When're you going to give her conduction anesthesia?"

Jerome glanced up, masked and gowned and slightly irritated, his gloved hands engaged between Jenny's spread legs.

"A caudal block?" He sounded exasperated. "What in heck for?"

"What for?" Numbed, Than closed his eyes and shook his head. Feeling as if his mind were playing tricks on him, he struggled to fight a rising panic. "Why, to dull the pain, of course."

"Now, Doctor!" Jerome straightened out and stared at Than irately, sounding exaggeratedly patient, like an adult talking to a child. "Thee knows the meeting's unequivocal stand on pain in child-bearing! We've had that out before!"

Than stood before him, pained, unable to move. "Jerome." He tried to laugh; maybe this was all some huge unfunny joke at his expense. "This is Jenny. And, Jesus, an *RSA*. With an RSA it's essential to have the mother's cooperation in bearing down. You can't have her exhausted with pain!"

Jerome's chuckle was slightly off-key. "Listen, Friend, thee'd be surprised how much a woman can endure. Why, I've seen some natives . . ."

Than closed his eyes. "Jerome, I don't care what the hell you've seen! This's Jenny we're talking about, remember? *Jenny!* Not just some poor hapless . . . *black* woman!"

There was a shocked silence. Then Jerome said carefully, "The one, Friend, is the same as the other in the eyes of the Lord. Even as God levies no favoritism in man's equality, so we cannot go making distinctions among ourselves."

"But, Jerome, for Chrissakes!" Than stared at the man wildly. "You know she can't take much more! Just give her something— *anything* —to ease the pain!"

"She has a good Christian endurance," Jerome said calmly. "And *thee* doesn't have enough faith. The child will be born spontaneously by lateral flexation, and with the help of God, we'll manage it. And the body has its own safety valve. She'll pass out when it gets too much to bear!"

Than walked out then. He stood in the cool darkness, convulsed in despair, while Jenny began to scream again; the sound carried on and on, reaching hysterical proportions, splitting his mind. Finally, in blind driving anguish, he rushed back into the sluice room, found the key and unlocked the drugs cupboard; he selected a vial of pethidine and put a hypodermic syringe into a kidney bowl.

Grace looked up expectantly as he reentered the delivery room. Jerome and Ingrid were crouched over Jenny's spread legs. Without a word, Than held the vial to the light and introduced the hypodermic needle, drawing off a hundred milligrams. He saw Grace's eyes expand with surprise. For a moment he thought she would contest him. She said nothing, but when Than approached the table, she stood dumbly blocking his way. Then suddenly, surprisingly, she averted her eyes and stepped aside. Quickly, Than pulled up the cream calico gown. He swabbed the side of Jenny's small white buttock with alcohol and swiftly injected the pethidine. Jerome and Ingrid drew back and stood watching him in astonishment. Ingrid's eyes had turned cold, but Jerome said nothing. There was the familiar resignation in his pained eyes. And there was hardly time for remonstrations now. Jenny was fully dilated and in a moment Jerome's eyes were down again, his hands busy as Jenny's failing reserves of strength were gathered in a last strangled cry.

Than left as wordlessly as he had entered. He stood on the veranda step outside, shivering in the darkness, listening numbly as the obstetrics team implored Jenny to a strength she no longer had.

And the drug, introduced so late, seemed to have hardly any effect, serving only to make her more confused and incoherent. She didn't even have the strength to scream anymore. And martyred to this endurance (it seemed like poetic justice somehow), Than listened to her delirious mumblings and exhausted crying and thought specifically about the dangers involved. Besides those to the mother, fetal mortality was always much higher in breech births. There was aspiration in delayed delivery, intercranial hemorrhage, fracture of the skull, and asphyxia. And as the long night dragged on, Than found himself fervently hoping that Jerome had deservedly overreached himself this time. That this blight on Jenny's life would pass from her, dead, at birth.

She made only feeble kitten sounds now. Then there was a sudden startling silence and Than thankfully closed his eyes; she had finally passed out from the pain. He heard grunting sounds of exertion and a satisfied gasp. Then there was a chorus of glad cries, and Grace and Ingrid were murmuring together, their voices maternally tender. Than knew then that the child had been born. And its sex lost priority to the color of its skin.

"*It's a miracle!*" Grace was saying, her stunned voice thick with emotion. "*He's white!* Oh, praise the Lord! *Pure white!* And the *straightest* black hair!"

Jerome gave a funny relieved chuckle. "Why, coming through all that, he's just a strong, strapping, healthy little man-child."

A soft breeze suddenly stirred and Than looked up and saw with surprise that dawn was breaking above the hazed horizon. In that moment, he heard the baby's first cry, and sitting on the cold step, all smoked out of cigarettes, staring dimly through gritty eyes and so tired he was numbed by it, his blood turned cold. He straightened his Stetson (worn a habit in haste) and closed his eyes, letting the stirring realization wash through him like pain.

A man's sins come home to him. *My son is born . . .*

15

The next day, the whole world knew that Dag Hammarskjöld was dead. His Swedish aircraft had crashed in the bush nine and a half miles from Ndola Airport, instantly killing him and all but one of his crew, who later died. Although subsequent exhaustive investigations of the strewn wreckage by various official bodies revealed no reason for the strangely off-course landing, an angry world was ready to level hysterical accusations at Tshombe, Sir Roy Welensky, and the British government. In Léopoldville there was an immediate call for war against Rhodesia in revenge for the "murder," while there was rage in Delhi and Cairo, and the Ghanaian government called it the "crime of the century"—all this anger illogically aimed at men and ministries whose best interest would have been more palpably served by the man's survival. The Federal premier's position in particular was an exasperating one, since he naturally desired peace in the neighboring Katanga and the suspicious United Nations authorities had declined to reveal their clandestine flight arrangements, even to him. Taking a wreath to the church in Ndola where Hammarskjöld, grand master of the order, lay in state before being flown back to Sweden, Tshombe, whose desperate hope of peace now seemed to have ended with the man's life, looked sad and defeated. Puzzling a blurred newspaper photograph, Matthew thought he glimpsed the suffering of all Africa in the black man's intelligent eyes. The whole wasted interlude saddened him greatly. His lingering depression haunted the hot September afternoon when he visited Jenny, whose baby, born on the eve of the secretary-general's death, cried lustily for the expressed milk that was impersonally fed him through sterile bottles by bored black nurses.

Matthew tried to explore the injustice of it all as he held a self-conscious one-sided conversation with Jennifer, who lay silent, shivering and shocked in the wake of traumatic birth. As white as the sheets she lay upon, she acknowledged Matthew's mutterings with dazed haunted eyes. Jerome Dooley, uncomfortably aware of Than Profane's disapproval of his handling of the delivery, worried about her feverish flushes, and haunted by the old ugly scourge of childbed fever, gave her five hourly penicillin injections to ward off possible infection, running circles around her in an effort to revive some will to live. He introduced two pints of blood and gave her iron intravenously; the other missionaries brought sweet-smelling flowers, orangeade, and awkward condolences. But nothing, it seemed, could coax Jenny from her gloom and failing strength. The replacement of lost blood brought no pink to her cheeks or sparkle to the flat eyes; she pushed away food and never spoke of the baby. And although this disinterest worried Matthew vaguely, he was grateful for it. It made their job easier, after all. For in a few weeks, when the tiny babe was old enough to travel, a light aircraft had been chartered to fly it, accompanied by him and Teller, to the government welfare department in Ndola, which had undertaken to arrange a suitable adoption.

"Oh, Than, I almost forgot. There's a letter for thee." As the family trooped into the lighted living room after First-day evening meeting, Katherine handed Than an envelope that had been propped up on the mantelpiece. He tore it open while Jayne and Suzannah looked on with absent interest. It was a disquietingly ill-timed belated birth-day from his illegitimate daughter in San Francisco. He scanned it absently.

Dear Uncle Than, the childish scrawl read. *Our letter was returned from the hospital where you worked. Then Mama met a friend of yours and that's how come we know where to send this greeting. You must be real good helping all those poor sick negroes out there. I go to school now. Mother says thank you for the money you send and why don't you write us sometime? Hugs and kisses, Cindy Lee.*

"A birthday card?" Katherine smiled at the scenic picture in Than's hand. "Who's it from, dear?"

Than looked up guiltily as Suzannah came to peer over his shoulder at the inscription. "Uh . . . just the little daughter of a woman I knew."

He handed the card to Katherine, who set it on display amid the ornaments on the wooden mantel.

"How sweet," she said uncertainly, and Suzannah eyed him with sudden skepticism.

"Yeah. Positively charming. A woman you know? Doesn't the little kiddy have a father?"

"Jesus, how should I know? I only got to meet the mother!" Than stalked out onto the dark veranda and lit up a cigarette. Suzannah and Katherine trailed out after him.

"Well, maybe she's illegitimate," Suzannah purred sweetly, reaching up to transfer the cigarette from Than's mouth to her own, eyeing him cannily as she exhaled smoke in the dimness. "Like our little Jenny's babe."

"Jenny's baby?" Than turned angrily on her. "Can't we talk of anything else around here but Jenny's baby?"

"Well, new babies tend to bring out the broody instincts in women, dear," Katherine sat down in the wicker rocking chair and started to rock. "And besides, it's kind of a touching situation, con-sidering . . ."

"Considering what?" Than hedged uneasily, not trusting Suzan-nah's simmering smile at all.

"Considering the poor little soul's likely to turn out a crissy-haired little nigger," Suzannah supplied, arms impatiently folded as she stood feverishly smoking, staring disinterestedly out across the dark mission. "With God knows what kind of mentality. Doesn't the Bible say how the sins of the fathers are visited upon their children?"

"Well, yes, that's so, dear," Katherine conceded, committed to the Good Book's defense. The old chair creaked accommodatingly as she slowly rocked. "However, I'm quite sure that goes double for inherent good. And with Jenny being the good Christian soul she is . . . well, I'm sure that's bound to outweigh the sins of the father, God forgive him, whoever he may be."

"Well, I don't see how." Suzannah spun around, mildly indignant. "No matter how spotless our little Miss Solomon, you can't tell me that the mark of some big black randy buck, with foul seed spilling from his filthy loins, isn't going to . . . what I'd like to know is how they hope to find someone white and respectable willing to adopt him!"

There was a moment's silence. Then Katherine stopped rocking and sniffed sorrowfully into a lacy handkerchief in the shadowed circle of her bonnet.

"There is no evidence," she said softly, "that respectability is limited only to whites or that black or half-breed colored people are averse to adoption. There are quite a number of coloreds on the Copperbelt. I believe they are reputed to be a charitable, home-loving people. And I believe all potential parents are carefully screened by trained welfare workers."

"Good Christ!" Than snapped, startling them both as he spun around, glaring. "I wish to God you women would stop talking about something you know nothing about! Who said anything about blacks or coloreds?"

"Yes, dear," Katherine smiled placatingly up at him through the moon-softened shadows. "I realize the child is white. But Dr. Dooley says in all fairness the whole history must be given. After all, if the color comes out in future generations, it could cause untold anguish in a white family. Whilst we, of course, would bear no discrimination against a blameless offspring, there are unfortunately others in the wider world less tolerant."

"Did you say he's *white*?" Suzannah's eyes had widened in disbelief.

Katherine nodded, and in her shadowed bonnet, her tender smile rearranged shining touches of moonlight. "It's true. Didn't Than tell thee? White as the driven snow! Thee see, the good Lord, in his benevolence, has been merciful!"

"But that doesn't seem possible!" Suzannah whirled on Than,

staring at him incredulously, eyes narrowed in odd indignation. "Is that true? What does he look like?"

Than stared down at the gold signet ring on his clenched fist. Besides everything else, he had a little daughter who thought her father was dead. Suddenly sick at himself, he closed his eyes.

"I don't know," he said gruffly. "I've never seen him."

16

One night, three days before the chartered plane was due at Mwinilunga to take the doomed little baby from the mission forever, an agitated African night nurse came hurrying to Matthew's house to report that Jennifer, still in the hospital pending her emotional recovery, had disappeared from her bed. It was late (the generator had just shuddered into silence) and Matthew slammed on his pith, snatched up a lantern, and went to search for her. On his way to the hospital he bumped into Than Profane, who was out walking his leopard with Jayne. Handing Bathsheba into his sister's keeping, the Boy came with Matthew at once. At Jenny's private room, they found that her slippers were missing, and Matthew relaxed infinitesimally. (At least this must mean she had left voluntarily and not been carried off into the night by some nameless black fiend!) The Boy stood staring at her empty bed for several moments. Then he suddenly turned and strode from the room, striding down the dark screened veranda. Sensing his purpose, Matthew hurried after him with Cuss at his heels. The lantern enveloped them in a halo of golden light all through the dark silent precincts of the sleeping hospital, drawing curious black disembodied faces like moths to the empty windows as they passed. They passed the two female wards, and when the Boy stopped at the room where the premature babies were kept, Matthew understood his reasoning at last.

The Boy opened the door and Matthew followed him inside, bringing his light into a little room that jumped with shadows. On the long table that ran the length of one wall stood a row of small basket cribs, a few of which were lined with blankets, filled with tiny, pale, pucker-faced African babies. Young babies had always been terrifying things to Matthew, and now he held himself nervously in, standing stiffly aloof with the lantern aloft in his hand. He saw that one basket pooled with blue blankets lay vacantly gaping.

Then he turned, and there she was, appeared like magic: little Jenny in a corner, sitting on the floor in her white cotton nightgown, a tiny baby held swaddled in her arms. The Boy's knee joints clicked as he crouched beside her, and Matthew drew in a ragged breath. But Jenny was oblivious. Her long dark hair, tumbling around her shoulders, had her face partly in shadow, and when Matthew lowered the lantern, they saw the look on her face, and it was rapt and glorious. It quite took Matthew's breath away, and he felt suddenly, humbly, like some mere mortal catching accidental glimpse of the bliss of angels. For her expression, in all its naked innocence, was surely something that only they, in their infinite joy, could wear. And Jenny was talking to the tiny thing, murmuring in the soft expression of love that needs no language.

"Jenny," the Boy said softly. She stiffened instantly. Then she slowly raised her head, her hands tightening perceptibly around the tiny bundle in her arms, her face transformed with a wary protective look.

"Come to bed now, Jenny."

But she drew back as the Boy reached for her child. "Come on, Jenny." he coaxed softly. "Give him to me. He has to go back in his crib now."

But the girl's hands seemed rigid and frozen, stuck in their covetous possession, and there followed the most heartbreaking tug-of-war Matthew had ever seen. Her face was dumb and pained, like that of a despairing animal, and she clung to the child with a desperate defiance. The Boy pulled gently, trying to disengage her locked hands, but she pressed back, crouching over her baby like a mother wolf protecting cubs in a lair. Her eyes flashed despairingly and the dark curtain of her hair fell forward, covering the tiny form.

"No," she whispered. "Oh please, *please* . . ." For a moment she seemed to Matthew, half demented with her mother love. Then the Boy spoke sternly, and the baby, almost in the same instant, began its retching, jerky, ear-splitting wail. Matthew, avoider of babies, felt his hair stand on end.

"Jenny, you'll frighten him," the Boy said disparagingly. And that seemed to do the trick. At once Jenny slumped back and simply sat, a harrowed despair on her face. Her blank eyes staring dumbly, she made no move to stop the Boy when he took the baby carefully from her arms. Then the night nurse, who had come in behind them, took the squalling infant, and the Boy said:

"Come, Jenny." He took her arm and pulled her gently to her

feet. She was crying now, the quicksilver tears just streaming down her pale face. As Than Profane led her out of the little room, Matthew caught a glimpse of his face and it was tight with a controlled, devastated fury, which scarcely fit the situation. As Matthew stood peering perplexedly after him, another baby awakened and began to cry, and a chain reaction set up. In a moment the room resounded with a lusty howling, which sent the night nurse scurrying around, murmuring endearments. And to Matthew it was a nightmare; cooped up in the little room with half a dozen tiny lungs bellowing in unison, he felt trapped in the midst of an air raid with the siren going off in his ear. Cuss, wise dog, had bolted at the first eruption, and now Matthew hastily followed him, stumbling out into the cool corridor on quaky legs, feeling like a shock with his white hair on end.

Leaving his lantern at the disposal of the night nurse, he felt comforted by the cloaking darkness as he hurried along the black corridors with Cuss at his side, guided by the moonlight, which shone through the long fly screens. He crossed a junction of corridors and, coming out onto an open quadrangle, might have blundered right past the Boy, who sat on the steps of the veranda outside Jenny's room, had not the glowing red ember of his cigarette, moving disembodied, caught his eye. Then he stopped in surprise. For the moonlight lit up the Boy's raised face as he stared searchingly heavenward, and in that unguarded moment his expression betrayed a pain so raw that Matthew was flabbergasted. Then the Boy dropped his tousled head, drew on his cigarette, and the expanding glow revealed him half-naked in those raggedy old denim bermudas, wearing an arrogance more protective than clothing, his sleek chest rippling with muscle and glistening with sweat as his narrowed eyes prowled the night darkness, as unconsciously aggressive as a preying animal's.

Thank the Lord he's on our side, Matthew though inanely, spooked for a moment. Then he was ashamed of his awe. For although the Boy had few of the gentle Quaker graces and no inhibitions, although he was stubborn as a mule and liked you to think he was heathen as Satan, Matthew had always sensed an innate, distant, disquieting good about him. Something deep down that was wholesome as raw earth. Some hidden basic quality that Matthew kept getting glimpses of just when he despaired of ever finding a virtue. In this way, chasing good in Than Profane was a little like being a prospector sifting a pan in the sunlight. In that teasing puzzling way, he kept seeing flashes of pure gold that always just eluded him. For although the Boy's way of going about things seemed often downright un-Christian, the end results were almost invariably, surprisingly wise and good. It was just his patently provocative presentation that jarred the other missionaries so. If only he weren't always such a rebel about everything. With a little more tact and humility, he might have been accepted. He reminded Matthew of some penned wild animal, continually charging at fences that held him captive. But in this instance, the fences were of the Boy's own making. If he would only stop fighting, he might realize that there was really nothing to fight about, that everybody, given the chance, only wanted to feed him and be friendly.

Matthew sighed in his exasperation, and the Boy, vigilant as a cat, looked up at the sound, and Matthew froze, caught silent and staring. Surprise hardened the Boy's eyes, and he adjusted his expression to appear merely piqued.

"Well," he drawled, questioning Matthew's prolonged presence with a wry sarcasm. "What're you waiting for? We found her, didn't we?"

"Er . . . yes, boy, I guess we did at that . . ." For a moment, Matthew stood rigid and irresolute. The Boy stared challengingly at him till, in the queerest retaliation, Matthew felt his own hackles rise.

All right, boy . . . easy now. I don't want to lock horns with thee . . .

With a conscious concerted effort, Matthew gathered his wits about him and strode fretfully away, tail between his legs and feeling foolishly that he might be jumped at any moment.

17

Somewhere in the duration of the night Jenny changed. When she awoke the next morning, she made a calm announcement that stunned them all. She would not, *could not*, give up her child. With a stubbornness unlike her, she stuck to this decision and nothing Matthew, Teller, or the Dooleys could say would change her mind. It was as if she only half heard their anxious dissuasions. She smiled at them gently, comforting their fears, as if she, the confused child, were really the older and wiser. And if rape and birth had left her physically ravaged and mentally maimed, the thought of keeping the product of these associated sufferings gave her a quiet strength and stirred new riches in her eyes.

"He's my baby," she said simply, smiling tenderly, as if washed of all her tragedy in this single decision. "I will love and care for him."

And that was that. Her desperate would-be dissuaders drew back from her in a quandary of doubt. For how could they further badger that poor girl to act against her maternal instincts and a conviction that was so obviously welded in the heart? How could they take away her one hope of happiness when she had already suffered so much?

In Matthew's mind, it was settled then. Cloistered in the sheltered and kindly atmosphere of the mission, she would bring up the child among them. But unfortunately, not without vehement opposition. The elder ladies reacted to the news with shocked repugnance, and Than Profane, in unusual alignment, supported their protests with a white-faced fury.

"Matthew, she can't! You can't let her keep it!"

When Matthew refused to further interfere, the Boy began to hound Jenny, rationalizing and imploring; he succeeded only in reducing her to tears and was so persistent that Jerome Dooley eventually had to ask him to cease, to preserve the poor girl's sanity. And the Boy, thus thwarted, became moody and truculent as a wounded animal, so that a body risked his head in simply asking the time of day.

But Matthew was convinced that all his fury and the ladies' protests would fade with time. Bolstered with this belief, he sent a radio message to the welfare authorities at Ndola, canceling the adoption plans. Then, relieved of this abortive task, and assailed of a quiet excitement, his mind began to play tricks of truth and it occurred to him that the little child—the offspring of a rapist—might in fact be God's compensation for its mother's suffering, and he was filled with a radiant optimism for the future. Now instead of the cloak-and-dagger plane ride that had hung over him like a cloud, he saw, stretched ahead, a whole sunny childhood for him to guide and observe. His own sons, who had ascetically settled, unmarried, into middle-aged life, seemed unlikely to provide him with grandchildren. Now in his mind he foresaw long golden days in which he, a grandfather by association, would take upon his knee a solemn little dark-haired child and patiently teach it right from wrong.

And so, feeling foolish and tickled, he fed on the idea, until, by the time he arrived home, he was bloated and entranced by it. And that was not all; the radio report that Moise Tshombe over in the Congo had finally managed to pin the United Nations down to an official cease-fire further buoyed up his mood. For the moment, Matthew felt that sanity had prevailed in the world.

Pending the new baby's arrival, there was an upsurge of activity in the Tomlinson household. Teller began to knit little soft oddments of clothing, and Matthew, with a suppressed excitement and a practicality unlike him, found an old oval basket, took up strips of wood and white paint, and proceeded to create a tiny crib, which, once lined with absorbent cotton and decorated with bows and frills by Teller, was hard to believe. He was so proud of his handiwork that he was quite mortally struck when Grace Dooley sent across the jaded old cot, fitted like a cage, which had served her entire family, right down to the rosy little triplets.

For a time Matthew was quite unreconciled to it. He criticized the flaked paint, the ingrained dirt, and the tiny half circles of teeth-marks in the soft wood.

"Why, I wouldn't put a *monkey* in that, let alone a dear child!"

But Teller gently consoled him, admonishing lightly, "The babe will soon grow out of the crib, and we can clean it up. Remember—the good Lord himself was laid in nothing more than a manger, and thy own two boys were weaned in nothing less—and I don't recall thee complaining."

She was right of course, and Matthew subsided, feeling himself fortunate that Teller was so wise and tolerant a woman. No doubt she felt as vaguely disturbed as he by the unnaturally favored view he gave the child. To the exclusion of even his own children, he felt clouted with a dumb adoration that was hard to explain. In elusive moments of stealing grandeur, he even imagined that this little child of a rapist would somehow embody the brilliance of a redeemer, and he plotted and prayed to mold the young soul to this end. For by virtue of its beginning, he knew that it would have sorrow in its eyes. And with sorrow there came soberness and dignity, the two virtues that Matthew sorely missed in his own two scalawag sons, who had grown up sturdy and strong, prone to fat and hilarity. They had none of the dignity and backbone that Matthew felt became a man; corpulent and uncouth as a couple of hogs, their rollicking rowdiness was a perpetual thorn in his side. Try as he might, he had not been able to knock the natural noxiousness out of them and remold them in his own bony dignity. By nature and by feature, they were a mockery to him, and before they were sent home to Indiana, he had spent most of his days in despair of them, wondering how so refined a lady as Teller had presented him with such contrary creatures. That he was fond of them both surprised and annoyed him. They were not of remarkable intelligence and their simple antics both amused and disgusted him. For a man did not want offspring to laugh at, he wanted sons to be proud of. And to a man of Matthew's own natural dignity, the observance of his given sons was almost painful. He felt exactly like the noble eagle finding gawky goslings in his nest. They were clearly not his own, but who would believe him?

When the Chitemene farmers were preparing to fertilize their fields, burning dried pyres of pollarded trees so that the hot October bush was filled with the nostalgic smell of woodsmoke, Jenny came home. She looked bewildered and frail with the little blue-wrapped bundle of her baby in her arms. Matthew and Teller had never been so happy and preoccupied; they determined to make up for the suffering that had started the baby's life and wrapped the little blind girl and her illegitimate son in a warm cloak of love that no outside disapproval could penetrate.

Although she could never hope to see it, Jenny endlessly explored the tiny baby with her gentle hands and never tired of hearing their descriptions of his appearance. The fact that she was able to nurse him herself increased her sense of closeness and added to her joy. With her blindness, there were initially many minor mishaps, and besides employing a black nanny to help her, Teller spent many patient hours helping her to master the craft of motherhood. Matthew, terrified and touched, watched from a safe distance, happy to run errands like fetching talcum powder or filling the tub with warm water.

And taking upon himself the role of grandfather, he felt all the giddy pride that this implied. Just as any stray lost pup had always moved him to the fiercest love, so this little foundling child, with his murky blue eyes and thick thatch of dark hair, aroused in him a delirious devotion. But his celestial bliss, not shared by others, was quickly brought down by them. One day, shortly after the baby's homecoming, Clara Fotch accosted Matthew with a grievous face and a grim voice, jolting him, started and hurt, from his nebulous state.

"Friend." The woman caught at his arm with tightly gripping fingers. "I must say that I am appalled and astounded that thee, of all people, should be the one to shame this mission so!"

Matthew stood, uncomprehending, for a moment.

"Thee knows very well what I mean!" The woman eyed him narrowly. "And in the future thee must expect to see less of Orville and I at thy house. For by allowing that . . . that *illegitimate* child to grow up in the home of thine own Christian children, *thee makes a mockery of all this mission stands for!*"

For a moment they stood eyeing each other in the shocked silence. Then Matthew slowly wrenched her hand off his arm. She drew back, offended.

"Dear lady," he said calmly. "I see thee standing before me with thine eyes all screwed up with vindictiveness and hate, and I feel shame for thee. I hear thy words and I pray for thy forgiveness. For by condemning an innocent little child, *thee* makes a mockery out of Christian charity! Now good day to thee, Friend. And I pray thee— chew on that stick of sentiment for a while!"

Clara stalked off in high indignation, but Matthew knew it was he, actually, who suffered more from the encounter. Seeing the situation through the eyes of others, he was deeply hurt. He wanted all the missionaries to feel as he did and strove, at every opportunity, to win hearts for the child, as though this, where compassion failed, would justify to them the babe's presence. But without Than Profane's support in this usual division of feeling, he felt oddly insecure. Now, shaken by Clara's savage denunciation, the Boy's angry words came back to him.

"You could have dissuaded her, Matthew, if you had really half tried! She would have listened if you were firm! She's nothing but an insecure little girl! A body can't say boo to her without her bursting into tears. And it's more than the normal postnatal depression. She was brutally raped; she's blind and unmarried. Can you call those suitable qualifications for motherhood?"

"But she *loves* him!" Matthew had struggled.

"Yeah." the Boy's smile had been bitter. "Don't little girls always love their dolls?"

Now, trudging across to the boys' primary schoolyard, Matthew stared despairingly up at the sky. "Oh, Lord, I am afraid . . ."

Afraid that they had given a live baby, as a plaything, to a winsome child . . .

* * *

But what was done was done. And despite the disapproval that raged all around them, they gave the baby a biblical name. Matthew had always cherished a secret fondness for Matthew, Mark, Luke, and John, and Jenny, respecting his feelings as Teller never had, made her own sure choice of the four apostles. And little Luke, blessed with this saintly label, solemnly stared and kicked in his crib. His accompaniment of toys, powder and pins, bibs, and diapers infected the big old house with a cozy family domesticity that had long since left it; in the stagnant October heat his poignant cry and soft crooning revived its old tired walls with a feeling like spring. And as the weeks passed, Matthew watched, fascinated, as the gamin infantile ugliness faded. The thin limbs grew sturdy and strong, and the tiny fingers became clutching little crabs that clung tenaciously to any offered object; the baby's soft skin turned pale bronze in the sunlight, and his face firmed into startling beauty. And right from the start, the angel-faced child seemed appropriately blessed with a saintly disposition. It seemed to Matthew that unless sick or sorely discomforted, he seldom fretted to the extent of other babies. After the first uncertain weeks of settling down, he slept long hours, murmuring only vaguely for his mother's milk-ripened breast before falling asleep again. Long-limbed and never overly plump, he gazed at the world out of solemn blue, black-lashed eyes, curious and content, a peaceful placid child whose hard-won and beauteous smiles became Matthew's dearest prize. And then the black hair thinned out and replenished and stunned them all. The soft down grew out the color and sheen of palest gold. The child was blond. And this, after all, was the whole and completion of Matthew's miracle.

18

In November, along with the first fierce sweet rains, two English missionaries, Creighton and Queenie Gladstone, arrived to start a secondary school at Mambundi in Barotseland. Their baptism into Africa was one of fire. The conservative old *Litunga* had thus far avoided political conflict in his protectorate by summarily deporting all agents of UNIP, Congress, and BASMO (the Barotse Anti-Secession Movement). However, one detractor proved a trifle difficult. He responded to a summons to appear before the Barotse tribal *kuta* by arriving with a vociferous crowd of supporters, who grew so unruly that the police, summoned from Mongu, had to disperse them with tear gas.

The riot, the first ever in the peaceful white-rule history of Barotseland, came as a severe shock to the *Litunga*. The British administration, and many missionaries, who had likewise failed to sense the growing disillusionment of the Barotses in their native government, were bewildered and dismayed. Others, including Homer Haskel and Matthew, had long seen the storm coming. At their subsequent yearly meeting, which was held that year at Mambundi, the conflict was clearly distinguishable in their own congregation. While most of the Lozi elite continued to decry UNIP, the paramount chief's royal rivals, and many commoners, pointed instead to the sins of the European administration. Their mouthings were disturbingly reminiscent of the nationalists' criticisms, and the missionaries felt suddenly conspicuously white, the confused middlemen in a national controversy.

The meeting was further unsettled by the news that in the Congo, the Congolese Central Army, breaking the cease-fire, had been joined by United Nations troops in a battle for Elizabethville against the Katangese troops, who had been conveniently rendered officerless by the United Nations order. For two weeks a battle raged for possession of the beautiful city. Hundreds of bombs were dropped on the suburbs, killing soldiers and civilians alike. Tshombe, attacking America for alleged interest in the economic ruin of Katanga, appealed to President Kennedy for peace. The United States President began preparations to end the hostilities, but in the meanwhile United Nations troops continued committing atrocities in Katanga. By nightfall of December 18, Elizabethville was in United Nations hands. The following day Tshombe arrived in Northern Rhodesia, disheveled and exhausted. He was subsequently flown back to an American-arranged meeting with Premier Adoula of the central government. What further pressures he would be subjected to there remained to be seen. But Matthew held out little hope for the survival of exhausted Tshombe and his clung-to ideals.

BOOK FIVE

THE CHRYSALIS: A NEW NATION EMERGES

·1962·

1

IT WAS A GLORIOUS DAY in Barotseland; the resplendent blue sky was mirrored in the sun-scintillating endless sea of the Zambezi, which had flooded its banks to swamp the great Barotse plain. Its waters lapped the *mutete*-reeded sloped bank on which Matthew stood, flanked by Than Profane and Benedict Poe, surrounded by hundreds of sweating Barotses who were massed along the long bluff. Uniformed policemen stood in the crowd, and here and there, colored umbrellas bobbed, protecting prestigious persons from the sun as they awaited the arrival of the paramount chief in the traditional exodus from his summer capital in the flooded lowlands. When news had reached Shonona that the *kuomboko* ceremony was to coincide with their visit into the territory this year, it was too much for Matthew to resist; although it was several years since he had last witnessed the stirring pageant, its enchantment had never waned for him. Poe, hatted and resplendently outfitted in his black Prince Alfred–suit to impress the prestigious *Litunga*, had never missed an attendance in all his years in the country; Than Profane had been lured the twenty-odd miles from the clinic at Shonona by the prospect of a multitudinous gathering that would doubtless include many sick.

It was a momentous time in the country on any account. The British government had finally announced its latest constitutional deal. Now, its neutralized conditions seemed to offer hope of winning to no one party; however, aware of the possibilities of amalgamation with other parties to achieve victory, each party (doubtless worn out by the long months of bitter wrangling) had reluctantly agreed to accept it. A general election under this new constitution would be held in Northern Rhodesia before the rains, on October 30. In preparation, the United Federal Party had begun to woo the more moderate Congress Party, while UNIP flirted with the Liberals. And in London, a relative of the *Litunga* appealed for a separate Barotseland within the Federation.

Now, as they stared out across the great "lake," with a fresh breeze blowing in their faces, straining for first sight of the flotilla, Matthew had to suppress a rising excitement. The flood was a predominant feature in Lozi life; it covered and uncovered crop fields, watering and fertilizing the soil; it dictated the methods of fishing and pasturing of the cattle. On the plain, all life advanced and receded before it; for weeks now the people had been living in increasing discomfort, plagued by snakes, frogs, flying insects, and soldier ants, fleeing the flood. The royal drummers had nightly sung of their hardships, entreating the *Litunga* to begin the mass migration onto high land. Finally, after the full moon, offerings had been made at the royal graves, and the *Litunga* began to pound on the national drums, followed by his councillors in order of rank. Lastly, the young men had struggled for the honor, and as the drums thundered out across the plain, men from all around the capital had come hurrying to escort their paramount chief on his voyage.

Now, here at Limulunga, a shout suddenly went up; with the thunder of the national drums faintly preceding it, the distant dots of the flotilla began coming into sight. A spontaneous cheer went up as the canoe carrying the hunting and war spears preceded the splendid royal barge. Zebra-striped, with a domed white canopy shielding the paramount chief and the provincial commissioner, the barge was swiftly propelled across the water by some forty oarsmen, all princes and councillors, dressed in bright cloths and caps with magnificently plumed headdresses. Behind the *Litunga*'s shelter, his personal band played; its monotonous music was alternated by the thunder of the national drums, which, representing the people, were transported in a separate barge, paddled by princes and councillors wearing reedbuck skins and lion-mane headdresses. These two main barges *fumba'd* in the flood, expertly zig-zagging, followed by a fleet of lesser barges: the queen's barge, the chief's councillors, the king's baggage barge, the councillors' baggage barge, and an escort of the canoes of commoners, crammed with their possessions and livestock. It was a colorful, compelling sight. With the thunder of the approaching drums increasing in volume and tempo, excitement reached fever pitch, and as the massive royal barge drew up alongside the crowded banks, the crowd held high their arms and shouted the royal salute: "*SHANGWE, SHANGWE, SHANGWE!*" Then they squatted on their haunches and clapped.

390

The first to alight were men bearing the war and hunting spears. Then came the *Litunga* and his entourage; as the procession alighted, a crackling loudspeaker system relayed the speeches of local dignitaries, including the resident commissioner, welcoming the paramount to his winter capital. The *Litunga*, with his sad-sack long sagging face, emerged in the resplendently plumed and tassled uniform of a British naval admiral that Lord Chamberlain had presented to his father in 1902. Lining the bank, distinguished local dignitaries, both black and white, in traditional and Western dress, waited to greet him. With a small thrill Matthew realized that Benedict had positioned them along the *Litunga*'s route. Self-consciously dusting off his shirt, he stepped respectfully back. Would the dignified old man remember him? he wondered. They had met only twice over many years, and then the solemn old aristocrat had merely nodded at him pleasantly. Beside him, he was aware of Benedict Poe removing his hat, straightening up stiffly in his good frock coat, twitching his boot-lace bow tie into place, while Than Profane, eyes narrowed against the sun and frowning in the shadow of his Stetson, frankly stared.

The *Litunga*, grand in his ancient perfectly preserved uniform, stared straight ahead, nodding distantly at the missionaries' gestured greetings. Then about two paces from their party, he suddenly stopped, and without turning back, uttered a surprising aside. For a moment, Matthew could scarcely believe his ears; it took the Boy's hat-tipped reply to confirm it; that, coupled with Benedict's stiffening soured silence. And Matthew could hardly blame the man. For while Poe had for years futilely bowed and scraped to install himself in the paramount's favor, the audacious Boy, never having met the *Litunga*, and without even trying, had insidiously reached the royal notice with a transilient reputation. "I see you, *Njumwaice!*" the *Litunga* had said.

2

One hot March day, during his consulting hours, Than looked up to see Matthew Tomlinson. Interrupting him between patients, the professor stood awkwardly in the green-curtained little office, clearing his throat elaborately, averting his modest eyes from Than's bare chest.

"Friend." He turned his pitch helmet nervously in his bony

hands. "It grieves me to bother thee at thy work, but the ladies, as overseers of this meeting's morals, have come to me with a complaint about thy wife, which, as senior elder, it is my unhappy duty to relay to thee."

"*My wife?*"

Matthew nodded mournfully. "Thy good lady is apparently laid out upon the river bank. Sunbathing, I believe. In one of them . . . er . . . *newfangled* things. A *bi*-kini I believe thee'd call it."

"A b . . ." Than's face cleared in comprehension. He closed his eyes. "Oh *Jesus Christ!*"

He tore from the hospital with Matthew stumbling miserably after him. From the high point of the swing bridge it was easy to see where she lay across the river. She was surrounded by a milling crowd of Africans, mostly males, who had flocked to her exposed body like flies to uncovered cake. Than ran so recklessly that the rope bridge rocked wildly in his wake. On the opposite bank, he ignored Hannah Rothchild, Clara Fotch, and Cherish Sinclair, who stood glowering furiously, removed from the gathering natives in a prim little knot. Pushing through the milling black bodies, Than stopped when he reached Suzannah, for a moment too pent-up with air and anger to speak. The natives, obviously fearing his outrage, blundered back, but did not disperse; they stood in a wide loose circle, compulsively staring.

And there she lay, draped across the spiky yellow grass, her face shielded by sunglasses and a floppy hat, her golden oil-sheened body as good as naked before this gloating group of Africans, who had probably never seen much beyond a white woman's ankles before, her decency barely protected by the skimpiest black bikini Than had ever seen. Well, anywhere else it might be fine. But out here her spectators were no genteel gentlemen of the diplomatic order. They were full-blooded, largely uneducated raw rural Africans, to whom instinct might just be tendency and rape a matter of opportunity. Than thought of the defilement of Jennifer Solomon and felt sick.

Suzannah, ostensibly dozing in the heat, did not seem to realize his presence; she writhed sensuously amid the leering crowd of Africans, who must betray their presence by sweaty body stench alone, let alone their soft lewd laughter. Than stood for a moment, fighting down his anger. Then he reached down and whipped up his wife as if she were a piece of rag. Her hat and sunglasses fell off and she dangled from his grasp with a look of stupid surprise, spluttering indignantly.

392

But without allowing her respite to retrieve her hat or glasses, Than pushed through the crowd. While the censorious group of old ladies looked on in nose-raised contempt, he dragged Suzannah after him up to the house. Struggling to break free of his biting fingers, she protested furiously all the way up the slope, up the garden path, and into the house.

Inside, Than dragged her up the stairs. In the musty dimness of their room, he slapped her twice, viciously, across the face. She went sprawling back onto the floor, shocked and weeping.

"You . . . you *bastard!*" Her face crumpled, and she began to cry like a child, all curled up in a knot against the wall, touching her crimson-welted face with shaking hands.

"Now just what the hell were you trying to prove?" he snarled softly, closing his eyes, face awrack. "Get yourself raped? Lady, they wouldn't even ask your name!"

"Listen, you bastard! I did nothing wrong!"

"Oh Christ, no! You were only lying there half naked, making those savages pant. Letting them sniff your body like some bitch in heat! You were enjoying all hell out of it. I guess you're just the common garden variety of cock-tease, baby! You get some curious sick pleasure out of making men drool. And it seems . . ." He stared down at her, white-faced with fury. ". . . it seems you don't care whether they're black or white!"

She gave a little scream of rage and leaped to her feet, fists clenched. "Oh sweet Jesus! How narrow-minded can you get? What's wrong with a bikini?"

"Well the natives seemed to like it just fine!"

"Oh, you poor bastard!" she spat at him furiously. "You've gotten just like them! Those sourpuss old women. Reaching for the smelling salts if a man takes off his shirt. Just about fainting if . . . *Jesus*! It's rubbing off on you too!"

"Suzannah," Than said tightly, still heaving with rage, "a white woman is a white woman is a white woman. She is an unknown and forbidden quantity to the black man."

"I don't care! I don't care!" she said defiantly, putting her hands over her ears. "I'll do what the hell-all I like! You don't *own* me. It's a free world!"

"Well, what I want to know," Than said in a voice deceptively soft, "is why you just didn't take it all off? Why didn't you show them what a white woman is like through and through?" He reached across and grabbed at her bra top. With a terrific tearing wrench, he ripped it off her body, making her squeal, leaving her breasts bare and white, shaking like jelly.

She stared up at him, shocked and white-faced.

"Oh, *you!*" She leapt at him like a wildcat, clawing and spitting and screaming her outrage. She pounded with her fists and slashed him with her long nails.

But his stony immobility under her attack was unnerving and ominous. She backed off slowly, eyeing him uncertainly, staring at his set face and the scratches on his cheek and chest, dribbling bright red blood, which diluted with his sweat and streamed down his bare bronzed chest. She must have seen the murderous feeling on his face, for she looked frightened for the first time.

"Listen, you," she mumbled weakly. "You don't own me. I'll do what I like. And if you touch me again, I'll . . ." The threat hung feebly in the hot humid air of their room.

"You and who else?" he said softly, and stood there heaving, dripping sweat and blood, still not moving, facing her quietly, topless as she, but taller and browner and a whole lot more muscular. "I'm bigger than you, remember."

She began to back away from him, eyes wide, slightly stooped, her pale breasts hanging soft and tender. She brushed the blond hair out of her eyes, whispering distractedly, *"You wouldn't dare!"*

But he was advancing on her slowly.

"You've been baiting me for a long time, Suzannah. Maybe this time you've pushed a little too far. The Continentals have a theory, that if you beat a woman, it makes her good and obedient."

"I'll scream!" she hissed at him. "The other missionaries . . ."

"Scream," he said quietly. "Something tells me they wouldn't listen. The way you've been behaving, they'd probably smile on it. Wife-beating is probably a whole lot more preferable in their books than native-baiting and smoking in church."

"Native-baiting? Listen, you bastard. You're lucky I just don't take it into my head to sleep with one!"

He saw red then. He reached for her and his mind went blank. For a while he was aware only of her broken crying and the whacking sounds of his own open-handed blows. Then, gradually, his mind cleared. Through a hazy dimness, and with a strange detachment, he saw her lying huddled on the bed. She was bruised and broken, her hair disheveled, almost too weak to cry, her arms protectively clasped across her bare breasts.

He stared down at her dispassionately, breathing hard. He felt curiously elated, triumphant; there wasn't a spark of repentance inside him. He went to the pitcher on the washstand, dabbed a towel into the stale water, and carefully wiped the streaks of blood from the scratches on his face and body. Then, almost casually, he went to the door. Suzannah lay on the bed, curiously silent now; she seemed to be hardly breathing. For all he knew she might be badly hurt. But without a backward glance, he left her. He took the stairs two at a time and almost bumped into Jayne, come home from school to fetch some forgotten trifle. She stared at him oddly.

"Why, Than, what's wrong? Thee're bleeding. Thee looks so strange."

He touched his scratched jaw self-consciously, smiling at her beatifically.

"Nothing's wrong at all."

He liked to think that. But after a while there arose inside him a curious ache; the feeling of elation went flat as stale soda pop, and he went through the rest of the day in a bewildered daze.

By the time he came home in the evening, his bitterness had worn out of him and self-reproach ached dully inside him. He dropped off his white jacket, scarcely worn, at the hospital laundry and walked wearily home, avoiding the Dooleys and Ingrid and Denise Smith, wanting to smart alone. The soft cool of dusk soothed him a little, leaving him feeling oddly naked; without the heat and storm of his anger, he felt small and shamed and woebegone. His skin was clammy with sweat and the cool breeze revived his tired eyes and singed his cheeks with burning coolness. He passed Matthew Tomlinson and Ratchet Cathcart, who were all agog with the latest news leaked to the press—that the new colonial secretary had flown to Barotseland last month to receive a document calling for the protectorate's secession; the *Litunga* had apparently accepted the new constitution, and bowing to pressure from the boma, confident of his people's support, had agreed to allow political parties to campaign in the protectorate for the October elections. The old professor, talking intensely of the implications, seemed to have forgotten all about Suzannah's scandalous breach of mission etiquette. And the day, being forgiving, made Than forgive. He remembered the way Suzannah had looked lying twisted and still on the bed, and he shuddered, rueing his own blind rage. She was reckless and spoiled and uninhibited, sure; but had her deed been that bad? Enough to make him side with the whole mission against her? Enough to make him raise his hand?

In the stifled dimness, the silence of the big house frightened him unbearably. He hurried lightly up the stairs, suddenly afraid to find her gone or, even worse, seriously hurt. God knows, he had no idea how badly he had beaten her.

Cautiously opening the door, he went weak with relief. For the last dusky daylight dimly revealed her as she lay uncovered and still half nude, right where he had left her, curled up like a cat with her legs doubled against her body. And she was soundly asleep, blond hair tousled and her flushed skin all shiny with sweat. She wore an absurd sulky expression on her face and her thumb was tucked into her plush mouth, giving her the helpless look of a child. She sucked at it even in her sleep, her puckering lips betraying a deep insecurity that stemmed from her childhood. But her breasts made him feel most brutal. Her tender pink-nippled breasts, vulnerable and defenseless-looking, which a man could so easily crush with his bare hands. They were the symbol of woman's very helplessness, of motherhood and fair sex. Staring at them, he felt a wave of agonized tenderness wash through him, a shame and remorse at what he had done to her frail female body in all his superior male strength.

A breeze picked up the dying day and billowed the curtains at the open window. He felt the rapid dropping of the temperature and took a quilt and covered her with it gently, wanting suddenly, fiercely, to protect her again.

She awoke, smoky-eyed and bewildered, in his arms. When her senses had settled, she struggled to shed him, but he shook his head at her and hung on, gentling her with his hands and seducing her with his sucking mouth. At last she collapsed, crying, against him, and he took her and defiled her with his love, moving with a gentle restricted passion.

Afterward, he discovered that her body was covered in marks and welts from his hand. A horror of his own cruelty jarred inside him, and he soothed her with ointment and kisses, vowing silently never to punish her that way again.

Later, lying a little aloofly in his arms, she said in a dazed strained little voice, "I want to go home."

He stiffened immediately. "You mean back to Salisbury?"

"Yes." She nodded, beginning to cry again. "It's the only place I feel I belong. I'm a misfit here. You know that. I can't stand it any longer."

After a moment, he sighed, nodding. He drew slightly away from her; they were glued by sweat in the oppressive atmosphere.

"You know it!" she insisted, shaking him.

"Yeah." He exhaled slowly, resigned. "I guess I do. Maybe you're right. You go back for a while."

She ran a hand lightly across his chest and looked appealingly up at him in the dimness. "Just for a little while."

He nodded, saddened and disgruntled, feeling oddly like a small boy, forced by common sense to give up a pet his heart desired. "Just for a little while . . . you go."

She did. But the length of her visit had not been discussed.

3

The news that Chief Kadesha had agreed to allow Than Profane to set up an out-clinic in his personal village had surprised no one. Although the chief was a devout Catholic, the nearest Catholic hospital was many weary miles away; his salmon and gray Zephyr Zodiac was often seen on the Mwinilunga road ferrying the urgently ill to the hospital, but gas was expensive, and the chief understood the needs of his less fortunate people. He was a tolerant and democratic leader who had many times politely exchanged religious views with fervent Friends from Suseshi while faithfully clinging to his chosen Catholicism. Although his allegiance to the white fathers was never in any doubt, he was always pleasingly grateful for the community services of any other denomination. As it happened, the clinic at his village was completed rather timeously. A week after the Boy's first session, Kadesha's villages were overrun with kindred Lunda tribesfolk fleeing the war in Katanga. Many were wounded, others footsore and starving. The Northern Rhodesian Government rushed in emergency food and medical supplies. The Boy did what he could. What casualties could not be accommodated at Suseshi he assigned to the Catholic and Plymouth Brethren hospitals in the province.

The haggard black refugees told him horrifying tales of residential areas, schools, and even hospitals being bombed at Kolwezi, Luilu, Le Marinel, and Elizabethville. To Matthew it was evident that Tshombe was being mercilessly driven to the wall by the military might and psychological pressure of the United Nations. Previous to this, a Congolese battalion of the central government had massacred and eaten thirteen Italian crewmen of United Nations aircraft and butchered twenty-three missionary fathers. A Katangese garrison had kept these murderous marauders at bay until the United Nations prevented supplies from reaching them. It was a sobering classic example of the absurdities and ineptitude of outside interference. But the perpetrators of a preposterous "peace-keeping" policy that allowed such barbarians free reign seemed unwilling to learn by the embarrassing incident. They continued to sabotage ruthlessly the ceaseless peace initiatives of the Congo's one orderly state. But Tshombe refused to be beaten. After exhaustive efforts, he had finally managed to pin Premier Adoula of the Central government down to another meeting to investigate cooperation between their states. However, even this much Matthew found hard to believe in. Astute old Chief Kadesha shared his views that Adoula jumped to the command of men who were diametrically opposed to the successful secession of Tshombe's Katanga.

And in Northern Rhodesia, Tshombe's record of respectful reliance on whites was denounced by the more radical nationalists. UNIP despised the man's ability to recognize the usefulness of the old imperialist overseers. In Mwinilunga, Matthew felt it was mainly the kinship of the Lundas for their tribal ally Tshombe that had bitterly influenced them against UNIP. But he was pleased that despite Benedict Poe's awesome pronouncement against any political involvement, more and more of the Lunda members of Suseshi Meeting were now openly admitting an affiliation with the more moderate Congress Party, which significantly was more kindly disposed toward their kindred Tshombe.

4

"Matthew, I need a guide to take me out to Chief Jahaliso, and I believe you are one of the few people who knows the way."

Than Profane's poser did not surprise Matthew; nothing the young doctor did surprised him anymore. Apparently he had heard that the Lunda chief was now almost blind with incipient cataracts, and fearful that he might turn to the witchdoctors to have his condition corrected, he had decided to seek out the chief and urge him to accept their more "scientific" aid. Well, Matthew was uneasy; their brush with the brutal Balubas last year had somewhat shattered his nerve. Jahaliso was a known UNIP patron and markedly anti-white. He might not welcome their interference, and the trip into his chiefdom was a long one, through territory where whites were no longer welcomed as the harbingers of goodwill. Indeed, in the present political climate, they might be stoned or harassed. However, since the spiritual and physical welfare of thousands of Lunda lives lay under Jahaliso's awesome influence, Matthew shelved his misgivings and agreed to accompany the Boy.

And on this occasion he had no illusions as to who would be in control; since the doctor's easy acquisition of Mulaisho's favor and affection, he knew well enough that the Boy called the tune. And now, as they packed a Land-Rover to depart in the dusky dawn, it was Matthew, gritting his teeth at being primed by a subordinate, who was duly cautioned and cajoled.

"Matthew, this Jahaliso seems a pretty cynical fellow, so for God's sake don't go whipping out any Bibles ahead of time." The Boy shoved a cardboard carton of medical supplies into the back of the Land-Rover. "From what I can tell, the chief classes missionaries as self-important prigs who make a hobby of patronizing natives, saving souls to boost their personal prestige. Well, I'm not sure he's altogether wrong on that score. But whatever, just for Pete's sake let's not rush in there and give him good grist to place us in that category right off the bat."

It was as simple as that. And if Matthew belonged to the aforementioned old school of missionaries who had a compulsive calling to save the indigenous souls of godless Africa, he swallowed his wounded pride and said nothing. He could scarcely object, after all. None of his own fancy theorizing, or that of his colleagues, had achieved a fraction of that accomplished by the Boy's more practical methods. And if the Boy had little faith in the power of the Gospel, he had an amplitude of belief in himself. Besides taking along a mountain of medical provisions, he had brought Teapot back from Eshalakali Hill to assist him with the medical ministrations he expected to be called upon to perform. And to Matthew's acute discomfort, his pet leopard was to be another member of their party. It seemed bad enough that the feline's periodic bouts in season had induced a succession of hair-raising nocturnal visits from an amorous wild male leopard, whose restless "wood-sawing" panting pulsated the nervous nights while it rhythmically skirted Bathsheba's sturdy outdoor pen, leaving pugmarks of an unsettling size. However, aside from the fact that the young leopard's presence prohibited thefts from the Land-Rover, the Boy had learned that she was a far more potent crowd drawer than penicillin had ever been. Well, Matthew had lost his ease with the beautiful creature at about the same time as she lost her milk teeth. Now, as they headed out into the smokily stirring early bush, his nervous apprehension of the great cat, whose supple considerable weight indented the canvas roof above them, was matched by that of the incredulous African tsetse-fly control officer who stopped them on the Mwinilunga road, spraying their vehicle with pesticide from a safe if ineffective distance before hastily raising the road-barring boom to let them through.

The rising sun streamed through the trees and the road ran over rackety old bush-pole bridges, crossing Zambezi-bound rivers and streams before plowing on through the wind-whipped feathery weeds that swamped the woodland. Before reaching the administerial outpost of Balovale, they turned into the bush. Slapped by the springy branches of endless trees, the vehicle waded through soft thick grass that scratched and hissed against its undersides as they twisted and turned, following interminable paths into a remote corner of the country, bordered by Angola. It was sparsely scattered with large villages comprising huts of unimpressive, squalid constructions. They came upon old men out hunting with dogs and bows and arrows, and women in colorful dust-dulled cotton dresses, who gracefully balanced incredible loads upon their cloth-swathed heads, or tended cultivated patches of bulrush millet and cassava. And to Matthew's mind, these once friendly people had been patently soured by Federation and spoiled by nationalism. They all stared sullenly; a few surly youths made threatening motions with stones. Matthew, all tensed up for trouble, was relieved when the bush opened out into a great tree-scattered grassy savannah. On one side, a curving spine of hazy blue hills bounded the village of Chief Jahaliso.

The large concentration of conical thatch huts looked pleasantly picturesque, with orange Canna lilies and purple plumes of bougainvillea. As they parked beneath a shady acacia tree, dogs ran out barking and the village inhabitants emerged and began crowding around the vehicle to gape at the leopard, which hissed threateningly from its lofty perch. While the Boy was fettering the cat to a Land-Rover door, the senior Lunda chief himself pushed through the milling throng.

"Good morning, gentlemen." The tall young autocrat greeted

them haughtily in English. He shook hands formally as he puzzled dimly at them through his cataract-clouded eyes. His uniquely European blue jeans and a flashy imitation ruby necklace were quaintly at odds with his ethnic regalia; a leopard-skin kaross flapped over one broad black shoulder, and his neck and arms were tassled with protective charms and status symbols, the most cardinal of which, the grizzly *lukano* bracelet, was symbolic of supreme Lunda/Lwena seniority.

The chief was gracious; leading them to a large multiroomed thatched hut made of mud bricks, with well-carpentered doors and glass windows, he brushed past the family pharmacopoeia of feathered fetishes, calabashes, and cupping horns that hung from the overhanging outer eaves and invited them inside. Here, the furnishings again reflected the conflicting cultures of old Africa and the West. In the main room, doubtless tortuously transported from the Copperbelt, stood a sagging old maroon and gray lounge suite, a cluttered glass-fronted display cabinet, and an elaborate walnut radiogram (electrically operated and thus of little use save as ornamentation out in these backwoods). On the dusty bookshelf were musty tomes of improbably intellectual English titles, and on the littered wooden table stood an impressive cut-glass wine decanter encircled with a set of shiny tumblers, while a fruit-fly-hazed gourd of honey-beer stood beside a full bottle of finest Johnny Walker Scotch Whiskey.

Already seated on the spring-humped settee, dressed in a shabby shirt slung with a colorful African-print toga, a bespectacled African gentleman was arrogantly introduced as being a UNIP official, canvassing in the area in preparation for the general elections on October 30. Instantly on his guard and puzzled by the man's vague familiarity, Matthew finally recognized him as an ex-boma clerk who had been dismissed by the D. C. at Kabompo for theft. He swallowed uncomfortably; well, it should hardly surprise him. According to D. C. Horn, an uncommon number of nationalist agents were petty criminals, malcontents, and misfits whose picayune real and imagined grievances they worked out in racialist rhetoric, brutal intimidation, and incitements to riot. If the majority of the people were moderate and content with their lot, it was unfortunately these few radicals who would make themselves heard. And this man, with his dirt-grimed collar and cuffs, with his round, oddly Oriental-looking bespectacled black face and inscrutable smile, seemed to Matthew curiously akin to the Communist Chinese whose propaganda and finance reputedly helped fire and fuel the nationalist cause.

Matthew sat uneasily on an armchair opposite the man, but Than Profane was at ease as usual; he had already shed his shirt in the sticky heat, and casually hunkering down on a native-made cloth-covered chest, he offered around his pack of cigarettes. Chief Jahaliso, obviously used to accepting the white man's free bounty since childhood, took two; he was evidently not easily impressed. Indeed, the Boy's offer to restore him to reasonable eyesight aroused little gratitude. As their visit progressed, Matthew was disconcerted to realize that his own presence was almost completely discounted, while, if *Njumwaice* at least had the impact of personal charisma and reputed medical prowess, it was, at most, a dubious imprint, for Jahaliso, by cagy conversation and sarcastic innuendo, was yet judging the young doctor, and still wary, he would not agree to an operation on his ailing eyes.

"Why not?" the Boy pried. "You afraid we'll take them out and use them for medicine?"

"You say you can help me," the chief hedged, smiling abashedly, obviously disarmed by this direct reference to popular local superstition. "However, my grandfather lost his sight when his eyes were operated upon by a white doctor many years ago in the Congo."

"Maybe so," the Boy conceded. "But things have changed since then. We have better instruments, methods, and sterile conditions today. We no longer take the same risks of injury and infection."

The chief nodded musingly. He had noticed the Boy's interested scrutiny of his bracelet of interwoven dried human flesh and seemed to take malicious delight in explaining that each of the flabby components was comprised of human genitalia, added by successive chiefs upon their ascension.

"Jesus." The Boy smiled slowly, blue eyes narrowed with awe. "Genital parts? Whose genital parts, if I may be so indelicate as to inquire?"

"Ah." Jahaliso's mocking smile broadened. "That is a secret. But some say that at least one—this lighter, more insipid specimen, no doubt—belonged to a white man long ago." He turned to include Matthew in the cynical speculation of his derisive smile. "He is said to have been a Christian minister, a particularly unpopular missionary, I believe."

Now it was Matthew's turn to blanch. In the process of testing the tone of Than Profane, the young chief was doubtless merely mocking them both. But their recent experience with the Balubas had unnerved him completely; now, alone with these akin contemptful black men, miles from the nearest civilized white outpost, irrationally afraid, he began to sweat uncomfortably. In the fly-buzzing stillness, Than Profane smiled musingly, meeting the chief's mocking gaze with a cool appraisal.

"I have yet to add my own contribution," Jahaliso said carefully, gauging their responses with narrowed eyes. "And the people have begun complaining that it is time another *white* link was added to the sacred *lukano*. Such a contribution would surely make very powerful medicine."

He drew on his cigarette and exhaled the smoke through his broad flat nostrils. "Tell me, *Njumwaice*, have you been circumcised?"

Though Matthew drew up in shocked indignation, the Boy's expression did not change; Matthew was able to detect nothing more than a slight narrowing of his smiling eyes as he considered the African's outrageously personal probe.

"Well," he drawled finally. "I find your keen interest in my anatomy somewhat disconcerting, Chief. I get the feeling that I'm being sized up for the cooking pot."

To Matthew's relief, after a studied moment, Jahaliso burst into his bright booming laugh.

"Ah, a missionary with humor," he spluttered, slapping a knee. "I have found that 'men of God' can seldom laugh at themselves. Perhaps in your good-naturedness, O *Njumwaice*, you would voluntarily consent to add another link to the *lukano*?"

The Boy's smile did not waver. "I see you too have a good, if chilling, sense of humor, Chief. Thanks, but no thanks. I must confess that over the years I have become a trifle attached to the part you now covet."

Jahaliso and the UNIP agent laughed softly together with polite cynicism, and Matthew was relieved when an agitated rap on the door interrupted their sinister speculation. The young chief strode to the door; he talked for some moments with a raggedly dressed man who stood humbly on the threshold, before turning back to them with a broad smile.

"Gentlemen, it seems Dr. Profane has ventured among us at a most opportune moment. This man reports that a youth has been badly trampled by a rogue hippopotamus. Perhaps, Doctor . . ."

The Boy was on his feet instantly. "Of course. We'll go right away."

He went out, and Matthew, anxious not to be left alone with the chuckling UNIP agent, hurried after him. As they approached the speculative crowd that still milled around the Land-Rover watching the leopard, the Boy called out to Teapot. The dresser, with the quasi-confidence that came from its handling since cubhood, stood boastfully preening beside the great cat. The animal stood up at sight of the Boy, warily craning its neck to watch his approach.

"Teapot, will you just take Sheba . . ."

But Matthew could see at once that the dim-witted fool, as usual rushing to conclusions as if they had a limited lifespan, had misunderstood the Boy. At Eshalakali Hill, at the end of his labors, such a call from the doctor was his cue to release the young animal into its master's keeping. But while the ritual might be perfectly safe under the deserted mango trees at the Hill, right here and now, amid this unstable boisterous crowd, before the sedating heat of the scorching summer sun had started to tranquilize the vigilant vixen into a sleepy pussy cat, it was positively insane. Matthew stopped short in dawning horror as Teapot stooped, fumbling with Bathsheba's collar; as the dresser's intentions became obvious, the crowd's chatter suddenly ceased and the Boy's footsteps faltered. Before anyone could stop him, Teapot had unclipped the chain and released the leopard.

The shocked spectators instantly backed away; Matthew, with eyes riveted on the animal, glimpsed their terrified tumbling for cover. Then the Boy, quickly recovering himself, called to his pet; clicking his tongue, he patted his thigh and whistled softly in a customary coaxing, which twitched the cat's ears. For one frozen moment all proximate witnesses ceased to breathe. Then, in a series of great gamboling bounds, with a spectacular liquid grace, the young animal streaked in a yellow-black blur before their eyes. And then it sprang. The petrified natives gasped in shock. The leopard struck the Boy's midriff with a stunning force that almost knocked him off his feet. But, braced to receive her, he caught and held the beautiful animal, his strong arms linking across the supple spine while the flexed hind legs, with deadly claws safely sheathed, slid down to lever against his blue-denimed groin. Purring loudly, the great cat rubbed its blunt whiskered head with fierce affection against the young doctor's throat and bare golden shoulders. Laughing huskily, the Boy turned his head from a flurry of feline kisses; his hat was knocked off as they nuzzled and pressed faces in sheer joy of each other. Then finally, staggering under the increasing pull of that spring-coiled weight, the Boy released the young animal. She slid to the ground, and rearing up on her hind legs with her front paws on his chest, she was a fine specimen, almost as tall as to reach his collarbones, licking the fine sheen of sweat off his golden skin with a pale pink sandpaper tongue.

As the Boy called for the cat's chain, Matthew slowly released his bated breath. Turning to Jahaliso, he noticed that the chief's cynicism had been broken at last; it seemed to him that the young African was looking at the white doctor in a distinctly different way.

5 From the Congo there was news that the Central premier, Cyrille Adoula, had waited for Tshombe to fly home from their talks (a draft communiqué in hand, and assured of their success) before declaring to the world that all peaceful means to end Katanga's secession had been exhausted. He called upon the United Nations to "resume" its responsibility. When the new secretary-general, U Thant, announced that as a result of this "breakdown" of the talks United Nations troops had been put on the alert, it seemed evident to Matthew that another major crisis was looming up, with the United Nations peace-keeping force straining at the bit to oblige the country's blood lust. After all their hopes of a final peaceful solution, this reversal was deelpy depressing, and Matthew, morosely musing on the matter as he walked to his office that morning, hardly paid much attention to a dust-dulled big battered black Chevrolet sedan that pulled into the mission.

Parking outside the hospital, the car emitted a tall powerfully built young African man in a dark suit and sunglasses who was escorted to the outpatient department by an attentive entourage of several men. Such was his charisma that the milling crowd parted as he walked, the long lines quickly fell away for him, and within minutes, the news was all over the mission; Jahaliso, dissident senior chief of the Balovale Lunda, had arrived to be treated for advanced cataracts.

Well, if the summons of the disdained Mulaisho had put the elder ladies in a flap, the unexpected arrival of this highly prized young chieftain had the missionaries excited and confused. When they gathered during the day's first recess, the ladies, armed with Bibles and tracts, considered going straight over to the hospital to confront him with the Quaker truth. (Matthew suspected that only the memory of the young chief's scathing denunciation of them after the humiliation of his V.D.-afflicted brother kept them no more than teetering on the brink.)

"Thee go, Matthew!" they decreed finally. But even pushed by their insistence, Matthew could go no further than the hospital grounds. Fearing the Boy's belligerence as much as the young chief's rejection, he settled for a mere inquiry about the patient's condition. News of a quite lengthy stay in their hospital to have the offending cataracts removed gave him a temporary reprieve.

Two days later, when the Boy had operated, Matthew was still pondering a fitting approach. He awaited news of the delicate surgery with a knitted brow. And he was not the only one. There had never been an operation more closely followed by the missionaries. Last heard of, Jahaliso was cautiously courting Catholicism. But there was a perfectly good Catholic mission and a neutral government hospital even closer to his home. His sudden arrival here had them all itching with curiosity. Had he fallen out with the Catholics? Discovered them shallow? Only Matthew had little doubt as to the real reason for the young chief's choice. Although the chief himself had apparently sheepishly conceded that part of his prompting stemmed from the experience of another, similarly blighted, relative, whose visit to a witchdoctor had left him permanently blinded, Matthew considered that Jahaliso had come here for no better reason than his faith in *Njumwaice*. It was this belief that held Matthew back from any undue optimism as to his convertibility, when he finally went to see the young black man in the male surgical ward, clutching a bunch of zinnias snatched from his own sparse garden.

Jahaliso's handsome black face was half-obscured by bandages as he lay indolently on top of his bed, looking surprisingly civilized in clean striped pajamas and a silk dressing gown, sharing a cigarette and casual conversation with Than Profane. Feeling vaguely vexed at the doctor's open and confiding manner (his habit of approaching pagans casually from his own easy level smacked of a permissive acceptance of their ways, which was not exactly conducive to Christian conversion), Matthew said courteously in Chi-Lunda.

"Good afternoon, Chief. It is I, Professor Tomlinson. I have brought thee some flowers."

"Professor Tomlinson?" The blindfolded man reached out for the posy. Remembering their vile smell, Matthew winced as the chief sniffed the flowers appraisingly.

"Why, Professor, have you come to influence me to your Quaker religion? You have brought roses!" Jahaliso said sarcastically in his impeccable English. And although he had heard them increasingly over the years, such eloquent English-speaking Africans still seemed to Matthew an absurd propriety, disarming him oddly, like animals in clothes. He tugged at his collar uncomfortably.

"Er . . . well, Chief, we heard thee had joined up with the Catholics."

"Ah, the Catholics," Jahaliso's white teeth flashed as he smiled. "Even now I remember the fishhooks, safety pins, and little slates which, years ago, they used to so charmingly persuade us children to see their particular truths."

"Indeed?" Matthew drew back stiffly. He was sure of it now; the young man was mocking him, with sly, feigned innocence, throwing the notorious missionary patronization back in his face. He parried politely. "I trust they are still doing such good?"

The young chief burst into his bright booming laugh. "Perhaps they are. How should I know? I myself prefer the Mohommedees, who understand a man's need for several wives. Even as a strong bull is put to cover many cows, cannot you Christians see that a man must leave his seed in many women?"

"Er, that's debatable!" Matthew blushed, annoyed by the Boy's ganging-up amused grin. He mopped his brow with his handkerchief. Well, at least the chief was not embroiled in Catholicism; even if he was, by the sound of it, treading on far more dangerous ground, at least they could openly combat such overt evil without any guilty sense of stealing from other Christians. Matthew cleared his throat. "I must say, Chief, I am surprised. I should not have thought that a man of thy particular standing would choose his 'God' according to the particular 'benefits' it bestowed him."

"Then you do not know me, my dear professor. If you did, you would understand that the only thing that promises freedom of expression to our people is nationalism—the new religion of Africa."

6

In July, a ceremonial parade was held in Elizabethville to celebrate the second anniversary of Katanga's secession. The United States State Department denounced Tshombe, while U Thant arrogantly called him and his government "a bunch of clowns." Still, although now desperately tired and torn, the Katangan premier worked for conciliation, summoning the foreign consuls in Elizabethville to put forward yet another hopeful plan for peace. Matthew marveled at the poor man's untiring innocent belief in human nature. His greatest grief was that his own admired countrymen, the aspiring young President John Kennedy, had apparently failed to grasp Tshombe's true worth.

As he sat sadly speculating on the matter in his rondavel office, Matthew was rudely interrupted by an irate African man who waved a mechanical appliance in his face and demanded to see Orville Fotch.

"Mr. Fotch is busy teaching a class." Matthew eyed the man cautiously. "Perhaps I can help thee."

The man was so upset that it took Matthew some time to get any sense out of him. Then he could scarcely believe his ears. The man claimed to have been sold an appliance by Orville which did not work. Well, as the appliance, a pop-up toaster by the looks of it, was meant to be operated by electricity, Matthew was not the least surprised it did not work out here in these unwired wilds! What did surprise him was the claim that Orville had done the defrauding. Horrified and intrigued, Matthew questioned the man more closely. What emerged was a campaign of petty profiteering that shocked him completely. The man claimed to be only one in a long line of customers who had previously extracted full benefit from Orville's surreptitious sales. In the past, the missionary had apparently successfully hawked clothing, cutlery, and canned foodstuffs. The African's indignant revelation was so obviously honest that Matthew drew back, positively scorched by the frightful truth. Finally, uncertain and upset, he took charge of the offending toaster and dismissed the man after magnanimously guaranteeing the total reimbursal of its cost. For a long time he merely stared into the air, unable to believe it. For the accusation had crystalized in his mind, an old vague lingering suspicion that was terrible in its implications. He remembered the bulky, secretly shielded packages regularly received by the Fotches over the years; always the couple had evasively passed them off as being "presents" from home. But now Matthew began to wonder.

By the time he reached home late that afternoon, he had already reached an unhappy conclusion. Going into the dim little boxroom he rifled through the piles of innocent little Quaker monthly magazines, *The Friend*, beginning a scrupulous search, which was finally rewarded. Here and there over the years an innocuous-looking little advertisement had appeared in the personal column, asking all good givers to kindly contribute whatever goods or money might be spared for "the impoverished children of Central Africa," such goods to be addressed into the benevolent keeping of O.P. Fotch of Suseshi Mission, P.O. Mwinilunga, Northern Rhodesia. For a long time Matthew merely stared. The implications sickened him, and he stood impotently convulsed in a wretched torment. In his timid tenderheartedness he felt incapable of hurting another, even in the case of so obviously deserving a designate, who would defraud and befuddle ignorance and poverty for his own gross gain. The man, however, could not be allowed to continue such a disgraceful trade. Something had to be done. Without saying a word to anyone, Matthew went across to the Fotches' house.

He found Clara having a conversational tea with Ezra Peabody and some Bible students; she waved him vaguely through to find Orville, who, she intimated, might be encountered clearing excess baggage from the curtained alcove off the front porch in preparation for the imminent arrival of Orville's widowed mother and the son of his younger brother, who had both been recently recruited by the board. Matthew climbed a long propped ladder into the roof attic, to find Orville counting a dubious wealth in the light of a lantern. The sudden appearance of Matthew's head through the trapdoor made him start with fright; for several shocked moments, he hastily pushed a pile of goods behind himself, before finding the composure to frown with irritation.

"Matthew! *Thee startled me!* Whatever does thee want?"

But Matthew was not fooled by his innocent air; he had seen two identical pop-up toasters among the heap of clothing and gadgetry that Orville had so guiltily swept from the lamplight, and the man's avaricious nature he knew of old.

"Orville, I'd like a word with thee, please."

Grumbling impatiently, Orville followed Matthew down the ladder. He stared stupidly when Matthew handed him the brown paper packet containing the toaster. One glance at its contents stopped the muttering dead on his lips; he turned a sickly color and stared sullenly at Matthew, trying to disavow all knowledge of the thing. But Matthew was in no mood for shifty evasions. The whole thing sickened him, and he wanted it over and done with as soon as possible. Quickly, without emotion, without sparing either of them, Matthew told Orville what he knew. He demanded that Orville return the money he had fraudulently extracted for the toaster, that he reimburse any other persons similarly defrauded, and that he re-frain in the future from engaging in such shady transactions ever again.

Well, obviously not understanding the narrowness of his escape from re-call, Orville was hard to convince; evading Matthew's grave gaze, he protested his innocence and decried the devious deceit of men (doubtless the parent of some schoolchild he had failed) who would brand him with such a nonsensical fabrication. Wildly, he blustered and blamed, and Matthew was finally forced to silence him with the simple suggestion that they should ask the board to look into the matter. It was enough. Orville, spluttering that Matthew should not bother such an important body with such trivia, wrenched the toaster from his hands; promising gamely to see the man and dispel his delusion, he saw Matthew off. Well, Matthew direly doubted it would be a delusion so easily dispelled. He rather imagined that Orville would be compelled to buy back the toaster to hush up the issue. Whatever the case, when he heard no more from the defrauded African, he concluded with relief that justice, in the form of Orville's remuneration and repentance, had been served. He returned to his life sadder but wiser.

7

Several weeks after Chief Jahaliso's discharge from the hospital, a surprise visit from him caused another flurry of excitement among the missionaries. The tall young chief, peering shortsightedly through a thick pair of plus-10 spectacles, was on his way to the ophthalmologist at Kitwe Government Hospital to have his adjusting eyes tested and fitted with more accurate permanent lenses. He had brought the shank of an arrow-shot reedbuck for Dr. Profane, and since he ostensibly had no further business with the hospital, the elder ladies immediately jumped to excited conclusions. But as it happened, the chief's stop-off at Suseshi had less to do with a grate-ful conversion to Quakerism than with the enshrinement of Than Profane, as Matthew learned later that afternoon when he stopped off at the hospital's classroom complex, where the Boy was busy lecturing the medical students.

Than's sister, Jayne, was among the year's new students who sat in the front row; with Katherine and Matthew's careful coaching,

Jayne had successfully passed her O-level cambridge exam last year; she was now fit to begin a career. However, although young Tom had graduated to secondary school in Southern Rhodesia this year, Katherine still refused to have her only daughter venturing alone out into the world, and Jayne's life-long obsessive interest in medicine had secured her enrollment right here, in her brother's medical assistant course. Matthew watched the girl as he waited to talk with her brother; the only white girl among a class of all black males, she sat serenely composed, a straight-laced little Alice-in-Wonderland with a white pinafore over her candy-striped long lilac dress, lustrous long hair tied back, and pretty face rapt and attentive as her brother forcefully expounded, enthralling his audience with an arresting eloquence and his own ardent passion for medicine. When he had finished, he stepped outside with Matthew to confide privately the details of Jahaliso's visit.

"Well, it's like this, Matthew." He lit up a cigarette and inhaled. "That poor jasper is so pathetically grateful he wasn't blinded like either of his relatives that he wants to make me his blood brother."

"His *blood brother?*" Matthew stared at the Boy in stupefaction. The natives sometimes rewarded extraordinary friendships or services among themselves in such a manner, but Matthew had never heard of a white man being bestowed the dubious honor. He stared at the Boy cautiously. "Er . . . thee declined him politely, I trust?"

"I saw no reason to refuse," the Boy said mildly. "Furthermore, it'll give me an honored opportunity to set up a few out-clinics in his region."

"Thunderation, Boy! Blood brotherhoodship involves a blatantly pagan ceremony!" Matthew snapped severely. "In the interests of thy own reputation, not to say thy Christian soul, I strongly advise thee to forget the whole thing!"

Exasperated at the Boy's stubborn stance, he stalked angrily off. But in spite of himself, the more he thought about it, the more it intrigued him. He knew that the other missionaries would never understand, and he excused his own indecent interest on the grounds that Jahaliso's short hospital sojourn had hardly certified his Quaker conversion; (anyone who could so shamelessly weigh up religion according to the benefits personally offered him would doubtless use their medical facilities with little residual sense of obligation). Therefore, if they wished to make use of this fleeting fraternization to extend their evangelical and medical outreach into the Balovale, it was expedient that they reinforce contact with the chief while the

Boy's medical ministrations were yet recent enough to render the chief kindly disposed. Perhaps, Matthew mused as he walked absently home, if they were to swear the chief to secrecy and say nothing of the matter to their own colleagues, well, then . . .

8 On a carved wooden stool, in company with Jahaliso's elders, Matthew sat in the long yellow grass amid a sea of hundreds of seated natives. They watched while Than Profane and Chief Jahaliso, both bare-chested and seated cross-legged opposite each other on the ground, underwent *kasengo*, the gory ritual that would make the young doctor the chief's blood brother and heir apparent. Not a breath of air stirred out on the sun-baked savannah, and the oppressive stink of surrounding sweaty bodies made Matthew's nostrils twitch as he watched, wincing, while a ritually decorated witchdoctor made cuts on the joined hands of the white man and the black man, on the pits of their stomachs, their right cheeks and foreheads. The streaming blood was then captured with a blade of grass and stirred into two cups of maize beer. Waving away the drowsy flies, Matthew felt a squeamish nausea as the Boy calmly followed Jahaliso's example, draining the cup containing the other's blood. Then, while the unstemmed blood still dribbled on their faces, bellies, and hands, as tradition dictated, they solemnly warned each other of imminent danger known to them. (Jahaliso warned that *Njumwaice*'s prowess and popularity were fermenting ill-feeling against him among jealous witchdoctors, while Than Profane cited the rumor that the government might chastise Jahaliso by removing his chieftainship for so overtly indulging in nationalist politics). Then they exchanged gifts; the Boy gave the chief a gold-plated cigarette case and matching lighter, bowing his sun-streaked head while the chief formally adorned him with a necklace of lion's teeth and a fine kaross of silver jackal skins. From now on, whatsoever belonged to the one would belong also to the other, providing he was able to extract it. As an honorary chief, the Boy was to have at his disposal his own band of olimbo players and was at liberty to call upon the tribespeople for hunting, labor, or any other help.

Finally, it was done. The people leaped to their feet, and a great cheer arose as the chief stood up with his great amulet-adorned arms jubilantly raised. When he asked his assembled subjects to accept *Njumwaice* as his *mulangumu*, the crowd sank to a reverential curtsy and gave a soft double handclap. It was amidst this respectful acknowledgment that Matthew, noticing the sudden distraction of the foremost few, turned to see a group of white people briskly approaching along the path from the village. He squinted in surprise, his befuddlement turning to cold shock as he recognized the long dresses and made out the Fotches and Ezra Peabody, with the Cathcarts and the maiden ladies bringing up the rear. Well, he had known they were spending the Saturday evangelizing at nearby Eshalakali; doubtless getting wind of their excursion into Jahaliso's prized chiefdom, they had decided to cash in on the Boy's privileged accordance. The chief turned in surprised annoyance as, picking their way through the packed natives, the missionaries panted up, squinting bewilderedly at the crowd in the fierce October sun. Their eyes immediately fell on the white man who sat with his back to them in the center of the crowd. Even with his broad shoulders covered with the jackal-skin kaross, there could be no mistaking that streaky-blond head, and in the suffocating heat, Matthew felt decidedly faint as the Boy slowly stood up and turned to face fully the glowering group.

A barefoot savage in his raggedly denim bermudas, he looked positively pagan in the lion-tooth necklace and the jackal-skin cape, with his sweat-shiny deeply tanned face and body still horrifically red with his own dribbling blood. The little group gasped; sickened by the gory sight, Orville turned, clamping a hand over his mouth. But Clara very soon found her voice.

"Dr. Profane, what on earth is going on here? I believe thee owes us an explanation."

"No, ma'am, I don't believe I owe you anything," the Boy said solemnly through the smeared blood. His brilliant blue eyes flashed defiantly, and he gestured cordially. "Oh, I don't believe you've met my brother, Chief Jahaliso."

"*Thy brother?*" the group quailed in unison.

Then Ezra's eyes narrowed. "So that's it! Thee've been engaged in some pagan ritual joining thee in blood brotherhood with the chief! Well, I must say I am deeply shocked and surprised at thee, Dr. Profane!"

Then Hannah Rothchild spotted Matthew; there was no place to run, nowhere to hide, and he stood, wishing the ground would open and swallow him, miserably twisting his pith helmet in sweaty hands as his colleagues turned to castigate him with righteous wrath.

"No . . . no . . ." he struggled feebly, stumbling forward in anxious apology. "Thee has it all wrong! I can explain."

"Perhaps thee'd better!" Hannah barked furiously, her hard horseface screwed up with demented indignation. "We came out here innocently expecting to help thee decently preach the Christian Gospel, only to find . . ."

"SILENCE, MAMA!" Jahaliso boomed. He had been watching with outraged incredulity, and now, perhaps remembering the dry old spinster's prominent part in the humiliation of his syphillis-ridden brother, he regarded her with haughty disdain, frowning with annoyance. "You have intruded my domain and interrupted a sacred tribal ceremony! What is the meaning of this?"

Stunned by his wrath, (his blood-streaked black face looked positively fearsome!), the group stood stupefied for a moment; Ratchet Cathcart's bushy eyebrows shot up and down like busy caterpillars, and frizzy-haired little Cherish Sinclair, who daily rose and fell, a barometer to the prevailing mood of her fellows, started to whimper woefully. Then Ezra drew himself up pompously.

"It's quite simple, Chief. We have come to preach the Christian Gospel."

"My people have no need of your Christian Gospel!" Jahaliso snapped. "I ask you to leave now!"

"Now see here," Ezra objected, waving off a bothersome fly. "Thee has no right to deny us! This is a free country. It is for thy people to decide whether they would hear us or not."

After a moment, Jahaliso nodded abruptly. He turned to face his people; his grim sweat-oiled blood-dribbled black face looked coldly brutal as he called across the sea of black heads.

"ANY OF YOU PEOPLE WHO WOULD HEAR THE WORDS OF THE CHRISTIANS WILL NOW SPEAK OUT!"

Ezra nodded righteously. But in a moment his confidence dissolved. For as the people rose to their feet and pressed forward in a hum of discussion to stare curiously at them, their faces were sneering and sullen; many were scarred with the old tribal cicatrices, their sun-squinting grimaces showing filed teeth uncomfortably reminiscent of the barbaric Balubas. Also, Jahaliso and many of his people were known to be blatant supporters of the reputedly vicious and anti-white UNIP nationalist party. And perhaps the recent propaganda put out by the opposing parties to discredit UNIP in the wake of the elections, citing its record of criminal brutality, had impressed the missionaries, for Matthew saw that they shifted uneasily in the surly silence. But the indomitable Hannah Rothchild would not be intimidated.

"Very well," she said acidly. "But if we are being asked to leave, what about *him*?" She pointed a bony betraying finger, and all eyes went to Than Profane.

The tall tanned young man turned and faced his adversaries with a magnificent majesty which far outdid his ludicrous dress.

"Yeah," he said softly. "What about me?"

"*He too is a Christian!*" Ezra burst out, conveniently contradicting his own oft-hinted belief in the opposite. "As a missionary, it is also his duty to convert thy people to Christianity! He *too* is one of us!"

There was a terrible silence. Then Jahaliso slowly turned to face the young white doctor, his oddly enlarged bespectacled eyes blank in an expressionless black face.

"Is this true, *Njumwaice*?" he said quietly. "Do you speak for these people?" In the stretching silence, with Matthew's entire career hanging on his reply, Than Profane said carefully,

"Chief, I guess a man can only ever speak for himself."

The missionaries drew back, outraged. And Matthew winced, waiting for it.

"*So!*" Ezra charged mightily, flapping his leatherbound Bible at the Boy, his chubby face pious with a look of grievous injury. "At last we see thy true colors, Friend! Thee would side with these heathens against thine own brethren!"

"*I said* I speak for myself." The Boy's blue eyes were uncaringly cold, and Jahaliso nodded with satisfaction.

"Then it is good." He waved his carved staff at the other missionaries. "My brother *Njumwaice* is welcome among us. But you others must go! We want no Christian indoctrination here!"

But the little group stood all bloated with air and outrage that had to be let out. Overriding Matthew's anxious attempts to intercede for them, they babbled indignantly, accosting the chief in a clamoring chorus. But Jahaliso was no vacillating Sakapuchi who could be browbeaten into submission. The missionaries' voices trailed uneasily as he turned contemptfully and heatedly conversed with an attendant witchdoctor.

"This man will exorcise our unwanted guests," he announced grimly. Then the *ngaka*, horrifically decorated with stripes of red ocher and white clay, clad in a bark-strip kilt, animal skins, beads and feathers, and wearing the vacant-eyed head of a maned lion-skin upon his woolly black skull, began a curious wailing, accompanied by a high-kicking dance that rattled the seed pods around his ankles and sent up puffs of red dust from the hard earth. Clutching a zebra-tail fly switch, he began to advance upon the huddled missionaries with his ritually decorated *gano*, or ceremonial spear, pointed menacingly in their direction. Cherish let out a terrified screech and turned to flee; she collided with her dumbfounded fellows, and there was a confused flurry as the witchdoctor shook his fly switch mockingly in their fearful faces. Still feigning alarmingly with his spear, he took a step forward for every one the missionaries bumbled back. Finally, abruptly abandoning their martyred stand, they turned tail and fled. Followed by the jeering laughter of the crowd, they ran gasping, furious and frightened, their dignity in shreds, disappearing down the path to the village, while Matthew, stunned witless, stared stupidly after them.

9

Later, when Than finally got in from Jahaliso's village with Matthew, it was already dark. As he trudged wearily up the garden path, carrying the jackal kaross and his medical bag, he spotted Jayne in her white nightgown, waiting for him up her favorite frangipani tree.

"Jaynie?" He shook his head bemusedly. "Didn't anybody ever tell you? Refined young ladies don't climb trees. One of these days you're going to grow a tail."

"Oh I will not!" She pouted at him through the moon-dappled branches. "Only monkeys have tails."

"And you think you're human?" He raised a disbelieving eyebrow.

"Oh hush, thee!" Giggling, she leaped at him straight from the bough; they fell on the ground, wrestling in a heap. "Ouch!" Jayne squealed. "Thee cracked my fibula!"

Having grown up perusing medical tomes for light reading matter, her quaint speech was appealingly peppered with such formal medical terminology. She never had a headache, but a pain in her cranium; her menstrual cramps were, more properly, dysmenorrhea. A regular little Florence Nightingale, she was doing exceptionally well in Than's medical-assistant course, and he loved her dearly. They were playfully entangled, laughing helplessly, when an outraged gasp alerted them to the formidable specter of Hannah Rothchild standing on the pathway, looking shocked and forbidding in the light from the house.

"*Miss Rothchild!*" Jayne sat up abruptly, disentangling herself. She straightened her nightgown to cover her long bare legs, mumbling with embarrassment, "I—I was just . . . saying hello to my brother."

"Indeed?" Hannah said stiffly, her arms, in their leg-of-mutton sleeves, rigidly akimbo.

"Yes . . ." Seared by the old maid's palpable disapproval, Jayne shook Than's shoulder. "Say hello to Miss Rothchild!"

Lying sprawled on the cool grass amid the scrambled kaross and his medical bag, Than raised himself up on an elbow; he spread a casual hand. "Howdy, ma'am. Nice weather we're having."

Hannah's nostrils flared threateningly, and for an ugly moment the prickly silence held them all transfixed. Then Katherine came out of the house. Coming down the veranda steps, skirts trailing, she seemed to assess the situation.

"Hannah!" she blurted. Then: "Oh, Than, Jayne, for goodness' sakes! Jayne, get thee inside this minute. I declare! Waylaying thy brother like that!"

Holding up her long nightgown, Jayne scampered obediently indoors, and Katherine turned apologetically to Hannah. "She just monopolizes her brother so! Why, he hasn't even had a chance to take supper yet. He's just got in from the bush."

"Oh, I am very well aware of that, Friend," Hannah snapped caustically. "In fact I have come to inform thee of a meeting the staff is holding this very night to . . . to *chastize one of our members* for the most disgraceful and grievous lapse of Christian propriety!"

She turned haughtily and affixed Than with such a scathing stare that he felt moved to retaliate. Chewing on a weed stem, he thoughtfully fingered the lion-claw necklace that encircled his throat.

"Miss Rothchild," he said, dimpling audaciously. "You seen any good witchdoctors lately?"

"*Oooooh!*" With an outraged cry, Hannah picked up her skirts, turned on the path, and strode away. The old gate creaked and they heard her furious snorting down the length of the cherry-pie hedge as she dissolved into the night.

* * *

Matthew knew all about the meeting when the Fotches, the Cathcarts, Ezra Peabody, and the maiden ladies arrived to convene it at his house. As he sat trying to swallow a heated plateful of dried-up supper, they came hurrying up his path, flush-cheeked with the sensation of sin, bursting with an outrage that was too hot to hold till morning. Crowding into his parlor, they accused Matthew of condoning Than Profane's disreputable actions and sat sumptuously pulling the pair of them to pieces like roast pork on a spit.

"Now see here!" Matthew broke in fretfully. For what they implied, without so many indelicate words, was as much as heresy! "Thee're all mistaken! There is nothing contrary to Quaker conscience in the Boy becoming the chief's blood brother. It is merely a social tie, quite devoid of religious significance! And as for myself, well, as a historian, I felt it my duty to record . . ." He saw their faces and hurried on. "Oh, to be sure, I regret thy ordeal today! And I made it my business to tell the chief as much. But that was none of Dr. Profane's doing! Oh I'll admit, in some ways he's a rascal to be sure . . . but . . ."

"That he most certainly is!" Hannah rasped. "And what I saw tonight most thoroughly confirms it!" Her narrow-set small eyes grew shifty and she lowered her voice to a sinister sibilence, looking around to greedily measure the shocked faces. "*It was he and his sister; the pair of them . . . lying together upon the ground!*"

There were scandalized gasps, and Hannah crowed triumphantly, "Lacking his wife, he now corrupts his own sister!"

"Hannah!" Face monstrous with indignation, Matthew rose from his seat like a jack-in-the-box. "*That is unfair!*"

"Well, it's true!" Hannah raised her jaw defiantly. "And that . . . that *sickening* display, coupled with the disgraceful events at Jahaliso's village today, must prove to us once and for all just what kind of a black sheep we are harboring in our midst! Why, to lay upon the ground with a member of the opposite gender! And him having grown up apart from that impressionable child!"

"Now see here!" Matthew struggled again. But his words floundered feebly in the backwashing tide of so many derisive eyes, against steeled hearts and made-up minds, against a company that still smarted from humiliations endured earlier in the day. They went on to cite the long list of the Boy's trespasses. But whatever the validity of their other accusations, Matthew refused to believe the hint of incest. He knew that the affectionate sporting of which Hannah spoke was merely an expression of the Boy's warm-blooded

418

nature. Matthew had personally observed him caress his wife, cuddle Jayne, and pay sedate court to his stepmother. And he had this way of kissing in passing, that hungry sensual mouth seeming always avid to fasten on to some lush female thing! Although Matthew had no doubt it was mostly in fun, his defiant derisive way of taking such personal liberties in full view of all had raised shocked brows and given the elder missionaries more perverse entertainment than they had enjoyed in years.

And yet, conversely, while he warmed to the touch of his female kin, the Boy spun from any casual male touch, as though contaminated. Ezra, always exuberant and gushing, had very soon found this out. He had a compulsive way of slapping backs and patting shoulders; in patronization and piety, he grew grabby as a child. Just once he had laid his hands on Than Profane, and then the Boy froze where he stood, holding still under sufferance, his face growing wracked as the clamp of those chubby hands sent him into a quivering seethe; Matthew had seen the blue eyes turn sulphurous and the soft mouth set hard. "Ezra," he had said in a voice deceptively soft, dangerous in its very control. "Get your hands off me." But Ezra, embarrassed, had loftily continued his conversation, still gently patting, until, shuddering unendurably, the Boy shook off the plump paw, spitting venomously: *"Don't touch me, goddammit."* After that impassioned command, Ezra had needed no further reminder. These days he kept his hands at bay and walked a three-foot ring around the Boy. Maybe they all did. But that didn't stop them from using missiles more underhanded and telling than patronization. It was wounded pride most of them suffered from. And Than Profane, serenely successful, rebellious and proud, was a fitting scapegoat for most of their failures.

But there was no way that Matthew could make these people see this now. Pushed finally too far, they were ripe for revenge, and the most he could do was to try to moderate their mood. And Teller, equally alarmed, tried to soften with solicitude, scurrying around offering comfy chairs and cups of tea. She had wheeled out the cup-laden tea trolley by the time Than Profane arrived with Katherine. Their arrival set off a deathly hush, and Katherine looked worried and stricken as the pair sat down in stony silence. Jenny, measuring with her hands in the ingenious way of the blind, prepared and poured the tea. Teller passed around the cups and set out the sugar bowl, trying to warm the chilly atmosphere with inconsequential chatter. But Matthew, for one, was so sick and distracted that it was not until he put his cup to his mouth that he noticed the anemic pallor of its contents; then he realized at once that poor Jenny, obviously likewise distracted and upset, had forgotten to spoon the tea-leaves into the hot water. But if he might have happily swallowed the watery milk to protect the young blind girl's feelings, Orville Fotch had no such compassion.

"*Yech!*" He pulled a face, whining in disgust, "Is somebody trying to poison me? *This is not tea!*"

In the horrified silence, Jenny, realizing her mistake, burst into embarrassed tears; she leaped from her seat, knocking over the umbrella stand and blundering into the half-closed door in her haste to escape from the room. Teller rushed to help her out, but Orville was unperturbed. In sneering silence, he and his league rose to haughtily replace their cups. And it was their unkind coldness that finally fully evoked Matthew's ire. Judge the Boy they might, but this cruel humiliation of Jenny was an unnecessary last straw. And that supercilious Orville, pretending a spotless piety that was nothing more than a hypocritical facade! Thinking upon it, Matthew felt a steely resolution straighten his spine with new angry strength. And secure in the sudden realization of his power, he bided his time, hearing out the committee's searing complaints in calm insulation (after all the Boy might even profit from a little castigation!). He waited while the Boy sat grimly silent, and Katherine, Grace, and Teller, hushed in white-faced consternation, until finally Orville pompously proposed informing the board of the doctor's "*outrageous acts of barbaric heresy!*" Then Matthew rose.

"I don't believe thee'll do that, Orville," he meaningfully intoned.

"Oh?" Orville smirked like a boastful child. "And just why not?"

"Well, for a start," Matthew said quietly. "I beg thee to consider that we *all* make our mistakes."

But Orville, thick-skinned as a rhinoceros, was hard to inform.

"Mistakes!" the man hooted. "Why, these were deliberate misdemeanors. A slap in the face to the Society of Friends!"

"Well then." Matthew said, clearing his throat, (even now merciful, he hoped to spare the man a more explicit disclosure), "let me put it this way. I'll give it to thee in one word. That is: *toaster!*"

"*Toaster?*" The entire company stared at Matthew as if he were mad; Hannah and Ezra began to babble as much, but Orville froze somewhat. He mumbled evasively, "I . . . er . . . have no idea what thee means . . ."

"Haven't thee, now? Well, let me elaborate." Matthew eyed the man shrewdly. He lowered his voice and, leaning forward, said definitively, "*Pop-up* toaster!"

"Pop-up toaster!" Hannah howled gleefully, leaping from her seat, slapping her knee. "Doggone it! Always suspected thee were mad. Now I know it! See how thy dalliance with the devil has affected thee—thee cannot even think with sanity!"

Grinning dementedly, she and Ezra turned to the Fotches; but the support they expected never materialized. Clara's face had taken on a closed evasive look, and Orville was sweating, looking decidedly sick.

"It's . . . it's my heartburn." He rubbed frantically at his plump chest. "I—it's particular bad; feels like I can scarcely breathe! G-guess I'd better hurry on home and take some *muti*!"

"Yeah? Sounds like an acute case of pop-up heartburn to me." Than Profane mused drolly. But the Fotches, making panicked preparations to leave, were not amused. As they stood up, their colleagues stared at them in puzzled astonishment.

"Er . . . we'd best discuss this some other time," Orville blustered back at them as he hurried out of the door after his disappearing wife. *"I feel pretty deathly!"*

The meeting broke up directly. The Boy's friends wandered away looking bemused; Ezra, the Cathcarts, and the maiden ladies stumbled off with mortified, befuddled faces. Aside from Matthew's own household, only the Boy and Katherine remained. She and Teller coaxed the red-eyed Jenny from her room. Katherine came out crooning, carrying little Luke in her arms; the solemn little blond baby, who had recently turned a year old, was still the apple of Matthew's eye. But tonight, intent on discretion, he left the ladies fussing over the shy toddler while they cleared away the tea things and went out onto the dark veranda. But very shortly the Boy followed him out. He leaned against the doorframe, measuring Matthew with a canny little smile.

"Samunyati, you old rogue!" He shook his head with amused admiration. "What's all this toaster nonsense about? Some kind of occult cant to silence Orville?"

"Oh never thee mind about that," Matthew sniffed. "Let us just say I have my ways and means, quaint at times though they may seem . . ."

10

Thankfully Matthew heard no more from the Committee on the matter of Than Profane's blood brotherhood. How the Fotches managed to justify their sudden change of heart to their colleagues Matthew never heard, but the abortive meeting was followed by a deafening silence on the issue. Orville, however, was not without his petty revenge, and Matthew came home the following day to find his water switched off. Since Orville was the jealous keeper of the generator and the pump house who in the past had proved himself particularly fond of venting his spite in so unmajestic a manner, Matthew knew just whom to turn to. He strode over to the Fotches' house to learn that Orville was mysteriously "busy" somewhere. Suspecting him lurking guiltily behind the door of an adjacent bedroom, Matthew ominously warned the haughty Clara that upon her husband's return, he should take immediate steps to resume the water flow to Matthew's house or else he, Matthew, might feel compelled to take steps of another kind. And although he never seriously intended such action, the veiled threat worked. Matthew returned home shortly to find a steady stream of river water spurting from his faucet. Well, Orville's dishonesty had at least provided him with a way of controlling the man, he wryly reflected.

But others were more devious; denied the chastisement of Than Profane, Ezra Peabody tried to upstage him. Talking loftily of rallying new converts for the Lord, the man, resplendent in his best dove-gray suit, hat, and gloves, trailing Clara Fotch and an awed auxiliary of Bible students, went out to rout and reform the "heathens" in the surrounding villages. Their grand crusade ended ignominiously later in the day, when Ezra, doubtless piqued when his eloquent evangelizing evoked none of the idolization enjoyed by Than Profane, petulantly overturned a forty-four gallon drum of kaffir beer that was competing for the natives' attention. The mission party arrived back at Suseshi shortly afterward, looking somewhat harried. In time they were followed by the wronged natives, who had been joined by inhabitants of the villages en route, forming a vociferous crowd that flooded, on bicycles and on foot, onto the school football field. When Matthew went out to remonstrate with them, they demanded Ezra's blood and an outrageous remuneration for the spoiled beer. Ezra, shaken but all puffed up with pride and piety, churlishly insisted that they be denied any such satisfaction, claiming haughtily that a mission of God would not deign to pay for the "Devil's doings"! When the position began to look impossible, with no side willing to back down, Matthew hurriedly radioed the district commissioner at Mwinilunga.

By the time D. C. Horn and his small force of black district messengers arrived with Chief Kadesha and his two *Kapasus* (rural policemen), the mob had swelled to almost two hundred, rhythmically shouting *"Kwacha "* (freedom) and hoisting crude signs which screamed in scrawled charcoal: GO HOME WHITES! WE WANT SELF-GOVERNMENT NOW! and CONGRESS FOR POWER! What had begun as a civil disturbance had quickly blown up into a political demonstration. And the furor was such that the mission came to a standstill, the missionaries adjourning classes and abandoning their labors to stand fearfully huddled on the outskirts of the field.

The district messengers, immaculate in their red-bordered navy-blue tunicked shorts and tassled red fezzes, spilled off the truck that had transported them and fell into military marching formation. They stood stoic-faced before the fearsome gesticulating crowd while first the chief then D. C. Horn, that stern and kindly little man who had been known to weep for the tragedies of these, his chosen people, tried to reason with them. When neither was able to calm the crowd, Matthew felt the old Congo terror begin to tingle in his veins. By now Ezra's hasty agreement to pay the outrageous remuneration demanded was met with defiance; now nothing would do but that they be recompensed with another barrel of the same beer. Since this commodity was obviously impossible for a temperate Quaker mission to obtain summarily, Matthew understood at last that these people did not wish compensation. No indeed, this display was a palpable manifestation of the nationalist fever that was disrupting the country all around them. After all their years of selfless service, it seemed they were to become scapegoats for the venting of centuries old racial resentments.

When the mob began stoning the adjacent classrooms, smashing the windows, D. C. Horn read the riot act through a megaphone, ordering the people to disperse in the name of the queen. When his order was ignored amid a roar of abuse, the commissioner detailed two of his sturdiest messengers to arrest the ringleaders. When others in the crowd began to grapple with the men, impeding their progress, he ordered his small force to charge the crowd. Thus, armed with nothing more than batons and the ethos of the old order, the brave band of less than twenty black men, some of whom had nothing more than graying temples to show for up to twenty years of sterling government service, fearlessly faced the crazed mob. It took three such concerted charges before the mob finaly began to break up and disperse, but eventually they did it, the small contingent of men wielding the mighty mystique of the boma against a voracious crowd which might easily have overwhelmed them.

When the dregs had finally dissolved into the dimming dusk light, Matthew stood with his colleagues, shivering and shocked on the edge of the deserted mud-churned field. Even more incredible than Ezra's stupidity was the numbing realization that familiar faces and former Friends had numbered amongst the mob. He finally saw that after their years of unchallenged supremacy, the mission was no longer the omnipotent edifice it had once been to the natives. No indeed. Their privileged position had been usurped; the natives were now looking to the nationalists for guidance and direction.

11 After operating half the night on a seriously ill man with a ruptured urethra, Than was lying exhausted on his bed in the festering heat one Saturday afternoon when he felt a sudden cool touch on his bare back. Rising up with a jerk, he stared, utterly surprised to find Jenny's small blond baby at his bedside, dressed in nothing more than a diaper, gazing placidly at him with brilliant blue eyes.

"Oh Jesus," Than said softly. The baby's eyes flickered, and he made a possessive grasp at the silver pendant that swung on a chain around Than's neck.

"Uh uh," Than admonished gently, unfastening the little soft hands. Still staring wildly at the solemn child, he slid off the bed and backed to the open door. His eyes fused with the baby's placid blue gaze. Unable to let go, he called out: "Kathy! I've got a baby in here!"

"Well, for goodness' sake; there he is!" Katherine appeared in the doorway, looking relieved. "I just missed him this instant, and I thought he might have tried the stairs!"

"You're looking after him?" Than said warily.

"Why, yes." She smiled. "Isn't he sweet? Jenny's busy with her weekend Braille class and his nanny's got the flu. I've been busy mending and he wandered off when I wasn't looking. I'll take him back."

"No!" Than stopped her, surprising himself. He saw the look on her face and tried to smile. "It's all right. I'll play with him a while."

"Well . . . if thee're sure thee want to . . ."

"I'm sure."

When she was gone, Than closed the door carefully and simply stared. The baby, seeming as fascinated as he, stared back. In the close dimness of the bedroom, they gazed at each other, spellbound. The tall little child stood emblazoned by the daylight that flooded through the opened french doors off the balcony; his fair soft hair was a haze of sunshine, and he stood solemnly unmoving while Than slowly advanced. Feeling his heart beating crazily inside his chest, Than crouched on the floor before the small boy and with a deliberate effort contrived a smile. The baby smiled back. And a catastrophic explosion occurred in Than's heart. It left him bleeding internally and in shreds.

"Oh my God." Than merely stared, dumbfounded and doomed. For, conceived in a chicken coop, of a blind mother, the fair solemn little child had the face of an angel. His smile was pure bliss. Than stared at the child through a radiance of brimming tears that never would fall.

"Hello, Luke," he said softly. Then he took the child in his arms, and with his eyes tightly shut, fiercely embraced him. The baby's diaper was half falling off, ammoniac-smelling and heavy-wet with urine, and Than ripped the garment off and tumbled the baby naked onto his bed. Then, with a face as solemn as the child's, he took off his pendant and, in a grave, ceremonial gesture, placed it around the neck of his baby son. The pendant reached to the bed on a surplus of chain and lay against the baby's genitals. Luke gazed interestedly down his puffed cheeks and turned the silver disc in small explor-atory hands.

"Oh God . . ." In a rush of tenderness, Than pushed the child over and crawled up beside him on the bed, holding the soft plump form reverently in his aching arms. And lying there in the stagnating heat, in a mindless heady spasm of wonder, his hands spread and touched the perfect wholeness that was his firstborn son. With an anguished joy he moved his trembling fingers over the soft-lashed eyes, the tilted nose, and the smooth pink cheeks. He gently explored the fat dimpled buttocks, the sturdy long legs and arms, hands and feet, and he tugged at the tiny penis and smiled in a surge of absurd male pride. Feeling the rhythmic jerk of the child's heart against his chest, he pressed his mouth against the softly downed head, his nostrils filling with the warm milky smell. Lying there with the child quiet and contented in his arms in the stifling atmosphere, he fell into a somnolent daze of pain and bliss. Bliss became abyss. And when Jayne found them later, they were both fast asleep.

"Well, good afternoon to thee!"

The next thing Than knew he was staring into his sister's clear gray eyes. It was late, the day had gone dim, and he was drenched in sweat and urine, worried by a drowsily droning fly, the baby stirring in his arms. He struggled up on the bed, shaking his head to clear it.

"Well, I never saw a picture so sweet!" Jayne was smiling. She had brought him a cool drink, which she set down on the bedside cupboard. "Thee and little Luke fast asleep together. Why, thee looked so alike, so sweetly aslumber, it quite took my breath away!"

Than snapped up his head and stared at his sister in a sick panic. *Out of the mouths of babes and angels . . .* He rolled quickly off the bed and stood up, his jeans damp with a patch of seeped urine, his bare sweat-sheened back turned toward her.

"Take him away," he growled softly.

She was silent for a moment, seeming surprised. Then she picked up the naked baby.

"All right," she said sweetly. "Just as thee wants."

"He wet my bed," Than said defensively.

"Yes. I guess he's a real bad little boy."

She smiled quizzically up at him as he turned and stared back at her, charmed and exasperated by the picture she in turn made, holding the little blue-eyed wonder in her arms. They too looked so alike that the resemblance filled him with fright and pain. She looked more his mother than Jenny herself.

"Take him away!" he repeated gruffly, turning away again. He relaxed abruptly when he heard the door close behind her. Then he groaned. *Take him away. He has wet my bed, invaded my life, and broken my heart. . . .*

12

On October 30, Northern Rhodesia went to the polls under its new constitution. The voting climaxed the most strenuous registration and election campaigns the country had ever known, enrolling nearly twenty times as many voters as had been enfranchised by the 1959 constitution. Although the schools were closed, the day at the mission was rather harassing with relays of workers taking time off to be ferried to and from the boma at Mwinilunga to vote. To make matters worse, Orville's mother and nephew were due to arrive by chartered aircraft at the Mwinilunga airstrip in the afternoon, and Orville continually interrupted intense political discourses to speculate excitedly on this event. Not that anyone gave him much notice. Aside from the hospital staff, whose work never ceased, most of the missionaries congregated at the dining *Chitenje* to dissect the crucial situation and the ponderables at stake in this cardinal election. And there was much to ponder. While the predominantly white United Federal Party had begun to praise its old enemy, Congress, as being the lesser of two evils, holding it up as the epitome of black moderation and a party with which it might be possible to conciliate, it put out thousands of leaflets warning voters of UNIP's record of vicious intimidatory murder, arson, and assalt. The white Liberals in the meanwhile had also abandoned UNIP, denouncing its extremism. And UNIP, left to its own devices, had gone all out to capture the needed white votes; its leader, Kenneth Kaunda, had canvassed Europeans at special meetings and cocktail parties around the country, promoting the doctrine *Look to the Future and Unite!*, projecting a harmonious multiracial image by having its few white candidates campaign with blacks.

Now, on voting day, acacia-seed pods cracked in the suffocating heat and the bush roads were lined with blacks walking or cycling to or from the boma, where they recorded their votes. The vast majority went to the polls for the first time; special personnel had been detailed to instruct objectively befuddled illiterates, assuring them of the strict secrecy of their choice to counteract the intimidations of the nationalist campaigners.

The day passed in searing heat and a strange silence. To Matthew it was a vexing interruption when Tallulah Fotch and her grandson arrived from the Mwinilunga airstrip. He knew Orville's mother of old. Over the years, the widow had wafted between Africa and Idaho, completing several tours of duty at Suseshi. A large fat woman who looked little short of ludicrous in traditional Quaker dress, she was unfortunately fond of loud and outlandish poke bonnets, and now as she waddled to the *chitenje* to greet the missionaries, her prohibitive bulk, swaddled in long skirts, put Matthew unkindly in mind of an elephant entangled in a circus tent. The woman's grandson he found equally as unendearing. Fauntleroy Fotch was a big strong strapping boy of nineteen or twenty, prone to chubbiness, with a spoiled, girlish mouth and a thatch of wheat-brown hair over a short forehead, which gave him a dull Neanderthal appearance. In a gawdy Hawaiian shirt, he chewed gum sloppily as he shook the missionaries' hands with a huge sweaty paw.

Tallulah had not changed. She seemed annoyed to find her arrival upstaged by the national elections and did her damnedest to steal the limelight, interrupting their speculative discussions with personal anecdotes, all delivered in her monotonous nasal whine. When she found no one but Orville listening much, she joined in the political discourse and proceeded to dominate the conversation, discussing aspects she could know little about. When she discovered Matthew's tolerance for the Congress Party and his personal respect and sympathy for the UNIP leader, Kaunda, she was on home ground amongst friends. Clara and Hannah joined her vindictive onslaught on his views, carping so continuously that Matthew finally left them in disgust.

From late that night through to the next day, he dogged his radio as the results began to come in. By evening it was obvious that the Liberals had been obliterated and that no one party was likely to win a clear majority. By November 3, when all the results were in, the United Federal Party had won fifteen seats, Congress five and UNIP fourteen. The question now was: would Congress honor its pact and unite with the federationists to form a government? Or would the old racial resentments and the unanimous African abhorrence of Federation finally prove insurmountable? In a deathly pent hush, the nation waited and wondered. After the amazing results of the election in Barotseland, it seemed to Matthew that anything could happen. There, apparently even UNIP was patently surprised at the outright victories of its three candidates. But if Benedict Poe was stunned, Matthew sadly saw the defeat of the tribal conservatives as a measure of the people's growing resentment in their *Litunga* and his antiquated totalitarian rule.

Throughout November it became increasingly apparent to the missionaries that Congress's hinted "pact" with the federationalists was by no means guaranteed. In fact, true to Matthew's dire predictions, the moderate nationalist party, suddenly finding itself holding vital national seats that could give either the UFP or UNIP the necessary majority to form a government, began playing "hard to get" as each side desperately competed to lure its allegiance. The national newspaper, *The Northern News*, succinctly summed up the situation with a cartoon depicting the Congress leader, Nkumbula, dressed in a wedding dress, being courted on either side by the kneeling suitors Kaunda and John Roberts, the local Northern Rhodesian UFP leader. It was anybody's guess whom Congress would align with in the end. Most of the missionaries spent their mealtimes endlessly speculating on the suspenseful jockeying for power. Matthew had grown averse to offering his views, since his theories were usually immediately shot down by the argumentative Tallulah Fotch, whose opinions seemed automaticaly opposed to his.

In fact, the minute she discovered Matthew's sympathy for the beleaguered Katangese president, Moise Tshombe, she proceeded verbally to demolish the man at every opportunity, showing her susceptibility to the propaganda of the popular American press when she loudly lauded the United Nations secretary-general's latest plan for Katanga. With obviously little knowledge of Tshombe other than what she had read in brief biased articles, she sneered that the man had only accepted the plan to save face, and further, that it was the man's incompetence, and not American interference (as Matthew argued), that had resulted in the open war now raging in north Katanga. The woman's views were consistently stereotyped and so devoid of justification and obviously contrived to bait him that Matthew finally refrained from discussing politics in her presence.

And her grandson he found equally exasperating. Matthew's innocent assumption that the youth had come out to Africa to volunteer his evangelical services was quickly dispelled. Leroy seemed bored in meeting, and outside of it he was loud-mouthed, uncouth, and lecherous; he burped at table, slopped his food, and openly ogled Jayne Profane. He had formed an instant affinity with the sly Sidney, who had finished his education and now remained slothfully at home, parasitically living off his parents with no other career apparently in sight. And while Sidney by himself had at least remained unobstrusive, the youth now took courage from his cousin's company. The pair together quickly became a perpetual nuisance, interfering in the lives and legitimate labors of others. Since Leroy's only practical asset turned out to be an ability to drive, Matthew was at a loss to understand his recruitment in the first place. It was some days before he heard from Teller, who had heard it from Hannah, who had filtered the facts from Clara, that Tallulah had persuaded the board to take on the young man to get him away from "bad company" back home in the States. Well, the kind of sterling references that must have prompted such an unpractical recruitment were as clearly misplaced as the widow's palpable adoration of the loutish youth.

His first apportioned task—that of driving Than Profane to his out-clinics (thus leaving the doctor fresh and free to tend any patients ambulanced back to Suseshi)—ended when Chief Kadesha bitterly complained that Leroy had tried to "touch" some native girls bathing naked in a river. The Boy was furious and disgusted. He warned Leroy specifically off his sister and refused to have the lewd youth accompany him again. And since he had taken so long to cultivate his clinics and harmonious relations with the people, Matthew hardly blamed him. By now Molly Dibb had left Suseshi to take care of the lepers and the sick at Eshalakali Hill. Since she was a capable nurse and quickly learned to cope, there was no longer need for Than Profane to make the trip to the little mission so often. He informed Jenny at table one evening that Leroy would in the future ferry her to the Hill for her weekly Braille classes. And if that at least gave Leroy some justification for receiving his salary, Jenny hardly seemed pleased. Matthew was struck by her stricken look, but the Boy seemed oblivious that their weekly trips together had come to mean so much to her.

The first time that Leroy took her to Eshalakali, Matthew accompanied them to show Leroy the way. While Jenny conducted her Braille class in the little church, Matthew went to talk with the Townsends. A while later he walked down to the leper colony to see how Molly Dibb was coping with her new work. He strode hurriedly past the line of lepers to find Leroy inside the little clinic hut lolling on a chair, hands behind his head and crossed feet up on the examination couch.

"Say, who would have thought they would assign such gorgeous dames as you to nurse lepers out in these backwoods. What a waste!" he quipped.

The thin plain English girl, obviously unused to such attention, blushed and cooed coyly back, "Oh, I imagine thee says that to all the girls!"

Embarrassed at having unwittingly eavesdropped such personal asides, Matthew quickly backtracked. After heralding his approach with a loudly cleared throat, he reentered the little hut to find Molly Dibb studiously tidying a shelf while Leroy was properly seated, his spoiled mouth girlishly prim, looking pious as a haloed angel as he stared serenely off into space.

13

On Thanksgiving Day in November, after the long unrelenting months of heat and drought, the accumulating clouds blackened and blotted out the sun. As the day darkened and the sweet scent of rain suffused the hot air, an irrepressible restlessness arose in Than, and he abandoned his stuffy little consulting office and the long lines of waiting patients, stumbling off the veranda and across the straw-grassed hospital yard. On the knoll of the slope, he pulled off his white jacket and lay back in the long grass, smoking and staring up at the cool cloud-swirling dark sky, feeling indescribably lonely, aching with a vague yearning he could not quite fathom.

Suzannah had been away from him for over seven months now. His last brief letter from her, a good three months ago, had been bubbling impatiently with news of diplomatic parties and the high life of Salisbury. Well, she was a willful girl; if she wanted to socialize, escorted by the embassy staff, there wasn't a thing he could do about it at this distance. His own reply to her had been relatively simple: *Just for God's sake keep your legs crossed!* Whether she took his advice or not had been a source of some worry to him. But over the months he had grown accustomed to the separation and immune to the hurt. The worst part was that he felt he hardly cared anymore. But while he might no longer miss her, he had never ceased to need the solace of her body. He was a red-blooded healthy male, and he had begun to fear that the prolonged repression of his natural sexual libido would give him a psychoneurosis.

As he lay on his back, his mind floated like a cloud. His forehead was burning like fire and, faintly emanating from the school across the river, he heard children singing in English Matthew Tomlinson's favorite old classic: "Shenandoah."

> *Oh, Shenandoah, I long to hear you,*
> *Go away, you rolling river . . .*

The words filled him with a nostalgia as searing as pain, and as thunder rumbled awesomely, echoing across the skies, the first welcome drops came spattering down, smacking into the dry hard-baked earth. He flared his nostrils and drew in the delicious fragrance, lying blinking beneath the rapidly increasing raindrops, which pelted into the hollows of his eyes, his mouth and ears, running cool and sweet all across his hot bare torso, finally fizzling out his cigarette.

And then there was Jenny; he couldn't think of her without anguish, that dark-haired young girl blundering blind and bewildered through the long days, saddled with an illegitimate child she was hardly equipped to take care of. *His* child. Well, he had opened a bank account in her name and intended regularly contributing money toward the child's well-being and education over the years. But with the secrecy necessarily surrounding their relationship, there was little other practical help he could give her.

"*Than!*"

He looked up to find Jayne, alluring in her seventeenth year, holding up her checked pink gingham skirt as she came running to him through the rain, laughing and barefoot, her long blond hair streaming in the breeze. With a daring so like her, she had escaped Denise Smith at Than's medical-assistant school to perpetuate this traditional First Rains meeting, which had become an annual tryst between them. With a single joyful bounce, she tumbled straight into Than's arms and they rolled on the ground and came suddenly to a frightening stillness. Panting sensuously against him, she had her arms unself-consciously around his neck, and as he held the precious female softness of his sister's body tenderly against him, Than closed his eyes, horrified to feel the rampant stirring of his own starved flesh, devastated by the sudden cramping hunger he felt for her firm, golden, beautiful body, for her buoyant little breasts, for her smooth coltish legs and the secret solace between them.

Across the slope, the schoolchildren were still sweetly singing: "*Oh, Shenandoah, I love your daughter . . .*" After a long agonizing moment, Than pulled carefully away from her, gently disengaging her arms.

"Butterfly," he said huskily. "You shouldn't lie with me this way."

"Why not?" The pixie teasing faded from her puzzled gray eyes and her soft mouth fell open; she pushed herself up on an elbow, flicking the long wet hair out of her eyes, blinking at him, squinty-eyed under the pelting raindrops. "That mean old Miss Rothchild is nowhere in sight. And besides, thee're my *brother*!"

"Yeah." Badly shaken by his own sudden incestuous arousal, Than tried to smile. "But that doesn't exactly make me a teddy bear."

Embarrassed and achingly aware of the hot straining erection that made a hump like a mountain in his blue denim bermudas, he sat up slowly, linked his arms across his raised knees, and stared seriously up into the massing rain clouds, wincing and ashamed. He flinched as she bumped against his side and laid her tawny damp head against his shoulder, slipping her small hand around his flexed bicep.

"Jaynie?"

"Yes, Than?"

There was a throbbing in his loins and his skin burned with her touch, but she had no way of knowing this and he couldn't tell her to lay off again without hurting her feelings.

He frowned. "Oh nothing . . ." They remained silently together, and gradually, in the drenching rain, his blood cooled and the tensions eased inside him. He stared at his hands and tried to justify it all to himself. The rain hung in drops from his lashes and ran down the tip of his nose, and he blinked and sucked the cool wetness into his mouth and told himself it was a natural thing to happen in an unguarded moment like that. It had been unconscious and unwilled, but hell . . . old John Thomas had no discrimination and no ethics at all. He closed his eyes and shuddered, because the revulsion against it was so inbred, because thinking of screwing your own sister was a little like thinking of eating human flesh. The fact that he was frustrated as hell didn't make it any less despicable. He sat stunned for a moment, appalled at himself.

Then her fingers moved lightly across his arm, distracting him, and he looked up; she smiled at him and all at once his torment melted. Staring into her sweet freckled face, he knew that he could no more touch her than defile his own mother. He smiled tenderly at her and they wrinkled noses at each other through the pelting rain.

"Jaynie!" He put his mouth close to her ear and yelled above the roar. "We're pretty well baptized now. Let's go on inside."

She grinned at him through her streaming hair, shivering as they trudged up the slope, huddling together for shelter and warmth. The rain tapered off as suddenly as it had begun; in the cooled atmosphere, missions of flying ants on their annual nuptial flight feebly fluttered from an ant hill, dive bombing them blindly. Jayne laughed, waving them off, and from the fading black sky thunder rumbled, distantly withdrawing like a forgiving father. Than felt the penitent ache in his testes and was at peace again.

14

Congress waited until its pact with the UFP had secured it more seats in the December 10 by-election (increasing the UFP and Congress seats to sixteen and seven respectively) before it finally came out into the open and declared its decision to unite with UNIP. Apparently, racial allegiance and abhorrence of Federation had proved the stronger incentives in the long run. As it became apparent that the two nationalist parties together had a clear majority to form a government, the stunned missionaries were filled with distressed disbelief, while their African Friends bubbled with mindless joy. The news caused a sensation at yearly meeting, this year held at Suseshi, where white Congo Friends were full of dire predictions (two and a half years after independence, the Congo had yet to achieve any reliable measure of stability and peace). And there was more trouble in the bedeviled Katanga. The United Nations had moved the greater part of its forces into Katanga, and declaring that they intended arresting him and his ministers to paralyze the administration, Tshombe had demolition charges placed at mining installations and threatened a "scorched earth" policy.

Here in Northern Rhodesia, Matthew found that the transcendence to political power had caused a curious change in many of their genial African Friends, who overnight became quasi-Europeans, full of outrageous demands and airs and graces; it seemed that after years of subjugation to whites, suddenly finding their race master of its own destiny, they demanded a back payment in familiarity and respect, which was reckoned to be long overdue. Like their Congo kin before them, they had been promised the white man's prestige, privilege, and possessions on nationalist ascension. Now, innocently expectant, they waited to reap individually these auspicious rewards with an audacious attitude to match.

It was in this climate of political change that the missionaries learned that Elliot Moke and Loreley Haskel had been quietly married; Edith Haskel was peculiarly ambiguous as to the exact date the couple had passed meeting with the help of the local D. C., but by the looks of Loreley's dress-straining bulging belly, Matthew had a feeling it was none too soon; his unhappy suspicion was shared by Than Profane, who shrewdly calculated the girl as already being several months' pregnant. Ah me! Matthew mourned, would the day ever arrive when a yearly meeting exposed among its members nothing more contentious than spiritual progress?

BOOK SIX

FORTY DAYS IN
THE WILDERNESS

· 1963 ·

1

THE DAWN of 1963 saw Katanga in an increasingly perilous position. Tshombe had refused an ultimatum to withdraw his troops from Elizabethville, and the mounting tension between his army and the large United Nations forces building up in the city had flared up into a series of skirmishes. Amid rumors that the United Nations planned a renewed assault, Friends of the Congo Gospel Mission, obviously tempered to steely strength by the continuing strain of the chronic secession situation, coolly informed Suseshi that the annual Missionary Alliance Conference would take place at Lusinga as usual this year. Horrified at such arrogant normality, Matthew, who had hitherto attended almost every year, felt simply too nerve-worn this time. But to his consternation, he found that every other likely candidate felt the same way; his colleagues all found imperative reasons for staying behind at safe Suseshi. In the end, far less afraid of facing the conflict than of admitting his fear of it, Matthew swallowed his misgivings and left with Than Profane as usual.

Tshombe's gendarmes, in evidence at the border post and strategic points along the route, asked them for cigarettes and were guardedly friendly. The beautiful Elizabethville was tragically battlescarred and crawling with United Nations troops. At Lusinga, Matthew was disconcerted to find that the Ruanda-Urundi delegation, far more forthright, had declined to attend. Their Congo colleagues, too, seemed less confident than they had sounded; they went around with strained harried expressions, looking nervously alert, as if dissidents of the notorious national Congolese army and the United Nations troops abounded behind every bush. All in all it was a troubled conference, disturbed by black refugees from the city streaming through the mission en route to their tribal homes and by the noise of gunfire from Elizabethville on clear nights. But the delegates persevered. Then one night Louella Breckenbridge began screaming for no apparent reason. The conference was quickly rounded off and terminated, and Matthew and the Boy returned to Northern Rhodesia, taking the high-strung young woman back with them for a recuperative rest.

When they reached home, they learned that Tshombe's cabinet ministers had retreated to Jadotville when Elizabethville's electricity and water supplies were cut by Tshombe's jumpy officerless troops. United Nations troops attacked Kolwezi airfield, but Tshombe, evading arrest, once more slipped through their clutches into Northern Rhodesia. He flew to Salisbury to liaise with Sir Roy Welensky, and by the time he rejoined his ministers, an Indian contingent of the United Nations force, had set out for Jadotville. After driving back Katangese gendarmes and two mercenary platoons with mortars and jet fighters, it crossed the bridge-blown Lufira River. Amid talk that the Katangese planned to implement Tshombe's "scorched earth" policy, the smelting plant was blown up at Shitiru and vital parts were removed from the Sogelec electric grid. But in the final analysis, Tshombe's civilized instincts must have proved too strong; when the Katangan government retreated to Kolwezi, the vital mining installations were left intact. By January 3, the Indian forces were in full control of Jadotville. For a while their advance was held up by the fear that Tshombe would blow up the Delcommune Hydro-Electric scheme between Jadotville and Kolwezi; besides destroying the road that crossed it on a long causeway, this would flood the valley and deprive the whole area of electricity. Thus, for the time being, Tshombe and his ministers and their uneasy military force remained safely under seige at Kolwezi near the Northern Rhodesian border.

But across it, they no longer had certain friends in the Northern Rhodesian government. The new nationalist coalition government was divided in its feelings for Tshombe; while the Congress leader, Nkumbula, had become an outspoken admirer of his, UNIP remained scornful of his conciliatory multiracialism. And this schism was only one of many that became quickly apparent in the uneasy amalgamation. Despite Congress's inferior strength, its unique bargaining position had enabled Nkumbula to insist that the six ministries be equally shared. But he and the UNIP leader, Kaunda, past bitter enemies, found it hard to conciliate now. Nkumbula repeatedly threatened to resign amid rumors that he planned to unite again with the United Federal Party, which, since the nationalist ascension, had rerallied under a new, less inflammatory name—the National Progressive Party.

Jahaliso's enthusiastic invitation to Than to set up two out-clinics in his area extended the mission's outreach to the Balovale. With the young chief's hearty endorsement, Than expected no trouble soliciting the sick from the surrounding villages. Setting off on his out-clinic tour with copious provisions to service his little clinics extending to and from Barotseland, he passed a convoy of huge Union Miniere trucks carrying frozen meat to Tshombe and his ranks, beseiged at Kolwezi near the border. He was still musing on the Katangan leader's desperate plight when he turned off to Eshalakali Hill to pick up Teapot to assist him. Since Molly Dibb now had the help of a trained nurse-aid at the Hill's leper colony, she could afford her junior assistant for the week that Than needed him.

At Jahaliso's village, they found the chief and a score of anxious Africans awaiting them. Than was setting up his equipment in the clean new sparsely furnished hut built for him by the villagers when an agitated man came hurrying in from the bush. He was ragged and wet, and pushing past the long line, he begged Than to help his wife. After giving birth five days ago, she had failed to expel the placenta and was now very ill, he claimed.

"*Jesus!*" Than stared in disbelief; he was surprised the woman was still alive.

He and Teapot climbed into the Land-Rover with the man and left immediately. When they had traveled some miles into the bush, they came upon a bridgeless river that was too deep to cross in the vehicle. While Than and Teapot were stripping off their clothing to wade across, their companion began scurrying around on the sandy bank, ripping up the roots of a scrawny looking bush. He broke three into near equal sizes and handed one each to Than and Teapot, retaining one for himself. Than stared at his in surprise.

"What in heck is this for?"

"Hold between teeth," the man grunted. Then he pointed to the opposite bank.

"*Crocodile!*" Than sucked in his breath. He could make out about six of them, large repulsive-looking reptiles that lay basking in the sun. "*Ker-rist!* Are we supposed to go in there and tangle with those fellows?"

"Bwana, that is the reason for the sticks," Teapot explained with an anxiously furrowed brow and an air of exaggerated patience. "If-y

441

a person carries the root of a *muzeze* bush in his mouth, the spirits of the ancestors will protect him."

"Oh come now, Teapot, you don't believe that!"

Teapot stared self-consciously down at his big black feet. "Bwana, one should not offend this man."

"Offend!" Than burst out laughing. "Teapot, you old rogue! You actually believe it!"

Teapot looked pained. "Bwana, this man says he has-y crossed the river many times. Always with a root, he has remained unharmed. Other men with roots were unharmed. Then one time a man forget and the crocodiles take him. All others with sticks were safe."

"Oh shit!" Than frowned. "Some protection! No, whichever way it's meant to be, I don't guess a piece of root will make one iota of difference to my fate or his feelings. Now let's go."

The stranger went first. Not bothering to disrobe, he began to wade into the murky water. Glancing anxiously back at Than, Teapot moved after him. Than, still wearing his hat and holding his bundled clothes and the medical bag above the water, swallowed hard and followed. He waded cautiously into the river, eyes pinned on the crocodiles on the opposite bank, his confidence diminishing with every step he took.

The water swirled cold and bleak around his legs; as it inched higher up his naked body, gruesome pictures of crocodile injuries he had attended flashed through his mind and he found it easy to imagine a crocodile, submerged, making straight for his flanks. The slimy river bottom sucked at his feet, and each trailing piece of vegetation, dragging against his flesh, made his blood turn cold. When he had gone a few yards, a quickening of movement caught his eye. He glanced up and saw one of the crocodiles waddling on short fat legs down to the water's edge. There was a smooth splash as the creature submerged.

"Oh Christ," he hissed softly. "We got company."

The stranger, by now almost mid-river, with water up to his chest, turned and stared dispassionately. Then, seeming unperturbed, he averted his gaze and moved slowly, stolidly onward. He was either inordinately brave or had good reason to feel profoundly confident of the stopping power of his stick.

Than backtracked in a hurry. Teapot turned and watched him in pained surprise. Searching in the reeds, Than found his discarded stick and bit on it aggressively, grinning abashedly as he waded back to meet his assistant. Now it was his turn to look sheepish.

"I guess you were right, Teapot," he gritted through clenched teeth. "There's no sense in offending the man's beliefs!"

To his enormous relief, they reached the opposite bank without being attacked. Drying out in the tender sunshine, Than stood on the bank and stared at his stick in the dumbest consternation.

"Damn superstition!" he said crossly, and placed it reverently on the ground.

Than found the stricken woman in a poor condition in a dim smelly hut. He anesthetized her with chloroform dripped on a wad of absorbent cotton and, wincing at the putrid smell, removed the decomposed placenta manually. She would have to be hospitalized; while the villagers were constructing a pole litter to transport the woman to the Land-Rover, the grateful family brought Than and Teapot mugs of sweet tea and an enamel plate of sour doughy bread. In the cicada-shrilling, shy silence, it seemed to Than that the entire village came to stare at them as they consumed this frugal repast; among them he noticed a vaguely familiar middle-aged man, who turned guiltily from his gaze and hurried away. Only later, as they readied to leave with the woman and her baby lying on the bamboo litter hoisted by four men, did Than suddenly remember where he had seen the man before. Intrigued, he singled out the sullen and embarrassed African and examined him in amazement. The last time he had seen the man had been at Suseshi Hospital, where he lay dying of positively identified abdominal cancer. When Than had been unable to give him any practical relief, the man had disappeared from his bed one night, never, Than had thought, to be seen alive again. And yet here he was looking strong and healthy with no sign of the cancerous mass that had previously hardened his belly.

The man's explanation was simple; he had visited Kwoyisho, a witchdoctor in Barotseland who was famed for his successes in the treatment of such ailments. After partaking of his *muti* for several weeks, all pain had left him, and now, several months later, he had lost all his former symptoms and felt completely well.

"This witchdoctor?" Than stared at the man in awe. "Can you tell me where I can find him?"

The man shook his head; he had heard that the *ngaka* had recently fled into the Congo to escape prosecution by the police for indulging in witchcraft in infringement of Northern Rhodesia's Witchcraft Ordinance.

Than let out his breath. "Well, if you ever hear he's back, let me know. There's a few questions I'd like to ask him."

2 The secession of Katanga was ended. Matthew and many of his colleagues heard the news on January 15 with heavy hearts. After holding out at Kolwezi for several days, Tshombe had finally capitulated to the pressure of the United Nations forces. Arriving at Elizabethville without warning, he declared he had come back to work for peace and the rapid application of the U Thant plan. The Congo flag was hoisted in place of the Katangan emblem, and the commander of the surrendered Katangan gendarmerie swore allegiance to the Congo president.

With the uneasy peace that now reigned there, Louella Breckenbridge, looking a lot less nervous, returned. She had no sooner left Susehi when Loreley Haskel (the new Mrs. Moke), now protuberant with pregnancy, arrived with her mother to be delivered of her baby at the hospital. A little mite was duly born to her with minimal difficulty one rainy February evening; it was a scrawny little boy, whose future, with a backward mother and an oddball father, Matthew could only wince at. He was relieved when Elliot arrived to take the doting grandmother, sullen, indifferent mother, and homely little baby back home to Mambundi.

Now that Cosmo had become an able surgical assistant and Than Profane had three white nurses to aid him in his other endeavors, he finally persuaded Jerome and Grace Dooley to go home to America for their long deferred furlough. This meant that his out-clinic schedule had to be curtailed for the duration. But Zelda Clayton, whose staff had increased to include a capable African dresser, had promised to periodically oversee his Barotseland clinics. Molly Dibb had reopened the "top" clinic at Eshalakali Hill, and with the help of two nurse's aides, was delivering pregnant women from Mulaisho's villages in the small maternity block that had long lain empty. Since the Boy deemed neither nurse competent enough to diagnose and deal with the myriad diseases they were likely to be faced with, he had given them copious written instructions including lists of symptoms to watch out for. Still, trusting no one but himself, he worried and fretted. Each Wednesday, when Jenny was taken to conduct her Braille class at the Hill, he waited impatiently for Leroy to bring back Nurse Dibb's report on the running of the clinic. Often the gum-chewing youth was put to good use ambulancing from the station the seriously ill or pregnant women who might need Caesareans at Suseshi.

But if Matthew was glad that they had at last found some meager justification for Leroy's presence on the mission, the youth continually complained. The roads were bad this rainy season, and when the Land-Rover got stuck in the mud or punctured a tire, loath to pit his back in unrelished labor, Leroy never let them hear the end of it. And he grumbled that the long drive was becoming increasingly dangerous besides; en route, they were often jeered at or threatened with stones. Well, Matthew was hardly surprised. Although the natives had at last achieved their promised autonomy and the new government's resolution to "secede now!" from the hated Federation had resulted in an aggressive delegation going to London, incidents of assault and arson had soared all over the country these past months. Matthew put this renewed violence down to the tensions within the new coalition government; the constant interparliamentary squabbles of the two nationalist leaders were reflected in more brutal battles between their followers. And now, still pent for a gargantuan struggle to achieve an ideal that had ultimately come with disarming ease, restlessly waiting to reap personally the white man's riches so rashly promised them by their politicians, the people languished in anticlimactical aimlessness. The vastly outnumbered Congress members had an anxious time on the Copperbelt, while out here, where the two groups were more evenly matched, both vented their frustration and loss of purpose by insulting whites and stoning cars.

In fact the situation had lately become so tense that one of the specialist riot-fighting mobile police units had recently been billeted alongside the boma at Mwinilunga, and that Wednesday, when Jenny went to Eshalakali Hill with Leroy, Matthew anxiously awaited their return. When they were late, he paced his veranda till the mud-splattered vehicle finally growled in. The occupants were safe; there were no patients on board, but for some reason Molly Dibb had accompanied them. However, although assuring Matthew and Teller that they had encountered no trouble, Jenny seemed nervous and strained. She took Luke from Teller and retired straight to her room. When she later declined to accompany them to supper, they put it down to weariness and the fact that little Luke was teething.

At the dining *chitenje*, Matthew was puzzled by the pompous air of injury that accompanied the arrival of the Fotches and Molly

Dibb. For once they ate in silence (if it could be called such; Tallulah, Orville, and Leroy sopped bread in their gravy and were sloppy eaters, masticating audibly!). Tallulah and Clara sat grievously smirking, and Leroy seemed nervous, stuffing his face with food as if a world famine were imminent. He appeared relieved to hear that Jenny would not be joining them, and after the meal, when Clara did not bring out her needlepoint and Hannah made no move to fetch the Scrabble set, Matthew sensed that some contentious issue was in the offing. And indeed it was. In a moment, prodded by his kin, Leroy stood up momenteously.

"Er, Friend Tomlinson!" he hedged uneasily, running fat freckled fingers through his corn-colored fringe. "I'm afraid I have a rather unhappy disclosure to make to thee, sir! I am well aware of the kind of wild stories Jenny will have been making up about me, and I'm afraid I cannot allow her to thus sully my reputation any longer; that's why I fetched Molly here back with me. I want her to tell what she saw and prove to thee that everything Jennifer's told thee is just a pack of lies!"

"*What?* Whatever is thee talking about?" Matthew gaped incredulously, and Leroy paled.

"Er . . . thee mean she hasn't . . . er . . . *said* anything?"

"No." Matthew leaned back in his chair. "*Should* she have?"

"Well . . ." Leroy trailed off uncertainly, ". . . in that case perhaps I'd best not say anything either."

He started to subside onto his seat but was elbowed up again by his grandmother and Clara, who sat on either side of him looking angrily righteous.

"*Thee must!*" Tallulah commanded, turning to the other missionaries with her fat face, framed with straggling wisps of gray hair, righteously drawn. "He has a duty to his family to protect his reputation, after all. In my opinion his gentlemanly wish to protect Miss Solomon is sadly misplaced since her behavior is none of our responsibility!"

"Jenny's behavior?" Matthew stared. "Just what is thee getting at?"

"Well, sir," Leroy said with studied reluctance. "It's my unpleasant duty to inform thee, as the senior elder of this mission, that the young woman thee harbors in thy home, Miss Jennifer Solomon, to be exact, has been . . . well . . . let me say that I feel her unfortunate experience in the Congo has weaned her onto *wanton* ways, if thee gets my drift, sir. See, she . . . er . . . threw herself at me today, I am sorry to say; begged me to make love to her!"

"*WHAT!*" Matthew rose from his seat in incredulous indignation; his patent disbelief made Leroy flinch. He blustered, "Why I've never heard such nonsense, and I'll thank thee, young man, to retract it immediately!"

"He most certainly will not!" Tallulah snorted, spraying spittle. "If anything, Fauntleroy is to be commended for his honesty! He's said nothing but the truth and he's entitled to tell it!"

"That's right!" Leroy nodded earnestly. "I knew thee'd be shocked, Professor, and it grieves me to be the one to break such distressing news of thy . . . thy houseguest, but Molly Dibb here will bear me out how she saw Jenny make a pass at me in the church up at the Hill! Isn't that so, Molly?" He turned anxiously to extract the prim, plain girl's vengeful nod. "So thee see . . ."

When the youth's expression suddenly grew wary, Matthew turned to find Than Profane approaching. Leroy froze to uncertain silence as the doctor entered the *chitenje;* nodding absently at the company, the Boy stepped over the communal bench and sat down between Katherine and Jayne. Apparently preoccupied with medical problems, he began to fill his plate from the steaming bowls of food that were passed to him by willing hands along the table. Finally, he began to eat, seeming unaware of the charged atmosphere he had intruded upon. Apparently anxious to keep him in such ignorance, Leroy sat down abruptly. But Matthew, shaking with suppressed rage, would not allow the matter to so ignominiously rest.

"Pray continue, Leroy," he snorted through his moustache. "I am sure Dr. Profane will be most interested to hear the scandalous news thee has chosen to so publicly disclose."

The Boy looked up, and Leroy mumbled evasively, "Uh no . . . I wouldn't want to bother the doctor."

"On the contrary, I'm sure he'd be most intrigued." Matthew met Than's questioning gaze with a grim face. "The fact is, Doctor, Friend Leroy here has accused Jenny of . . . of making an *indecent* pass at him!"

"You're kidding?" The Boy stared incredulously. He set down his fork and looked around, breathing a bitter laugh. "Is this some kind of a tasteless joke?"

"It's true, sir," Leroy got to his feet and stared earnestly through his wheaten fringe. "And considering what she went through in the Congo, I guess it's hardly surprising. Why, we all know about that Congo nun who was ravished, and after the taste of it, it turned her into a lustful woman? Well, it seems like the taste of the sensual

447

pleasures of sex has driven Miss Jenny wild for more! Well, naturally I held her off, as Molly here will testify, and believe me I'd just as soon keep mum on the whole matter, but it occurred to me she might try to shift the blame. And my grandma here warned me how dangerous it could be to just leave things lie. After all, she might start trying to solicit the natives and . . ."

Something in Than Profane's expression made him stop and hurriedly modify: "I guess it's not her fault, and naturally I pity the poor girl but . . ."

"WELL MAYBE THEE DOES, BUT I FIND THE WHOLE MATTER *DISGUSTING* IN THE EXTREME!" Hannah Rothchild shrilled, leaping to her feet, nostrils flaring.

"My sentiments exactly!" Clara carped with sneering distaste, turning to her fellows for confirmation. "To think that a member of our mission could so behave *sickens* me to my very stomach. I for one will not rest until this whole disgraceful affair has been exposed and that girl expelled! By her sinful debauchery she is sullying the very name of this mission, and I fail to see how we, as decent people, can stand by and allow her to . . ."

The Boy stood up. The pale livid seams of his healed Blood Brotherhood scars gave his taut tanned face a cruel contempt; his scathing look silenced even the unsilenceable Clara, who slowly subsided, seeming to shrivel in her seat.

"Mrs. Fotch," he snarled quietly, "I guess you've never forgiven Jenny for getting raped and showing you and your husband up for the grasping individuals you are! I guess it must be a source of delight to you to have Leroy give you this chance to imply she deserved as good as she got. Well, ma'am, I for one am not falling for it. And the best I can say for you and your kind is that you're a bunch of malicious bitches! And as for Leroy; well, his ego sure is screwed up if he thinks for one minute that Jenny would even deign to hold his hand. She's blind, not retarded! And as for you, Nurse Dibb, you have a clinic and maternity ward to run back at Eshalakali; instead of pandering to your boyfriend's egotistical sex fantasies, I suggest you get your ass right back there and take care of your patients!"

There was a shocked indrawing of breath; in the stunned silence, Matthew, for once, was too gratified at this loyal defense to take umbrage at the language it was worded in. While the entire table sat still shocked speechless, the Boy, apparently angered out of his appetite, wiped his mouth, threw down his napkin, and stepped back over the long bench.

448

"One more thing," he growled. "I wouldn't repeat this slander if I were you. There's not one of you here fit to throw the first stone. Jennifer Solomon happens to be the finest lady I've ever known. And any one of you who wants to say otherwise will have to answer to me first."

3

But for all Than Profane's intimidating anger, Matthew knew that the matter would not end there. Unfortunately, the Boy had told too many home truths about the Fotches for them to drop the matter now. Now, more than ever, they would be determined to discredit and disgrace Jenny once and for all. After the doctor's angry departure, the Fotch family left in a haughty huff, muttering furiously about discussing the matter in committee and exposing Jenny's behavior to the board. Well, Matthew would have preferred to spare Jenny the embarrassment, but with these ominous plans afoot, he and Teller had no option but to broach the subject when they returned to the house. Phrasing Leroy's accusations as delicately as possible, Teller sat opposite her on the bed in her room and gently invited her to supply the real truth.

At first, while sturdy little Luke, pink-cheeked with fever in a toweling jump-suit, stood restlessly stomping and grizzling on her lap, she merely stared at them, looking dazed. Then, as she soothingly stroked the tow-headed toddler, her blue eyes filled with tears and, hugging the squirming baby against her, she whispered: "Leroy said that? Oh please, you must believe me—he's lying!"

"We know that, honey," Teller murmured, patting her hand. "But he has that silly Molly Dibb eating right out of his hand, supporting the ridiculous story. So perhaps thee'd better tell us what really happened so we can set them all straight."

"Well, it was Leroy," Jenny swallowed. "Right from the time he first started taking me to the Hill, he—he was always . . . well, he was always touching me and paying me compliments. I always pretended I didn't notice or changed the subject . . . and then today, after I finished my class, he came and sat beside me in the church. He started talking to me about that . . . *that day* in the Congo." Struggling to keep from crying, she closed her eyes and swallowed.

"Dear heart, don't upset thyself!" Teller murmured, but Jenny shook her head, regaining her composure.

"No, it's all right," she sniffed, smoothing away a tear. "I suppose I should have said something before, but I was embarrassed and I didn't want to cause any trouble. I kept hoping that if I ignored Leroy he would stop it after a while. But he didn't. And then . . . then he started telling me awful things . . . about what happened to me in the Congo . . ." She started to cry, pressing her anguished face into the baby's body. "H-he told me about some missionary nun who had . . . well, he just said that he knew how much I must be . . . *wanting* a man . . . and . . . well, he started to kiss me and I pushed him off. That was when Molly Dibb walked in. She was angry and Leroy jumped up and told her the same thing he told you. I tried to tell her the truth, but she would only listen to Leroy. Then I told him that I was going to tell you how he had behaved toward me, and I refused to go home alone with him. I said I would speak to the Townsends. That's when Molly agreed to drive back with us. I—I didn't know then that their intention was to have her back up his lies about me to you all."

She raised a tear-glistening, despairing face, rocking the whimpering baby in her arms.

"I didn't really intend telling on him. I just wanted to frighten him into leaving me alone. But I suppose he believed me and wanted to get in with his story first."

"Evidently." Matthew nodded. "Well, that kind of figures with my estimation of Leroy's character, I'm afraid. Only trouble is, my guess is that infatuated Nurse Dibb would rather believe anything than the fact that Leroy could be . . . er . . . attracted to anyone else. I'm afraid she'll back his story all the way."

"You think so?" Jenny stared in horror. "What must everyone be thinking of me?"

"Anyone who really knows thee will know thee is innocent, my dear," Matthew consoled stoutly. "The rest are not worth worrying about. Oh, and if I were thee, I'd have nothing further to do with that . . . *Leroy*. It's obvious to me that besides being a dangerous lecher and a liar, he has very few scruples to speak of. I'll see if I can arrange for someone else to transport thee to Eshalakali each week. Tell thee what, if worse comes to worse, I'll take thee myself!"

"Oh thank you." Jenny gazed at him gratefully through her tears. "I don't think I could face going with Leroy again."

But despite his reassurances to Jenny, Matthew was seriously worried about the matter. By their grim tenacity, he knew that the

Fotches and Hannah Rothchild would do their utmost to make the most terrible trouble for her. For some reason, right from the start, Jenny's handicap had a way of showing up their meanness. By now they had a whole backlog of humiliations to avenge, and avenge them they evidently intended. The way Matthew heard it, they proposed awaiting the next quarterly committee meeting to enlist the backing of Benedict Poe before taking the matter further. In the meanwhile, they pointedly ignored Matthew, Than Profane, and Jenny herself, all the while treating Leroy with the exaggerated solicitude due a hero returned. Fetching and carrying for him, they indulged his slightest whim till the chubby young man grew smug and pompous, and by the affronted way he began greeting Jenny's presence at mealtimes, Matthew guessed that the youth had begun to believe his own lies; reveling in the role of innocence offended, he took pride in the piety his doting kin pretended for him.

Well, if his relatives wore blinkers, Matthew did not. And faced with this psychological onslaught, Jenny remained polite and reserved. She spoke when spoken to but refused to be baited by the sly provocations that were daily flung at her. Unfortunately, before Matthew got a chance to inform Leroy he was no longer required to transport Jenny to Eshalakali Hill each week, the young man made a public issue of flinging a pious refusal in her face. Well Matthew tried to tell him that Jenny had long ago decided to forgo the "privilege," thank thee, but by then his hasty disclaimer sounded like nothing so much as a grasping retaliation. Leroy subsequently made a further point by taking the long way around the table to avoid passing Jenny's seat. Though her lack of sight mercifully spared her this added humiliation, Matthew was hopping mad. And that was only the beginning. When their elder relatives were not around, Leroy and Sidney took to sniggering in Jenny's presence, seeming to take particular delight out of mocking her thus in front of Matthew. Although this infuriated him and obviously upset Jenny, they held their heads high and did not deign to respond.

But for Matthew this control grew harder each day; Leroy's blatant obnoxiousness grew so malicious and marked that he took to escorting Jenny to her Braille classes to save her the stress of any chance encounter.

One Saturday afternoon, two weeks after the incident, he escorted Jenny to Suseshi meeting house, where she gave weekly Braille classes to a group of blind adults from Mwinilunga. Later he was surprised to see the students, distinctive with their walking sticks and guiding companions, fumbling their way home well before time. Puzzled, he approached them.

"The bwana has told us to leave; there is no class for today," a man informed him.

"Impossible." Matthew frowned, perplexed. "Thee's made some mistake. I took the *dona* there myself." Then a chill thought struck him, and he turned back to the group. "This bwana who sent thee off—what was his name?"

Apparently no one knew, but a sighted guide was able to offer a description. Young, chubby, with light brown, "yellowish" hair. It was as good a picture of Leroy as a body could get, and Matthew stood a moment in uncomprehending shock. Then anger engulfed him, bitter and black, fogging his reason. What were things coming to when that young pup went around cancelling Jenny's classes! Well, this time he had gone too far. This time Matthew would not let the matter go. He had no idea what he would do, but shaking with rage, he felt capable of murder. He might have rushed right off and done something rash, had he not, just then, caught sight of the only figure of authority Fauntleroy seemed to respect seriously. Than Profane was out walking his leopard on a lead. These days, with his tight schedule in Jerome's absence, he could only afford the time to exercise the animal outside her enclosure for short periods a few times a week, and with Bathsheba presently in heat and thus doubly dangerous, he was afraid to trust her even with Samson, the Profanes' garden boy and her customary native handler.

Despite the big cat's fearsome proximity, Matthew hurried after the Boy, hailing him urgently. Than turned with irritated eyes; the strain of overwork was etched on his tanned face, and he made no effort to silence the hissing leopard. As always, the spectacular dazzle of Bathsheba's beautiful dappled coat quite took Matthew's breath away, her bared curved canines stopping him short of the range of her lead. But in his anger, he was not long restrained. While the Boy stood frowning, straining against the leopard's tugging lead as she urinated and rolled languorously in the bushes, amorously uttering gruff sawing sounds, Matthew poured out the provocations of the past weeks and now this latest presumption.

"You say Leroy's dismissed her class?" The Boy frowned warily. "Where's Jenny now?"

"Well now . . ." Matthew ran his fingers through his rumpled white hair. "Come to think of it, with her class gone off, she should have come home by now. Why would she stay in the meeting house?

Unless . . . by golly, I hope that obnoxious Leroy hasn't started *pestering* her again!"

"Jesus," the Boy said. He wasted no more time speculating, but started for the meeting house with the great leopard bounding along beside him. Matthew hurried breathlessly after them. On the high ground above the river, the big stone-facaded building stood ominously quiet in the late afternoon; it had started to shadow and cool with the receding of the sun. While the Boy stopped to harness his leopard to a tree outside, Matthew rushed around to the front; he opened one of the big double doors and, suddenly cautious, slipped silently inside. In the dimness of the big empty hall, struggling to suppress the ragged breaths that still shrilled in his ears, he waited while his eyes adjusted to the cool blue gloom of the vibrant stained-glass windows that lined the long walls. Jenny's antiquated Stainsbury Braille machine still sat on the central rostrum table, while the little portable tables bearing hammers and awls, the crude writing tools of the blind, still lined the inner square of benches around it. A bulky pile of Braille books were on one bench, but otherwise the pews appeared empty. Matthew felt relieved. Then, as he started stealthily up the aisle, he heard a sound. He stopped, straining his ears. And then, coming from the back pews, he clearly heard it: short panting breaths, murmurs and giggles. He couldn't mistake it: it was *Leroy. Leroy and Sidney Fotch!* As he crept quietly closer, he heard Jenny talking.

"Give me back my cane." Her voice sounded curiously dull. "I know you've got it. I heard you throw it on the floor beneath these pews."

"Aw, come on Miss Jenny," came Leroy's coddling voice. "I've looked all over for it. 'Pears to me thee're mistaken. This here floor's pretty cold, but seeing as we're all down here together, cozy as can be, thee might as well be nice to old Uncle Leroy. Thee ain't had a real man till thee've had me, baby. And I'd better warn thee, my aunt and uncle aim to report thee to the board. Think how it would shame thy daddy and the whole mission if they was to throw thee out in disgrace? But if thee're real nice to me, maybe I'll back down with my story and get them to leave thee be. So it's up to thee, Sugar-pie. And after what thee've been through with all them stinking black niggers, a nice clean white boy should be a breeze, a real treat in fact! So, come on now, honey lips, pucker up and stop playing hard to get. I know how bad thee must be wanting it!"

"Let go of me," Jenny said breathlessly. *"Let go. . . ."* There was the sound of a small scuffle and ripping cloth. Then Jenny, bonnet bedraggled, staggered up from behind the pews; Leroy leaped up on one side of her while a grinning Sidney surfaced on the other. Leroy was pawing at Jenny's dress, and as she struggled to push him off, her tearful gasp finally snapped Matthew out of his stupefaction, and he bounded forward, bellowing in outrage:

"STOP THAT! DESIST! LEAVE HER THIS MINUTE!"

Just then the side door parallel to them burst open; it slammed back against the wall and a shaft of golden daylight spotlighted a flinching Leroy as he stood in one of his gawdy Hawaiian shirts, guiltily frozen with a shocked, disheveled Jenny in his arms. Silhouetted in the doorway there could be no mistaking the tall tanned blond-streaked figure in a white medical jacket, blue denim jeans, and embossed Western boots. Glancing frantically from Matthew to Than Profane, Leroy babbled sickly, "I can explain! See it's just like I told thee all! She was trying to seduce me again! Siddy will tell thee how I tried to restrain her, but she just . . ." He swallowed, releasing her, his hands dropping self-consciously away. "She just ripped open her buttons and came at me!"

"*Indeed?*" Matthew sneered sarcastically. Fists clenched and quaking with his cold anger, he snorted, "And I suppose after dismissing her class and searching the mission for thee, that child, blind and all by herself, dragged the pair of thee here, kicking and screaming!"

"W-well no sir . . . we can explain!" Leroy turned. His feeble smile faltered and the short hairs seemed to stand up on the back of his head when he saw Than Profane, moving with a curious, stunned, sleepwalking slowness, starting along the first row of pews toward them. In the sudden deathly hush, there was no sound but the comment of his boots on the concrete floor, his slow steady footfalls relentlessly advancing. Matthew, subsiding shakily, stared at him in fascination. He had never seen the young doctor look so strange. The Boy's handsome face radiated a towering terrible rage that seemed too huge for him to contain; the ritual scars were livid on his sunburned skin, the small muscles flickered furiously in his clenched jaw, and blindly blinking with it, he struggled to suppress his heaving breaths enough to speak. When he finally did, his velvet voice was dangerous in its very control.

"I'm gonna kill you, you know that?" he said quietly, his calmness curiously at odds with the context of his words. "You motherfucking maggots, I'm going to kill the pair of you with my bare hands."

"Now, Doctor, don't be hasty!" Leroy held up a plump placating hand. He was pale and his soft lower lip twitched nervously as he earnestly indicated the ferret-faced Sidney, who had shrunk back in fright. "Siddy will back me up in this! He saw it all, didn't thee, cousin? And see, she . . . she . . . *listen, thee've got to believe me!*"

But the look on Than Profane's face as he continued approaching with such deadly, deliberate, unnatural slowness was too much for Leroy. With a yell, he turned and tumbled for the door. Sidney, quick as the ferret he resembled, streaked after him. The doctor dived out after them, leaving Matthew and Jenny alone in the meeting house. Stunned, Matthew looked at her for the first time. Silent tears streaked her dazed dusty face, her long hair hung awry over her dangling bonnet, and there was an ageless sadness in her big blue eyes as she stared sightlessly, her hands ineffectually holding together her button-burst bodice, which had been ripped open to reveal a little white lace-fluted brassiere. With a crushed and aching heart, Matthew started tremulously toward her. Then he heard a shout and the fleshy percussion of bodies outside, and he left her and rushed out to avert the cold-blooded murder he had seen blazing from the Boy's hate-blinded blue eyes.

Outside, he found his worst fears realized. The Boy had hold of Leroy, and the youth struggled to free himself with a desperate wrench that ripped his palm-patterned orange shirt. Panting heavily, he gabbled between gasps:

"*Hey!* Lemme go . . . thee got it all wrong!"

But the Boy was not listening; the blue eyes were blank beyond seeing as he slammed viciously with his fists into Leroy's face and stomach, knocking the breath and bluster out of the hefty youth so that he buckled, gasped, and went stumbling backward, nose and mouth streaming blood. But the flurry of blows finally got up Leroy's ire; regaining himself, he rushed at the Boy with an outraged yell, flailing with his thick fists. The Boy dodged and grabbed him; grappling, they lurched around locked in a macabre embrace, in a desperate shirt-shredding struggle which Matthew's pleas could not penetrate. The leopard, chained to the branch of a nearby tree, stood hackles risen and hissing as the two men furiously tangled. Matthew was so beside himself that he hardly noticed the natives who came running from all parts of the mission; keeping cautiously clear of the snarling leopard, they gathered around, mouths agape as the bwana doctor and Fauntleroy Fotch tried to kill each other. When Matthew

455

finally looked around, they were surrounded by an awed audience of houseboys, meeting elders, members of the permanent board, and even Boniface, the good-for-nothing mission hunter (otherwise never to be found!), who rushed up brandishing the rifle he seldom put to serious use.

They all watched in disbelieving fascination as the Boy caught Leroy's jaw with a brutal upper cut, which knocked him off his feet. When he staggered groggily up again, shaking the corn-colored fringe out of his glazed eyes, the Boy hit him again. Leroy stumbled back, then, eyes wide and whimpering breathlessly, he charged, lashing out with a furious flabby-handed blow that spun the Boy's head. When the following fist, delivered with desperate strength, sent the Boy sprawling, Leroy turned to flee. But the Boy was up in a trice; the crowd fell away as he took a running dive at the escaping Leroy. The pair skidded down on the hard earth, the breath jarring out of them. They rolled on the ground a few feet from Bathsheba, who crouched, hissing and snarling, moving her paws restlessly, working up into a veritable frenzy of feline agitation as she saw her master manhandled by this stocky stranger.

"Stop!" Matthew cried. "Please! Thee've got to stop!" But he might have entreated the trees, and when he looked up there was more trouble coming. The cowardly Sidney had evidently enlisted outside aid in the form of Ezra Peabody, Ratchet Cathcart, and the Fotches, who hurried up, followed by the skirt-clutching maiden ladies. Their outraged yells bruised the air from several yards off. Orville and his mother panted up first; looking to Matthew like monstrous twins, childishly overdressed, their plump similar faces were pink and pursed with anger and exertion.

"How dare he!" Tallulah hooted from a horrendous purple poke bonnet. "This is an outrage! Fauntleroy is a pacifist Quaker! Get that disgraceful doctor to stop that this minute!"

She waved a fat hand in Matthew's harried face, evidently unable to believe he was as helpless as she in the matter. Then Clara and Hannah Rothchild, demented with indignation, rushed up and vented their frustrated fury in a frenzied chorus.

"*Outrageous!* The board will hear of this! He's attacking Leroy!"

"Beg pardon, ladies," Matthew mopped miserably at his perspiring brow. "At this point it appears to me they're attacking each other, and lessen we can figure out some way to stop 'em, somebody's likely to get seriously hurt!"

Just then the Disneys arrived and the valiant Virgil and Lars

Wikstrom tried to break up the brawl. But the pallid pair, pacifically trained, scurried around, hesitating timidly; the sprawling men seemed impossible to lay hands on, and Virgil and Lars leaped fearfully back as they fell around like nine-pins. The crowd gasped as they rolled within range of the leopard, who backed up against the tree trunk, tail nervously switching and her ear-flattened head lowered as she snarled in a rumbling sonorous growl, which gave Leroy the necessary incentive to break free of the doctor; he scrambled up, followed by the Boy.

"*Oh no!*" Jayne Profane, in her pink gingham dress, had burst through the throng. She was joined by Katherine, who stood staring in despair.

"Uncle Matthew, *stop them!*" Jayne implored, whisps of blond hair and tears in her eyes, and Matthew, fretting helplessly, (why did they all always look to him?) paced around, brandishing his pith helmet and bellowing for them to stop. By now the Boy looked a little bushed. He was smeared with dirt, grass, and blood; his white jacket hung on his golden chest in tatters, but he shook the lank sun-silvered hair out of glazed blue eyes that still flamed with fanatical feeling, and Leroy, his own shirt ripped to riotous ribbons, tottered drunkenly on his feet as Than mercilessly continued brutally battering his swollen bloodied face till the ladies squealed, turning squeamishly away, and the Africans *aaaaaaaahh-ed* in awe. Then Leroy, stung by this treatment, rallied in rage; with an ear-splitting shriek he barreled heavily into the Boy, pushing him backward, aiming a kick at the Boy's groin. He missed, but the lowly tactic seemed to snap something in the Boy. With a furious growl he fell on Leroy, encircling his throat with strangling fingers.

The outraged roar that went up was the final catalyst. The big crouching cat, finally provoked beyond endurance, suddenly sprang. As she launched through the air like a lightning strike, the small branch encircled by her steel lead snapped like a twig; it flew after her at the end of the chain, and for Matthew time stood suddenly still as the awesome animal landed on Leroy's haunch with a rapacious roar. In the sudden shocked silence, Jayne screamed; Lars had to hold her back from running to her brother. Gasping in terror, the crowd stumbled back, and the Boy, finally shaken to his senses, released Leroy and grabbed the cat's collar.

"*Sheba!*" he yelled, struggling to pull the leopard off. The impact of her weight had taken Leroy to his knees, but eyes wide with terror and screaming like a woman, the youth was alert with desperation. He drew back a fist and began pummeling at the cat's silken flank. With a shock of disbelief, Matthew realized that he held a knife in his hand. Blood had begun to stream down the beautiful dappled pelt as he punctured the animal's side again and again. She loosened her grip, and as the Boy yanked her off, Leroy tumbled free. Immediately aided by his clustering kin, he staggered up, howling horrendously, but to Matthew's relief, his buxom buttock appeared merely deeply scratched through his trousers. Bathsheba, however, seemed more seriously hurt. With her yellow eyes maddened and opaque with pain, she turned unseeingly and transferred her fury onto the next nearest; Jayne slumped in a dead faint as the cat leaped, snarling, at the Boy. Her flexed hind legs embedded the deadly claws deep into his thigh, and surprised and exhausted, he went down under the onslaught. Grappling with her desperately, holding her off by the throat, he rolled on the ground with the cat snarling on top of him.

By now most of the crowd had dispersed in total terror, the limping Leroy and his family and friends, bundling off with unbecoming haste, to barricade themselves in the meeting house. Those few who remained out of concern for the Boy were held back by trepidation, and helpless to help him, they demonstrated desperately, screaming and shouting to scare off the cat. But the din only further confused Bathsheba. When the dim-witted mission hunter, who had been one of the first to flee, crept fearfully back and tried to get a bead on the writhing animal, Matthew had no idea what might have happened had not the ever-practical Ward Disney snatched the rifle from his hands and fired it into the air. The deafening shot, followed by a barrage of blows from Matthew's pith helmet, finally disarmed the crazed cat. She left the Boy, turned, and bounded off; dribbling blood and dragging the leafy branch at the end of her trailing chain, she lurched around the meeting house and disappeared into the long grass of the bush beyond.

For a moment, in the sudden silence, they were all too stunned to react. They stared at the Boy, whose chest and one thigh were raked with deep blood-seeping scratches. He had made no sound during the mauling; he made no sound now. As he struggled to sit up, spreading blood darkly stained his jeans and his white jacket, and their sensibilities returning, they all rushed to aid him. Leaving Lars cradling the stirring Jayne, Katherine sank down beside him, tears coursing her pale cheeks.

"*Than*. Oh, Than, thee's hurt!"

Matthew, Teller, and Ward bundled around him, but he ignored them all, pushing off their hesitant hands. Matthew watched in horror as he rolled onto his hands and one knee; dripping blood from his lacerated chest and dragging his left leg, which was raw and bloodied as fresh meat through the shredded denim of his jeans, he raised a wracked face and called out to the skies,

"Jesus!" It was like an entreaty to God, and as they watched, dumbfounded, he began to crawl painstakingly toward the meeting house.

"Son, son!" Matthew croaked. "what are thee doing? Give me thy arm! Lean on me, I'll help thee . . ."

But the Boy shrugged off his hand. "Leave me!" he snarled, and he was deadly as the leopard in his intent. Reaching the stone wall of the meeting house, he leaned against it as he struggled up; finally he stood triumphantly poised on his one good leg, swaying precariously in proud independence while all those who cared stood around him, unable to help, fenced off by his spitting wrath.

"Now," he panted. "Give me the gun."

"No!" Matthew spluttered. "Thee cannot! What is thee thinking of? Thee're in no condition to . . ."

But the Boy held out his hand with such stoic command that Ward handed him the rifle without a word. Boniface rushed forward to give him bullets, and they all watched in white-faced wonder as the Boy fumbled to load the gun with grazed, shaking hands.

Dully digesting his intention, Katherine wailed: "But thee needs medical attention! Oh, honey, if thee must—let someone else go after Bathsheba!"

But he ignored her; holding the rifle, he began hobbling painstakingly around the meeting house, wincing with pain and limping badly on his lacerated leg. And in his concern for the Boy, even despite his own fear, Matthew was forced to follow him and Boniface into the bush. It is well-known hunter's lore that there are few animals more dangerous than a wounded leopard, and as Matthew walked, the last in line, into the long clutching grass, his spine prickled in awful anticipation of a leaping attack. At first the cat was nowhere to be seen; the trail of her blood was difficult to follow in the long grass, and Matthew began to hope they would not find her. Then the Boy, who had been stumbling slowly along a little ahead of them, suddenly stopped. He squinted into the grassy scrub a few yards ahead. Boniface pointed, and puzzling at the spot, Matthew saw a flicker of movement. It was the cat's tail, thrashing like a snake in the shade of a tree. Staring intently, Matthew was able to make out the exquisite pattern of black rosettes, perfectly camouflaged in the shade-dappled tawny scrub.

As they cautiously approached, the leopard began to growl; the deep sonorous rumbling made Matthew's hair stand on end, and the Boy and Boniface stopped. Then, almost overbalancing as he struggled to stand still on one leg, Than softly slapped his thigh and clicked his tongue coaxingly. He began talking gently, reaching out to the animal with love and familiar phrases. As his murmurous voice softly coaxed, Matthew saw some misty memory move in the beautiful yellow eyes, and when the Boy took another few lurching steps forward, the cat lifted her head to follow his movement, her golden gaze fixed on him, the loose skin of her throat pulsating as she panted. Her tail still slashed ominously in the long grass, but the growl was petering, and the Boy, struggling to suppress the exerted heaving of his chest, continued his encouraging crooning as he hobbled closer.

"Sheba . . . it's all right girl. It's me! I won't hurt you."

And then it happened; Matthew had seen it before. While lesser mortals trembled, the Boy could go into the cat's cage while she was snarling savagely over her food dish and practically take the meat right out of her mouth. The magic worked now. The leopard, finally calm and comprehending, allowed the Boy to approach her. Matthew's heart was in his mouth as Than carefuly set aside the rifle and, holding his injured leg stiffly extended, crouched beside her, awkwardly balancing on his good leg. The cat, softly *owling* with all her former affection, nuzzled her blunt whiskered head against his tenderly stroking hand, licking the fearless fingers with a rough pink tongue that was flecked with blood-speckled foam.

For several moments he gentled her, talking softly. Then, edging precariously closer, he leaned over and tried to explore her wounds. The leopard grew nervous as he touched her knife-punctured flank, and caught edging warily closer, Matthew stopped dead. But her low warning growl turned into a piteous yowl and she moved her paws fretfully before convulsing and vomiting up a mouthful of bright red blood. She began to whimper and pant distressfully, and even to Matthew it was obvious that the poor creature was mortally wounded and in awful anguish.

"Sheba." The Boy smiled tenderly. He caressed her beautiful head, pressing his mouth to her furry brow. Then he drew back slowly, lifting the rifle. He placed the barrel squarely between the big cat's trusting, great golden eyes. As his finger tightened on the trigger, Matthew turned hastily away; he shuddered as the shot echoed out in the still air. Afterward, when he turned slowly back, the Boy was bowed in eerily still infinite anguish over the slumped inert form of the dead leopard. Trudging wearily to him through the snapping grass, Matthew reached out and wordlessly touched the tense, shivering shoulder.

At the edge of the bush, the others waited. The gunshot had alerted them to the worst, and Katherine began to cry as she saw the truth on the Boy's dazed, pain-wracked face. He stumbled as he reached them, and Ward, Kathy, and Teller reached instinctively to help him. But ignoring their hands, he regained his equilibrium and hobbled haughtily on through their midst.

"Lean on me, son!" Matthew implored.

But even then, pale, perspiring, and panting with pain and exertion, he growled through gritted teeth: "I can help myself!"

And then it began. The long lonely walk. Using the rifle, buttdownward, as a crutch, the Boy limped along the slope, dragging his lacerated left leg in an awesome supreme effort, executed in proud suffering and pain.

How he ever got across the tremulous swing bridge in that condition was a source of amazement to them all. And yet, unaided, he did it. Slowly and painstakingly, limping gingerly, he dragged his torn leg and the trail of his own blood across the bumpy wooden slats. Following cautiously in his lurching wake, Matthew warned the others not to shake the ropes he depended upon for support; he anticipated the Boy's plunge into the swirling river below in wincing trepidation. But the Boy, through sheer will, defied this likelihood, and displaying remarkable stamina, began the long haul up the opposite slope to the hospital. At his approach, an alerted orderly came running. With maniacal stubbornness, the Boy warned him off and continued making his own tedious way, swaying and toiling up the slope, trailing a silent awed audience, which increased as he went. Finally, in the short-grassed hospital yard, Nurse Wikstrom, alerted by the cries, came hurrying to the scene. She stopped dead when she saw the blood-splattered Boy, her face crumpling in horror.

"*Njumwaice!*" she gasped, hands clasped to her mouth. "Can this be?"

He stared at her dully, blinking bewilderedly.

4

It took three orderlies to carry the unconscious Boy to the treatment room. Matthew waited beside the curtained cubicle while they laid him on a high white table, which was quickly stained with his blood. They pulled off his boots, and Ingrid, with shaking hands, began to cut away what was left of his jacket and jeans. Once he was naked on the table, she informed Matthew tightly that he had lacerations to his chest and his left thigh was extensively mauled. She cleaned carefully deep into the wounds with gauze dipped in iodine, tied off the blood vessels, and introduced plasma intravenously to combat shock and make up for the loss of blood. Leaving the wound open in case of infection, she taped the torn flesh together and covered it with sterile gauze before bandaging; she injected penicillin to fight the deadly bacteria found in scraps of rotted meat left in the claws of carnivorous animals. Then she and the rest of the mission watched over him and waited.

In the meanwhile Leroy was being subjected to similar treatment; although his lacerations were less serious, infection could be transmitted through a simple scratch, and the moaning, sweating youth was given penicillin injections and kept in the hospital. Due to the hostility between them, he was placed in a separate room, which was, unfortunately, adjacent to Than Profane's, and the following morning Katherine was distressed when the Fotches refused to exchange civil words with her in passing; they walked away from her commiserations about Leroy with noses in the air. Their sneering avoidance exemplified a corrosive un-Christian attitude, which Matthew resolved to remedy before it spread to infect their work.

Fighting down his own reluctance at the concession, he took a bottle of Teller's homemade orangeade to Leroy at lunchtime the following day. His cautious greeting was met with surly silence from the youth's rallying relatives, and Leroy, who lay on his stomach moaning affectedly, hastily shut his eyes the moment he saw Matthew; his black-eyed, beaten face had a piggy puffiness and his bandaged backside made a minor mountain under the bedclothes. He pretended not to notice Matthew, ignoring his stiff commiserations, and finally, stumped to inanity by the silent hostility surrounding him, Matthew turned to leave.

"*Do not imagine thee has seen the end of this matter!*" Clara burst irrepressibly as he reached the door. "Aside from being most brutally assaulted by that . . . that *shameless excuse for a doctor*, Leroy might have been killed by his accursed leopard! And you may be sure the board will hear about that!"

"Madam," Matthew said patiently, "the leopard thee speaks of is now dead, and the doctor was himself severely mauled; why not let the matter rest at that?"

"Never!" Tallulah snorted. She waddled around the bed in her swaddling skirts. "A doctor who goes around *brutalizing* pious Quaker pacifists is a barbarian who makes a laughingstock of all this mission stands for!"

"Friend, if thee'll beg pardon, the doctor can hardly be accused of making a habit of such behavior, and in this instance he was most sorely provoked."

"Indeed? And just what does thee mean to imply by that?" Orville pouted sullenly. "I suppose the doctor has been dreaming up excuses to cover his disgraceful behavior!"

"Indeed he has not." Matthew was indignant. "If thee had taken the trouble to find out, thee'd know he is presently in no condition to worry about such temporal matters! What's more, I need no explanations from Dr. Profane since I happened to witness the entire fracas myself."

"Oh?" Orville looked a trifle wary now; (nobody could doubt Matthew's long-established integrity). He said uneasily, "Well, I'm sure that's merely a matter of opinion."

"Not at all," Matthew said flatly. "I heard and saw exactly what happened."

"And exactly what might that be?" Orville hedged haughtily, looking away.

"Why don't thee ask Leroy?" Matthew said, and the youth, who had fallen silent and had one eye open as he strained to follow the conversation, abruptly shut it and began moaning again.

"Or Sidney." Matthew suggested sinisterly as they all stared helplessly at the moaning Leroy. "Thy son was there too. Why don't thee ask him? I'm sure the board would be particularly interested to hear his story. . . ."

Turning to go, Matthew stopped at the door. "Oh, and to be on the safe side, I'd keep the pair of them well out of Dr. Profane's way once he recovers. . . ."

He left with a grand flourish, sinfully, sumptuously enjoying the shocked, uncertain silence that followed him out.

Within twenty-four hours they knew that all Ingrid's precautions had not been enough; Than Profane had acute osteomyelitis, the destructive inflammation of hard bone tissue and the bone marrow, of his left femur. His temperature rose to 104 degrees, and his pulse was rapid. His face had a toxic flush and he was so dehydrated from vomiting continually that Ingrid introduced intravenous feeding, alternating glucose and saline. She gave him regular massive doses of penicillin to combat the infection, and drugged to kill the pain, he drifted in and out of a feverous delirium, hardly recognizing Katherine or Jayne, who hovered almost constantly at his bedside. And during his rare moments of sanity, he had a craving for vengeance that matched his raving for water.

Matthew was shocked at the Boy's deteriorated appearance when he stopped by for a visit. He lay on the high hospital bed looking pale and very ill, his body swathed in bandages and connected to a saline drip, his eyes in the sick sallow face dull with sedation and dark with pain.

"Matthew . . ." he whispered, talking so weakly that Matthew had to strain to hear him. "Listen to me . . . those two . . . two . . . *bastards* . . . we've got to get them! Report them to the board . . . get them off the mission . . . away from Jenny. . . ."

"Hush, boy," Matthew said anxiously, patting the bandaged hump of a knee beneath the bedsheet. The Boy immediately flinched and caught at his breath, face clenching with pain, and Matthew hastily withdrew his hand. "I'm sorry, son. Maybe thee should rest. This is no time to worry about . . ."

But breathing heavily with the exertion of talking, the Boy shook his head. "Matthew . . . you *have to* . . . promise me that."

"Now, now . . ." Matthew mumbled. "Don't thee worry about Jenny. She'll be fine. Leroy for one is presently in no condition to harrass *anybody*."

"*Jesus* . . ." the Boy whispered, closing his eyes. "*I should have let Bathsheba make a meal of that bastard!* . . . I should have . . ."

Matthew was horrified at the hatred on his face, so engrossed that he jumped when Ingrid entered the room, white-clad and officious.

"Professor, I am afraid I must ask thee to leave now. We cannot have our patient overtaxed."

"Surely." Matthew mumbled, standing up as Ingrid took a thermometer out of her breast pocket, shook it, and stuck it into the Boy's protesting mouth. Taking his free wrist, she began to consult her watch.

"Matthew . . ." the Boy lisped around the tiny glass tube, his urgent blue eyes seeking reassurance. "I'm . . . relying on you . . . you got to promise me . . . !"

The nurse clucked him into silence and Matthew, obediently backing out, stopped. "Yes, boy. Just thee rest assured."

He saw the Boy's face compose in relief; the heavy-lidded eyes closed, and he lapsed into fitful sleep again.

But Than Profane's condition worsened, and gravely ill, he rambled insensibly through long feverous nights. He called repeatedly for his wife, and Katherine, who had cabled the young woman immediately after the accident, waited impatiently for some response. But a brief letter was all that ever came. Katherine confided the contents to Matthew as they walked home one night after visiting the Boy.

"Oh, Matthew, I feel to blame." She raised tear-flooded eyes. "Perhaps, in my wish to spare her undue anxiety at that distance, I did not adequately convey the seriousness of his condition. She sends her love to him but feels unable to join him due to a . . . a *previous commitment.*"

"A previous commitment?" Matthew frowned incredulously.

"Yes." Katherine sniffed into a handkerchief. "Apparently she is presently fulfilling a modeling contract that cannot be broken without great financial forfeit. Also . . ." Katherine's sigh was totally without bitterness or censure; like her eyes, it was merely sad. "She feels an obligation to her agents, who rely on her."

They stopped and stood for a moment, struggling with the silence. Matthew turned away.

"I see." He nodded stiffly.

"Oh, Matthew!" Katherine pressed her handkerchief to her mouth. "What will I tell him?"

But Matthew had no better idea than she; he patted her shoulder ineffectually and they stumbled home together, silently mourning the matrimonial mess that the Boy was a party to.

But if Than Profane's own wife felt too indisposed to fly out to see him, many Africans who had only the barest acquaintance of him rode battered bicycles or walked weary miles to inquire after his condition. His family were heart-warmed by the increasing crowds that came to keep silent vigil outside the veranda of his room every day. Fauntleroy Fotch's quota of visitors was conspicuously small in comparison.

"Isn't it touching!" Tallulah enthused, loud enough for Matthew to hear as she and Clara walked ahead of him along the hospital corridors to visit Leroy. "They're worried about Leroy! Why, I declare that lovable scamp's become popular in so short a time! The natives dote on him!"

Matthew gritted his teeth at this arrogant distortion of the truth.

But there were other visitors the Fotches would not dare or deign to claim. Chief Jahaliso, bearing a hunk of fresh eland meat, was one of the few allowed in to see the sedated doctor; Kadesha, another, brought the condolences of his people, while Mulaisho, probably either too ill or intoxicated to come himself, sent commiserations with Furanswa, his head witchdoctor, a dubious emissary who had become a particular friend of Than Profane's. When Matthew arrived during an afternoon visiting hour, the mangy little man had tied his pet hyena to a tree and was busy spreading a variety of ritual symbols on the ground before the open veranda.

"Oh, Matthew, thank heavens thee've arrived!" Katherine met him, wringing her hands. "When I explained to this man he couldn't see Than, he started setting out his spells right outside here! And when the Fotches saw it, they hurried straight off to fetch Ezra. Something tells me they intend using this incident to create the most terrible trouble for Than! Trouble is, I can't get this man to understand that, and I don't relish hurting his feelings. I'm not sure Than would want me to, either. After all, he means well; his chief has apparently given him an injunction to cast out the evil spirits he believes are causing Than's illness."

Matthew understood her distress, and he was angry. Even while the Boy lay seriously ill, the feelingless Fotches fermented against him, and he noticed that while they had no compunction about claiming the more respectable of the Boy's beneficiaries as Leroy's, when it came to heathen witchdoctors, they were suddenly superciliously selective.

"Well now, Katherine," he mused thoughtfully, "I'm not so sure we should deny this man access to the patient. After all, as thee says, he means well."

While she stared incredulously after him, he stepped into Leroy's room. The youth was peacefully snoring as usual, and after quickly pulling the curtained screens around his bed, Matthew invited the surprised witchdoctor inside to cast his spells around 'the bwana who has been injured by the leopard.' While Katherine looked uneasily on, the grizzled little *ngaka*, earnestly agreeing not to disturb the sleeping patient, gathered up his grisly paraphernalia and entered

Leroy's room. He was well into an involved spiel and had just begun a low wailing incantation when the Fotches arrived with Ezra Peabody.

"Where is he?" Ezra panted up, looking wildly around. "Well, just listen to that heathen cant right in the doctor's room! Well, I sure never thought I'd see the day when *thee*, Katherine, would stand blithely by while this consecrated ground is being desecrated by the like of that . . ."

"Well, since Leroy is not her relative, Kathy hardly liked to interfere," Matthew answered for the dumbstruck woman, and Ezra squinted around at the Fotches in bewilderment.

"Leroy?"

Just then Leroy's door widened, and Furanswa, looking supremely satisfied, walked out. A wildebeest-tail fly switch tucked under one arm, he wiped his hands matter-of-factly, nodding at the stunned missionaries before strolling off, with a flounce of his tail-tassled kilt, to fetch his hyena and depart. Abruptly thawing from her shock, Tallulah gave a squeal of outrage and hurtled into Leroy's room; Orville hurried after her. In a moment, scraps of feathers, bones, a cock's head, and other odious objects were frenziedly kicked through the doorway before Ezra's disbelieving eyes. It took sundry prayers, glowering glances at Matthew, and a whole bottleful of Clara's meanly treasured lily-of-the-valley perfume before Leroy, rousing innocently to the furor all around him, was thought to be sufficiently sanctified again. Matthew, though secretly deeply shocked at himself and his shabby deception now that the dastardly deed was done, hung on to the frail hope that under the circumstances, the good Lord in his mighty mercy might not judge him too harshly.

5 Aggravated by excruciating pain, Than Profane's delirium brought his anxieties to the fore; obsessed with unfinished procedures, he struggled weakly to get out of bed to continue his medical work, ranting insanely about surgery to be performed and patients to be treated. The way Matthew heard it, Ingrid had to increase the sedation to keep him quiet. And all the time the infection raged. He had pseudoparalysis and muscle spasms.

And without a doctor's help, with the responsibility and running of the hospital added to her burdens, Ingrid was at her wit's end. What help was volunteered by the other missionaries was insufficient to relieve the strain. Jayne came to help out in the outpatient department, and the rest of the medical students became her auxiliaries. But with no supervision, Ingrid, Cosmo, and Mbiya were constantly on call, and Lars began to ferry the most urgent surgical cases to another mission hospital, near Solwezi. Ingrid operated on minor cases herself with the help of a trained black nurse while Cosmo, whose skill as a surgical assistant was now established, operated the anesthetic machine. All other surgical procedures were suspended indefinitely.

But the African patients were not Ingrid's most pressing concern. As the days passed, Than's condition continued to deteriorate, and she grew hollow-eyed and distraught with worry. Continuing the administration of penicillin to fight the toxemia, she immobilized his leg in a plaster cast to prevent pathological fracture due to the softening of the bone. Leaving an opening for the draining of pus from the medullary cavity, she covered the open wounds with sulphanilamide powder, packed lightly with petroleum jelly gauze. However these precautions did not prevent septicemia, which had developed four days after the injury, and near breaking point, she came to Matthew for counsel and prayer.

"I simply do not know what to do," she confessed wretchedly, staring fixedly down at the hands clasped tight in her lap. "I—I feel completely helpless . . ."

Matthew gave her a fatherly pat; not being medically minded himself, the only comfort he could give her was limited to his own blind faith.

"There, there, Friend, why not leave matters in the hands of the Lord?"

"In the hands of . . ." Ingrid stared at him stupidly. "But Professor, thee does not understand. It is not that simple. I have to make the decision myself. Now. The illness is so severe that I am afraid his heart may be damaged by the toxins. I may have to amputate the leg."

"*Amputate?*" Matthew started at the young nurse, stupefied with shock.

Ingrid nodded tightly. "In order to check the toxemia and septicemia and to prevent development of pyemia, which could be fatal."

"Dear Lord!" Matthew passed a hand across his face. "Oh surely there must be some other way? Could we not get a doctor down here for a second opinion?"

"Second opinion?" Ingrid stared at him dully. "Thee knows that is not possible. And anyway, it is a straightforward case. I have seen it many times before in cases of animal attacks. Usually, though, we can save the limb. But sometimes, as in this case . . . well, the organisms seem to be insensitive to antibiotics."

"I see." Matthew sat staring at the girl in stony acceptance. "And if thee . . . *does not amputate?*"

"If I do not amputate," Ingrid said with weary resignation, "then ultimate death is a very real possibility."

"I see." Matthew swallowed hard. He looked earnestly up at the girl. "And can thee perform this operation?"

"Amputation?" She stared at him blankly. "Well, I have assisted in the procedure often enough. And it's a fairly straightforward operation. Man has been performing it since ancient times."

"I see."

They sat for a moment in appalled stillness. No Quaker silence had ever been so tortured or stricken. With death the only other terrible alternative, Matthew was forced to the advice he gave in God's name.

"Then," he swallowed painfully, "I guess thee has no choice. The Lord has already decided for thee."

"Yes." Ingrid nodded stiffly, sighing. "I guess thee is right. Pray for me, Professor. I will need it."

She rose to leave the cozy comfort of his living room, unconsoled but instilled in her duty.

But both they and God had reckoned without Than Profane's manic stubbornness. The following morning, when Matthew and Ingrid were holding meeting for the Boy in his room, he suddenly opened his eyes and stared at Ingrid with a surprising lucidity. "Hi," he said.

"Thee!" Ingrid spun around in surprise. She tried to smile, but it was a tight-lipped effort and she choked on her own casual words. "Well, good morning to Thee! And how are thee feeling?"

"Pretty bad." He barely mouthed the words.

"I know." She nodded stiffly at him, and he stared at her steadily for a moment, as if trying to analyze her expression. "Don't look so worried," he said softly. "I'll be all right."

She looked up sharply then. *"No!"* she mourned wretchedly, shaking her head. "No, I am afraid thee will not."

He closed his eyes, face contorted.

"Just . . . just hold on to your nerve," he enunciated carefully, obviously struggling to keep his voice calm. "And keep on with the penicillin."

"Keep on with the penicillin?" Ingrid stared at him hopelessly, tears springing to her eyes. "Don't thee think that's what I've been doing? Don't thee know? But it's just no good. Thee still have pain and pyrexia. Thee have gone into the chronic stages and thee have septicemia."

"Yeah, I know. But that just means you have to prolong the treatment. We'll win out in the end. And my guess is, the drainage is inadequate. Also, there's probably separated bone tissue down there that you'll have to remove surgically. It may also help if you drill into the bone." He spoke slowly and carefully, gently, as if she were the patient and he the administrator. She stared at him in fright and he sighed, closing his eyes. "Nurse, you're starting to panic again."

"Panic?" she snapped, swallowing hard, closing her eyes fiercely tight, nodding. "Yes. Yes. I am panicking all right. But then I am only a nurse . . ."

"Well," the Boy said, smiling faintly, "that's the first time I ever heard you admit it."

". . . And thee, thee are no ordinary patient! And thee seem to forget the risk!"

"Ingrid!" he snapped, turning away, face awrack. "You're not going to amputate my goddamn leg, so just you forget it."

"Oh! How can thee say that!" She all but wept. "The responsibility is on me! It's easy for thee!"

"You think so?" Then he saw her face, and sighed, relenting. "Listen, I guess you're pretty tired and overworked. But I know what I'm talking about. So you don't have to worry."

"Not worry!"

"Ingrid! Are you ever being a bad nurse to me. Listen." He tried to smile. "Cosmo can help you, he's gotten pretty good and it's a simple operation to remove the bone slough."

"Simple for thee, yes! But thee forgets the other risk. I only wish I had thy confidence! Can thee not see? . . ."

"How long have I been ill?" he interrupted.

"About three weeks."

470

"Well, at this stage, the dead bone should be clearly distinguishable from the living."

She gave a harsh skeptical laugh. "Thee make's it all sound so simple."

He smiled faintly. "Listen, just give me a local anesthetic and I'll watch the procedure and give you and Cosmo directions."

"Directions?" She stared at him dumbly. "But thee cannot be serious. Thee cannot give directions for surgery upon thyself!"

He smiled at her dimly. "Ingrid, just you watch me. Who's the doctor around here, anyway, you or me?"

But Ingrid's reassurance at having the Boy's sane opinion behind her was short-lived. Within hours he had lapsed back into delirium, and she confessed to Matthew that unsupported, she felt full of doubt again. And in his delirium the Boy's fears were revealed. He became crafty and crazed, suspicious of her intentions and insanely obsessed with the idea that everyone was plotting to cut off his leg. He fought the black orderlies with insane strength, and they practically had to straitjacket him to continue treatment. But his desperate defensiveness had the desired result; by the following day, Ingrid was resigned to risk the lesser operation.

Than, although weak and very ill, awoke with a clear mind. He refused sedation, suffering the increased pain in order that he might retain his senses during the surgery, which Ingrid had scheduled to take place immediately. He was wheeled into the small OR room in a cold sweat of agony that became acute as he was moved by the orderlies onto the high OR table.

"Hey." Through gritted teeth, he smiled wanly at Ingrid. "Now I know what it feels like."

Ingrid nodded. Without a word, she administered a local anesthetic. Than was propped up on the table, and with the help of a strategically placed mirror was able to clearly view the wound site, as Ingrid, aided by Cosmo, worked slowly and uncertainly; he gave her instructions and encouragement when she wavered.

At last, to the great relief of them all, the operation was completed. A section of separated dead bone (sequestrum) was removed and the living bone drilled into. Than was wheeled back into his room in a thrall of pain and strain. He was given sedation and slept heavily throughout the day.

The following day, the first improvement could be detected in the subsidence of his temperature. And slowly, as the days went by, Ingrid and Than's family, in a rapture of relief, watched over him with bated breath as his condition gradually stabilized and the tremendous risk in not amputating the limb was proved worthwhile. Than developed a normal appetite and a renewed craving for cigarettes. The pain decreased and he began to pick up weight. The penicillin began to have effect, and the improvement was then so rapid that Ingrid was able to suture the wounds in two weeks. It was then that her greatest problem began. Freed of the sickness and delirium, Than was freed also of weakness and caution and would not resign himself to a lengthy convalescence in bed. With the aid of a pair of crutches enticed from an orderly, he began to slowly limp the long wards to review his patients. Ingrid, fuming fretfully, was no match for his stubbornness. She hurried along behind him, whispering chastisements as, smiling obliviously, he conducted his ward inspections, more interested in the record charts than her anger.

"Ingrid, will you for Chrissakes quit bitching and pay attention. Now, I want four or five of our worst surgical cases. Tomorrow, we operate."

The next morning, while Than stood propped up on his crutches, Ingrid, grim-faced, angrily handed him instruments, and he slowly and painstakingly performed a Caesarean section. His hands shook and the sweat popped out on his temples; he cut crookedly and fumbled with the sutures, but he worked doggedly, taking his time but doing fair work.

But one patient was as much as he could handle that first day; swaying on his feet, dizzy with pain, he had to be helped to a chair.

The next day Than got up, cleared out his locker, and discharged himself. Using the crutches entreated from Cosmo, wearing a dressing gown over his father's old pajamas, he limped home to get a fresh change of clothes. Today was Saturday, and Kathy fussed anxiously around him while he washed up, shaved, and changed. She made him coffee and flapjacks with maple syrup "to build up his strength." Finally, feeling suddenly shaky and sick, he limped into the kitchen, prepared to give in to his stepmother's motherly ministrations. He stopped in the doorway, surprised to find Jennifer Solomon sitting at the table, spread with its lemon gingham cloth, near the window, where a fresh morning breeze billowed the frilled matching curtains. Lifting the steaming coffee pot off the big black coal stove with a cloth, Kathy smiled at him fondly.

"Jenny's just come over to ask how thee are."

Than leaned the crutches against the wall, engineering himself awkwardly into a chair. "Oh? Well, as I recall it, my door was always open."

Jenny colored at once. "I—I didn't like to intrude on the family when you were so sick." She looked up earnestly. "But I prayed for you. Every day!"

"Well, Jenny, I don't know what you're worried about." Than scooped up a forkful of the syrupy pancakes and chewed listlessly. "My own wife never bothered."

Then he saw the pain on her face and he was instantly ashamed, surprised at his own bitterness. Suddenly depressed, he sighed, setting down his fork. "Listen, Jenny, it's no big deal. Just forget it, huh?"

But she stared sightlessly down at her clasped hands and he knew he had hurt her deeply.

6 At the end of 1962, Britain had accepted Nyasaland's right to secede from the Federation. Now, at the London Conference of Northern Rhodesian Nationalists, the *Litunga* of Barotseland urgently repeated his call for the secession of his protectorate, and amid the nationalists' demand that Northern Rhodesia be allowed to secede from the Federation, Sir Roy Welensky made a desperate last stand for the ideal he had so long cherished. But it was a pitiful petition and he stood alone; in the last election, his party had been defeated in all three territories of the Federation he had worked so long and hard to create and perpetuate. Well, that was the way it went; but now that the noisy native nationalists were finally top dog, Matthew's sympathies, ever for the underdog, severely shifted; he felt acutely sorry for the white man, who was, he felt sure, well-meaning and just as much a victim of upbringing and circumstances as were the blacks.

Than Profane's recovery filled Matthew with relief; only now did he feel able to devote himself wholeheartedly to his mission duties again. And these were many. Besides building a one-block teachers' training college (one of his own long-cherished dreams), he and Ward Disney had to supervise the building of an airfield for Suseshi;

apart from the fact that the Congo troubles had showed them the necessity for such a rapid route of travel, Than Profane's ambitious dream of eventually initiating a flying doctor service, centered at Suseshi to facilitate speedy visits and the ferrying of the seriously sick from his out-clinics, had apparently impressed their last annual batch of visitors from home. Two businessmen, forming a "concern" for the project, proposed raising money for the purchase of a light aircraft. In the meanwhile the mission board, still shocked at their narrow escape in the Congo and nervous about their safety in their own area now that the country was to achieve black rule, had sponsored the building of a runway to facilitate it.

The long days and nights passed and gradually Than was able to resume more and more of his medical work. Although he was easily exhausted and suffered constant pain with his leg, he battled doggedly on. The muscles of his left thigh had healed shrunken and twisted, so he was left with a limp. The leg was stiff and sore and Ingrid made him exercise it and gave him a daily massage to loosen the stiffening muscles. Gradually he progressed and was able to move around more nimbly and for more prolonged periods, providing he took brief, intermittent rests. Ingrid played constant nurse over his health, aggravating him like the pain in his leg. Her advice, for all he listened, was as good as not given at all, and he continued to work and overwork. Suffering sleepless nights due to his pain, he would head for the hospital, often finding Ingrid or a night nurse wrestling with some problem he was better able to handle.

One night he was rudely awakened from the rare oblivion of sleep, summoned by Mbiya to a premature birth. Despite all he could do, the undernourished, prematurely aged mother gave stillbirth to a gray malformed child, then promptly died herself, swamped in a hemorrhage that drenched the obstetrics table and dripped onto the floor. Than and Ingrid stood back finally, besplattered in blood, bludgeoned with failure and fatigue. Exhausted, they stood silently side by side and stripped off their soiled white overclothes. Leaving the two pitiful bodies laid out beneath a sheet while a night nurse mopped up the blood, they left the dark hospital and stumbled silently home, leaving behind anguished relatives, who had carried the woman miles to this quick ugly end.

The night air breathed on them with soft chill breath and somewhere in the deep dark bush a jackal caterwauled like a courting cat. They walked across the softly swinging rope bridge and up the dark moon-touched slope, moving close together in a shared comfort, jostling against one another as they encountered the ruts and rises of the uneven ground. In the cold air, Than's bad leg pained him badly and he limped heavily, gingerly testing the black shadows. Before going his own way, he escorted Ingrid to the little boxlike house that sat high up on the slope, looking prim and unpretentious as the brother and sister it housed. At the door, Ingrid turned and looked at Than with concern.

"The leg, I can tell it is bad. Come inside awhile. I will give the massage."

Than began to protest, but subdued by a numbing lethargy, he gave in to the firm capable pull of her hand.

"Lay down on the couch," she said matter-of-factly, leading the way confidently into the small dark living room. He stood watching her fumble with some matches at the white globular sphere of an oil lamp.

"Don't light it," he said softly. "It's restful in the dark."

She shrugged and led him to a low skin-thonged kaffir couch. He lay down on the lumpy cushions with his aching leg stiffly outstretched. Kneeling beside him, she began to knead and rub at the scarred tender flesh of his thigh through the rough denim of his jeans. He gasped a little at the hurtful release.

"Don't you want my pants off?"

"No, no." She was breathing a little heavily, sounding flustered; what was sanctified in a hospital would be improper in the home. She had to work doubly hard through the material, and he sighed as he felt the sore stiffness gradually let go. The pleasurable release mellowed into a warm languor that pooled, specifically, deep-seated, in his loins, and he opened smoky eyes, now accustomed to the darkness, and stared at the thin boyish woman who leaned over him, with a frank lust.

"Ingrid?" He took hold of one of her thin supple hands and moved it up his thigh, holding it pressed, against her will, over the hot straining hump at his crotch. She drew back in shocked surprise, and he held her hand in a grip of iron.

"Feel it?" he said softly, voice husky with desire. "I guess I want you."

He tumbled off the couch at her, bowling her over so that they lay panting and entwined on an Impala skin rug, shivering and shocked, fumbling in conflicting intentions.

"No! No! What is thee doing?"

But he shut off her protests with the soft sucking pacifier of his mouth. His probing tongue was stopped at the cold defensive barrier of her clenched teeth, but his hands, moving down, sought softer pastures. At first he caressed only lightly, countering her contesting hands. Then gradually, as her breathing changed to soft panting gasps and her tugging hands seemed to lose conviction, he gave up all pretentious playing and brazenly unbuttoned the top of her white ether-smelling smock, pressing his mouth against one small hard breast. She gasped, stupefied, sagging against him in sudden surrender. And lying on the stiff brace of his bad leg, the throbbing pain coursing it became the aggravating impetus driving Than on to this mindless madness. He ripped aside her hands and buttons, and pulling down her bra, found a stiff shocked nipple with his mouth.

"No. No," she murmured, but he could tell her protest was only token now, and she lay rigid and lifeless beside him, mesmerized by the pleasurable suck of his mouth, holding his head pressed close as an infant at feed. But some of her supine, sacklike surrender left her as his hands moved down and began to wrest with her bloomers. Then her free hand, coming to life like a guard caught napping, was instantly resisting, tugging at his hand with clawlike ferocity, denying entry to the sacred cotton-armored spheres of her undeflowered maidenhood.

"*Oh Jesus!*" he whispered vexedly. His leg was a raw pain beneath him. "Don't fight me now!"

Then, in desperation, sensing her reasserting sensibilities, he wrenched at the tight denim of his own pants. He ripped and fumbled, finally bringing forth the silken-sheathed conscienceless rod of his own warm living flesh. He took her hand and her fingers felt soft and cool cupped around him, her inexperience and surprise as exciting as sin. She made no move to draw away, but lay beside him, breathing catchily, thrashing a little, her knees drawing up against his thighs in sensuous distraction, gasping softly through her mouth. And then, as shocking as a bull crashing through a china shop, a voice broke into their perverse preoccupation, invading their light-headed lunacy, welding them with horror. It was Lars, calling from a back bedroom.

"Ingrid, is that thee?"

The two on the floor went into a rigor of shock. *Oh damn him, damn him, damn him!* In that moment, the hair-trigger catalyst, so sensitive through long denial, was set off. Than gasped silently as the paroxysm of release rippled through him, convulsing his body, ejecting warm wetness that spilled over their clasped hands. Ingrid was pulling away from him even before it was over, her harsh voice grating against his mood like salt rubbed into a raw wound.

"Yes! Yes! I am here!" she called out, sounding breathless and guilty, her wet hand pulling away, as slippery as a fish through Than's urgently retaining fingers.

"Are thee sure? Thee sounds . . . strange." There was a quality of listening in Lars's cautious voice.

"Yes! J-just tired!" Ingrid scrambled to her feet and fumbled to light the lamp. Than, left lying on the skin mat, closed his eyes in an anguish of frustration and shame. Soiled with semen and an unsatisfactory climax, he numbly made himself decent, dragging himself awkwardly up onto his good knee just as the lamp blossomed glaring light, aggravating the soured feeling inside him. He stood up slowly, suddenly bewildered.

How had this mindless madness suddenly overcome them? There was no accounting for it now in the sallow light of sanity and the oil lamp. Ingrid was staring at him stupidly, wiping her soiled hand frantically against her smock with a look of distaste. Well, what did she think he was made of anyway? Stone?

"I guess I have to thank you, Nurse." He smiled at her wryly. "You massaged me real good."

After that, surprisingly, he found her far easier to handle. Much of the stiff Swedish starch had gone out of her cool impartial manner, and he had only to stare into her pale blue eyes to get her flustered, breaking down the armor of indifference she had previously used against him.

7

Than Profane's insistence that the Dooleys were not to be told of his accident and illness had been ignored by Matthew, who had anxiously watched him grow thin and emaciated under the increasing strain of his failing health and an abominable workload. And as he had known they would, the family, full of concern, arrived back at the mission, fatter, fit, and rested, fully two and a half months ahead of time. Matthew saw the shock on Jerome's face as the Boy limped into their living room to greet them. And despite his protests, Jerome was adamant; the Boy should take off to his wife in

Salisbury for six weeks' rest. But the Boy was equally as adamant. He was going nowhere; Jerome would need him at Suseshi. He seemed to feel no one but himself capable of running the hospital, and even Jerome's allusions to his "pigheaded egotism" failed to move him. He was staying right where he was needed.

Such was his vehemence over the issue that they were all surprised and mystified a few days later, when the Boy meekly rescinded his objections and agreed to take the time off. It was only later, when Matthew came upon him packing his car a day before departure, that he began to understand. He stared at the Boy's luggage in surprise. His medical bag, sleeping bag, and food and medical supplies were amongst the paraphernalia he stashed into the trunk along with a large haversack.

"Well, now," Matthew sniffed suspiciously. "What have we here? Doesn't look to me like thee're off to a peaceful vacation in suburban Salisbury. What is thee up to Boy?"

The Boy straightened. "You sure you want to know?"

"I'll risk it."

"Well," the Boy said, shutting the trunk. "I'm off to seek out a certain witchdoctor, name of Kwoyisho, who just may hold the key to the cure for cancer."

"Kwoyisho?" Matthew stared stupidly. "I've heard of him; he's highly thought of amongst the natives, but thee doesn't for one minute believe . . ."

"I don't believe it, but I've seen it," the Boy said, and he was dead serious. "And if he can cure a cancer-riddled man whom we had given up as hopeless, then he knows something I'd like to know. Apparently he's been over in the Congo for some months, evading the authorities on some charge under the Witchcraft Ordinance. I've just heard he's recently returned and is presently holed up on some secluded island on the Zambezi River, apparently preparing to train some novices in his craft. I aim to join him there."

"But that's ridiculous!" Matthew spluttered. "Thee has to rest. Thee told Jerome . . . I mean—*thee can't do that!*"

"Oh can't I?" By the grim determination on his face, Matthew knew that it was useless to argue.

8 At Jahaliso's village on the Balovale, the young Lunda chief waited with an African guide he had procured for Than as a part of the free service engendered him by their blood-brotherhood pact. Leaving his car parked at the village in the chief's care, Than and the shabbily dressed guide took up his equipment and set off through the Balovale bush on foot. Hot and sweating, scratched by underbrush and bedeviled by insects, they reached the wide blue Zambezi River, where the guide, Basubila, a Barotse basket weaver who commuted to and from the North Western province to sell his wares, had a handmade canoe secreted in the undergrowth. After loading it with their provisions, the man took up his position in the bow while Than sat astern. As they paddled out into the main stream, Than had to concentrate to maintain balance in the precarious craft; carved and cauterized in one piece out of a tree trunk, the shallow fifteenfoot-long narrow and knobbled dugout wobbled alarmingly at his every movement, threatening to summarily overturn with any sudden lurch. But gradually, as he got the feel of it, Than relaxed and began to enjoy the breeze on his face and the passing panorama.

Thick *miombo* bush rose up on either side, lush, green, and majestic with palm trees, spreading tamarinds and great wild figs, some of whose spiderous roots kissed their reflections from eroded banks. One or two other craft traversed the river and they passed occasional riverside villages from which native bathers and fishermen stringing nets, seeming fatalistically indifferent to the crocodiles in these murky waters, waved to them from the plume-tossing papyrus banks. By the time dusk fell, heralded by the shrill clamoring of birds, Than's exposed skin stung with sunburn and his unaccustomed arms were beginning to ache from the continious paddling. He was relieved when they tied up at a fallen tree trunk, preparing camp on a bushy bluff that overlooked the river. At a small smoky fire they ate warmed-up corned beef and beans. Then Than crawled into a sleeping bag, the guide curled up in a blanket, and they spent the night swatting off frenziedly whining giant mosquitoes while the cool evening air was horrendously rent with the snapping smashing of foliage and the furious bellows and savage snarls of a pair of dueling male hippos, which sounded ominously close.

It seemed to Than that he had scarcely drifted into a troubled slumber when the muffled booming of hornbills and Basubila's polite shake snapped him awake again. The pearly pink sheen of the fresh cloud-streaked dawn sky was reflected in a glass-smooth river shrouded by hushed breathing mists that wafted ethereally from the warm reeded banks. A skein of the graceful great white egrets were magically mirrored as they soared along above the river, and as Than and the guide pushed off in the laden canoe, a magnificent fish eagle, the black, white, and rufus king of the African skies, swooped to snatch a wriggling fish from the waters. By now Than's strained arm muscles had started to stiffen, and the river, swelled by the Kabompo and the sluggish Lungwebungu tributaries, required more dexterity; stiff little waves were whipped up by an early wind, the surging waters channeled through confusing labyrinths of reeds, and around a blind bend they were suddenly pitched into a sun-basking herd of hippopotami, which floated like a clump of gigantic boulders in the green water. The beasts are notoriously aggressive, and Than, furiously paddling, endured a heart-stopping moment when an enormous bull suddenly surfaced alongside their canoe, blowing and snorting; its little pink piggy ears twitched as it yawned monstrously, displaying, at terrifyingly close range, a monumental mouthful of blunt tusks in huge jaws that could snap their crude craft with a single bite.

That evening, serenaded by the wild lonely screams of settling fish eagles, they beached at a special camp for river travelers; since the river formed part of the "labor route" used by migrant mineworkers recruited at Mongu, several such shelters dotted the banks at appropriate intervals, and in the cleared communal campground they were joined by two canoe-loads-full of laughing young Lozi men, who chattered excitedly about an imminent airplane ride that would take them to Bechuanaland, from where they would be entrained to the gold mines of South Africa. They gave Than some herbal insect repellent and invited him and his guide to sup with them on fish baked with onions and wild bananas in leaves baked in the fire's coals. It was a succulent meal, and since the night was cool and clear, sweetly scented with wild water-lilies, Than slept out in the open under an immense black star-twinkled sky. The insect repellent proved effective, and he awoke the next morning feeling satisfyingly fed, rested, and refreshed.

While the forest around them resounded with the song of wood pigeons and little green doves, he shared a steaming pot of coffee with their companions before they parted company, setting off ahead of the Lozis into sun-shot swirling pink and gold mists, disturbing early wallowing flocks of sandpipers, herons, and softly whistling pygmy geese. As they drifted on through the day, the river constantly changed; in the steep banks, colonies of brilliant carmine bee-eaters were a pinkish dazzle of wing-whirring activity, and from the placid, lotus-fringed stretches, they were tossed around on churning currents and had to veer to avoid great green islands, their beaches strewn with basking crocodiles, while floating patches of tangled sedge and great clinging clumps of the mauve, white, pink, and blue water hyacinths threatened to clog up their passage.

In the hot afternoon, they heard the plaintive *pula pula* of a forest bird, before a sudden storm blew up from nowhere; before they could reach shelter on shore, the sky had turned black and the tortured heavens, splintered with brilliant whiplashes of lightning, opened above them with a thunderous roar, releasing a stinging staccato of rain that dimpled the surging gray river and swiftly soaked them to their skins. The damp set off a bout of rheumatism in Than's bad leg, and the storm delayed their progress, so they failed to reach the next sheltered camp before nightfall. Than spent the night sleepless and chilled, clawing at his aching thigh as he lay, wrapped in his jackall skin kaross, shivering and huddled beneath his rubber ground sheet under leaf-pattered wet trees, which dripped dismally.

The morning broke fresh and sunny, and as they penetrated Barotseland the remote banks grew sandy and the vegetation receded, gradually flattening as the great river melted lazily to swamp the vast Barotse Flood Plain to the horizon. Here they had to row for miles to camp on shore at night, using long bamboo sticks to pole through shallowing waters past protruding tree tops and a deserted village of water-lapped stilted huts and patches of maize treacherous with clinging clusters of virulent red ants and slithering scores of hissing swaying snakes trapped by the flood.

After a time, as they traveled on and on, the days merged into one in Than's mind. His guide was a serious man who seldom smiled or spoke, and out in this awesome wilderness, growing instinctively in tune with each other's unspoken needs and moods, they fell into a companionable silence, into a strange timeless limbo that was like nothing Than had ever known before. Soul-stirred by the stupendous sights and sounds of this wild lonely landscape, by the surrealistic splendor of the flaming sunsets and the hushed iridescent dawns that sandwiched the cold uncomfortable nights and the hard hazardous days, his senses seemed to expand and he developed a rapport with the river and its environs, intuitively assessing its mores and moods as he sat alertly astern, in constant vigilant anticipation of rapids, rocks, hippos, or the swirling whirlpools that could turn any unsuspecting moment into a furious fight for survival.

Once they left the plain, gigantic barricades of basalt catapulted the lazy flow of the flood plain into riotous rapids and the cascading cataracts of the inspiring Sioma and Ngambwe falls, all of which forced them to make long portages through thick bush around the rocky straits and deep gorges. On the river again, they reached broken sparsely wooded mopani country; on one bank lay the Caprivi Strip of South West Africa. Here a solid phalanx of black rock barred their passage and they were bedeviled by the tiny insistent mopani flies as they once again toiled with the hoisted canoe and their luggage through the bush near Katimo Mulilo. After this the river flowed tranquilly through wide bush-blurred imposing banks and they waved back at colorfully uniformed African children being ferried on a pontoon to school at Susheke on the Northern Rhodesian bank. They rowed on through low malarial marshes interspersed with little tree-covered kopjes, where a pack of baboons foraged in the swamp grass, a couple of these incuriously watching colorful characters casually copulating as they paddled past. Further on, on the broad Susheke plain, Basubila pointed out scatterings of the rare red lechwe, and out on the open vlei they saw boiling black herds of wildebeest and buffalo.

They portaged past the Mambova rapids, and after the confluence of the Chobe River at Kazungula, the frontiers of Northern Rhodesia, Southern Rhodesia, Bechuanaland, and South West Africa met. Flowing on, the swollen river quickened as it neared the cataclysmic leap of the Victoria Falls, and paddling with desperate dexterity, they shot a succession of unruly rapids that alternated wide smooth stretches. Narrowly negotiating tumultuous channels between thickly forested islands and sand spits encrusted with crocodiles, they encountered an awesome entourage of stately gray elephants along the left bank. Then, several miles from the falls, Than suddenly discerned a faint faraway roar above the liquid rushing of the river and looked up to see a distant smudge like smoke that increased as they grew closer, soaring massively several hundred feet into the air to form *Mosi-oa-Tunya*, The Smoke That Thunders, the immense rainbowed shroud of spray and mist caused when the mile-

and-a-half-wide river, in full flood, poured down a 335 foot chasm to form one of the seven natural wonders of the world—the Victoria Falls.

About three miles from the lip of the mighty canyon, Than and Busubila fought the careening accelerating current to beach their canoe on a large forested island reputed to be the secluded retreat of the legendary Kwoyisho. The roar of the falls carried clear on the still air and the day was thickening into dusk as they alighted and tentatively began exploring the vegetation-shrouded rocky island. There was the swaying motion of monkeys in the high trees, and the ominous clawed slithers of crocodiles marked the sandy beach; otherwise the place seemed silent and deserted. Than was just beginning to feel disillusioned when they smelled smoke and Basubila pointed out a cluster of little clay water gourds and a reed-screen half-hidden in the foliage. Then, at a sudden snapping of twigs, they turned to find themselves confronted by a line of about a dozen traditionally dressed surly men and one bare-breasted woman, who stared at them in suspicious hostility.

One of the young men held an ancient tower musket. He warily fingered the highly polished bead-decorated butt, and Basubila had to talk persuasively for several minutes before the men relaxed their vigilance, staring curiously at Than. Informed of their mission, they grudgingly invited them to be seated at the site of their habitation, a utensils-littered spot screened with reed fences beneath the gloomy shadows of trailing mopani trees and tall vegetable-ivory palms where two small fires were boiling the evening meal. A man went off to find Kwoyisho, eventually returning to inform them that the famed witchdoctor would see them in the morning; in the meanwhile they were invited to share their food and shelter for the night.

By now there was a decided chill in the air, and exhausted and aching, his bad leg paining him badly, Than ate a little of the *nshima* and fish offered them before curling up in his sleeping bag under a thatch shelter among a dozen other blanket-swaddled sweat-smelling bodies. Thus, amid these snoring companions, lulled by the roar of the great waterfall, he fell into a restless sleep in which he dreamed that Kwoyisho turned out to be his own dead father, dressed like a native, who proceeded to reveal to him the amazing herbal cure for cancer. In the midst of this Than looked up and saw Bathsheba; she looked at him, whimpering pathetically, but when he tried to approach she growled reproachfully and disappeared. He awoke with a throbbing head and an aching leg, feeling uneasy and disorientated.

After a brief wash and a mug of coffee, he and Basubila were escorted along a deep moldy-leafed path to a dilapidated little hut set among thick shrubbery on the other side of the island. Out of this edifice Kwoyisho stepped into the early sunlight. Dressed in skins, beads, and feathers, he was a spry-looking gray-haired old man, surprisingly frail-looking for his awesome reputation; his sensitive face was finely wrinkled, and he smoked on a small clay pipe and stared serenely at Than out of wise and serious monkeylike bright brown eyes. Softly clapping his hands in the traditional native greeting, Than introduced himself and Basubila.

"Please enter my house and we will talk," the old man said concisely in the Chi-Lwena Than had addressed him in. "Your name has come before you, and I have heard many men talk of your powers of healing."

In the dim little hut, seated around a small smoky fire among piles of skins, horns, gourds, and other curious utensils, Than and Kwoyisho talked for almost three hours. Than countered the old man's quiet refusal to impart any secret of his traditional craft to an uninitiated stranger with desperate pleas for him to relax the ruling in the universal interests of science and medicine. Sadly, the old man told him that the decision rested not with him but with the dead ancestors who guided and controlled the work of all herbalists and diviners from the world of spirit; these had long ago decreed the rule that excluded Than. Unable to penetrate the solemn old man's implacable resolution, Than finally left him and broodily prowled the island, acidly angry with his huge disappointment. Suddenly, in the midst of his frustrated fuming, the dream of his father resurfaced, and remembering seeing his father dressed as a witchdoctor, he was struck by a preposterous idea that was powerful in its potential. He hurried back to Kwoyisho's hut and the old man regarded him patiently as he asked to be trained as a witchdoctor along with the other novices under tuition on the island.

"I am sorry," Kwoyisho sighed regretfully, removing his pipe. "I am not given authority to instruct people who are not of my own tribe and race."

Than stared at the man in a slump of despair; he had almost given up hope when a sudden thought sent him hurrying back to the novice camp. He fumbled in his bedroll for the small sack of items he had so fortuitously decided to bring along, finally reentering Kwoyisho's hut feeling as shy and irrepressibly proud as a schoolboy with top grades in his class. Kwoyisho stared at Than's lion-tooth necklace and the jackal-skin kaross with renewing interest; his bright monkey eyes and small wrinkled black hands brooded upon the carved wooden fetish that had broken up a raging Baluba rebellion in Katanga three years ago.

"You see," Than touched the healed cuts on his face and held up the necklace triumphantly, "my scars and these trinkets prove me to be the blood brother of the Lunda chief, Jahaliso, and therefore an honorary African. Also I have been told that you yourself are of half-Lunda parentage; we are therefore tribal brothers. And last night I dreamed of my dead father; he too was dressed like you and he promised to show me the cure for cancer."

Knowing of the superstitious African prerequisite that just such a dream of an ancestor should serve to appoint a novice and give legitimacy to his training, Than was innately grateful that the peculiarly opportune dream enabled him to speak truthfully. The old man was obviously impressed. He tugged on his worn pipe, his liquid eyes thoughtfully narrowed in the fire-flickering gloom. "You must go away and allow me to think on these things now. I must speak with my ancestors."

Than left his regalia with the old man. He sat with Basubila, idly watching the activities of the trainee witchdoctors as he impatiently awaited Kwoyisho's decision. Before nightfall he had his reply. It was a smiling Kwoyisho who invited Than back into his hut at dusk. The spirits had assented, and if he could meet Kwoyisho's fee and certain other requirements, Than Profane would become the first white man in Africa to be trained as a witchdoctor.

9 Kwoyisho's fee for the training was set at one ox; this fee was not normally formally revealed before the training was completed, but as Than's circumstances were markedly different from those of the usual initiate, Kwoyisho candidly answered his questions and seemed happy with the offer of fifty pounds, which was all the money Than had brought with him and considerably more, he judged, than the current market price of a Barotse cow. With the business aspect thus prematurely settled, it was decided that Than's course would begin the next day. The aged *ngaka* agreed to instruct

him for a period of four weeks, after which time Than would be formally initiated with the other novices and free to practice the ancient craft throughout the land. Than's guide, Basubila, who had an injunction from Jahaliso to look after *Njumwaice's* every need, had to be convinced he would not be needed in the interim before he left for his home at dawn, promising to return to the island to fetch Than on the appointed day of his initiation. Than watched the solemn, quiet man paddle off into the early mists with the feeling of parting with an only friend; he turned back to find Kwoyisho, in his tailed skins and feathers, silently awaiting him on the damp mossy path.

Thus began a period of intensive training that seemed to climax the absurd in Than's life. While Kwoyisho, a reasonable man, was prepared to make modifications where obvious differences demanded these, he would not bend on the ruling that Than was to eat, dress, and live like his native companions during the period of his training. Of his Western garb, Than was not even permitted to retain his undershorts, and under Kwoyisho's watchful eye, in the little smoky hut, he quickly stripped off his clothing and dressed himself in items from Kwoyisho's own varied wardrobe. Finally he stood clad in a kilt of striped genet tails over a skimpy skin breechclout, a short black and white cowhide cape, python skin amulets filled with medicines, seed-pod anklets that rattled around his bare feet as he walked, strings of beads around his waist, and a cowry shell necklace, which was worn with his prized string of lions teeth. He had been given a *jusango*, or rattle, comprising a round seed pod tied to a stick; an ancient blunt *gano*, or ceremonial sword; a bead-bedecked zebra-tail fly switch, a cupping horn, and various old containers: bottles, tins, gourds, a kudu horn, a skin bag, and a tortoise shell, in which to store his medicines. Finally fully kitted out to Kwoyisho's frowning satisfaction, Than felt heathenish and strange, conspicuously white and naked.

Kwoyisho's teaching commenced every day at dawn, hence the novices were expected to be up before the sun had broken through the trees. The old man began each lesson by talking to the other novices in their native Sikololo; since they were more advanced in their training, they then went their separate ways, seeking out herbs and concocting such medications or fetishes as Kwoyisho requested, returning at intervals to extract his inspection and approval. Than, however, remained at first at the old man's side as Kwoyisho gave him an intensified course of instruction, which began with aspects of ancestor worship and divination, progressing on to herbal remedies and their concoction, which, as an herbalist, were Kwoyisho's specialty.

Than found the first few days tough and tedious; he felt uncomfortable in the unaccustomed skins and fetishes and found it difficult to converse continuously in Chi-Lwena. The strange food, which he was expected to help prepare, he found even more difficult to adjust to. In the damp atmosphere his injured leg constantly ached with rheumatism and he limped around, shivering in the shade in his semi-naked state, once the sun sank below the trees. And the nights, on a pliant reed mat and a hard wooden headrest, were no less easy to endure. However, gradually, as the days passed under the hot sun of their secluded island retreat, he became accustomed to the arduous and rigorous routine, and submerging into the strange world of nature, witchcraft, and herbalism, Than forgot himself; his skin burned a deep glossy bronze and the stubble grew on his chin, and oblivious to all else, he fell under the spell of Kwoyisho, with his quiet melodious voice and his calm wise face, as he learned of antiquated customs and a bush lore that began to fascinate him. He watched Kwoyisho tremble in a trance and talk in a variety of strange voices, giving accurate directions as to where certain herbs could be found; these, if mixed with certain others, would certainly cure such and such ailments. Than was skeptical and awestruck. Kwoyisho, in the manner of a good teacher, cross-questioned him continuously to ensure his comprehension, and Than learned more about native lore in a week than he had learned at the mission in years.

In the second week, he was taught about African herbs and their action and interaction on the human body, and Than's climbing interest quickened. So as not to forget the myriad details, he took to surreptitiously jotting them down on a small notepad he kept stashed in his unused bedroll, during the time and privacy allowed him to go into the bushes to perform his private toilet. Now, as the days went by, his excitement grew and he could scarcely await each dawn to begin embarking on new trails of discovery. On the tenth day, when Kwoyisho declared him finally fit to accompany the other novices on their hunt for herbs, he felt as excited as a new intern again. He was allowed to keep clippings of the plants and roots used, and these he kept in his mongoose-skin pouch, which had been specially made for the purpose, meticulously marking each with name tags that corresponded with his secret notes of their properties and popular usage.

*   *   *

In the first days he learned the African cure for such common ailments as dysentery and diarrhea, decreased lactation in nursing mothers, headaches, bronchial and lung complaints, and asthma, and excessive menstrual bleeding.

On the fourth day, the nature of their needs required a trip to the mainland, where the "ancestors" decreed a certain rare plant would be found in the rain forest of the Falls. In four dugout canoes they crossed to the Northern Rhodesian bank, where they left the canoe, walking through the thick green bush the three miles to the Falls. Its roar increased as they went, the cloud of spray now an awesome formation that loomed high above them in the blue sky. Taking a tangled, slippery-wet, prickly path through the underbrush, they finally reached it. Than stood on the eastern cataract and stared in utter awe. Twice as high and one and a half times as wide as Niagara Falls, this magnificent sweep of water was truly stupendous. The wide river, now a reddish gold with the sand sediment of the full flood, was compressed into a narrow channel before it burst over the ledge of a 335-foot-deep, long and narrow zig-zagging fissure in the earth's face, pouring five million gallons of water per minute into the yawning chasm with a titanic roar and reverberation that stunned the senses; the rebound alone was awesome, the huge cloud of fine spray falling in an eternal rain upon the luxuriant gleaming green forests directly opposite, and through the swaying dripping tropical palms and ferns, amid the tangle of riotous growth, Than stared in wonder at the fantastic formations of white foam as the great river churned tumultuously over the edge. The other novices, obviously used to the spectacle, were amused at his awe. While they began their search in the dripping wet undergrowth, one of the young men, curly black eyelashes bejeweled and blinking in the falling mist, pointed out the different sections of the immense cataracts, which were colloquially known as the Eastern Cataract, the Rainbow Falls, the Main Falls, and the Devil's Cataract. Than shook his head in the fine rain, deeply impressed. With the roaring immense spectacle so close, he found it difficult to concentrate on their herbal search and kept looking up to feast his incredulous eyes on the stunning view through the veil of mist and the tropical tangle of vines and monkey ropes.

It was while he was thus preoccupied that he became aware of a small group of white people standing on a path across the wide slope from them; they wore raincoats, and by their cameras and binoculars, he realized they must be tourists. Their awed gazes must have skirted the width of the stupendous view before they turned to find him there amid the like-clad group of Africans. Yet even swamped by the magnificent roaring natural spectacle, they were staring at him, mouths agape in astonishment, and he suddenly realized the strange picture he must present. Steeped in his present psychology, he found it hard to remember that near here there was a civilized thriving tourist town, named Livingstone after the legendary missionary discoverer of the Falls—and the contrast in standards made his position so ludicrous that he felt acutely uncomfortable. Staring compulsively back, he was glad when Kwoyisho, leading the search, turned and hailed the group onward. Than followed obediently; when he looked back, the tourists, oblivious of the miracle of nature that roared in foaming thunder over the gigantic gorge, were still staring after him in nonplussed amazement.

Back on the island, at the familiar-growing camp among the great gloomy trees, Than felt himself finally fully identifying with his African companions. Somehow the white tourists had seemed strangely alien, worlds apart from him, and the forming of a particular friendship in the group had helped him to feel conformed; the pleasant-faced African who had so politely shown him the Falls and helped him to find his herbs turned out to be Katende, Kwoyisho's youngest son, a young Barotse apparently destined to follow in his father's footsteps.

The next day Than awoke with vaguely aching limbs and a headache; by midday he knew he had another bout of malaria coming on. Katende found him shivering and took him to his father. The old man ordered that a great fire be built and sat him beneath a tree. While Than warmed himself, Kwoyisho got busy preparing a herbal remedy. Trying not to think about the chloroquinine in his medical bag that was his for the taking, Than girded himself to test the efficacy of the African brew being prepared for him. By dusk it was ready; Kwoyisho brought him a gourdful of murky-looking liquid that smelled vaguely of cat urine and had bits of tree bark and leaf floating in it. However, by then Than was feeling so bad he might have drunk the undiluted urine of any animal without a qualm, providing it might ease him.

With his raging thirst helping him, he glugged down the whole acid-tasting gourdful. In half an hour, he began to feel strange; through the warps of his dizziness, he noticed the grins of the other novices and realized they expected what was coming. By nightfall his pain and discomfort were gone; the other novices piled skins and blankets on him, and as his shivering sweat subsided, he experienced strange hallucinations, which were less like the delirium of malaria than a fantastically realistic movie show in which he took part, at the same time remaining aware of his whereabouts and companions. He felt as if he were rising above his own body, in fact, looking down upon it; then he seemed to enter a kind of dark tunnel and in the light at the other end he found a fantastic land of beauty and light. He saw other people and became absorbed in them and their setting to the exclusion of all else.

He awoke in the morning feeling nauseated and sick; he remembered his pleasant experience of the night before and begged Kwoyisho for some more of the liquid. The old man nodded and brought forward another gourd; however, this time it contained a different liquid and its effects were less remarkable. Than found himself feeling better, but remarkably sane and sober; so much so that he was able to continue his studies under the old master. However, by nightfall the chills and the aches and the nausea had once again returned. This time Kwoyisho gave him the same urine-smelling concoction of the night before, and very shortly Than felt his shivers cease and he was soaring again, up into space and light and untold adventures. The next morning it was the same; he felt even worse, but Kwoyisho seemed unperturbed and gave him some more of the second liquid. By nightfall, when his chills and aches again produced a gourd of the urinelike liquid, Than began to understand the plan in the old man's treatment. The one liquid made him feel temporarily well and gave him the strength and lucidity to see through the day's tuition, while the other gave him an equally temporary relieving diversion into fantasy; neither was lasting, both were fascinating in their implications. And Than began actively to enjoy the alternating routine.

His days, feeling well and full of learning, were spent in eager expectation of the adventures of the night, when he journeyed into some subconscious world, which each time grew more fantastic and bizarre and was not always pleasant. He was often terrified and confused as his consciousness wandered strange dark netherworlds and encountered terrifying spectacles. In these hallucinations he often saw actively portrayed Kwoyisho's folk tales and he began to see and hear the ancestors the old man talked of. When he told the witchdoctor of these surely subconscious encounters, Kwoyisho merely nodded mildly as if all were well. It was now the days that began to take on a sense of unreality, while the nights were horrifically real. Than

490

digested his lessons with a still obedient mind, yet somehow he felt
above it all. It was during the nights, after partaking of the bark
liquid, that he began to truly live and sensate. Vaguely, behind it
all, he realized that the days were passing and the hour of his initiation approached, yet strangely, even despite his sickness and recurrent hallucinations, he knew that he was doing well. Katende had
helped him with much of his work, and Kwoyisho, he knew, was
well pleased with him.

On the night that Kwoyisho informed Than that his initiation,
together with those of the other novices, would take place on the
morrow, Than had the most fantastic hallucination of all. He
dreamed, vividly, that he met another self, a Than Profane who was
twice as big and twice as evil as he; the two together underwent a
titantic struggle for supremacy. Than the real and good won; yet as
he overpowered his magnified image, his own size increased while
that of his evil decreased. He sensed in some way that it was a symbolic struggle of good and evil within him, and when he awoke,
feeling vaguely light-headed in his physical body, he felt supremely
satisfied with the outcome. In some strange way he felt that he had a
better self-knowledge; it had been a baptism of fire, but he had
emerged tempered like steel. . . .

Gradually, as his consciousness fully returned, he realized that
he was sitting beneath a tree, cross-legged, in a peculiarly Eastern
meditative pose. Directly ahead of him he could see the stupendous
mist cloud of the Victoria Falls, and such was his sense of atunement
and well-being that he felt strangely at one with it and all nature.
The events of the night had somehow climaxed a pinnacle; this had
been a chrysalis; now he was emerging with wonder like a wing-
spread butterfly from the fog of a cocoon. He shut his eyes again and
sat in a serene daze of supreme bliss for he knew not how long; he
might have happily stayed that way forever if a sudden premonitory
sense of uneasiness had not caused him to open his eyes and focus
properly. In a few moments he realized that he was staring at a
crocodile. And it was real and alive, its creamy-gray horny crenu-
lated body gigantic and so close he could see the strange yellow of its
opened mouth between the evil, crooked, tooth-stubbled grin. He
realized that it was watching him too, and as its short webbed claws
began slowly waddling toward him, he was instantaneously catapulted back into the real earthy world with a jolt that shook his
senses. He realized that the crocodile was coming for him and, with
a tremendous swish of its great tail, coming for him fast. With an

animal cry, Than reached back and clawed frantically in the grass beside him; he found a few pebbles and some sand; it was a feeble rebound, but after his deathlike stillness, his yell alone was enough to halt the creature's accelerating rush. This gave him the needed time to find a fistful of sand, which he flung into the reptile's beady little eyes. Blinded, it turned instantly and thrashed off through the undergrowth, its great armored body swishing out of sight. Than stood up slowly; he was shaking with fright, but the malaria had left him and he was alive and well and with the world again.

10

That day, Basubila and his relatives were among the small crowd of friends and relations who came across to the island in canoes to witness the mass initiation of the novices. Beer, which the novices had been brewing for days, was now ready, and at sunset Kwoyisho prayed in his hut while the guests gathered around it for the ceremony. When Kwoyisho came out, he spread a reed mat on the ground and honored Than by calling him forth first. He invited Than to sit on the mat and placed on it the various pieces of equipment he had been allotted over the past weeks, together with two pots of beer. Then Kwoyisho stood up and solemnly addressed the gathering, first in Chi-Lwena, then in the Sikololo of his own people.

"I have asked you people to come here so that you may know that this man has qualified," he said solemnly. "He has completed his course of instruction, he has with him sufficient equipment with which to treat diseases, and I am sure he will carry out his duties well."

At this, all the men began to clap their hands and the women cupped their mouths to make the shrill *lulutu* sound. There was drumming and dancing and the people began to drink the first of the two pots of beer. During this celebration, Katende explained to Than that after each had been initiated, at dawn tomorrow, there would again be much music, dancing, and singing, after which the new young *ngakas* would become possessed by their healing spirits and be ritually dressed by Kwoyisho. Than had no idea how he, as a skeptical Westerner, would perform such a feat, but he decided to take things as they came. He was less worried about such facets of

492

the ceremony than he was about the promised revelation of Kwoyisho's jealously guarded secret, the ancestor-inspired cure for cancer. His weeks of travel, struggle, and toil would then suddenly be given sense, and he could scarcely contain his anticipation enough to sleep that night. He was wide awake in the early hours of the morning, when there was a shout. Than had barely struggled out from under his kaross when one of the guests came running, pointing wordless.

Than found Kwoyisho collapsed outside his hut. A cursory examination showed that he was suffering an acute heart attack. Than's attempts to restart his heart by manual percussion were hampered by Kwoyisho's son, who failed to understand the therapeutic value of the repeated blows. In any event, it was useless, and the old man, eyes feebly fluttering, lay dying in Than's arms. The last words he could have heard were Than's frenzied entreaties: "Tell me! Tell me now! The Secret! The cure for cancer!"

But in the cast of wan moonlight that fell through the trees, the old man looked mildly surprised at such a suggestion; he closed his eyes, his aged, fine sensitive face composed as his head rolled and he was dead.

For a long moment Than simply sat, vaguely aware that Kwoyisho's son, dazedly staring, was crying. There was inside him at that moment such a cataclysmic mingling of emotions that he was speechless. After a moment, he laid the old man upon the cold ground and stood up unsteadily. He patted Katende's shoulder before he turned dazedly away.

"My father! My father!" Katende was rocking and moaning with his anguish. "What shall I do . . . what shall I do?"

"You can come back to Suseshi with me," Than said dully, in English. "Jesus." He shook his head. "If you have any sense of justice at all, you'll come back with me and be trained as a white doctor."

II

In June, approximately six months after the secession of Katanga, Tshombe, deprived of his personal bodyguard, with indefinite detention and the vengeance of the notoriously murderous national army hanging over his head, suddenly departed for Europe. He left amid rumors that he and his cabinet had massively embezzled from the Katangan treasury to facilitate a comfortable nest egg for themselves in this eventuality. Well, the man and his ministers had existed, tenuously, in a society and situation where ordinary ethics had ceased to apply. But his rule had been based upon deathless ideals, and Matthew privately hung on to the flickering hope that Tshombe, buoyed by the love and loyalty of his people, had set aside enough currency and courage to bide his time and rise again at a more opportune moment. Whatever the case, the despairing and disillusioned man left behind fear-ridden followers in the sad shambles of what had once been the most prosperous, well-administered, stable, and racially harmonious state in the Congo.

The same day that they learned of Tshombe's voluntary exile, Than Profane came back to Suseshi out of a clear blue sky. Although he emerged from the familiar big yellow Thunderbird, Matthew hardly recognized the darkly tanned, long-haired, and bearded stranger who only vaguely resembled the sick, wan, and weary young man who had left. Like a prophet returned from the wilderness, he limped across the mission slope with blue eyes blazing with fanatical fire in the glowing bronze face; he had the silent intensity of a man who had undergone some profound religious experience. And indeed, his experience had been profound, if not religious in the manner Matthew would have wished. The revelation Matthew was greeted with made him deeply regret his own innocent asking.

"I've become a witchdoctor, Matthew," Than Profane said quietly. And Matthew shuddered; sometimes he suspected that the renegade Boy laid such outrageous truths on him merely to make him suffer. Now, an unwilling party to the knowledge of the Boy's unquakerly deviation, he was burdened with the evidence of a heresy that sheer Christian ethics should compel him to denounce and reveal to the board and his fellows. Instead, sympathy reduced him to a stance of sinful secrecy, even worse, to a perverse complicity, in that it was *he* who urged the Boy to remain silent on the issue. To his own uneasy horror, he found that he understood and even condoned the Boy's reasons for undertaking the bizarre training, even if God's disapproval might be seen by some as embodied in Kwoyisho's ironic death before a satisfactory end could give sense and justification to the Boy's unorthodox means. . . .

It seemed to Matthew that during the first months of its office, the new African government was largely concerning itself with throwing off the shackles of the old imperialist colonial rule. The official dissolution of the Federation was set for December 31, and the government, bitterly resentful of the centuries-old imperialist rapine of the country's natural resources, had begun negotiations to buy back its mineral rights, which had been sold to the British South Africa Company by Lewanika I of Barotseland in 1890. In such outside issues the coalition government was fortunately of one mind, but in other areas they were irrevocably divided; the growing discord between the two leaders was increasingly reflected in bloody battles between their opposing party members. A string of murders was climaxed in a mine township on the Copperbelt when one hundred people were injured and seven men brutally hacked to death with spears and axes. A commission of inquiry into the incident blamed unemployment, the lack of educational facilities, and a sense of anticlimax and dissatisfaction that the people had failed to immediately reap those bogus benefits so rashly promised them by aspiring politicians. The commission further blamed the indecisive outcome of the 1962 general election and the unsatisfactory coalition government that had resulted. It recommended that a new constitution be exercised in another general election as soon as possible. With an African government now firmly entrenched, the British government had no option but to enfranchise the great mass of the African people, and the governor announced that fresh general elections would be held in January. It was hoped that the registration, which was to begin immediately, would occupy the people and help to resolve their frustration.

In the meanwhile, in Barotseland, that old die-hard, the *Litunga*, had not yet given up the hope of securing the separation of his protectorate. Even notwithstanding the fact that UNIP had just won all twenty-five seats in the Barotse National Council, the Barotse native government sent a memorandum to the British government, putting forward an original new line and asserting that Britain could not transfer her obligations to Barotseland to the "new state" of Northern Rhodesia. As the next general election would give Northern Rhodesia complete self-government, the matter was urgent, and the awkward little clause precluding the holding of elections in Barotseland without the *Litunga*'s permission probably spurred the British government into arranging a conference on the matter at the Victoria Falls. But as usual, little more than argument evolved. However, the *Litunga* agreed to allow the holding of the elections in Barotseland.

In Barotseland, Shonona clinic was rapidly expanding; since Than's initiative on the plain, the plainspeople had begun coming in droves, so much so that a new wing had recently been added to cope with the influx, a new white nurse had flown out from Britain, and Than reluctantly relinquished Cosmo Mlongoti, himself a Barotse, to service and take charge of the out-clinics Than had established in the protectorate. The new nurse, Gladys Miffon, was a matron in her fifties with years of experience in an English nursing home; Zelda, although younger and less experienced, had served in Africa and knew something of the people and the language. Thus the question of seniority was uncertain, and since Shonona had been chosen as this year's venue for yearly meeting, Than accompanied Cosmo to Barotseland a little ahead of time to settle the young dresser into his position and sort out the situation.

They found Zelda, now confidently in control of her clinic, brusque and authoritative.

"Cosmo, I have some urinalysis tests you can take care of in the lab." She dismissed the dresser the first morning after their arrival, and Than and Cosmo exchanged looks. They both knew her own capable African dresser customarily took care of such tasks.

"Cosmo's not here to do that kind of work," Than said shortly, and Zelda colored.

"Well, maybe not all the time. But I thought, while we're holding our meeting . . ."

The two nurses waited expectantly; apparently, as whites, they expected to decide all issues without the black staff. But this country was undergoing rapid changes. It was preparing for an election that would be based upon universal adult suffrage, and it was presently governed by natives who were not all helpless primitives without initiative. It seemed to Than time they realized that.

"Cosmo doesn't have time for that," he said quietly. "He's attending the meeting with us." Since Than was medical director of the Friends' mission, the two nurses could hardly argue, but Zelda and Gladys Miffon stared at him in undisguised horror.

Later, in the staff meeting, which included the Poes and the Haskels and the Gladstones, who had come across from Mambundi to help prepare for yearly meeting, Than's calm announcement that he had decided to appoint Cosmo Mlongoti medical director of their growing Barotseland service was met with shocked silence. Then Zelda sprang to her feet and started to babble; his idea was unthinkable, she ranted. In terms of years, she was senior nurse in Barotseland; in terms of outside experience and qualifications, Sister

Miffon outranked them all. They both had training qualifications superior to Cosmo's, she pointed out indignantly. But Than was adamant. He had given the matter serious thought, and all things considered, Cosmo remained his irrevocable choice. Finally Zelda stormed out, weeping furiously. But she had friends in the meeting. Sister Miffon, Benedict Poe, and the Gladstones sat in stony silence.

Finally Benedict scratched his head and said deliberately: "I think somehow, Doctor, that the board will agree with Nurse Clayton."

Than knew then that he had trouble coming; his opponents evidently intended taking the matter further, and over any distance it would be difficult to convince the board that Cosmo, though of lower education and less formal medical training, was a responsible, well-balanced African who had a natural flair for medicine. Under Than's informal daily tuition, his diagnostic and surgical abilities had blossomed unbelievably; furthermore he had years of experience among the African people, and best of all, he was fluently trilingual and completely understood the complex African mind.

Than awoke the next morning with vague misgivings and an aching wrist. He was rubbing it fretfully when a man was carried in from the plain in terrible pain. An examination revealed that he had the common African complaint—a strangulated hernia. Unless he received immediate surgical attention to remove the blockage, he could die within hours. Than ordered that an impromptu surgery be set up in the lab. He and the two white nurses and Cosmo robed themselves and scrubbed up in the lab sink before quietly assembling around the moaning man. Than administered chloroform, and while the patient was succumbing, the nurses and Cosmo closed their eyes in the customary silent Quaker prayer. When they looked up again, Than was rubbing his wrist.

"It's pretty sore," he said mildly. "I don't want to strain it further." He looked at Zelda. "Sister Clayton, would you mind doing the operation?"

Zelda, who had seen him uncomplainingly operate under worse handicaps, stared at him, aghast.

"For goodness' sake!" she spluttered, flustered and confused. "Thee knows I haven't been trained to perform surgery myself!"

An inquiring eyebrow cocked at Gladys Miffon evoked the same flabbergasted refusal, but Cosmo, the last invited, simply smiled under his white mask. The two white nurses stood stumped into disbelieving silence while, without any aid or prompting from Than, the young African dresser flawlessly performed the entire operation with the two stunned nurses assisting. By the end of it, Than knew he had won. But if the two nurses frostily acceded to Cosmo's superior ability, they would never forgive Than his compunction in recognizing and rewarding it above their own white status and superior qualifications. Than attended yearly meeting, regretfully knowing that he had surely cemented two more bitter enemies, who pridefully, indiscriminately, opposed the status-eroding action of change. . . .

BOOK SEVEN

THE CRUCIFIXION

· 1964 ·

1

ON DECEMBER 31, the Federation had passed away peacefully; now January 1964 saw developments its adherents could not have dreamed possible in this decade. In an election that enfranchised one million, as compared to the minuscule seven thousand in 1959, special symbols had to be assigned to each of the three political parties competing to aid the great mass of illiterates. UNIP was represented by a hoe, Congress by a lion, and the People's Democratic Party by a corn cob. As each voter left an election booth, his thumb was dipped in red ink to record that he had voted. Although the day passed in pouring rain, many people walked for over twenty miles to their nearest polling station.

The reformed Federal Party's strongest victories were in the Copperbelt towns, where there was a high concentration of conservative whites of South African origin, but UNIP received more than one-third of the European votes and all of the Asian. On the main roll it was unopposed in twenty-four seats and won thirty-one others. Although it made no inroads in the Southern province and at Mwinilunga, which were Congress strongholds, it was victorious in the Northern, Luapula, and Eastern provinces. Kenneth Kaunda, the party leader, became the country's first prime minister; at thirty-nine he was the youngest premier in the British Commonwealth. He and more than half of his thirteen-man cabinet had served prison sentences or terms of detention in the pursuit of their political beliefs. Now, finally in power, they sought a constitution that would have a president as its executive head and aspired to make Northern Rhodesia the independent republic of Zambia, on October 24, United Nations Day. Well, Matthew reflected somewhat sadly, with ultimate frightening swiftness, the day of the whites was finally over. . . .

*　　*　　*

In order to inspect the progress of the new secondary school at Mambundi, Matthew accompanied Than Profane on his clinic run into Barotseland. The Zambezi was in full flood, extending like a massive blue sea to the horizon, and in the bush, native women were reaping sorghum and millet. Matthew was relieved that at the mission, Sidney and Leroy Fotch were conspicuously absent; he had no doubt the errant pair would remain out of sight for the duration of the doctor's stay, and if the Boy had gotten wind of their exile to this lonely swamp outpost, he was kept too busy tending the increasing scores of sick who flocked to see him to do much about it. Matthew went straight over to the fine new secondary school block, which Homer had built, to consult with the two new English missionaries. Creighton and Queenie Gladstone were an ingratiating gracious couple who had immediately adopted the mission's idiom and mode of dress. At recess, Queenie poured them tea in the neat new paint-smelling staff room, and after politely enthusing about their work for several moments, she suddenly set down her cup and clasped Matthew's hand, leaning forward with a conspiratorial air.

"Oh my dear professor—how I do sympathize with thee!" She crooned in her upper-class, cultured English accent, chestnut curls piled atop a thin face that was intense with seeking sympathy. "We all understand how difficult it has been for thee trying to keep the peace and decorum, trying to preserve the very dignity of this mission while that . . ." she shook her curl-heaped head as if lost for words ". . . that *dreadful* Dr. Profane goes about dressed like a common tramp, smoking and blaspheming, sullying just about everything decent the Friends' mission stands for! No, no . . . don't deny it! We realize that as senior elder, thee have long been suffering in silence, bearing the brunt of his actions, but the talk is all over the mission. The Poes and the Fotches are particularly distressed, and at yearly meeting, the poor little spinster ladies admitted to me how his immodesty and disrespect have caused them agonies of embarrassment. We realize that with the hospital at Suseshi so sorely in need of his services it has been impossible to have him expelled in the past, but we wish to reassure thee, thy troubles are finally over!"

"*They are?*" Matthew stared sickly at the woman.

"Certainly!" The portly Creighton Gladstone patted Matthew's knee. "It's our joy to inform thee, Friend, that way is now open for thee, as senior missionary in the field, to insist upon Dr. Profane's recall! Thee sees, Queenie's young brother, Dr. Cedric Fotheringill, a trained physician and devout Quaker of the highest caliber, is fully prepared to come out to Africa to take his place!"

502

The couple sat back and stared at Matthew in eager triumph. There was a long stunned silence before Matthew, mortified, could bring himself to reply. Then, abashed by the couple's quizzical, expectant smiles, he croaked awkwardly:

"Er . . . well, er, it's most gratifying to hear that thy brother is willing to come out here and doctor the natives, Mrs. Gladstone. And I'm sure that once the clinic at Shonona has been expanded sufficiently to warrant the services of another doctor, he will be most gratefully received. It's most kind of thee to be concerned, I'm sure. However, until then, I must set thy mind at rest and assure thee that Dr. Profane is doing an entirely adequate job at Suseshi. In fact neither Dr. Dooley nor myself have hitherto seen any need to have him replaced."

The couple drew back as if stung, their kindly expressions of commiseration turning cold and soured as Matthew, growing red in the face, hurried fretfully on: "And as for moves to have him recalled, I must say I am dismayed to hear of it in as much as I consider him to be a valuable member of the Friends' medical team in this country."

Queenie's face turned suddenly mottled, and in the uncomfortable stricken silence that followed, Matthew, acutely embarrassed, groped for his pith helmet.

"Now, if thee'll both excuse me, I—I think I'll go on over and visit with Homer."

2   Matthew returned from Barotseland deeply disturbed that the antipathy toward Than Profane had chrystalized into talk of recall. Nothing the stubborn renegade seemed likely to do would ease the tension, and, brooding on the portends, Matthew met Cuss's cold crusty nose and Teller's affectionate kiss with an absent frown, which only the night's sleep and the shy wiles of little Luke finally smoothed out. The toddler was invariably silent and aloof with strangers, but as usual, after a few moments alone with Matthew, he opened up and chattered solemnly. After Saturday morning meeting, they meandered the mission together, trailed by the mission dogs, talking loftily of God and leaves and ladybugs and other awesome things. At noon they went to the *chitenje* so that Matthew could catch the midday news on his transistor before lunch. He left Luke

playing with ten-year-old Glen Dooley who was home from Sakeji convalescing a tonsillectomy. Lenius had begun pounding the dinner drum that hung from the big bush tree beside the smoke-billowing kitchen hut a few yards off, and several of the other missionaries had begun arriving for lunch, when a frantic voice entreated, "*Help!* Uncle Matthew, *help!*"

Matthew hurried out of the *chitenje* on the heels of Hannah Rothchild to find Glen Dooley up the big bush tree that shaded the kitchen hut.

"Uncle Matthew, me and Luke can't get down," the small boy gulped tearfully, staring down through leaves and a mass of sandy freckles. "There's a green snake slithered right past me down below us!"

"A *green mamba!*" Matthew gasped. His head snapped back and he felt the bottom drop out of his stomach. For there, in the topmost branches of the tall tree, almost overhanging them on a thin bough that dipped with his weight, was the two-and-a-half-year-old little mite in Matthew's charge. His solemn golden face was framed by nothing more than a thatch of corn hair and empty blue sky.

"Well, will you look at that! Spunky little kid." Than Profane, hands on his hips, stood staring up at the child in frowning admiration.

"Well, don't just stand there!" Matthew blustered. "The child is in mortal danger! *Do something!*"

"Sure," the Boy said easily. "You come down first Glen. You'd better jump if there's a snake below. You're not too high up. I'll catch you. Hey, I wasn't college champion in basketball for nothing!"

But, deliberating the ten-foot drop, Glen seemed more awed by such aggressive confidence than assured by it. He burst into a hoarse sobbing, which set the branches precariously swaying, almost giving Matthew apoplexy and disturbing a hornbill that flew off noisily squawking.

"I want my daddy! I ain't jumping to nobody but him!"

The horrendous howling went on until Jerome arrived at a run followed by his wife, Teller, and Jenny.

"Now, Glen, take a hold of thyself, son. Just thee jump down, I'll catch thee!" Jerome panted. And in a moment the small sturdy boy let go of the tree and leaped like a toad. He almost knocked Jerome off his feet with the impact. He slid squawling through his father's arms and threw himself against his mother, who embraced and consoled him.

But Matthew's relief quickly faded; a serious silence settled over the group as it backed away and stood staring intently up at the little boy still clinging to the treetop. Only the child's mother stood staring straight ahead; she was white-faced.

"Make him come down," Jenny said quietly, and Than Profane called cautiously, "Listen to me, boy. Ease out and climb carefully down till you reach the big branch Glen was on. Then you jump and I'll catch you."

They waited, breath-bated, while the child scratched his freckled nose and stared coolly, consideringly down at them. Matthew felt dizzy and sick watching the tiny child swaying in his precarious perch against the cloud-scudded sky.

"Come along, son," he implored. "Thee be a good boy for Grandpa now. Climb down and jump."

"*No!*" The word hit Matthew like a bullet, and Than Profane parried with a studied casualness, "Aw . . . why not?"

"I want my daddy." The simple reply floated down to them, the implications hitting them like rocks in a landslide, stunning them where they stood. For there was that stubborn shy lonely little boy, imitating, as children will, a standard he had just seen demonstrated. In his innocence asking for the one thing in the world that was most completely denied him.

"I wan' my own daddy for me," he continued calmly, in a perfect American accent, so unlike his mother's, talking in the sweet voice of deathly determination that Matthew had come to know and dread so well. That little soft speck of a boy wielded a will that was lethal as a weapon in his tiny hands. "I jumping to my daddy."

"Has nobody told the child?" Hannah Rothchild whined in a voice of pained ire that Matthew found particularly unforgivable at that moment. *Told him what?*

It was then that Jerome stepped forward. "Tell thee what, son— I'll be thy daddy. How's that?"

The small boy frowned suspiciously down through the leaves. "Thee promise?"

"Sure," Jerome laughed flusteredly. "Anytime; thee can count on me!"

And then, while Matthew watched with pent breath, the child, calmly disregarding the anxious directions shouted from below, groped and shinned along down the branches. He stopped on the bough ten feet up. Then, in perfect trust, he sailed down through empty air into a proxy father's arms. Bundled against the good man's breast, he slithered to the ground and struggled free, a tall tiny little blond boy in patched red corduroys, frowning fiercely up at the father-figure before him.

"Thee my daddy?" He demanded, and was met with an idiotic grin.

"Sure son," Jerome tousled the soft blond hair, his eyes brightly atwinkle.

"Daddy?" the small boy tested the word on his soft sweet mouth, his brow perplexedly furrowed as he looked up with clear blue eyes that held the sky and all eternity inside them. "Daddy," he instructed softly. *"Thee stay by me!"*

In the wonder of the moment, it was awhile before Matthew realized the significance of the popping explosive sound behind them. Then he heard Jayne's horrified hiss and turned to see Than Profane standing white-faced in the *chitenje*, his hand dripping water and blood, the remains of a drinking glass shattered in shards that stuck to his flesh.

"Oh, honey!" Katherine advanced on him, eyes wide with concern. But the Boy backed away, seeming strangely preoccupied, disposessed of the slashed bleeding hand.

"Well!" Hannah Rothchild expostulated furiously, while the others stared in dumb astonishment. "I never heard of a body holding a tumbler that hard!"

The glass was one of a community set, which had lasted the practical missionaries almost twenty careful years.

En route to Lusinga Mission to attend the annual Missionary Alliance Conference in the Congo with Matthew, Than Profane stopped at numerous wayside villages to sell Aureomycin eye ointment in tubes decorated with ritual symbols to local witchdoctors, many of whom were probably the very incompetents who had previously blinded their patients with acid concoctions. The Boy's new status as a full-fledged member of the dubious fraternity encouraged the *ngakas* to deal with him openly, and their eagerness was indicative of his growing reputation as a Great Healer in the territory. Although Matthew felt a little uneasy at his conspiring with such blatant heathens and doubtless devil worshipers, he consoled himself that the medicine would certainly save many who might otherwise be blinded, and he said nothing. After bribing a difficult black customs officer with a ten-shilling note at the border post, they crossed into the Congo, and Matthew was deeply saddened by the air of desolation and decay that hung over the once beautiful city of

Elizabethville; the carefree continental capital had become a forsaken backwater, a virtual ghost town whose harried inhabitants hurried around with frightened furtive faces.

The umbrellas of the pavement cafés hung in mildewed tatters, and along the littered streets, they drove past dirty derelict buildings; the Congolese flag flapped forlornly over Tshombe's former palace, but although many of the city's buildings were cracked and pitted, its byways broken and neglected, giant billboards bearing the exiled ex-premier's sad smiling face had incredibly survived the United Nations occupation. L'ESPOIR DU CONGO! they poignantly proclaimed: Hope of the Congo. And in the empty, tree-lined boulevards it seemed to Matthew that the cheers of the adoring crowds that had once thronged to see Tshombe echoed silently in the sad soughing wind.

Meanwhile, in Northern Rhodesia another bid for secession was being unceremoniously ended. The new UNIP government had made it clear it would tolerate no partition of the land, and following the independence conference in London, it was ruled that Britain should cease to retain any responsibility for Barotseland; the last ties of the "special relationship," first honored by Queen Victoria, were summarily broken, and the little river kingdom was made an inseparable part of Northern Rhodesia forever.

In June Than drove his senior medical students to the government hospital at Lusaka, where they sat for their final examination. Three days later they returned triumphant. Than's two best students had received overall percentage marks in the seventies; five others had scored in the sixties, while the majority scraped over the fifty-percent pass mark to qualify for the government diploma. Only two were demoted to do the year again.

Arriving back at the mission at midday, Than was troubled to hear from Denise Smith, at the hospital, that two Africans who had been asking to see him had been chased off the premises by Hannah Rothchild and Clara Fotch, who objected to their "indecent" tribal attire. Than went immediately across to the dining *chitenje*, where most of the missionaries were taking lunch. He was about to tax the haughty-faced ladies on the matter when he spotted two bedraggled skin-hung figures distantly departing down Disney road. As their vague familiarity dawned on him, he left the *chitenje* and began limping furiously after them, yelling for them to stop. As he approached, the pair turned warily. Seeing him, their closed black faces broke into wide white-toothed smiles.

"*Katende!*" Heaving with exertion, Than greeted Kwoyisho's son with a joyous handshake. Beside him, proudly bare-breasted amid looped strings of beads, stood Ngwani, the woman who had shared their tuition under the old master. Than remembered then that today was the earliest date he had given for the enrollment of the year's new medical students. Ignoring the angry stares from the *chitenje*, he defiantly led the shy pair triumphantly back into the mission.

3

One overcast morning in mid-July, a group of spear-carrying Luchazi people from a village at the Manyinga River, near the Angola border, arrived at Suseshi. Discounting one other mission on the way, they had walked day and night for almost five days, living off cassava root and what they could forage off the land, covering some two hundred fifty miles of rugged bush country to reach Suseshi. Then, in a steaming of lightly labored breath in the chill winter air, they decamped in front of the hospital, shivering in their drab bark-cloth blankets as the men and women alike sat in the dry grass, sullenly smoking on long-stemmed metal pipes. They were the *vaka ndonga*—the river people. Their chief, a wrinkled old man with a fine dignity and a grizzled gray beard, smoked an old-fashioned hookah with an enormous bowl and a stem three feet long. When Matthew arrived, he looked up and quietly spoke the legendary name: *Njumwaice.*

The Boy had recently returned from his clinic run into Kabompo, the Balovale, and Barotseland, where, with the help of accommodating chiefs and headmen, he had successfully installed several of his newly graduated medical assistants to take charge of some of his bush clinics; retaining two to work at Suseshi. Now, summoned to the scene, he walked slowly down the veranda steps, set apart from the other missionaries by his distinctive limp, Stetson, and stethoscope. The Luchazis recognized him immediately. Many fell to their knees, stretching out their hands, impassive black faces taking on sudden animation as they called to him anxiously.

"They say there is sickness and death in their villages," Matthew translated. "Many of their children have gone blind. They have heard of thy medicine and seek help from thee. They have brought many gifts. . . ."

Even as he talked, the men were standing up, opening their ragged blankets to bring forth scores of objects; there was a bolt of bright *chitenga* cloth that depicted a full-maned lion rearing against an unlikely background of colorful flowers; a scrawny white fowl, hung cruelly upside down, its claws tied by bark string, and enough *mukwa* wood carvings of animals to fill a market stall.

"Tell them to put that stuff away," the Boy said. "I'll see the sick."

Matthew translated and there was a shuffling and a fierce whispering before a small frightened-looking girl was carried forward on a crude pole litter. The litter was set on the ground, and the doctor knelt and removed a thin blanket to examine the child. She was naked underneath; with hands clutched under her chin, she shivered convulsively and there was an impression of fever and suffering about the little matchstick-body bared to the winter air. Her eyes were dull, the hopeless face streaked with the chalky marks of dried tears, and the Boy stared in awe at the raised rash of pustules that peppered her skin. He pulled up the threadbare cloth to cover the pitiful puerile nakedness, and there was a breath-caught hush when he slowly stood up.

"What is it?" Matthew said, and the Boy looked at him with vague eyes.

"Well, there's only one such disease I know of that blinds and kills. I've seen it in textbooks. You ought to know it, Matthew. There was an epidemic of it here in your time."

Suddenly recognizing the strange sweetish smell that hung about the people, Matthew closed his eyes. "Yes," he said softly. And from long ago the familiar chill came back to him. He knew it, all right. *Ichingwali*. It was smallpox.

Matthew immediately radioed the D.C. at Mwinilunga. By the time the man arrived with the medical officer, Than Profane and Jerome Dooley had positively identified the disease, pronouncing eleven of the Luchazis as being afflicted with *variola majora*, the most virulent type of smallpox. The medical officer agreed with their diagnosis; he approved of the strict aseptic precautions Than Profane had instituted in the isolation and treatment of the sick and further decreed that the remaining Luchazis stay at Suseshi, installed in a special quarantine camp, for the requisite twenty-one days. He ruled that the schools be immediately closed and that all mass gatherings be banned forthwith. The first batch of vaccine, which had been radioed from Lusaka, would be flown in on the morrow, at which time the vaccination and revaccination of all the Luchazis and the mission personnel would begin.

It all sounded cut and dried and simple, but it involved radical reversals in the mission's routine, and the district commissioner and Matthew spent hours trying to make the primitive Luchazis understand why they should remain isolated from outsiders until their conditions could be verified. Finally, bewildered and fearful, looking trustingly to Than Profane, they set to work constructing a camp in the bush near the hospital; all afternoon the air rang with the sound of axes chopping down trees, and by nightfall they had dug several pit latrines and erected crude sleeping shelters; the village was staked out and stockaded with enmeshed trees and bushes. Since the clan would be legally confined within for the next three weeks, all their living requirements, including food, and water for drinking and washing, would have to be brought to them. Matthew raided the storeroom for maize meal, oil, and beans, entreating cooking pots and utensils from the hospital and school kitchens. The government would recompense the mission once their requisitions had gone through the proper channels; until then, they would have to improvise and do the best they could.

The missionaries, numbed by the swift descent of this devastatingly deadly plague, stared at each other dumbly. As soon as the schoolchildren had been vaccinated, they would be sent home; until the disease had been controlled, the missionaries could not hold mass meetings. Smallpox, they knew, was a particularly vicious disease, causing hideous disfigurement, blindness, and even death; it was wind-borne and transmitted through droplets. And suddenly conscious of the very air they breathed, the Fotches, Ezra Peabody, and the maiden ladies fanned their faces and surreptitiously breathed into their handkerchiefs. Most of them made excuses to hurriedly leave the table when Than Profane, who was one of the few directly treating the isolated cases, came to eat. (Although assured that the most stringent aseptic precautions were being taken, they had yet to be revaccinated, and how could they be sure?) It was a sinister situation that infected them all with nameless fear. And all through the night the village drums relentlessly throbbed: the dreaded *ichingwali* was upon them. *Epidemic* had begun.

4 The small Cessna bearing the precious smallpox vaccine was the first plane to land at Suseshi's windblown bumpy new airfield, which stood on a grassy plain a mile from the mission proper. After Than had inoculated the Luchazis in the quarantine camp, he had the black hospital workers vaccinated, then all the schoolchildren, the black mission staff, and their families. Lastly he revaccinated the missionaries and their families. The residue of vaccine he used to inoculate some of the panicked people who came pouring in from the bush. When the lymph solution finally ran out, they had to turn dozens away, urging them to return when the next batch of vaccine was due to be airfreighted to Suseshi. While they waited to see if the first vaccinations had taken, two children and a woman showing signs of the disease were brought in from Eshalakali by Nurse Dibb. When six more followed, they were seriously worried; the disease was spreading fast, and the new cases posed a serious problem: the hospital's isolation rooms were already crammed to capacity with smallpox patients, and the hospital, full as usual, could afford no more space.

The two doctors consulted urgently with Matthew. They had to have the meeting house; Than Profane was quite unequivocal about it. The empty school classrooms were too small and segmented. It would be easier to monitor strict sterile safety precautions if the smallpox victims were confined to a single, self-contained building with a capacity to take large numbers. Well, Quaker meeting houses were traditionally practical, Matthew conceded; indeed, theirs was regularly used for Jenny's Braille classes. Unfortunately the Fotches and Ezra Peabody were pettishly put out by his arbitrary decision; although mass meetings were banned, *they* had still been able to worship in the meeting house. But Matthew knew that they argued more out of fear and bewilderment than any real sense of right, and their churlish voices fell to a stricken consensus as they watched African cleaners move the pine pews out of the huge hall to make room for the piles of mattresses and bedclothes that, in the absence of beds, would be used to accommodate the sick on the meeting house floor. When the entire building had been swept out, scrubbed, and sterilized to the satisfaction of the two doctors, smallpox patients on stretchers borne by masked and gowned hospital staff were transported into the meeting house, transforming it from a cathedral of worship into a house of healing.

As the days went by, smallpox sufferers continued to trickle into Suseshi in steadily increasing streams. Five were referred from Than Profane's out-clinics, and since the rash closely resembled chicken pox to the inexperienced eye, the Boy was proud at the vigilance of his newly appointed medical assistants. Mwinilunga boma was in constant contact with the mission concerning the apprehending and treatment of the sick, and for once there was no delay with the delivery of requisitions. Emergency supplies of mattresses and bedding, of medications and bandages, arrived promptly from the Copperbelt and Lusaka; more vaccine was flown in in batches as it became available, and from the government clinics, inoculation teams set out to scour the villages to the Manyinga River, from whence the Luchazis had sprung.

All contacts had to be quarantined, and since they and the smallpox victims themselves required prodigious comfort and care, the missionaries rallied to cope with the influx. Teller, Katherine, Jayne, and the other medical students helped with nursing; Ward Disney and his sons were constructing another quarantine camp, and Matthew, Lars Wikstrom, and Ratchet Cathcart, self-consciously donning long white overgowns and masks that hung at the entrance door, ventured uneasily into the quiet blue gloom of the meeting house to tell the sufferers about Jesus. Jenny too did what she could for the sick; she comforted the newly blind and told Bible stories to calm the frightened and homesick children.

The hospital staff worked in shifts to keep the smallpox patients under constant surveillance, and some, like Than Profane, seemed to take little rest; he alternated between the hospital and the meeting house, and he was seen working with the patients during both the day and night shifts. He did all he could, but it was not enough. He told them dully at the breakfast table one morning that two of the Luchazi children had died during the night. He looked haggard and exhausted, and Matthew took up his Bible and went with him and Cosmo to report the tragic loss to the Luchazi people.

The Boy was brief and as gentle as possible. The Luchazi leader, nursing a sore swollen arm from his vaccination, shook his old gray-bearded head with disbelief, his eyes filling with tears. Despite Matthew's awkward attempts to give what comfort he could, the awful heartbroken wailing of the parents rose from the makeshift hovels while the Boy mechanically examined the rest of the camp for any sign of the disease, checking their vaccinations to be sure they had taken. He had Cosmo escort a woman and a child manifesting early signs of the disease to the meeting house, but a cursory examination of an adolescent girl who sat shivering in terror told him that her light rash was only a reaction from the vaccine. He reassured her, applied ointment to her sores, and left the camp with Matthew directly, eager to escape the searing sounds of grief that rent the silence.

Two days and one death later, morning revealed the quarantine camp standing uncannily quiet. Two messengers entrusted with ferrying essential supplies to the incarcerated inmates returned with disquieting news: *the Luchazis had gone.* The two doctors hurried to the scene; in a short while they realized that the Luchazis, obviously losing faith in their methods when several of their already infected members fell ill despite inoculation, had fled, but not before stealing into the meeting house, past the sleepy night-shift nurses, to ferret out and carry away their own members among the diseased. They would doubtless take to the bush to consult their own healers again.

Matthew immediately notified the district commissioner, and the boma police were sent out in pursuit. But by nightfall the camp still stood empty; the Luchazis, it seemed, had disappeared without trace.

"Oh dear," Teller murmured fretfully as she sipped her soup at the supper table. "I do hope thy chastisement did not unduly upset them, Ezra."

"*Chastisement?*" Than Profane, who had been hauled to the table by Katherine to face a sustenance he only picked at, set down his fork and stared at Ezra dully. "*What* chastisement?"

And then, by dribs and drabs, the truth was forcibly dragged from the truculent-turned man. Matthew was stunned, equally surprised to hear that while others had been solely concerned with the solace and succor of the sick, Ezra, in league with Hannah Rothchild and the Fotches, had conducted a sneaky after-dark campaign to convert the Luchazis. Matthew could just imagine the scene: while the Luchazis, grief-stricken and crazed with fear, cowered within their constricting enclosure, the disembodied voices of Ezra and his erstwhile conspirators had floated over the leafy stockade to warn of eternal damnation for the undelivered, of flaming hell-fire lest they believe. He was shocked by the crass insensitivity of it, and the more Ezra and Hannah and Clara blustered to defend it, it came through as a sickening coercion, self-evidently shameful by its very secrecy and deceit. Now, through their crafty cupidity, the Luchazis had run off to untold destruction, leaving an intangible trail of death and disfigurement in their wild wake.

"*Jesus Christ!* You goddamn interfering, crazy fool!" the Boy snarled.

Matthew had never seen him so angry; he sprang off the bench, tore around the table, and wrenching Ezra bodily from his seat, began shaking the chubby man furiously. Ezra, gasping and flabbergasted, struggled to free himself. It took four of the men, belatedly coming to life, to drag the Boy off and hold him till he came to his senses. Rushing to pat and pacify the shocked Ezra, who was almost in tears and swaying on his feet, Hannah, Clara, and Cherish tore at the Boy with shrill hysterical voices. The Boy stared at them dazedly; when he suddenly relaxed, the men released him, and without a word he turned and walked away. The shrieks of the three viragos followed him into the night.

5   In the early hours of the morning Than finally stumbled home to the dark silent house. He let himself in at the front door and groped his way to the stairway in the dark. Halfway up, suddenly overcome, he sat down on the step with his shoulders hunched and his head hopelessly hung.

"Why, Than dear—whatever's the matter?"

Than turned and stared dully up at Katherine's white-gowned form materializing out of the gloom. He sighed. "It's nothing, Kathy; go back to bed."

"Now, honey." She settled on the step beside him. "Trouble shared is trouble halved!"

"Oh, Kathy." He started to laugh bitterly, shaking his head. "Poor little Christian. I guess I'm an eternal trial and a puzzle to you."

"No," she said softly, frowning in the darkness. "No, thee is not."

"Kathy—you're a noble liar."

"Oh, I admit thee worries me at times. But only a little. And in spite of all they say about thee, I . . ." She looked aghast at her slip. "What I meant was . . ."

"Oh shit, Kathy, will you shut that sweet mouth of yours and listen a moment. It's not *them* I'm worried about. If you have to know it—I've got the Luchazis on my conscience. They've gone running off to disease and death and God knows what. Oh, I know Ezra Peabody probably played a large part in their flight, but they would never have run off if I had lived up to their expectations and given them something concrete to hang on to."

He stared at her searchingly in the dimness. "They regarded me as some kind of a god, you know that, Kathy? They and a lot of other natives. I don't know how they got hold of the notion, and it's not what I claimed to be. But by misguided reputation or whatever, it's what they believe me to be. And when enough people believe it of you, the confidence rubs off a little and you start to believe it yourself. Almost."

"I see."

"But the awful part is, Kathy, I've failed them. You see I've discovered a disturbing little fact: God help me—*I have feet of clay!*"

There was a small silence then Katherine stirred; she gazed at him intensely in the darkness, her face luminous with compassion. "Hush now," she whispered. "Feet of clay are no shame, dear. They, like most earthly afflictions, are a common malady of men."

The next day a further shock awaited them; the night nurses came wailing to report numerous abductions and desertions of patients from their beds, and the hospital yard, which usually teemed with the sick from early morning, stood silent and empty. The few natives who remained in the wards stared at the missionaries with uncertain eyes. No amount of questioning could extract from them the reasons for the departure of their fellow patients, but that afternoon Chief Kadesha arrived and confided to Than Profane that it was being whispered in the villages that the Europeans, instead of trying to cure smallpox, were in fact causing it. Apparently, the soreness and the light harmless rash that followed vaccination in some cases had sewn the first seeds of doubt, the same doubts that had unsettled the Luchazis, whose final desertion had clinched the suspicion for everyone else. Now, fueled and inflamed by the perfidy of jealous witchdoctors, the rumor presently raging was that the white administration behind the bomas, outraged by the African as-

cendancy to self-government, was sending out inoculators in a deliberate program of genocide, to thin out the population and regain for
the Europeans their position of power.

It was a preposterous assumption, and Chief Kadesha fortunately
had the sense to see it as such. (He and his family, among the first to
be inoculated, still thrived healthily.) Unfortunately, the majority of
his people were not so refreshingly sober and sane. Those who had
not yet been vaccinated had begun ignoring his advice and running
off when the boma inoculation teams arrived. Since no cases had
been discovered in the Mwinilunga district as yet, this abstention
was not presently so serious. But the news from the boma that Chief
Mulaisho's people, apparently motivated by the same fear, were refusing inoculation had them really worried. Several smallpox cases
had already been reported in the old man's region; furthermore, the
infected Luchazis had traversed the area en route to Suseshi; they
had doubtless returned the same way. Therefore the need to have
the dissident Chokwe clan inoculated was of the utmost urgency.
Than Profane abandoned his hospital duties and left to see the old
chief immediately; Matthew accompanied him, and they took with
them the little blind boy, Africa, whose healthily fattened frame and
comely clothing should convince the old man of their continuing sincere good intentions toward the Chokwe people.

Beyond the tree-shrouded escarpment, the bush stood strangely
quiet in the dry-season cool. This was the traditional time of the year
for the felling of trees to be dried and burned for the fertilization of the
gardens later in the year, but no trees were being cut or pollarded; the
village gardens stood untilled and deserted, and in the villages, what
solitary souls they saw disappeared at their coming. At Mulaisho's
village, only pigs and chickens listlessly rooted, and the scrawny dogs
ran forlornly out to meet them through the thorn boma, which had
sagged into shabby disrepair. At the sight of them, children, caked in
mud to ward off the winter cold, ran screaming, and skin-hung scowl-
ing adults disappeared like flitting shadows. Matthew, in his good
Prince Alfred–style suit, leading little Africa, who was dressed in a
charming little bow-tied suit that had once belonged to one of the
Dooley boys, felt a veritable monster to be regarded with such trucu-
lence and terror. Than Profane, in his faded denim jacket and jeans,
limped resolutely to the old chief's big circular hut. There, a trembling youth with a spear tried to bar his way.

"For Chrissakes, quit playing games," the Boy said wearily,
pushing the spear aside. At the same time the chief shouted out, and

although it was a debarment, the Boy took off his Stetson and bowed through the low doorway. "Come on, Matthew," he called, and Matthew, somewhat uneasily, did as he was bid.

Inside the dim hut the firelight flickered on the gnarled old chief as he lay sprawled on his skin-covered ornamental brass bedstead. He glared at them with apprehension, and one of his concubines, a plump young wench, gave a little scream and cowered down behind the bed, as though they might take her and forcibly inoculate her with the dread disease right then and there.

"All right," the Boy said quietly, sitting down on a crude creaking chair, which swayed under his weight. "Let's stop this pretense, old man. Is *Njumwaice* no longer welcome in the villages of his Chokwe friends? There's a smallpox epidemic presently raging in these parts. Why are your people fleeing from the boma inoculators?"

The old man hummed and hawed; he denied that there were any sick in his villages, maintaining that his people refused smallpox vaccinations simply because they had no need of them. And that was that. The Boy appealed and cajoled; he threatened with disfigurement and with death, with government and with God, and still he was thwarted, shaking his head at the folly of an old man poisoned with suspicion, pinioned by age-old superstitious ignorance. Finally, seething with impatience, he stood up to leave, and Matthew, turning, discovered little Africa gone from his side. The forgiving little fellow, forever filled with gospel zeal, must have gone to impart Christianity to his own people. Matthew hurried from the chief's hut in a panic; they had intended using the child merely to demonstrate their benevolence, for although the little mite had been inoculated against smallpox, his vaccination had refused to take; now they still awaited the results of a second attempt.

Matthew scurried through the squalid village calling his name. He was enormously relieved when the little fellow gave a shout and crawled out of a ramshackle hovel. Matthew pulled him up by the hand and hastily dusted off his little seersucker suit. As they walked off, the ghastly death dirge of a woman keening with grief rose like an ill omen, confirming their worst fears, and the Boy stopped dead.

He questioned Africa about the conditions he had encountered, and the woeful little one-eyed child suddenly broke down and started to weep. Two of the children he knew had died since he had left the village, he stammered through heaving sobs, smearing snot across his little black face as he wiped at the tears streaming from the disfigured orb of his one eye; many of the others were seriously ill, and one well enough to talk had told him a terrible tale of sickness and suffering. On the instructions of the witchdoctors, none of the sick were being allowed to sleep at night, which was the time when evil spirits were expected to snatch them away in death. Thus, as they struggled, feverish and sick, to sink into the momentary merciful oblivion of sleep, drums and calabashes were pounded and clanged, and cold water was poured onto them in the freezing winter air.

Well, with that kind of treatment, if the pox did not get them, pneumonia surely would! Matthew was horrified and deeply afraid, as much for Africa as for the afflicted, for in his blind, groping way, having obviously sustained such particularly direct contact with the highly infectious disease, it was clear that the little boy's own life was now in God's hands. But Africa was not afraid for himself, and when they wanted to leave, he begged them to take the other children back with them to the mission, where they could learn of Jesus and be made well, just as he had been. When Matthew gently explained about the dreadful misapprehension under which Mulaisho's people labored and the awful consequences of direct contact with the disease, the small boy was undeterred. Was not the Lord Jesus looking after him? he queried. With the Lord to guide him, he would ferret out the sick children and lead them secretly to safety. Matthew started to shake hopelessly his head, but the Boy stopped him; a thoughtful frown creased his face, and Matthew felt he could read his mind. After Africa's impulsive visit to tell of Jesus, what did they have to lose, after all? If his vaccination was due to take, he was immune; if not, he was very probably doomed to the disease anyway.

"Maybe he's right," the Boy sighed. "It would mean leaving them to die. Maybe he can do it."

They parked the Land-Rover beyond a thick clump of jesse and waited for nightfall. Then, in the chill drum-throbbing darkness, with the aid of discreetly shielded flashlights, they stumbled back to Mulaisho's village. There, an aura of evil hung over the place; the weird looped calls and insane giggling of hyenas tantalized the frosty night, and Matthew's hair stood on end when a pair of the mangy spotted animals, doubtless feeding off the stinking village refuse, bounded from their path; the pulsating drums had a wicked abandonment, and through the bedraggled thorn boma they could see the drunken swaying of figures around the fluctuating night fires. Well, if the smallpox epidemic had interrupted work in the fields, it had surely not interfered with the brewing of beer, Matthew reflected bitterly. By the sounds of it, the people were drowning their sorrows in gallons of the foul stuff. Their incapacity finally convinced him that what they were doing was right. How could they leave the poor defenseless children to the meager mercies of such drunken degenerates, after all? Childhood among such primitive pagans was in any case a seldom-survived cruel transmission of unmitigating hardship; sickness only added to their suffering.

Than Profane tied a handkerchief around little Africa's face to protect him from the smallpox germs. Then he and Matthew pulled aside the collapsing thorn boma and waited behind it while the little blind boy crept into the village on all fours, his cautiously patting little hands testing the ground ahead of him like sensitive antennae, searching for known landmarks to lead him to the village paths he had come to know by touch alone. Watching him crawl cautiously out of sight, Matthew was beset with awful fears and doubts. But he consoled himself that Africa was accustomed to feeling his way around the village in his private darkness; he was black, and amid the drunken carousing, with his good clothes scuffed with dust and cloaked by the night, he would likely go unnoticed.

It seemed a small eternity before the child came stumbling back; Matthew squinted through the tangled thorn boma, staring hard to make out the little humped figure that faltered toward them, tapping with a crude stick. Calling softly to guide him, they pulled aside the loose thorn hedge, and when he reached them, Africa slumped, panting with exertion; the Boy caught the weakly clinging child who slipped from his back. By the cupped light of his torch, he quickly examined the pitiful scrap, a small girl whose little black face was plainly peppered with the smallpox pustules. The Boy carried the sick little girl to the Land-Rover while Africa crept back to fetch another child. The game little fellow went back again and again, creeping into hut after hut, waiting to be told the coast was clear before he staggered off with the next fearful little smallpox sufferer. He left nine times, blundering bravely back with as many sick shivering children borne upon his little bowed back. Finally, gasping, his once-spruce little suit scuffed and soiled, he collapsed, and the Boy decreed it was enough. Africa was exhausted, and dawn was breaking over the horizon; discovery now would jeopardize the safety of those already rescued. They left just as the first soft light was starkly silhouetting the inky-black artistic frieze of the surrounding trees.

519

6

One of the children they rescued from Mulaisho's village was beyond help. The sick little stranger died in Than's arms the evening of the day they brought him in. The others were faring better, but little Africa's vaccination had failed to take. Upon their return, he had been thoroughly washed and disinfected before being placed in one of the quarantine camps. When it was realized he was not immune, he was revaccinated immediately, and when Matthew Tomlinson accompanied Than on his daily visits, they both anxiously studied the little boy for some sign of fever or the dreaded pox.

In the meanwhile, D. C. Horn conveyed the news that the infectious fear had spread further south, ahead of the inoculation teams. Now the tribes in Kabompo and the Balovale, claiming that the vaccine blinded adults and caused instant death to children, were refusing inoculation as well. The boma officials were at their wits' end to know what to do. As soon as Than heard, he left to see Jahaliso. There, the villagers stared at him with suspicious hostility, and even the arrogant young chief seemed discomfited by his presence; unable to look Than in the eye, he admitted his people were refusing inoculation but denied that there was anything he could do about it.

"But they'll listen to you! They respect you!" Than exploded. "You can have yourself vaccinated and *prove* to them it's safe. If you don't care about catching the disease yourself, then for Chrissakes at least think of the ones worst hit—the children!"

But Jahaliso was looking at Than strangely. "It is the children we are most afraid for," he said quietly. "And it is not for me to prove the harmlessness of the vaccine, brother—it is for *you*!"

With those words Than realized for the first time the enormity of the hold that superstition and suspicion had over the African mind. If even the more enlightened Africans like Jahaliso were forced into sitting on a fence over such confused confabulations, they were in trouble indeed.

"All right," Than said slowly. "Maybe it is. But in the terms of our blood brotherhood, I ask you to at least ensure I get an audience to prove it to. Deceive them if you have to; tell the people that a great witchdoctor is coming who can cure the disease—and it will be the truth. And I want the witchdoctors present too. I want to share my knowledge and to work with them! I want the Lunda and the Lwena and the Chokwe people to hear and see the truth of what I have to say! I want . . ."

"I hear you, my brother," Jahaliso's thick lips spread in a slow smile. "And it is done. I see that you at least *believe* that the stuff the Europeans are sending out from the boma is harmless and effective. I cannot promise that the people will heed my words, but I will tell them of the 'powerful witchdoctor' who has healed me in the past, and I will urge them to come to hear you speak. I will talk to the witchdoctors and the chiefs . . . and I will tell them to bring their children."

7

Matthew saw Than Profane immediately upon his return to Suseshi, when he came to Matthew's house to divulge his plan. Here, the first white child the Boy laid eyes upon was little Luke Solomon. And Matthew had to agree the child seemed a perfect choice to use in the demonstration of the smallpox vaccine. His vaccination had taken well, so he was immune, and despite his dubious genealogy, the child, now almost three, was fair-haired and blue-eyed, about as young and European-looking as you could get. Jenny readily agreed to his use, and when they received word from Jahaliso that "all was arranged," the Boy obtained permission from D. C. Horn to hold a meeting, which would take place in the bush, somewhere between Mulaisho's chiefdom and the Balovale. And Matthew began to pray earnestly. So much depended upon it, after all. If Than Profane failed to sway the people, many more would die and there was a very real danger that the disease would spread to the rest of the country.

According to the news media, the new black government already had enough to worry about; apart from concerning itself with the bartering back of the country's mineral rights, it was even more urgently engaged with the subjugation of the Lumpa church, a pacifist religious sect led by a self-styled modern-day prophetess, Alice Lenshina, a plump village matron who commanded the allegiance of many thousands of simple villagers. Since the advent of the black government, the sect, which refused to indulge in politics, had been subjected to continuous intimidation at the hands of local UNIP members. These, apparently piqued that such dissidents, indifferent to Kaunda's rule, should thrive in his home district of Chinsali, assaulted and killed them, burned their churches and grain bins, and barred their families from clinics and schools. Unfortunately, the new government failed to denounce these terror tactics, and finally, in self-defense, the persecuted people banded together in huge fortified villages.

According to news reports, the tense situation had exploded when police entered a Lumpa village to arrest members suspected of beating an outsider to death. The Lumpas, apparently equating the government police with their enemy, UNIP, attacked them with spears and arrows. One white policeman, two black constables, and forty Lumpas were killed in the following foray, and the prime minister flew immediately to Chinsali to appeal for a peaceful surrender. He ordered that the sect's settlements be disbanded and that the Lumpas return to their old villages. But, terrified of more intimidation, the Lumpas refused. When the police and security forces finally stormed the sect's central headquarters of Sione, some seventy men, women, and children taking refuge in a church were mercilessly mown down by overzealous African soldiers with automatic weapons.

Two days later, the survivors, desperate with despair, overran several UNIP-loyal villages and the Lundazi boma at night; their leader had written them "passports to Heaven" lest they be killed, and with cries of *"Jerico!"* they ran amok, killing all they could. As the shock waves echoed throughout the country, Kaunda declared that Alice Lenshina was wanted dead or alive and temporarily banned the religion, pending a peaceful settlement. Meanwhile the fighting continued and hundreds of refugees fleeing the slaughtering Lumpas massed, under troop protection, at a Roman Catholic mission and the boma. It was a tragic situation, which, had the Lumpas been handled with more tact and understanding, might have been avoided. Now too many had needlessly died, and as the fanatic, grief-crazed Lumpas continued to resist, massing in their thousands in the bush for further retaliation, Matthew feared that many more innocent lives would be lost.

By the time Matthew and Than Profane arrived at the great plain for the *ndaba*, droves of people, coming in from all directions, trampled the wheat-white winter grass and snaked in along the dusty footpaths in continuous streams. Their very numbers and haggard, harried faces bespoke the despair and desperation that had brought them here today. Most had walked the many miles in their bare feet; some came crammed in old trucks, while still others rode bicycles: they passed one man laboriously peddling his entire family atop a battered *jinga*, the mother athwart the crossbar while numerous children clung, monkeylike, to both parents.

The thickening crowd parted for their Land-Rover, staring at them in evident surprise. Matthew espied the large anthill that would be their platform; shrouded with trees and bushes, it was mounted with a small open thatch *nsaka*, the sheltered dais upon which UNIP agents had formerly addressed their Balovale supporters. With relief, he recognized Chief Kadesha's salmon-and-gray Zephyr parked beside the bigger battered black Chevy of Chief Jahaliso, and at the foot of the anthill Kadesha himself, dressed in traditional finery, stood beside Jahaliso, who wore a colorful African-print toga. As they drove past, Chief Mulaisho was jostled up upon the primitive kingly conveyance of a bamboo machila borne by four stalwart servants; he raised himself upon an aged elbow and regarded the Land-Rover with sooty suspicion. Many in the crowd had begun to grumble and gesture in their direction, and Matthew knew they had a mighty battle coming to convince the people of their good intentions. As the Boy parked the Land-Rover beneath a bush-surrounded solitary tree, Matthew said gravely:

"Well, Doctor, it appears to me these people have been thoroughly poisoned against us; they'll take a deal of persuading."

"You think so?" The Boy climbed out of the cab, and Matthew lifted out Luke and followed the Boy around to the back of the vehicle.

"I do. And I've been thinking, if we could just use a little tact and ingenuity . . ." he paused, watching absently while the Boy removed a swag bag from the vehicle and took it behind the bushes. "Well, what I mean is, remember what thee said about . . ."

There was a scuffling from behind the foliage, and Matthew stared in mild surprise as the Boy's blue denim jacket flew over a branch, followed shortly by his shirt and jeans.

"Yeah?" the Boy grunted, and Matthew snapped to and continued earnestly:

"Well, what thee said about appealing to the natives from their own level—it has occurred to me we might do just that. I mean, thee has, after all, been initiated in their 'ways,' and whilst I would normally frown upon such practices . . . well, with the eyes and lives of especially little children at stake, I am sorely tempted to believe the good Lord in his mercy might forgive it, just this once, if thee were to . . ."

He broke off, nonplussed, as Than Profane stepped out from behind the bushes adjusting a bedraggled string of genet tails around his hips; he was shockingly half naked in a skimpy skin breechclout and the feathered fetishes of a witchdoctor.

"Tut tut, Professor—you're not suggesting I appeal to the people in my capacity as a heathen witchdoctor, are you?" Dimpling at Matthew's mortification, the Boy draped his silvery jackal-skin kaross over his bare shoulders. The string of lion's teeth and a cowry shell necklace encircled his throat; he wore python skin amulets on his wrists, and made a strange figure, distinctly pagan, with his ritual scars and lurid streaks of black, red, and white paint desecrating his golden face, and a bunch of guineafowl feathers dangling from his streaky blond hair. Squinting up at him, sheer astonishment prompted the shy little Luke to splutter:

"Mister—what in tarnation is thee dressed like a *muntu* for?"

"*Mister?*" The Boy spun on the child with odd indignation. "My name is Than. I thought everybody around here knew that."

"Fan?"

"Yeah. And don't you forget it."

"Okay, Mister," Luke stared dubiously up at the Boy. "But thee sure do look funny."

Matthew and the Boy looked at each other and started to laugh.

"Mister yourself!" The Boy tousled the child's soft blond hair. He picked up his medical bag, and Matthew hauled out the heavy old hand megaphone D. C. Horn had loaned them, and they set out for the anthill.

Strings of dried seed pods rustled around the Boy's ankles as he walked, and the crowd fell away before them, staring incredulously at the bwana doctor in his primitive costume. The silvery seams of scars snaked across his golden chest, and the deeply gouged, muscle-twisted mutilations the leopard had left on his left thigh were sporadically visible through the swinging striped tails of his kilt as he limped along. They joined the two chiefs and began to scramble up the steep bushy mound to the sheltered dais, which stood some twenty feet up, commanding a panoramic sweep of the surrounding saffron plain.

Inside the small dusty shelter, among spider webs and shales of dead leaves, stood a long knobbled bench; the Boy sat between the two chiefs and Matthew, who perched on one end with little Luke on his lap. There was a crumbling clay wasps' nest high up one of the support poles, and Matthew, with the nervous vigilance of one who has once been stung, kept his eyes riveted upon the two ominous looking inhabitants that lurched around the air near them with long black-and-yellow striped legs dangling and slender evil black bodies imbued with sinister needle-thin stings. But none of Matthew's companions seemed concerned.

Jahaliso adjusted his Pan-Africanist toga, took the megaphone, and stood up to speak. His great booming voice, amplified many times, achieved instant quiet and attention as it echoed out across the wide open plain, over the upraised black faces of the great multitude beneath them.

"I KNOW THAT MANY OF YOU WILL FEEL YOU HAVE BEEN DECEIVED BY THE PRESENCE OF WHITE MEN AMONG US TODAY," he said gravely. "BUT YOU HAVE NOT. ONE OF THE MEN IS MY OWN BLOOD BROTHER, *NJUMWAICE*, WHO HAS, UNDER THE EXPERT TUITION OF THE GREAT NGAKA *KWOYISHO* BECOME INITIATED AS A WITCHDOCTOR IN OUR TRADITIONAL WAY. SO WE SEE HERE WE HAVE A EUROPEAN WHO DOES NOT CONDEMN OUR WAYS, BUT RATHER SEEKS TO EMULATE THE BEST OF WHAT HE FINDS IN THEM, AND WHO IS IN HIS OWN RIGHT A GREAT HEALER, POSSESSED OF POWERFUL MEDICINE. WAS I NOT MYSELF ALMOST BLINDED BY THE MALADY OF THE CLOUDED EYES? WERE NOT TWO OF MY OWN RELATIVES COMPLETELY BLINDED WHEN THEY SOUGHT TREATMENT FOR THE SAME THING? AND WAS I NOT, THEREFORE, GREATLY AFRAID OF LOSING MY OWN SIGHT?"

He paused to slap away one of the wasps, which dangled menacingly in the air in front of his face. When the evil insect immediately lunged back, Matthew saw the stubborn extent of African stoicism: the chief swiped at the insect and crushed it in his bare fist, contemptuously tossing away the crumpled body. If he had been stung, his inscrutable black face expressed no pain as he continued:

"BUT I TELL YOU THIS—MY BROTHER NJUMWAICE PROMISED TO RESTORE MY SIGHT, AND AFTER MUCH DELIBERATION I DECIDED TO TRUST HIM. AND YOU SEE HERE TODAY HOW MY TRUST HAS BEEN REWARDED. AND SINCE THEN HAS NOT *NJUMWAICE* LIAISED WITH OUR OWN DOCTORS AND GIVEN THEM A POWERFUL *MUTI* WITH WHICH TO CURE INFECTED

EYES? AND IN THIS DID HE NOT ALSO TALK THE TRUTH? ARE
NOT OUR OWN *NGAKAS* NOW CURING EYE AILMENTS AS THEY
WERE NEVER ABLE TO IN THE PAST? THEREFORE, I SAY UNTO
YOU—DOES THIS NOT PROVE TO US ALL THAT *NJUMWAICE* IS
INDEED A BROTHER TO THE AFRICAN PEOPLE? A BWANA
MKUBWA WHO ASPIRES TO SHARE WITH US HIS KNOWLEDGE
AND HIS MEDICINES?"

He nodded emphatically and sat down abruptly, his last words
eddying in diminishing echoes across the plain while the crowd
stared up in mesmerized silence. In a moment, Kadesha, gathering
his long cloth *kanza* about him, stood up to speak. The thin, gray-
haired elderly man held the heavy megaphone with an unsteady
hand; addressing the people slowly, with his customary quiet dignity, he told them that his personal acquaintance with *Njumwaice* had
led him to regard the young doctor with almost the affection of a
father for his son; he told of *Njumwaice*'s years of work among the
Lunda people, of his great competence and integrity, and above all,
his sincere concern for the African people. He testified that he and
all his family had already been vaccinated against smallpox at Suseshi and had suffered no ill effect. He said he believed that the
rumor that the vaccine caused blindness and death was nothing but a
falsehood encouraged by enemies of the African people, and he
urged them to ignore such evil, ignorant assumptions and to gain
immunity through inoculation.

When he sat down, Than Profane stood up and took the megaphone. He greeted the people and told them simply, humbly, that
he was their friend and wished to help them. He told them that their
real enemy was not the smallpox vaccine, which would give immunity to the terrible disease presently raging among them, but the
twisted rumors that slandered it, explaining that the very people
who, however unthinkingly, perpetuated such slander were in fact
indirectly promoting much of the blindness and death they so
feared. He paused, then circling his head to gaze upon the vast assembly arrayed beneath him, he told them he was prepared to prove
the harmless efficacy of the vaccine that the boma inoculators were
using; he would use the solution to inoculate one of their own white
children, and he asked all the *ngakas* present to step forward to examine his methods and *muti* to be sure he perpetuated no trickery.

There was a murmurous speculation as the missionaries and the
two chiefs scrambled and slithered down the anthill through the
thick shrubbery. At the foot of it, Than Profane hoisted little Luke

onto the roof of Jahaliso's dusty black car so that the child was visible above the crowd. Then he handed Matthew his medical bag and motioned nearer an inquisitive collection of colorfully clad herbalists, diviners, rain-makers, and witchdoctors, who stepped warily forward to watch the proceedings. Among them stood Furanswa, surly with suspicion, pulling his huge hump-backed hyena along on a crude leather lead.

"Now, Matthew, I want you to hand me my equipment as I need it, as we rehearsed." The Boy heaved himself onto the car beside Luke. "And make sure these *ngaka* gentlemen get a good look at everything as you pass it up."

He crouched to address the small boy. "Luke, I want you to take off your jacket and bare your arm for me, boy. You've had a vaccination before, so you're not afraid are you?"

"No, sir. I a big boy. I ain't feared," Luke said stoutly.

"Good." The Boy stood up. The roof indented with his weight, and Luke stared curiously up as the white barbarian towering above him shook a zebra-tail fly switch and began the curious wailing soliloquy of a traditional curative song, which had obviously been taught him by Kwoyisho. Since smallpox was a relatively rare disease, the song had undoubtedly been composed with some other ailment in mind, but the Boy substituted the word *ichingwali*, at appropriate places, and to Matthew it sounded authentic enough and seemed to convince the crowd, which was hushed with awe, watching avidly while around the white child this incredible white man did a small ritual dance. An impressive figure with his deep glowing tan and muscular body, his ritually decorated face was solemn, the seed pods rustling and tails tossing, as he moved with a native precision and grace. Finally, completing the spiel, the Boy knelt before Luke. Matthew handed him a ritually decorated buck horn filled with common commercial alcohol. He watched nervously, holding his breath with the rest of them while the Boy dipped a wad of absorbent cotton into the liquid, and then, moving deliberately so that everyone might clearly interpret his actions, sterilized a patch on Luke's arm. He waited until the alcohol was dry before placing a drop of the precious smallpox lymph solution upon the spot. Then, taking up a sterile needle that was decorated with beads, he made three careful scratches in the child's pale skin. Then he sat back on his haunches, studying Luke's face.

"How was that? That hurt you any?"

"No, sir."

"Fine. Then I want you to turn and give all the people a great big beautiful smile just to let 'em know you're all right."

"Sure." Luke turned with a shy self-conscious smile, and Than Profane stood up and searched the upturned frowning faces arrayed beneath him.

"YOU HAVE ALL SEEN THAT THE CHILD HAS BEEN INOCULATED WITH THE VACCINE AND IS STILL WELL," he shouted. "NOW WHO AMONG YOU WILL STEP FORWARD TO BE THE NEXT TO RECEIVE IMMUNITY FROM BLINDNESS AND DEATH?"

As the crowd hesitated, Matthew heard a man near him mumble that perhaps the *muti* was only fatal to blacks. He knew that unless a sufficiently confident volunteer was immediately forthcoming, such infectious fear would spread to destroy their good work. As the Boy turned on the car roof, eyes frantically seeking, the silence stretched on. For one terrible moment it seemed that all was lost. Then a man spoke up, raising a powerful black arm. It was Chief Jahaliso, and his broad black face was impassive as he asked to be honored to be the first treated. He climbed solemnly onto the car beside the Boy, toga flapping in the breeze as he offered his muscular black arm. Releasing his breath with relief, the Boy performed the inoculation while the tall young chief looked on with a tense, sober face. When the simple procedure was completed, Jahaliso stood silently considering for several moments. Then his black face broke into a broad tooth-flashing smile, and he raised his great amulet-adorned arms and triumphantly boomed:

"*NJUMWAICE* SPEAKS THE TRUTH! I AM WELL!"

It was enough. The roar of surging hope-heartened voices washed over them like a warm rain, tingling Matthew's flesh. There was dancing and jubilation in the crowd all around them. *They had won!* But when Matthew turned to congratulate Than Profane, the Boy was not listening. Crouched on the car roof, he had reached across to embrace little Luke. His shaggy blond head was bowed over the child as he held him fiercely tight; his eyes were tightly shut and there was about his paint-smeared, oblivious face, a beautiful anguish that was so oddly out of place, that Matthew was disturbed.

He stood puzzling on it vaguely while the people surged forward, begging to be inoculated; the desperation with which the witchdoctors pushed to be among the first attended was indicative of their own dismal failure to conquer the disease. And so it began. Before the sun went down, Than Profane vaccinated some seven hundred and fifty persons; his fingers ached with the pressure of the needle, but only the final running out of the solution made him stop. And then he promised the many remaining the same service if they would journey as soon as possible to Suseshi or their nearest government clinic.

By now Matthew and the Boy could barely stand with their weariness; but it was a pleasant exhaustion, and they drove home in a stupor of contentment, with little Luke curled up between them, sound asleep, with his fair, tousled head nestled trustingly on the young doctor's thigh.

8 Over the next week, people flooded into Suseshi and the boma clinics all over the province to be inoculated; among the hundreds of healthy came the afflicted. The meeting house, which had been slowly emptying as its inmates died, swiftly filled to overflowing, and another quarantine camp had to be constructed to contain the "contacts." Demand for the vaccine quickly overtook the sporadic supply, and in desperation, the Boy initiated arm-to-arm inoculation, taking strict sterile precautions to avoid secondary infection when he used a number of natives, whose vaccinations had taken, to directly impart the cowpox virus present in their blood to their uninoculated fellows.

But they had their failures. Despite Matthew's fervent prayers, little Africa developed chills, pain, and fever, followed in a few days by the distinctive watery blisters mainly on his forehead, neck, and wrists. Furanswa, Mulaisho's head witchdoctor, was another who came down with the disease; since the *ngakas* had been the ones most actively involved with the disease, it was hardly surprising. The funny little man had brought his pet hyena to the quarantine camp with him, and to allay his anxiety, they kept the unsavory creature in a crude log cage and fed him kitchen scraps through the bars. This much to the disgust of the guiltily sulking Ezra Peabody, the Fotches, and the maiden ladies, who had scurried squeamishly off when asked to work with the sick.

However, since even the medical officer, the normally dour Dr. Goudie, was patently delighted with Than Profane's work in bringing about such a massive reversal of public opinion, there was very little they could say about it. The Boy had wrought a small miracle, after all, and Matthew began to feel that they were winning the battle to contain the dread disease in their own province, although several apparently unrelated cases had sprung up among the refugees fleeing the crazed Lumpas in the northern districts. There, the black government's efforts to disband the dissident Lumpa sect had flared into what the foreign press had dubbed Zambia's Holy War. By now, upward of seven hundred people lay dead; Alice Lenshina had surrendered, and rehabilitation camps were being set up to house the rest of her followers, who had responded to her call, via plane-dropped leaflets, urging them to surrender, by painting white circles of affirmation around their villages.

In the chill night air Matthew walked wearily across to the meeting house. He had never grown used to the ordeal of witnessing so much suffering; he still dreaded his daily visits, and now the prospect of entering the hall at night seemed even more formidable. But there was no help for it. It was getting late and he must fetch Jennifer home. She had remained at Africa's side all day; the child had become an earnest pupil of her Braille classes, and she, like many of them, had developed a special affection for the little blind foundling. And she was not the only one worried. The little boy was rapidly deteriorating, and Matthew had begun to fear that he was dying.

But if he was afraid, the child was not. As he grew weaker, little Africa was transformed with a strange other-world serenity that glowed like a light from his little one-eyed face; yet he must know that his grip on life was frail, for in a hoarse whisper, he asked constantly what heaven was like and smiled and sighed with the contentment of a homesick child going home when told that there the blind would see, the lame would walk, and all good believers would nestle in the lap of the loving Lord forever. It was heartbreaking, and Africa was only one of many little children who teetered on the brink of the Valley of the Shadow.

Fear for them kept all the mission workers going long after natural energy should have run out. Grace Dooley hadn't seen her own children awake for days; Jerome's shifts of duty even overtook hers, and overwork had reduced Ingrid Wikstrom to a pale, gaunt figure. The black staff never flagged or complained despite the added demands on their time and vitality, and Katherine Profane fretted that her tall young stepson hadn't touched his bed in days. No one had seen him take a meal in all that time, and the fact that he was still going, looking dazed but grimly determined, was a tribute to extraordinary strength. Though his nerves took the toll and he was snappy and short with his colleagues, with the sick he had endless patience and was always mysteriously calm, serene, and solicitous.

Teller, Katherine, and Jayne, with the medical students as auxiliaries, worked different shifts to relieve the regular hospital workers. They had grown adept at bathing the smallpox lesions with warm water, swabbing sores with a solution of potassium permanganate to prevent infection and, when the crusts formed, anointing the pustules with carbolated Vaseline to relieve the itching and make the pitting less severe. To prevent spread of the disease, the Boy had ordered that all fecal matter passed by the patients be mixed with three times its volume of a strong phenol solution and left to stand for two hours before being disposed of; all urine was mixed with an equal amount and left for an hour before disposal, while all other bodily discharges were collected on soft paper and burned. Bedclothing or linen worn was soaked for three hours in a tub of phenol before being taken away for laundering; all dishes used were likewise soaked in the solution before removal. Even water that had been used to bathe the patients was mixed with chloride of lime and left to stand before being thrown out.

Now, as Matthew entered through the only door in use, he saw the long trestle tables that bore the covered pans of such fermenting masses and, in large tubs beneath, the soaking soiled linen. He took one of the long white gowns that hung in a row from the wall to be worn by every person entering the hall; an adjacent table bore bowls of soap and water and a disinfectant solution, in which, upon departing, each person was expected to wash and rinse his hands. The whole painstaking disinfection routine was instituted not only to protect outsiders from the disease, but also to guard the patients against secondary infection. In the flickering glow of countless candles (used to save generator fuel), Matthew stared around the huge high-roofed hall with its rows of stained-glass windows blacked out by night as he slipped conscientiously into the gown. After a night nurse had tied a mask on him, he moved cautiously into the distressing sights and sounds.

Men, women, and children, lying swaddled in bedclothing on reed mats upon the bare concrete floor, were roughly divided in groups, and the nursing staff scurried around them, using portable bed screens for privacy. Than Profane was present, doing his rounds, moving from patient to patient, examining and counseling, administering penicillin injections to fight bacteria that might be present on the skin, and setting up glucose drips to introduce intravenous nourishment in cases of continual vomiting. The mission drum had long since sounded the supper hour and the patients had been fed their milk, *nshima* gruel, and fortifying fruit juices specially prepared in the hospital kitchen. Yet even despite these precautions and all they could do, the disease had taken a terrible toll. Those who were not blinded were left horrendously pockmarked for life. The little malnourished children were usually the least fortunate. Some had convulsions and went into fatal comas; others merely grew drowsy and sleepily died. A whole family of five children under the age of seven was wiped out, and the Boy delivered two women who gave birth to tiny babies covered in the dreaded pox.

As fast as the dead were removed, new cases replaced them while the blankets were still warm. To accommodate the dead, a new graveyard had been started in the bush, and Matthew had recruited a special detail of gravediggers; none was able to afford the luxury of a coffin, and the bodies were unceremoniously wrapped in cheap cotton cloth dipped in an antiseptic solution to prevent the spread of the disease from the dead to living flesh. Matthew had said a prayer over each sad little mound. He had never prayed as earnestly or as often as now. He prayed in the graveyard, in his home, and most of all, he prayed in the meeting house.

The huge hall had become a torrid world of anguish and death, by day, bathed in the unearthly blue light of the stained-glass windows, by night in the soft guttering glow of countless candles. Here, within its cathedral confines, all time seemed to stand still, and it seemed impossible that outside the birds still sang and the seasons shifted as normal, the chill breath of winter giving way to the fresh flush of spring; shaven heads and the wretched lament of mourners had become common sights and sounds within the precincts of the mission, and it seemed to Matthew that they all wearily trespassed a great darkness, haunted by the anguished groans of the afflicted and the rows of scab-encrusted faces. Now, children wept pitifully for their mothers, and the coughs and moans and distressed cries arising from the rows of litters reminded Matthew of a dawn chorus of the injured and dying after a battle. He spotted Jenny kneeling beside Africa, and feeling ghoulish in the long white overgown, his old bones heralding his coming with a decrepit creaking, he went to her.

"Jenny child?" When he stooped he realized with surprise that, sitting back on her heels, she was sound asleep on her knees. Dwarfed by one of the long white gowns, her white-masked face was bowed, long-lashed eyes shut as she clasped one of Africa's little black hands. The child too was asleep, his wry little scab-spotted face looking serenely at rest, mouth slightly agape in a mysterious little smile, the disfigured white orb of his one eye half closed. Matthew patted Jenny's shoulder and she came to with a small start, bewildered blue eyes staring vacantly up at him over the white mask.

"Come on home to bed now, child. Thee's done enough for one day."

"Oh." Jenny started to replace Africa's hand, then froze, frowning. "He's so cold," she murmured thickly through her mask. "Professor, why is he so cold?"

"*Cold?*" Matthew leaned forward; as he was squinting anxiously at the child, Than Profane joined them. Looking fatigued in a soiled white gown, arrogantly unmasked, the Boy he knelt to examine the small, still form; pulling down the blanket, he pulled up the white jacket and placed his stethoscope against the little black chest, listening for a heartbeat. Then he took the child's free hand and felt for a pulse. After a moment he replaced it and sighed, sitting back on his haunches.

"He's just got a chill, Jenny," he said gently, his signet ring flashing in the flickering candle glow as he carefully disengaged her hand from the limp black fingers. But when he looked up, his eyes were unnaturally bright and Matthew felt a dull, crushing, disbelieving pain begin to burn at his heart as the doctor pulled up the thin gray hospital blanket and tenderly covered the poignant little one-eyed face, with its scab-encrusted features so blissfully arranged in death.

"Matthew's right," the Boy said softly. "You go on home to bed now, Jenny." ·

9

The witchdoctor Furanswa died the next day. He had asked that his pet be allowed to accompany him to the "spirit world" should he die, and in accordance with his wishes, when he closed his eyes for the last time, Than Profane fetched the mission rifle and shot the slavering animal through the head. That afternoon, sharing a grave with his horrendous pet, Furanswa was buried at the same time as Africa. It was the one funeral the Boy took time off to attend. Matthew, with tears streaming down his wracked face, conducted the meeting for burial before the two open graves. He asked God to forgive the witchdoctor his ignorant idolatry, and paid heartbroken tribute to the courage and compassion of the little blind foundling whom the Lord had entrusted into their keeping and who had so trustingly gone to meet his beloved Lord Jesus.

While he talked, Ratchet Cathcart, his bushy brow mournfully furrowed, busily blew his nose, Jenny, with tear-bright blue eyes, stood dazedly shivering, and the other ladies wept. Hannah Rothchild, who had deigned to attend, stood head haughtily averted from the grave of the heathen Furanswa and his hyena, and the Boy, hat in his hands, stood pale and expressionless, swaying slightly on his feet before the two deep pits. It was only when it was all over, when the shoveled sand of the gravediggers had obliterated the cloth-swaddled bodies, that Matthew got some insight into the extent of the strain the Boy had been laboring under. The sudden respite had apparently allowed the ceaseless toil of weeks to catch up with him, and as they were walking away, he suddenly buckled at the knees and keeled over in a dead faint.

With a cry of anguish, Katherine knelt down at his side; cradling his unconscious head, she brushed flecks of grass and dust from his hair and anxiously stroked his pale, perspiring face. When he came around, he was dazed and disoriented; too weak to protest, he limped along through the bush, supported by Katherine and Matthew. At the mission, they took him to the dining *chitenje*, where, against his faint protests, they eased him into a seat and made him rest while Jayne ran for Dr. Dooley. While they waited, he accepted a glass of water with shaking hands and gulped it down. He was staring dazedly off into space when Ezra Peabody, the Fotches, and Cherish Sinclair arrived.

At first, numbed with grief and agitated with his concern for the Boy, Matthew was bewildered by the vicious rage that warped their grim faces. He listened uncomprehendingly to their furious vituperations for several moments before he finally understood. Then their righteous wrath at Than Profane, whose heroic fortitude and courage had undoubtedly saved so many lives, seemed so incongruous and undeserved, he had the hysterical desire to laugh in their faces.

They had apparently just learned of the Boy's posturing as a witchdoctor in his effort to win the fearful masses over to inoculation. And if this successful ruse was evidenced and excused by the many who now camped in the quarantine camps and convalesced in the meeting house, these pious Christians apparently cared little. Demented with rage at the revelation that the Boy had actually studied divination and herbalism under a heathen native, they castigated him mercilessly, with shrill hysterical voices vowing vengefully to bring his aberrations to the attention of the mission board. The Boy, made humble and vulnerable by utter exhaustion and despair, winced visibly as their outraged, denigrating accusations, allowing him no respite, flailed into him like so many rawhide whips.

"Why, it's positively satanic! The mere idea sickens me to my very soul!" Hannah Rothchild shrieked, sneering as she joined in with the spiritual demolition with evident enjoyment. "Why, the very idea! *Masquerading as a witchdoctor!*"

The Boy looked up, and in infinite weariness, defiant to the very end, said quietly: "That was no masquerade, ma'am; didn't they tell you? *I am one.*"

"*Oooh!*" Came the babble of affronted voices. "Has thee no repentance? No shame? *Heathen! Heretic! Disciple of Beelzebub!*"

Under this stinging onslaught, too stunned to react, the rest of them were helpless to help the Boy. Even Matthew, guilty himself of having encouraged the fantastic fiasco to woo the people, stood dumbstruck at the thought of how it would sound to the board. Over any distance of time and space, the board's upright, sober members, however broadened by the world, could never in a thousand years be expected to understand the legitimate logic and integrity of a white Christian missionary enacting a heretical heathen ritual. No. No matter what the ultimate goal or the lives at stake, he knew it would sound like a shameful renunciation of all that others had worked long years to achieve. . . .

10

Rest, Jerome prescribed for Than; complete rest away from the mission. And this time, feeling simply too weak to deny he was of no use to anyone in his present condition, he obeyed. On the return flight of the next aircraft that ferried more vaccine and medical supplies to Suseshi, he flew to Lusaka. From there he flew to Salisbury; he took a taxi through the 5 o'clock rush of home-bound traffic and arrived at the ambassadorial mansion just moments before the ambassador himself. He was just greeting his surprised father-in-law when Suzannah squealed into the driveway in Magdalena's cherry-red sports car. She parked it behind her father's black Cadillac.

"Daddy, just wait till you see what I bought today!" Seeming unaware of Than's presence, she emerged with her arms full of brown paper packages. "I got a new dress for the ball, new shoes, a new bag and . . ."

She froze in her tracks when she saw Than, her plush pink mouth falling open. For a moment they both stood mesmerized. The ambassador chuckled and moved away; they heard the front door close behind him. Then, looking white-faced and weak, Suzannah walked right past Than as if in a trance. He turned and watched as she stooped to place her packages on the ivory-tiled steps, subjecting him to a stupefying view of her lacy panties over a shapely rear. Then she straightened up and turned; their eyes met and she bit her lip, looking suddenly yearning and frightened as an errant child, serene and beautiful with her hair grown long now, the shiny blond tresses resting in curls on her slender shoulders. She wore a short tight pink dress, and her skin was tanned a glowing honey-gold.

"Than . . ." she whispered hesitantly, coming slowly toward him, reaching out to tenderly touch the ritual scar on his cheek. He held mutely still, giving her no help, and then she was against him, touching him, her delicate perfume filling his nostrils. *"Oh, Than!"*

He closed his eyes and he was lost. Somehow, suddenly, in spite of the recriminations of months, she was tightly wrapped in his arms, his cigarette tossed irrelevantly aside. For a small eternity they remained clinging together in mutual speechless need. Then slowly, gently, she drew back, loosening herself from him. "Oh, honey, honey—I can't believe it! When did you arrive?"

But he was staring at her dumbly, hardly comprehending, aware only of the raw aching physical need pulsating within him. Smiling tenderly, she drew him, limping, up the ivory steps. "Oh, darling, I just can't wait!"

In the flower-arranged entrance hall, when the black butler had carried off his luggage, Than silenced her with his mouth, pushing her into a corner, surreptitiously petting her right there, where anyone might find them. They were finally split apart by the ambassador's cautious throat clearing, and they turned guiltily, flush-cheeked and panting.

McQueen grinned, looking a trifle embarrassed. "Sorry to break up the party, but there's someone I'm sure would like to see you!"

Magdalena had a bad cold; she lay in a big double bed, in a lacy pink bed-jacket, her stylishly cut chestnut hair freshly brushed. Than just stood in the doorway, giving her his famous dimpled smile.

"*Than!*" she squealed, reaching out to him. He sat down on the bed and kissed her cheek. She had written him a get-well card and several consoling letters while he was ill, and he felt a fondness for this effusive French woman which did not extend to her husband. "Oh, Than, but this is wonderful! And about time too. It is not right that a man and his wife should be parted so long! How are you?"

"Oh, fine."

"But you have got so thin! You are not telling the truth. You have scars on your face, and I can see it in your eyes. You have had a bad time, a lot of pain."

When he was finally able to break away from her, he found Suzannah impatiently foot tapping just outside the door. He followed her along the carpeted landing to her room, bundled her in, and shut the door. They stood for a moment staring searchingly at each other in the dusk dimness. He began to back her toward the bed with his awkward limping gait. Finally her calves struck it and he gave her an offsetting little push and they both went down in a smoky haze of passionate oblivion. Shaking with impatience, he ripped down her panties and made love to her fully clothed with her dress all hooked up. Slightly impeded by his aching leg, it was a brief, furious coupling, and they fell asleep finally, wet, tangled, and sweating in each others arms. When they awoke later, it was dark outside and they heard the household quickening.

"It's suppertime." Suzannah raised a hand, but he caught at it. "Daddy . . ."

"The hell with supper!" He kissed her, silencing her with his mouth. "To hell with Daddy."

He undressed her tenderly, then began to unclothe himself. He hopped awkwardly, taking off his pants, and when he finally kicked them away, standing naked, she snapped on a lamp. He stood frozen for a moment, aware of the unsightly hairless scars on his abdomen and thigh. *I hate sickness and deformity!* Her stinging words came back to him, but he held brazenly still, letting her see him as he was.

"Oh God!" She flopped onto her stomach amid a welter of pillows and gazed at him dreamily. "You're so beautiful! I'd forgotten how much. And those scars look so sexy!"

He closed his eyes, exasperated. While he might strike her as being esthetically more appealing this way, his leg didn't service him quite as well as it had before. She saw his expression and was instantly contrite.

"Oh I know, honey. I can imagine how it must have hurt. But you just look so sexy that way. And you're so goddamn well endowed, I'm surprised the rest of you doesn't faint through loss of blood when you get an erection!"

"Well." He smiled at her frailly. "Let's not let a good thing go to waste!"

They fell asleep exhausted in the early hours of the morning. When he awoke around noon the next day, he found his arms empty. She had gone off to her work, leaving a note pinned to her pillow. He was just reading it when Magdalena knocked and entered with coffee and toast on a tray.

"Good afternoon!" She smiled at Than bewitchingly. "Had a good sleep?"

"I died. How's your cold?"

"Oh, seeing you again cured it! Now I am all well and ready for the ball tonight. And I have taken the liberty of hiring you a dress suit. You'll be accompanying us, of course."

"What ball?" Sipping the coffee, Than stared at her bewilderedly.

"Oh," Magdalena chuckled. "Suzannah forgot to tell you! Well, it's a big charity ball; all the very best people in diplomatic circles are going to be there! I find the social life of Salisbury most stimulating. I'm going to miss it. Did Suzie tell you Aaron is being transferred to the diplomatic mission in Djakarta in two months? Goodness knows what she will do then. Indonesia is miles from you, or anywhere. And Suzie seems to thrive on neon lights and nightlife, I'm afraid."

11 When Suzannah came home, her hair was tinted a smoky blond and set in a charming Cinderella style, piled high on top with three unleashed locks resting on one shoulder. She was all set on going to the ball, and although Than would have preferred an evening at home alone with her, he felt he could hardly disappoint her. She chattered excitedly about the event as he took a shower in the luxury bathroom adjoining their bedroom. When he came out with a

towel around his hips, she was sitting on the bed in a peach-colored satiny slip, just drawing on her nylons. There was a knock at the door, and the ambassador's voice came muffled through the wood: *"Suzie!"*

She sprang off the bed, patted Than's crotch as she walked by him, and opened the door. Her father's voice sounded low and anxious and some sixth sense made Than strain his ears in eavesdropping.

". . . Carl Steiner . . ." He heard the mumbled name with a stab of shock. "Didn't you tell him?"

"Oh shit!" Suzannah muttered vexedly. "Clean forgot. Tell him I'll be right down."

When she closed the door and turned, Than was waiting for her, eyes narrowed and wary.

"Tell *who* you'll be right down?" He eyed her challengingly, but she swung past him, breezy and evasive, pulling on a padded pink robe.

"Oh, it's nothing, honey. Just a little misunderstanding. Be with you in a moment." She kissed him clingingly as she walked past. *Too clingingly.* It was as if she were trying to placate him, to divert from him other issues, to hide from him—what?

For a full minute after she left him, Than stood frozen in wariness. The aura of other men, an unsettling precognition of other times and trysts, was heavily upon him. It made him a little lightheaded and dizzy, sick to his stomach. Slowly, in a numbed thrall, he began to dress. After pulling on his pants and socks and taking great care tying his shoes, he was seized with sudden impatience when it came to his shirt. The silence downstairs was suddenly unbearable, and leaving his shirt hanging loose and unbuttoned, he tore out of the room. he limped down the stairs, his bad leg, affected by his emotions and the weather, suddenly paining him viciously. He stopped halfway down the elegant curved stairway, just in time to see Carl Steiner, with a cased corsage of orchids in his hand, leaving huffily. He didn't see Than, but Suzannah, turning around just then, stopped at the sight her estranged beau had missed. And maybe irate husbands were a little more ominous than jilted boyfriends, for the secret little smile she wore froze on her face when she saw him, her tawny eyes growing appealingly wide with fright.

"Oh, honey," she stammered, beginning to climb the stairs to him. "You're almost ready."

"Pretty good-looking guy, is Carl Steiner," Than said hoarsely, his words, heavy with implication, making her wince as she stopped before him, looking suddenly uncertain and sick.

"Well, I never thought of him that way." She smiled up at him weakly. "He's just Daddy's junior third secretary. Very junior. And he's not a patch on you where it counts."

"You know that?" He eyed her woodenly, and she laughed, flustered.

"I meant his looks. What else would I . . ." her words trailed, and her eyes were guiltily downcast. "Listen, the fact is I didn't know you were coming, did I? And he was taking me to the ball. Naturally, I had to go with someone. Maggie and I couldn't both drag in on Daddy's arm. And Daddy approves of Carl. He's respectable embassy staff, and . . ."

"And a man." Than eyed her stonily. "What'd you let him have, pussycat?"

She froze, pretending to misunderstand.

"Well, you don't mean to tell me a guy like that—that all-Godly pompous prick Steiner was wasting his time escorting a married woman to all the best places just for the honor of being seen with her!"

"Honey, I don't understand you." She shook her silken Cinderella head at him, amber eyes filling with hurt tears. "I don't understand you at all."

She brushed quickly past him, proud and evasive, acting hurt. But Than wasn't reassured; reading guilt in her gravity, he thundered after her, following her into their bedroom, slamming the door shut behind him. He stood with his back pressed against it, breathing hard.

"You have to tell me, Suzie," he said gently. "You have to tell me now."

She spun on him furiously, tears sparkling in her eyes, struggling with a china lighter to light up a cigarette. When it would not ignite, she threw it down again, furious and frustrated, her cigarette unlighted. "Well, yes, if you must know, I let him kiss me. And just what the hell is wrong with that?"

"Nothing." He shrugged a little, smiling beatifically, hiding the terrible gnawing hurt that had begun to tear at him deep down, disarming her with tenderness when she expected rage, softening her up for the final admission. "Nothing at all . . ."

But she still didn't quite trust him. She snatched the lighter off the bed and this time caught a light, drawing furiously. She withdrew the cigarette and threw up her delicate hands, ranting.

"You forget this is not that Victorian hole you came from! This is civilization! Out here there's such a thing as *platonic* friendship!"

"They were platonic kisses?" Than ventured carefully. He approached her cautiously, and when she spun around, he smiled gently, feeling the screaming hurt as smoky as bliss in his eyes. She stood fuming uncertainly, eying him in a mesmerized way, like some defenseless little bird, petrified by a cat. She nodded stiffly. But her expression was guardedly grave and new lines of wariness were etched for him, clear-cut as confession on her face.

"But that wasn't all, was it, Suzie?" he said softly, gentling her with his voice, raising her chin, making her look at him. "I guess that's easy enough to figure out. I know how it must have been, darling. You're a healthy woman and you love it. You let him love you, didn't you, pussycat? You put out for him. You let him get between your legs."

"Yes," she whispered then, her lips trembling, the word falling from her mouth as softly as the simultaneous tears that splashed onto her cheeks. It was the expected admission; the gentle confession that exploded in his face, leaving his world in shreds.

"You let him . . ." he repeated numbly, shaking his head, frowning wryly, in perplexity, feeling dazed. "You let him . . ."

"*Yes!*" She burst out crying then, her face all screwed up like a child's. "If you must know it—*yes! yes! yes!* But it would never have happened if you weren't always so goddamn far away! If you had been here! If you had come home to me once in a while like a good husband should!"

"You let him . . ."

"*Yes, goddamn you!*" she screamed at him. "I told you! I let him do everything, do you hear? *Everything!* And it's all your fault!"

He stared at her numbly, vaguely aware of the gnawing hurt deep down in his gut, of the random urges that took him by storm only to be dulled by bewilderment. Urges to sink his fist into her soft stomach, to take her by her slender throat and strangle her until dead. It was rage dogged by need of retribution, swelling up inside him only to deflate again through the holes of hopelessness, dissipated by disbelief, leaving him lost. To his own surprise he merely stared, hurt and horrified, irresolute, while a sense of isolation expanded inside him, so vast it roared in his ears, so infinitesimal, it puzzled him vaguely. It was the echo of emptiness washing up on the shores of his soul, an erosion of reality, leaving him dumb.

"Stop looking so shocked!" She was crying helplessly, hiccoughing like a child on her sobbing breaths. "Can't you understand how it was?"

"Yes," he said at last, dimly, distantly, through the roar, beginning to back away. "I guess."

"Then you stop looking that way! You're a doctor! You know about people and their desires! You always said that old double standard was hypocrisy, anyway! That women were as liable and entitled to sexual excursion as men! You always said . . ."

"I know what I always said."

And yet, somehow, it didn't apply anymore. The years at Suseshi must have changed him subtly; indefinite exposure to that religious climate must have honed down his liberal edge, rubbing a little of that abundant morality off on him. It was an old-fashioned wholesomeness of values that rode in on jealousy and accused them both.

And maybe his face spoke something of what he thought, because she was staring at him strangely, distraught and aghast. Maybe she could see him fading away, withdrawing before her very eyes, because she began to panic then, sobbing deeply, screaming and weeping, spewing up her fear, crying so hard she could hardly speak, hardly breathe, and he could hardly bear to look at her.

Shrew! Whore! Faithless woman!

He turned suddenly and limped furiously into the adjoining bathroom. Slamming the door shut behind him, he leaned back against it, raising a wracked face. Suzannah's fearful howls stabbed into him like knives and his thigh pained him agonizingly. He dug his fingers frantically deep into the tormented scar tissue, cursing under his breath. Then gradually his fingers fell still as a deeper hurt swelled up inside him, encompassing his heart, restricting his breath. Suzannah's negligee was hanging from the door and he turned abruptly and buried his hot tortured face into its cool perfumed delicacy. His throat contracted then, and he closed his eyes, wanting suddenly, very badly, to cry . . .

At seven-thirty, Than came down the stairs in the fine black dress-suit Magdalena had hired for him. He was calm and controlled, holding a cigarette in a perfectly steady hand, and the ambassador and his wife looked up at him in surprise. Aaron McQueen bulged out of an expensive dress-suit, and Magdalena looked beautiful, glittering in a sequined cherry-red gown.

"Suzie's in the study," the ambassador said warily. He grabbed at Than's arm as Than made to move past. "Listen, fella, you'd better take it easy with her."

"Oh Jesus!" Than shrugged off the man's hand, smiling deprecatingly. "Stop looking so worried. I'm not about to do anything—except take her to the ball."

"Well just go easy on her, boy," the ambassador gave grudgingly. "It's not entirely her fault, you know. The unnatural circumstances of your marriage, for a start . . ."

"Unnatural circumstances?" Than stopped; he turned and faced the man with cold eyes, smiling bitterly. "Well you ought to know, ambassador. I'll give you that much. It was a marriage you engineered!"

McQueen blanched; his face congested and swelled up like a frog above his tight white collar. Then he seemed to relent, passing a hand across his brow. "Listen, I expect you to be there in good time. With my daughter *intact*. Oh, and you'd better take the Cadillac with the chauffeur. We'll take Maggie's car. You'd never find the place."

"Fine." Than left them and opened the study doors. He found Suzannah curled up in one of the fat leather chairs, thumb tucked into her mouth, her drawn face pale and streaked from crying. She was still wearing the peach-colored petticoat, and there was a bottle of vodka with a half-filled glass on a small table beside her. At the creak of the door, she spun around toward him, snatching her thumb guiltily from her mouth. Cowering back in the seat as though he might strike her, she reached instinctively for the glass. Striding swiftly across, he snatched it from her hand, sniffed it, tasted it, and came back wincing.

"*Jesus!* Neat."

She covered her face with her hands and started to cry. Her fine Cinderella hairstyle was all mussed up.

"You little lush," he said. "You go up and get dressed. Cinderella's going to be late for the ball."

When she came sweeping down the stairs thirty minutes later, skilful makeup and rearrangement had repaired the havoc of her face and hair. She looked tragically beautiful in a long peach-pink gown, studded with colorless rhinestones at the low neckline. Her anxious eyes were startlingly large, fringed with long false black lashes, and her beautiful breasts looked soft and lush squeezed into the tight cups of her bodice. She flinched slightly when he took her hand, apparently unnerved by his unnatural composure. In the back of the big black ambassadorial Cadillac, they rode to the ball in a frigid silence.

The ball was held in a huge flower-bedecked hotel hall, a prestigious affair with a seven-piece orchestra, thronged with dress-suited foreign diplomats and local politicians and their long-gowned ladies. Most of the senior diplomats with larger diplomatic missions had found their jurisdiction suddenly excised from Northern Rhodesia and Nyasaland with the dissolution of the Federation; here in Southern Rhodesia, the government ministers were still white, and over caviar and alcoholic drinks they tut-tutted condescendingly about the black Northern Rhodesian government's "greedy grab" to regain the country's mineral rights and the savage mess they were making in trying to chastise the recalcitrant Lumpa sect. As Than sat with Suzannah at the sumptuously set long banquet table, drinking wine and eating roast duck and cherries with a strawberry soufflé for dessert, it all seemed light-years away from Suseshi with its heartbreaking hundreds of diseased and dying.

Though the McQueens and Suzannah were watching him nervously, Than was on his best behavior, in fact so elaborately attentive and polite, he knew he had them all worried. Though he drank a little too much, he was gallant, ignoring the gnawing ache of his bad leg to dance, awkwardly, twice with the ambassador's wife and any number of times with his own. And Suzannah, in corresponding control, was as graciously contrite and as petulantly polite as a spanked baby. Distant in his arms, she danced with tears in her eyes, a tragic beauty. But if he was coldly immune to her charms, other men were less wooden. She was as appetizing as frosted cake, and everywhere she went, men's eyes dogged her like flies.

Everything went well until Than went off to fetch them drinks; when he returned, he found Carl Steiner with her. They were talking agitatedly, Steiner nursing vodka and a sneering smile. Then he turned and saw Than. The smile fell from his face in a quiver of fright, and they faced each other, hackles up, in the ageless combat of rival males. The orchestra stopped playing and their looks clashed and locked, like combatant horns, in a terrible thunder of deafening silence. Than stood barely conscious of the people around them staring at him strangely, of Suzannah tugging imploringly at his arm. For the stealing isolation was upon him again. The vast hall dimmed and diminished, the roar was in his ears, and only Steiner's face loomed before his dulled eyes. He felt a growl of outrage coming from deep in his gut and he wanted to emit it, but no context would form. And Steiner, snug in alcoholic insensibility and protected by the seemliness of things, quickly regained his composure. The deflated smile rose mocking and malicious, and he faced Than with a cockiness which screamed its own challenge.

"Well, well, look who's here! Little boy lost. How are ya, Doc?"

Than stiffened with an involuntary jerk that had his nerve ends tingling. The two glasses of brandy and Coke began to shake in his hands, and he stood gasping silently from the impact, fighting down a rage, which was transformed from fathomless feeling into a sensory wallop that took his breath away.

"Ease off, boy! Back down!" He was shaken back to sanity by the ambassador's gruff voice. The man took the glasses from Than's hands, grunting furiously: "You too, Carl! I want no trouble here."

And suddenly the danger was past. In the release of tension that followed, a small crowd of fascinated observers broke up. Steiner obediently evaporated with them, but Than remained frozen where he stood, a fool left holding the fizzled fuse of explosive feeling. His breath subsided slowly, his vision clearing. He turned slowly, aware of Suzannah and Magdalena staring at him strangely as he stood, face burning in proud shame, shaken by his own white-heat intensity of a moment before.

"Get your ass out of here and cool down!" the ambassador grunted through his fleshy jowls. "This is a public place."

"I'm not your goddamn junior third secretary," Than said dully. But he turned and stalked off. The orchestra started up again as he wended his way through the milling people. Outside, in the cool car park, he located Magdalena's little sports car, and as he was striding toward it, he heard the light tapping of high-heeled shoes hurrying after him. When he turned, Magdalena slammed into him. He steadied her, and she stood staring up at him in the dark, panting lightly, sequins glittering in the moonlight.

"Please, Than, do not do anything foolish. Suzannah told her father about it. I know how you must feel. But Suzannah is still a child at heart. An impulsive girl who grew up without a mother's direction!"

"Christ, Maggie!" Than turned away from her. "It's bad enough having to take it from McQueen—but you too!"

He opened the car door and climbed in behind the wheel. He

started to feel for the keys, then sat slumped in inanity. He climbed slowly out again and faced her.

"Maggie, do you have the keys?"

"Yes . . . no . . ." She flashed him a guilty look. "Than, I mean I do not wish you to go rushing off. I saw your face. I am afraid you might . . ."

"Christ, Maggie—*give them to me!*"

"No, Than, I do not have . . ." But she moved her sequined evening purse behind her back, innocent as a child in giving the clue.

And then he did a curious thing; lacking other cudgels offhand, he stooped instinctively to the old infallible persuasion. She stood mesmerized, eyes and mouth shining up at him in the dark, holding infinitely still as he bent and gently, caressingly, kissed her glistening parted mouth. The gesture was so unscrupulous, so flagrantly calculated, that she capitulated immediately in a kind of defense. The fleeting pleasure of the moist contact surprised even him, and he felt vaguely bereft when she drew back before he was finished. And she would not look at him. Her own obvious guilt told him that she had enjoyed it as well. Too well; the vague associated accusations of incest and adultery screamed at them both. He stood a moment in shamed wonder; for the first time her effusive warmth and concern came home to him as something else. Opening her purse, she took out the keys and flung them at him. He caught them against his stomach and looked cautiously up at her.

"Do you want them that much?" Her voice was angrily tearful. "Would you seduce me to win a point? Are you that unscrupulous?"

"I'm sorry." He shrugged in shame. "Habit, I guess."

But she stood heaving with her back to him, silent and unforgiving. After a moment, he climbed back into the car. As he started it up, revving it furiously, Magdalena turned and stared down at him with a wracked despair on her face. She lifted a faint hand.

"Take care, *mon chéri*," he heard her whisper before he engaged the gears, reversed, and roared away in a reckless squealing of tires.

12

Two days later, like the proverbial bad penny, Than came back. He turned up at the ambassador's house with a raging hangover, a two-day stubble on his jaw, a blank patch in his memory, and a dent in Magdalena's car he couldn't account for. Magdalena greeted him with a relieved, tearful embrace. Her face clouded when he asked for Suzannah. The girl, she explained, had been phoning hospitals and the border posts, so out of her mind with worry that they had persuaded her to return to her work to get her mind off him. Than went up to their bedroom, washed up and changed, then went to find her at the address Magdalena gave him.

He went up the narrow stairs of a musty old building and along a dim passage to the shabby little two-room photographic studio of the modeling agency that employed her. Against the pointed request of a receptionist for him to wait in the outer office, he obeyed his own driving urgency and burst unannounced in on a photographic session. In a room crammed full of props and photographic equipment, he found his wife posing for a seasonal calendar. Sitting on a rustic swing against an artificial background of pale-blue sky and orange autumn leaves, three of which, strategically placed, covered her, she sat otherwise as naked as the day she was born. She glanced up as he entered; her eyes widened when she saw him and she stood up off the swing with a little exclamation of shock. Without a word he turned and left.

Three hours later, in a house discreetly vacated by the McQueens, he trudged wearily up the stairs and found Suzannah warily waiting for him in their drape-drawn room. As he opened the door, she leaped to her feet. He closed it behind him, and there in the carpeted dimness, alone at last, they faced each other frankly. She began to come toward him, her beautiful face knotted with concentration, looking desperate for forgiveness. But his look cut her short.

"Suzie," he said quietly, "I want a divorce."

"*A divorce?*" she whispered incredulously. All keyed up for reconciliation, she looked devastated with shock.

"Yes, it's the only way."

"You can't mean that!" she whispered in horror, staring at him disbelievingly, white-faced, shaking her head as though her wits were deserting her. "Oh God, you can't!"

"I do," he said resolutely, turning away, suddenly impatient of the emotional appeal he suspected he had yet to endure. Tears welled up in her eyes as he threw a suitcase down on the bed and began to empty her drawers of his clothing. She stood staring at him with a look of stricken sorrow, agonizingly beautiful in this sudden soulful sincerity, her hands twisting, mouth soft, and eyes wide. She wore knee-high white cotton socks, a pleated skirt, and a Peter-Pan collared blouse, and with an Alice band through her long blond hair, she looked appealingly childlike, angelic and lost, reminding him more of Jayne than he cared to think about at this moment.

"You're going. Oh God, you're really going!"

"Suzie, I'm not waiting around to count your lovers."

Unmoving, she watched while he swept up indiscriminate handfuls of clothes and threw them into the open suitcase. She spread her hands uncertainly, staring distractedly. "Just like that?"

He stopped what he was doing and stared up at her. It surpised him that he felt nothing more than weariness. "It's best this way. Maybe you can see a lawyer and take out papers for a separation. I'll be the fall guy. Just say I deserted you . . . what the hell you like—I'll go along with anything just as long as you don't go dragging out things that will hurt my family."

"*Your family!*" She burst out, staring at him through heaving breaths. "Your precious family! They're all you ever really cared about. Katherine and sweet little Jayne! You poor slob, are you so blind you can't see your own sister's in love with you? Well I've seen the way she looks at you, and Jesus! Sometimes I swear she'd like to do it with you!"

He stepped back, aghast. "Don't you . . ." He swallowed. "Don't go fouling up something fine with your filthy thinking. I guess you just can't understand pure, innocent love!"

"She always did stand between us." She shook her blond head, staring at him reproachfully through brimming tears. "But you used to care. You used to *need* me. What's different now? I told you how it was. I said I was sorry! You *know* I won't do it again. I promise!"

Than stared at her despairingly. Her childlike belief that everything could still be the same was hard to believe.

"Suzie, it's not just Steiner. It's everything. It's our whole damn togetherness. We just don't suit. I'm not saying it's your fault, but the whole damn setup's a rotten mess!" He snapped the suitcase shut.

"Where are you going?" she said nervously.

He looked up expressionlessly. "Back to Suseshi."

"*Tonight?*" She stared at him in fright, shaking her head dazedly. "But aren't we going to talk it over or something? I don't understand. . . . W-what is it with you? I mean what is it *really*? Is it my modeling that's bugging you? Is it the nudity that rattles you? Would you like me to stop that?"

He gave a weary sigh. "Suzie, it's just no good."

"No good?" She stared up at him.

"This is good-bye, Suzie."

"Good-bye?" A slow horror expanded in her amber eyes. "But you don't understand. Don't you know how it is? *I love you!*"

"Tell that to your next husband," he said and saw the pain and panic fill her face.

"Please," she said softly and the tears splashed onto her cheeks and slid silently down her beautiful face. "Oh *please, please,* I'm begging you."

He averted his eyes. "Suzie, for God's sake, don't do this."

"Don't you want me anymore? Can you look at me and say that?"

He turned away.

"Look at me!"

He looked. And what he saw filled him with more disgust than desire. She was frantically unbuttoning her blouse, the tears streaming down her face. Her breasts heaved with convulsive sobs and she had gone demented. Laughing hysterically she began to rip off her blouse, pulling down her bra, standing before him with her golden breasts bursting from the white lace, resorting to the only enducement she knew how to levy.

"Suzie, you don't want to do this! Put your blouse back on."

"You want me." She began to sob. "I know you do! You're just angry. I hurt you and I'm sorry! But it'll be the same again! You'll see."

"Suzie!" He turned away from her but she threw herself against him, cleaving her lithe body to his, begging him with every fiber of her being, entreating him with flesh. He turned and jerked down her arms, thrusting her away from him, coldly immune. "Suzie, I'm going now."

She fought against him, hanging on. Finally, he had to throw her down on the bed. But she came back up at him, weeping and hysterical, ripping at her clothes. Something snapped inside him then. He slapped her face and she fell silent and whimpering, dazed on the bed.

"You sniveling little whore!" he seethed at her. "Don't you degrade yourself that way again. You can't give me anything I can't get in a cathouse. And if that's all you have to give, baby, it's precious little!"

She fell finally silent. They stared at each other in shocked stillness. After a moment her throat began to work, she moved her mouth with effort and articulated carefully. "I . . . I can't live without you."

Then she got up shakily, her clothes all awry, and staggered through to the bathroom. She closed the door behind her. He stood for a moment struggling to feel relieved. Picking up his suitcase, he left the room and started down the stairs. But it was no use. Halfway down he was assailed with manic fear. *I can't live without you. . . .*

He flew back up the stairs into their bedroom and wrenched at the bathroom door. "Suzie," he enunciated cautiously, swallowing down his fear, trying to stay calm. "Open this door!"

There was no reply. He felt the panic burst inside him and began to hammer and push. "Suzie, do you hear me? For God's sake, *open up this door!*"

There was a long silence. Then she began to laugh insanely. It scared the life out of him. "Suzie, will you quit playing!" But her laughter fell to a silence that only scared him more. "*Suzie, goddamn you! Open up!*"

In a halfhearted attempt, filled with fear, in irresolute panic, he rammed at the door a couple of times with his shoulder. But it was solid and locked tight. *Take a hold . . .* he thought. *She's trying to frighten you. She's not doing a thing in there but smugly smiling!*

Backed up with this theory, he tried to leave a second time. But the uneasiness hung over him like a cloud and he couldn't quite make it. He sat down on the stairs in the empty house and felt the gloomy premonitions invade his bones. He had misjudged a girl's suicidal resolutions once before. Finally, after enduring twenty minutes of ghastly silence, he could bear it no longer. He raced up the stairs, reached the bathroom, and began to wrench violently at the door with the serious intention of breaking it down. The wood had already begun to splinter and snap when he heard the sound of glass breaking inside.

"*Suzie!*" he shouted, stiffening in strained listening. "You open up this door this minute! *You hear me!*"

To his surprise, she complied. He heard the click of the key turning, and stood frantic, breath-bated while the door slowly opened.

"*You bitch!*" He was furious, shaken, and angry. But she stared at him strangely, her eyes woozy and wide, a sleepy little smile on her beautiful face.

"Good night," she said softly. She took two faltering steps forward and collapsed, limp as a rag doll in his arms.

She had taken twenty sleeping pills, inducing a dangerously deep sleep, which left him with a horror of what might have happened if he had left her that night. As it was, he had to work frantically to bring her around. He gave her no peace, making her vomit and walking the floor with her. Finally, when she had slept off the last effects, she awoke, weak and woozy, to find him watching, white-faced, over her.

"Suzie," he said, turning away, acid in his throat. "I ought to break your neck."

She turned her face into the pillow and began to cry softly. He sighed.

"Suzie, I guess we're going home."

"*Home?*" She stared at him incredulously through her tears.

"Yeah." He sighed. "Home to America."

He held her in his arms while she cried.

13

Leaving Suzannah in Salisbury, Than caught the earliest plane he could charter back to Suseshi. Twenty minutes after he arrived, he was back at work. The first thing he did was to look in on the smallpox patients in the meeting house. Shivering slightly with the remembered horror of it, he donned a sterile gown and mask at the door and went warily into the awesome cool and quiet of the long dim hall. Mbiya, likewise draped, was wheeling a dressings trolley down the aisle and Than joined him, rifling through the treatment book and medical charts, examining the patients and administering their injections while the dresser spooned out medications, changed dressings, and dabbed the softening sores with calamine lotion.

Jerome burst in on them just as Than, crouched beside one of the floor pallets, was injecting penicillin into a thin listless youth.

"Kid," Jerome said tensely, shrugging on a gown, still minus a mask, his gray eyes urgent. "I heard thee were back. I'd like a word with thee."

There was such gravity in his voice that Than stood up. "What is it?"

Jerome sighed. He looked deathly pale, and there was anguish

551

and weariness etched in every line of his haggard face. "It's little Luke. I've admitted him to the hospital."

Than felt his heart begin to jerk painfully hard inside him.

"Yeah? . . . What is it?"

"Well, it's hard to tell and I may be wrong. God knows I hope I am. But I think . . . I think it's a complication of the vaccination. I think he's developed . . . *encephalitis.*"

Inflammation of the brain!

Than felt all his reflexes loosen and let go; as he stood there, the hypodermic syringe slipped unchecked from his fingers and tinkled to the floor. Neither of them made a move to retrieve it, and Than stared at Jerome in a senseless thrall.

"Jesus," he heard his own voice come out in stunted parenthesis above the turbine pounding of his heart. *"You can't mean that!"*

Jerome looked up with pain-filled eyes; the breath sighed out of him like a mournful wind. "I wish I didn't. But the fact is . . . well, Jenny called me to see him the day you left. The symptoms are pretty marked: fever, dizziness, and tremors. Also, a generalized aching in the muscles. Well, I don't know what to think. But in light of that inoculation . . ."

The only white child in a ward full of black children, Luke lay looking pale and very small in one of the white steel cots. Jenny and Teller were seated tensely at his bedside, and Than dismissed them both with a meaningful nod at Teller. As they moved away, the small boy opened bewildered blue eyes and squinted vacantly up at Than. Than reached over the bars and with a trembling hand gently stroked the pale baby-soft cheek.

"Hello, Mister," he said huskily, and tried to smile as the child stared sleepily up at him with a tiny perplexed frown furrowing his fair brow. Than swallowed. "Aren't you going to say hello to an old friend?"

"I . . . I sick," Luke said listlessly, squinting as if to concentrate through dimming eyes. "I can't see good. I's sick."

"I know, boy. And maybe I can help. But first you'll have to tell me all about it. And then . . . then we'll take a few tests. . . ."

A short while with the child was enough, and Than, correlating his own and Jerome's findings with the drowsy little boy, stood up abruptly and walked from the ward. He did not want to accept the truth; it was too much to bear. The implications ate at his heart and the great weight of it almost crushed him. He tried desperately to find alternatives—to find some basis for rejecting the sum of his investigation—but there was no discounting the symptoms, and he stood unmoving in the screened corridor, horrified by the prognosis.

After a moment Jerome came out of the ward behind him. They stood together for a moment without talking, staring sightlessly out across the drab hospital yard, weighted with tragedy, while all around them life, uncaring, went casually on. The orderlies were wheeling out the lunch trolleys; children laughed, a baby's dismal cry hung in the air, and outside, a distant spire of smoke rose from the horizon. Flies buzzed and bickered around the dusty screens.

"I can't believe it," Than said softly, bowing his head.

Jerome merely stared; after a moment, he turned away. His emotion-charged voice near breaking, he said carefully:

"You know it always worried me how we'd ever find the words to tell him the truth about himself—about his *origin*. Well, it seems that now we may never have to." When he looked up, his graying sandy hair was rumpled and his twinkling green eyes were suspiciously bright. Than averted his eyes and they stood for a moment in uneasy silence. Then Jerome ventured disconsolately:

"Thee'll have to take care of him—thee knows that, kid. I'm too personally involved." He looked up at Than and all his defenses were down. His cheeks were wet with tears.

"I can't do it," he whispered. *"He's like a son to me!"*

Than closed his eyes. For a long time he could not move. He tried to speak and found a great dryness. Finally he broke it and his voice came out lifeless and dull, devoid of feeling.

"Yeah," he said softly. "I know what you mean, man."

He walked out into the world and showed his uncaring with a blissful smile that shone like tears in his eyes.

14

Matthew was relieved to hear that Than Profane was back at Suseshi, looking refreshed; with little Luke so sick and the smallpox epidemic still in process, although dying down, the Boy's incapacity and absence had troubled him greatly. But his relief was short-lived. He was busy with administration matters when Clara Fotch brought the mission mail across to his office. She singled out a long white envelope, an odd little smirk on her face.

"Here's·a letter that should interest thee."

It was addressed to the committee's secretary, from the mission board, and forewarned by Clara's inquisitive stare, Matthew waited until the woman had gone before he tore open the envelope with quaking fingers. The letter, concerning Than Profane's most recent breaches of mission etiquette, devasted him completely. Yet, reading through it, he wondered vaguely why he should be so shocked; he had, after all, for so many years, feared as much. In anticipation, he had recently written the board a long letter in mitigation, listing the Boy's achievements. But despite all he had said, its members apparently were not impressed. It seemed so unjust, another awful outcome of the epidemic, and Matthew wondered dully when the horror erupting all around them would end. Feeling old and tired, worn out by the accumulating worry of weeks, he sat for the rest of the afternoon, staring at the wall in a numbed daze. Having trouble accepting the board's censure himself, he wondered how he would find the words to break the unutterable news to the Boy and his family.

As it turned out, he did not have to. For Clara had kept a second letter up her sleeve. This epistle, addressed to the Boy himself, she presented to him with a vengeful relish at the supper table. Matthew felt ashamed of the air of suppressed excitement with which she, Orville, Tallulah, Ezra Peabody, and the maiden ladies, gloating perceptibly, awaited the Boy's reaction. He wore a worried frown, apparently still preoccupied with his patients (though the body be at bay, the truant mind yet walked the wards!), and while he sat for a moment staring absently at the envelope, Matthew stared at him bereftly, with the extraordinary fondness inherent in a last farewell.

They were moving into summer now, and in the full heat of the afternoon, the Boy had removed his medical coat; in the descending evening chill he had slipped on his blue denim jacket. It hung unbuttoned over his bare bronzed torso, and the silver disc depicting his sign of the zodiac glittered on his chest. *Virgo, the virgin:* The implication alone was a terrible sarcasm, the blatantly pagan pendant another small, casual audacity that vexed the elder ladies still. Nothing much had changed, and Matthew had the feeling that if he but blinked his eyes and squinted at the scene askance, it would be yesterday, all those years ago, when the Boy had first arrived. Now, as the Boy opened the envelope, there was a hushed indrawing of breath from across the table, where the row of eyes measured him greedily. As he read, his eyes narrowed incredulously and the color drained from his face, and Matthew realized with a pang of pity that despite the threats following his numerous scrapes and indiscretions over the years, he had honestly never believed that his errant actions and the antipathy of the other missionaries would come to this. But perhaps it was only the strain of weeks of overwork that made his hand shake, for he looked up with a strange composure, with a strangely compassionate, melancholy gaze.

"It's from the board," he said quietly, looking around at them all. "I think you'd all better know it: I've been recalled."

There was a shocked exclamation from Katherine, Grace Dooley spluttered, and Jayne stared incredulously.

"But that's impossible!" Ingrid gasped, and Jerome Dooley shook his head, aghast.

"*No! Thee've done so much! It's unjust! They can't do that!*"

"They can and they have," the Boy said gently. "And I'm afraid they have a legitimate point. I don't fit in here; I've never been representative of this meeting's ideals. And the fact is, I've come to accept that my time here is running out. . . ."

He sucked in his breath and turned to his stepmother with an arrogantly lifted head, a despairing face, and a heartbreaking humility. "I'm sorry, Kathy. I never meant to bring this on you."

"*No! It's not fair!*" Jayne burst into grieving tears, and Katherine struggled up from her seat, blond bunned head raised in proud loyalty.

"Thee has nothing to be sorry for!" she choked, her voice tremulous with emotion. "No one has done more for this mission than thee. And if thee are not considered good enough to work here—then neither are we! If thee has to leave, *then so shall we!*"

"Now, Kathy." The Boy took her hand and urged her down beside him again.

"No, she's right!" Grace, in equal outrage, cried through her freckles and wisps of red hair. "It *isn't* fair! We all know that! How can they make such a judgment? On what grounds?"

"Here, read it for yourself." The Boy handed the letter across.

But by now sniffing and unable to see or talk for her tears, Grace passed it on to Matthew. He felt for his reading spectacles as he smoothed out the pages. His own throat ached and he tried to straighten his furrowed face while, with a sick, stricken heart, he read aloud in a quavering voice:

"*Dear Dr. Profane, it is this board's unpleasant duty to inform you that following numerous complaints from your fellow workers, we feel it in the best interests of all concerned to recall you forthwith. We base this decision, arrived at after long and prayerful discussion, upon the testimony of not one, but several of your colleagues in the field. Apparently, aside from joining the natives in the celebration of their heathen rituals, you have treated the sick without regard for the spreading of the Christian Gospel and without obligation to unconverted Africans. By distributing the mission's benefits so freely, we feel you have removed a valuable inducement for heathen sinners to come to the Lord. As for your adopting the role of a pagan witchdoctor and enacting uncouth primitive customs, we feel this has brought the Society of Friends into ridicule. A colleague at the mission has petitioned us on your behalf, but since it is a Christian Quaker mission you represent, we are unable to excuse your behavior and feel we can no longer risk the harmony of the mission and its good name and works by allowing you to continue your work in the field. We must inform you that Dr. Cedric Fotheringill (brother of the Gladstones presently serving at Mambundi) has been recruited to take your place, and we will be grateful if you will be good enough to remain until he has been installed in October. We must warn you that this decision is final, and hope you will accept it with good grace. We wish you well in your future employment and . . ."*

Unable to continue, Matthew set the letter down. He removed his spectacles and rubbed at his eyes, unable to erase from his mind's eye the image of the Boy, with dark circles of weariness under his eyes, stumbling silent, unsleeping and uneating, through the long dark days as he ministered the smallpox sufferers with a singular devotion. He had been exhausted but tireless, arrogant but innately humble, worldly but a shining example of selfless service: a champion of good for its own sake. He knew that the board's members had decreed what they sincerely felt best under the circumstances. But nothing was as simple as they imagined. Morality had many shades. Perhaps the Boy was a different species of Christian, but his selfless dedication and devotion, *his work*, if not his words, had proved him one. They did not know. Over any distance they could not hope to know. And suddenly seared by the injustice of it all, Matthew rose, uttering a gruff growl of outrage.

"Friends," he said hoarsely, slamming his bony fist on the table, "I would have thee all know that I, for one, cannot agree with the board's judgment in this instance! I feel they have been sadly misled by those Friends among us who have chosen to speak out against Dr. Profane. And I say unto ye all, even as Christ said: *Who among ye is fit to cast the first stone?* It has been claimed that Friend Profane has acted out of compliance with this mission's principles—yet are we not a Christian institution supposedly based upon the example of Christ? And even as Christ fraternized with the shunned prostitute, did not our Friend administer to Mulaisho's forsaken heathen people? And even as Jesus forgave and gave special audience to the tax collector—did not Dr. Profane give undiscriminating attention to the heathen witchdoctors and radical nationalists spurned by ye all? These are those who have most need of us, and it occurs to me that Friend Profane has been the only one of us with Christian wisdom and courage enough to know this and act upon it! As such, I regard it as an honor to have served with him, and far from ushering him off in thankless disgrace, I take this opportunity to commend him for being, if a little unorthodox in method and demeanor, in terms of service at least, as fine and exemplary a missionary as it has been my pleasure to . . . to . . ."

He sat down abruptly, so full of anguish and outrage he thought he might weep. There was a stunned silence; all those who cared for the Boy sat dully staring, eyes glistening in the lantern light. The Boy himself sat with his streaky blond head humbly bowed; he must have been affected by Matthew's words, for his throat contracted and, face contorted, he shut his eyes tightly, unable to speak. But if he was speechless to respond, Hannah Rothchild and Clara Fotch rose up with a furious squawking and Ezra Peabody bounded to his feet with a bellicose bellow.

"Friend Matthew! I think we have heard quite enough of thy mealy-mouthed kowtowing to a member who has all along shown the gravest contempt for all this mission stands for! It sickens me to hear such a . . . yes! A blatant *heretic* whitewashed into a veritable saint! If by thy sly insinuations thee implies our criticisms of Dr. Profane to be unwarranted, I'll remind thee that I am no schoolboy novice! I know Christian ethics when I see them, and the demon dalliance of Dr. Profane most certainly does not qualify! So don't imagine thee can befuddle *me* with thy clever words, Friend. Thee speaks here to a man whose religious writings have been acclaimed by countless Friends the world over!"

He stood for a moment, heaving importantly, glaring around at them all.

"Ezra," the Boy said quietly, in a disconcerting tone of infinite boredom. "Your tie is in your soup."

And so it was. With an embarrassed gulp, the man sat down,

face contorted with humiliation and anger as he dabbed furiously at the flashy adornment with a napkin, muttering heatedly under his breath while he and his ilk glowered at the Boy with detesting anger. But if they had expected a return of wrath, he stared back at them with a bewildering weariness that completely discounted their presence, with a haunting unseeing stare that was somehow, inexplicably, more hurtful than hate.

15

The following day, the horror of Than Profane's recall was overshadowed by an even darker cloud. Matthew and Teller were accompanying Jenny to visit little Luke at the hospital when Dr. Dooley intercepted them, leading them into his office. Than Profane was there; he did not greet them but sat perched on the desk top, drinking a glass of water, staring at the wall. And as Jerome spelled out Luke's condition, Matthew suddenly understood the Boy's strange dispassion over his recall the day before. He had already known the worst about Luke, and from his odd insular serenity, Matthew realized it must be bad. And it was. Encephalitis, Jerome explained, was a dangerous, damaging disease. And as if this were not enough, a complication had arisen. Luke had developed an abscess on the brain.

Matthew did not want to hear any more. Weary to the bone of the grief and despair that had raged all around them these past weeks, he left Jenny and Teller with the two doctors. Stumbling from the clinical little office, blinded by his tears, he walked dazedly across the hospital yard, desperately hanging on to his fast-waning faith with the dregs of his sanity. Finally finding himself at his little rondavel office, he went inside, closed the door, and fell to his knees. "Oh Lord," he moaned, "not this one! Not this child! Whatever our sins—hasn't thee punished us enough? The graveyards are full! Any other, Lord—*take me!*—but please, *please*, not this one!"

But God remained stonily silent, and the most Matthew or anyone else could do was to carry on. And they did. Suspended on the hook of hope, like spiritless puppets performing the same empty acts, they went through the motions of daily living. And in between eating, sleeping, and working, they prayed. Than Profane was to perform a craniotomy, a complicated brain operation to drain Luke's abscess, but other than this drastic treatment and their own constant beseeching prayers, there was no specific treatment for encephalitis, the main affliction. It was a virus that attacked the central nervous system, causing small hemorrhages in the brain. In this instance the encephalitis had almost certainly been caused by the inoculation that had been given to the child to demonstrate the harmlessness of the vaccine to the natives, and even in his terror and despair, the bitter irony of it was not lost on Matthew. Used as a model to save many others, the child had ultimately become a sacrifice. According to the doctors, encephalitis had been known to leave permanent damage to the body, mentality, or personality of the victim; even if the little boy recovered from the acute stages of the disease, it was doubtful he would ever be the same again. . . .

On the day scheduled for Luke's operation, two other surgical emergencies came up to delay it. First an old man was brought in in agony with a strangled hernia, then a young girl in labor required a Caesarean section. By the time she was safely delivered of a healthy child, it was eleven-thirty. While the theater was being washed. down and the instruments resterilized, Than went to see Luke. The little boy had been prepped earlier that morning; his shaven head was covered in antisepticized gauze and a Tubagauze cap, and he lay swamped in a large white hospital gown and long cotton socks. Grace Dooley had just finished administering the premedication, and the child stared woozily up at Than, looking so small and defenseless that his heart contracted and he turned away hurriedly, feeling an ominous ache starting in his throat. Outside, he passed Jenny and the Tomlinsons waiting on the screened veranda. The unanticipated delays had clearly unnerved them too, and catching the old man's urgent eye, Than hesitated. But there was nothing he could say to them, and he moved on. The old man hurried after him. He latched on to Than's arm, and when Than turned, his pale eyes were crinkled with care.

"How is he?"

"He's fine," Than said tightly. He had to steel himself against the compulsive urge to shake off the hand. Then the fingers loosened of their own accord and dropped away, and he relaxed infinitesimally. He became aware of the old man gazing at him with such a look of reverence, with such desperate hope, that he blanched inwardly.

"*Thee'll do it!*" Matthew said with irrevocable sureness, shaking his erect white head with every staunchly delivered word. "I have faith in thee!"

Than closed his eyes. *Please—not this again!* Not that misguided old delusion of unconquerable ability.

"Hey, now . . ." he said softly, musingly, shaking his head. "I'm not being facetious, but you have to remember that I'm not . . . not *God*! I'll do my level best, but that's pretty much short of infallible."

"*Thee'll do it!* I have no doubt."

"Matthew . . ." Than sighed hopelessly. For there were no reasonable words to explain how doubt of the human element in him would have been infinitely more reassuring to him at this moment. He gave up without trying. "Yes," he said softly. "Maybe I will. Now, if you don't mind, I have to scrub up."

"We'll pray for thee!" Matthew's determined voice echoed after him down the corridor, and Than nodded to himself.

Yes, old man, you do that. It was added insurance he didn't mind at all.

16

It was almost noon by the time Than, freshly scrubbed, stepped back into the operating theater. He was helped into his gown and mask by Mbiya, who was acting as circulating nurse for the operation. Outside, the hospital generator throbbed, feeding them power; everyone stood at their posts and four instrument trolleys and a small instrument table had been placed in position. The sterilized instruments on them had been carefully arranged, checked, and rechecked. There were piles of compressors, cups and trays, and sealed containers. Wires had been taped to the floor, drugs prepared, and dressings counted.

Luke lay on the high table, his soft baby form looking pathetically small and out of place in the highly mechanized world around him. He was almost unrecognizable for the tubes and needles that fed into his tiny body. He was soundly anesthetized, having been injected with drugs to induce sleep and muscular relaxation. A tube had been inserted into his mouth and down his throat to facilitate endotracheal anesthesia. It was packed into place with sterile gauze, and two strips of Elastoplast had been fixed under his nose and throat to prevent any excessive escapage of gas. Now Grace Dooley, sitting behind a sterile curtain, breathed for him, squeezing a rubber breathing bag to pump oxygen into his lungs from the induction machine.

On Than's instructions, Jerome had performed a cut-down on the child, exposing the large saphenous vein just below the skin, inserting a flexible plastic tube which had been guided up the vein into the child's abdomen. This was to guard against the risk of circulatory collapse, to facilitate ultra-rapid blood transfusion, or to feed drugs directly into the opened vein should an emergency arise.

An intravenous drip of glucose and saline had been set up at the foot of the operating table and connected to the tube fixed to the catheter. The blood-pressure cuff had been fixed and a self-sealing Gordh needle had been inserted in the boy's left arm, to allow for an emergency injection of muscle relaxant should it be required. A diathermy plate, to ground him during the use of the hospital's new electric cautery machine, had been laid below his leg. Every foreseeable precaution had been taken, and Than stood for a moment, taking silent stock of the preparations. He stared at the inert figure lying prone and small beneath the bright overhead light and, lastly, at the anxious assembly of white-masked faces.

"Everything okay?" he asked cautiously.

"Fine. I didn't try to position the head for thee," Jerome said tensely. "Thee never can satisfy the other guy."

"Fine." Than squinted across at the X-ray plates mounted on the wall across the room in their strip-lit panel. Then he bent and stared down at the bald white dome of the small boy's head, mentally correlating the one to the other. "Okay," he said grimly, flexing his fingers and lifting his feet in their nonstatic overshoes, like a bull pawing earth. *"Let's go."*

He went to the scrub sink in the room and briskly resterilized his hands and arms before returning to the table.

"Prep trolley, please."

"Prep trolley!" Ingrid snapped, and Denise Smith, masked and gowned, wheeled it to the table. It held swabs, one gallipot of Cetavalon and another of Hibitane.

"Okay to start now?" Than looked toward Grace Dooley, sitting behind her sterile curtain at the induction machine, keeping vigilant watch over her clock and dials.

"Yes," she said lightly. "He seems fine."

"Okay. Gutta-percha, please."

"Gutta-percha," Jerome repeated, and Ingrid handed the eye-shield to Than. He positioned it carefully across the child's brow, to protect his eyes while he washed the scalp with the strong antiseptic solutions. Using a fresh swab with each stroke and working methodically from the front to the back of the head, he swabbed on first the Cetavalon and then the Hibitane. As he steadily worked, the only sound in the room was the soft gasping of the respiratory bag and the ticking of the alarm clock on the shelf.

"How's that drip?" Than said grimly, and Grace glanced at the intravenous standard from which the mixture of glucose and saline flowed into the unconscious boy.

"It's flowing fine."

"Good." After a moment, Than stepped back. "All done here."

Denise Smith stepped forward and removed the prep tray.

"Now I want that hot swab, please."

Mbiya withdrew a steaming swab from the sterilizer unit beside him; he carried it over with a Cheatle's forceps and Than took it and placed it firmly around the edges of the eye-shield, forming a perfect seal. Then he stood back to study the scalp, glancing from it to the X-ray viewing panel. When he finally turned, Denise Smith was waiting with a battery-operated headlight, which she fixed to his bowed head, making sure it was comfortable and correctly placed.

"Thanks." Back at the head of the table, Than took the small boy's head and turned it slightly. "Okay." He turned to Ingrid and she slapped a scalpel into his hand. Using the blunt end, he made a rough scratch mark around the area to be incised. Then he traced the line with the sharp edge, and a thin line of red blood followed his course.

"Procaine!"

Ingrid handed him a syringe that had been prepared with the local anesthetic and this he injected into the skin beneath the marked area. The flesh puckered under the effects of the drug, which would act as a hemostat when the cutting proper began.

"Gauze, please." Than took the soaked pad and placed it over the marked area. "Towels!"

Ingrid and Denise brought forward the antiseptic towels and began to arrange them over the small prone patient.

"Blood pressure one-oh-five—a little high," Grace interjected in a tense voice.

Than looked up briefly. "Yeah, check."

As the nurses stepped back, he inspected the towels, clipped into place.

"That's fine." He glanced across at Grace again. "How's the pressure going?"

She looked up. "The same."

"Fine." He went to the scrub sink and once again went through the rigorous ritual of scrubbing up. As he worked, Ingrid silently laid out all the instruments that would be needed. Denise Smith connected the sucker tube to the suction machine, which would be used to suction away and exactly measure the amount of blood lost in the operation. Mbiya connected the cautery lead to the machine, which would be used to seal off cut vessels. Back at the table, Than wriggled his hands into the powdered rubber gloves Ingrid held out for him.

"You ready?" he said, and she nodded.

He took the scalpel and cut deeper along the etched line. Blood began to spurt, and Jerome took artery forceps from Ingrid and began to use them. Than worked steadily, cutting the flesh and ligating the severed blood vessels with clamps. Swells of sweat rose on his brow, and above the *wooshing* of the respiratory bag there was no sound but the clicking as one instrument after another was discarded, to be removed by Mbiya.

"Clamp." The request rang out time after time, until the line of the wound was festooned with the instruments. "Clamp!"

Than glanced up at Grace. "How's he doing?"

"Pressure's still steady at one-oh-five."

He nodded, and called again for a clamp. Then: "Irrigation, please."

He waited while Jerome used disinfectant solution to wash the wound clean to keep the field clearly visible. "Okay. Next clamp." He worked steadily on, all his movements anticipated by Ingrid as he tied off vessel after vessel.

"That looks like it," Jerome ventured finally, in a breath-caught voice, but Than shook his head.

"Uh-uh. One more . . . two!" He tied the vessels off deftly and eased back a little. "Guess that's it. Irrigation, please."

When the area was washed clean, there was no sign of bleeding, and Than nodded in satisfaction. Then he bent and with slightly shaking hands began to pare back the skin flap. Ingrid handed him an antiseptic pad, which was placed over the raw flesh.

"Sweat!" Ingrid was leaning across to mop his brow even as he spoke. He glanced across at Grace again. "Okay, how's he taking it?"

"Fine. Pressure's steady at one-oh-five."

"Good." Than rinsed his gloved hands in an antiseptic solution, flicking off the excess water. "Okay—diathermy needle, please."

Ingrid handed him the needle, which was connected by the lead to the machine at the foot of the table. "Cutting at four," Than said, and Mbiya nodded and moved to the machine and turned the switch to the desired reading, sending electrical current into the needle.

"Cutting at four, Bwana!"

"Right." Than took the needle and began to cut through the pericranium—the flimsy layer of skin which covered the bone. "Irrigation," he grunted, and Jerome sluiced the area with the antiseptic solution. "Perforator!" Ingrid handed him a steel brace with a cutaway V-pointed blade attached. Than hesitated a moment and took up a position in readiness for its use. He stood legs braced and slightly apart.

"Get back!" he snapped as Denise Smith and Mbiya leaned forward, encroaching the table area with interested eyes. He wanted no distractions. They stepped back immediately.

"That's better." Than bent his head and began to use the instrument; after drilling two or three turns into the bone, he stopped. It was impossible to judge the thickness of the skull beforehand. He had to feel his way.

"Irrigation." He waited while Jerome washed out the small hole. "Okay. Dural hook." It was slapped into his palm as he spoke, and he took the instrument and began to probe into the burr hole to judge how far he had drilled. He found no crack and resumed drilling again. After another few turns, he repeated the probing with a dural hook.

"Through!" he grunted triumphantly and stepped back to allow Ingrid to collect the skull shavings in a small gallipot; the dust would be used to refill the holes at the end of the operation.

"Right. Irrigation!" Than snapped, and Jerome carefully sluiced the burr hole again to prevent any of the bone dust from getting into the dura matter, which lay directly underneath—a membraneous covering of fibrous tissue over the brain.

"Burr, please!" Than took the instrument and proceeded to perforate another hole. He started with fright when Grace suddenly wailed:

"The blood pressure's dropped! Heart's stopped. Oh no! He's in *cardiac arrest!*"

Her chilling voice, quivering with fear, rang through the little theater, turning them to stone.

"*Jesus . . .*" Than snapped upright; he stood for a moment bludgeoned with shock at this, the most dreaded of all operative complications. He was aware for a split second of the whole team standing stock-still on caught breath, frozen with fright, while the clock ticked away the precious passing seconds. He struggled out of his own binding numbness with a physical jerk. "Grace—are you sure?"

"Yes! Yes! Oh God!" She was weeping, blinded by her tears.

"Then listen to me! All of you! *Hold on to your nerve!* We've got three minutes!"

If he failed to reestablish the blood flow to the brain beyond that time, the danger of permanent damage would arise. If he didn't succeed in five minutes, the thought and speech processes would be permanantly affected. Any longer than seven minutes and the child would be dead.

"Switch off the anesthetic!" Than shouted, but Grace, regaining her composure, had already done this within the first ten seconds. She had started to ventilate Luke's lungs with pure oxygen, and Than snatched a hypodermic syringe of adrenaline from Ingrid's hands and injected several milligrams into the I.V. tube.

There were two forms of cardiac arrest that Luke could have suffered. Ventrical standstill, in which the heartbeat suddenly ceases, or ventricular fibrillation, in which the heart goes berserk before coming to a stop. The problem was that each type was treated differently. In a standstill, the heart has only to be restarted. In fibrillation, it must be brought to a dead stop and then restarted. Than had no way short of lengthy tests to determine positively the type of arrest the boy had suffered. He had to trust his own intuition. He decided on ventrical standstill.

"Thirty seconds!" Grace began the terrible countdown marking the passing of precious time. By now it was clear the adrenaline had failed to restart the heart, and Than snatched a second syringe of the solution from Denise Smith; Ingrid had pulled the child's gown up around his neck and he stooped and injected a stiff dose of the adrenaline directly into the heart through the chest wall.

When nothing happened, the theater was pitched into a practiced emergency routine. The instrument trolleys and dressing trays were wheeled back from the table. Jerome quickly covered the boy's exposed scalp with antiseptic pads. The two black nurses stood waiting expectantly, ready to act on any request that might suddenly be sprung on them. All eyes were fixed on the tiny prone form on the table. The little boy, so recently past babyhood, lay wan, white, and naked under the stark overhead light, the long cotton socks reaching up to his groin. There was a heartbreaking pathos about his tiny genitals.

"Forty seconds!"

There was no time now for sterile precautions; nothing mattered but speed, and the only essential was a knife. Than found the required instrument in his hand, magically slapped there by Ingrid's forethought, racing ahead of the need. He bent over the body and made a large slash over the lower ribs and began to cut down through the layers of tissue. There was the steady hiss of the induction machine as Grace oxygenated the child's lungs; the clock ticked on. But despite the pressure of time, Than, with a high strange rock-like calm worked carefully, cutting his way through the pectoral muscles, another layer of connective tissue, and the final layer of tough tissue—the periosteum, which adhered to the bone and gave anchorage for the muscles. There was no bleeding—a clear sign that cardiac arrest had occurred. Carefully, he parted each layer, giving a deceptive appearance of slowness in a practiced caution, which had Jerome Dooley impotently gnashing his teeth.

"*Hurry! For God's sake!*"

"Seventy-five seconds!"

Than said nothing; he cut through the membranous periosteum and finally the ribs were exposed.

"*Periosteal elevator!*" he grunted, and snatched the instrument from Ingrid's hand; using the elevator, he began to strip the covering away from three ribs.

"Rib shears!" He tossed away the elevator and grabbed the next instrument, already waiting in Ingrid's hand. With quick sharp cracks, he cut off sections of the ribs and removed them.

"Ninety seconds!"

Time was working against him and the strain surfaced a sweat that fell like rain from Than's face. He shook off Ingrid's hand as she reached across to mop his brow.

"One hundred five seconds!" Grace stammered as Than pushed his gloved hand through the hole he had made in Luke's chest; he eased his fingers around the tiny heart and began to massage it, squeezing it rhythmically eighty times a minute to get the blood flowing to the heart. Over two minutes had passed since the onset of the crisis and he had just seconds in which to restart the blood flow manually before permanent damage set in. Grace kept the oxygen flowing into the small boy's lungs and Than worked steadily, rubbing the heart with the palm of his left hand.

"Beat, goddamn you!" he pleaded through the mask. "*Beat!*"

"One hundred thirty-five seconds!" Grace called out, and she was weeping.

566

"Hold on!" Than closed his eyes. *"Please God! Hold on!"*

And standing there, eyes tightly closed against the cloistered reality, he drifted into a mindless euphoria, into a vague warm vacuum of feeling and sound, aware only of his rhythmically clenching hand. He held the whole enormous sum of his world in his palm, and it refused to pulse without him. Time stood still for an eternity and there was a soundless roar of oblivion in his ears that went on and on with the steady, untiring clenching of his hand.

"Three minutes gone!"

He was vaguely aware of Grace's hoarse sobbing; losing her nursely decorum, she was the first to break. There was the risk of damage to the speech and thought faculties now, but still, blindly, stubbornly, Than carried on and on. He had worked the trick so many times before, and now, when he most wanted it . . . he refused to give up because it was life that he fought for; life, love, and a little three-year-old boy, never saying *Daddy.*

"Five minutes!" It was Jerome, and his voice sounded strange—gruff and coldly despairing.

And still Than worked on and on, paying no mind to the ache of his flexing fingers. But he was brought up short by Jerome tugging at his shoulder, shouting:

"Eight minutes! *It's too late! Do y'hear? Let him go! Let him go! It's too late!"*

And when he opened his eyes, he saw that it was. The conduction mechanism of the heart had failed; there was still no bleeding in the wound, and Luke's skin was a strange color, his tiny fingernails a smoky blue. The little heart would never beat again. Than stared dumbly down at the lifeless organ in his still palm and thought irrelevantly that his hand looked inordinately big inside the small mutilated chest. When he looked up, he became aware of the whole surgical team staring at him strangely, and he realized that he had been single-mindedly carrying on with the massage, doggedly trying to restart the circulation long after all hope of saving the child as a human being with any intelligence had been passed. In his fanatical bid, he might have heedlessly revived a mindless vegetable.

"He's dead!" Jerome ripped off his mask and stood staring dazely. *"Dead! Don't you know that?"*

Than stared bewilderedly around at Ingrid, his good right hand, and her anguished gray eyes told him the same truth. They filled with tears that splashed down onto her surgical mask. She reached across and took his hand, easing it gently from the chest opening. He stared dazedly around at Denise Smith, at Mbiya and the black nurses, and found the same stark vacant shock staring back at him. He struggled with the enormity of reality as it descended, swamping him like a morass—standing lost for a moment in his own sense of loss; vaguely bereft—aware that just a few short minutes ago an irreplaceable part of his life had faltered to an end.

But even in the midst of unbearable sorrow there were things that had to be done. They saved him.

"Yes." He squared his shoulders, and while all around him helplessly stared and wept, he worked with painstaking care to put what mortally remained of his son back together again. And as he worked, he raised his head in wry bewilderment, in an attitude of listening.

Life, oh indiscriminate dealer of sorrow and strife, you have dealt me too much!

17

Carelessly wrenching off his surgical whites, Than stumbled out of the operating room, and on the veranda outside, the cool-aired rushing reality of the world hit him like a sobering slap. He faltered and stood dumbfounded up against the wall of waiting that met him. For upon seeing him, Matthew, Teller, Katherine, and Jayne rose up of one accord, leaving Jenny, unknowing, behind on the bench. They hurried along the passage and stopped, silently arrayed before him, blocking his way; Matthew in his good First-day suit (occasion inviting God's presence was occasion for dress!) and the ladies brushing the polished floor with their gracious Quaker dresses. They stood speechless with their fearful hope, beseeching him with harrowed eyes.

But being unable to tell them what they wanted to hear, Than could not speak at all. It was Matthew who made the first faltering move; he reached out a gnarled brown hand, and his eyes, like a forsaken old dog's, silently implored: *Please do not fail me!*

"Son . . ." he croaked, but Than could only stare.

It was the Dooleys who saved him. Than leaned against the wall as they came out of the induction room behind him, moving past him, still in their whites, arms linked and supporting each other in their grief. Jerome, face awash with tears, was white-faced and dazedly calm. Grace stood glassily staring; her freckled face was swollen and red from crying.

"*No!*" Matthew wailed, glancing from Than to the couple. He must have had some warning from the strange sum of their silence and stupefied staring, for he turned suddenly, deathly pale. He closed his eyes.

"It's all over," Jerome told them in a quaking voice, raising his pain-filled eyes. "There was nothing we could do . . . nothing."

Matthew's eyes snapped up in outrage. He stared at Than in stunned disbelief. Than stared dumbly back, his brow clenching infinitesimally, in a vaguely remembered far-off distress. *I tried to tell you, old man. You see! You see! I have feet of clay. . . .*

"It was cardiac arrest," Jerome was saying, and Matthew stood rooted like rock while the women beside him, finally digesting the truth, emitted small choked cries over their wrung hands, slumping, stunned, in their grief and despair.

Than walked woodenly through their ranks. Then his footsteps faltered and he stopped instinctively, parallel to Jenny on her lonely bench, still sitting there waiting, silent and blind. And deliberately submitting himself to this ultimate endurance, he turned to her, a young dark-haired girl, looking expectant and anguished, the hands clasped tightly in her lap. Detecting his presence, she raised her beautiful blind blue eyes at him, inquiring and afraid; and nothing in his life had prepared him for that moment. Her sightless look shattered him like a bullet, and he knew that after this, there was nothing worse that he could feel. . . .

He didn't know how long he stood there, but terrorized speechless with suspenseful waiting, Jenny's eyes filled with tears, her soft mouth began to tremble, and eventually Jerome, strong of necessity, had to move past Than to take up the task. He took up her hands and gently raised her.

"Jenny, oh my dear . . ." he said brokenly, face harrowed as he cast mentally for adequate words. "I—don't know what to say but that God works in strange ways. We may never understand why, but . . . Jenny, Luke died twenty minutes ago. His heart simply stopped beating and there was nothing—not a thing in this world— that we could do. . . ." His words, frail and bereft, stole ineffectively into the strange afternoon.

"He's dead, Jenny."

Something went out of her eyes then. Quite suddenly the fright and the fear, the hope and the horror, melted away, leaving them vacant and dull. She stared blankly up at Jerome, still frowning in that baffled puzzled way, like a small bewildered child trying desperately hard to understand.

"Jenny, are thee all right?"

But she did not reply. The rapt look of blank bewilderment remained on her face. She did not cry out or faint, but stood sightlessly staring. Jerome took her arm and urged her gently forward. He glanced up at Than and their looks communicated. She was in deep shock.

Outside, clouds had hustled the sun into premature twilight; a swirling wind had arisen and thunder coughed and grumbled distantly from the smoldering skies.

Teller Tomlinson, her gentle face softened with sorrow, took off her old brown cardigan and moved forward to place it over the girl's slender shoulders; Matthew, with tear-blazed eyes and crumpled face, came to take her. Red-nosed and sniffing wretchedly over his snowy moustache, he reached out his arms and wordlessly enclosed her. He held her with anguished eyes tightly closed, tears streaming down his wracked face. *"Jenny child! Oh, Jenny child!"*

Dull-eyed and dazed, she was with family. As they made to lead her away, she made no protest, and went with them meek as a lamb. She was shivering.

"Keep her warm." Jerome raised his head. "I'll come across now to give her a sedative. . . ."

Than stood on the open veranda, outside the outpatient department, leaning up against one of the supportive poles, watching as the huddled little group moved away. The Dooleys left too, and it seemed that the whole hospital was emptying away from him as one by one, people, black and white, stepped off the veranda and left his charged proximity. In the end, there was only Ingrid, and she, looking lost and alone, stared at him with such yearning that he touched her absently as he moved away, sensing his own indescribable need also in her. . . .

18

There was a curious swift change in the atmosphere; the heavy clouds smoldered on the horizon, thick and black as smoke, and the sky shimmered with a queer bright unnaturally sustained silvery light. Wind whispered in the trees, playing tricks with dry leaves and loose sand, and birds soared in panicked flight, their piercing warning cries splitting the silence of the wide open sky. The first brilliant whipsnap of lightning fragmented the windblown clouds and the awesome drumroll of thunder climbed and racketed around the immense firmament with a deafening reveberation that seemed to quake the very earth.

The First Rains. And coming early, they came with a vengeance. Than stared across the dry-grassed slope of the mission that fell away to the dank vegetation-shrouded river, which mirrored the gray scudding clouds as it surged silently to its own eternity. Than had never been so painfully, acutely, aware before. On the swing bridge, he felt the rough hessian prickle of the ropes under his fingertips; felt and heard the dry wooden slats as they swayed and clacked softly under his moccasined feet. The scent of rain was in the air, rising in waves as the humidity touched the steaming earth. He found a cigarette he couldn't remember lighting smoking in his hand, and he tossed it into the far-below swirling waters of the river. He could hear the rain coming, distantly echoing over all the vast forests of the bush, approaching in a muffled roar that descended on him with frightening rapidity. He blinked under the first kissing wet drops, squinting up at the swirling gray skies as he began pulling off his shirt. He dropped it unheeded on the slats, walking over it, leaving it wistfully hanging above the river, meeting the downpour with a bare chest, wordlessly begging: *Harder! Harder! Hurt me! Distract me! Wash away my pain. . . .*

He reached the far bank and, without knowing how or why he had got there, found himself wandering drunkenly toward the mission vegetable patch, which lay parallel to the river, high up on its bank. Limping unmindfully through Matthew Tomlinson's gardens, he felt his feet sink deep into the soft soil, artichoke seedlings crushed heedlessly underfoot. He stooped and went into the dry dimness of an open creeper-covered arbor he had never been in before. It was raining hard now, the staccato rattle of rain exploding in a roar on the corrugated-iron roof as he stumbled, shivering and wet, into the cool shelter and the dank pungent smells of honeysuckle and fertilizer. Eyes squinted against the gloom, he found an upturned wheelbarrow and sat down on it, pulling off his muddied shoes and socks. Thunder rumbled hollowly over all the earth and he watched lightning splinter the sky through the hanging wall of honeysuckle vine; the tangled green arms were dark-shadowed and grotesque against the gleaming rain-streaked silvery daylight and the vine shivered and swayed, sheltering him, binding him in, holding him hostage to his moment of truth. Through the hanging curtain of foliage, a fine spray of rain reached him on a breeze and the damp cold seemed to seep to his very soul.

He felt small and afraid and indescribably alone, and sitting there, an inertia of despair fell on him, a desolation so empty and ageless that he thought he would die of its effects. He stared into space while the random irrelevant thoughts just tumbled through his mind like windblown leaves before a storm. And when he blinked, the day had gone. It was dark outside and he shivered feverishly and wondered where his mind had been. He was smoking absently, staring thoughtfully out into the spitting black night, when it hit him.

My son is dead.

As he struggled dazedly to digest it, the terrible familiar warmth was upon him again; he felt the ache in his chest spread like a fire through his body until he glowed with heat, with an excruciating warmth that intensified with every second, becoming so intense that he could scarcely endure the scorching wave that enveloped him as the slow full realization exploded in his mind. First he saw his cigarette hit the ground, white and insignificant, and then, somehow, he was on his knees on the damp earth, hugging a wooden pole. His eyes were tightly shut, he could scarecely breathe through the wracking convulsions that shook him, and the alien animal choking that filled his ears was the sound of his own sobbing. . . .

My son is dead!

For as long as he lived, he would never forget the feeling.

19

Two weeks before his third birthday, they buried the little boy in a small *muku* wood coffin. The sun was appropriately overcast the day of the meeting for burial; a high clear stillness, as delicate as mist, lay on the mission like a mantle. Since Jenny's father was presently convalescing from major abdominal surgery in hospital, her family had been unable to attend, but all the houseboys in their short khaki suits and white aprons, the hospital dressers and nurses in their white uniforms, and the rest of the black mission staff crowded with the missionaries around the open grave. The woebegone singing of "Amazing Grace" rose mournfully from the grieving throng as the little coffin, with its frail weight, was lowered into the red earth.

"Suffer little children to come unto me . . ." Matthew could not finish the text for his inconsolable weeping, and Ratchet Cathcart, with timid fortitude, continued for him. When it was all over, they stood staring at each other, as bewildered as new chicks just out of their shells. There was a general air of disbelief, and few faces were without tears. Jenny's was one of them; she stood in her blue dress and bonnet with Teller's old black shawl over her shoulders, looking mesmerized and dull. She had not uttered a word since the child's death, and no food had passed her lips. Though she did all she was bidden with a lifeless meekness, she showed no signs of emotion or even presence of mind. The missionaries watched over her with worried eyes; Matthew and Teller, in particular, cosseted her with loving care, leading her from the graveside to a house that stood heartbreakingly silent. Teller made coffee and there was fresh apple pie, but the visitors were a disconsolate group and Matthew's aching heart lay under earth behind the ruins of the old brick meeting house. He rose, furtive as a shadow, and stole out into the settling dusk, where an iridescent sunset flashed saffron and cerise along the winding face of the river; meandering drunkenly along the slope like one deluded, he wended his bewildered way to the haunted silence of the mission cemetery.

There, beside the pathetic little flower-covered mound of newly turned soil, a shadow moved, and silhouetted against the pink glow of the twilit sky, Than Profane, in his best Sunday suit, stood tall and alone. There was desolation in every line of his body, and across the terrible weight of his own sorrow, Matthew felt a great transcending compassion. Before he could stop himself, the words burst from him:

"'Yea though I walk through the Valley of the Shadow of Death, I will fear no evil, for thou art with me!'"

The Boy stiffened but did not turn, and Matthew whispered fervently: "*I know, I know—-it is in me also!*"

The Boy raised his head and in the last glow of the sky Matthew detected the bitterness in his eyes.

"Listen to me, son," he croaked, his voice sounding old and tired as he felt. "I too have tried to understand the reason for it all; why that little . . ." he swallowed the rising lump in his throat ". . . why that little morsel of clay was born at all. Hour upon hour I have ceaselessly plagued the Lord for the plan of His judgment. And then suddenly, at the graveside, it came to me. And it seems so simple now, I wonder I never understood it before. The vaccination which they say caused his disease saved many other lives. He had a blessed, merciful mission, like the Lord! *He was born and he died that others might live!*"

After a moment the Boy stirred. Smoking as he stared out into the distance, he said softly: "You think so, Matthew?"

"*I know so!* And a soul never died for a more noble reason' Like the cross of Jesus, he was privileged, a blessed child'"

"I envy you, Matthew," the Boy said huskily, and   ᵗᵗᵃᵣ-ness glittered like contempt in his eyes as he threw down · cigarett‹ and crushed it underfoot. "You can believe all that."

"But it's true, I tell thee! And thee must not try to   blame, son. No one could have known the reaction that vaccination would have! It was a chance in a million! And as for the . . . the *operation* . . . well, everybody knows there is no better surgeon than thee. If thee could do nothing, there was nothing that could be done! So thee see, son, he died because . . ."

"Matthew, the reason he was born and he died had less to do with God than with me! I know why he died! *You all know!* And there was no divine plan behind it."

It had begun to rain lightly, the drizzle spitting down at them from the immense blackening sky. The Boy looked up then, and in that moment Matthew saw such a depth of despair as he had never seen before. Although the Boy did not verbally enunciate his unutterable belief, it glowed in pain-filled eyes which shouted his terrible torment: *He died because I killed him!* The rain whispered between them and ran like tears across the Boy's proud anguished face. . . .

The numbed hours turned into days; the days slowly passed, dragging like loath feet in painful chains. It had been a season of death and it left them burned out and black and bitter as a razed field. For a while they were thoughtful and silent and cynical of God. But life, unrelieving, went on. It was the saving of them all. There were the schools to be tended (with the epidemic finally ebbing, they had been reopened), and at the hospital, more people died and babies were born. Though the Dooleys waned and bowed under their grief, the Boy worked like a man possessed to carry the extra load. For there was much still to be done; though the worst had been weeded out by death, the last of the smallpox patients lingered on; those who had not deteriorated to the graveyard still needed attention; in their diminished numbers they were transferred back to the hospital's isolation block, and the meeting house, never more needed, was reclaimed by thankful worshipers. It rang once more with prayers and promptings; ostensibly it housed their faith and repulsed fear. The hours of solitude and meditation oiled their grief like balm.

Oh God, our help in ages past . . .

But still there were the long desolate nights, the endless distracted days. The empty wind echoed with a little boy's laughter and the sunny blue skies mirrored his eyes. Matthew could not bear it. He crumpled in anguish.

"Oh Lord! Help me! Help me! I cannot go on!"

But he did. Of necessity, he rallied and sheltered the little blind girl. He gave some token pretense of normality; he even gave comfort to others, but inwardly he marveled at God's apparent cruelty. (To give so vilely, and then so cruelly to take away!) Although he was outwardly the rod of strength he had always been, inwardly he felt the very foundations of his former faith shift beneath him.

He thought of his own sons, fat and rowdy, and felt no comfort in their sparing. *Thee might have taken them, Lord,* he calmly accused, and in his wooden state felt no guilt at this concession—*and I would not have blamed Thee.* . . . And many times he stood in tortured solitude at the sad little grave and ceaselessly searched the inexplicable avenues of life for some light-shedding meaning. There he stood. And he wept at the dawn and the dying of every day, wept so that the unfamiliar tears fell plenteous and free and a dry sobbing wracked his frail chest. For the world was not the same. It never would be again . . . God had plucked his fairest flower. Child of a rape and indescribable sweetness! He stared at the small silent grave through a brimming radiance of tears.

Oh, little unwanted boy—thee are wanted now!

20

Gradually, above his own consuming grief and concern for Jenny, Matthew began to notice that a change had come over Than Profane since little Luke's death. He had gone into a strange penal state of isolation. He went dutifully through the motions of daily living, pushing himself and working harder, if that were possible, than he had ever done before. But he was a haunted shadow of his former self and a great silence had fallen on him like a blight. He was thoughtful and withdrawn and had taken to staring motionless off into space for long periods of time. He often did not hear when spoken to, until the speaker, in exasperation, reached out and touched him. Then he would turn in dawning surprise: "Hmmmmm?" And for a split second you might catch the pain in his far-off eyes before the false shutter of indifference came down.

Matthew's heart cried out for him for, of them all, the Boy's burden was greatest. The torment that went on inside him was something that others could only guess at. Katherine reported that he cried out in his sleep at night and strange muffled sounds penetrated their bedroom walls. She fretted when he would not eat and stayed up late into the night. But as much as she fussed and tried desperately to comfort and console him, he was unreachable. Even Jayne could not woo him with her trembling smile. He had turned overnight into a cold stranger. The old wall of aloofness was around him again, and he suffered alone where no mortal could help him.

But Than Profane was not Matthew's only worry. Jenny's state of mind worried him more. As far as he knew, she still had not cried, and she grew pale and thin and vague as a shadow; daily she grew more withdrawn into herself and spent hours on end just staring into space. In a dazed monotone, she answered when spoken to, but otherwise, she neither spoke nor smiled, and ate only what sustenance Teller managed to force on her. Jerome visited her regularly and as the days went by and she failed to revive, he grew more alarmed. Finally he called Matthew aside.

"We have to do something, Matthew. She's withdrawing into herself, rejecting reality. It's a psychological adjustment, and I'm very much afraid, if we don't do something to snap her out of it pretty soon, she may need psychiatric help. She's gone into a kind of paranoic melancholia. It's lack of the will to live. People sometimes die of it—virtually of a broken heart. And if she continues with this no-eating fad . . . well, once you have to start intravenous feeding, the mental outlook is pretty bad."

"I see." Matthew stared off into space, digesting this additional sorrow. He raised his anxious eyes. "What . . . what may we do?"

"Well, I think we have to get her right out of this environment. She's basically a brave and intelligent girl, and I think that given time and the right circumstances . . . well, I've written to her father, Matthew. He should know Jenny better than any of us. Maybe he can reach her. You know how it's always a great comfort to be with family in times of sorrow? Well, I know he's written thee that he'll be coming here to see her as soon as he's recovered from his operation. But I believe she needs to be back in her old circumstances, in the surroundings of her childhood, when her life was less . . . *burdened*. Anyhow, I've asked him to communicate with me on her progress. He's an intelligent man; he should be able to handle the situation with tact. And I want her to leave as soon as possible, Matthew. I've told her father to expect them."

"Them?"

"Yes." Jerome looked up. "I thought Than could take her. The kid needs to see his wife and settle up his affairs before he leaves for America. But that's not the whole of it. The fact is, I think he needs to get away as well. He's dropped weight so rapidly, I'm afraid his health will suffer. You know how he blames himself? Well, I guess that must be pretty hard to live with. And God knows he's carried the burden long enough for us all."

Matthew glanced up. "Can thee manage without him?"

Jerome smiled tiredly. "If I have to."

"Has he agreed?"

"No. And I know I'll have to fight him. But I'll use Jenny as my argument—that way he can't refuse."

21

Than agreed reluctantly. He felt honor-bound to help in any way he could, but these days he hated just being with Jenny. Seeing her lost and alone reinforced the reality of Luke's death, intensifying unbearably the sense of his own great guilt. Now, perversely, he was grateful at least for her silence and inability to respond. They left in the early morning and rode in silence until, at a lonely little sub-boma in the bush halfway to Solwezi, he stopped to refuel. While an aged African laboriously operated an antiquated handpump to fill his car with gas, Than escorted Jenny to the little brick toilet tucked away behind the petrol tank and storeroom. The pump attendant had finally completed his painstaking task and Than was paying him when a European family arrived in a dusty sedan; the sunburned, boisterous children rushed straight off to the toilet. Fifteen minutes later Jenny still had not emerged, and when two of the children returned and Than overheard their mother ask the pump attendant for another key to extricate her three-year-old, who had apparently somehow locked herself in the toilet, Than knew instinctively that something was wrong. While the parents went off to summon a boma official, he limped around and entered the dim dusty little toilet. As he had feared, the single toilet door was firmly locked; Jenny was nowhere in sight.

"Jenny?" He knocked tentatively. "You all done now? Open up, please."

When there was no response, he said brusquely: "You better stand back. I'm coming in."

Two of the children watched big-eyed while he rammed at the door with a shoulder, throwing his weight with restrained force against the steel lock until it burst open with a resounding *thwack*! against the opposite wall. Than peered cautiously into the dimness. And there, in that small smelly toilet in the middle of nowhere, an ageless sadness, chilling as a wind, stole over him in the hot listless quiet. Jenny stood pressed back into a cobwebbed corner beside an open lavatory bowl, looking guilty and aghast, caught out in a secret shame. She stared dumbly beyond him, holding a solemnly staring child in her covetous arms.

"Jenny," Than lamented softly, shaking his head in hopeless despair. "Oh, Jenny . . ."

For it was shades of yesterday. When was it? A little blind girl holding desperately on to a baby she couldn't let go of. There was no appearance of Luke about the child, but it was roughly the same height and similarly built, with brown hair cropped short as a boy's. To a sighted person the similarity might never be noticed, but kinesthetically—*touch-wise*—to the blind . . .

"Come on away, Jenny," Than said softly. "You have to give that baby back to its mother now. We're going home. . . ."

For twenty miles Than drove in a furious silence, irrationally angry with Jenny. Finally the car ground to a halt with the engine seized and the radiator hissing clouds of steam. Disgusted at his own negligence, Than took a jerrican out of the trunk and limped around to open Jenny's door.

"Come on, Jenny. We need water. I spotted a village a ways back; looks like we'll have to walk for it."

She came meekly, with sleep-walking slowness dragging along after his impatiently pulling arm, down the rough rutted road. As they broke through the trees, the village dogs and children came out to greet them; the village teacher, dignified in a threadbare suit, offered to take Than to a stream, while his wife, a rotund matron with rouge-reddened lips, cosmetically bleached skin, and hair fuzzily straightened in the European-aping modern fashion, served Jenny tea in a little earthen church cum schoolroom. On the way to the stream, Than and the teacher passed a crowded rural market, with fly-festooned vendors hawking piles of stinking dried fish, vegetables, and an impressive array of basketware and mats. Returning with the jerrican dripping with murky water, they heard the blaring of a car horn and a furious bantering of raised voices. Immediately the milling market crowd began to race for the village. When the teacher too took off, Than marveled anew at the excitability of the African temperament; their volcanic tendency to spontaneously erupt into a frenzied blood lust, accounted for the high rate of hit-and-run accidents in the country; when Africans were the victims, even Europeans usually drove off rather than risk a summary stoning.

By the time Than reached the village, a pushing, pulling, tightly packed congestion of bodies had clogged up the village center. As he pushed through the sweat-stinking clamor, he saw a fish trader's dilapidated truck, and catching odd words in the argument, realized that the driver had run over a goat; now the angry owner demanded compensation, while the trader, adamant that the fault was not his, obstinately hooted to clear a passage through the village. The crowd meanwhile grew ugly, pushing, pounding on the truck, and threatening the driver with physical harm. The discordant sight and sounds and the oppressive press of so many belligerent black bodies was to Than uncomfortably reminiscent of the Baluba attack. (Even now, almost four years later, he still awoke sweating from related nightmares.) Now, as he fought to break free, he suddenly noticed the teacher's wife in the crowd; he looked wildly around, but Jenny was nowhere in sight. Struggling to suppress a rising panic, he battled his way through the clinging morass of humanity; with the roar of the crowd ringing in his ears, he limped frantically to the little thatch church. Dropping the jerrican in one of the open doorways, he squinted into the stifling windowless dimness within. His eyes gradually adjusted and he sagged with relief to find Jenny, distinctive in her long dress and bonnet, sitting on one of the thin log benches that stood in crooked rows, embedded in the earthen floor. He began limping toward her. But she was sitting strangely still, staring so starkly that his footsteps faltered and he stared at her in sudden eerie alarm, instinctively aware that the terrifying rabid roar of the mob had penetrated her stoic state, the frightful familiar noises of mad men and hooting unearthing the awful buried memory of the barbarous Balubas. He saw the fear frozen on her face and instantly understood that she was finally remembering, reliving the untold total terror of being deserted by her friends, dragged blind and bewildered into a darkness that was both sensual and temporal, pushed, pulled, and pawed by the unseen hands of alien animals who had borne her down, bludgeoned and bleeding, to ultimately invade her very body, shattering her sanity.

"Jenny?" Just then he kicked over a stack of school slates; the tumultuous clatter started her screaming. She screamed and screamed. The sound was unbearable, and desperate to silence her, Than hurried toward her, calling: "*Jenny, it's me!*"

But his words were muffled by the rising roar of the crowd outside, and she was hysterical, beyond reason. When he sat down to placate her, his hands were the hands of the Balubas, and she fought him like a wildcat, pushing him off with desperate strength. Caught off guard, he fell over backward and cracked his head on the bench behind. By the time he had regained his senses and his Stetson, she was in the aisle, whimpering mindlessly as she crawled frantically toward the dimly perceived light of the nearest doorway. She had struggled to her feet and was running blindly into the bush by the time he reached the threshold. He watched, wincing in horror as she slammed into a tree and spun to the ground. Then, half-stunned, she struggled to her feet and began fleeing again. It was like watching a bewildered bird dashing itself to death against a windowpane; he saw that in a few moments she would reach the solid resistance of more trees, and he began limping furiously after her. He took a desperate running dive and the breath grunted out of her as they thudded to the ground in a sickening, flesh-scraping slither. Panting and gasping, she turned and began fighting him desperately. Withstanding the feeble pounding of her fists, Than jerked her into his arms, struggling to still her against him, shouting:

"*Jenny!* It's me, Than! You're safe, hear me!"

All at once the rage seemed to seep out of her, and she sagged against him, staring up at him strangely.

"It's okay," he said gently. Her bonnet had spilled off and he stroked her disheveled hair reassuringly. "I've got you. You're safe. No one can hurt you."

She buried her face against him with an anguished sob, and he pressed her head to his chest and held her tightly, murmuring: "Yes. You let go now; you cry . . . for everything."

He eased back down onto the prickly grassed earth, caressing her gently, stroking her hair with his grazed fingers, silently encouraging as she went through the rusted motions, making little disjointed spastic sounds into his shirt, until, there in the long grass in the remote bush bounding a lonely Lunda village, the forgotten function was finally remembered and she began to cry wrenchingly. She cried heartbrokenly, with such raw, audible pain that it hurt him to hear her; it seemed to him that she cried for them all and it was not nearly enough. While she sobbed, the soft white flickers of butterflies fluctuated around them and long shreds of golden grass, emblazoned by the sun, waved in blurred focus above them. She cried until all the tension seeped out of her taut body and the sun sank into swirling cloud, cosseting the bush in a deep and cool humid gloom. Then, suddenly aware of the itching grass and his bad leg aching beneath him, Than released her and struggled up onto his knees; he helped Jenny up and they sat facing each other, sitting back on their heels. Her dress was covered with dust and part of the gathered skirt had ripped free of the bodice. There was a graze on her left temple, her eyes were red and swollen from crying, and she looked pale and exhausted, the dusty streaks of drying tears on her scratched cheeks.

Her fine dark hair snapped around her in the rising wind and there was a look of infinite love on her pretty face that terrified him dumb.

"Jenny?"

She dropped her head in a sweet shyness and he raised her chin and made her face him; he took her hands and raised them to his face.

"*Look* at me, Jenny."

For several moments she stared up at him vacantly. Then slowly, with great trepidation, she spread her trembling hands and began to explore him. Her seeking fingertips passed gently over his mouth, nose, and closing eyes; they tenderly traced his blood brotherhood scars, trailing hesitantly through his hair, through his forelock, and down his sideburns. They left a trail of fire, and when he opened his eyes, the blinding brightness of her rapt face dimmed the dizzy world into pale insignificance. Tears shone like lights in her blind blue eyes, and she stared solemnly straight up into his soul.

"*Njumwaice*," she whispered fervently, frowning, mouthing the words with great deliberation. "I love thee!"

He closed his eyes, humbled. "Yes," he said softly. "I know."

For suddenly he did. And looking back across the years he realized that he had always known. She was staring at him dully, a lackluster look of sorrow and shame in her beautiful, long-lashed, expressive eyes. And he stared back, mute with his caution. For there was no answer inside him. He was trembling on the brink of some great heart-stopping realization, but it was all-pervading and elusive as air and he could not quite grasp it. He resolved the silence the only way he knew how. Leaning forward on his knees, he bowed his head and gently brushed her soft surprised lips. His searching mouth nuzzled and then clung in sudden rabid possession. And there, in the sallow gloom of the clouded bush, without otherwise touching, they remained that way, kneeling opposite each other politely as Orientals, joined at the mouth and desperately kissing. As they kissed, the village clamor suddenly ceased and a great silence grew and engulfed them; it seemed that all Africa wheeled around them and time itself stood still as the kiss went on and on until it bewildered them both. Finally he broke it, watching bereftly as she felt around and struggled shakily to her feet. Then, awkward and stiff, bruised and smeared with blood, sweat and dust and the burning imprint of her kiss, he fetched the jerrican, and leading her protectively, stumbled slowly back to the car, aching and dazed, speechless with unfathomable feeling.

22

A sophisticated tarmac road, the main artery of the Copperbelt, took an S-bend through the bush, then leveled into a softly lawned entranceway that was lined with flowering trees and shrubs. Bisected by a little languid river, the small mining camp of Luanshya had earned its awesome African title, The Valley of Death, in the early days, when scores of pioneer miners from the adjacent Roan Antelope copper mine had died here of blackwater fever. Now, like most decomposing masses, the rich dead past had given rise to something good. Blazing with blossoms, the town was tropical, open, and pretty. The long tree-lined avenues of identical brick mine houses were alphabetically named after the flowering trees and shrubs that flamed in every garden. A stranger directed Than along a great curving road to a newer part of town; here, Kerria Avenue was a picturesque winding road, lined with beautifully gardened bigger modern houses that skirted the bush. It was late afternoon by the time Than pulled into the long driveway of Jenny's father's home. The three-bedroom house looked attractive and new; a brilliant blaze of scarlet poinsettia, splashes of orange canna lillies, and multicolored petunias flourished in the graciously lawned half-acre garden.

Mr. Solomon came out to greet them with his two younger daughters, Julie and Sally; a rust-colored Rhodesian ridgeback almost knocked Jenny over in its enthusiastic welcome, and Than held the excited dog off while Jenny's family embraced her affectionately. When they were through, there were tears in all their eyes, and struggling to regain his composure, her father led them along the concrete garden path, to a cool fly-screened veranda. Inside, the house smelled of floor polish and boiling vegetables. In the modestly furnished lounge, the blinding blaze of the late afternoon sun slanted through the long floral curtains, catching on a framed photograph of Luke on the wooden mantle above an ornate stone fireplace. Than looked hurriedly away, grateful that Jenny at least was spared this poignant reminder. After he had helped the houseboy to carry Jenny's luggage to her neat bedroom along a long cool passage, the company sat on the veranda and the girls brought out a tray of iced drinks and a tall foaming glass of Lion lager for Than. He savored the welcome coolness of the ice cold beer while Jenny sipped at a glass of orangeade. Her sisters, shy pretty girls in their late teens, wore the mid-calf stiffly petticoated dresses that were currently in fashion, and beside them in this modern setting, Jenny's full-length Quaker skirt seemed odd and out of place. When she had bathed and come out changed into her long lilac dress and matching bonnet, her family's obvious discomfort reminded Than of the artificial antiquity of a lost little world he had come to regard as real.

The sky had clouded into premature twilight and thunder rumbled distantly while Than scrubbed the dust off his skin in a good tepid bath. Later, over a fine steak supper prepared by Jenny's sisters, the two girls and Mr. Solomon laughed delightedly at his anecdotes of mission life. They kept a Braille typewriter at the house so that they could write Jenny letters she could read; they seemed as generous and kind as Jenny herself, and Than was grateful that she had this fund of love to come home to. Some of her father's natural diffidence melted when he discussed the political situation, a topic of conversation that was currently the most popular in the country.

Apparently here in towns, the changes caused by the new African administration were most discernible. With the Congo massacres still so recent, most whites had seen the nationalist ascension as the beginning of the end. Many, reluctant to leave a land and a life they had come to love, adopted a wait-and-see attitude, while the more fearful had resigned their jobs and started a steady exodus south. Their departure left convenient vacancies for the fulfillment of the new government policy, which urged that all jobs presently held by white expatriates be nationalized as soon as possible; to appease the impatient people, the mining companies had begun paying off still other white veterans with "golden handshakes." Inevitably, production and the economy would suffer, Douglas Solomon mourned; already this indiscriminate dispensation to unqualified Africans had led to the resignation of white officers in the army and police force.

The results had soon been seen; now led by incompetents whose qualifications were often only the color of their skin, the law was no longer the dependable edifice it once had been; black constables, promoted to top positions they were incapable of handling, became petty tyrants who used their positions to exploit their ignorant fellows and expiate their hatred of whites. Cases of Europeans being arrested or beaten for trivial traffic offenses became common; since the next in command was often equally as black and biased, there was no platform to redress such wrongs, and the whites simply tried to stay out of trouble's way. But this was often difficult to do. It had become the sport of certain UNIP officials to roam the European townships, provoking whites with familiarity and insolence; failure to buy UNIP party cards was a dangerous infringement; failure to properly respect the prime minister, his portraiture, or the national anthem, a criminal offense. "One Zambia, One Nation!" was UNIP's rallying call, loosely interpreted as "all are equal and united." And indeed they were made thus. These days blacks in appropriate positions were being moved into houses in the white areas, and the clubs and organizations that had once been the privileged domain of whites were being flooded with blacks whose main purpose seemed to be to flaunt their newfound "equality" or to subjugate and humiliate their old superiors.

Under this new reversed order of things, the black man was always right; to call one "boy" or "kaffir" (terms they hated) was to risk imprisonment or even deportation. Douglas Solomon shook his head angrily, and Than could understand his helpless exasperation. The massacre of the Lumpa sect in the Northern province had been the colossal crowning incompetence that made you fear most for the future: soldiers with automatic weapons mowing down men, women, and children in a church. The long years of the black subjugation to whites was reaping a bizarre and bitter harvest indeed.

23 They were dawdling over coffee, watching TV, when the brewing storm suddenly broke; Than looked up and listened with relief as the rain roared down on the roof above them. Thunder exploded deafeningly and Mr. Solomon switched off the television and rushed out to close his car windows. When the houseboy came to clear their coffee cups, Than excused himself; followed by the dog, he walked out into the wafting cool of the veranda. He had been allocated the bed there, and without switching on the light, he sat down on the quilted divan and pulled off his shirt and boots and stood up to feel the rain. The furious deluge, with the creaking of crickets and the guttural croaking of thriving frogs, fanned through the dusty screens on a fresh breeze, billowing the curtains and kissing him with a fine wet spray. He inhaled the scent of saturated earth and stood rapt with a vague longing. *Oh God, will it never go*

away? He closed his eyes and stood once again far away on a car roof on an open plain, surrounded by a black multitude while a little blond boy fatefully bared his arm and was not *feared* of the consequences he could not know awaited . . .

Than felt a touch on his arm and tumbled breathlessly down to earth again. He turned and it was Jenny, blindly groping to his side. Without a word he took her hand and they stood in harmonious silence, just listening to the rain. The front door opened and Douglas Solomon burst dripping wet onto the veranda. Jenny snatched away her hand, and her father stopped in surprise when he saw them there in the darkness. He smiled awkwardly.

"Well, I'd better say good night. I'm wet through! It's quite a downpour."

He left them hastily as lightning snapped and a horrendous bombardment of thunder blasted their eardrums. Jenny flinched involuntarily, and Than put his arm around her shoulder and drew her close. They stood together, sharing warmth, she, shivering against him as the storm played itself out in a fury of sound and spectacular displays of forked lightning. As they waited, the thunder gradually receded and the rain trailed to a hesitant dripping on the enormous rubbery elephant-ear leaves outside. The dog chewed a bone on the linoleum floor, and in the house the African gray parrot whistled sketchily from his perch. *"Joseph!"* the screeching summons rang repeatedly, and the houseboy mumbled a disillusioned reply. Than watched as one by one the lights of the big house, lying in squares of light in the rain-glistening garden, were snatched up from the darkness. The lounge light behind them went out before the houseboy slammed out of the back door; Jenny's sisters called good night as the last light popped out and the house enclosed them at last in complete darkness. A silence, precarious as breathing, settled over all, and they stood in a thrall, burning at the touch. Finally Than stirred.

"Jenny, I have to leave tomorrow. Suzannah'll be waiting. Kathy cabled her."

"I know." She lifted her chin and stared straight ahead.

He looked down at her proud profile.

"This is all we'll have—you know that, Jenny? This is all there ever can be."

She nodded, and for a moment they both stood stumped, at a loss to begin what could not continue. As the silence stretched on, he tightened his grip on her small hand. Jerking her toward him, he

586

pulled her roughly around, into his arms; they fell together, like old lovers going home, wracked with their love, too overcome to speak. Finally he found his voice.

"*Maseccasecca*," he whispered huskily into her hair, and his throat contracted and started to ache. "*I love thee!* Oh God, how I love thee!"

And there it began.

24

They spent the night under the quilt on the divan, lying fully clothed in each other's arms. The fresh night air was sweetly scented with the blossoms of a yesterday, today, and tomorrow bush outside, and the thin liquid piping of frogs pulsated the silence. The bed was a little lumpy, but although Jenny was little and Than was long, she fitted snugly under his arm with her head cushioned on his bare chest. Her nearness filled him with a powerful protective love he had never felt before, with a great awkward anguished tenderness he ached to express. He felt enobled by her goodness and he longed to love, pamper, and protect her, to spend the rest of his days making up, in some small measure, for the loss and pain of her tragic life.

"I must be dreaming," she whispered wonderingly, touching his chest self-consciously. "I can't believe you can really love me . . ."

"Angel, I just thank God you can love me too."

"I wish I could see you," she whispered desolately. "My sisters say you're very handsome."

"Aw, Jenny, don't believe them," he chuckled, stroking her hair. "They're just being polite. The truth is I'm kind of homely. Got these buck teeth and I'm a little cross-eyed. I have to face it; without my powerful personality, there's just no way I could win a beautiful lady like you."

But she wasn't laughing. "You don't look like that at all," she said shakily, and he was instantly contrite.

"I don't mean to make fun of you," he said seriously. "But I'm just an average guy; the fact is you're not missing much."

"I know Luke looked like you," she said softly, and he stiffened and drew back to warily stare down at her in the dimness.

"Who told you that?"

"Nobody did. Nobody had to. I just knew."

They were treading on dangerous ground; he felt the pain begin to rise inside him, and he cupped her face gently with his hand and bent to kiss her, lingering fervently on her lips with a burning tenderness that seared his heart.

"Don't talk," he said huskily, fighting the ache that throbbed in his throat. "Please. Just love me. Be with me. Don't say a word."

She let him caress her little breasts through her dress, but when his hands moved down, gently tugging at her clothing, he could feel her tensing and growing fretful and he stopped. The recently revived memory of her rape, he knew, might take years and endless patience to overcome. Until then he would have to love her as sexlessly and tenderly as he might love his own sister. It was hard for him; his testicles ached, but her talk of Luke had put an emotional brake on his physical feelings, and denied natural consummation, they lay bereftly in a celibate daze of bliss, chastely kissing and caressing through the long night hours. But being transitory and stolen, their joy was precarious; it trembled between them fragile as a bubble, and they lay in dread of the inevitable pinprick of dawn. By the time the first soft light had begun to glow green through the plastic curtains, he knew that he would move heaven and earth to stay by her side. He started to believe there might be a way.

While it was still dark, they parted with a discipline they had foreordained themselves. Later, without touching or talking, they sat uneating at the breakfast table with Jenny's family. Unendurable love and lack of sleep had left them in a stunned limbo, and they sat under this spell, strong because their love was strong. When her father and sisters had left for their work and study at the Roan Antelope mine and the town's little technical college, Than phoned Suzannah in Salisbury to postpone his arrival. And all at once his paper dreams came crashing down. The disremembered reality of his wife's voice stunned him and he registered her words with sick disbelief, hanging on to the phone while the world rocked around him.

"Pregnant?" he echoed dully. "Oh God, Suzie—are you sure?"

"Sure I'm sure!" she was crying furiously. "I'm five weeks gone, so you better stop talking about damn delays and get down here quick. You got that?"

"Yeah," he sighed. "Sure, I'll see you." He dropped the receiver back in its cradle, and when he finally turned, Jenny was standing behind him, a look of horror frozen on her face. As he watched, she turned and walked slowly away. When he had regained his composure, he found her in her bedroom, staring sightlessly out of a window.

"Jenny," he said gently. She bowed her dark head, and when she would not turn, he embraced her from behind. As his crossed hands cupped her small breasts, an aching tenderness rose up inside him and he kissed the back of her neck, teasing her gently: "Itty-bitty little things, ain't they?"

When he turned her around, her sad face was wet with silently streaming tears.

"Oh God, Jenny, don't!" He gathered her gently in his arms and tried to kiss them away, but they fell as fast as he could erase them.

"I'm sorry," she whispered distraughtly, turning her face from him. "It's just that . . . *what we're doing is wrong!*"

"No." He shook his head at her. "Nothing this good could be wrong. Marriages were made by men. Love like ours belongs to the angels."

"But . . ."

"Hush! Listen, Jenny. My wife is a thing apart from us. She can never touch what we have."

"But it's her I'm thinking about!" Jenny raised a wracked, tear-stained face; the graze from her fall had turned blue on her temple, and there was a terrible torment in her blind blue eyes. Cheating was not her way. "It's wrong to her."

"Aw, Jenny, believe me, she'd never give you the same consideration."

"But she's going to have your baby!"

That silenced him. He took her in his arms and held her tightly. After a time she stopped crying and he kissed her and buried his face in her soft, scented hair.

"Darling, listen to me: I'll try to come back!"

To you, to your love! But they both understood there could be no promises. They came from two different worlds, just touching in passing. The complications of his former life tugged at him like a network of wires; the way back to her lay through this bewildering maze, and for the moment they could not see beyond the dark pain of their parting. . . ."

25

A little after six the following evening, Than arrived at the McQueen house. Feeling hot and tired, he was thankful to find that the ambassador and his wife were away attending some official function. As he climbed from the car, the face-slapping shock of Suzannah's beauty was an aggravation to him; he was aloof in deference, and they kissed dryly as strangers. He followed Suzannah up the stairs to her room in a frosty silence. There, in the drape-drawn, hot, sticky dimness, she flew at him verbally like a shrew, crying and wailing in the release of pent-up panic.

"It's all your fault! You told me it was safe! You said I couldn't fall!"

"Suzie." Setting down his suitcase, Than looked tiredly away; he had anticipated this. "No one contraceptive is one hundred percent sure."

"Now he tells me!" She threw up her nail-varnished hands, a smoking cigarette between her fingers. "All right, so they're not sure! Now what are you going to do about it? That's what I want to know! You *put* it there! Now you take it away!"

"Now wait just a minute!"

"I've waited long enough already! And it's your responsibility! You did it to me!"

"You sure it was me?" he said coolly, but she spun on him with such honest outrage that, convinced of his paternity, he regretted the implication. He had promised not to mention Carl Steiner again, and now he no longer felt jealous enough to risk a row by breaking his resolution. He smiled at her bitterly.

"Well, there's an old man back at the mission who'll tell you on good authority that it was God. God does everything—didn't you know? And I must confess that just this once I'm tempted to let Him take His rap!"

"Have you been drinking?" Suzannah eyed him skeptically; she approached him, sniffing disdainfully, and he leaned forward and breathed brandy fumes shamelessly all over her.

"I stopped at a bar to get bolstered up to meet you. But you needn't be upset; I've still got my senses."

"Well, you could have fooled me! You behave as if we're not

married and I'm trying to pin it on you. We parted friends, re-member?"

"Yeah. Friends and lovers. Oh, I remember we parted. We parted and we parted and we parted."

"Well I don't recall you complaining the last time!" She stared at him wretchedly through angry tears.

"Well, I guess I finally wised up. And I don't guess you've missed me much. You don't even want my baby."

"That doesn't come into it. It's just I've had this little experience before—and now I want out!"

"Poor baby," he said sarcastically. "I guess you can't stand the inconvenience."

"I just don't want any little *monster* wriggling round inside me!"

"*Monster?*" Than stared at her in wry, wondering amusement. "Yes, that would be just about your gauge on life."

"You're drunk!" She eyed him uncertainly. "And you're just like any other goddamn male: all honey when he wants it, then a regular rat when he's left some evidence!"

But he was staring at her vaguely, losing the train of his thought. "Did you know," he said dully, "that little Luke Solomon died?"

Suzannah looked startled for a moment; for just a second a reaction flickered in her eyes. Then they went bland with disinterest, and she shrugged. "Kathy wrote me. Oh, it's sad I suppose, but maybe it was for the best. He was illegitimate, after all. And his mother is blind."

"For the best?" he whispered incredulously, staring at her in dawning horror. "Because he was illegitimate and his mother is blind? *Je-sus Christ!* You really believe that?"

"Well, I don't know what you're going on about! It's got nothing to do with me!"

"No," he said quietly, and staring at her, it seemed to him that some soul-deep muddiness had dredged through her beauty, dulling it like dirt. It made him sick to look at her. He shook his head numbly. "I don't guess it has. Poor little pussycat. It must be lonely to be so emotionally divorced from the woes of the world!"

He lit up a cigarette, and she stubbed out the tail end of her own and snatched his away. Doggedly, he lit up another, blowing the smoke deliberately into her face.

"Don't." She turned away, wincing. "It makes me feel sick."

He eyed her inquiringly: "And your own smoke doesn't? You're smoking like a chimney; it's not good for the baby."

"I don't care what's good for the baby; I don't want . . ."

"What'd your doctor say?"

Her eyes snapped up at him, filled with outrage. "That's just it! He refused to help me! I told him how you said it would be dangerous for me to have a child, but he took some tests and big-heartedly assured me that if I was sensible and terribly careful, I could bear this . . . this *brat*, with hardly any trouble at all. He said he didn't see any reason to take it away now that it was started. He said that I was married and financially secure; I have a doctor for a husband and could afford the best possible care! I went to doctor after doctor, and they all said the same! There are just no good old back-street abortionists in this damn place! Everybody is so goddamn noble. And of course I couldn't let Daddy or Maggie know what I was up to; they would have thrown a fit if I was rushed to hospital under shady circumstances; the adverse publicity, after all!"

She looked at him expectantly. "You can work an abortion, can't you?"

"Oh sure," he said drolly. "I can cut open your tummy with a kitchen knife and take it out in the true tradition of all good surgeons. It'd be easy as pie."

She stared at him balefully. "What d'you mean? Well, can't you?"

He turned exasperatedly away. "Listen, pussycat, I don't happen to have the necessary drugs and instruments right here!"

"But you *have* to do it!"

He shook his head tiredly. "Suzie, I'm not exactly overwhelmed with joy myself, but my hands are tied. I don't *have* to do anything."

Staring at him in horror, she said in a tiny frightened voice, "Then what am I going to do?"

He thought for a moment. "Why don't you try that old-fashioned thing invented by little old ladies for irate housewives? A steaming hot bath and a whole bottleful of whiskey. All you have to do is get blind drunk and shake your tail around."

"Ooh!" She tossed a pillow at him, and he ducked.

"Shit, Suzie," he said, smiling deprecatingly. "Your aim's getting lousy!"

She slammed out of the room, and he slumped down on a bed and fell instantly asleep, drugged by the heat, alcohol, and his own nervous exhaustion. When he awoke, the room was dim with the dying of day. He eased like a mole from under his pillow and found Suzannah sitting on the bed beside him, in a black nylon half-slip. In the dim light, her honey-gold skin glistened with a fine sheen of perspiration and her smoky hair was let loose, tumbling in half curls in the hollows of her collarbones. Her golden breasts burst from the low-cut black lace bra (just the flesh pink tips tantalizingly visible over the top) and her long smooth beautiful legs were drawn up on the quilt. She was smoking a cigarette with an expression of boredom on her exquisite face; her pouting mouth, puckered kissable and pink, and her honeyed eyes flashed fire in the gloom.

She was beautiful and he knew that, Oh God, he was still tied to her by the shackles of his body, by his own betraying biological urges. He felt himself stirring even then with an irrepressible need that was as cramping as pain. Flushed with sexual heat, he stared at her through the smoky haze of his desire. She was a *woman*, she excited him sexually, whereas Jenny, in her sweet way, would only ever be a girl.

"Suzie . . ."

"Hmmmmm?" She pouted sultrily at him.

"You come over here."

He went to her at the same time and they met in the middle of the bed. And it was an explosion of feelings. The warm clinging softness of her cushioning body sent fire through his own. He wriggled out of his pants in frantic haste and made love to his wife feeling like a traitor to Jenny, a fornicator in his mind. And after long abstinence, the high fine exquisite sensation almost blacked him out. It was a rapture delirious; an erotic encounter that staggered him and very soon even the guilty nagging died away. His whole consciousness was reduced to the single animal state, to the practiced thrusting of his pelvis; to the strumming pleasure bursting unendurably inside him. And when he finished loving her, he wanted still more. He knew he would always want more.

But, feline eyes flashing, she was in a truculent mood, spitefully teasing him, as surly and unstable as a captive cat.

"Not yet again!" She wriggled breathlessly from under him.

"Why not? For God's sake! We haven't seen each other in weeks."

"Yes," she said bitterly, "and last time you left me with a little memento."

"Well, Jesus! I can't make you pregnant twice!"

"Well, you made me pregnant once! And I don't see how you can be so casual and unconcerned about it. You're horny as a mountain goat! And I'm in this godawful condition!"

She stared angrily down at her satin pink fingernails.

"My doctor said I shouldn't make love during the first few months. He said it would be dangerous for me to do anything . . . *strenuous.*"

Than raised up slowly on the bed. He should have known that; it was a consideration he might have levied her.

"Well," he said sarcastically, "I don't see what you're so worried about, then. Maybe this will do the trick."

"*Maybe!* I don't want any *maybes*!" She stared furiously at him, her fine breasts heaving. "I want something positive done about it. Here and now!" She stared at him challengingly. "And *then* you can love me all you want!"

It was the ultimate intimidation; the little sex tease bartering her greatest asset. Her words rang through the stifled dimness and he stared dully up at her as she picked up her lacy black panties and bra and began to put them back on with all the practiced coquetry of a stripper. After a moment, he scratched his nose, smiling at her sourly. "That an ultimatum?"

"Listen, I mean it!" She flicked her gold lighter and drew on a cigarette. "Wouldn't a knitting needle do? I've heard . . ."

"Oh sure," he said sarcastically, rolling onto his back. He reached up and snatched the lipstick-smeared cigarette from her mouth. He drew on it, staring up at her with smoldering eyes. "A knitting needle is just about the finest instrument. I wouldn't be at all surprised if some of those damn things are actually made these days with abortion in mind. They sure do the job all right. Knitting needles have helped many a little girl out of her difficulties, but permanently. Yeah, I'd say it does a very effective job, ripping blindly into the womb, piercing the membraneous sac . . ."

"Don't be funny!" she snapped quietly. "I mean it. Now, are you going to help me or . . ."

"Suzie, I told you. So listen to me good, once and for all. The way things are now, I can't do a goddamn thing to you without endangering your life. And you'd better believe it. Now, if you don't care about your life, I happen to care about my medical reputation. And I'm not throwing it all away just to give you . . ."

"But you said it was dangerous for me to carry a child!"

"I know that, and I'm sorry about it. But like the guy said, if you're pretty careful . . ."

"I don't want to be careful!"

"Well, that's your decision. But I'm not about to play around with your life under imperfect conditions." He closed his eyes and thought for a moment. He sighed. "Under different circumstances, I might do it. If I could just get hold of . . ."

He opened his eyes and stared at her exasperatedly. "Shit, Suzie, I've got no hospital privileges here and it can be messy and complicated, even in a hospital. You ever seen a fetus that's come away? Man, some of these little things are so perfectly formed, it makes you feel like a murderer." He closed his eyes. "Well, I don't guess I have the heart for it anymore."

She stared at him in an unmoving daze; tears blurred her eyes. "You've got no right to be so uninvolved!" she whispered furiously. "No right!"

After a moment, she got up and went through into the adjoining bathroom. She closed the door carefully behind her.

"You could always have it adopted!" he shouted after her as a parting shot. He thought he heard a sob escape her, but after a moment it was quiet. When the minutes ticked by, he began to puzzle vaguely when there was no sound of running water. He got up and pulled on his jeans. Then, frowning in mystification, he opened the bathroom door.

And there she sat, crouched on the tiled floor, her golden thighs spread apart. Beneath her, she held poised in her hands a sinister gray knitting needle that was smeared with her blood. She gave a start of fright when she saw him and he stood paralyzed with shock. She looked dully down at her hands.

"I've done it," she said slowly. Then, looking up at him with terrified eyes, she began to cry, guilty and fearful as a little girl caught cheating. "Oh, please don't be angry. *Help me!* It hurts!"

In a daze he took the needle from her hands and carried her through to the bedroom. He antisepticized his hands with pure Dettol from the cabinet, then crouched before her on the bed and began to examine her gently. He could feel the ragged point of intrusion where the needle had pierced, but he couldn't tell how bad it was because even as he blindly fumbled, the blood had begun oozing up, hampering his investigation. Finally she was hemorrhaging quite strongly. He raised her hips on a pillow, wadded a towel between her clamped thighs, and went to the phone. He picked up the phone book and began to run his finger along the listed names to find her doctor's number. His mind kept going blank and his hands shook. Finally, he called Salisbury General Hospital for an ambulance. While they waited for it to arrive, he sat holding her hand, trembling inside, unable to stop thinking about a young girl he had seen in the States who had died after just such a self-inflicted abortion. Suzannah looked terrified and he smiled at her sickly.

"It's okay, baby. It's going to be all right."

26

That night when it was all over, he tiptoed into her private room to see her. She lay looking pale, beautiful, and chastened on the high white hospital bed, an I.V. tube feeding blood into her arm. And he had to tell her that—wouldn't you know it?—her doctor had managed to save the baby. She wept silently so that the silver tears seeped into her pillow, and he stared at her and couldn't help marveling at it all.

There were some lives that just battled all hell—the greatest odds—to be born. Suzannah, with her weakened kidneys, had very nearly died; there was still some concern about her, but the baby, amazing all the experts, had stubbornly clung to life. And he had to think that maybe something that struggled so hard, an unwanted tenant in the house of its mother, deserved to live. It at least deserved more welcome than they had spared it.

Her father hadn't even known she was pregnant. He had sounded stunned when Than phoned him from the hospital. Than assured him he had spoken to the hospital authorities; fortunately her doctor was willing to hush up the incident. Understanding Suzannah's state of mind, he had accepted that she had inflicted the wound on herself. And there the matter was narrowly resolved. In a few short hours Than's whole life had been planned, placed, and decided for him.

"Than?" Suzannah looked at him with soft, terrified eyes. "You'll stay with me, won't you? I'm so afraid."

He held her hand and looked away, speechless, while the knot of emotion rose up in his throat. Just a little while ago he too had been afraid, and of losing something he no longer personally wanted the burden of—her life. He knew now that she couldn't make it without him, and he was resigned. She would need him, vigilant and ever-present through the long months of her pregnancy; the birth would be the greatest trial. Then, when it was over, the baby, the new little life, would need someone. Suzannah might turn it away at birth, so it had to be him. Twice he had denied his own children; Luke would never know him as a father, but this third little child would find him waiting.

"Don't cry, baby." He sighed and a great transcendental weariness came over him. "There's nothing to be afraid of. I'll take care of you."

But his distant eyes went to the window, and he watched a mythical dream fly away. *Good-bye, Jenny, good-bye . . .*

And he had to think that maybe it was all just an illusion after all. Maybe he didn't really love Jenny. Maybe it was guilt or pity or both. Whatever it was, he couldn't logically assess his feeling right now. For the moment, it was Suzannah, real and proximate, who needed him. In loyalty, he loved her and he shut little blind Jenny out of his mind.

27

Matthew was as surprised as everyone else when, even before Than Profane returned, Jenny's father brought her back to the mission. His fears that it was too soon for her to resume her work were dispelled by her tremulous smile; though the sadness still lingered in her eyes, something had changed. She had come to terms with Luke's death, and though it still hurt terribly, she wanted to be back at Suseshi to diminish her pain in helping others less fortunate. The courageous girl had become like a daughter to Matthew and Teller. They assured her anxious father that he could return home with an easy mind; they would take care of Jenny and all would be well.

Two days later, Than Profane's replacement arrived. Almost as tall as his predecessor, Dr. Cedric Fotheringill was a fair-skinned, slender young man with thin girlish arms; he had brown hair, an arrogant aquiline nose with nostrils that flared when he was in earnest (which was often), and a tight-lipped determined mouth. From the first, Matthew had the feeling the young man had been reading too many African novels.

"*Jambo!*" he pompously greeted the assembled hospital staff, and Mbiya, jealous of this man's usurpal of their beloved *Njumwaice's* position, answered in arrogant English:

597

"Sir, we do not understand that language here. However, on behalf of my colleagues, allow me to extend you a most cordial welcome to Suseshi."

But if the resentful black staff were silently antagonistic, Ezra Peabody, the Fotches, and the maiden ladies rushed to celebrate the man like some holy occasion. He moved in with the Dooleys, pending the departure of the Profanes, when their house would become his own, but he was so wooed by the Fotches' flattery, that he spent most of his spare time there, privately complaining about the rowdiness of the Dooley triplets. Doted upon by his elder sister, Queenie Gladstone, who had come up from Barotseland to see him settled in, he was a brisk, efficient, assertative young man who was already firmly in control of his new position by the time the old occupant came back.

At first meeting, he and Than Profane stared at each other, visibly bristling in instant dislike. Reaching across the supper table to shake the seated man's hand, the Boy "accidentally" upset the gravy boat, drenching the clean white tablecloth and the man's white sleeve. Dr. Fotheringill drew back, cringing with distaste, and the Boy expostulated:

"Oh shit!" In the fulminating October heat, he had just completed an arduous car trip back from Salisbury, but Matthew, mindful of the dregs of his reputation, said stiffly:

"Doctor! Thy language! Kindly remember the ladies present!"

The Boy was instantly contrite; he turned to Grace Dooley, who, to Matthew's mortification, was struggling to suppress a fond amused smile. "I'm sorry, ma'am; I just get so pissed off!"

Matthew winced; it got worse and worse. But if the Boy had spent some six-odd years antagonizing the other missionaries with his personal idiosyncrasies, he wasn't about to change one whit for this new medical paragon of virtue. He stripped off his shirt in the sweltering heat, smoked, swore, and damned the Lord with all his old happy abandon. Antagonized and appalled, Dr. Fotheringill countered his California casualness with elegant airs and a stiff English etiquette. Matthew knew the kind of tales the Fotches had been telling when the young English doctor arrived at Matthew's house. His sunburned skin was raw, red, and peeling, and he spoke with the conspiratorial, sanctimonious air of a tale-telling star pupil seeking a pat from the teacher.

"My dear professor," he said haughtily, sitting gingerly in Matthew's shabby wing-backed chair, cautiously generalizing. "I am well aware of the strain a certain "Friend" has put thee through in the past, and I wish to inform thee that thee need fear no such reprehensible behavior from me. I, sir, will at all times conduct myself with the utmost decorum and regard for the good name of the mission. I will . . ."

Matthew nodded knowingly; that was exactly what he had feared. Only half listening, he struggled to contrive a suitably gratified expression and to pay proper attention as the doctor continued loftily.

"I have only been working with this so-called Friend for two days, but already I can see what an embarrassment he must be to thee all. The man is an opinionated, blasphemous, ill-mannered lout, and callous besides! I have been shocked to learn that he expects the diseased lepers to work their own gardens, and as for that young blind lady, Miss Solomon, I could not help but notice the way he treats her; he has no pity for her handicap and cannot even be bothered to acknowledge her presence!"

Well, he was right on that score: whereas once the Boy had treated Jenny with elaborate consideration, these days he seemed to shy from her company. Matthew had seen her eyes fill with tears at the Boy's abrupt behavior. This avoidance had begun after Luke's death; clearly, the Boy's feeling of guilt made him uncomfortable in her presence. And this attitude had worsened since his return. Though Jenny had apparently benefited from the change, the Boy had come back with an increased aversion to her that was obvious to all.

"That's all I wanted thee to know," Cedric Fotheringill finished, and Matthew snapped back to the present with a jolt. "So please rest assured I will at all times conduct myself in a manner befitting a devout Quaker missionary."

Well, Matthew did not doubt it; he smiled thinly, nodding awkwardly as he saw the man off. Well, he should feel pleased. The man was right, after all. How often had he lamented Than Profane's unorthodox behavior and worldly ways? Now at least he could rest easy nights, knowing no new row was brewing to disrupt their meetings. It was a peace and harmony he had longed for since the Boy had first appeared on the scene. And even if Dr. Fotheringill patronized the natives and was impatient of their ignorance and uncleanliness, he worked hard and was always strictly correct; he turned up at the hospital positively glowing in spotless white, he regaled each patient with the Gospel, and was more concerned with saving souls than broken bodies. He was always on time for meals, had impeccable manners, and neither smoked nor swore. To the ladies' delight, he was congenial and sociable; he could be depended upon to stay for Scrabble and *never* returned to the hospital after hours if he could help it. He prayed eloquently in meeting and sank soulfully into meditative silence. Yes! All things considered, there could be no doubting it. Cedric Fotheringill was everything Than Profane should have been but wasn't. He was the glowing epitome of a good Christian Quaker, and Matthew's days of refereeing community quarrels, of hushing up horrendous trespasses, were thankfully, finally over. It was the peace and quiet he had so long yearned for. And yet . . . and yet . . . he could not shake the vision of a blue-jeaned cowboy leading a leopard across a sun-shot saffron plain; of a shining-eyed young man holding a tiny baby he had just delivered in a remote Lunda village; of a muscular, sun-bleached white savage in skins and feathers casting a witchdoctor's spell . . . and he knew, sadly, that things would be a little duller that way.

28

On the evening of October 23, the Independence stadium at Lusaka was filled to capacity with thousands of Africans gathered in an atmosphere of awe and expectancy, to see the official end of Colonial rule and to usher in their own independence. At the prestigious podium, among a distinguished array of heads of states and their representatives from all over the world, the British secretary of state for Commonwealth relations presided to officially relinquish the old imperialist reign. From midnight, Kenneth Kaunda, the shock-haired young prime minister of Northern Rhodesia, wearing his distinctive purple toga over an impressive Western suit, would become the first president of the newly independent state of Zambia.

Now, in the floodlighting that focused on the center of the stadium, the British flag gave a few last feeble flutters in the wake of midnight. There was a hushed collective gasp of awe from the crowd as the stroke of midnight plunged the scene into pitch darkness. After a few moments, when the lights went on again, the old Union Jack was down. In its place, the green, red, black, and orange flag of the new Republic of Zambia was slowly hoisted up the flagpole. A colossal cheer reverberated the night. The era of British rule had finally ended; *Zambia* was born.

October 24, the first day of the independence of Northern Rhodesia, dawned bright and fair; the eleventh-hour news that the British South Africa Company had finally accepted the government's last-ditch offer of a paltry four million pounds for the country's mineral rights gave the day an added triumph. But to Matthew it still loomed like the end of the world. For today, after being joined by the Boy's wife in Salisbury, the Profane family were due to fly home to America forever. First, however, there were farewells to be made.

At morning meeting, Matthew paid an earnest, emotional tribute to Katherine and the Boy for their good works during their long years at the mission. If his humble homage was somewhat spoiled by Hannah Rothchild's glares and Ezra Peabody's long-winded enthusing about the "rising new nation," the Fotches, incredibly, made up for it with ingratiating gushes. Considering the vital part they had played in securing the Boy's banishment, their pious appreciation of the family now was about as insincere as it was out of character. But Matthew was hardly surprised. The couple's attitude had undergone a radical reversal since Kathy had begun giving away household items they no longer needed. Now Orville had fixed a gleaming covetous eye upon the big yellow Thunderbird; nobody knew what the Boy intended doing with the car, and Matthew had noticed the hopeful Orville secretly admiring it, possessively shining up the chrome in passing, in between hopping helpfully around the Boy, his ulterior motive about as evident as that of a vulture hounding some dying animal.

After meeting, the family placed a last bouquet of hibiscus blossoms on Tom's grave before loading up the car and driving out to the mission airstrip in convoy with the rest of the missionaries. At the great windswept grassy field, the chartered Cessna had landed and a surprise awaited them: the long clearing was thronged with thousands of Africans; Matthew was stupefied by the black immensity of people who lined the runway to pay their last respects to Than Profane. The condescending Cedric Fotheringill peered perplexedly around, nostrils flaring, evidently so misled by the Boy's detractors that he was unable to believe him capable of commanding such respect and affection.

"Good Lord, I see these poor blighters are still in awe of the great bird from the sky'!" was his patronizing assumption, and Matthew wondered how he accounted for the huge hoisted banners expressing the people's love for Than Profane and their innocent hope for his return, in the poignant, muddled phrases: GOOD-BYE HAPPY FATHER. WE WAIT FOR YOU AGAIN. A great cheer went up as the Boy climbed out of his car, looking calm and handsome in his good navy blue suit and white Stetson. After a senior from the girls' primary school had handed Katherine a bunch of arum lilies, Mr. Katima, the headmaster of the boys' school, conducted the assembled children in a moving song that incorporated the tune and chorus of "Kumbaya," with custom-composed words of stirring tribute to the young doctor and his work among them. Katherine and Jayne burst into tears, sixteen-year-old Tom junior, stood blinking ominously, and it was too much for Cosmo Mlongotti who had traveled up from Barotseland for this last farewell; his eyes ablaze with tears, the quiet young dresser stepped forward and emotionally embraced his mentor.

"Bwana, you are my mother and my father!"

It was the highest praise an African could bestow. Beside him, also in a white uniform, stood the gray-haired old Jeremiah, looking more mournful than Matthew had ever seen him. The captain of the lepers, Teapot Kapendula, who headed a humble group of his leonine-faced charges from Eshalakali, hurried up to add his own accolade as the Boy was helping to haul the family's luggage from the car. Sniffing and wiping his broad flat nose on a sleeve, he diffidently dumped a bouquet of bougainvillea into Katherine's already laden arms and pressed a crumpled note into Than Profane's hand. Matthew squinted across the Boy's shoulder to read the careful scrawl expressing the young orderly's "unsurpassing" love for his "supreme father," for whom his heart would cry, without ceasing, until his return. The Boy swallowed; his eyes glittered strangely when he looked up, and Matthew, fighting a constricting lump in his own throat, was relieved when Chief Mulaisho was jostled up on his creaking bamboo machila, supported by four of his subjects while a fifth carried a gay orange sunshade over his royal head. Upon being set down, the wizened old rascal alighted unsteadily. Proudly wearing the grubby old greatcoat the Boy had given him so many years ago, he walked shakily with a haughty flourish across the field to formally decorate Than Profane with a skin-thonged duiker's horn filled with *muti* and a doctored skin bracelet, which, he stoutly declared, would ward off all evil during the doctor's hopefully temporary sojourn away from them. Obviously deeply moved by these humble tributes, the Boy was just completing a small speech expressing as much when the crowd parted and a battered black Chevy squealed up. A smartly suited Jahaliso, who was shortly due to fly to Lusaka for the independence celebrations, tumbled out with four traditionally dressed companions; these turned out to be the Boy's personal olimbo band, and they hurried through the crowd onto the field, furiously playing their neck-slung instruments. Jahaliso babbled breathlessly:

"Brother, I apologize, but the bloody car broke down again!" Then he turned, straightening his flashy zebra-striped toga over his suit, adjusting his thick spectacles as he formally addressed the crowd.

"FRIENDS, TODAY, THE DAY OF INDEPENDENCE OF OUR GREAT NATION, IT IS A GREAT SORROW FOR ALL THE AFRICAN PEOPLE THAT WE ARE TO LOSE MY BROTHER *NJUMAICE*, WHO HAS SERVED SO LONG AND WELL AMONG US. NO OTHER WHITE HAS DONE SO MUCH FOR OUR PEOPLE, AND I KNOW THIS— EVEN LONG AFTER HE HAS GONE, HIS NAME SHALL LIVE AMONG US! HE IS A BWANA MKUBWA: AND I ASK YOU NOW TO HONOR HIM WITH THE GREETING TRADITIONALLY ACCORDED SO GREAT A CHIEF!"

At once those seated in the crowd rose to their feet; a forest of fisted arms rose in the air and the crowd roared as one: "*SHANGWE! SHANGWE! SHANGWE!*" It was a stirring salute that made the goosebumps rise on Matthew's arms, and he stood tingling with emotion as the people completed the spiel, crouching on their haunches and softly clapping. When the clapping finally died down, the Boy, obviously too overcome to speak, nodded his thanks. He took a bunch of keys from his pocket and tossed them to the tall young Lunda chief; Jahaliso caught them and looked up at him uncomprehendingly.

"My car," the Boy said huskily. "I have no further need for it."

Jahaliso, jubilant, embraced the Boy while the crowd broke into a spontaneous cheer. When the chief broke free, his bespectacled black face was oddly wracked; he stared at the Boy in fond anguish, and declared: "*Njumwaice*, I have decided. If Quakers are like you, *then that is what I wish to be!*"

The milling missionaries were still staring incredulously when Mulaisho spoke up. "Perhaps, *Njumwaice*, if I am also to become a Quaker, I am abled to dress like you! Of all things about you, Bwana Cowboy, I admire most your fine white hat!"

"Be my guest." Bowing his head, the Boy transferred his Stetson reverently to the chief's grizzled gray head. Another cheer went up as the gnarled black face wrinkled endearingly into a gum-gaping gamin grin of pure delight. Then Kadesha too stepped forward; in his flowing *kanza* the dignified elderly chief, with eyes aglow with quiet sadness, shook the Boy's hand, European-style.

"The Lunda people are forever indebted to you, my son. We beg you to return someday, and if you do, you will find me also sitting in the church of the Quakers."

Matthew could scarcely believe his ears; culminating in a single day, without ever having preached a word of the Gospel, their disgraced delegate, by his selfless deeds alone, had earned this influential allegiance to their God. He had reaped, threefold, in years what the rest of the missionaries combined had failed to achieve in as many decades. With his uncanny knack, the Boy had turned this infamous departure into a distinguished deliverance. But there was no time to ruminate the achievement now. The aircraft had been loaded with their luggage, and the pilot, glancing at his watch, asked his passengers to board. It was the moment Matthew dreaded; fighting to control his emotions, he stood in line with the other missionaries to wish the family good-bye. Across from him, while the soured Fotches, mourning an automobile, pouted surly valedictions, Peter Disney was embracing Jayne. At nineteen, looking a lovely young lady in a pale lemon bonnet and dress, with long blond tresses flowing free, she was weeping as she broke from the bereft young man and unloaded a clinging little gray fur ball onto the wet-eyed Teller's ample maternal bosom.

"Aunt Teller, take care of Jasper!" Then she threw herself on Matthew and hugged him fiercely. "Uncle Matthew, we'll miss thee!"

Tom, looking tall and grown-up in a tie and long trousers, shook Matthew's hand and mumbled an awkward good-bye in a gruff, breaking voice. Then dear Katherine, ever dignified in her Quaker-gray dress and bonnet, stopped before Matthew with such a look of love that he was touched and embarrassed. She kissed his leathery old cheek with a gentle reverence that almost broke his heart. He was relieved when she left him to scramble aboard the little six-seater plane after her children. The pilot was gesturing frantically at his watch, and Matthew, infected with the shrill underlying hysteria of haste, turned agitatedly. But the Boy was still busy; Matthew spotted his streaky-blond head surrounded by the Dooleys. He was crouching while the red-headed five-year-old triplets he had brought into the world tumbled adoringly all over him, as playful as puppies. Then Jerome extended a hand and the Boy stood up and the two men fell silent as they shook hands, their serious eyes bespeaking a respect and affection that needed no words. Grace, however, was less easy to leave; she clung to the Boy, crying into his shirt. Ingrid Wikstrom, with typical Swedish starch, extended a formal hand; the Boy ignored it and kissed her soundly on the mouth. Apparently fearing the same treatment, little Cherish Sinclair turned shrinking violet, averting her scarlet face as the Boy shook her timid hand. Hannah Rothchild, however, refused to bury bygones; she ignored his hand, haughty nose in the air. But Ezra Peabody, finding himself the next in line, dimpled chubbily in an embarrassed insincere smile, awkwardly reciprocating the Boy's gracious, ungrudging farewell. Then there was only Matthew; he cleared his throat awkwardly.

"Well, son, looks like this's the end of the trail."

But the Boy, already sweating in his suit in the hot morning sun, was shrugging off his jacket, looking frantically around. "Matthew—where's Jenny?"

"Jenny?" Matthew looked around himself. "Why I . . . I reckon I missed her. Must be *somewhere* around though. Surely somebody thought to . . ."

Even as he spoke, the pilot impatiently started up the plane; the gunned engines filled the air with a deafening roar and the propellers made a few hesitant revolutions and began to spin. One of the passenger doors still hung open in beckoning to the Boy, and Katherine and Jayne were calling him from the interior.

"Jesus—she's not here!"

"What's that?" Matthew strained to hear above the noise. He put out a hand to catch hold of the Boy, but the Boy slipped through his fingers.

"Come back!" Matthew yelled hoarsely above the roar. "IT'S TOO LATE, D'YOU HEAR? TOO . . ."

But his voice dropped in hopeless dismay. For the Boy was gone, pushing frantically through the crowd. Matthew saw him snatch his car keys from the surprised Jahaliso before he sprang into the big yellow Thunderbird and roared off, tires squealing amid a spume of red dust. The plane engines droned on and on; turning, Matthew saw Jayne inside it, tugging urgently at the pilot's shoulder.

29

At the mission, Than parked at the Tomlinson house and leaped from the car. Frantically calling Jenny, he limped up the overgrown path. The silence that came back at him was more than he could bear and he hurried along the open veranda that encircled the house, searching desperately. But around every corner, the cushioned wicker chairs stood unoccupied and quiet, and he pushed open the screened front door and went into the musty-smelling dimness. But her neat bedroom, with its lonely toys, the heartbreaking legacy of little Luke, stood empty and still, and he rushed from room to room in a daze. The cold answering silence of the rambling old house filled him with panic, and he stumbled out again, skipping down the polished green veranda steps. He stood for a moment, panting, closing his eyes and struggling to compose his thoughts. Then an idea struck him, and without waiting to catch his breath, he plunged down the path and on again, limping frantically along the green-grassed slope. In some objective part of his mind he realized that Suseshi had never seemed as beautiful as now; the tall borassus palms waved in the breeze, the shady flamboyant trees were just bursting their brilliant red blossoms through the fringed green foliage, and the river reflected the placid blue of the sky. But none of this mattered; Jenny was gone, and he knew that his heart was breaking.

His thigh ached unbearably, but with the silent echo of the plane roaring intimidatingly in his ears, he ran furiously, favoring his bad leg in awkward undulating strides. The duiker's horn swung rhythmically around his neck as he labored, lungs bursting, past the silent empty building of the boys' school and on past the new meeting house to the ruins of the old one. He limped through the scattered blackened bricks, where the long green grass had succeeded the dusty ash, and through the line of fir trees that surrounded the graveyard, where the bunch of bright hibiscus blossoms were already wilting on his father's undistinguished, cross-demarcated grave. Then he stopped dead, and it was suddenly all worthwhile. For there she was. Jenny. In the long lilac dress he had come to know so well, she was kneeling with her back to him in the sand before the sad flower-strewn mound of Luke's little grave. He let out his breath. Suddenly nothing else mattered; time itself was irrelevant, and he waited until the fire faded from his laboring lungs and his breath gradually regulated before he limped toward her. Stones rolled under his boots and she must hear his approach, but she did not move. He stopped behind her.

"Jenny," he said gently. "I've come to say good-bye."

Her back stiffened, and it seemed to him she took a deep bracing breath; when he touched her shoulder, she turned slowly around. Though her cheeks were shiny-wet and he could hardly see her beautiful eyes for the brimming tears that hung like diamonds from her long dark lashes, she raised a sweet face that was radiantly smiling. *Maseccasecca:* One Who Smiles . . .

"Oh baby!" he groaned softly, shaking his head. He tumbled to his knees, reaching for her hands, face contorted with his anguish as he whispered: "Did you think . . . did you really think I could leave without seeing you?"

That was where Matthew finally found them. He left the Land-Rover parked at the house, and aimed by instinct, went scurrying along the slope, through the ruins of the old meeting house, to the graveyard where Jenny was so often to be found these days. He burst blindly through the fir trees and stopped when he saw them, struggling to fight down his demented breath. Then, mesmerized by what he saw, he stumbled slowly on toward them, staring perplexedly. For there was something in their attitude that struck him as strange. They stood absolutely still, heads drawn together and clutching hands as solicitously as lovers, so rapt in each other that they appeared not to register his presence, their tender faces radiating such love that Matthew felt strangely moved. And the Boy was talking softly; his face was solemn and by his controlled voice you might never know it, but he was crying. If that little blind girl could see, she would observe, as Matthew did now, the glistening tears that streamed down his proud golden, defiantly scarred face. And he was saying things that even Matthew, after years of judging the Boy, found hard to believe.

"Listen to me, darling; I'll come back someday," he lied valiantly to make it easier for them both. "That's my covenant to you, Jenny. Wait for me. And no matter where I am, whatever I do, every minute of every day I'll be loving you, Jenny. With all my heart, till the day I die."

Matthew stared at the pair in a shocked thrall of compassion. For this surely was the Impossible Dream: to love pure and chaste from afar. He watched as the Boy loosened his tie and unbuttoned his collar; he was pulling something off from around his neck. The silver medallion flashed in the sun as he placed it tenderly over Jenny's bowed head. He lifted her dark hair and gently kissed the chain where it lay against her fair skin, tucking the small disc down the top of her dress, between her young breasts. And then they were in each other's arms, embracing as if they would never let go. The Boy's face was wracked with a terrible torment, such torment as Matthew had never seen before, and he saw in that bowed blond-streaked head a picture of yesterday. When was it? On a car roof, amid a jubilant throng; the Boy fiercely hugging a little child. Realization hit Matthew in a bright starburst of pain, and he stood in sudden dark shock. Of course! Why had he never admitted the resemblance before? That little illegitimate child—*Luke*—was the Boy's own son. . . .

The Boy left Jenny at the grave. His limping slowed when he saw Matthew, and he must have seen the truth in Matthew's aghast face, for he suddenly stopped. Then he took a great breath and continued advancing toward him.

"Yes, Matthew. Luke was my son."

Matthew was weeping against his knuckles, and the Boy closed his eyes in shame.

"It happened the night we were stranded on the Barotse plain. I got a little high on the headman's liquor, and Jenny . . . well, Jenny wasn't in any state to hold me off. It only happened once, and neither of us intended it. So now you know. We love each other, Matthew."

At the airstrip, Jayne tumbled thankfully into the Boy's arms, and he was verbally set upon by a crowd of chastising missionaries. The pilot, standing outside the plane, was furiously smoking. He dropped his cigarette when he saw Than Profane and climbed back inside the cockpit. And now that departure was imminent, the Boy, carrying his suit jacket slung over one shoulder, battled a clamorous throng of natives to reach the plane; the crowd had surged forward, anxiously calling him, reaching hands straining to touch him one last time. But he pushed obliviously through the multitudinous press of sweaty bodies, shouting to Matthew over the desperately craning heads and clamoring voices.

"You take care of her, hear? I'm counting on you, old man. Jesus, I . . ." he closed his eyes. *"I love her,* Matthew! So much it makes me ache inside."

But time was tugging at him, insistent as the hands, and he prattled briskly on. "And remember—I'll be depending on you to set up that marble angel I want for Luke's grave, with any words Jenny wants."

He stopped at the plane and looked suddenly uncertain and afraid.

"But most of all . . . *take care of her, Matthew!"*

Then he turned. He scrambled into the aircraft after Jayne; the metal door was slammed shut, the engines were gunned, and the propellors revolved and spun. The crowd stepped back, watching in awed silence as the sturdy white aircraft ran the bumpy length of the strip, then lifted on short wings and took off into the wide blue October sky.

Just as abruptly as he had come, the Boy was gone. The other missionaries started to drift disconsolately off with the crowd, but Matthew stayed behind, staring up at the sky long after the speck of the plane had faded from sight. Then, shaking his old white head to stir himself, he turned and began to trudge despondently back to the emptiness that remained.

In the cloistered atmosphere of the little cabin, Jayne was crying in the seat behind Than; she reached out to touch him, but he did not respond. His forehead was pressed against the cool windowpane, and as they flew over the mission, he stared down at the buildings, lying miniature and remote beneath them. White-clad figures came out of the hospital and waved up at the plane; Cedric Fotheringill would return there soon, asserting control in Than's place. The winding river gleamed lead-colored beneath them. *Suseshi.* The name sang in his mind. And looking at it through the eyes of love, how different it all seemed from the day he had first seen it. He saw the scattered school buildings, the line of old missionary houses and, beyond the new meeting house, the little mission graveyard. Jenny was there, and its good African soil covered so much that he loved. His father and his son. And away in the bush to the north and to the south lay more graves, the graves of Tanda, Kwoyisho, Africa, Furanswa, and all the countless African victims of disease, neglect, and deprivation. He looked across the leafy canopy of the green bush, the myriad trees dimensionally projected above their moving shadows, and he knew that he left more than old bones in Africa. He left Jenny and his heart. And he was departing a little more quietly than he had come. Africa, grief, and a leopard had taken their toll of his body and soul, and it was with a chastened heart that he now limped bereftly home. Back to the States, where the Indians and the backwoods had been tamed, where money was plenteous and the women were permissive.

The plane circled and flew off over the gleaming green Kabompo River, on and on till it crested the wide blue Zambezi. And under cover of the multitudinous trees, a rising new state passed beneath them: Zambia. Throwing off the shackles of the parent country, the adolescent nation was starting out for richer or for poorer, for better or for worse. The masses were fiercely independent, eager to cast off the influence of their old overseers, and in their unbridled haste to be rid of their white mentors, Than wondered how long the mission would last. In this climate of speedy progress and change, the little Christian institutions that thinly dotted the vast landscape were fast becoming unwanted anachronisms. For although the politicians spoke tongue-in-cheek of harmony and goodwill between the races, hatred was in fact the deep-seated reverse. The undercurrents of resentment rumbled through the land, and in the towns myriad trees and telephone poles bore the angry sign of the times: WHITES GO HOME!

Well, Than was doing just that. And for him it was over all too soon. As he stared yearningly down over Africa, a great transcendental compassion stirred in him, and he was dumbfounded by the racially unrequited love of a people. And as they flew on, away in the Dag Hammarskjöld Stadium at Ndola, Africans were singing with fervor and with hope: "*Nkosi Sikelele Africa!*"

God Save Africa. *Africa and my love.*